Worldwide Pr
of John Patrick and STARbooks!

"If you're an avid reader of all-male erotica and haven't yet discovered editor John Patrick's series of torrid anthologies, you're in for a treat. ...These books will provide hours of cost-effective entertainment."
— *Lance Sterling, Beau magazine*

"John Patrick is a modern master of the genre! ...This writing is what being brave is all about. It brings up the kinds of things that are usually kept so private that you think you're the only one who experiences them."
— *Gay Times, London*

"'Barely Legal' is a great potpourri...and the coverboy is gorgeous!"
— *Ian Young, Torso magazine*

"A huge collection of highly erotic, short and steamy one-handed tales. Perfect bedtime reading, though you probably won't get much sleep! Prepare to be shocked! Highly recommended!"
— *Vulcan magazine*

"Tantalizing tales of porn stars, hustlers, and other lost boys...John Patrick set the pace with 'Angel'!"
— *The Weekly News, Miami*

"...Some readers may find some of the scenes too explicit; others will enjoy the sudden, graphic sensations each page brings. ...A strange, often poetic vision of sexual obsession. I recommend it to you."
— *Nouveau Midwest*

"'Dreamboys' is so hot I had to put extra baby oil on my fingers, just to turn the pages! ...Those blue eyes on the cover are gonna reach out and touch you..."
— *Bookazine's Hot Flashes*

"I just got 'Intimate Strangers' and by the end of the week I had read it all. Great stories! Love it!"
— *L.C., Oregon*

"'Superstars' is a fast read...if you'd like a nice round of fireworks before the Fourth, read this aloud at your next church picnic..."
— *Welcomat, Philadelphia*

"Yes, it's another of those bumper collections of steamy tales from STARbooks. The rate at which John Patrick turns out these compilations you'd be forgiven for thinking it's not

"Pleasure is the only thing one should live for."
— Oscar Wilde

Pleasures
of the Flesh

A Collection
of Erotic Tales
Edited By
JOHN PATRICK

STARbooks Press

First Edition Published in the U.S. in June, 1999
Second Edition Published in the U.S. in April 2006
Library of Congress Card Catalogue No. 98-96880
ISBN No 1-891855-71-9

Books by John Patrick

Contents

Editor's Note

Most of the stories appearing in this book take place prior to the years of The Plague; the editor and each of the authors represented herein advocate the practice of safe sex at all times. And, because these stories trespass the boundaries of fiction and non-fiction, to respect the privacy of those involved, we've changed all of the names and other identifying details.

"I don't regret for a single moment having lived for pleasure. I did it to the full as one should do anything one does. I wanted to eat of the fruit of all the trees in the garden of the world. I lived on honeycomb!"
— Oscar Wilde in *"De Profundis"*

- - -

"The great pleasure of the debauched is to lead others to debauchery."
— Andre Gide

- - -

"I've often felt that certain great pleasures require that we first must be deprived of a pleasure of a lesser sort...."
— Marcel Proust

"In the garden he picked flowers and taught me to name them in French, but I quickly forgot all the names. I could only remember what his mouth looked like as he said them. What else do I recall? His bare hips, slightly turned as he lay in bed beside me. A glimmer of sweat limning the hollow of his back. Night, its gradual onset, and then our long slow recline. The boy ... turned to me across the bunched pillows and let his soft chin rest on my shoulder. His nipples had softened and lay flat. His skin was warm from an increasing fever. I think it's okay for you to take pleasure in these things. ...He took my hand in his and drew it along his ribs to his belly and hip, and then he let my fingers touch the perfect lip of his shallow belly button, where I stopped for a moment to dwell. ...You must never forget that I truly and impossibly did love him."
— Matthew Sadler, *"Allan Stein"*

The epitome of the pleasure principle: popular Las Vegas-based escort and porn star Pagan Prince, courtesy Studio 2000

INTRODUCTION PLEASURE: A PAGAN IDEA
by John Patrick

"I think that the realization of oneself is the prime aim in life," Oscar Wilde said, "and to realize oneself through pleasure is surely finer than to do so through pain. I am, on that point, entirely on the side of the ancients the Greeks. It is a pagan idea."

To demonstrate Wilde's paganism, at his trial over a hundred years ago, as documented in the play "Gross Indecency: The Three Trials of Oscar Wilde" by Moses Kaufman, it was noted that Alfred Taylor, an ex-public-schoolboy who had, by the age of thirty, squandered his inheritance, ran a delicate and peculiar commercial service introducing gentlemen to their social inferiors from his rooms behind Westminster Abbey. Taylor introduced Wilde to "about five" other youths. When asked what their occupation was, Wilde replied, "I do not know if these particular young men had occupations." Wilde admitted giving them money or presents, and that he delighted "in the society of people much younger than myself. I like those who may be called idle or careless. I recognize no social distinctions at all of any kind; and to me youth, the mere fact of youth, is so wonderful that I would sooner talk to a young man for half-an-hour than be well, cross-examined in court."

One of the boys, Sidney Mavor, testified, "One day, Taylor said to me, 'I know a man in an influential position who could be of great use to you, Mavor.'"

Wilde testified, "People thought it dreadful of me to have entertained at dinner these men, and to have found pleasure in their company. But then, from my point of view, they were delightfully suggestive and stimulating. It was like feasting with panthers. They were to me like the brightest of gilded snakes, their poison was part of their perfection. I did not know that when they were to strike at me, it was to be at another's piping and another's pay. I am a lover of youth. I like to study the young in everything. There is something fascinating in youthfulness. The 'Love that dare not speak its name' in this century is such a great affection of an elder for a younger man as there was between David and Jonathan, such as Plato made the very basis of his philosophy, and such as you find in the sonnets of Michelangelo and Shakespeare. It is that deep, spiritual affection that is as pure as it is perfect. It dictates and pervades great works of art like those of Shakespeare and Michelangelo, and those two letters of mine, such as they are. "...I am placed where I am now. It is beautiful, it is fine, it is the noblest form of affection. There is nothing unnatural about it. It is intellectual, and it repeatedly exists between an elder and a younger man when

the elder man has intellect and the younger man has all the joy, hope, and glamour of life before him. That it should be so the world does not understand. The world mocks at it and sometimes puts one in the pillory for it."

While Wilde shepherded his beloved Bosie (Lord Alfred Douglas) through the world of letters, Bosie took Oscar deeper into a milieu less refined, but more immediately stimulating. Increasingly during their relationship, Bosie brought recklessness to a fine art: he would never take the hazardous option if a suicidal one presented itself, and his attitude to sexual intercourse wherever, whenever, whomever and love of danger began to excite and entrance Wilde.

Stephen Calloway, in his book *Oscar Wilde*, states, "Although Robbie Ross had introduced Oscar, on occasions, to rough trade, the lower-class boys who made up the lowest rank of the underworld, Douglas had a friend able to provide an endless supply of such creatures, whose bodies and even their souls could be purchased for a pound and a meal.

"Wilde was fascinated by the inhabitants of Taylor's dangerous world. They 'were wonderful', he was to say of two of the dubious acquaintances he made there, 'in their infamous war against life. To know them was an astounding adventure.' But neither Taylor nor Wilde knew then that many of the boys had discovered for themselves a lucrative side-line in extortion, thanks to the Criminal Law Amendment Act of 1885, which, for the first time, had made all sexual acts between men illegal, and became known as the 'Blackmailer's Charter'. For the moment, Wilde enjoyed, perhaps in genuine naivete, the pleasures of seeking out exotic and novel pleasures according to Paterian principles, which he called 'feasting with panthers.'"

Wilde was no novice to liaisons with young boys. In Paris in January 1883, he took up with William Wordsworth's great-grandson, Robert Sherard, blond, twenty-one, masculine and obtuse. "Sherard was one of a long series of bewitched young admirers whose attentions Oscar so savored, though until his seduction by the young Robert Ross in 1886, Oscar seems not to have given physical expression to his desire for youthful male bodies," according to Jonathan Fryer in his book, *Andre and Oscar*. "Indeed, Robert Sherard later maintained that he had been completely unaware that there was anything odd about Wilde's interest in him, despite the fact that Oscar once kissed him full on the lips. Comradely affection and the use of endearments between men were much more common between Englishmen before Wilde's disgrace than they are today. Besides, Sherard was dazzled, as so many other young men had been and would be. Oscar, for his part, delighted in having such a sturdy acolyte...."

Wilde saw Sherard every day; he enjoyed shocking the lad and used him as a confidant perhaps realizing that his confessions would be recorded for posterity. "...Wilde was addicted to the presence of intelligent but preferably adoring youth, who were as much an intellectual as a physical stimulation. As he wrote in *The Picture of Dorian Gray*: 'The only people to whose opinion I listen now with any respect are people much younger than myself.' Oscar was intrigued and attracted by the seventeen-year-old Robbie Ross, with his Puck-like

2

features, lively personality and precocious knowledge of the world. That knowledge extended to the art of homosexual love; Robbie had no doubts about where his proclivities lay, and he proceeded to seduce the fascinated Oscar, who was nearly twice his age. This was almost certainly Oscar's initiation into the physical side of homosexuality, however often in the past he might have been stirred by the sight or idea of beautiful youths. It is unlikely that it was Robbie's deflowerment. Ross's mother and Constance Wilde must both have been unaware of the sexual relationship that existed between Robbie and Oscar, as the following year, 1887, Robbie moved into the Wildes' home... He stayed for three months, while his mother was away... In view of the fact that homosexuality between men had been made illegal in England through the Labouchere Amendment just over twelve months previously, and that Robbie was still a minor, Oscar's recklessness in arranging for his young lover to move in is breath-taking. Perhaps he felt that such an inadvisable liaison was best kept hidden from public view within the sanctuary of his household a precaution he would have been well advised to take in the future. But it seems that already Oscar enjoyed dancing with danger. At the same time, the arrangement demonstrated an extraordinary lack of concern for his wife's feelings. One can imagine Robbie and Oscar rather enjoying the situation, like naughty schoolboys, exchanging knowing looks across the dinner-table.

"...Oscar undoubtedly found adulation an aphrodisiac, especially when it came from young men who fell within his preferred age range of approximately seventeen to twenty-five. Having Robbie in the house probably prevented Oscar from looking for commercial sex from the numerous rent-boys who plied their trade in Victorian London, operating openly around Piccadilly Circus, inside several theaters and pubs and on other cruising grounds. Given widespread poverty, prostitution of all kinds was rife in the great metropolis, despite all the legal and social constraints.

"...As Oscar became more prosperous, his entertaining became more lavish, including dinners at the Savoy and the hiring of private rooms at Kettner's restaurant in Soho, where a cuddle could be indulged in between courses. He began to distribute inscribed silver cigarette cases to particular favorites as liberally as a more cautious man might hand out cigarettes. Oscar found nothing strange about his thirst for new encounters, despite his marriage and his parallel relationship with Robbie. Years later he joked that he had been married three times in his life, once to a woman (Constance) and twice to men (Ross and Douglas), but these core relationships did not deter an accelerating interest in promiscuous sex with youths, several of whom became objects of infatuation, at least for a day. He became adept at seducing them in the most unlikely, and inappropriate, places, including his own publishers' offices.

"...Ross, who perhaps had more legitimate reason to be offended by Oscar's new associations, seems to have taken a very tolerant, philosophical view of his lover's philandering, at least when youths of a lower social and intellectual standing were involved. Robbie set no great store by physical fidelity; sex was

3

fun. He even seems to have accepted Wilde's relationship with a handsome young poet of some talent, John Gray, who liked to style himself 'Dorian', with Oscar's indulgence.

"...Unscrupulous youths on the game could, by accident or design, often 'rent' their clients twice over, first being paid for sex, and then extracting further payment from them under the threat of public exposure. (Wilde) had a long-standing fascination in the activities and psychology of the criminal classes, and the prospect of rescuing a young lord from disaster was as romantic as some of the plots of his own fairy tales."

As Andre Gide himself was to point out in his memoirs of Wilde, so Oscar himself acknowledged that the gods had given him almost everything: "genius, a distinguished name, high social position, brilliancy, intellectual daring," but he had spoiled himself by surrounding himself with smaller natures and meaner minds.

In *Wilde's Last Stand*, Philip Hoare reveals that in late middle-age, Douglas retained the looks of a ravaged beautiful boy: "His thick silky blond hair was barely touched with grey, his figure was slender, his skin pale and delicate with a tendency to flush rosily like a boy's. He dressed simply, with a liking for heavy boots rather than shoes and a habit of wearing battered hats. But the physical portrait betrays a certain neuroticism. His voice was delightful when he laughed but shrill when he was angry; and Douglas was often angry. To Croft-Cooke, who met him in 1922, he looked like a hurt boy. The eyes were brilliantly expressive, often merry but sometimes pained and resentful. The features that in boyhood were so delicately modeled had grown pronounced, the nose formidable, the corners of the mouth turning down petulantly.

"In the years after the Wilde trials, Douglas had sought domesticity, marrying Olive Custance in 1902, with whom he had a son, Raymond.

"...As a married man drawn towards Roman Catholicism, Bosie had conceived a distaste (which later became a loathing) for his own homosexual past and those associated with it. He attempted to drop Ross quietly, but Ross would not go quietly. The affair began to escalate when Douglas wrote in his accustomed intemperate manner his father's legacy, telling Ross: 'I no longer care to associate with persons like yourself who are engaged in the active performance and propaganda of every kind of wickedness, from Socialism to Sodomy.'

"...For the next five years, the spat between Ross and Douglas was a social skirmish for the upper hand. In 1913, it became open warfare. Arthur Ransome had published a biography of Wilde, written with Ross's help. Douglas, annoyed by the way he had been portrayed in it, took out a libel action against the book. Through Ross, the unpublished section of *De Profundis,* Wilde's open letter to Bosie, was produced, although it was supposed to be kept secret, at the British Library, until 1960. It destroyed Douglas's case, being clear evidence of his homosexual relationship with Wilde. Douglas felt posthumously betrayed by Wilde when he heard the new portions of *Dc Profundis,* and the trial had the effect of turning Douglas violently against Ross and Wilde just as his father had

turned on Wilde. Douglas would have been better advised not to have brought this action.

"...Somewhat relishing their effect, (jurist) Hume-Williams read yet another of Wilde's letters to Douglas: 'Bosie, you must not make scenes with me ... They kill me, they wreck the loveliness of life. I cannot see you, so Greek and gracious, distorted with passion. I cannot listen to your curved lips saying hideous things to me. I would sooner be rented than have you bitter, unjust, hating ... I must see you soon. You are the divine thing I want, the thing of grace and beauty.' Douglas replied, 'That is the letter that was produced by my father in his effort to smash up Wilde to save me, and that has been the result. My father comes before the Court to save his son, and you lawyers come here twenty-five years afterwards to spit it up again for money? because you have been paid to do it.' To this, Hume-Williams replied, 'When did you cease to approve of sodomy?' 'When did I cease to approve of sodomy?', retorted Douglas. 'I do not think that is a fair question. That is like asking: When did you leave off beating your wife?' Now a third letter was produced (it was said that Sir George Lewis kept a file full of stolen letters, lent to those in litigation with Douglas). 'If you show me letters in my handwriting,' said Douglas, 'I give you fair warning that I shall tear them up. It is a stolen letter, stolen by a blackmailer, and you having it there makes you a partner in that theft and blackmail: you yourself are a thief and a blackmailer if you make use of such letters.' (That was bad enough but) it was the next letter that would completely undermine Douglas's testimony. Dated 9 June 1895, it was a reply to accusations from the editor of *Truth* that Douglas had abandoned Wilde and that the 'acts which resulted in Wilde's incarceration are not practiced by others'. On the contrary, Bosie had written, 'I personally know forty or fifty men who practice these acts. Men in the best society, members of the smartest clubs, members of Parliament, Peers, etc., in fact people of my own social standing ...' Many contemporaries of his at Oxford 'had these tastes', and he would produce a translation of a pamphlet written by 'Professor Krafft-Ebing, the celebrated Austrian physician (he was in fact German, but took a chair at Vienna in 1889) ... a special plea written for the express purpose of obtaining a repeal or modification of the law on this subject in Austria, and which has been to a very large extent successful. It is designed to prove what I maintain, viz., that these tastes are perfectly natural congenital tendencies in certain people (a very large minority), and that the law has no right to interfere with these people, provided they do not harm other people; that is to say when there is neither seduction of minors nor brutalization, and when there is no public outrage on morals ...' He went on to cite favorable conditions under French and German law. 'England alone has refused to take any cognizance of the now known and admitted facts of modern medical science.'

"... 'The period which you hoped for in which sodomy, unchecked by the law, will flourish, has not arrived?' said Hume Williams. 'Yes, I do think it has,' said Douglas, 'At the time I wrote that letter, sodomy was condemned by all decent

5

people.' 'You were not a decent person?' 'No, I was not,' admitted Douglas, and I have said that. Much good may it do you. Douglas set off accusing 'Prime Ministers, judges, lawyers, and everyone' of conspiring to support the perverts, and said that the reason why he was attacked was because he was no longer one of them. Douglas's affair with Wilde had placed him outside society; his row with Ross had done the same, and he felt it. He said, 'I say there are several judges, and many people in the highest positions in this land, who protect sodomites all in their power, and actually give them public testimonials. I have said it. I have written it to the Prime Minister. I will prove it in the dock with the greatest of pleasure in my life.'

"...It was a difficult time for Douglas: his wife left him, and he was allowed only limited access to his son."

It appears Bosie's most pleasurable days were those he spent with Oscar.

And speaking of pleasure as we are, in David Leddick's delightful novel, *Sex Squad*, the hero, a young dancer named Harry, spends a night of incredible pleasure with his quasi-lover, fellow dancer Rex. For the first time, Harry tells us, Rex decides not to "regulate his penis."

Harry says, "Soon it had pushed its way above that blue-and-white band all by itself. Foreplay was not Rex's long suit. It was that Italian blood. He told me that Italian foreplay was 'You ... there.' He wasn't far off the mark.

"He stood up on the bed and pulled off his underpants and threw off the robe. I knelt in front of him. I could see us in the big mirror on the wall by the window. (I had found it in the street very nice mahogany frame.) We had the lamp on the dresser on, so his body was lit with yellow light from the lamp and blue light from the television. A marble faun. Not classic. Renaissance. Did you ever see *The Sleeping Faun* in Munich? Like that not overly long legs; but the slope of the thighs in one direction and the whole triangle of the shoulders down across the flat pectorals and the even flatter abdomen, directed everything to the cock.

"He moved it in and out slowly. He didn't shut his eyes ... He looked at me, but in a very absent way. Dancers have strong stomach muscles and very flat. His were like some cabled bridge, holding up the weight of his outstanding penis as though it were very heavy and straining to drop. Occasionally, when he took me from behind, I could feel his abdomen slapping my buttocks and it felt good, flat and hard and powerful.

"He pushed me down on the bed and lay down beside me, his head in my crotch. He took me in his mouth while forcing himself in and out of mine and started probing my anus with his fingers. Hard. Like some animal trying to eat you and tear at you at the same time. Rex didn't usually let himself go like this.

"'Hey,' I said gently, taking him out of my mouth. He stopped, pulled himself up to me, took me in his arms, and started kissing me, equally hard. He slipped his cock between my legs and we lay on our sides, him holding me in his arms, his mouth and his penis probing deep, deep, deeper.

"'I have to have it,' he said, and turned me on my back. I pulled the pillow

under my buttocks. He knelt between my legs, pulling at himself slowly, downward, as though making it as long as possible. He wasn't masturbating, more checking the wonder of it. I always kept Vaseline under the pillow. I rubbed a handful up between my buttocks and used that hand to join him in pulling down on the swinging curve between his legs. He lay down on me and slowly pushed in.

"'Easy,' I said.

"Rex knew what he was doing. Not roughly but steadily he pushed his way in and began rhythmically pulling in and out. He could do this a very long time. Rex enjoyed the feelings of his penis in another body as much as, if not more than, his orgasm. He was never in a rush to get there. It wasn't your pleasure he was concerned with. Never. But his pleasure was my pleasure. The more he relished those deep plunges into my flesh, the more pleasure I had. Not so much the thrill of the feeling of him in me, but the pleasure of giving him pleasure.

"I heard a famous painter say, once, 'I think homosexuality is envy,' and maybe it is. Maybe I was loving his doing this leisurely penetration because he was my surrogate. He was having the pleasure for me. Surely I have never had an equal pleasure in penetration. It's okay. The orgasm is good. But I never felt the luxuriant writhing about, the seeking to get that cock in as deeply as possible so every little millimeter could have the pleasure of being immersed in warm interior flesh. He loved it, and his rich pleasure was something I could share. Since I was the rich pleasure, how completely ego-satisfying.

"I had gotten pretty good at holding off my own orgasm until Rex came. I had to put my hand over my penis sometimes to keep the regular thrusting of his hard stomach from forcing an orgasm out of me. As he approached orgasm, he lost control of himself completely and the thrusting became frantic. You could tell that he held himself back from the edge as long as he could, and when he irrevocably slipped over that edge, he crashed down that slide to orgasm totally abandoned. It was pretty exciting. I took my hand off my penis and let his body push me over my own edge.

"'Hold me,' I told him. 'Hold me very tight.'

"It felt so dangerous to be slipping into that oblivion. I didn't want to be there all alone. His arms clamped about me very tightly. His lips forced my mouth open and his tongue was deep inside me also. His buttocks worked furiously and then his mouth came off mine, his head went back and he groaned very loudly. He held his pelvis very tightly against mine. He was pulsing hard inside me without any movement. I was aware of this at the same time that I was out somewhere in the midnight sky, falling and falling and falling. His strong arms kept me from falling into many small pieces, difficult to pick up again. He collapsed on me. I put my arms around his back. He was soaked in perspiration. Slowly he eased his way out, almost automatically.

"'Let's get cleaned up,' he said.

"He pulled away from my body and, crawling to the edge of the bed, he put on my terry-cloth robe and went into the kitchen. I couldn't move. It was all right

that his arms weren't around me, but I couldn't move my arms and legs and lift my head and be Harry. Not yet."

THE PLEASURES OF THE FLESH
by John Patrick

Rome was to be different for me this time. My parents had taken me with them on vacation when I was only 15. As much as I wanted to, I could not indulge in the pleasures of the flesh. Now it would be different. It was four years later and I had achieved a small amount of success as an actor. I had started out as a little boy in TV commercials, learned my craft playing Shakespeare in summer theaters, and had even done a stint on a soap opera. I had paid my dues, on the boards and in the beds of some of the powerful and the not-so-powerful. I was ready for my big break. Against my agent's advice, I took the lead in "Spring of Passion," a movie-within-a-movie being directed by the famous, or infamous, depending on whose stories you believed, Carlo Giovanni. The film was sold as a sort of poor man's version of "Death in Venice." In Carlo's version, the older man manages to sleep with the Tadzio character, who was now an American. Since I could easily pass for fifteen, I got the role over fifty other youths.

In the lead part played by Dirk Bogarde in the original, Carlo signed another noted British actor, Godfrey Duncan. He was still quite handsome, I thought. In his twenties he was almost too much so. His pale skin and delicate features, his thick, curly, red-blond hair, his laughing gray-green eyes, his tall, slender figure made a distressing contrast to my dark, muscular appearance. He dressed up to his appearance, too in beautiful designer suits and colored shirts. The switch of having the boy be the stud in the new version, and the composer be the vulnerable one seemed odd to me, throwing the whole thing out of balance from the original Thomas Mann concept, but Carlo said that was the whole point.

Four years before, it had been summer in Rome, stark, glaring, hot on the Piazza del Popolo. Now it was a cool and rainy spring, and, inexplicably, I was even hornier than I had been at 15. I suppose that is why when within a few hours of our meeting at the Luxor Studios, where were filming the interiors, I gladly consented to drive off with my co-star.

The air was damp but the sun was shining brightly as Godfrey and I rode back to the hotel in a cab, and flowers were vivid everywhere. There were pots of pink azaleas all the way up the Spanish Steps and carts with blue delphiniums along the entire length of the Via Bourgognona. On the corners, street vendors were selling bunches of roses and irises and gladioli. Even the daisies looked fresh and appealing although Godfrey said he had never liked daisies. "Their smell is rank," he said, "and their stems are weedy."

"Can't have a weedy stem," I joked.

He thought I was mocking him, and gave me a stern look.

When we arrived at the hotel, the cabdriver asked for twelve hundred lire,

although the meter indicated only seven hundred. Godfrey said, *"Non e possibile."*

The cabdriver broke into a stream of Italian well beyond even Godfrey's comprehension, but it was clear that he was repeating his demand. He was young and tough-looking, and I wondered what Godfrey would do.

Godfrey shook his head, stern as ever.

"Allora," the driver concluded furiously, holding up ten rigidly outspread fingers. Then he said something else. It was clear he was cursing us.

"Bastard!" Godfrey said, starting to walk away. "I'd have given him the thousand," muttered Godfrey, "but no way now."

The hotel doorman and several passersby were watching with interest by now, and I realized that the cabdriver was trying to make Godfrey lose face. He suddenly broke into English. "I no take less than thousand," he declared, hands waving.

Godfrey held out his hand again. "Sure!"

The driver spat out the window and put the car in gear. Godfrey shrugged. The cab lurched forward and drove away, tires squealing.

"That was amazing," I said as we entered the plush lobby. "He ended up with nothing!"

"His choice," said Godfrey.

"What a bummer," I said, but I really thought it had been the most exciting event since my arrival and made me look upon Godfrey in a new light.

We had returned early to "practice our lines." Godfrey suggested lunch first. It was quarter to three by the time we arrived at the restaurant in the hotel. The waiters were sullen and slapped down the plates. To make matters worse, Godfrey smelled something heavy and unpleasant, and we turned to see a vase of daisies by the cash register. We laughed about this and started drinking the wine. Godfrey quickly grew cranky waiting for our food. A downpour started outside and we sat watching the people scurry for cover. Before dessert, suddenly, all the lights went out. The waiter calmly reached for a kerosene lamp and lit it. Temporary blackouts were apparently common in Rome: this was the third since my arrival. They lasted only a few minutes but the downpour might last another hour.

Two tables away, two American girls were drinking mineral water and complaining about how much their feet hurt. I wondered whether they ever had any fun: they looked so plodding and dull. One of them looked especially pitiable: pink, rubbery face, fat arms, wispy hair. Godfrey said he also found them pretty pathetic. "We know how to live, don't we?" he said, patting the top of my hand.

I smiled back, realizing it really did take one to know one, and although I had proof of this fact nearly every day, it always amazed me when it happened.

The pasta arrived, warm and bland, and Godfrey ate purposefully for several minutes.

He ordered another bottle of wine. Then the antipasto occupied Godfrey for

10

the next few minutes: he said he loved the cold cuts and olives. The wine made me expansive and detached. He told me the reason he was in the movie at all was because American filmmakers had cast him in some comedies that made money, none of which, I had to admit, I had ever seen. "They have a motto in Hollywood now," he said, "'write Yiddish, cast British.' Now I'm well-off enough to take one of these pictures every once in a while."

"These pictures" were the weird ones that no one in America would probably ever see but that would add to his status as an internationally acclaimed "artist."

"I heard there were other reasons you've done well in Hollywood," I dared to venture, now that the wine had gone to my head.

In gay circles in Hollywood, Godfrey was "the new catch of the day" a decade ago. The legendary proportions of his prick were noted time and time again. Some had said that he had to have it strapped down to the side of his leg so that it didn't show in some of the costume pictures in which he appeared. Some said that he wore a metal cup to keep his perpetual hard-on in place. It was rumored that, while he had abundant sex with women, usually to further his career in some way, it was boys he lusted for.

"I didn't know you cared." Godfrey smiled, then patted my hand, which was nervously tapping on the table.

"I don't. I mean, I do," I blubbered, "it's just, well, interesting "

"You fascinate me so, you know."

"I do?"

His hand covered mine now, as if he were attempting to hold it, right there in the restaurant. "Oh, it's no secret I didn't agree with Carlo. I didn't think you were right for the part. I would have preferred an Italian boy, but now I'm convinced. An American in Rome. What could be more decadent?"

With my free hand, I gulped down the rest of my wine.

"Why don't we go upstairs and rehearse?" he suggested.

"Rehearse?"

"Rehearse our love scene, dear boy. You know, you will be called upon to kiss me."

I hadn't forgotten that part, certainly. My agent told me that would end my career. I had my misgivings about it, but now, with a chance to rehearse it, I was warming to the idea.

"You certainly can play rough trade," Godfrey said, pouring me another glass of wine, which I certainly didn't need, in his room, which was three times the size of mine and with a grand view of the Rome skyline.

"Oh?" I sighed, taking the wine glass from him. I had never considered myself rough, or trade. I was simply gay. "Well, thanks. That's a real compliment coming from you. I think you and I understand each other." Looking at that bright, mobile face, which seemed to be growing younger by the minute, I sighed again.

"Sit here," he said, patting the cushion beside him on the couch.

11

"No," I countered. "That's too far to walk in my condition. I'll just sit...here." I dropped to the bed, spilling wine on the spread.

"Very well. I'll just sit here and admire you."

"Likewise." I sipped my wine, but decided enough was enough and set the glass on the floor. I struck a pose and stared at him, right at his crotch.

He snickered. "You are quite handsome, dear boy, in a rough sort of way. Perfect for the role."

"I'm getting sleepy. I suppose if we don't start rehearsing soon I'll fall asleep." I stretched my legs in front of me, displaying that I had, despite the booze, sprung a boner.

"I can see you're ready to start rehearsing, all right. I have problems in that regard. Takes a lot to get me going."

So, the rumors of a perpetual hard-on were false; I wondered what else was myth. "Oh, well, we're only going to rehearse a kiss. Just a kiss."

He stood up, obviously less affected by the wine than I, and stepped over to the bed. I expected him to just stand there, letting me indulge myself, investigating just how true the rumors were. But, no, he stunned me by dropping between my legs, tipping the wine over onto the carpet. He ran his hands up my thighs and started rubbing my bulge. I leaned back on my elbows and watched him in silence.

"Trade-y, very trade-y," he said. "Perfect."

As much as I wanted to be anything other than trade at that moment, I knew I needed to feel someone's mouth on my swollen prick. I had never been hornier, of that I was sure.

My fingers softly guided Godfrey's roving hand to my zipper. In the smoky light, I could see those dazzling green orbs searching my own, an unspoken agreement passing between us. We both smiled that we knew what we wanted, but Godfrey was determined to have his first. Godfrey's fingertips were dancing lightly until I began pressing into him. Godfrey kissed the bulge through the fabric. I began gyrating my ass. Soft moans began escaping my parted lips; my eyes fluttered and clamped shut. His teasing fingers finally slipped beneath the shorts and were met with a cock oozing pre-cum. With his free hand, he tugged my shirt up, and inhaled deeply. "God, you are gorgeous," he said, and then his mouth tackled my nipples voraciously, his fingers stroking my prick. The intensity of my sudden spasms surprised Godfrey, so that he had to steady himself to keep from being knocked off balance. He stroked the cock, intermittently kissing it, as the spasming subsided. He wiped the excess cum from his mouth and laid his head on my thigh.

"I want to suck you, Godfrey," I whispered, gently pushing him away. But I was met with a brief flash of temper. "No, no. It's okay," he whispered, caressing my cock with a tenderness expected of a more familiar lover. "I love your cock, dear boy."

I smiled in the semi-darkness, feeling that, at least for a few minutes, there was someone who cared only about my pleasure. Still, I couldn't hide my

12

disappointment. "Okay," I said, "if that's the way it is. I guess the rehearsal is over."

"Yes," he said, leaning back against the bed while I pulled up my pants. "But that was just a rehearsal."

Confused, feeling a bit betrayed, I muttered my thanks for everything he had done, knowing that words somehow weren't enough, and hurried to my own room.

- - -

If I had even considered having an "affair" with Godfrey, such notions were dispelled quickly. He never seemed to take anyone seriously after he had made his initial and usually successful effort to charm them. He mocked the world, but most of all he mocked himself. He had no enemies and no intimates. He existed only to please himself.

Then, suddenly, a youth from America arrived to "visit" Godfrey. My humor upon hearing this was not improved by seeing Gilbert, looking outrageously young and almost flamboyantly gay in a green velvet jacket, at the restaurant that evening. Gilbert went to buy Godfrey some cigars, giving Godfrey a chance to impress me with the boy's attributes.

"Oh, Gilbert's such fun at parties," Godfrey said. "He's not always talking about how hard he works, like the other boys. He despises drudgery." He smiled coyly. "Isn't he fantastic?" Even in the gentle haze that the wine had created, I could sense Gilbert's undeniable appeal if young blonds were your thing. They had never been mine, and I doubted they could be. Still, he was cute, I had to admit.

"What *is* his work, exactly?" I asked.

"He's a poet. He has been published."

"Poet or no poet, isn't he a bit young?"

"It's not only a question of age, dear boy." After a tense, stiff little pause he continued, but in a more relaxed tone. "He's insatiable."

Sometimes it seemed as if Godfrey wasn't pursuing men or women at all, but the elusive orgasm, and that if he ever found the person who could release him he'd never, never, never leave. Godfrey went on, his long, strong fingers massaging my genitals under the table. They were firm and gentle fingers, daring and frightening. Over and over, I had pictured Godfrey on his knees between my thighs, sucking, sucking, until my cock ached, and I coming in his mouth. Now I pictured him between Gilbert's knees, doing the same. How could it be that the guy with the legendary endowment couldn't get off, that his greatest joy was getting others off? As the king said in my favorite musical, it was a puzzlement.

Later, in Godfrey's room, they descended on me, running their tongues over my sensitized skin.

13

Their shirts were off by then. Gilbert had his pants unzipped and they had begun to slip down his legs, making him look slightly ludicrous. Godfrey was the most dressed, the most composed of the three of us. His pants were still closed; his belt was even yet to be undone. How like him, I thought. It kept him in control to the last. I reached for his belt buckle and loosened it in two swift movements. Then I opened the fly of his slacks, pulling them down to his knees so that he too looked totally absurd. I laughed at the sight of the two of them. Retaliation was immediate. They went at me as if I were a rag doll, pulling and tugging. I began to fear I'd be dragged about the room, but their actions weren't violent or hostile just silly, yet incredibly sexy. They halted their mock attack of me long enough to remove their dangling trousers. They were free now. Wearing only their briefs, they renewed their attack on my body. Godfrey, the larger and stronger of the two, lifted me up under the arms, swinging me off the ground, while Gilbert pulled off my briefs. Godfrey returned me to my feet. I stood there as they circled me. "Isn't he gorgeous?" Godfrey said, just within reach, twisting my right nipple.

"Yes," said Gilbert, as he moved in just a little closer and brushed the inside of my leg. "I think I like this best of all," said Gilbert with a glancing touch to my cock, which was now fully erect. Around and around they went, coming just a fraction of an inch nearer with each rotation, commenting on my body as if it were a thing independent of personality, touching me just barely, but with increasing intimacy. I stood motionless, getting off on all this adulation.

Then Gilbert was in front of me, Godfrey behind. Gilbert caressed my inner thighs with his hands, then started sucking my cock. Godfrey massaged, then started kneading my buttocks, as if they were two rounded loaves of bread he couldn't wait to bake, then consume. I gasped as Gilbert worked on my cock, barely able to stand under the assault. They stopped only long enough to remove their own briefs. Then they lifted me into the air like a sacrificial virgin ready to be flung into a volcano. They laid me onto the bed, surrounding me on either side. Hands, lips, tongues touched me everywhere. And then they began going from me to each other. Reaching across my prone body they embraced, kissed, deeper, deeper, their mouths locked together. I was fascinated. Repulsed. Aroused. Even jealous.

They separated, their hands reaching for the other's penis, fondling, stroking. I couldn't tear my eyes away from the sight of their cocks. Gilbert's cock was cut, smaller than mine, and stiff. Godfrey's cock was very long, even though it was only semi-flaccid, and his foreskin covered the cock head completely. Then, as if set off by some internal signal, Gilbert climbed on top of me. Just as quickly, Godfrey crawled behind and mounted him. Gilbert began sucking me and suddenly groaned at the violation of his ass as Godfrey began jamming his not-quite-fully hard prick into him, but the expression on his face was one of ecstasy, and then Gilbert returned to the expert sucking of my cock.

I was overcome with the need to be fucked as Gilbert was being fucked. I spread my thighs and begged Gilbert to do it. "Oh, yes," he said, and went to

14

work on my asshole with his mouth before inserting his prick.

Soon I was engulfed, crushed by the weight of the two of them. I was also excited beyond anything I could ever have imagined. Our bodies moved as one entity, thrusting, undulating. Gilbert plunged into me with piston-like regularity in response to Godfrey's motion, which was not sustained for long. Godfrey drew back and the pressure eased in Gilbert's anus. I was sure it must have been painful for him, but he uttered no complaint during it. Now he concentrated on fucking me. He pounded harder into me while he jerked my cock. It was so grand there was no way to prolong my orgasm. When Gilbert realized what was happening, he came as well, filling me with his cum.

We separated wordlessly, and Gilbert went to the bathroom while Godfrey climbed between my thighs.

I was happy to be alone with the actor, to at last examine the fabled cock up close. I noticed a thick vein that trailed down along the shaft of his big meat, branching out as it meandered into his spicy foreskin. I started nibbling his overhang, rubbing it against my lips and digging inside it with my tongue.

His balls filled his bag like a couple of lemons, the left one hanging higher than the right. I glanced down at my own crotch and saw my cock was beginning to point high in the air once more. I started pumping his cock. I focused all my attention on pleasing this man. Sweat was running down his sleek, nearly hairless body, and I rubbed it into the skin while I took the long cock into my mouth. I was unable to look him in the eye, feeling a certain shame for what I was doing to this man I had been working with on the set every day. As I continued to suck him, my shame lessened, as the urge to make him come became overwhelming. My prick surged, I gasped, and my ass cheeks flexed. I really wanted him to come up my ass.

Just then, Gilbert returned. "Oh, yeah clean it up, pretty boy, clean it good. After he's fucked me, he's filthy." I glared over at him, then up at Godfrey. He was looking at me intently. "You want it up your ass," Godfrey said. "That's what you want, isn't it?"

"Oh, yes." I watched in amazement as his big dick started to swell and twitch, slowly rising up from between his thighs like old-growth timber. Now that it was fully erect, it looked about a foot long. The knob on the end kept swelling up bigger and bigger till it popped out of his foreskin, gleaming in the soft light.

Gilbert snickered, "Yeah, give it to him good. Finish what I started."

"I think you'd like it better on your belly," Godfrey said, rolling me over. Then he straddled me, planted his hands on either side of my head, and started rubbing the cock head along my crack. He grunted when his thick prong popped through my ass ring. His stabbing thrusts hurt at first, then began to give way to ecstasy as his balls began bouncing off my sweaty cheeks. I moved back against him, savoring the heat and the incredible size of him. I could hardly believe that Godfrey was finally fucking me, but the evidence was impossible to deny.

Gilbert moved to the bed and was crouching beside us, watching Godfrey go to town over me. I reached up and wrapped my fingers around the pulsing shaft

of his cock, and gave it a squeeze. I kissed the head of his prick. I took a deep breath and leaned into him, opening my throat and taking him in down to his pubic hair. His hairless thighs tensed, and he tangled his fingers in my hair. I breathed in his freshlyshowered scent. After I'd licked every inch of his cute little cock, I grabbed his dangling balls.

"I don't know if I can take much more of this, boys," Godfrey said.

"Let him have it," Gilbert said, shoving my mouth over his cock.

And, of course, Godfrey did let me have it with gusto.

Each of us fell into a deep sleep that didn't end until nearly noon the next day. Always one to insist on the last word, Godfrey woke me while Gilbert remained asleep. Despite my sleepy protests, he insisted on fellating me, and wouldn't give up until I ejaculated in his mouth.

How quickly extraordinary things became the norm. Our little menage a trois continued for the duration of the filming, each time becoming a little less interesting than the last for me, anyway. Our configurations varied only slightly from that of the first night. The preliminaries became increasingly predictable. At the end, I was glad it was over, because of the knowledge that they were far more enchanted with each other than they were with me.

Yet, as I was preparing to leave for California, the shooting having wrapped, Gilbert came to my room while Godfrey was at the studio filming all day. I could tell he wanted one last fuck. I put up no resistance as he dragged his mouth downward. There was no need for him to tell me what he wanted. I knew. He tugged at the waistband of my briefs. He pressed his cheek against the nylon. I wanted to be sucked, and he, as usual, was tenacious. I pushed at his head as he pulled the briefs down, tantalizing himself as he slowly uncovered more skin. I lifted my ass to make the removal of the briefs easier. He pulled them off, and I suddenly felt so bare, so decadent with someone else's lover about to suck my cock.

I lifted my knees, opened my thighs wide, then hooked one leg around him to draw him in. He bent to it, as I moaned with pleasure. Soon I had both legs hooked around his back, my thighs wide apart, my cock completely available to his hungry mouth. Before long he was stroking his tongue up and down, around the head. I whipped his cheeks with my erection, and then he started to suck it. His desire was intense, suffocating, relentless. I couldn't take too much of it, and I pulled at his hair. He raised his head. My heart beat wildly as I watched him take hold of my erection with his hands and give me a coy look. "Fuck me," he begged.

How could I refuse?

I backed away, made room for him to get on the bed on his belly. Now his lovely round buttocks were visible. My pulse raced and my cock throbbed as I took in the beauty of his ass again. With a groan of desperate excitement, I lowered my face to run my mouth over the curve of a springy buttock. He whimpered, responding with a gentle wiggle of his hips.

16

I treated the boy's ass with reverence. I so envied Godfrey this ass. The skin was like ivory, the flesh beneath it both firm and resilient, smooth and soft and warm. I knew how much Godfrey must have enjoyed having this around all the time. I manipulated both buttocks with my hands, and he responded as I raised him up, nuzzled in the crack. Using both hands, I opened his ass, pulled it apart, and buried my face in it, licking, tonguing. With a groan, he arched his ass upward another few inches. His knees slid farther apart, his ass gently rolling. My mind was in a whirl. Below the split between the two buttocks, his balls and cock were begging for attention. "Fuck me," he begged.

I became the substitute lover commanded, and heat seemed to radiate from the two globes. For a brief moment, I felt an urge to rebel against Gilbert's desperate need to be serviced, to be unfaithful to his lover. But then he bumped his ass upward and I couldn't resist it; I went back to tongue-fucking, probing vigorously and then relaxing to a mere delicate fluttering at the entrance.

Finally, I could stand it no longer. I rolled him over, and slammed into him as quickly as I could, pushing it. As my cock slid in all the way, I thought that now he belonged to me, at least for a while, anyway. I felt terribly slutty, yet the feeling was wonderful, my body keyed up to a high pitch of anticipation. I began kissing him again, slowly, a romantic pecking, kissing and licking his mouth, then fluttering my tongue down between his nipples, over the rib cage and into his navel.

He moaned, "God, I just love getting fucked. I can never get enough." And he came, quite suddenly, jerking his cock with his fingers, the cum running everywhere. We kissed after that, his ass gripping my cock till I came as well, my body shaking, the cries coming out of my throat as I kept the cock moving as long as I could.

I leaned over and kissed Gilbert on the cheek, and his eyes were as embracing as his smile.

"I think you're special, Gilbert. Really special. I wish I could have gotten to know you better."

He swallowed. "Ha! How much better could you know me?" "We'll see whenever you get back to the States."

"I'll look forward to that," he said, and I didn't try to hide my desire. I loved getting dirty like this with this beauty. How different Rome was for me this time, so different than I had ever imagined: I came looking for Italians, big, uncut, with raging hormones, and I ended up with a blond American who was my co-star's kept boy!

His fingers moving slowly, he pushed against me, gripped my cock, holding it in him.

"Just a little more, please."

So, of course, I gave him what he wanted.

THE LASCIVIOUS LIFEGUARDS
by John Patrick

I was above them all from my stand, where my eyes scanned the beach like a beacon. I could see the old man who had had a heart attack and walked with small weights in his hands, up and down the shoreline, every day. And the girls, who never seemed to tire of buying me Cokes and potato chips. And there was Brett.

All summer long, when he could sneak away, Brett came and sat at the base of my lifeguard stand and talked about the old days. Brett had been my teacher for Red Cross training and taught me what I know about riptides and undertows and sudden changes on the surface of the sea. I wanted him to teach me other things, too, but he avoided ever being alone with me. I felt a connection, but thought it was just because I wanted him so badly.

He was only twenty-six that summer when I became a lifeguard, but he used to say, as bronzed girls handed me Cokes or asked if I needed more oil on my back, "Man, you don't know what it is. You don't know what you've got." He'd always say it in the same way, so finally one day I said to him, "What is it, Brett? What've I got?"

He extended his arms as if to encompass the beach. "You've got all this. It's yours."

I laughed, not understanding what he meant. "You know," he went on, "I've got this bitch of a wife, this shit job, working for my father at the damn paint factory, and I think to myself how I wish I were anywhere else doing anything else, but what can I do?"

Just then one of my girlfriends, Cindy, appeared, with a hot dog for me with everything on it, one I hadn't even asked for, and she handed it up. Then Peggy strutted by in a bikini, and Brett whistled between his teeth. "You don't know," he said, "just how lucky you are."

I was beginning to. In fact, I felt luckier just then than I ever had in my life. I loved my body that summer. I loved its firmness and its bronzed skin. But mostly I loved the way it was admired. Girls I didn't know would come up and talk to me. I loved to stroll the beach among the girls who wanted to have me, but, more than anything, I loved how Brett looked at my body, and told me how lucky I was."

The most difficult part of lifeguarding was just sitting on my ass in my chair. Your eyes should be set on the sea. You watch for nothing, really, and sometimes you begin to see things. And then I would see things that aren't there at all. Lifeguard mirages, Brett said, and they happen to anyone who looks at one thing too long. But at times it was hard for me to keep looking out, and so I looked forward to Brett's visits. I was happy the girls admired me, wanted me to fuck them, or at least take them out, and I did take many of them out. But I knew

I was gay from birth and it was Brett I wanted. Brett was what I had wanted from the moment I laid eyes on him. He was "the lifeguard" as far as I was concerned. He was a dead ringer for Sam Elliot in that old movie about an aging lifeguard, and he always chuckled when I talked about that movie.

Near the end of summer, on a day of particular calm, a Saturday when a gentle southwest wind blew, when the waves hardly lapped and it was almost hypnotic for me to keep my eyes fixed on the sea. Brett stood beneath my lifeguard stand that afternoon. He stood there and said, "You know what, man, I've been thinking. I could do something else with my life. I mean, I could go to night school, get my teaching degree, become a coach."

"You'd be a great coach."

"That's just what I've been thinking. I've been thinking about it a lot."

Cindy came by with a Coke; Brett winked and drifted away. "Catch you later," he said, and he went back to his towel not far away.

I didn't have to look; I could feel his eyes on me as Cindy kept reaching up for me, and I pretended to pull her up to my stand.

Later, as the sun was low in the sky, Brett came over and said good-bye. He said he had to go home and fix his own dinner. "The bitch has gone to her mother's for the weekend. Thank god I didn't have to go. I think I'll get drunk tonight, kid." He stood before me, tall against the summer-gray sky. My sex god, glistening. He was taunting me now, for the first time. It was as if he was saying, hey, time is running out, kid, you'd better make your move. But I just told him I'd see him soon.

That night I dreamt of Brett, drunk or not, fucking me. It was so violent a fuck that it woke me from my sleep, leaving me sweaty, the sheets twisted around me. I threw the window open, and my mother, who never slept well in the big bed after my father died, shouted, "Are you all right? Is anything wrong?"

"Yeah," I replied. But there was something wrong. I kept thinking about Brett, at home, alone. I went downstairs. I sat in my father's old chair in the darkened den until I knew what I wanted to do, what I had to do. I found the address in the phone book. Then I got on my bike and pedaled along the ocean road until I was a block short of his house. I still wasn't sure if I could go through with this.

The breeze was kicking up off the ocean, and I knew a storm was coming, so I made up my mind and hurried along the beach, then turned down the street until I reached the house where Brett lived. The lights were on upstairs, but I stood for a long time on the porch. Then I knocked on the door, softly at first, then louder.

"Yeah?" he said, his voice warm like a breeze.

"It's me," I said.

He slowly opened the door, only partially at first. He looked at me oddly, as if he couldn't believe it was me. "You look like shit," he said.

"I couldn't sleep. I had a dream. A dream about you."

I don't know how long I stood there like that before he smiled and reached for

20

me, pulled me to him, wrapped his arms around mine. He smelled of shampoo and oils, not the salt and sand I'd expected. It was the first time I felt what it was supposed to feel like to be in the arms of another man, not the girls whose breath steamed my car when I got the nerve to take them out.

But then he let me go. "You'd better go, kid."

I grabbed at him, trying to hold on. But without a word he went inside.

"Wait," I said, "come back."

"No, kid. We can't do this. Really."

I knew I would never want anyone or anything as much as I wanted Brett right then, and I found myself becoming angry as he released me back into the real world.

He closed the door and I stood there, my eyes tearing. I pounded on the door, "Please," I said desperately.

At last he opened the door again.

"Okay," he said.

And there we were, standing in the darkness, in the silence of the house he shared with his wife. "Look, I've never had anyone here before. It's kinda scary."

"It's scary for me, too."

"I know."

"I've wanted this for so long."

"Me, too. But...."

I could smell beer on Brett's breath as he rubbed against me, his tongue seeking to unravel me completely. My breath came quickly and my cock throbbed without even being touched.

Brett lifted my tank top over my head and tossed it on the floor. Then he drew my nipples into his mouth one by one, urging them alive. He ground his face from tit to tit, biting softly on my nipples with his teeth. He opened my thighs and maneuvered one knee between them. Breathlessly, I rode it. He pulled away from me and fell to his knees. I noticed that my erect cock had left a dark wet spot on my shorts, and it made me feel embarrassed that he could see the power he had over me.

As he unfastened the zipper of my shorts, they fell to the carpet like a discarded flower. Suddenly exposed to the air, my cock felt both hot and cold at the same time. It stood out proudly, defiantly. It was soon covered by his mouth.

He sucked it hard, looking up at me with those wicked, dark eyes. I was swooning with the mere thought that I had Brett on his knees in front of me, licking my cock as though his life depended on it. That alone was enough to send me plunging over the edge, but I held it in.

When I could take no more, I pushed him away and drew him up into my arms. My pre-cum tasted sweet on Brett's lips. I kissed him, simultaneously releasing from his BVDs the most perfectly formed cock I'd ever seen. Smooth, slick, mushroom-headed. At the base, a hairy, heavy sac. I buried my nose in his pubes, and his hips bucked uncontrollably as I slid my mouth up and down

21

along the shaft. I swirled my tongue around the head, flicking the dew of pre-cum from the tip. Then I took his balls into my mouth and pursed my lips around them. Every time I felt his body surging, I stopped. When this became too much for him, Brett scooped me into his arms and eased me onto the carpet. It felt rough against my skin. I lay on my back, legs spread, my ass throbbed in anticipation.

Wordlessly he turned me onto my hands and knees. "It'll be easier this way," Brett said. He kissed my shoulders, my neck. "Stay here, just like this." He stepped into the kitchen and returned with a bottle of hand lotion. He smeared it all over his cock, then squeezed some into my crack.

He slid a finger in and wiggled it around. "Scared?" Brett asked.

"No," I gasped.

"I think you're terrified. I can feel it in your ass." It was true I was terrified. I was being finger-fucked by Brett.

But fear aroused me: the unanswered questions, the shreds of doubt. My breath came in ragged chokes. I was helpless. I wasn't responsible for my actions.

"Yeah," he said as I began to relax, pushing my ass back onto his fist.

"It feels good," I moaned weakly.

He pulled out his fingers and soon replaced them with the head of his cock. Slowly he shoved it in. I bit my lip as inch after inch went in me until there was no more left. The pain lasted only a few moments. He was gentle with me, slowly sliding his cock in and out.

When Brett bit the back of my neck, I could feel him smiling.

As he rocked from hip to hip, swirling into my ass, goose bumps covered my flesh. My hungry body clung to every inch of his cock. Lightning flashed in the sky, followed by a distant explosion of thunder.

I groaned.

"Do you want me to stop?" he asked.

"No," I told him. "I like it."

Brett held onto my ass cheeks and pumped. Sweat dampened my face. Thunder boomed, closer this time. Brett wedged his dick deep in me, as far as it could go, and left it there for a few moments. One hand pinched my nipples, while the other massaged my swollen cock. Lightning flashed again and I started to spasm. Just as I began coming, Brett started to slam into me. He, too, was caught up in the moment.

I bowed my head and began to climax strongly, battered by sensations, sounds and emotions.

I screamed my orgasm into the night. Seconds later, I felt the knob of Brett's cock swelling inside me, and knew he was spewing his cum into me.

Finished, we lay there silent, motionless, for a few moments. His cock plopped from my anus, and just then, thunder boomed again and broke the magic.

Stumbling into the bathroom, we turned on the jets in the shower until the

22

water was warm. We jumped into the shower, rubbing warmth into each other's flesh. It was odd; we didn't speak, really, just smiled and scrubbed each other. Then Brett turned off the shower and pushed me out. When we stepped out onto the cold tiles, he grabbed a towel, got down on his knees and dried my legs, my feet. He worked his way up to my cock. He looked into my eyes as he slowly sucked my cock into his mouth....

Years have passed since that first night with Brett, and I am old now but the memory of it never fails to arouse me. I know two things: I never enjoyed getting fucked more, and I have never looked at another lifeguard in quite the same way again.

THE BEAUTIFUL AND THE BETRAYED
by John Patrick

The taxi pulled up to the hotel, a huge, early nineteenth-century palace, built in colonial British style. The architect had obviously been influenced by the white palaces of the Raj.

Tom, hit by the humidity as he climbed out of the air conditioned cab, asked the elderly black driver to take his bags up to the desk, then leaned against the car, his Panama hat firmly down on his head. He lit a cigarette. He'd given up smoking a year ago because his doctor had asked him to, but this was his fifth cigarette since last night. Nervous about this quickly arranged getaway, he sucked on his cigarette gratefully.

Suddenly, a tourist bus pulled up beside Tom. An odd group disembarked: Japanese, mainly middle-aged and nervous; laughing Americans, from the Midwest, Tom guessed; a group of giggly English schoolgirls; and one lone young man. He was so stunning a young man that he took Tom's breath away. He dropped his cigarette to the ground as the boy turned and looked at him. Tom stared; he couldn't help it. There was something vulnerable about the lad's persona that attracted him. He was small with dark hair, and his fragility created a grace about him. And he was alone. Tom carefully projected the more handsome side of his face as the youth walked past, pulling at his suitcase. The boy ignored Tom. This disaffection plunged Tom into a further depression. He wasn't used to being ignored. The cab driver whistled to get his attention, irritating him further. The days of respect for one's customers were definitely on the decline.

Tom entered the hotel. The foyer was spacious and cool. Ornate, with high marble ceilings, it had an atrium in the center, around which the building had been designed. His suitcase sat by the desk. The concierge, an extremely handsome young man of mixed blood, was busy chatting flirtatiously with the beautiful youth, his rucksack plunked unceremoniously on top of the desk. If Tom hadn't seen the youth first, he would have found the older fellow more captivating. He was tall, with brown skin and, Tom noted bitterly, unusual green eyes for a mulatto. The concierge said something that made the boy break into laughter.

The room clerk extended his consonants in the attractive Caribbean way, pushing himself forward as if to display to the youth his obvious masculinity. Tom couldn't help noticing the lush growth of thick brown hair on the boy's head. With a pang of jealousy he was reminded of his own thinning pate.

"Any chance of some service here?" Tom hated the sound of his own rudeness but he couldn't help himself.

"I'll just finish with the boy, sir." As the room clerk handed a key to the lad, Tom noted his unusually large hands. Probably hung like a horse, Tom mused

bitterly. Tom thought he was equipped with an average-size penis and always envied those with big dicks. Seeing these two, Tom felt suddenly old. Doubt about his proficiency as a lover crept in slowly through all the other doubts.

"Room seven, it's a lucky number," the room clerk said to the boy, with a broad suggestive smile. The boy smiled back.

Tom thought it was about time to intervene. "Tom Smythe." He leaned back, hoping that the boy would turn around, acknowledging his presence, but he just walked off.

"Yes, Mr. Smith," the room clerk said. "Sorry to keep you waiting."

"No, it's Smythe. With a 'y' and an 'e'."

"Of course." The man's charm, Tom saw, extended to older men as well. As Tom signed the register, the clerk got his key.

"Room twelve," the clerk said, handing the gold key to Tom, "the presidential suite. Our very best, Mr. Smythe."

"Well, thank you," Tom said.

While he always had a suite when his publisher was paying the bill, on his own Tom was normally frugal, but his agent had been able to arrange a deal with the hotel chain for him so that he would "enjoy" his vacation.

When Tom saw the accommodations he silently thanked his agent: The bedroom was magnificent large with a huge four-poster bed hung with silk. It was mock antique, elegant but comfortable. Beside the bed sat a small table, along with phone, fax and remote control for the huge video screen sitting opposite. Tom moved over to the small bar fridge and opened it. It was stacked with strawberries and mangoes, his favorite fruit, ones he always requested when we was on a promotional tour. For the first time in forty-eight hours he smiled. He reclined on the bed, realizing that the silk doubled as a mosquito net. The sound of children playing in the distance drifted in through the huge bay window, along with splashes from the pool below.

Tom closed his eyes for a second, only to be confronted yet again by the sight of the boy from the tour bus. Then the room clerk. Then the two of them, fucking. But not just fucking; with them it would be fucking with gay abandon. The black over the white, naturally, impaling him with his huge dick. Then Tom pictured Joey, back in Chicago, with his new lover, also a black man. Oh, god, it was too disgusting. Joey storming out of the apartment, shouting epithets. But how was Tom supposed to react? Sexual betrayal is one thing, but in your own domain? Joey must have known what the consequences would be. But he allowed the black to fuck him in their bed anyway, and Tom just happened to return at the wrong moment. Or was it the right moment? "Get out! Get out!" Tom screamed at Joey. And Joey did.

Tom needed this vacation. He needed to clear his head. Start afresh. And who should he see on his first day but a young beauty who reminded him of Joey, flirting with a black man? It was all too disgusting!

He opened his eyes and grabbed the remote control for the television. He pressed it and CNN flashed on; images of an earthquake intercut with footage of

the minister pleading for more aid flickered silently across the screen. He switched it off, and reached into the small bedside cupboard, pulling out the brochure found in all hotels, the one starting with Swedish masseurs and finishing with high-class escorts. Even on this small island they'd managed to create a flourishing industry judging from the quality of the paper. Most of the prostitutes were black and beautiful. He thumbed through the photos with their accompanying descriptions in German, French and Japanese. He had considered hiring one of these woman several times in the past, just as a novelty. But, no, he didn't need that now. He needed romance. Oh, occasionally, when stress had reached an intolerable level, he'd hired a boy to suck or suck him off; it had been good, but the perfunctory nature of sex without emotion held no charm except physical relief for him. What he craved now was romance. He wanted to have an affair. With the boy on the bus. Yes, he thought, that would bring him out of his depression.

He reached over and phoned down to the desk. There were no messages. None. His mind wandered back to Joey. He had actually been hoping Joey had called and left a message: "Return immediately." Ha! Fat chance of that, he laughed. What really disturbed him, a fact that kept tugging at him, was the extreme virility of the black man Joey had chosen to seduce. Perhaps he was really too old for Joey. More than anyone, Tom knew the incredible power of sexual potency. He just hadn't been able to satisfy his young lover. It was just that simple. He ran his hand across his forehead. There were permanent furrows on his brow. His jawline, once referred to as having the classical edge of an Eastern European prince, was now definitely jowly. And then there was the question of his belly. Although a fairly decent tennis player, he didn't get enough exercise. Perhaps if he promised to diet, to spend more time in Chicago....

Night had fallen and a chorus of crickets had started up, punctuated by the occasional tree frog. He went to the window. It smelled balmy outside. The scent of the sea was just discernible under the scent of frangipani and orange blossom. None of this cheered him up; if anything it fed his melancholia, the nostalgia that lay embedded under the incredible anger of being betrayed. He was too old for this kind of thing. With that thought, he slammed the window shut and went in to have a shower. It was bedtime for this novelist from Chicago.

Later, washed and in his favorite blue silk pajamas, he pulled back the spread and got into bed. It was too hot for blankets. He contemplated leaving the fan on, but decided that he wouldn't be able to sleep with the noise. He switched the fan off with the remote and lay flat on the bed, the sheet pulled high up over his ears. After a moment his hand crept down to his cock, softly curled against his thigh. Comforting, a friend that had accompanied him over a long, hard journey. When erect it was the most unwrinkled thing about him. Normally he was proud of this fact, and had often used it as a pick-up line. Tonight the thought depressed him. Joey's black man was so huge, he had evidence of that as the

man pulled out of Joey and ran into the bathroom. He was convinced that was what Joey had secretly craved. Big, thick cocks.

He felt vulnerable and protective of his own now, cradled in his palm. He'd always thought his was of respectable dimensions. He stroked himself thinking about Joey sucking on it. He wanted to feel Joey's lips caressing the base of his cock in fthe renzied way he had, begging him to come. Ah, Joey, a totally instinctive lad who was able to orchestrate the small strokes, the quick bites and gentle sucking perfectly. Tom stiffened. Then the image of Joey, not sucking but on his stomach in their love-bed with the black over him suddenly loomed up, a jarring note that instantly upset him. He tried to think back over the years, but he couldn't remember anyone complaining about his size, and he'd had over a hundred boys.

He turned restlessly in his bed, contemplating the sleeping pills he always had with him. A light came on in the room opposite, and for a moment Tom's bedroom became a shadow play of mysterious shapes. He sat up on one elbow, peering across. Just visible in the window opposite he could see the boy from the bus getting ready for bed. He stood for a second, his face even more beautiful in the flattering light; he was a vision in his boxer shorts. He had a good body, Tom thought. He wished to see it in the nude. The light went off and the boy was lost in the shadows.

In the middle of the night, he woke abruptly. His room was awash in light. The electric clock glowed one A.M. He went to the window and opened it. The lights were on across the court, in seven. He could not see anyone, but he could hear the unmistakable sounds of love-making. He leaned against the window, listening. The breeze blew the curtains in seven out the window. God, Tom reflected mournfully, it sounds like the time Joey and the black were having at it. As Tom walked down the corridor to the bedroom, the sounds intensified, becoming so incredibly loud they seemed to push out the walls of the bedroom and made them pulsate.

Then the image of the black man pulling out of Joey and running scared filled his mind. The hugeness of him. Like Joey, there was something about excess that has always appealed to Tom's satiated taste buds. When you're with a stud like that, he thought, it was as if you were surrounded by cock. There was no ambiguity, just sex in all its viscous glory.

A sudden scream that was almost a roar made the hair on his arms stand up. It was coming from room seven. It was not just an orgasm, it was a mega one. Could it be that the room clerk was in the room with the boy?

If only he had been able to hear Joey coming with his black lover, to see just what the black did to get a cry like that.

There was another shout, followed by a series of bumps as if the man was dragging the boy over to the bed, reducing Tom to further despair. How many orgasms can a boy achieve in one night? Maybe he just hadn't ever cared enough, been in love enough, to really consider the other guy's needs.

It was his generation, he reflected dourly. It wasn't until he was twenty-four

that he enjoyed sex without feeling guilty about it.

Now there came again a series of low-pitched grunts. Perhaps if Tom went to the lobby and cornered the black tomorrow morning he could get some advice from him? Tom had respect for technique, and considered craftsmen in any field to be masters in their own right. He wasn't above taking lessons. Lessons from a black stud. He began to stiffen. He noted with a certain amount of returning confidence that perhaps his cock wasn't all that small. Now, thinking about the black man fucking that boy has made him harder than he has been in months. He soon found himself in the middle of a fantasy involving this stud giving him lessons. At one point, he found the black staring at his cock. "Lesson one is how to extract as much pleasure from the male organ as is humanly possible."

Tom hated the stilted way all his characters sounded in his fantasies, but he never had the necessity to rewrite them since they existed only in his mind.

"It is a blunt instrument of torture, a tool of pleasure...." the black said as he reached out and stroked Tom's hard-on very gently. A glistening drop of dew appeared at the tip. Tom groaned; the black's practiced touches excited him greatly. Then Tom stroked the black's mammoth organ, which was at least four inches longer than his, and very thick. Tom's face became an exclamation of surprise at the softness of the velvety head of the monster.

"You can lick it; it won't bite." Shyly, Tom lowered his head. Eyes closed, Tom stuck out his tongue and ran it along the whole length of his throbbing organ. He looked up at the black, who was staring expectantly at him. Tom knew he wanted him to suck it, to show him how good a cocksucker he was.

Another groan came from across the court. Tom interrupted the fantasy and looked up, hoping to see the boy or the black. In so doing, he stopped himself from coming. Tom waited a few moments, but heard nothing more, saw nothing more. Tom closed his eyes and returned to the fantasy. Leaning backward on the bed, Tom began to whimper, then his whimpers turned to moans of pleasure as the black started to lube Tom's ass, then his cock. Looking down his body and across his own erection, blinding tightness built up in the back of his head, rolling as it gathered momentum, drawing pleasure from every pore in his body, as skilled fingers prepared his anus, then stroked his balls.

"You're very naughty," the black said, "a very naughty man."

Tom flushed, staring into his dark brown eyes and realizing that he knew how long he had waited for this moment. He'd never been forced to admit to it.

"If you were mine," he said, drawing out his words, lazily, "I'd fuck you every day." He spoke in an unbelievably calm voice, but his words made Tom shudder just the same.

"I'd fuck you wherever we were, simply bend you over the nearest chair, table, sofa, and slide right into your tight ass."

Tom stared, unbelieving. He didn't know this man, couldn't comprehend the fact that a stranger, a black man, was speaking so boldly with him.

"This is what you want, right, man?"

"Oh, god," Tom sighed. There weren't many words after that, because the

black was in Tom, quickly, the door to the bedroom wide open, the shades open as well.

"Oh, yes," the black hissed, slamming deeper inside Tom. "You like it."

"Yesss...!" a moan.

"You asked for this."

Each word was punctuated with a thrust, a slip-sliding thrust of the phenomenal phallus inside him, of the black's hips driving against Tom's. They were rocking the bed, forcing it forward and against the wall.

"Yes," Tom murmured. "I think about this all the time. But never...."

"From now on, then," the black said, "this is what you will want."

And then he pulled out and came all over Tom's chest.

Tom came, jacking himself. He came loudly, much louder than the black had.

Tom's eyes snapped open. The fantasy was over, the reality was at hand. Tom felt a pain in the pit of his stomach, and with a shout he came, ejaculating for real all over his fingers and the sheets. Balls aching, cock shriveling, he was jolted back to reality. Somewhere, as consciousness flooded back, it became the shouting and roaring of the boy across the court. He seemed to be finally coming. It was the most extraordinary orgasm Tom had ever heard. An impending and now overwhelming sense of inadequacy overtook him. He felt pathetic, an old man wanking over the prosaic fantasy of a size queen. He, Tom Smythe, successful, well-known author of historical fiction, reduced to this. He would never be a lover like the black next door, or the one Joey wanted. He would never be able to take a boy to those kinds of heights. Never again would he lie against his body after hearing that little whimper, the tender clutching at his cock Joey's orgasm. The scent of Joey, familiar, comforting, his and only his. Once upon a time. He wiped himself with the sheet and got up.

To his annoyance, he saw the room clerk, slim and extremely majestic in his muscularity, climb out of the youth's bed as the boy caught him with his naked arms, pressing him against his chest. They kissed. God, Tom thought, they looked beautiful together, and so vibrant in their youth. Coffee and cream. Tom smiled. He was right all along. He knew what was going on down at the front desk. No, Tom wasn't born yesterday. He knew his way around.

Down in the breakfast room he ordered fat-reduced yogurt and fruit, rejecting his usual black coffee and croissants. A waiter brought him copies of *The Times*, the *Guardian* and the *Observer*.

Tom flicked a grape off the table. He felt terrible. His eyes ached from too little sleep, and the overwhelming sense of loss still gnawed at his intestines. He badly wanted to talk to Joey. Joey was always so good the next day, soothing away his fears with a dismissal. Perhaps he should ring him up: "Forgive me, Joey, all is forgiven. I'm flying home tonight." But he couldn't he had lost face and that was unforgivable. The schoolgirls filed into the breakfast room, neat, with their school uniforms pressed crisp. As they walked past he tried smiling at an exceptionally beautiful girl, a vivacious brunette, but she was too busy

30

glancing shyly at a handsome black youth serving at the buffet. It was no good. Tom would have to resign himself to approaching old age and auction off what remained of his sexuality. A middle-aged woman sitting alone at a table opposite him glanced across and smiled at him. He averted his eyes, looking down at the papers.

At the desk, the room clerk was humming to himself. Something with a calypso beat. There was a certain smugness about him, the air of the conqueror, the recently laid, that irritated Tom greatly. "Any messages for me?" Tom asked him.

The room clerk smiled brightly at him. In his paranoia, Tom thought he detected a gleam of pity in the black's eyes.

"No, sorry, man. Expecting something from the wife, yes?"

"My agent actually," Tom replied curtly. If there was one thing Tom abhorred, it was being pitied.

"Have a good night, Mr. Smythe?" the room clerk inquired.

"No, I was kept up for most of it. The couple across the way, they were, well you know ... and one of them just couldn't stop screaming, shouting."

"Oh?" The room clerk had a broad grin on his face.

"You know very well...." He turned angrily away.

"Tonight," the black called after him. "Tonight I promise I will visit you."

Tom did not look back. He shook his head in dismay. He kept walking ahead, but, for the first time in two days he started to feel a little more optimistic.

A NIGHT WITH THE COACH
by Leo Cardini

"Coach Douglas!" Norm blurts out, nearly jumping out of his skin as we descend the back stairs of Chaps, bare-chested and sweaty from discoing our buns off at the Sunday tea dance.

Yes, there he is in the flesh, Coach Douglas, our high school gym teacher and football coach, dressed in a tight, white tank top and snug-fitting Levi 501 cutoffs. The outrageous mound of soft dick and big balls imprisoned against his right inner thigh fulfilled every juicy daydream I'd ever had of him when I was bored to tears in algebra class and needed something that would really stimulate my mind.

"I think under the circumstances you can call me Steve," he says to Norm with a wink, mobilizing the rugged features of that handsome, all-American face of his that always made me think of a shaving commercial.

"Yeah. Uh...hi, Steve."

By now we'd just stepped onto the dirt sidewalk that faces the back of the Boston Public Library. Steve surprises Norm by pulling him into an embrace, and Norm tenses up, which I guess makes sense, considering. I mean, how often is it you're taken by surprise outside a gay bar by your high school gym teacher? Especially when it's the first time you've ever been to a gay bar!

Oh not me. Norm. Hell, I've been sneaking into gay bars long before we graduated from high school last year.

Now, this is back in the spring of '77, when Norm and I still lived in the same neighborhood we grew up in, back in Jamaica Plain, which is actually part of Boston. Very working-class. Mainly Italian (like me), Irish, and Polish (like Norm). Everyone knew everyone else's business, which is maybe why it took Norm so long to come out of the closet.

"Uh...." Norm utters as he pulls away, blushing bright red that Steve would kiss him on the cheek right out in the open, "...remember Tony?"

Coach Douglas looks me up and down, and then lets his gaze linger on my crotch.

"Tony Bielli?" he asks, like he was interrogating my dick.

"Yeah. Hi, Steve."

"Well, I'd expect to see you coming out of a gay bar...." he says, finally addressing my face.

You see, all my life everyone's assumed I was gay. Truth to tell, I used to be a real sissy. But then in high school I started going to the Back Bay Health Club because I heard a lot of gays went there. Once I saw what went on in the Jacuzzi and in the steam room, and the type of guys who got the most action, I really got into developing my body. By the time I was a senior, older men in their forties down at Napoleon's Bar and I mean men with good taste and lots of culture

well, they were always saying I looked like this statue called Michaelangelo's David. Actually, I finally got to see a copy of it at this hairdresser's elegant townhouse in the South End. Frankly, my dick's bigger than his was.

"...but, Norm? Well, this is quite a surprise."

At a loss for words, Norm gives him one of his cute, dumbass smiles to die for that makes you realizes how boyishly handsome he is as Steve hungrily takes in inch by tantalizing inch of Norm's six-foot-two, broad-shouldered mass of muscular perfection. I watch Steve's eyes descend Norm's bare chest below his well-developed, nipple-crested pecs, following the thin trail of brown hair that crosses his rippled abdomen until it finally disappears behind those tight, faded blue jeans of his noticeably straining against the dimensions of that huge sausage stuffed inside.

"Yeah," he finally continues, his eyes glued to Norm's crotch. "Quite a surprise indeed!"

"Oh. Well, you see...what kinda happened is, uh...."

What Norm's not doing a very good job of explaining (he's not very bright; sometimes he even makes me look like an Einstein) is that until several weekends ago he was a complete virgin, hanging around with the same dumb jocks he hung out with in high school, drinking beer and talking about girls. But you could always tell he wasn't exactly like them.

Like he let his hair grow long. So now he's got this gorgeous mane of dark brown hair he parts in the middle that's always spilling over his forehead.

And for another thing, he even smoked grass with me. Which is how I got to suck his cock.

Yeah, I did! You see...but that's another story.

And then yesterday, he fucked me! But I suppose that's another story too.

I guess the point is, I don't care how stoned you get, you don't let another guy suck you off, and then three weeks later give into the urge to fuck him unless you at least think you might be gay.

Which Norm did get to thinking yesterday. And I could tell it was really bothering him. That's when he brought up working out with me at the Back Bay Health Club, which he knew from me was where a lot of gay guys went.

Well, it could've turned out better, because after our workout, when we're sitting together butt-naked in the steam room, in walks Mike Franzi, this hunk of a football jock we knew before his family moved away to Malden, and he tries to put the make on us. Well, to make a long story short, Norm nervously escapes to take a shower, and I try to explain Norm's sexual confusion to Mike.

"Oh, he's gay all right," Mike says, as sure as can be. "Believe me, I fucking grew up in locker rooms. You get to know these things. All he needs is a good shove out of the closet."

"And jocks are my specialty," he adds with a wide grin as he exits the steam room, heading for the showers. "Especially jocks with big dicks."

Well, before you know it, the three of us end up in the same shower stall, with Norm fucking Mike, while Mike fucks me. And then later, when we're all

34

getting dressed, Mike invites us to join him at Chaps for tea dance, tempting us with the promise of a big surprise that whetted our curiosity.

So that's how we ended up here, losing Mike about fifteen minutes back when he followed the kid he was cruising into the men's room in the hopes of making it with him in one of the stalls.

Well, before I can begin to explain any of this to Steve, there's Mike stepping out onto the back steps. He spots us instantly, dashes down the stairs, and surprises me and Norm by running right into Steve's arms, giving him a great big kiss, tongue and all.

Breaking their embrace and slapping Steve on the ass, Mike turns to us with, "This is the surprise I said I had for you guys. Steve and I are kinda like...well, somewhere between lovers and fuck buddies."

"Fuck buddies?" Norm asks me in a quiet aside.

But before I can explain, Mike continues with, "Isn't this wild, Steve? I ran into them over the Back Bay Health Club. And guess what?"

He holds out his hands, palm facing palm about a foot apart.

"Both of them."

"Hmm," Steve says with an interested smile. And then he switches to, "So what's it like inside?"

"So packed," Mike improvises, "you could get gang-banged at the bar while waiting to order a beer, and no one would notice."

"Shit! I hate it when it's that crowded."

"He's just saying that," Mike explains to us, with a teasing glance at Steve, "as an excuse to invite you guys over to smoke some grass and down a few beers."

"Well, why not?" Steve asks with an irresistibly eager gleam in his eyes

So I go "Okay!" and Norm mumbles a somewhat apprehensive, "Sure."

Well, the four of us stroll over to Steve's place, shortcutting behind the Prudential Center as we gossip and get the low-down on each other in constantly shifting twosomes, and I encourage Norm just to loosen up and go with the flow.

Once I see Steve's place it overlooks The Fens I recognize it immediately. It's one of those grand old apartment buildings with fancy masonry and stone lions out in front, and marble hallways and a wrought iron elevator inside. I once tricked with this writer named Colin who lives on the third floor, and on another occasion with this college student named Bob on the first floor.

Anyhow, Steve's apartment's on the top floor, and his front windows look out onto the Fenway with a view to die. Not that you could make out any of the action in the bushes, though I tried.

We settle into the living room, and while Steve goes into the kitchen to get us some beers, Mike takes down an elaborately carved wooden box from the mantelpiece over the fireplace. He raises the lid, revealing a potent-smelling stash of grass, and proceeds to roll some joints.

Well, fifteen minutes later we're all working on our second beers, and we're all stoned out of our gourds. Turns out Steve's got really, really good grass. And

its yakety-yak grass, so one moment we're explaining to Norm what fuck buddies are, and the next Steve, Norm and Mike are fondly reminiscing about after-practice locker room stuff back in J.P. High, like who had the biggest dick, who liked to parade about in the buff and who was always getting hard-ons in the showers.

Then suddenly we all stop talking. Uh-oh. I've been through this scene before. We're all horny and no one dares to make the next move.

That is, until Mike grabs our attention by extending his arms out into a long, drawn out stretch, and then smelling his sweaty pits.

"Ewww!" he goes, crinkling up his face. "Anyone want a sniff?"

Well, we all laugh and go "Eww! Gross!" and Mike rises to his feet and says, "So, I'm gonna shower off. Anyone care to join me?"

Norm rises from the sofa like he's about to take him up on his offer, and I think, "Oh boy! If he does, I will too." But he suddenly turns stoned shy and says, "That's okay. I'll wait til you are done."

"Aw shit. But suit yourself."

And with that he heads for the bathroom.

"So, any requests?" Steve asks, getting up and thumbing through his collection of LPs.

"I didn't know if he was joking or not," Norm whispers to me.

"Don't worry about it," I whisper back.

"Well?" Steve prompts, standing by the stereo.

"Oh." Norm says. "You have any...you know...Betty something?"

"Bette Midler? Sure do," he says, pulling out *The Divine Miss M* and setting it on the turntable. "You know, I actually saw her perform live at the Continental Baths."

"Really?" I say, betraying my admiration, since I've never even been to New York City.

Well, of course Norm wants to hear all about the Continental Baths, and before you know it, Steve's got us hot and horny with his descriptions of all the sex-on-premises places he's been to in New York City, like the Club Baths, the Anvil, and what really got my cock squirming the Mineshaft.

"Well, I see someday I'll have to take you guys on a field trip," Steve concludes, clearly relishing the thought.

I can barely begin to ponder the pleasures of a fling in New York City with these guys, when there's Mike standing in the doorway in nothing but a jockstrap that sags with the effort of supporting his huge Italian-stallion dick

"Okay. Bathroom's all yours," he says to us as he towels off his hair, setting the contents of his jock pouch all ajiggle. He catches us staring at his crotch and explains provocatively, "I figured, why put on my smelly clothes again when I can borrow one of Steve's jockstraps. Maybe these guys would like that too, huh?"

"It'd be sorta like hanging out in the Mineshaft, wouldn't it?" Norm asks eagerly.

36

"I can already see you there," Steve says as he leads us into his bedroom. He rummages through his bureau, and then pulls out two well-worn jockstraps, which he tosses to us with, "Here. Catch. Found these in the locker room. Jesus, the things you guys leave behind there."

Just fingering its well-worn pouch, I can feel my dick stiffen as I contemplate the unknown jock who once wore it, curious about what he had to stuff into it that stretched it so.

Well, Norm and I head for the bathroom together. Once inside, the sight of Norm naked once again brings me to full erection, but that's cool because I see Norm's got a big fat boner, himself.

Unfortunately, the shower's in one of those old-fashioned clawfoot tubs with a plastic curtain. Norm and I step in together and try to fool around, but because of the close quarters and difficulty with a temperamental nozzle, we give up, and I quickly finish my shower and step out to towel off.

I don't wait for Norm because I've learned from his two recent visits to my apartment the blowjob visit and the ass fuck visit he's one of those guys who spends forever showering. Instead, I slip on the jockstrap it's a Bike Medium over the hard-on I don't seem to be able to get rid of and make my way out down the corridor towards the living room with my stiff rod poking out over the loose waistband.

I guess I'm not really so surprised at what I see. Steve's sitting on the couch, leaning back with his hands clasped behind his head. His cutoffs are down around his left ankle, and his tank top's pulled up over his head behind his neck. He's got his legs spread wide apart, and there's Mike kneeling between them sucking him off, one hand dug deep into his jockstrap, stroking his dick like there's no tomorrow.

They've both got their eyes closed, looking as blissful as can be, like two nasty angels.

Even at thirty-whatever-he-is, Steve's got a fantastic body. It's trim, tan and hard as rock a real he-man's body with a gorgeous spread a black hair fanning out across his chest and encircling his tight little innie of a navel. And below, Mike's bobbing head teases me with partial glimpses of his outrageously huge, rugged hard-on sticking straight up, looking two sizes too big for the rest of his body.

Mike surprises me, since his eyes are closed, by waving me over with his free hand.

When I approach, Steve unclasps his hands and reaches out as if he's got radar to detect any dick within reach, grabs my hard-on bulls's eye right through the jock pouch.

"Jesus!" he says, opening his eyes as if to confirm its really as large as it feels in his hand.

He wastes no time in pulling the jockstrap down to my knees, deep-throating me with surprising ease. You see, most guys go into a fit of gagging when they try to swallow too much of me too soon.

While Mike dismounts Steve to watch him sucking me off, I give into the sweet feelings of his expert blowjob, all the time thoroughly mesmerized by the tantalizing sight of his oversized dick. It's gotta be a good ten inches, with a riot of thick veins bulging all over the expanse of his brown cock shaft.

But Steve's almost too good a cocksucker (if there is such a thing!) and I can already feel the countdown to orgasm churning away deep within my nuts. So I jackknife assbackwards to slide my dick out of Steve's mouth, and get down on my haunches next to Mike.

Steve stretches his arms along the top of the sofa, slides forwards a few more inches, and spreads his legs as far apart as they can go. Ah, such a spit-shiny monster of a dick! But before I can fully appreciate its rugged beauty, Mike goes down on him again, so I zoom in on his baseball-sized ball sac, brown and furrowed, clinging close to the base of his cock.

I reach in between his legs to touch it. At the feel of my inquisitive fingers Steve lets out an appreciative groan. I move my mouth in, below Mike's bobbing head, stick out my tongue and lap Steve's nuts until I've got the hairs that cover them nice and wet.

I coax one big ball into my mouth, swirling my tongue all around it while giving it a gentle tug. Then I maneuver the other one in, wondering how it is that no matter how big the balls, or how snug the ball sac against the base of a guy's dick, I can always manage to get the whole of it into my mouth. I guess it's just a gift I have.

Anyhow, I'm licking and tugging on Steve's nut sac, and Mike's going up and down on his cock with noisy, showoff suck strokes, when I decide to abandon his balls in an attempt to sample some of his dick for myself. After all, I think, Mike's sucked Steve off countless times, I suppose, so it's only fair I should be able to make use of this rare opportunity to blow our high school gym teacher, just like I always dreamed about so many times during algebra class. Which is probably why I got a D minus.

When I abandon his balls and move my mouth close to Mike's, he immediately dismounts Steve's dick, and pushes it over to me with his tongue as he opens his eyes and stares directly into mine. This cock sharing, eye-to-eye intimacy sends a sensual shiver of excitement through my body.

I stick out my tongue and flick the tip of it across Steve's piss slit. Mike does the same from the opposite side of Steve's dick, looking deep into my eyes as our tongues spar with each other along the underside of Steve's cock head, greedy for the pre-cum that begins to ooze out in abundance.

"Ohhh...shit! You guys are soooo fucking good," Steve utters in a throaty whisper. "Oh, yeah. Yeah! Fuck, yeah!"

Each "yeah," and the ones that follow, attest to our progress down Steve's cock as we tongue the stiff, veiny territory of his shaft, until I feel the tickle of his pubic bush against the side of my mouth.

"So suck on it, man!" Mike encourages me, and I waste no time in deep throating this Mount Everest of dicks, plunging into the pleasure of working my

way up and down as much as I can take in while Steve keeps going "Yeah! Yeah!" until his words dry up and I sense a shift in his attention.

"So Norm," he says towards the doorway, like it was the most natural thing in the world to remark at that moment, "I understand you're still a virgin."

Well, Mike and I pull ourselves out of Steve's crotch and look over to see Norm dressed in the jockstrap Steve had lent him, his towel dangling from his grasp as he stares at us in amazement.

He blushes in response to Steve's comment. Shit, he looks so cute standing there with that hunky body, that over-stuffed jockstrap, clutching his towel at his side like a little boy with his teddy bear.

"Who told you that?"

"Mike. Tony. I forget which. On the way over here."

"I've been rimmed. Does that count?"

"You have?" Steve asks, so deeply interested he grabs his dick and strokes it.

"Yeah. Tony. The day before yesterday."

"You lucky dog," Steve says enviously, looking down at me with an admiring shake of his head.

And then, returning his attention to Norm, "If you only knew how may times, seeing you butt-naked in the locker room, I dreamed about what it'd be like to get you alone, force those creamy-white ass cheeks of yours wide apart, and drive my tongue all the way into your hole. Yeah, if you only knew."

"Would you like to try it now?"

This takes us so much by surprise, the three of us just stare at him. Which embarrasses the hell out of Norm. I don't think he's aware of it, but he slides his free hand slowly across his jock pouch as if to protect himself.

"I mean...uh..."

Steve sits up, pushing me and Mike from out of his legs and waves Norm closer with "Commere."

He steps over in front of Steve, looks down at him, and asks, "Do you have any poppers?"

Norm's just one surprise after another today.

"Sure thing," Mike says, jumping up and darting out of the room, preceded by his huge stiff dick flopping out of control in front him. Jesus, a runaway cock that big could hurt someone.

"Tony turn you onto poppers, too?" Steve asks.

"As a matter of fact, yes."

"Well, while Mike gets us some..."

He pulls down Norm's jock pouch, and his huge, pale dick falls out, heavy-hanging in its semi-hardness, the most succulent piece of fat Polish sausage you'd ever hope to see.

"Jesus," Steve says to me in utter amazement. "You guys sure grow them big in Jamaica Plain."

But all I can think to reply is "Mmm," as I watch him lean into Norm's crotch, tongue-lift his huge, mushroom-shaped cock head into his mouth and slide his

lips down around the generous dimensions of Norm's cock shaft.

Never in a million years, not even in my wildest algebra class daydreams, did I ever expect someday I'd be watching Coach Douglas sucking cock. The chiseled features of his face mobilize with his blowjob efforts, making cock sucking look like one of the most he-man things a guy can do.

And without skipping a single suck-off beat, he looks me in the eyes and pats the portion of sofa by his side, indicating I should get up off the floor and join him. Which of course I do.

Then I kinda pull myself out of the moment and watch the two of them while at the same time I look into my thoughts.

So much has happened between me and Norm these past few days, what with me rimming him and him fucking me, and that threesome this morning with Mike in the shower stall at the health club. And now Coach Douglas! I mean, even this morning, if I'd thought of him, he'd be that hot high school gym teacher I used to strip naked in my mind, who I was sure wouldn't even give me the time of day because I was such a sissy. And now he's just invited me to watch him sucking on Norm's dick!

But now he dismounts Norm's juicy piece of meat, which throbs for more attention right in front of our faces. Turning to me and placing a hand on my thigh, Steve asks "You want some?"

Coach Douglas is asking me if I'd like some of the cock he's been sucking on! "Would I ever!"

And in the way Mike and I were just sharing Steve's cock a few moments back, we now feast on Norm's glorious nine-plus-inches networked with thin blue veins that emphasize its alabaster whiteness.

It seems like we'd hardly begun working on it when Mike announces his presence again with, "Shit! You leave the room for ten seconds...."

"Oh, shut the fuck up," Norm interrupts good-naturedly, "and pass us those poppers."

Which Mike does. Then he sets down a tube of K-Y, which I guess is foresightful on his part.

We each take a hit and pass the poppers back to Mike. As the popper high begins to wash over us Steve says to Norm, "Now turn around and bend over."

He obediently rewards us with the close-up view of his beautiful, ivory-white butt. Steve pulls Norm's firm ass cheeks apart, exposing his pink, puckered butt hole and moves his face into Norm's ass crack, sticking out his tongue and flicking it against the rim of Norm's hole.

Norm's responsive groans are immediate as he melts into the pleasure, thrusting his butt out towards Steve's face. As if Steve needed an incentive to snake his tongue inside and explore where only I've ever been before!

Once Steve's working his tongue in and out with expert ease, Norm reaches up, blindly seeking out Mike's crotch. He finds it, digs his hand into Mike's jock pouch, grabs him by the dick, and yanks him around in front of his face to wrap his lips around Mike's half-hard log of a cock. But he's in a difficult position for

cock sucking, let alone not very well practiced in it (yet!), so once he steadies himself with his hands on his thighs, Mike helps him out by planting his hands on either side of Norm's head, carefully sliding his cock in and out of Norm's stationary mouth. In seconds he's sucked into a full hard-on, which Norm seems to be managing with surprising ease.

Eventually, Steve pulls his face out from between Norm's ass cheeks to examine his moistened butt hole, which Norm repeatedly clenches as if to lure his tongue in again. Steve smiles, then pushes my face into Norm's ass crack.

"Yeah. That's it, Tony. Stick your tongue all the way in. Loosen him up so's I can slide my dick inside to show him what it's like to be a man taking a man-sized load of cock up your ass."

"No," Norm protests. He has abandoned Mike's dick, surprising us all. "Tony."

"Huh?" Steve asks.

"Tony. I want Tony to be the first guy to fuck me. He was the first guy who ever sucked my cock, the first guy to rim me, and the first guy to let me fuck him. If it wasn't for him, I'd still be spending the afternoons hanging out behind my father's gas station drinking beer with all those other dumb jocks I used to hang out with, big-talking a lotta bullshit. So it's gotta be Tony."

"Well," Steve says slowly after a pause, "that's damn decent of you. But then, you always were a good kid. Sure it'll be Tony. But you wouldn't mind if I coached you through it, would you?"

"I might be kinda dumb, but I don't think I need a coach to learn how to get fucked."

"You probably don't, but think how much fun it'll be for all of us."

"Tony?" Norm asks me.

"Sure."

"Then," Mike says, "I make a motion we move into the bedroom."

Which we all do, poppers, lube and all, discarding the few articles of clothing left on us, so we step into the bedroom absolutely naked with our heavy-hanging hard-ons bouncing all over the place.

Steve orders Norm up onto his king size bed ("sleeps three comfortably," he brags) so he's on his hands and knees with his feet dangling over the side.

"Just remember," Norm says, craning his neck around to face us, "It's my first time, so...oh!"

Steve's already got his tongue up Norm's asshole again.

And before you know it, he's got me and Mike taking turns rimming Norm while he sits on the bed next to Norm coaching him to relax his butt hole, telling him not to worry about a thing.

"Okay guys," he finally says, reaching for the lubricant. "Now to ready Norm for his first fuck!"

He squeezes some K-Y onto his fingers and slathers it all over Norm's butt hole. While he's busy doing this, Mike grabs the K-Y from him, squeezes a huge gob of it into his palm and wraps his fist around my dick, twisting it up and

down my cock shaft, getting it nice and slippery.

Once Norm's hole gleams with lube, Steve slowly slides his index finger inside.

"Ah!" Norm goes, tensing up.

Steve stops at the first knuckle with a soothing, "Just relax, Norm."

While Norm visibly unclenches his hole, Steve continues in up to the second knuckle.

"Oh!" Norm says in wonderment, "So that's why you guys like to get fucked so much!"

"Yeah, the trick is to stay loose," Steve advises, working his finger in as far as it'll go.

"Do you think," Norm asks, craning his neck around, "you could manage another finger in? I mean, Tony's got such a big dick, I've gotta be ready for it. Oh, Jesus! Careful! Yeah! Fuck, yeah! How about a third?"

Which Steve willingly gives him. And before you know it, he's sliding three fingers in and out of Norm's hole with no difficulty at all.

"Think you're ready?"

Norm twists his head around again, casting an apprehensive glance at my dick, though what he says is, "Yeah, I think so."

"Good. Get him a pillow for his head," Steve orders Mike, who reaches up, grabs one by the headboard and doubles it up.

Slowly sliding his fingers out of Norm, Steve says, "Now, lie down on your back and rest your head there. Yeah, that's it. Now pull your legs back."

He and Mike get up on the bed on either side of Norm and together lift his knees up to his shoulders. Mike grabs a second pillow and slides it under Norm's lower back to prop up his ass.

"That'll make it easier," Steve assures him.

And then, grinning at me, "Okay, Tony. He's all yours."

So I get up on my knees behind him, stunned by the breathtaking sight of him in this position of ass-vulnerable availability. I'm surprised that he's still maintained his hard-on, which he slowly strokes, his huge ball sac rising and falling above his exposed butt hole.

I plant my hands on the back of Norm's hard-as-rock thighs and press my cock head against his butt hole. Still stroking his cock, Norm looks up at me, trustfully.

I give a little push and my cock head slides into him with no difficulty. Norm reacts with an audible inhalation, like he was toking grass, making it unclear whether he likes it or not.

I push in the first few inches of my cock shaft. The sensations of slow entry explode along my dick like a million and one firecrackers.

"Ah!" he exhales. I'm still not sure if he likes it, but I take the chance of sliding in another inch.

"Ohhh!" he moans, slowly twisting his head to one side.

"You okay?"

42

"Of course! Just keep going!"

I give him another inch, extracting an "Ow!" during which he momentarily tenses.

But then he relaxes again, his accelerated cock strokes broadcasting his enthusiastic reception of the rest of my cock as I gradually sink it all the way into him.

Steve manages to knee step behind Norm, taking control over both his legs so his dick's hovering above Norm's face.

"That's it Norm," Steve says, looking down at him. "I'll bet you never imagined someday I'd be coaching you through your first fuck. Well, you're doing just fine. Just hang loose and let Tony do the work. That's it, Tony, in and out, nice and slow. Nice and slow."

You can tell Steve's really getting off on talking us through this ass fuck.

"Why, I remember when Tony was nothing but a skinny little...but look what he's done with his body. You've got to admire a guy like that, huh, Norm?"

"Yeah," Norm says in a voice shaky from his jack off strokes.

"Enough to wanna have him fuck you, huh?"

"Uh-huh!"

I find the rhythm I need to give Norm a smooth, steady fuck and the four of us fall into sync: the aftershocks of each plunge into Norm's butt setting Steve's dick bobbing out of control above Norm's face while Mike looks on in silent appreciation, stroking his dick with one hand while his other one wanders about our bodies, sampling a nipple here, a bicep there, probing into crevices and gliding along the muscular contours of our sleek, straining limbs.

Suddenly, Norm shifts into high gear, jacking off a mile a minute.

"Yeah, Tony!" he practically shouts, like I'm force-fucking the words out of him. "That's it! Pump it up my ass! Pump it up my fucking ass!"

This takes me by surprise, but how well I know the feeling of some hot and horny stud pounding away at your hole, so I begin to really ram it in him. Norm shows all the signs of orgasmic transport; his breathing's labored, beads of perspiration cover his forehead, and wide-eyed and open-mouthed he stares up at Steve's huge, swaying dick. What a sight that must be to see it from below, each downswing bringing Steve's pre-cummy cock head so close to Norm's mouth he actually manages to lick off some of the coach's clear-liquid ooze.

The humid intensity of the moment exudes an aura that wraps itself around the four of us, like we're all a part of the same orgasm. My nipples sting, my dick feels honey sweet and I can feel the jism churning around in my nut sac, accumulating, the pressure increasing until oh, my God!

My body's taken over by the uncontrollable onrush of orgasm and I pump in and out of Norm like there's no tomorrow, practically screaming, "Ah! I'm going to come!"

"That's it baby," says Steve, "Shoot it up his ass. Shoot it up that fucking beautiful ass of his!"

"Yeah, man," from a less articulate Mike who's clearly captive to his own

43

fast-approaching climax, his rigid body one beautiful mass of sweaty, straining muscle.

Then it happens. As the bed begins to shake like a raft on rapids, the cum explodes out of my dick and up Norm's ass.

Norm welcomes my butt-pounding outpour of jism with "Oh! Oh! Ohh!" And then, with one final strangulated "Ohh!" he tosses his head from side to side as he lets loose with a violent outpouring of cum that spurts all over his chest.

Mike joins in with an "Ah! Fuck!!!" shooting his own load up into the air, his scalding hot jism landing indiscriminately all over the place. So much cum! So much sweat and strain! And after I empty myself of what feels like quarts of cum, I collapse onto Norm's sticky chest just as Steve releases Norm's legs to grab his own swollen dick.

I drive my tongue into Norm's receptive mouth, but it doesn't stay there for long, since we hear Steve yell, "Ahh, Shit!" and quickly look up at him. With his body tensed, he furiously strokes his outthrust dick, aiming it at our faces.

"Yeah, Steve," Mike encourages, giving his butt a loud smack. "That's it! Give it to them!"

"Ohhh!" Steve roars as the first powerful discharge of cum explodes from his dick.

Reflexively, we squint our eyes closed as spurt after spurt of his hot jack off juice splatters all over our faces.

And then, once Steve's drained his nuts and his cum begins to slowly river down our faces, he goes limp with a "Whew!" resting his head on Mike's shoulder just as Norm rolls over on top of me.

"So, Norm," I hear Steve say, after we've all somewhat recuperated, "it hadda be Tony, huh?"

"The first time? Yeah."

He kisses me gently on the lips. I think I'm falling in love with the guy.

As Steve stretches over to once again slip a finger up Norm's butt hole, Mike leans into my ear, whispering, "I think I know who's going to be second. So what do you say we leave them alone and slip off to the Fens to suck some fresh cock?"

I struggle out from under Norm, sliding off the bed and giving him a quick peck on the cheek.

"We'll be back later," Mike whispers from the doorway, like he doesn't want to disturb them.

But they don't seem to care. Steve's busy poking his fingers up Norm's hole again, and all Norm can do is squirm his beautiful butt in receptive appreciation, moaning, "Oh, Coach! Oh, oh!"

HIDE AND SEEK (A Boyhood Memoir)
by James Wilton

I grew up in a typical middle class suburb. Next door lived Mrs. Burroughs who was widowed with three young boys, spaced two years apart. Jamie, the youngest, was my age. He was very musical and spent lots of his free time practicing the piano and other instruments he played. Don, the middle, was bookish and read away much of summer vacation. Bob was the outgoing one. He was athletic and congenial, spending most of his time playing outdoors.

Our neighborhood had a disproportionate number of boys. The oldest in our playgroup was Bob Burroughs. The boys older than him hung out with their own peers so Bob was father to his brothers and camp counselor to our gang. Even as he got into his teen years, he always had time for his brothers and their friends.

Without our realizing it, Bob got his growth spurt and began to look like an adult among us boys. It didn't bother him and he was as ready as ever for a game of hide and seek or softball. I remember fondly the times he would let me hide with him under a bush or behind the trash barrels. He used to fold me under his arm and lean over me to keep as low a profile as possible. Even before I had any sexual feelings I used to love being held in those strong arms.

As we grew up and Bob got his license, a car full of us would occasionally go to a drive-in movie. In his mom's Buick, we could pack four in the back seat and three across the front seat. On one particular night, I had the front seat, next to Bob. The movie was of no interest to me and I began to doze off. As my head got heavier, I leaned to the left and rested my head on Bob's shoulder. Just as I slipped into sleep, I heard him laugh as he put his arm around my shoulders in a fatherly gesture. When I woke up I found that I had curled into him and was resting my hands on his upper thigh.

As I began to stir, I realized that there was a hard tube of flesh along the leg under my hand. Since I was thirteen and already masturbating myself, I knew what I had in my grip. I gently rocked my hand back and forth along the rod without giving any indication that I was awake. I am sure that I heard a very slight gasp and moan over the soundtrack of the movie. Suddenly Bob sat upright and pushed me aside, saying that his arm was asleep and that I would have to sit up. I tried to keep my hands on his erection but he firmly took hold of my wrists and pushed me away. Thankfully, no one else in the car figured out what had happened.

When the movie ended we drove home. Every time we passed a street light, I looked down and saw that my plaything was still hard against the driver's leg. Bob stopped at the top of the driveway to let everyone out as usual. I didn't move and chose to ride to the garage with my big friend. When the car doors were closed, I asked Bob why he had broken off my massage of his member. He laughed and said that we would both have been sorry if the others had figured

out what was happening. I don't know where I got the balls to ask it but I told him I could see he was still hard and wondered if we could continue the action somewhere away from the others.

It's a wonder that Bob didn't either soundly reject me or even punch me out. Instead, he looked me right in the eye and said that my hand felt real good on his dick but that he could get in real trouble having sex with a youngster. I asked if we could resume our session when I was eighteen. He laughed and agreed, without any concept of how seriously I took his assent.

Six months later I was fourteen and got the usual card from Bob. In it I wrote "Four more years." I slipped it in his pocket the next time I saw him.

As he took it out and opened it he laughed and promised that he wouldn't forget. Each year we followed the same routine and each time Bob made light of the note.

During this time, Bob had gone to a local college so that he could live at home to help his mother and be with his brothers. When he graduated, he got a job not far away and set himself up in a small apartment about a mile from us.

My eighteenth birthday came in January of my senior year in high school and I was still a virgin. I knew that I wasn't interested in girls and never got into that maybe-I-can-become-straight-if-I-just-fuck-the-right-girl game. Despite all the boys around me, I hadn't experienced sex with any of them since none of them gave off the right signals and I wasn't about to expose my inclination to my classmates.

I still saw Bob several times a week as he stopped by to have dinner with his mother who was now living alone since the younger two boys had gone away to college. A few days before my big event, I approached Bob to remind him of his promise. Other than the birthday cards, this was the first time we had talked about our arrangement. He gave me a piercing look and said that he certainly hadn't forgotten. All this time he had been hoping that I was serious about my desire but hadn't dared show too much interest in case I had been putting him on. He admitted that he had enjoyed watching me grow from a gangly preadolescent into the developed young man that I had become. We agreed that my actual birthday wouldn't work so we set a date for the next night at eight o'clock.

I fell into sleep every one of the next nights with a hard-on as I recalled every intimate contact I had with Bob, especially that aborted session at the drive-in. My actual birthday wasn't a real event, it was a prelude to a date I had awaited over four years!

At eight on the dot, I rang Bob's doorbell with a sweaty hand. I was buzzed into the building and found his apartment door slightly ajar. I opened it, calling out my hello. He answered that he was in the back room. I shut the door behind me and slipped off my coat, dropping it on the floor in my haste. I stepped through the hall and saw my childhood buddy lying on his bed, hands behind his head and legs spread wide. I looked at him and realized that the big kid I had grown up with had turned into a masculine, handsome twenty-two-year old

hunk. He wore a tight T-shirt that showed off his broad chest. His sleeves were rolled up so that his biceps were fully exposed and the hair in his armpit showed. His tight jeans revealed his sizable thighs and basket. Just like that night in the car. His cock was hard and stretched out over his upper leg. His nostrils were flared and his eyes were glazed over in lust.

My throat went dry at the sight and I couldn't say a thing. We silently stared into each other's eyes for an eternity. Finally Bob opened his sensual lips to speak. His voice cracked and he stumbled over his words, showing that I wasn't the only one overwhelmed with the intensity of the situation. For those long years I had been looking forward to my chance to be taught the mysteries of sex by my handsome neighbor. Until this moment, it hadn't occurred to me that Bob might have been looking forward to initiating somebody.

After a few gulps, Bob told me that this was my evening and that I could do anything I wanted. Guessing that I was still a virgin, he reminded me that my first sexual experience would be something I'd remember all my life and that I should make this evening as fulfilling as possible. He then told me that he had fooled around in college and with some guys from his gym so that he knew what he was getting into and was willing to submit to my every whim. That speech made a drop of precum ooze out of my throbbing cock. I was still frozen in my tracks, looking down at this body I had before me.

To get things moving, Bob suggested that I return my hands to where they had been four years ago. I stepped forward and cupped his shaft. It felt just the same. The member was hard and I could feel it pulse in my hand. The warmth of it radiated through the denim. I felt a slight upward hump as Bob pushed into my palm. I looked up and saw his eyes closed in bliss.

Even though the crotch was my primary interest, I didn't want to arrive there so quickly, so I slid my hand up Bob's body. My movement broke his musing and he looked at me with an encouraging smile. His time at the gym had really bulged up muscles that were already well developed. I could both see and feel the rippled abdominal muscles. His pecs were so defined that there was a significant ridge where they arose from his belly. When I brushed the nipples Bob sucked in a short breath and his eyes rolled back. Those little buds quickly hardened and stood up under the cotton.

Next, I put a knee on the bed beside Bob's chest and reached out to grasp each bicep. They, too, were hard and huge; I couldn't even reach around half of their circumference. As I paused to enjoy these mounds Bob flexed slightly. My moan encouraged him to further display and he did isometric presses against the back of his head. The result was both amazing and arousing. I enjoyed every ripple of the brawn in my hands. Looking down into Bob's eyes, I smiled in appreciation and continued my travel along his arms.

At the wrists, I connected with his beautiful face. I cupped those cheeks in both hands and massaged the cleft chin with my thumbs. Bob must have shaved for me because his skin was silken smooth. I ran my fingers along that strong jaw line to his lips. As I outlined them with my index finger, they opened a

crack and his tongue brushed it. I felt as if I had touched an electric wire; the shock ran right down to my crotch. I continued my tactile exploration of this face I knew so well: his thin nose, the lids over those intense blue eyes, the thick brows, the wiry blond hair.

When I was done, Bob reached up and pulled me down to meet him in a kiss. This was the first time I had ever kissed a man. His tongue passing over my lips sent chills down my back. He forced my mouth open and invaded it. The contact between our tongues increased my sexual energy. I reached around him and tried to force his whole body into my mouth. I scrambled up onto the bed for more contact. Bob steadied my head with one hand and stilled my body with the other so that we could enjoy the kiss for quite some more time. When we finally broke apart, Bob laughed and commented that he was pleased to see that I was enjoying this as much as he had hoped I would.

My mentor suggested that he stand up so that I could have more thorough access to his body and, should I want, greater ease at removing his clothes. That comment brought a chuckle from me. There was nothing I had wanted so intensely except, possibly, my driver's license. As I stood up to get out of the way, Bob swung around to the side of the bed. Before standing up, he slipped off his sneakers and socks. Then he stood in front of me in the same pose he had on the bed.

I took him by the waist and turned him around so that I could look over his back. His musculature was as prominent as it had been on the front. There was a deep valley running down his spine from the broad shoulders to his round, protruding buns. I reached up and grabbed onto those shoulders as I had years ago when climbing onto his back for a horsy ride. This time was different, though, as I took my time and felt the strength under the skin. I put my thumbs into that trough and slowly descended the length of Bob's spine. The result was a prolonged moan as he bowed his back.

Once down below the belt, I couldn't resist grabbing a fistful of bun in each hand. They were as hard as all the other muscles on his body. As with the biceps, Bob showed off a bit for me and flexed his glutes. Again, I was impressed and aroused. My thumbs seemed drawn into the crack between those melons. I dug them as deeply into the jeans as I could and felt Bob spreading his knees to widen his stance and try to sit down on my thumbs.

Realizing that there was too much fabric to get between the buns, I surprised this guy by quickly reaching through his opening and cupping his crotch. As before, that dick was good and hard. I pulled him backward so that I could rest my cheek in that curve where the small of his back meets the top of his butt. Bob eased his stature and dropped both hands. One cupped my exposed cheek and the other gently rubbed the back of my hand over his basket.

After this pause in the action, I had Bob turn around so that I could begin the uncovering. I slowly pulled his tee shirt up, exposing that hard belly. As I knew, he had a good amount of blond hair on his body. There was that thick runner of fur extending up from his navel to his chest hair. His pecs were well covered as

48

was the breast bone. Once the shirt was off, I zeroed in on those nipples. As I tweaked and twisted, Bob grabbed my shoulders to steady himself. Evidently I had found two really intense buttons on this body.

As much fun as the chest was, I was looking right into something that promised to be much more interesting. I reached down and opened the belt and waist band. As I unzipped the fly, both he and I held our breaths. I was pleased to see that Bob wasn't wearing anything underneath. I was so eager to get to the goods that I didn't want to deal with another layer. The jeans were so tight that it took some doing to get them over his jutting buns but I succeeded. As the pants descended, more and more of his cock came into view. This splendid member that I had never touched but had seen innumerable times in changing rooms was standing rigid for my perusal. It was all I had hoped it would be. I already knew that it was cut and grew out of a generous blond nest. It never looked small but I hadn't realized how thick it got when hard. It was seven inches long, and much thicker than my erect dick, the only other hard-on I had ever seen. Once freed, it stood nearly upright, parallel to his belly. Both the cock head and belly were liberally smeared with precum, which he must have been oozing for much of the evening. The crown was slightly wider than the shaft so it looked more like a helmet than a mushroom. The balls were larger than I remembered, but the fur all over the sack was what I had pictured.

As I lowered the jeans, the hair on his thighs came into view. Beneath, the muscles were almost as well defined as his arms. He flexed an invitation to grab hold but I was much more interested in the cock above.

Having never seen or felt another man's erect dick, other than that experience at the drive-in, I was fascinated with the organ before me. I reached up and touched with one finger. This brought a chuckle from Bob, who told me that it wouldn't break if I grabbed it. So, I did just that. He sucked in a quick breath and straightened his whole body. As I held on, I could feel a slight forward move as he tried to fuck my fist. My other hand reached up and cupped those inviting balls. The skin was loose and pliable. The orbs felt as if they were floating in oil; just like mine felt. I palmed them around in their bag with one hand and began to slide the skin back and forth on his rod with the other. Before long, Bob warned me to stop or I might push him over the top.

I figured that this might be a good time for me to undress. As I stood up and reached for my shirt tail, Bob offered to do it for me. He began by feeling my chest and commenting that I had filled out nicely. Such a compliment coming from a toned hunk felt almost as good as his hand did. He lifted my shirt over my head and again explored my upper body. Without any preliminaries, he reached down, unzipped me, and lowered my jeans and jockeys. As my dick was exposed, Bob whistled in appreciation.

Later I found that it was longer and thicker than average but this was the first time that it was acknowledged.

He reached down and slid my clothing off so that we were facing each other nude and erect. That was when I had someone touch my penis for the first time

in my life. Bob started at the root and slid his fingers up the underside. He then slid them back down and closed his fist around me. The sensation was so intense that I exploded in an ejaculation. Bob was caught totally by surprise and jumped back as he felt my hot jism splatter on him. Even after he lost contact, I kept shooting.

When the flood was over Bob laughed, saying that he hadn't realized how close I was. The look on my face must have shown that I was crushed. First, I wanted the session to last. Second, the idea that I had disappointed my hero and made him laugh at me destroyed me. Realizing how seriously I was taking this, Bob pulled me into a bear hug and assured me that he was flattered that he had that effect on me. He also pointed out that after coming, I no longer had a hair trigger and could enjoy a prolonged second round. He took a towel off the side table and cleaned us both up. We were then ready to pick up the action where we had left it.

Bob, who was still sporting a semi-hard, held me by the shoulders and poked at my softee with his growing erection. The contact as well as the sight of my buddy's dick jabbing into my equipment got me back into the spirit. As my pole rose to full arousal, I reached forward and pulled Bob into another hug. This time, our cocks dueled as we humped each other's crotch.

Bob backed off a bit and pulled my staff down to just below his balls. He then leaned back into me and I found that my dick slid between his upper thighs and into a tight crevice. I began a short fucking motion and enjoyed the feel of my cock as it brushed the underside of his balls and the base of his ass crack. I was back in the mood.

Meanwhile, Bob had taken advantage of our closeness and was nibbling on my neck and ears. I had no idea that these body parts could be so tender and erotic. He had me writhing against him with all the attention. I thought I'd find out what happened if I tried these tricks myself. As I expected, they had a strong effect on Bob. He threw his head back and groaned. His arms tightened their hold on my chest and I felt the strength in those muscles. It was a real turn-on to see this brawny hunk be weakened by my tonguing.

My mouth was having such a good time that I decided not to detach. Instead, I licked my way down the chest to those sensitive nipples. My mouth was even more successful than my fingers in getting a rise out of those buttons. Bob moaned even louder than he had when I worked on his neck. The erect penis I felt bumping into my stomach beckoned me farther south. I followed that trail of hair past the navel to the pubic bush.

Bypassing the cock, I first made genital contact with the scrotum. It felt smooth on my tongue and the odor was distinctly masculine without being offensive. I lapped all around the balls, managing to get them into my mouth, one at a time. Then, I worked my way up to the base of the pillar. The upward rise of Bob's erection drew me up its length. As I neared the head, my attention began to cause his member to jerk to even stiffer hardness. I had to grab it to hold it still. I could feel the throb of his heartbeat in that turgid flesh. It stood so

upright that I was tempted to pull it down, away from his belly. I only got it a little way down when it was obvious that I was beginning to hurt it. I let got and watched it snap back to attention. It was so stiff that it didn't even slap his stomach as I expected. It just straightened right up.

After a few more bends and releases, I held it still and looked more carefully at the dickhead. There, I saw a drop of clear, fresh precum, newly emerged from the slit. I was ready to check out the taste and found it not at all unpleasant. I licked around the area, tasting the dried spots. In so doing, I was giving Bob a high-intensity head job. He warned me to ease off or face the consequences.

Figuring that Bob just wanted me to stop that specific action, I chose then to see what a man's prick would feel like in my mouth. I opened and went down as far on his shaft as I could. This time it was Bob's turn to surprise me with an unexpected eruption. Calling out that he had warned me, Bob blasted the back of my throat with a powerful ejaculation. I wasn't ready for this but knew that I wanted to taste a man's discharge, so I held on and swallowed as fast as I could. I wasn't successful in capturing it all and some of his seed dribbled down my chin but I did keep most of it. The taste was totally new to me but the conditions under which I acquired the liquid made it precious to me. As Bob's orgasm subsided, he reached down and hugged my face to his crotch. I held on to the dick and felt it soften in my mouth. Finally, as it lost its stiffness, I let it slip out of my lips and concentrated on the new flavor in my mouth. It was a taste I took an immediate liking to.

Bob reached down and lifted me toward the bed. He laid me back and went to work on my body, starting on my nipples. This was an area I suspected could give me pleasure but it took his expertise to make me realize the full potential. Mimicking my route, he proceeded to pay attention to my balls and then cock. Unlike me, he wasn't exploring but was giving me an overwhelming sensual treat. His tongue was obviously quite experienced and brought my nerves to the brink. After flicking all over my equipment, Bob finally went down on my rod. The feeling was indescribable.

All the talk I had heard of good fucks and good blowjobs hadn't prepared me for this. As he worked my shaft in and out of his mouth, Bob brought me closer and closer to my second orgasm. My panting and writhing gave him plenty of warning and he brought his hand into play. He fondled my balls and ran his finger down into my ass crack. All this added up to the stimulation I needed to cross the threshold. I sprayed the back of Bob's throat with another barrage of manjuice. He clamped down on the root of my dick and swallowed fast to catch all the liquid I had to offer. I nearly blacked out at the intensity of the ejaculation.

After I went limp in his mouth, Bob backed off and climbed up to give me a kiss. On his tongue I could recognize the taste of my offering to him. This time the contact was slow and leisurely, in contrast to our first one. As we broke away and replaced the deep kiss with brief pecks, I curled into a ball and Bob folded me under his arm. I fell asleep remembering fondly our games of hide

and seek so long ago.

A DAY AT THE BEACH (Naked Skateboard Boy II)
by Frank Brooks

Corey had spent most of the day at the beach trying to attract the attention of a muscular lifeguard he was sure had an enormous cock, but the lifeguard was surrounded by a flock of worshipful, giggling girls and gave no indication that he even knew that Corey existed. Still, Corey got so horny looking up at the man and imagining getting fucked by him that he almost went into the beach restrooms nearby, where he knew he could let off steam by getting a blowjob.

There were boy-hungry older men who sat in the restroom all day, waiting to suck off young surfers, or young skateboarders like himself, through glory holes in the stall partitions. Occasionally, when he was feeling really horny and frustrated, he would go in there and let one of them relieve him, even though, to tell the truth, he would rather suck cock than be sucked, and better yet, get screwed by a muscular older stud with a cock the size of a baby's arm, as he was sure the lifeguard had. That's what he fantasized about, that's what he wanted and needed, and a suck job by a glory hole cocksucker just didn't fit the bill this afternoon, so finally he threw in the towel and went home to jerk off while imagining the hunky lifeguard fucking his hot, horny little butt.

His hard on throbbed nonstop as he skateboarded toward home dressed in his baggy T-shirt and baggy shorts. His tanned feet were bare and, as usual, he had on his baseball cap backwards. As he slalomed along the sidewalk, his reddish-blond hair fell forward into his eyes. The summer was all but over and so far it had been one of sexual frustration. He'd got very little of what he'd been expecting and imagining he'd get after he had "come out" to himself last spring.

After that photo shoot with Steve early last spring he'd been on top of the world. Steve, in addition to being a photographer who specialized in shooting naked boys, was a handsome muscleman with a massive cock and had fucked Corey's virgin boy-pussy but good, and it was then that Corey had realized finally who he was and what he wanted. It was as if Steve's fucking had awakened Corey from a long sleep, allowing him to see himself at last as the cute young gay boy he was as a cute young gay boy who needed as much hard dick up his horny little butt as he could get. But knowing what he wanted and getting it were two different things. At first he'd expected Steve to meet all his sexual needs, but soon after that first photo-shoot Steve had left town.

Steve had gone on a so-called business trip to photograph naked boys around the world and had left Corey with an insatiable ache in his loins. He had promised that he would call Corey as soon as he got back, but five months had passed and Corey wondered if he would ever hear from Steve again. A man who made his living chasing around the world photographing and videotaping boys showing off their stiff pricks and horny asses and having sex with each other might not be the most reliable man around.

Corey nearly collided with another skateboarder who was coming at him from the opposite direction and they exchanged grins as they narrowly missed each other, then looked back at each other over their shoulders. Corey felt a thrill and was tempted to follow the boy a few blocks down the street and into the alley where, behind a dumpster, he and the boy had a few times exchanged blowjobs. He almost turned around to follow the boy, but the image of the hunky lifeguard was too much on his mind. What he really needed now was a dildo up the ass, a dildo he would imagine was the lifeguard's big cock fucking him while he jacked off. Without looking back again, he hurried home.

Since coming out, Corey had learned where to cruise to meet other boys, and he'd jacked off and sucked with a lot of boys his own age. He'd even fucked some of these boys and had been fucked by them, but none of them satisfied him the way Steve had. He wanted a *man* a handsome, muscular, boy-hungry man with a huge cock, but he wasn't sure where to cruise to find men like that. The older men in the beach restrooms were usually too fat and wimpy to appeal to him much, and usually all they wanted to do was to suck out his boy-cum. So, unable to find what he really wanted, he'd been doing a lot of jacking off lately.

Home at last, he was relieved to see the driveway car-free, indicating that neither of his parents was yet home from work. Now he could jack off in peace, making all the noise he wanted. The telephone was ringing as he let himself in and he tracked beach sand onto the living room carpet as he ran to pick it up.

"Corey, please," said a deep, resonant male voice.

Corey swallowed, his throat slightly dry. "This is Corey." The sound of a man's deep voice always flustered him.

"This is Coach Moore over at school. You left some things behind in your gym locker at the end of last semester. I was thinking you might want to come down here and claim them."

"Oh," was all Corey could say, tongue-tied at finding himself talking on the phone with a man who had always infatuated and terrified him. And what could he say about the gym gear? Like most of the boys at school, Corey had never bothered to clean out his gym locker at the end of a semester, leaving his soiled, sweaty, worn-out gym clothing behind for the janitors to discard.

"When can I expect you?" asked the coach. Even when asking a question, Coach Moore had a tone of command in his voice.

"Anytime," Corey mumbled.

"Good. Then I'll see you within the hour. Come down the back stairway off the playing fields. I'll leave the stairway door unlocked. Lock it behind you after you come in. I'll be in my office."

...

Corey skateboarded in a daze down to the school from which he had graduated a few months earlier, his mind going a mile a minute with images of Coach Moore, a man not quite as muscular as Steve, but hairier and more rugged. He would never forget the afternoon last spring when he and his

54

classmate Tim had been standing in the showers with erections and Coach Moore had walked in on them.

Corey had hid his boner before the coach could see it, but Tim, who always had an erection, dropped the soap intentionally, according to Tim and asked Corey to pick it up for him, and Corey, bending over, had, according to Tim, "rubbed his boy-pussy in the coach's face," and the coach's enormous prick had, according to Tim, stood straight out like a log or something. Corey, too shy and flustered to turn around when handing the soap back to Tim, hadn't seen the coach's supposedly erect monster. "Coach wants your sweet little boy-pussy," Tim had told Corey later, which, at the time, had thrilled Corey to death, yet, in a way, scared the shit out of him.

Now, months later, Corey's pecker was ramrod stiff and he was trembling as he opened the back door of his former high school the stairway door that led straight down to the locker room and as he stepped into the reddish glow of the EXIT light inside. As Coach Moore had instructed him, Corey locked the door behind him, then leaned his skateboard against the wall at the head of the stairs and tiptoed down the dark stairway on bare feet. He found the locker room dead silent and as dark as the stairwell except for a shaft of light that shone out through Coach Moore's open office door.

The school was deserted except for Coach Moore and himself, he realized, and the darkness and silence made him so nervous that he was tempted to turn back up the stairway and flee. He hadn't had to come here. He'd graduated from this joint and the coach no longer had any authority over him. But something inside him kept him moving forward until he was standing just outside the shaft of light and peering into the office.

Coach Moore was slouched behind his desk, his bulging pecs and abs, biceps and deltoids sheened with sweat as if he'd just finished pumping iron. He had his huge bare feet up on the desktop and was paging through a magazine and sniffing a jockstrap. Corey gaped at the sight. The coach's right arm moved rhythmically as his hand, out of sight behind the desk, apparently jacked his cock. Without intending to, Corey gasped.

"What the " The coach started, nearly tipping his chair over backwards, then stood, yanking up his gray sweatpants. "Who the hell…"

"It's me," Corey croaked. "Corey."

"Damn it, you almost gave me a stroke!" the coach said, coming toward the door. "Why'd you sneak in here like that?"

Corey couldn't say anything. He noticed that the man's sweatpants were tented as if with a Billy club.

"Well, come on in, I won't bite."

Corey stepped into the office and the coach locked the door.

"I'm sorry," Corey managed to say.

"Forget it." The coach handed the magazine he'd been looking at to Corey. "Real nice stuff, kid. I never knew you were a star."

Corey was stunned by the magazine cover, from which his own face peeked

back at him seductively over a naked shoulder, a smooth, skinny shoulder that he seemed on the verge of kissing. In the photo he had his back slightly arched and his smooth bubble-butt turned up. A caption under the photo read: NAKED SKATEBOARD BOY: HE WANTS IT! ARE YOU MAN ENOUGH TO GIVE IT TO HIM?

Although Steve had told Corey that the pictures Steve had taken of him during their photo shoots would be published in a gay men's magazine, Corey had never quite believed it. And never had he dreamed that Coach Moore would get hold of the magazine!

"Well, look inside," the coach said.

Opening the magazine, Corey found a whole spread of color pictures of himself. The first photo showed him dressed in his baseball cap, long-sleeved shirt, and jeans, his schoolbooks under one arm as he glanced cutely and seductively back over his shoulder, performing dressed the same pose he was doing naked on the cover. In all the other photos he didn't have a stitch on.

One photo showed him sitting sideways on his skateboard, his pink cock head pecking at his navel, his legs up in the air and spread in a V as he balanced on his ass, showing off his balls and silky-smooth crotch. Another photo showed him up on Steve's desk on all fours, his ass turned up, one hand reaching back to spread the cheeks, his moist, pink pucker fully exposed. His asshole looked so wet and fuckable because Steve had been licking it just before he'd snapped the shot. He expected when he turned the page to see Steve's cock buried half up his ass, as had happened soon after Steve had rimmed him, but instead he found a close-up of his bare feet, toes curled around the edge of his skateboard.

The next page showed him leaning back in an easy chair with one foot up on the seat, showing off his perineum and fat pink balls. He had his stiff dick in his right hand and was squeezing pre-cum out of it. His left arm was raised to show off a smooth armpit, which he was sniffing.

In all the photos he looked like a willowy, hairless, very-young boy with a stiff cock and an ass itching for a fuck. He found it both shocking and titillating to find himself looking so young and boyish, so seductive and sexy. He'd never realized just how coquettish he could appear. He felt slightly embarrassed that his own pictures turned him on so much and that he felt like jerking off over them.

Coach Moore, rubbing his hard on through his sweats with one hand, pointed with his other at the description of Corey printed in the magazine. "Is this stuff for real?"

Name: Corey Hanks
Age: 18
Ht: Five-three
Wt: 110 lbs.
Hair: Reddish blond
Eyes: Bluish green

Likes: Skateboarding, pizza, kissing, Getting fucked by very well-hung, muscular older men

Corey blushed, nodded. Yes, it was all true, except for the last name they'd given him. He wondered where they'd come up with Hanks.

"I thought they made all that shit up," the coach said. He took the magazine and paged through Corey's photo spread again, continuing to massage the swollen cylinder in his sweats. "Hot stuff, boy! Some of the hottest stuff I've ever seen! Enough to drive a man like me...." He tossed the magazine aside. "I don't play games, kid. I don't have time for it. Your pictures turn me on. *You* turn me on! Look what you do to me, baby! Look at this thing!"

Corey swallowed as the coach lowered his sweatpants and his naked cock sprang out huge, naked, and sweaty. It was incredible, a rod as big around as Corey's forearm and bulging with veins, with a gleaming, maroonish head half-hidden by foreskin. The magnificent tool stood straight out and throbbed, oozing dick-lube.

"Big enough for you, Corey baby?"

"Oh, Coach!" was all Corey could blurt, dazed and dizzy and trembling as the man knocked off his baseball cap and stripped him completely in a matter of seconds.

The coach kicked off his sweats and wrapped his arms around Corey, kissing him, shoving his tongue into Corey's mouth.

Corey felt as if he were melting. Trembling in the coach's embrace, he let the man take charge, let him do what he wanted, let him suck his juicy tongue, lick his moist hairless armpits, suck his small, boyish nipples. The coach lifted him as easily as a doll and perched him on the desk top on all fours as in the picture in the magazine then licked the soles of Corey's feet and sucked his toes, licked up his satin-smooth legs from behind, nuzzled and licked his ass crack, crotch, and tight fat balls. He bent Corey's stiff pecker down and backwards between his thighs and licked it, then let it snap back up tight under his belly. He licked and sucked and kissed Corey's asshole and drove his tongue deep inside it.

Corey nearly hit the ceiling. Going out of his gourd with excitement, he rotated his ass and moaned "Oh Coach!" again and again as the man's fat tongue darted and twisted in his ass. "Baby, you're a hot one!" panted the coach. "You've got one hot boy-pussy if I ever saw one!" He fumbled in a desk drawer, pulled out a jar of Vaseline, lubed up his cock and Corey's asshole, and, standing up close to the desk, mounted Corey from behind. With a deft thrust, he buried all nine inches of his rigid tool up Corey's pulsating ass.

Corey moaned, tears of lust and joy trickling down his downy cheeks. He couldn't believe it Coach Moore's dick up his ass! The sudden stretch was almost too much, almost painful, almost more than he could tolerate, but he was in heaven. He thought the man's arm-like cock would pop out of his mouth. It was so fucking long and thick! As the huge phallus pulsed in his depths, Corey quivered from scalp to toes and almost came. Even Steve's oversized cock

hadn't fucked him this deep. Tim was right: Coach Moore had a *fucking log* between his legs.

"Oh baby!" the coach growled, grinding his cock inside Corey. "Sweet baby-fuck!"

"Oh Coach!" Corey whined, writhing as the big man screwed him. "Coach, fuck me! Fuck me hard, man!"

The coach's greasy hands encircled Corey's waist and jerked backwards with each ramming thrust of his loins. "Christ, you're tight!" panted the man. "Fucking hot!" His thrusting soon became so wild that his muscle-bulging thighs banged against the desk, jarring it so that it inched with screeching jolts across the concrete floor.

Corey gasped with each grinding penetration of the man's battering ram into his guts. Moaning, he hauled back-handed at his own cock as fast as the coach was fucking him. He couldn't believe his luck! Finally, he was getting exactly what he wanted what he *needed*!

"Fuck!" the coach bellowed, his cock flexing inside Corey and nearly lifting him off the desk. "Christ - I'm coming!" He moaned so loudly that it was as if he didn't care if the whole world heard him, then shuddered as his spunk exploded up Corey's ass.

Corey jerked with each powerful ejaculation into his body. The man's fuck-cannon was not only blasting cum into him, but electricity and fire as well, and fuck sensation saturated every cell of his writhing young body. It was as if his nipples and toes, his nose and tongue, his fingers and scalp all of him had become cock-flesh and were was seized with orgasmic sensation. Yelping with boyish ecstasy, he shot streams of sizzling boy-spunk across the desktop. Behind him, still humping deliriously, the coach grunted like a bull, pouring bullets of man-spunk up his squeezing, spasming young asshole.

As their orgasms petered out, Coach Moore eased his cock out of Corey and lifted him off the desk, then leaned over the desktop and lapped up Corey's spunk. It was a sight! Coach Moore sucking up boy-jizz as if it were honey! Unable to resist the invitation of the man's muscular legs and buttocks, Corey squatted behind him and buried his nose in the man's ass crack and started licking it out. The coach moaned and lay face-down over the desk, turning up his ass as Corey rimmed him.

"Yeah boy, eat it out, boy! Do a good job!"

The man rotated his ass as Corey tongue-fucked it.

When Corey finally pulled his tongue out, the coach rolled over and lay face-up across the desk, his legs hanging off, his muscular feet on the floor, and Corey went to work on his enormous hairy balls and gleaming cock. The nuts were as big as lemons, the nut sac dripping sweat. The musky man-scent went to Corey's head and he jerked at his own cock as he slobbered over and sucked the coach's bull-nuts. Corey's ball-sucking caused the man's phallus to swell to full hardness again and to throb against his abdomen like a hooded cobra.

Corey lifted the heavy prick off the muscular belly and held it straight up so

58

he could study it and tongue it. "My god!" he cried. It smelled of Vaseline and the musky-sweet scent of boy-ass. He worked the tight foreskin up and down, fascinated by it. The shaft was so thick that he couldn't close his hand completely around it and, as he squeezed it, what cum still remained oozed out. Corey used both hands to wring out every last drop of man-spunk and licked it off. Then he opened his mouth as wide as he could and, holding the foreskin down tight, swallowed the naked cock head.

Coach Moore groaned and arched up, grinding his loins, flexing and extending his muscular feet as Corey pleasured his massive fucker, jerking the foreskin up and down two-handed as he sucked the succulent knob.

"Fuck yeah!" the coach sighed, writhing against the desk top, rubbing his muscular feet against the concrete floor, his toes clutching sensuously. "Oh baby, do it to me!" Arms clasped behind his head as he luxuriated in Corey's servicing, he watched every bob of Corey's blond head and every ripple of the boy's silky hot lips over the flange of his dickhead.

Corey growled like a hungry tiger, sucking and jerking, hungry for man-cum. As he sucked, he worked his nimble tongue under the man's foreskin, darted it into the huge, open piss hole. The man's cock-lube bubbled out as Corey slid the tight foreskin up and down and sucked hungrily at the throbbing, apple-sized head. Suddenly the coach arched up and grunted as he shot a torrent of thick spunk into Corey's mouth. Corey choked, surprised by the man's quick orgasm, cum oozing from the corners of his mouth as the coach fucked more spunk into his throat. Gaining control again, Corey began gulping the man's salty fuck-juice as fast as he could shoot it. Before the coach was done, it seemed that he'd fed Corey at least half a cupful.

With the coach lying there limp and dazed after two orgasms in a row, Corey stood looking down at him and jacking off. The coach looked hotter than that lifeguard on the beach. This was his former coach, for goodness sake! It was too much! His hand pistoning around his slender boy-cock, Corey felt the wonderful, mind-blowing sensations begin in his loins and his blue eyes rolled back as his body twanged. With a cry of pleasure, he shot streams of boy-jizz all over the Coach's hairy muscles.

Coach Moore laughed, rolling under the splashing torrent. "Way to go, baby! Drown me in the stuff!"

...

To his surprise almost shock Corey got a call from Steve the next afternoon and went straight down to Steve's studio in a remodeled warehouse near the beach, where he found Steve relaxing on a couch in front of a TV set. The handsome photographer was looking as muscular and tanned as ever and Corey flushed at the sight of him sitting there in nothing but a pair of tight athletic trunks.

"Corey the naked skateboard boy!" Steve said, putting his arm around Corey

as Corey sat down next to him. "How is my favorite cover boy? I'm tickled you could come right over." He kissed Corey's cheek and nibbled on his ear, which sent pleasant chills through Corey's body and made him shiver.

Corey kissed Steve's cheek, then his lips, and fed him some tongue.

"Phew!" Steve said. "You're getting me all hot and bothered! How've you been, darling? I missed you!" Before Corey could answer, Steve nodded toward the TV. "What do you think of those cuties? Some of my overseas models."

On the screen, against a background of palm leaves and brilliantly colored blossoms, a half-dozen naked bronze-skinned boys were performing a lewd, wiggling dance, their hard ons wagging from side to side and up and down. They laughed as they squirmed for the camera, showing off their smooth bodies and excited young cocks. One of them pissed a long golden stream from his hard cock and when he'd finished another boy, dropping to his knees in front of him, licked the end of his piss-dripping tool and went down on him. Two other boys started fucking, one bending over, one standing behind him and drilling his ass. The last two boys jacked off while kissing.

"Cute, huh?" Steve said. "I didn't even have to direct them. I just told them to act natural and do what they felt like doing, the horny little bastards. This was my most productive trip ever. I visited ten countries and caught at least 200 very-willing lads on film. *Very* willing!"

"Did you fuck them all?" Corey asked mischievously.

"Not all, but most," Steve said. "Certainly well over a hundred. Yeah, it's a fact: boys just can't resist a big cock. The sight of one gets them squirming and throbbing."

Corey couldn't argue with that. He reached over and started feeling up Steve's thick rod through his shorts.

As the bronze lads sucked and fucked and spurted on the TV screen, Steve pushed a magazine in front of Corey's eyes. "Voila, darling! Congratulations!"

"I know," Corey said. "I've already seen it."

"You *have*?" Steve sounded disappointed. "Darn! Of course, I feared you might have by now. I'm sorry, darling, I was hoping to get back earlier like a month ago so I could be the first to show it to you."

"It's all right," Corey said, more interested in feeling up Steve's cock than in talking about the magazine.

Steve leaned forward, picked up a cardboard box from the floor, and set it on Corey's lap. "Well, you've already seen the mag, but you haven't seen these."

The box was stuffed with unopened mail.

"All for you, cover boy. Your first batch of fan mail. I got at least half as many myself, from horny men all over the place begging for more pictures of you."

Corey stared at the horde of letters. "It'll take me a year just to read them all."

Steve stroked Corey's head. "I'll help you sort through them, if you want. In fact, I suggest that you let me act as your manager for a modest fee, of course. I have experience with this stuff and will look out for your interests. You don't

60

want to be taken advantage of. I've managed a lot of boys just like you."

"How will I be taken advantage of?"

"Like this...." Steve pushed the box off Corey's lap and started ripping off his clothes.

"Oh, I don't mind," Corey said, laughing as he squirmed.

"I never thought you would," Steve said, shucking off his shorts. "Which is why you need me. You don't want to give it away for free. You've got hundreds of horny men aching for a piece of your chicken ass, and that's where I come in to see that you cash in on what you've got."

Corey found himself being stretched out on the couch with the muscular photographer stretched out on top of him. "Oh Steve, I missed you!" he murmured.

"Well, I missed you too," Steve said, grinding his oozing prong against Corey's belly. "I've been thinking about your tight little ass the whole time I've been gone."

"Even while you were fucking those other boys?"

"Of course," Steve said, and slipped his juicy tongue into Corey's open mouth.

On the TV screen, boys with bronze skin squirmed and ejaculated. On the studio couch, Steve hooked his shoulders under Corey's knees and screwed his greased, rock-hard stud-meat to the hilt up Corey's throbbing young ass.

...

Steve was right on about the fan letters. Corey couldn't deal with them himself. How does an inexperienced boy, willing though he may be, handle a few hundred horny daddies who want to fuck him? He was glad that Steve was willing to act as his manager on a commission basis.

Corey had never realized that he was capable of turning on men so much that they were willing to pay, and pay well, for the chance to fuck him. Many of the men sent pictures of themselves in which they showed their big hairy erections, and Corey got so turned on that he jacked off while imagining them up his ass. He wanted them as much as they wanted him. There was no denying that.

Corey's first client wasn't a man who had written directly to him, but one who had written to Steve and had offered an outrageous sum of money for the chance to fuck Corey while Steve made a videotape of the action, a one-of-a-kind videotape the client would keep. His bid for Corey's body was the highest of all the offers yet made, so Steve and Corey agreed that he should have the first crack at Corey's ass.

For the occasion, Corey showed up at Steve's studio dressed only in his baseball cap and jeans. Anticipating the meeting, he'd had a nonstop throbbing hard on for the last 24 hours but had forced himself not to jack off. It was the first time in years that he'd gone a full day without shooting his load. He was used to three, maybe even four, orgasms a day. The thought of making it on

61

videotape with an older man excited him terribly and he was standing shirtless and barefoot on his skateboard and trembling as the man walked in.

The man had silver hair and looked to be in his late fifties, but was handsome and rugged for his age, like a cowboy dressed in a business suit. Corey was turned on by the looks of him and watched him closely as he stripped. His boy-cock jumped at the sight of a well-built physique and a thick cock of at least eight inches that stood straight out, throbbing as excitedly as his own. The man wasted no time. Once naked, he crouched at Corey's feet and began licking Corey's toes as Corey balanced on his skateboard and Steve videotaped the action.

The man spent a long time slobbering over Corey's tanned bare feet, licking and sucking Corey's toes as he slowly masturbated his uncut cock. Then he rose up to lick Corey's belly, nipples, and armpits. Standing, he kissed Corey deeply, licking out Corey's throat, then slid back down, unzipped Corey's pants, and pulled out Corey's stiff cock, which he licked and nuzzled for a few minutes before going down on it and swallowing it to Corey's plump, pink, hairless balls.

Corey, holding onto the man's shoulders for balance, his toes clutching the skateboard, sighed luxuriously as he wiggled his hips and thrust in and out of the man's wonderfully hot and talented mouth. What a way to make a living! he was thinking, imagining himself a professional hustler for life.

The man sucked until Corey was on the verge of coming, then let up at the last moment and released Corey's cock. Corey moaned with frustration. When Corey's cock had settled down again, the man resumed sucking it, rapidly bringing Corey again to the brink of ecstasy before letting up. Corey thought his nuts would burst. When Corey had again settled down, the man resumed sucking and again he nearly got Corey off before letting up at the last possible second. Corey thought he would lose his mind. He wasn't used to such teasing. Most men tried to suck him off as quick as possible so they could drink his load.

"Hey man, I wanna shoot!" he complained.

The client smiled, then licked and sucked Corey's nuts until his dick nearly jumped out of its skin, bubbling boy-lube like sap. The man bent Corey's prick down, engulfed it, and churned his fat, wet tongue at the sensitive underside of it. In two seconds Corey's eyes rolled back and he let out a whimpering yelp as the boy-jism surged through his cock and scalded the man's throat. Whimpering and humping out of control, Corey shimmied his hairless legs together as the delicious spasms pulsed through his loins and his cum shot again and again down the man's gullet. He felt hot spurts on his feet and he looked down to see the man jacking off onto them. When the man had sucked every drop of boy-spunk out of Corey, he again crouched like a cat and licked his own cum off Corey's toes and skateboard.

"Marvelous!" the man said, and they took a break for refreshments.

Steve was getting off on the scene as well. Corey couldn't help but notice Steve's uncut dick sticking out the fly of his pants, ramrod stiff and throbbing as

he videotaped the action and now as they sipped soft drinks. The client asked Corey about himself and was surprised to learn that he'd just graduated from high school.

"You look much too young," the man said. "You're such a smooth, skinny little thing. You could be my grandson."

Corey flushed, excited by the idea.

When the taping resumed, the client positioned Corey on the floor on all fours, but with his hands on his skateboard, then he got down behind him and started lapping up and down the length of Corey's ass crack and nuzzling and kissing his exposed, twitching asshole. Corey couldn't help but squirm and wiggle his butt, especially when the man drove his tongue up Corey's butt. As he ate Corey out, he masturbated his cock fiercely and soon was lubing it up with Vaseline. Then he kneeled up behind Corey, grabbed Corey's ass, and inserted his thick cock where his tongue had been. Corey sighed as the man's hairy belly met his smooth, upturned butt and as the man's prick, completely buried inside him, throbbed and flexed. "Fantastic!" the man breathed, sliding his rigid cock in and out of Corey. "What an incredible tight ass!"

Corey shivered, his body shot through with hot flashes and chills as the grunting man screwed his hot slab of uncut fuck-gristle in and out of Corey's sizzling boy-pussy. He'd never been fucked by a man this old, and it was thrilling, like getting fucked by his grandfather, except that this man was a lot handsomer, sexier, and well-built than his real grandfather, and his old cock, although not as massive as Coach Moore's or Steve's, was just as hard. And this grandpa man knew how to fuck! It took Corey's breath away as the big prong plunged into him again and again, the man's hairy belly jolting his up-turned wiggling little butt with each thrust.

"Fuck me!" Corey panted. "Screw me!" He was getting exactly what he wanted what he needed and he was getting paid for it! He could hardly believe it!

The man screwed in deep, then withdrew his cock completely, yanking it out of Corey's open ass and plunging it back in just as Corey's fuck hole began to close. Corey could feel air tickle his gaping asshole as the man yanked out, then the man's hot rock-hard cock stuff it again. He almost shot off each time the massive cock torpedoed into him.

Without withdrawing his cock, the man suddenly lifted Corey up off the floor and onto Steve's desk, where he rolled Corey onto his back with his ass at the desktop's edge. Standing in front of the desk, gripping Corey's ankles as he continued fucking him, he began sucking Corey's toes. Corey lay there squirming and half out of his mind as the man screwed him and simultaneously sucked his toes, his untouched cock flopping against his stomach and oozing pre-cum. The stimulation nearly drove Corey out of his mind and soon an electric spasm gripped Corey's loins and his untouched cock began to spurt jism.

"Uhhh!" he grunted, watching in fascination as the boy-spunk squirted from

his flexing cock and splashed on his stomach and chest. As he writhed with orgasm, the man continued sucking his toes and fucking his ass deep. As his spurts petered out, the man leaned forward over him and lapped the jism off his skin.

The man pulled out and climbed up on the desk to straddle Corey's chest. His greased cock looked incredibly huge, its open piss hole dripping, and Corey choked on it as the man forced it into his throat. Gripping Corey by the hair, the man rocked his loins and Corey felt the vein-bulging cock swell even larger in his mouth. With a powerful shudder it ejected a torrent of hot spunk down Corey's gullet. Though still half choking, Corey gulped, taking the grunting man's load and sucking for more. At the same time, he fisted his own stiff cock in a frenzy and in seconds felt the surging sensations of another orgasm drill through his youthful rod. Pointing his toes, squeezing his smooth legs together, he shot a surprisingly profuse load of boy-spunk against the man's back and ass as he sucked the dregs from the man's pulsing cock.

STATES OF AROUSAL
by John Patrick

The dark stranger seemed to be looking first at a cute blond standing near me at the bar, and then suddenly it seemed he had turned and was looking directly at us, at me and Mark. His eyes were deep pools of black at this distance, set wide on either side of a straight Romanesque nose. They gleamed darkly within the relative brightness of the youthful, broad-shouldered stud's face. He moved toward us. He smiled. Now he was smiling at me, ignoring Mark. He wore a white, long sleeve, silky shirt not tucked into his jeans, but still neat. The hair was dark, cut short. He was the sexiest thing I'd seen in months. He was someone I might fear if I saw him on the street, but here in the bar, he seemed relatively safe. His smile grew broader the closer he got, so why was I feeling as if I were a specimen under a microscope?

"Do you know him?" I asked Mark, who usually knows everybody in the bar, and had fucked anybody who was the least bit interesting.

"No. Wish I did," he murmured.

When the stud was so close I could almost smell his sweat, Mark whispered, "I'm not sure really. I don't think I've seen him here before, and yet." He sounded as confused as I felt. Poor Mark had fucked so many guys, but such a hot stud like this would be hard to forget even for him.

Then the stud passed by us on the way to the john. I thought he was going to introduce himself, but he was just teasing us. We sat down now, glum, without speaking, feeling the sensuous caress of the air conditioning on our cheeks drying the sweat that had covered our faces and necks from our dancing.

Mark ordered more beers. Suddenly, a strong, warm hand touched my shoulder. I flinched and jerked my head around.

"Don't I know you?" the dark stranger asked.

I was speechless, staring into those eyes, which I now saw were very dark brown, deep and luminous. I looked at him in awe and then at Mark, whose face was turned up to the stranger's. The air around the man seemed to stir, almost to crackle, with energy.

"I guess not," he said. I felt his hand brush my neck, so quick that all I really felt was a chill run down my spine. I turned my head and looked up at him again. His lips parted and his perfect teeth gleamed very white, but then he glanced over at Mark, who seemed even more enchanted with him than I.

The next thing I knew, the stranger had taken Mark's hand and was leading him away, onto the dance floor.

I sat there dumbly, feeling emotions wash over me in waves feelings I hadn't had in a long time. Mark usually got the guy, and that was fine with me. Mark and I had been lovers for six months and when it ended we still remained fast friends. He had even invited me to go home with him when his trick showed

some interest in me, but I always refused. I was looking for love, I said, not just sex. Now I was angry that I had acted so stupidly; I was frustrated that I'd let this dark stranger get away. He danced before me, sultry, graceful, as hard as iron. And he was dancing with Mark.

I couldn't take watching them any more; besides I had to pee. In the john, I stood at a urinal when a drunk threw his arm over my shoulder and began to stroke my crotch. I managed to slip out from under his heavy hand, but there was another one there to take his place, along with another one. I am small, blond, blue-eyed, easily threatened, and I was scared. I couldn't fight off one, let alone three. Then, suddenly, and practically silently, they backed away. The dark stranger had entered the john and was approaching me. He looked down at me and smiled, "Hey, it's time to go, baby."

I was already saying yes, yes, whatever you want. But there was Mark, waiting for us. Was this it? Was it going to happen at long last: Mark and me and the stud?

"You gotta be careful in there," the stud said. "That's worse than any john we got down in Miami."

Miami? He's from Miami. Maybe that was it. Maybe we had seen him when we went there a year ago. Yes, that was it, Mark confirmed, the man was a dancer at the Boardwalk. Mark had almost summoned up the courage to actually pay for it, but then he backed down and we went back to the hotel together, just the two of us. It was on that night that I let Mark fuck me again for the first time since our relationship had ended. We said it was just "recreational sex," that we were both horny and needed relief, but I knew things would be different between us after that. I was finally able to accept Mark as he was, and even enjoy the once-a-week screw he'd throw into me. At least I didn't have to see him every morning, masturbating in the shower because I wouldn't give him my ass.

Now, months later, here we were again, a potential three-way in the offing. Yes, I remembered now the dancing stud from Miami. His name was Rolando and he was a headliner there, but he traveled a lot, he said, seeing "friends."

In Mark's old Lincoln (a Mark, of course), while he drove, Rolando and I got better acquainted. Rolando was hot to trot, but he started slowly, with kisses and caresses on my lips and face, sending a delicious chill down to my cock. He reached out and touched my cheekbone with the backs of his fingers, causing me first to tilt my head a little away, then towards his hand again, trying mindlessly to make contact again. Rolando gave off such incredible sexual energy. Leaning into me, he whispered in my ear, "I want you."

It was surrender. Utter, total surrender. I had to stop struggling and listen to my body. He placed my hand on his groin. I felt the hardness there, the hugeness of it, and, for a moment, I actually felt fear and my body shook. He could kill me with a cock like that!

His lips had come to rest on the most delicate part of my neck, down by my collarbone. Then he raised his head and looked me in the eye. "Oh, god, I want you," he repeated.

66

I looked at his face and tried to read his eyes as he could read mine. The flutter passed through me, and then something was released. I heard myself groan as he lowered his head again, and I felt his teeth take my skin between them.

All this was driving Mark crazy. He sped up, anxious to get back to his place so he could get in on the action. He had a tendency to drive the old car balls-out when he was turned-on, so I was used to it, but Rolando was outraged when we hit a bump in the highway and he banged his head on the rearview mirror. He turned towards Mark. "Slow the fuck down," he growled, and Mark obeyed.

"You're actin' like a jealous lover," Rolando said, drooping his arm around Mark's shoulder.

"We aren't lovers," I piped up.

"Is that so? Coulda fooled me. You two look like you should be lovers. In fact, you look like you might be brothers."

Mark smiled. "We get that all the time. No, but that's how we met, actually...."

"Yeah," I interrupted, afraid Mark would make a long story out of it, "people kept mistaking us for each other so we had to meet...."

Mark wasn't going to give up easily. He had to elaborate. "And then we became lovers. But not for long. Now we're friendly rivals, I guess you could say."

"Well, don't you worry none, there's plenty to go 'round," Rolando said, patting his crotch with his right hand. I brought my hand on top of his and pushed down, anxious to feel the bulge again.

And Rolando was right, there was *plenty* to go 'round and it was free, at least as far as I could tell. Rolando said he had stayed on in town after visiting an unnamed man whom he had met the week before in Miami. "After one of those, I need to relax, have a couple a drinks, have some fun," he said.

While Rolando went to pee, I joined Mark in the kitchen to get some beers and I told him I was sure that Rolando wouldn't be charging us for the pleasure of his company. I told Mark what Rolando had whispered as we were walking up the steps to Mark's apartment, his hands stroking my ass: "I'm here for pure pleasure." That seemed to satisfy Mark, who refused to pay for it regardless of the package. This had been the major hurdle in Miami, and, besides, that night it appeared that Rolando had them waiting in line. We only managed a few minutes of his time that night after his sizzling strip. The sign out front had said Rolando was "direct from Rio," but the Brazilian-born stud said that was a joke, since he'd lived in Miami for ten years. Smiling, he quickly moved away from us when an older gentleman motioned him over for a drink.

Now I was guzzling my beer; Mark didn't believe in air conditioning and it was unusually warm for May. I felt sticky all over as if I had been smeared with semen. That was what I thought about as I listened to Rolando when he began talking about his nights at the Boardwalk. Smeared with semen....

My body pulsed. Rolando was in the kitchen now, beside me, drinking his beer. I felt a large, warm hand trail down from my ear, across my neck to my ass. A hand massaged my buns.

Mark had moved to the living room and turned on the stereo. "Careless Whisper" started; Mark loved George Michael. Rolando responded to the song, starting off slowly, then rubbing my ass faster and faster. My eyes closed, I visualized a sticky penis in my hands. I opened my mouth to receive either his tongue or his prick. I was thirsty and sweating. Faster. More. He was all over me. The song ended, another started. I opened my eyes, my mind reeling more from desire than from the half-finished can of beer. He stood before me now, his erection following the line of his zipper. Kneeling, I unzipped his jeans and tugged them over his ass, my hands trembling so badly that I was grateful not to have to deal with his underwear as well. He stretched and pulled off his shirt with one motion.

His cock was everything I had hoped it would be and more. I was fascinated by the smooth, soft feel of his thick foreskin as I slid it back and his huge prick head bulged out. It wasn't the longest cock I had ever seen, but it was incredibly thick. Just having the head enter me would probably make me come, I thought, and I licked away the pre-cum. As his cock slid between my lips, the music rang in my ears.

I sucked the magnificent cock for only a few moments before Rolando was lifting me up and tugging at my clothes. My jeans, along with a drenched and twisted tank top, made a small pile of abandoned clothing next to his.

I stepped back to gaze at him at the peak of his arousal, his whole body seeming to be wild with unreleased sexual tension.

Mark walked into the kitchen right then and gaped in amazement at the sight of the naked Rolando. Rolando smiled at him, but grasped my butt cheeks. His penis was soon shoved against my crack, and he moaned. Mark got the bottle of lotion he kept at the sink and came over to us. He reached out and stroked Rolando's hairy balls, then, as Rolando backed up, Mark slid his fingers around Rolando's penis, greasing it, then guiding it into me as Rolando held my ass still. I cried out, gasping, my body stretched tight with desire. The music swirled faster through my mind. As my cock began to throb, Rolando pushed deeper into me. I raised my buttocks to meet his hips.

Mark hurriedly tugged off his jeans. I watched him closely as he stripped. I felt a catch of pure lust in my throat and chest when he took my hand and brought it to his cock. "What are we going to do about this?" he asked.

I considered the question, maintaining direct eye contact. Mark knew how much I loved his seven-inch, cut cock; it was his insatiable desire, and consequent slutty ways I couldn't tolerate day in and day out. But now I was in the middle of it and there was serious heat going on here, unlike anything we had ever experienced.

Rolando pressed against me and I had to stretch to reach Mark's mouth for his slow, deep kiss. Out of the corner of my eye I saw Rolando smiling as he slowed

his fucking and reached out and lightly caressed my pecs, then gave my nipple an insolent pinch.

Mark pulled my hand deliberately down to press against his crotch. Heat flooded my face. I watched his response as I reached out to fondle him. I released his cock and gave it several upward strokes, felt it hardening, watched the lust grow in his eyes. I took the weight of his testicles in my hands and squeezed gently. His pubic hair was thick and wiry; his cock thrust hard against my cheek as he moaned. Pressing him against the counter, I kissed his tummy, then bent to take his cock in my mouth. I drew him deeply into my mouth with slow, easy movements. I used my hands and mouth together, moving more urgently, I was sucking deeply now, hands on each of his muscular thighs.

Mark leaned back, watching Rolando fuck me, and his body was soon tense with excitement. I moaned in response to the strong hands kneading my ass, spreading me open, fucking me, and I wriggled against Rolando. Mark sensed my pleasure, and he continued to watch with obvious enjoyment. He stroked my head possessively, sensually, then wrapped his large hands around my head and thrust his cock into my throat.

Rolando and Mark moved in hot rhythm together. It was glorious, but it was short-lived. Suddenly, Rolando pulled completely out of me with a lewd pop, and simultaneously Mark slipped his cock from my mouth, touching my naked shoulders as he lifted away.

I relaxed, looking only at Rolando, at the huge, uncut cock now bobbing before me, deliberately teasing Mark. There was more to this than would meet Rolando's eye: Mark had always wanted to watch me be fucked by someone else with full abandon, and I had given him this pleasure. Now he wanted to stick his cock where Rolando had been, which was fine with me, but looking at him, giving him permission, might break the spell, might prevent him from freely taking what he wanted.

Rolando reached down and swooped me up into his embrace. Mark pressed his sweaty body hard against me. He slid his sopping wet cock into me. Leaning back, my arms extended, I rode him hard. He lifted me up and down on him with ease, his orgasm close, heat rising from his groin. As Rolando played with my nipples, Mark came, hard, one of the hardest orgasms I'd ever seen him have.

Slowly, Mark withdrew and suggested we go to the bedroom. I followed Mark, clinging limply to Rolando, and fell towards the bed. I sprawled on my back as Mark leaned over and kissed me deeply.

Rolando got on the bed between my legs and toyed with my erection. He stroked my cock, spread me wide with both hands and guided his cock towards my ass. Mark watched with delight as I squirmed, then bent his head to my cock and tasted it. He lifted his face, forcing me to look at him.

"You want Rolando's big meat now, don't you?"

"Yes. I want to be fucked again. I want to be fucked hard, as hard as he can."

"You do, do you?" Rolando asked, shoving it into me without care.

I cried out. Mark moved up alongside me, leaning on one elbow as he looked down at Rolando's cock invading me. With his free hand, he continued to toy with my cock. Smoothly Rolando thrust into me. I responded by bucking against him, low growls emerging from my throat.

"God, look at that!" Mark gushed.

Pro that he was, Rolando fucked superbly, deliberately, lifting my ass in the air and drawing me to him. I could not bear it. He was controlling my movement, as he pumped slowly in and out. I writhed in his hands as I desperately tried to grind against him. Rolando stiffened; I saw in his face and heard in his groaning that he was going to come, and, sure enough, hot cum filled me again, and began to drip out of my aching asshole, spilling onto the sheet as he withdrew. He got on the other side of me and the two of them shared my cock.

Heat, even more intense than before, flooded my body. And I came in long, shattering spasms. Soon I was drowning in emotion and cum. Drawing back, Mark scrambled to his knees, got between my thighs and shoved his renewed cock into me. He looked at me as the cock slid in and said, his face and voice hot, "Tell me that you love me."

I moved with him, and that little explosion went off in my head again surrender. My arms and legs wrapped tightly around him, I bucked wildly, gripping his cock with my ass muscles, feeling his heat as never before. Rolando was there, on the bed, watching, but he didn't matter any more. This was just about Mark and me and our crazy love.

"Yes, I love you, Mark. Oh, god, yes, I love you. I'll always love you." I held onto him as he continued to fuck me, determined to come again. Finally, my cries mingled with his as he shot another load into me.

"You bastard," I said as he collapsed warm and solid against me.

- - -

For days after this, I noticed an elevation of energy, a bounce in my step. I felt almost weightless. We didn't talk at all about my lesson in giving up resistance. I certainly didn't mention how sexually aroused I had been with Mark and Rolando. I caught Mark studying me surreptitiously now and then, but he didn't say anything either. Gradually I floated back to earth. It was then that Mark suggested we spend the weekend in Miami....

BI-NIGHT
by Edmund Miller

With years of hands-on experience to my credit, I can report that there are two types of men. There are gay men guys who frankly enjoy the erotic experience of other men. I am happy to number myself in this group. And then there are straight men guys who fantasize about women's breasts while they are having sex with other men. I have never encountered any other types. But in recent years I am not encountering either type so often as I used to: the pickings are always better when you are young and beautiful, and it even turns out that the old wine of beautiful is no match for the bouquet of even an indifferent young.

But now that I have moved a few years away from young I have discovered a useful fact about the straight guys: they are far less moved than gay guys by the claims of either beauty or youth in another man. I do not know whether they feign indifference to convince themselves that looks only matter in a woman or they truly are indifferent. I do not much care either. I only know that they are far less concerned than gay guys about seeing what they are getting. This fact makes it a lot easier to reach them through personal ads addressed to the straight but curious.

Recently I tried a new ripple on this approach and learned something myself. I placed the following ad in *Swinging Singles*:

Mature GWM seeking attractive young straight
couple to explore new horizons. I am gray at
the temple but attractive and fit for my age.
I miss the muscular energies of youth: you will
have to coax me along: I have never been with a
woman or a male/female couple before. Box 708.

Hard as it may be to believe, I got over three hundred responses to the one ad placement, some of them coming in as late as seven months later. A few looked too weird, and three or four wanted money. Six were from incarcerated felons. And two addresses did not pan out. But I contacted all the rest, and thereby set myself up in a very active sex life for a whole year. This is the story of a recent encounter.

Marianne wrote the letter. She said she and her husband were in an open relationship, both preferring men for their outside interests but preferring to do things together most of all. They were both gym fanatics, often meeting men at the gym, and she got a good workout on such occasions, but Sean tended to watch rather than participate. Sometimes the problem was the other guy, but usually it was that Sean felt intimidated. He was hard and muscular but his body

was on the small side. She thought he might relax more with an older man, somebody who was not a body builder.

From this description of Marianne's I supposed that Sean really was short but thought there might be an additional shortage in the cock department accounting for his shyness. This possibility did not bother me. A small cock can be easier to handle and a lot more grateful. The picture of Sean she enclosed revealed a baby-faced beauty. His skin was pale white, his blond hair was parted in the middle and neatly fell to each side, framing his face. He had long eyelashes and full, pouty lips. She did not enclose a picture of herself. I took that as a good sign an indication that she understood I was really interested in the man and also that she was trying to show him a good time.

We agreed to meet on neutral territory, an elegant hotel bar. But the precaution was unnecessary. We hit it off right away. Marianne was perky and energetic. She had long auburn hair, which she wore loose around her shoulders. She had pale, clear skin and wore little makeup except for traditional dark red lipstick. Marianne did all the talking for the two of them when it came to setting up the ground rules for our encounter, but Sean was friendly enough in general conversation. His hair was paler and blonder than it had looked in the picture. His skin was paler too, but with a very healthy peaches-and-cream look. "Tell him how beautiful he is," she said; "he won't believe me." I told him, but he seemed unconvinced. He wanted to be reassured that he was "O.K." compared to other guys. Having put the words of that lame compliment into my mouth, he did seem willing to accept it from me. "See. What did I tell you?" she said, shrugging her elegant shoulders. When we stood up to leave, I saw that she was taller than her husband by quite a bit.

We went back to their place. She took charge right away when we got inside, directing us right into the bedroom. She lay back on the bed and raised one of her legs in a provocatively revealing way. Sean look a seat in the corner and crossed his legs. Not to be left standing in the middle of the room, I sat on the corner of the bed, being careful not to block Sean's view, and settled in to watch the show. But she was apparently not willing to let me just watch and pulled my hand under her skirt. I felt the softness of her legs through pantyhose. She pushed my hand up farther, and I felt even stranger territory, damp and wrinkled and hairy. I pulled my hand away.

Sean came over to stand behind me at the side of the bed. As Marianne unbuttoned and removed her blouse with deliberate slowness, Sean took off my jacket and opened and removed my tie. I reached around behind to grope him and felt hard thighs and a small hard round ass through his fashionably baggy trousers. He leaned over me or through me really pushing me down closer to his wife's dark mysteries. He reached under her skirt with his left hand while reaching up under my shirt with his right. She closed her eyes and moaned softly. He was rubbing and kneading the muscles of my back quite pleasurably, but after a few minutes of this I moved his hand around to my chest and helped him find my nipples. He pinched and tickled these until he got me moaning

72

softly as well. Then he moved his left hand up to play with his wife's nipples through and then under her bra. She turned a bit to the side and asked me to undo this garment. As I did, I saw a little tattooing of bumps and indentations laid out across her back. I ran my hand over these and found the skin strangely alien soft and smooth despite the lumps. As I was doing so, Sean reached back and removed my trousers with a single swift tug. As he moved to put these on the chair, he let his own trousers fall to the floor, revealing hard, muscular thighs and calves covered by a thin golden matting of hair. As he bent over to fold the two pairs of trousers, his shirt rode up a bit in the back, and I surmised from the hard round curves that peeked out below that he was not wearing any underwear.

Somehow while I was not looking, Marianne had removed all her clothing down to the pantyhose, which she was at this point rolling up, legs held high above her on the bed. Sean came back to his position behind me and reached over me to push her legs back still farther. His fingers disappeared into some mysterious place as I reached around him to cup his buttocks and lay a finger on his soft pucker. He pushed himself forward on the bed and sank his head forward between his wife's legs, arching himself up on the bed at the same time. I pushed his shirt up a little and ran my hands slowly over the flawless alabaster rear of a Greek statue. I reached to poke an index finger in his asshole, but he tensed up. I smacked his ass lightly with my open palm, and he relaxed as a faint red handprint appeared in all the whiteness and began quickly fading to pink and disappearing.

As his head bobbed furiously at the work it was doing, I slipped a finger into him, slowly but inexorably. It felt snug and at home there. I felt around under him and discovered a rock hard little rod pointing straight up and tight against his belly. I stroked it lightly and then, as he began moaning softly, I added another finger to his asshole. I pulled down on his cock, which resisted and hung back. It gave a bit at last like a rusty lever on an old machine and bent down a bit forward. The effort was rewarded as his ass arched up some more and opened to another half inch of finger I had not known I had.

Then Sean moved forward on the bed, squeezing my fingers tightly in his ass and dragging my hand along with him. After reaching over to the night table for lubricant and rubbers, he pulled my hand out of him and lubed us both up. He took my hand in his and brought the two of us together into her damp female place. It felt all loose, and the walls seemed to be alive and moving. I wrapped my fingers around his to hold on for dear life. Marianne let out a strange, unearthly sound and began convulsing, her whole body vibrating in a hot sweat. Sean pulled our hands out, put a condom on himself, and then without further foreplay knelt forward to enter her with his cock in a single smooth movement.

"Do it. Do it!" she was saying over and over again. Then I heard something else. "Do it! Fuck him," she said quite distinctly. "Fuck him! Fuck him!" Appreciating the significance of this invitation, I pulled a condom over my swollen cock and pushed the thing down the shaft as far as it would go. Then I

too knelt forward and tried to sink in with a stroke. But Sean tensed up on me again. I guided two lubed fingers back inside of him, where they encountered a huge distended lump. I stroked this a bit, pressing against it alternately with each finger the way a cat uses its paws to prepare a spot on your belly for settling in to nap. As I did this they both let out loud cries simultaneously and I leaned forward to thrust most of my cock into the waiting hole. My fingers were still wedged inside, and when I tried to pull back on them, I felt the lump pulsating against them and heard my two friends cry out in ecstasy again.

Eventually I did pry myself loose. I put some lube on my thumb and ran it around the rim of Sean's hole, pressing back the surface so that, inch by inch, I could sink deeper and deeper in. He moaned in pleasure at each advance. When I was all the way in, I started to pull back and encountered the resistance of an airtight vacuum. I had to press the side of his asshole with my thumb to let a little air in, but then I could pull back easily: in fact I had to pull his hips back against me with both hands to keep from being thrust back out of the narrow channel completely. Using my hands on his hips to control my thrusts, I then began to fuck in a more normal rhythm. I noticed that when I pulled back on him, he came completely out of his wife, and she let out a low whine each time and scrambled to help line him up again for the reentry. We kept at this for five minutes ten minutes, twenty.

Finally her convulsions became so extreme that he could not keep up with her. He began working her off with his hand, and liberated from the complicated rhythms of the scene, I was able to speed up my thrusts. With a guiding thumb up his ass and two fingers of the same hand stroking the base of his cock, I started to come and was gratified to discover that he was discharging over my hand at the same time.

We all fell back on the bed, exhausted. I closed my eyes and nodded off for a moment to some rhythmic humming.

When I started awake, I was momentarily disoriented, lost in some strange world smothering in soft cushions. Then I realized that I had fallen to rest my head against Marianne's breasts, now gently heaving to a regular, steady beat. I felt my way clear of the breasts, finding that they fell away at my touch, great lazy things. Sean reached over to suck on one of the nipples, and I noticed that even his full, dark lips failed to cover it. I joined him tentatively, licking up against his lips, darting my tongue in under the edge, glancing against his own tongue at work. But when I tried to kiss him full on the lips, he pushed me away. He would not even let me lap around in the vicinity after that, so I started working on Marianne's other nipple. Unlike a man's, it was soft and yielding, and it responded to the attention immediately.

As I tried to contain Marianne's breast with one hand as it seemed to keep retreating from my tongue whichever way I pushed, I reached around underneath Sean and discovered that he was hard again. I pulled him around behind me, and he thrust up against me in urgent little strokes. I put a condom on him, and he sank into me easily, all the way in on the first try. He thrust

74

eagerly, trying to go deeper and encounter my prostate just out of reach.

As I spread my ass cheeks to help him out, Marianne turned to face the base of the bed and took the tip of my cock in her mouth. She pulled the foreskin down and licked all underneath this and along the shaft. With a free hand, I urged her to suck deeper on my mounting erection, but she could not, having had no experience with anything of a size nearly on this order.

As Sean thrust home inside me, I had a sympathetic orgasm and discharged all over Marianne's face and hands and into the loose tresses of her auburn hair. When she got up to clean herself off, I moved a hand around behind Sean, who had left his spent cock resting in my ass, and thrust two fingers back up his ass, considerably looser after all the action it had seen.

Marianne came back over to the bed, on Sean's side this time. She was carrying a long rubber dildo with ribbed or, rather, fluted edges. It was only about an inch across at the wider parts although more cylindrical, not so wide as my cock in fact but it was the length that made it truly formidable. Except for a quick application of lube, she thrust this thing into Sean unceremoniously in a single thrust, sinking it seven or nine inches down at the stroke. He gasped in agony and went limp inside me in a second. He pulled out of me or fell out and reached around to remove the invader from his rear. Unfortunately, Marianne got in seven or eight rapid lunges before she even grasped that something was the matter.

"Hey, hey, you're killing him there!" I said. "Here, let me show you." And with that I took the offending appliance from her hand and pulled it back so that it just rested in the cradle of his pucker, throbbing now more in pain than in excitement. "A dildo up a man's ass serves a different purpose than a cock. Rapid thrusts are going to hurt with something as unyielding as hard rubber. The point of the sensation is the feeling of fullness, a quiet, calm feeling of wholeness and completeness. It isn't at all like fucking, where the frenzy of one's partner is part of the experience and where even the biggest cock has some give to it." Then I delicately soothed Sean's asshole with lube and imperceptibly eased the bulb at the head of the dildo inside. By working my fingers around the rim of the opening, I loosened him up so much that he sucked in another two bulges along the shaft as we watched. A little light pressure on the end of the dildo just to keep it in place and some more fingering at the other end eventually brought him to the point where he seemed almost ready to make the whole thing disappear up inside him. As I tugged back to prevent this from happening, he let out a moan of content and rolled over on his back where I couldn't get at it anymore.

I moved around to sit on his face, and Marianne sat down on his erection, reaching forward at the same time to play with my rearoused organ. After a few minutes of an intoxicating rim job I had to pull off or risk passing out and falling off the bed. Marianne seemed to be having the same problem, and we all just simultaneously fell over one another in a heap and fell asleep for more than an hour.

I see them regularly now, and Marianne has been learning to deep throat a big cock. With the secret of how to use a dildo on a man that she learned that first night she is a formidable force in a threesome. Sean will not see me without her, but he is completely uninhibited when the three of us get together. I have a few more tricks to teach him: sucking cock, kissing....

THE WEDGE AND THE VOYEUR
by Mark Anderson

"They call me the Wedge," he said proudly, then proceeded to prove the point. My ability to attract off-the-wall, kinky dudes was uncanny.

His zipper scratched downward in the dark, silent hallway leading from the bar to the smelly john. I waited, heart pounding against my rib cage. Dirty jeans were pulled apart boldly by even dirtier fingers. The aged jockeys, once white, held a promising package. Evidently, the exhibitionist was as excited as evidenced by the wet spots dotting the bulging, thin cotton.

"Wait," I said eyeing his crotch, as I groped at mine.

Message clear, he understood what the voyeur in me recognized, that his kinky nature required an audience. Following my request, he relaxed against the wall in the empty passageway as I did. We tried to assume nonchalant poses, but clutched and sucked too eagerly on our cold brews. A single chick, then a dude sauntered by more intent in emptying their bladders than paying us any notice.

In the relative dimness of the hallway between sounds of splashing piss and that of the raucous bar noise, we stood waiting, silently. My eyes traveled repeatedly from his crotch to his eyes. He watched me shamelessly, in anticipation. I felt the electricity of desire build then snap across the narrow space we inhabited. The cotton underwear at the open zipper glowed enticingly.

Slowly, ever so slowly, the bulged cotton expanded. Filling, the jockeys lifting then starting to stretch, pushing from the open fly, holding the promised, yet trapped flesh. Was the pounding music sending tremors through the building or had the cotton moved to a rhythm of its own bold immodesty?

When the scruffy chick exited the can, I noticed how my companion turned, giving her full opportunity to check out his crotch. Even though she neglected to look down, that simple, but calculated flash excited him considerably.

"Stay that way till the guy leaves," I said, enjoying his excitement and indulging my deviant curiosity.

Watching him facing the open doorway of the men's washroom I could see his chest rise and fall rapidly. How far would this guy go, I wondered? A dark shadow filled the doorway, then the dude appeared. Moving toward the bar he glanced down at my friend, snickered, but looked back as he passed to confirm what he had seen, before becoming lost in the bar. Turning to me as if I were a stranger, the exhibitionist arched his crotch, demonstrating what he had just flashed. The cock jutted hard, sideways along the inside of the flimsy cotton. Nuts, heavy with excitement pulled the briefs down over the zipper's lethal tab and were larger than I had expected. Was each defined orb a rival for the cock in size?

"I want you to stay standing like that, understood?"

The glazed eyes told me all I needed to know. We were players. Moving

toward him, I buttoned the top of his jeans, leaving the cotton bunched in a pouch hanging erotically from the open fly. Looking down at the bag outlined by the jeans, he enjoyed my alteration. Seeing his crotch, grossly accentuated, he was fascinated by my simple adjustment. His cock and balls were exposed yet safely hidden behind the thin, frayed pouch.

"Follow me into the bar," I said, then walked away.

Although it was crowded, I found a spot across from the bar, near a wall with a ledge to lean upon. Looking around the room, I saw my young friend parade through the crowds toward my side.

"Good boy," I told him. "Now go and get us some fresh beers."

Handing him five bucks, I watched his reaction. He realized that I had forced his hand. With a quiver of excitement he turned toward the bar, causing a few quick looks to which he pretended to be oblivious. Returning, his eyes watched where mine were centered. It was all he wanted. The pouch remained full with lust, fuelling his passionate need for indecent exposure.

"You forgot something."

"What?" the punk with sex-crazed eyes said.

"Show me the Wedge."

The husky voice said, "Ya, right," as his fingers lowered then quickly dug at the dirty, elastic waistband of the jockeys.

Pulling the cotton down, I saw the wide root of a cock. Excited at being told to expose himself in a crowded bar, his fingers tried to extricate the trapped flesh. As he grunted, with desperation, I heard the material rip. Cotton parted in tatters on either side of the sharp, cutting edges of the zipper. The unveiled cock sprung up and outward.

"The Wedge," he introduced, passionately, then removed his hand giving me or anyone in our vicinity visual access to the amazing sight.

"God," I said, shocked by the deformed beauty.

The base, at a quick guess, was at least three inches wide tapering down its eight-inch length. A bulging, finger-sized blue vein snaked down along the top of the shaft to a pointed end. The head of the cock, about three quarters of an inch wide, sat mushroomed on the narrowed end. Thus, a wedge-shaped dick. Although weird, it excited the hell out of this voyeur. Flaunting his dick in public caused it to grow, strengthening in rigidity.

"Leave it out," I said, unable to pry my eyes off the incredibly long, triangular-shaped, pink cock.

"Sure," he returned, stepping back, giving anyone who just might take a look full appreciation of the awesome Wedge.

He appeared relaxed in the crowded bar, unlike the presented Wedge which stood hard like a piece of iron. His eyes were a fire of desire. He turned casually left, then right, aware of the quick glances in the crowded bar by those who enjoyed the rakish, shameless display that had sent my cock erecting.

"You need to show your cock, don't you?"

A crazed smile was the only response I got.

78

"Ever heard of Jonny Toxic?"

"No."

"You are just like that punk rocker."

"Yeah?"

"Yeah. Check him out in the video world."

"You know a lot about him, I suppose being a voyeur and all?"

"Uh-huh, I'm a peeper, just what you want, no?"

"Yeah, man. Just talking to you like this, I mean with my dick all hanging out keeps me pumped."

"You got a weird but great-looking cock, man. You live around here?"

"No, next town, Burlington."

"Name's Mark, I have an apartment about five blocks from here. Woul dyou be interested?"

"Sure, not often I come across a true voyeur, if you know what I mean."

"Leave it out and we'll go get my car," I instructed.

Eager to continue displaying the Wedge, we finished our brews, pushed through the crowd to the lighted parking lot behind the grunge bar. The Wedge remained out on display.

"If I could," I told him, "I'd make you sit naked in the car while I drove to my place."

A porn aficionado, I have always been fascinated by the exhibitionist, or possibly envious of a guy who flaunts his sexuality for excitement, possibly leading to sexual gratification. How singularly excited he must feel in creating a shock value by his public display of his exposed genitals. Where I got off, sexually, was on secretly looking and hunting for sexual situations. The thrill of spying and seeking out lurid visuals. We both were working like Yin and Yang, feeding off each other for our own sexual release. So far we were working well at stimulating each other.

Alone, directly below a phosphorous light in the deserted parking lot, I stopped in front of my car for a cigarette. Turning, I maneuvered so he was forced to face the parking lot. My subtle positioning delighted him as he stood bathed in light, his dick arched hard from his jeans. The possible risk of being caught or observed was like a drug rush for the addict. Moving, trying to find the better light, his eyes scanned the lot excitedly hoping someone was watching, acting as if his display and posture were the most natural thing in the world. I saw that the small head of his dick had started oozing precum.

"You're leaking, man," I said.

"Ya, I know," he returned, excited by displayed arousal.

Reaching for my car keys I brushed the Wedge. His reaction was nil, as if it were expected of me. Encouraged, I reached forward and gave the Wedge a couple of strokes, then let go and stood away observing. Unable to stand still, he still posed as if nothing were amiss. I knew he could feel my excitement also. Hearing a car pull up the alley toward the parking lot, I partially sheltered him from view. Only when I was certain they were bar patrons did I step back. My

shadow disappeared, leaving him spotted again in light. Only one of the older guys noticed, tripping on a curb at the entrance to the bar.

"Let's go, man," I said, "but leave the Wedge out, all the way to my apartment."

Making sure I stayed in the left lane, I passed busses, trucks, and vans. All were offered a complete view of my passenger. The mental effect caused the dick to remain erect. Once in the lighted underground garage and parked, I did not have to tell him to leave the Wedge out. We headed toward the bank of elevator doors, with the Wedge bouncing in full view, leading the way. Standing behind him, I made him face the elevator doors as we watched the descending lights of an approaching car. What were the chances of anyone being on the car at such a late hour? I was struck by his calm display, even though the cock remained rock hard.

I held my breath as the doors opened silently, but the car was empty. Was his sigh one of relief or disappointment? I pushed him into the car, but before punching my floor's button I told him to strip. Was I crazy or what? No, just as excited as he, by observing how the flasher operated. I had pushed him far. Would anyone be waiting at the lobby level? The chances were stimulating enough to go for it. His T-shirt was shed and pants dropped to his ankles immediately. He assumed a nonchalant but suggestive stance against a corner wall. His glazed eyes revealed nothing was out of the ordinary. His only trouble was controlling the jerking exhilaration of the cock.

My smile to him was a challenge. His returned the smile, cunning, accepted the challenge. I pushed for the lobby, then my floor. The elevator lifted slowly. When the doors opened to the lobby I noticed a sudden contortion. The Wedge had started to ejaculate out of the door to the lobby floor. Bolt after bolt was released as he held onto the walls of the elevator. I was stunned. The door closed slowly on the empty lobby. The elevator continued to lift.

"Surprised ya, didn't I," he said.

"Yes," I managed to say watching him stand there naked with his cock still drooling, semi-soft.

The downward tilt to his cock had pushed his balls forward. They looked huge. I didn't dare touch them or my cock for fear of climaxing.

"Stay naked," I said when the doors opened on my floor. He followed obediently to my apartment door, clutching his clothes.

"Get rid of that stuff," I said closing the door behind us.

He walked into the living room naked, then stood surprised as I pulled open the drapes. Two apartment buildings faced mine. The implication clear, I watched his cock harden. The exhibitionist wasn't finished yet.

"Go ahead," I suggested. "The balcony has a wrought iron railing. Anyone wishing to, could see you."

Hypnotized with lust, he crossed the room cautiously as his cock, bouncing hard, led the way. His body cast a soft reflection from the single living room light. Turning to see if I was watching he became momentarily puzzled till he

80

spied me half hidden by the drapes. He realized the Peeping Tom was watching as I jacked off to his brazen boldness. The nude stranger on my balcony exhibiting his swollen cock for the world to see was a sight I would never forget. Pumping my dick, hidden from view, I had to hold back for fear of climaxing too soon.

Unconcerned, the nude punker sauntered back into the living room. Mindful of my hidden presence, but playing the game, he ignored the corner where I hid. Kneeling on the carpet before the open doorway to the balcony, he then reached behind and pulled his ass cheeks apart. A rosebud hole surrounded by dark hair opened, then closed. I became engrossed as the whole area grew, opening then expanding into a swollen pucker. Unable to contain myself I huskily said, "Yeah, I've got to fuck it, man."

"Oh, yeah," he responded desperately. "Please, fuck it!"

"Okay, okay!" I said, kicking my jeans across the floor then yanking my T-shirt off and sending it flying.

Squatting behind him, I touched the soft extended puffiness of the ass hole. To my surprise it pushed out further as he arched his back like a female cat in heat. My cock jerked sending precum flowing from my gaping piss slit to the carpet.

"Just a second," I said quickly getting lube and a condom.

"Hurry, man. My ass needs your big cock inside."

Smearing lube over the extended flesh, I caught him looking up out through the open door to the balcony. Shit, I thought, fuck the neighbors, let them watch if they want. It's what my friend wanted, desperately, to put on a show for someone.

"Shove it in," he groaned.

Snapping the condom over the head of my slippery dick, I rolled it down. I was ready to plow the hot, puffy hole.

"Yes," he begged, "fuck me hard. Yes!"

I could feel his smooth insides as I passed the hard nut of his prostate gland. He moaned again, backing up on my dick, which was buried to the root.

Before long, he began to fuck himself on my pole in frenzy never before known to me. It seemed he was completely caught up with the idea that someone might be looking at our display. Suddenly, my balls stopped swaying and pulled up tight against the shaft of my dick. I was about to shoot. I couldn't hold onto the fantasy any longer.

"I'm goinna cum inside you!"

"Ooowww!" he yelled, splashing his jism everywhere.

"Ughh...mmm...yeah," I groaned as my cum filled the condom.

Rolling from him, I lay face upward beside him; he remained on all fours. Leaning over, he kissed me wet and deep.

"Oh, man, that was the best yet," he said smiling down at me. "Now I've got something for you."

He reached over pulled the condom from my semi-soft cock.

"Look," he said, and as I did he poured the contents of the condom over my

mouth. "Lick it up...."

"What?"

"Lick it, take it in."

I did, tasting my own cum for the first time. Sweet, yet pungent, I thought, licking my lips, then smiled.

"You see?"

"Not bad at all."

"Not bad for a kid, eh?"

"No."

"Think of what we've got to look forward to in the future. We're only starting, man!"

"I'm thinking, I'm thinking!"

My young friend then planted a big kiss on the end of my fat knob.

"Let's go for a drive," I suggested.

"Only if I can stay naked," he responded with a wide smile. "That's the only way I'd take you," I said as we both rose. Our dicks were already thickening.

MY LATIN MUSCLEBOY
by Jesse Monteagudo

The month of October in 1973 is memorable for many reasons: The "Saturday Night Massacre," the Yom Kippur War; and rising gasoline prices. But for the crowd that gathered at Miami College auditorium, that month will long be remembered as the date of Miami-Dade's first annual Latin Teen Bodybuilding Competition.

After months of preparation, and weeks of preliminaries, twelve of our community's finest muscle boys stood in their posing briefs in front of adoring parents, relatives, girl friends and boy friends in search of fame, fortune, and the adulation of their fellow-men and women.

Since it was first announced, six months before the final match, the Competition was the talk of the town, or at least of Miami College. Every 18-or 19-year-old with a toned body and a drop of Spanish blood in him looked in the mirror, smacked his lips, and went out and registered. They had the full support of family members and friends, who were convinced that the prestige of their national, racial, religious or economic group would suffer if their favorite son did not put his muscles on the line. One very persistent girl, the reigning Homecoming Queen no less, solemnly announced that she would only go out with a contender, at which point a dozen boys signed their names upon the dotted line.

When I first heard about the Latin Teen Bodybuilding Competition I was at the campus gym, as usual, bench-pressing my guts out. My bud Tonio Moreno, who spotted me, let out a loud but not uncharacteristic yell that almost made me drop my weights. When I looked up to see what was the matter I was handed a flyer by a swarthy muscle boy in tight jeans and a painted-on t-shirt. Printed in both Spanish and English, the flyer announced what every red-blooded *Latino* muscle boy wanted to hear:

Do you have what it takes to be Miami's first Latin Teen Bodybuilder? Come show us what you got and we'll give you what you deserve: fame, fortune and perhaps the girl of your dreams. Forms are available at the Student Lounge.

I doubt there was a competitor in the gym who didn't think he had what it took, or who wasn't interested in fame, fortune, or acquiring the girl (or boy) of his dreams. Since fame and fortune (and girls) are hard to share, arguments soon broke out in English, Spanish and Spanglish over who was most qualified to be Latin Teen Bodybuilder. Not wanting to join in the fracas, I tried to toss my flyer into the nearest trash can, only to be stopped by the ever-watchful Tonio.

"Don't be an ass, Joe. This is your big chance."

"*Your* big chance, maybe, but not mine. I am no Mr. Universe."

"None of us. That's what makes it better. There aren't too many Latin muscle

boys in Miami, no matter what these guys say, which narrows down the field. In fact, it's more likely than not that one of us in this room will get the trophy."

"Then *you* enter!" Though I've been working out since junior high school, I didn't think I was in the same league as some of the boys in the gym. Even Tonio was bigger than I in the muscles department, though my body was better proportioned. "What makes you think that *I* have a chance?"

"For one thing, you are better proportioned than a lot of those guys. Or me, for that matter. Besides," he smiled, "you are a hot little *Cubano*, and some of those fag judges will cream in their pants when you trot on stage in your cute little posing briefs." As if to prove that I was cute, Tonio pinched my hard nipples. I jumped off the bench, more in surprise than in pain.

"Hey, watch it!" I said, nervously scouting around the gym. "I don't want these guys to know what's going on." Though Tonio and I have been fuck buddies for months, our sex life was something I didn't care to share with the guys at the gym. For a young Cuban dude and a young Puerto Rican dude to be workout pals was one thing; but the fact that the Puerto Rican dude fucked the Cuban dude's bubble butt on a regular basis was something the guys might not approve of. But Tonio only laughed at my embarrassment.

"You crack me up sometimes, Joe Martinez! In any case, I got a better reason why you should enter the contest. Sergio Ramos."

"Sergio Ramos? What does *he* have to do with all of this?"

"Plenty. He's going to be a guest poser at the Competition. And one of the judges. *That* should get you to register."

Tonio was right. Sergio Ramos, "the Puerto Rican Muscle King", had been every Latin muscle boy's hero since 1966. That year Ramos beat all of the competition to become, at the age of 18, the first Hispanic to win the prestigious Mister Cosmo title. With a handsome face to match his perfectly proportioned body, Sergio was the idol of young *Latinas*, who hung his photos in their rooms, and of young *Latinos*, who worshipped Ramos much more surreptitiously.

In fact, it was Sergio Ramos's unprecedented victory that started the body-building craze among Miami's Latin boys. Always looking for new ways to prove our *machismo*, Miami's young *papis* flocked to the gyms in droves, determined to transform scrawny or fat figures into reasonable facsimiles of *el Rey* Sergio. Even "brainy types" like Yours Truly began to work out with such a passion that, five years later, I was able to sport an impressive figure (if I may say so myself). But was it impressive enough to impress the judges? Or Sergio?

"I don't know, Tonio. There will be some stiff competition."

"Don't put yourself down, *puto*. Once Sergio takes one look at that tight little *culo* of yours, he'll want to fuck you right on stage. And wouldn't that be something?"

"I am sure my parents would love it. But what makes you think that Sergio will be after my ass, or anyone else's? According to the tabloids, he and Sylvia Pena are quite an item." Sylvia, a popular star of *telenovelas*, had just announced her engagement to *el Rey Sergio* on Spanish language television.

84

"She's just a front," Tonio replied, "like the chick who dated Juan Gabriel last year. Besides, no *heba* can compete with my hot little Cuban fuck buddy."

"Well, just because *you* think I am hot, it doesn't mean that Sergio will. After all, he's *Sergio Ramos*, the Puerto Rican Muscle King, the star of stage, TV and teenage bedrooms. You are just a Puerto Rican college boy with a big ego."

"And a big *pinga* to match, and don't you forget it! Which reminds me ... we haven't played around for a while. If you come over to my place you can polish my sausage before dinner."

"Thanks for the offer but I can't make it this afternoon."

"Why not?"

"'Cause I gotta register for the Competition."

For once Tonio was speechless.

- - -

The next few months were a blur of early morning workouts, late night workouts, protein diets, nutritional supplements and even more workouts. Gyms stayed open all night to accommodate the needs of would-be contestants. Social calendars were put on hold, to the dismay of parents, relatives and lovers of both genders. School grades plummeted to such an extent that the dean seriously considered banning the Contest from the campus. But hosting Miami's first annual Latin Teen Bodybuilding Competition was too prestigious an event to cancel and, lacking a credible basketball, football or soccer team, all that Miami College had to its credit was the fact that it had the most pumped-up students.

Those who were genetically indisposed to muscular greatness tried to get around this handicap by taking steroids. Though the results were impressive, the fad was short-lived, since the organizers made it clear that steroid use would not be tolerated. Those who still tried to get away with using steroids were set straight during the preliminaries, when two of the most promising contestants tested positive and were disqualified. I, of course, never used steroids. And, I presumed, neither did Tonio.

The day of the finals arrived, and by hook or crook both Tonio and I survived the preliminaries and the semifinals. After a good night's sleep and a final workout we arrived at the auditorium's dressing room two hours before the main event. As we twelve finalists removed our clothes, we looked at one another with trepidation, envy and, in some cases, lust. Here, I thought, are Miami's hottest Spanish muscle boys. What an orgy we could make, a dozen hot Latin boys queer for one another's cock, balls, tits and ass....

Tonio read my mind: "Put your tongue back in your mouth, Joe" he whispered. "Most of these guys are straight." Tonio was right. Most of the contestants would kill you if they caught you looking at them. Many of them turned their backs as they removed their shorts, not wanting their genitals to be seen by another male. On the other hand, I removed my underwear in full view of my competitors, and remained proudly nude as I oiled my body.

But even an exhibitionist has to dress sometime, and I was about to put on my posing briefs when the dressing room door swung open by Leo Devinzo, the Cuban-born organizer of the Latin Teen Bodybuilding Competition. A former champion bodybuilder himself and, I heard, a notorious chicken queen, Devinzo licked his lips as he gazed at my naked body. Fortunately for me, Leo was not alone.

"Boys, I want you to meet *el Rey*, Sergio Ramos, guest poser and judge." You could hear a pin drop as the Puerto Rican Muscle King strode into the room. He was a stunningly handsome mulatto, still in his prime at 25. Like me, he was five-six, about average height for Hispanic men. His close-cropped hair framed a handsome face, with two black eyes that burned like charcoal, a firm nose and sensuous lips. I couldn't keep my eyes off of this hot muscle *papi*. Even my pal Tonio could not compare with him.

"Take your clothes off, Sergio," said Leo. "Show those kids what you got." He smiled. "And don't be shy. These are all men here."

"You're the boss," laughed Sergio, in heavily accented English, as he stripped to the buff. Even the straightest one of us gasped as we took in the Muscle King's masculine perfection. Like the rest of us, Sergio's body was shaved clean, right down to his pubic hair. His brown body was perfectly proportioned and muscular without being grotesque, as would become the fashion in later years. His perfect physique made us puny by comparison, and we sighed with relief that we did not have to compete against him. But while the other contestants gazed at Sergio's muscular biceps, triceps, deltoids and pectoral muscles, I could not take my eyes off the Muscle King's imposing genitals: his thick brown cock uncut like the rest of us and his plump, low-hanging balls.

"OK, boys, stop gawking!" shouted Leo. "It's time to go on stage. Get going." As the other contestants followed Devinzo out of the dressing room, Sergio beckoned me to his side. Putting on my posing briefs, I went over to the Muscle King, who was still naked. After I introduced myself, we spoke in Spanish.

"You look like a smart kid, not like the rest of those bums. What are you doing in this Competition?"

"Just trying to show them how good I am. I've been working out since junior high school, the year you won Mister Cosmo."

"Yeah," Sergio noted, as he put on his posing briefs. "That was some contest. A day doesn't go by that I don't run into some kid who tells me that I changed his life." He paused. "But don't think this is the be-all and end-all. You might not know it but after I left Mister Cosmo I enrolled in the University of San Juan, where I hope to finish medical school next year."

"I know," I said. This, of course, was common knowledge, as was everything else about the Muscle King's life. He was no muscle-bound idiot, but a well-rounded man, with a brilliant mind to match a perfect body. "I too want to be more than just a body. That's why I'm going to school here. I plan to be a school teacher." And, I did not add, a writer.

"Don't worry, you'll get there. How old are you, Martinez? Eighteen?"

86

"Nineteen. I'll be twenty in May."

"*Cubano?*"

"Yeah."

"I like Cubans. We are like brothers, though we don't act like it sometime. I think Cubans and Puerto Ricans should get together more often." Did Sergio read my mind? Did he know that I was queer for hot 'Ricans, and that Tonio wasn't the only *Boricua* whose cock pleasured my hungry mouth and ass? Before I could learn the answer, Leo came barging in.

"Martinez! Get your ass out there. The contest is about to begin!" I went out quietly, but not without sharing one last private smile with the Puerto Rican Muscle King.

- - -

The Latin Teen Bodybuilding Competition was a smashing success. Sergio Ramos was stunning as a guest poser, and remarkably knowledgeable as a judge. We twelve contestants did our stuff well, posing to Spanish Musak before a cheering crowd. The winner, a small 18-year old Peruvian of Japanese descent, brought the house to tears when he spoke about his older brother, also a young bodybuilder, who died while defending his family from terrorist guerrillas. Though neither Tonio nor I won any prizes, we had a blast. Now it was time to party.

"Get your ass in gear, Joe," said Tonio, as he dressed in his best polyester suit. "Me and the guys are going out to celebrate!" For Tonio and his straight friends, "celebrate" meant a straight Latin bar in Hialeah. It was a nice club, with great *merengue* and lots of hot bods, but none that were available to me. And I had *another* idea.

"I'll join you later, Tonio. There's something I need to take care of." Tonio gave me a skeptical look, but shrugged his shoulders and left. So did the other contestants, the attendants, and Leo Devinzo, though not before Leo invited me over to his penthouse for a drink. After I gave Leo a friendly but firm refusal, I found myself alone in the locker room, waiting for *el Rey* to arrive.

It was half past midnight when Sergio finally came into the locker room, having spent over an hour warding off a horde of fans and reporters. Sergio was tired, glistening with sweat, and grouchy as hell. Happily, his frown turned into a smile or surprise when he saw me, sitting on a bench, as naked as the day I was born.

"Joe, what are you doing here? I thought you'd be gone by now."

"I thought I'd wait for you. I thought you might need some company."

"Actually, I do. But first I need a shower. Why don't you join me." Though I had already taken a shower, I did not mind getting under water for a second time. Not when Sergio Ramos was going to be there with me.

"Nothing's better than a good shower after a hard workout, Joe," Sergio added as we entered the now-empty shower stalls. "Don't you forget it." Nude, we

faced each other under the pouring water, two young muscle warriors who fought the good fight. As we took in one another's beauty, our thick cocks stirred, slipped out of their foreskins and stood in all their hard, masculine glory.

"*Tu me gustas, papi*," Sergio muttered. "Do you like me?" Without waiting for an answer Sergio moved next to me and kissed me passionately on the lips. Our moustaches meshed and our tongues explored each other's mouth, even as our hands took hold of each other's muscular torso. I grimaced as Sergio's strong hands grabbed my hard nipples and pulled them, mercilessly. As Sergio worked my tits, a sharp pain shot through my body, a pain that was soon mixed with pleasure.

"I knew we were queer for each other the moment I saw you, Joe. I got the hots for Cuban boy ass, and you've got the one for me. You got great pecs, too, which only makes your tits stand out more." Taking my left nipple in his mouth, Sergio sucked on it while he continuing to tweak my right tit with his hand. When he thought my left breast had enough, he began his oral attack on my right one, while focusing his manual dexterity on my left tit. Though my man tits had been played with by many a man, they had never experienced the savage workout they were getting from the Puerto Rican Muscle King. It was a workout that I was sure to feel for days to come.

But Sergio had more things on his mind than my tits. "You did not win the contest tonight but you'll get the big trophy," he said, as he placed my hand on his massive meat, "my hard, ten-inch *pinga*!" He grinned. "My cock is ready for you, Joe. Get on your knees and work on it."

The Muscle King's word was my command. I got on my knees, taking in the strong, masculine odor that no shower could erase, the pungent smell of a natural man. Without a thought, I took hold of Sergio's enormous prick, pulling back the thick foreskin to lick the massive brown head beneath. Sergio groaned with pleasure as my tongue licked his massive cock head, moved down the sides of his thick shaft and played with the sensitive spot where his cock meets his balls. I then took Sergio's balls into my mouth, working each sensitive nut the way that only a man knows how.

Having worked around the surface of his cock and balls, I took Sergio's massive man-muscle deep inside my mouth and down my burning throat. Sergio moaned with savage pleasure, holding my head firmly in place as I continued to deep-throat him. As I gave the Muscle King the blowjob of his life, my own thick prick stood at attention. This was my dream come true: the opportunity to service my idol's manhood with my mouth and with my hands. Though the shower heads continued to pour water on us, we were oblivious to it. We only cared for each other; two young musclemen who took pleasure from each other's hard body.

"Get up," Sergio ordered, as he pulled me to my feet. "It's my turn." As I leaned against the shower wall, my muscular lover got down on his knees, taking my thick hard cock in his mouth. I sighed with pleasure as Sergio began to suck my hot young *pinga*, pulling back the loose foreskin with his tongue

while taking the hard shaft in his mouth. Soon my pleasure turned into ecstasy, as my young cock went in and out of this young muscle stud's mouth.

"Suck my cock, Sergio!," I yelled. "*Mamame la pinga!*" As Sergio continued to blow me, his hands grabbed my plump eggs, driving me wild as he pulled on each tender *huevo*. I willingly surrendered myself to this muscular stud's experienced mouth and throat and hands. My own hands took hold of my erect nipples, giving them the same workout that Sergio was giving my thick cock and low-hanging balls.

"You got a nice dick and balls, Joe. Hard and thick and full of juice. But it's your hot young ass that I want. Now turn around!" Sergio's wish was my command. As I faced the wall, Sergio's strong hands grasped my bubble butt, pushing my muscular buns apart to expose the sensitive hole within. Using soap as lubricant, Sergio played with my tender rectum, teasing it and readying it and me for the savage fuck that was sure to follow. Sergio's experienced fingers pushed their way inside my manhole, finding their way to my tender prostate. I sighed with pleasure as Sergio massaged my sensitive man-gland.

"You have a nice, tight *culo*, Joe. I've wanted to fuck you since I first saw you. Tell me you want me to fuck you. Tell me!" My muscular lover continued to work his fingers deep inside my hole, stroking my glans and driving me out of my mind. I spread my legs wide and my cock stood in attention as Sergio continued to finger-fuck me, filling me with his pent-up erotic energy. I cried and whimpered like a baby, needing to be possessed by Sergio's powerful blockbuster. My own hard cock fucked the shower wall, adding to the sex-charge that flowed through my body.

"I want you to fuck me, Sergio," I screamed. "Not with your fingers but with your cock! I want you to fuck me, *papi*, NOW!" I didn't care that someone might walk in. Nothing mattered but my savage need, a need that could only be appeased by having Sergio's cock up my ass. "Please fuck me, Sergio," I whimpered. "Please!"

"You got it, Joe! You're going to get the fucking of your life." Now on his feet, Sergio pulled his fingers out of my ass. Taking his manhood into his own hands, Sergio pushed it deep into my tender rectum. Though Sergio had opened my asshole with his fingers, I was not ready for the sharp pain that shot through me as he took possession of my muscular young *culo*. I was a slave of the Muscle King, my asshole a tool he used for his own savage pleasure.

Having placed his cock deep inside my hole, Sergio began to thrust it in and out with ever increasing force. Like a muscular young warrior, Sergio drove me hard, taking us both to greater degrees of passion. As Sergio continued to fuck me, his hands worked on my nipples, giving them the same intense workout he was giving my ass. I held on to the wall with my right hand, while I pumped my own restless cock with the other.

"Fuck me!" I screamed. "*Chingame el culo!*"

And so, time stood still as we continued to fuck under the showers, oblivious to the world around us and outside us. Sweat dripped down our bodies, mixing

with the rushing water as it reached the floor. We rutted like two muscular young animals, caught up in the most primal of passions, man fucking man. Sergio's cock up my ass, his hands on my tits, and my own hand on my cock drove me beyond reality into another dimension, a world of savage and brutal mansex.

"Take my load, Joe!" shouted Sergio, as he held on to my tender nipples. "I am gonna shoot!"

With a savage thrust, the Muscle King shot his hot *leche* deep inside my ass. The force of Sergio's orgasm sent me past the point of no return. As my Puerto Rican lover held me in his muscular arms I stroked myself into orgasm, releasing gallons of jism out of my restless prick. Soon the shower floor was covered with our accumulated man milk.

"God, Joe," said Sergio, as we came down from our sexual high. "I'm glad I met you."

"And I'm glad I met *you*, Sergio. It isn't often that a guy gets fucked by his hero."

"How could I help it with a boy like you? Guys are going to line up to fuck your hot little bubble butt. But take it from me. You're not meant to be a bodybuilder. Keep your body in shape, for your sake and the sake of other dudes who'll want to fuck you. But use your mind, stay in school, and become the best damn teacher you can be."

Sergio was right. Bodybuilding was not for me. I was a nerd, pure and simple. Still, I had a body that turned heads, even Sergio's, and I meant to keep it that way. And I'll always have the memories of the night when the Muscle King fucked me beneath the shower. But now it was the time to say goodbye.

Sergio seemed to read my mind: "You're not going anywhere, Joe. I am not going back to San Juan until Monday, and I got all day tomorrow. Why don't you join me? I'll take you out to dinner."

"And then?"

"Then I'll take you back to my hotel room and fuck you raw. In my bed."

"It's a deal!"

THE PUNK
by Jack Ricardo

He was a punk: loud, obnoxious, and pushy. When the dressing room door opened and a guy walked out, this prick pushed in front of me and stomped inside. The son of a bitch! I pulled open the door before he had a chance to latch it.

"What da fuck ya doin', dude? I'm gonna try on these jeans!"

"And I've been waiting for fifteen fuckin' minutes to try mine on." I closed the door and locked it with both of us inside. A close fit. Maybe 4x4, with a mirror on one wall, a bench, and hooks. I unbuttoned my pants.

"What the fuck...." he muttered.

I toed my sneakers off and dropped my pants.

"Hey, man, come on, get the hell out a here. And put your fucking pants back on. I ain't takin off my pants with no dude watching me."

I looped my pants on a hook and adjusted the pouch of my briefs. "Tough shit, kid. Then wait in line outside."

He was small, had buzzcut sidewalls with spiked hair on his crown, was on the skinny side, and had cool clear eyes. If he weren't such an insolent bastard, he'd be one hot little fucker.

He stuck his chin in my face, or tried to, couldn't quite reach. His crotch brushed mine, or maybe it was only my imagination. "Hey, old man, you queer? Why don't you get the fuck out of here."

I grabbed the shithead by his oversized black T-shirt, shoved my nose to his. "Old man, huh? Listen, kid, I'm 52 years old, and I got a body you only dream about and a dick you'd die to have swinging between your legs, so don't fuck with me." I pushed him against the mirror. "And, yeah, I'm queer. What you gonna do about it?"

The kid huffed and mumbled nothing intelligible. He turned around, unhitched his black pants and dropped them. I was about to step into my new jeans when I stopped and stared at a taut and tiny bare ass, round and firm and creamy white. My mouth went dry. The kid stumbled trying to get a leg into the jeans and fell back. I held him up.

"Argggg," he growled. "Gonna break my ass with the two of us in here." I was holding him under the arms with both hands, his ass was pressed against the pouch of my shorts, and the stink of the perspiration from his pits was pumping blood to my head. I humped my crotch into his butt.

"Hey, dude, you're queer! That's cool. But I ain't queer."

He didn't try to move away. Not that there was much of anywhere to move.

I slipped one hand in front and groped him.

"Hey, hey, hey, hey...." He pushed my hand off his cock and balls, sprung around and stood up tall. Well, as tall as he could be for a short fucker. "Hey,

queerdude, I'm horny as hell, but I don't dig doing it with guys, okay, I'm straight, you know...."

My mouth was wet now, damn near drooling. Spiked hair didn't top his cut cock and his broad low swingers. Curly blond hair, a thick growth, a moist growth. The kind of cockhair you wanna snuggle your nose into, the kind you wanna whiff, the kind you wanna lap up. I drooled inside and pulled myself out of my erotic mirage. "Hey, punk, you ever make it with a man? You're so fucking impudent and brazen, come on, fess up you, you ever make it with a dude." I tried to sound both friendly, pissed, curious and challenging.

"Nope, never did and never will," he stated, lifting his chin, trying to look down on me. A short kid trying to be a big man. Cute.

"No, balls, huh?" I chided and grinned.

Whether he knew it or not, he took up the gauntlet. "No fucking balls? Yeah? What about these?" He was naive, defensive, daring, and tugging at an overflowing fistful of thick nuts and flabby flesh. "Those are fucking balls."

"Can't fight that, punk. Great-lookin' set of nuts," I agreed truthfully, my tone tinged with lust. My balls itched.

"Yeah, ain't they," he agreed right back, smiling, proud, still holding on tight.

"Goes with that great-lookin' cock and its helmet!"

"Helmet?"

"Dickhead," I emphasized, wondering how large that tomato head would grow inside my mouth.

Maybe the punk was thinking the same thing. He was fondling his balls, I was scratching mine through my shorts. I could smell the punk sweat. I could smell myself sweat. Aromatic fucking aphrodisiac.

"Hey, what you doing in there?" a voice yelled.

"Be right out," I snapped back. "Hold your water."

Without another word, both the punk and I got dressed. And we both left our new jeans behind. He followed me out the door of the store. I had him, I knew it. "So, where ya off to, punk?"

He started to say, "None of your fucking business," then thought twice. Long seconds passed. He eyed me, wheels were spinning beneath spiked hair. I watched, waited. He peered around like a spy meeting his handler for the first time. "Were you serious, queerdude?" he whispered.

"What?"

"About...well, you know?"

"No, I don't know."

"Shit, you know," he shouted at me. One hand swept over the front of pants that were about five sizes too large for his boyish frame.

I grinned facetiously, ogled him lewdly. "Yeah, I know. Come on, punk."

We subwayed downtown. We walked up six flights of stairs. The punk ambled in like he owned the place, looked around. "Hey, cool, dude, I never seen a bathtub in the kitchen."

The place was a dive and I wasn't here to talk about my combo bathtub/sink. I

92

grabbed his crotch. The punk was startled but didn't push away. "You're a fast cocksucker, you know that, and I'm fucking horny for a blowjob, dude. Yerah, I'm just gonna let you blow me. First time. First time with a dude that is. Hell, lotsa girls blow me." A braggart, and I doubted it.

I grinned, I hoped mysteriously, squeezed his nuts, then toed off my sneakers, unzipped my jeans, pulled them off, along with my shorts, and stood there naked. The kid didn't speak, but his eyes did a quick roll over a dick fast growing in eager anticipation. I again reached out and grabbed a crotchful of punkmeat. There was more to grab this time. The cock inside those loose-fitting pants was expanding, swelling, the balls heavy. Yeah, this straight little punkfucker was horny as a toad.

I unbuckled and unzipped him. His pants dropped to the floor and he stepped out of them. He was one fine fucking sight, this punk his Eraserhead hair sticking up like it was charged, his sides razoed to his scalp, his black T-shirt flopping on his chest and ending at those appealing blond cockhairs. His scuffed work boots and sagging socks finished the image. And a damn good finish it was. This punk was fucking hot with a capital EATEMUP. He grinned.

I sat on my haunches in front of him. My balls brushed against the heels of my feet. The grin the punk had on his face turned into a sneer of contempt. The shaft of his cock was growing tall and thin, his helmet matched the growth. I leaned over and nudged my nose into his musty cockhairs. They stank of sweat and tickled my nose. I inhaled the dank aroma and my cock leaped. I licked, I lapped my tongue over those hairs, gnawing, tasting, purring quietly. My cock drooled and jerked. His cock snapped up and hit my neck.

I sat back and wiped the sweat from my brow and the slobber from my lips. The punk's flesh-helmet was staring at me eye to eye. The punk's chest was expanding, contracting. So was mine. The punk's eyes opened wide, so did his mouth. "Suck me off, queerdude," he said, his voice a harsh and hurried demand in a small room. "Suck me off now, you filthy fag," he insisted.

I smiled up at him, sneered. Sneer for sneer.

I thought I saw a faint hint of fear behind those cool, clear eyes. It vanished quickly and was replaced by a jeer of haughty ridicule when I reached up and cupped his balls with one hand while pulling on my own balls with the other. Both felt damn good. All four, I should say. My own bags of juice and fun were hairy and full, the punk's hangers were fuzzy and damn heavy. I flopped his balls in my hand, glared up at him again, then bowed down and sniffed his balls, licked them. The punk began moaning softly. I slurped both nuts inside my mouth and gargled them. The punk bent his knees, "Yeah, you dirty, filthy fag, eat my fuckin' nuts! Eat 'em. Yeah...yeah...yeah...!"

I ate them, I ravished them, I devoured them, I swallowed them, I gorged on them, I made love to them, two large, baggy fucking balls with giant eggs floating inside. A fucking punkfeast! And I tickled his asshole with one finger.

"Hey, dude, I don't dig nobody playing with my ass," he quickly told me. "Nobody." I kept tickling. "Stop it," he yelled, angry and annoyed.

I stopped and swept my fingers up the crack of his fuzzy and creamy little ass, let his balls flop my mouth, and licked the punk's dickhead.

"That's better. Oh, yeah, queerdude, that's it, suck me off."

I sucked on his knob, fluttering my tongue over and around it. And also trailed my fingers back to his asshole. When one finger stayed and tried to pry apart that furrowed little hole, I felt the punk flinch and I knew his mouth was about to open in protest. I downed his cock to the root. "Yeowwwww...." the punk huffed. Not in pain, in pure pleasure as his dickhead tapped my tonsils, as I sucked back up and began worshipping a dickhead attached to one prime punk. The crown filled my mouth, my tongue measured its roundness, teased its piss hole and sucked up the slime leaking out. The punk was shaking. My fingertip inched into his asshole. The punk groaned. His ass was fucking tight and gripped my finger.

I flipped his cock from my mouth, pulled my finger from his ass, dropped his balls, stood up, turned the punk around, and pushed him against the tub. He leaned his arms on the rim to balance himself. I kicked his legs apart, sank to my knees again before he could protest, and kissed his ass.

The punk was startled but recovered quickly as I began to slide my tongue down the crack of that cute tiny ass. He clutched the edge of the tub with both hands and backed his ass up, crying out, "Yeah, eat my fucking shit hole out."

I sucked. I slobbered. I clutched his cheeks and pulled them apart, then rammed my tongue deep into his ass.

Now this kid literally went wild, wiggling his hot little ass, pushing back while I wormed my tongue round and round the inside of one creamy and tight and hairless asshole. I slobbered my spit both inside and outside that cherry asshole. The punk was moaning, he was groaning, he was growling, he was in fucking heaven. And I was about to give him hell.

I stood up. The punk was panting for air. He still kept his fingers gripped on the tub, his legs were still spread, but he craned his neck behind. "Why'd you stop, dude? Why you stop?" he cried, gasping for air. "Man, I was about to pop and I ain't even touched my cock. Come on, dude, I loved it! Eat my fucking ass out with your tongue again. You got a great tongue, dude! C'mon...."

The punk was pleading, and I was busy rolling a rubber down the thick shaft of my cock and lubing it with KY. His eyes popped open, so did his mouth. "Hey, no, man. No way, dude. Hell, No! No you don't, queerdude, you ain't gonna...." He spun around.

My cock was rubber-coated. I grabbed his shoulders and slammed him against the tub again. He tried to turn back. "No, no!" he screamed.

"Hold still, punk!"

I stepped behind him and aimed my cock between his legs until my dickhead was poking those delicious nuts of his. He was small, I was big. It was easy keeping him in line.

"Man oh man, oh man!" the punk wailed. I hunched my ass back, my cock slid under his legs, back, forth, gliding and leaving a path of growing pleasure,

94

for both the punk and myself. I slipped my hands under his arms and hugged my chest to the back of his black T-shirt. My cockhairs scratched his ass. I whispered in his ear. "Hey, punk, if you gonna make it with a queerdude, you're really gonna make it with a queerdude." There was a warning attached to the words. "With this fucking fag," I added, derisively. "Dicking another fucking fag."

"No," he cried. "I'm no fckin' fruitcake! Not me, man!" I felt his body stiffen. The punk was terrified. Of me, of my dick. My stiff cock pushed against a tight but slippery asshole and the head popped inside. The punk yelped like he was stabbed. I didn't want to turn the punk off, though. I brought one hand down and wrapped my hand around his balls. I fondled them, tenderly, gently, softly. The puck didn't try to pull off my dickhead. He was mooing. But he was still tense, scared. And fucking horny. His rock-hard cock was twitching against my wrist, his two balls were hunching up into one thick sac. My shaft began the long glide inside.

"Oh, no," the punk croaked. But it wasn't a croak to stop; it was a realization that he was about to get dicked in the ass for the first time in his life, and he was loving it. I yanked on his balls. The punk moaned, "Oh, no." My chest and brain were filled with sparks ignited by the tight muscles of this punk's asshole itching round my cock. I grunted, I moaned, I held onto his balls and shoved my stiff cock clear up the punk's ass. "Oh, oh oh, oooooooo," he crooned, like a cow with a stud bull inside her.

He leaned his head back. I cuddled my face into his neck, wiping my lips over his cheek, his face, reaching for his lips and finding them. The punk's tongue snaked from his mouth and flicked at my lips. "Yeah...." he said, as soft as a breeze. "Yeah," he whimpered. "Yeah," he sighed. It was a long, grateful sigh. I smiled.

I pulled my hips back and my cock came with them, bringing along needling sensations that stirred my balls and blew my mind. Then I plugged back into the punk. "Yeah," I grunted. "Yeah," I groaned. "Oh, yeah!" I shouted as rammed the little punk's ass. Back, forth, in, out, shaking, sweating, chewing the punk's neck while he swirled his head, pushed his ass back onto my cock and caught the rhythm.

I could tell the punk was floating on cloud fucking nine, what with my cock ramming up his ass, with my fist pulling his balls, with my mouth sucking his neck.

"Man, I'm gonna, gonna...goonnnnaaaaa..." he was meowing, crooning, sighing, gasping. His two balls became one rock-hard ball and his cock began trembling and shooting. I couldn't see it, but I could feel it in the tug of his ass muscles clutching my cock, begging my cock to dick him and dick him deep. I dicked that little bastard punk, deep and heavy, and stayed put, keeping my hard cock so far up his ass it damn near came out of his spiked head. And I fucking creamed that fucking punk's guts with my cum, globs and globs that were slamming out my dickhead and making me quiver all over. I was shaking, the

punk was quaking. And he was fucked.

It took me a couple of minutes before I ever had energy enough to pull out of the punk's asshole. When I did, my rubber was bloated. I tossed in the tub. The punk shot his wad over the side of the tub, over his feet, over the floor, a large load. He turned around and was embarrassed to look at me. I flopped down on the mattress in the corner. The punk was deflated.

"Come'er, kid," I said, patting the mattress. He looked up, he walked over, he sat down. I leaned back against the wall and pulled him into my arms. His face was cradled on my chest. His chest was still heaving. His dick was resting.

"Thanks, punk," I said softly.

He didn't say a word. But he wrapped an arm around my waist and kissed my chest lightly, considerately, gratefully. He whispered, "Cool, dude," and flopped his leg over mine.

FORBIDDEN FRUITS
by Peter Gilbert

The official name of the block was Ff. The sixth building on the sixth campus of the Academy for Entertainment. The staff called it "Double F." The boys accommodated there were all dancers and musicians. The latter group called it Fortissimo. To Robert the plastic letters on the wall meant "Free fucks". There were times when he worried about his activities there but not when he had one of the inhabitants of the block in his arms.

Ben groaned. Robert held on to his shoulders and thrust harder. Ben groaned again. Like all the musicians and dancers he was almost certainly a first timer. His ass had that agreeable tight resistance that Robert associated with boys who had held out despite the temptations they were subject to and to which they contributed.

"Nearly there," Robert whispered. He pushed in as far as he could. Ben's soft buttocks pressed against his groin. The muscles tightened and then relaxed slightly. For a moment or two Robert lay still to gather his energy and to think how lucky he was. Long-legged, handsome young Ben was the seventh boy he'd had since being appointed to the Academy staff. Other men had to go to a licensed establishment to slide their rods into well-worn passages. Robert got the first taste of forbidden fruit for free.

"It feels better now," Ben murmured.

"Even nicer soon," said Robert.

"Your legs are hairy. I can feel.... Ah! Ah! Ah! Ah!" Robert felt the boy wriggling slightly underneath him, trying to bring himself off against the mattress. A good sign....

"Ah! Oh! Ah! Oh!" Ben's movements became more and more frantic. It took all Robert's strength to hold him. He felt the boy's prostate; a tiny, hard lump in velvet, smooth and warm tissues. He was aware of a great muscular spasm. For an instant, his cock was gripped incredibly tightly. Then Ben let out a long sigh and relaxed completely. An instant later Robert came. Jet after jet of pent-up semen flooded into the boy. The air in the room filled with the scents of sweat and spunk. He kissed the back of Ben's neck. Ben was number seven. Who would be next?

"Stay in for a bit. It feels nice," said Ben.

"Better than singing about it, eh?"

"You bet."

"I heard you practicing this morning. You were good."

"Let's hope the audience thinks so. We've got a concert tour next month. Far too many illegitimate babies in North America they say."

None of the boys was fooled. They all knew, or soon realized, that Acadent (properly called the Academy for Entertainment) was a propaganda training

school. The New World Order had been established for more than a hundred years. Most of the world's population realized the dangers of unlimited and uncontrolled reproduction. Most were happy with the artificial insemination program but there were still odd cases of hetero-sex despite the death penalty. There had even been a case at the Academy itself. A boy in the dance troupe had been caught with a dirty picture. By all accounts he was an attractive lad and a good dancer but an undoubtedly bad influence. He'd been beaten and sent over the road for training of another kind.

The Academy musicians and singers with their songs, the Academy's dance troupe with their provocative costumes and long, shaven legs not to mention the establishment, always referred to as "over the road" were enough to convince most men that Central Government had the right idea.

The relative silence in the room was suddenly shattered by the sound of music from the next room. "That's Coq's latest," said Ben. "I like this one."

"Boys shouldn't be playing music at this time of night," said Robert. Ben laughed. "And my administrator shouldn't be fucking me at this time of night for that matter," he said. "Coq is good, isn't he? I wonder if I'll ever be a famous star like him."

"You might. You're already a star of another sort."

"I'll bet you say that to all the boys," said Ben, laughing.

Not all; just seven but Robert said nothing. His shrunken cock was making its reluctant, slippery way out. The music was so loud that every word Coq sang could be heard:

"My ass is itchin'
My cock is twitchin'
For you ooo"

Most of the boys were obsessed with Coq. It didn't do any harm. The Director maintained that it had a positive effect on their training. The fact that Coq had been a former student made them strive to emulate him. The message he put across was beneficial as far as their attitude training was concerned and, as for the posters that adorned their study walls Robert was surprised they didn't wank themselves to death. Coq was a lovely, blond twenty-one-year-old. He was always photographed in a provocative position and always wore the brief, almost see-through shorts that had become the latest teenage male fashion.

Robert said goodnight, dressed and left, but not before calling on Ben's next door neighbor to remonstrate about the volume. Chris was the boy's name. He was lying naked on his bed when Robert went in. He made a desperate attempt to pull the quilt up over him but not before Robert had caught a glimpse of a very erect and substantial penis. He turned round. Sure enough, there was a huge Coq poster on the door. Robert had seen it many times before. The star was sitting on a broken-down wall that must have been uncomfortable to his thinly clad behind. Privately, Robert was convinced that the enormous bulge in the front of the shorts was artificial.

"Sorry. I couldn't get to sleep," said Chris. As if to confirm the fact, Coq sang,

98

"There won't be no sleepin'
I know that you're keepin'
A place in your bed for me."

Chris reached for the control and turned the volume down.

"That's better," said Robert. "I guess you're worried about the tour, eh?"

"Er, yeah. I guess I am."

"You're a dancer, aren't you?" It was a totally unnecessary question. One look at the boy's smooth arms and shaved armpits was enough.

"Yes."

"Well, stop worrying and go to sleep. When I was a student and couldn't sleep I used to masturbate. Try that."

It was all Robert could do to keep a straight face. The lump in the quilt looked like Mount Fuji. Chris blushed.

"I'll pop into your rehearsal tomorrow," said Robert. He turned to leave.

"Do you like Coq? You could stay and listen to the rest," said Chris.

"I like cock very much," said Robert. "Maybe tomorrow evening, eh?"

"Sure."

"And you'll be number eight," Robert murmured to himself as he left the building.

- - -

Sam grinned a welcome as Robert entered the dance studio. An alumnus of the Academy himself, Sam was probably the best choreographer in the business. Robert smiled back and stood near the door. Sam came over to join him.

"They're coming along," he said. "They're not perfect by any means but they're not bad."

"They look pretty good to me," said Robert. Ten boys, dressed in the briefest of shorts, stood with their legs elegantly crossed whilst five others, similarly attired, danced to the inevitable accompaniment of yet another Coq song:

"'Ten boys are waiting,
Waiting for me....'"

"Not sexy enough!" Sam called. "Let's see those butts swaying! That's better. Can you do something about those shorts, Chris? They'll be round your ankles soon. Not that anyone would complain but the strip dance comes later on."

"They're too loose. It's this new diet," Chris explained.

"He's started to fill out in all the wrong places," Sam whispered. "Pity really. The audience went crazy over him on the last tour."

"I'm not surprised," said Robert. Paradoxically, the shorts, loose though they were, made Chris even more attractive than he had seemed on the previous evening.

"Want to see a preview of the final number?" Sam asked.

"Sure."

"You'll enjoy this," said Sam. He changed the chip. "Final number, lads," he

called. "Specially for Robert. Put all you've got into it. You can have a break afterwards."

"We'll need it," said one of the tallest and oldest of the troupe and all the others laughed. Smiling, they formed up in a line.

"You know me so well" sang the familiar voice as they danced gracefully from side to side.

"It's hard for a boy,
It's hard for a man,
Hard for a man; hard for a man...."

Each boy put a hand in his shorts and turned to face the rear wall. It was pretty obvious from the way their bottoms tightened and the movements of their shoulders what they were doing.

"Hard for a man. Oh so hard for a man,
Hug me. Hold me. Let me feel you.
Come into me. Come into me."

They waggled their butts provocatively and then turned round again. Fifteen pairs of shorts stretched tightly over erect penises. The boys smiled happily and the music continued.

"Left, right or center,
It's all the same to me
If it's really you, I'll let you see...
Left...."

They pulled down the left side of their shorts and turned round to expose a tantalizing glimpse of buttock.

"Right...." and the other side came down. Chris kept hold of his.

"Or center'
and the shorts fell. They bent over and clasped their ankles.
Do it to me slowly,
A happy lad I'll be,
I'll be your boy for ever,
If only you'll love me."

"Bravo!" called Robert, clapping.

"Not bad, eh?" said Sam. "Okay, lads. Fifteen minutes' break." The boys filed off the stage.

"You'll have to wipe it off the seats after the audiences have seen that number," said Robert.

"Providing I don't have to wipe if off the stage, I don't mind," Sam replied. "I'm not at all sure it's a good idea to stop them having it off. To ask a lad to dance around and display his attributes to get the audience randy and then expect him to live a chaste life is unnatural."

"The psychologists reckon it's a greater turn on that way," Robert replied. "It makes people fantasize about being the first to pick the cherry."

"That's ridiculous. If a boy hasn't been fucked too roughly, there's no way anyone would know."

100

Robert smiled. The image of Chris was clear in his mind when he left the studio. Long legs; a delightfully tight little bottom and, although he had only caught a glimpse of it on the previous night, the boy obviously had a substantial cock. He couldn't wait for the evening to come but he had to. There were two ways of relieving the tension. One would require him to go home. The other merely involved a trip over the road. The clinical, disinterested attitude of the people over the road was guaranteed to lower his pulse rate and his cock. He usually hated going to the place.

There was the usual hassle about getting in. The security system was actually designed to stop the boys from getting out but it worked both ways. The singers, musicians and dancers were allowed out. They were propositioned of course. That was only natural but they were generally intelligent enough to realize that their careers came first. The boys from over the road were different. On grading days when all the kids in a particular zone were graded, the last things the examiners looked for in a pleasure-house boy were foresight and intelligence.

Mike, the superintendent, was always pleased to demonstrate and explain his skills on Robert's rare visits.

"Come to see the new lot?" he asked.

"Didn't know you had a new intake," Robert replied, sprawling in a chair and hoping that his still-excited state wouldn't be too apparent.

"They're opening a new place next year," said Mike. "That new building they're putting up in Zone Five. God knows who's putting up the money. He or they must be loaded. All the very latest amenities apparently. Name your pleasure and you'll get it there. From what I've seen of the drawings, people's tastes are getting more and more exotic. There's even going to be a suite of flagellation rooms."

"And how do you propose to train them for that?" Robert asked. Whipping boys; especially boys as beautiful as Chris, would be an act of desecration.

"I'll have to think about it," said Mike. "Come and have a look at them. There are some nice ones."

"No thanks."

Younger boys did nothing for Robert. In fact the whole establishment was a damper as far as he was concerned. He'd seen it all before. Mike was never happier than when explaining his training techniques. A hundred or so sniveling boys were made to undress and were prodded and poked by the medical team. Six months later they were happier or seemed to be as they did their gymnastic exercises.

Whether or not they were really happy Robert didn't know. Like everybody else he'd been to a pleasure-house once or twice. The whole business of choosing a boy, doing what you wanted with him and then leaving was about as romantic and pleasurable as putting his numbered card into the time lock on the room he'd been allocated and paying the bill when he'd finished.

"An hour and thirty five minutes. That's three hundred and eighty Dhalers. Thank you. Have a nice day now." Eighty-five Dhalers would go to the boy:

payment for surrendering his ass and shooting his semen. The rest went to Central Government. It was small wonder that the demand for boys was increasing. Mike and his staff worked hard to provide them.

With the more-than-willing help of the older boys, they learned how to suck and be sucked. They learned the erotic potential of the anal region. Then came the vibrator practice. The first ones were as slender as pencils. As the months went by the size was increased. They stopped yelling after a few months. They grimaced, certainly, as bigger and bigger instruments were pushed into their resistant asses. After that they grinned, then closed their eyes and let their various fantasies take over as a man-made penis prepared the way for the real thing.

"You remember that lad who was transferred," said Mike.

"David? The dancer?"

"That's the one. He's a natural."

"A boy who has that sort of perverse stuff can hardly be a natural." Robert replied. "The Director showed me the picture. It was revolting. He's a hetero for sure."

"Come and look at him if you don't believe me," said Mike. "He's due in the studio about now."

Robert made a token show of reluctance but climbed out of his chair and followed Mike down the corridor to the studio. As it happened, the boy concerned was approaching from the opposite direction. Robert could hardly believe his eyes. He walked with the delicate grace one associated with dancers but that was the only vestige of his previous career. His cock pointed stiffly upwards and what had been smooth-shaven white skin now sported a dense black patch of hair.

"Hairy little bugger, isn't he?" said Mike.

"I wouldn't describe that as little," Robert replied.

"Always a good sign when they get a hard on beforehand. He's itching for it. That boy's ass is going to be a gold mine."

David went into the studio. They followed him. He got up onto the bench. The supervisor clamped his legs in the stirrups and swung them apart.

Just the sight of David's tightly closed little brown orifice made him remember the dance practice and Chris's white buns glistening in the footlights. It seemed wrong, somehow, to expose the most secret and, to his mind, the most exciting aspect of a boy to view in such a callous fashion. Those little knots of muscle were for tickling; for licking and stimulating until they opened. The attendant had no such qualms. Like many of them he was a convicted heterosexual on re-orientation training.

"Nice one," he said and thrust the spout of the oiler in as if he were lubricating some unthinking machine. David gasped.

"Want to do it?" Mike asked, with a grin. He handed Robert the vibrator. "The ultimate pleasure for people like you, eh?" he added, as Robert removed the plastic cover. In the circumstances, it was an unfortunate thing to say. If he only

102

knew it, the ultimate pleasure lay a few hours in the future.

At least Robert was more gentle than any of the resident staff. The boy moaned and his face contorted as inch after inch went in until all seven inches were inside him. Robert switched it on.

"He's eighteen but he'll probably take some time. They wank themselves to the point of exhaustion," the attendant said. "I've got time for a coffee. Want one?"

Robert declined and stared down at the boy. His eyes were closed and his tongue protruded from the corner of his mouth. Beads of sweat had formed on his forehead.

"Good one," said the attendant, sipping his coffee. "I wouldn't stand too near. They splash all over the place at this age. I got some in my drink once. Bloody horrible it was. What people see in boy spunk beats me. Fancy paying money to suck that stuff out."

Robert smiled. He didn't have to pay.

David had stopped grimacing and was squirming so violently that the stirrups squeaked. Finally, with a mighty upward heave, he came. The attendant was right. It jetted upwards and cascaded down over the boy, the bench and the floor.

"Have a rest, son," said Mike as the attendant pulled the vibrator out.

"You know we've got Coq coming next week?" said Mike after David had made an unsteady exit.

"No!"

"Another one who hasn't heard. No doubt our ever efficient, so-called Director will get round to telling you some time."

"What's he coming for?"

"Your guess is as good as mine. I guess getting his leg over is pretty high on the list. I might give him David. I think an eighteen-year-old virgin is a rarity."

"He might not be into eighteen-year-olds," said Robert. "A man with his money might well have more exotic tastes."

By the time Robert had returned to the admin. block, the notice had been posted. "In view of a possible hysterical reaction which would adversely affect their studies, I do not wish any boys to be informed," the Director had added.

Everybody on the staff seemed to take a vicarious view of Coq's sexual preferences. The acrobatic trainer from over the road had heard a rumor that Coq had once produced a baby by the forbidden method and that Central Government had hushed the matter up. One of the elementary trainers, also from over the road, knew for a fact that Coq liked very young boys. Sam was quite sure that Coq, in a hologram interview, had said he liked teenage boys with "long, sexy legs."

It was pretty obvious that not one of them knew what he was talking about. The best thing to do would be to consult a teenage fan. There were enough of them. One in particular would probably know the answer and what better excuse for an evening visit?

In fact, Chris wasn't a lot of help. He tried to be. Robert sat next to him as he

fed disk after disk into his computer. They read the articles together. Coq's houses were described as was his interest in water-sports and his humanitarian interests but the one thing that Coq kept quiet about was his sex life. Robert began to think the baby rumor might be true after all.

But it wasn't a wasted evening. As picture after picture of Coq appeared on the screen, the volcanic-shaped mound rose in Chris's groin. He tried, at one stage, to push it down but that volcano was particularly active and sprang up again, helped, it has to be said, by Robert's comments.

"No kid could possibly have a tool as big as that. It's got to be artificial," he said as they looked at a picture of Coq relaxing on his private beach.

"I think it's real. It's just as big in all his pictures," said Chris, gazing at the picture of his idol.

"If you had that in your ass, you'd know about it," said Robert, looking down at the growing mound.

"A friend of mine says it always hurts the first time. He contracted for life with a guy. He says it's okay now but the first night was agony."

"Are you thinking of contracting for life, Chris?"

"I don't know. I'd like to but...."

"But what?"

"Well, you know."

"Studies and professional career first, eh?"

"Yes...and meeting the right man. That's not easy when you're a dancer. My friend says that men like boys with hair on them."

"Whoever heard of a hairy dancer?" said Robert with a laugh. "Anyway, it's just not true. There are loads of people who'd go for you. You're good looking. You've got a good figure...."

"Do you really think so?"

"Sure."

"You don't think this new diet's made me too thin?"

"No, I don't think so. I wouldn't have noticed it if it hadn't been for those shorts."

"Funny, that. The whole troupe was measured for new ones this afternoon. Not just me. They're going to have sparklers sewn on to them. I can't think why they're panicking so early. The tour doesn't start until next month."

It was on the tip of Robert's tongue to tell him the reason but there were other priorities for the tip of his tongue at that moment.

Chris needed very little persuasion to get undressed. The musicians and vocalists were sometimes a bit hesitant. Ben, on the previous evening, thought Robert wanted to feel his diaphragm but pretty soon realized that the administrator's interest lay considerably lower.

Chris was absolutely stunning. There was no doubt about that. Like all the dancers he was in perfect condition.

"Sorry about this," said Chris, blushing and pointing downwards. "It's through looking at Coq's pictures. It always happens."

104

"Normal enough," said Robert. "I'm the same."

"So I see. That's the great thing about Coq. His fans are all ages."

"It's not just Coq who has done this."

"You don't mean...?"

"Sure. Why don't you come and lie on the bed?"

Chris hesitated. They all did at first. What if someone were to find out? Like all of them, Chris did not want to end up over the road. But, like all the rest, he succumbed in the end. The feel of fingers other than his own was almost certainly no novelty but it got him going. Whether or not other tongues had worked on his rigid shaft, Robert didn't know and Chris didn't say anything. All that Chris could do at that stage was to gasp. Privately, Robert was disappointed. He missed the feel and the scent of pubic hair. There was just a slight bristly feel at the end of his nose. Dense, sweat-laden hair would have been so much better but he had to give Chris top marks for his performance. With legs so far astride that they hung over either side of the bed, the boy squirmed and arched upwards, pushing his cock farther and farther into Robert's mouth. Then the taste changed, almost imperceptibly at first. The slightly bitter-sweet flavor of pre-cum. Robert stopped.

"Go on. Finish it," Chris panted.

"I intend to," said Robert, undressing as fast as he could.

"You mean...?"

Robert nodded. He took the tube out of his pocket and handed it down to Chris, who read the label and looked up at him, scared.

"I'm going to prove just how wrong your friend was," said Robert.

Chris turned over. He didn't want to at first.

"You really are a stunner," said Robert. It was small wonder that audiences went wild over the boy's butt, which rose gently from his smooth thighs and sank sharply to join in the hollow of his back. It looked good enough to eat which is what Robert proceeded, metaphorically, to do. There was no doubt that Chris enjoyed it. He spread his legs wider apart. Robert tickled it with his tongue and, joy of joys, found a couple of sparse hairs in there that the barber had missed.

It took a long time; a very long time, for Chris to open but tongue and finger turned fear into lust. Like the pupil of an eye presented to the dawning sun, his sphincter expanded; lubricant was applied and Robert entered. By that time Chris was in such a state of ecstasy that pain was indistinguishable from pleasure. He moaned. He even reached behind him to part his cheeks. Not that it was necessary. Inch by inch, Robert's penis slid into him.

Like Ben, Chris came first, groaning and sighing. Robert felt him relax and one of Mike's aphorisms came to mind. "Give a boy the gravy stroke just after he's come. That's when he's at his best." Chris certainly was. His buttocks were softer; his interior muscles were still tight but Robert could feel the grip on his cock relaxing. Just how many spurts there were in that particular ejaculation, he didn't know. Chris lay motionless with his face buried in the pillow as jet after

jet filled him.

"Not so bad after all, eh?" said Robert later.

"Mmm. Nice," said Chris. "You really love me don't you?"

The question took Robert by surprise. "You know I do," was all he could think of saying. He felt a warm affection for the boy. It had been good to talk about Coq and about music. Slipping into the building unobserved had been a great thrill and infinitely better than walking into a pleasure-house and consulting the computer.

"Preferred age range? Ethnic origin? 'Please wait. Your request is being processed. Select the boy of your choice from the following pictures and press the appropriate key. You have been allocated room 129. Charges start when the lock is activated."

So you didn't spend time talking to a pleasure-house boy. More often than not you left without even knowing his name, let alone what sort of music he liked and which star he most admired.

"I thought you did," said Chris and, to Robert's amazement, the boy leaned over and kissed him.

- - -

It rained on the day of Coq's visit. That was the least of Robert's worries. The Director was unwell. It was said that his aversion to teenage hysteria was the real cause of his absence. Thus, Robert was left to welcome the superstar and that wasn't his only worry.

For days, Chris had dogged him. He couldn't be in his office for more than a few moments before Chris showed up with a weak excuse. Fortunately, at the time the huge stretch hovercraft came to a halt and sank silently to ground level, Chris and all the other boys were in their respective studios, waiting to perform for the distinguished visitor who, rather disappointingly, was not wearing the famous shorts but a smart, glittering suit. The pictures hadn't lied. He was amazingly good looking. He also turned out to be an extremely patient man.

The choir and the soloists and musicians performed. Coq clapped enthusiastically after each number. Then it was the turn of the dancers.

"One thing I would ask," said Robert as they started their final strip number. "Can you make a special fuss of the one in the middle? The tall, blond one."

"Be glad to. Very glad to," Coq replied when Chris's shorts descended. "That's the neatest butt I've seen in years."

"I'm afraid admiring it is all that's possible," said Robert with a slight pang of conscience. Coq didn't answer.

True to his promise, he sent for all the boys and Sam to congratulate them and wish them well on their tour. He asked Chris to stay behind. They chatted for some minutes, or rather, Coq chatted. Chris was strangely tongue tied but managed to stammer his thanks for the promised gift of a complete set of autographed Coq disks.

"You sure are one beautiful boy," said Coq. "A feast for the eyes and no mistake. The guy who gets you is sure gonna be one lucky man."

They had lunch with all the staff, some of whom exceeded the boys' doting admiration. Numbers that Robert had heard them rate as "sentimental rubbish" were described in enthusiastic tones as "brilliant." The music teacher who had taught him and had described him as a "conceited little bastard with no musical ability who should have been sent over the road" had revised his memory. "I always knew you'd be a great star," he purred.

Robert introduced Mike. "It's you I really need to see," said Coq. "You're training my new batch."

Mike looked perplexed. "We thought you might like a boy but we didn't really know what you had in mind," he said.

"No, no. Not for me. For the new pleasure house."

"You mean the new place in town?" Mike asked.

"Sure it's mine. Didn't you know? I'm going to need about two hundred boys next year. Central have agreed."

"Two hundred!" Mike gasped.

"Sure. Biggest place in the country. No expense spared. With Central's backing and my name, hell, it can't fail."

Robert thought it best to excuse himself and stood up but Coq was reluctant to let him go. "I might need you," he said and so Robert went with them.

Coq applauded the acrobatic display. "Keeps them supple," the instructor explained as fifty inverted young faces grinned, framed in their owners' legs. The reason for the other exercises was self-apparent.

The new intake was paraded for inspection. Coq strolled idly up and down the line, stopping only occasionally to speak to a boy. He patted a few bottoms in a paternal sort of way, slid his hand down the front of one boy's shorts, said something which made the boy laugh and moved on.

"I hope he's not after one of them," Mike whispered. "They're not nearly ready."

Coq returned. "A good lot," he said. "I shall need many more though."

"For your own use?" Mike asked. The bulge in Coq's shiny pants said everything.

"Shit no!"

"I have got one boy who might be of... err... personal interest to you," said Mike. "Eighteen. Slightly older than these. He's ready for it."

"Pre-stretched you mean?"

Mike nodded. "He used to be a dancer," he said. "A nice- looking boy. Do you want to see him?"

"No way. I've already chosen one."

"Certainly. Which one?"

Coq turned to Robert. "What was the name of that blond dancer?"

"Chris. But as I explained...."

"Have him taken out of the dance troupe. I'll fix it with Central and send

transport for him. You'd better not tell him. He'll be good. Of course you wouldn't have had a virgin boy. You don't know what it's like."

Conscience-stricken, Robert shook his head. Mike looked aghast.

"Nothing like it," said Coq. "A bit like opening a bottle of champagne but you wouldn't know about that either. Neither are easy to open but both froth up. Young Chris is going to have the time of his life. So am I."

Robert could hardly wait for the man to leave the Academy. In a blind panic, he called on the Director at home. There was no doubt that Coq would be able to arrange Chris's transfer. That was bad enough. Worse was the undoubted fact that he would either sense or maybe Chris would tell him that he wasn't the first after all.

The director didn't look at all ill. He listened attentively to what Robert had to say.

"It comes as no surprise," he said. "I was Dean of Studies when he was a student here. There were one or two little incidents involving his fellow students that we hushed up because he obviously had star quality. I detest the bastard. The best thing to do would be to put out a story to the effect that Chris has been.... He hasn't of course, has he?"

"I ... er...."

The director smiled. "You're young. I guess it's natural enough. These midnight calls had better stop. What's that block called?"

"Double F."

"Forbidden fruits, Robert. Remember that in the future. Forbidden fruits."

NAVAJO JOE
by illiam Cozad

Joe, a Navajo Indian from Arizona, was in my freshman class in college.
I never thought much about him until I saw him in a culture awareness program. After that, I hardly thought about anything else. Since about half of the students in school were from different ethnic backgrounds, there was music, dance and readings from African, Latino and Asian students in their native dress.

But I was awestruck when I saw Joe on the stage. He was medium height with straight, silky black hair and brown eyes. He had high cheekbones, a hooked nose and thick lips. Bare-chested and bare-legged, all he wore was a buckskin loincloth. His body was smooth, red-skinned and muscular. He wore a headband with a single feather in the back. He chanted and danced on the stage to the sound of recorded drum music.

I didn't know what that was all about. All I knew was that when he moved around and the buckskin flapped, his dark ass cheeks were visible. I got a big hard-on. I wanted to touch and taste that ass of his.

The memory of Joe in the buckskin loincloth stayed in my head long after his performance. I could never hear the chant that sounded like "waya, heya, haya" over the drum that sounded like thunder.

I rushed home after the culture awareness program. I went to my room and sprawled out on my bed. Reaching down inside my jeans and shorts, I felt my throbbing dick. With visions of Joe dancing in my head, I stroked and squeezed my dick. I shot one of the biggest loads of my life, soaking my shorts with gobs of cum.

Joe was friendly in school. But he was kind of an outsider. In my English class, I sat a couple rows behind him. I couldn't concentrate on the teacher's comments or the student discussion. All I could do is look at that muscular red skinned butt in jeans and dream. When the teacher called on me, I had to ask her to repeat the question.

Then I went back to daydreaming about Joe's butt. Since I wasn't in his gym class, I'd never seen his jewels. I wondered what they looked like. He had a big dick, judging by the size of the bulge in his jeans. I became obsessed with him.

Out of the blue, one day after class I invited him to go to my house. I made up some cock-and-bull story about my interest in Indians and wanting to know more about them. Not a total lie, because I wanted to know more about Joe.

He walked home with me. I lived in the better part of town, because my folks earned a good income running their own insurance company. I knew that Joe lived on the other side of the tracks, literally the Southern Pacific tracks, where property was cheap and there was flooding from the winter rains.

At my house, I got a bright idea. I thought we needed to relax a bit, so I got us

each a soda out of the fridge and I poured some out and spiked them with whiskey from my folks' liquor cabinet. While I was fixing the drinks, I explained to Joe that my folks were away for the weekend, attending a seminar.

When I handed him his drink, he teased, "Firewater makes Indians crazy, you know."

"It makes me horny," I said.

I showed Joe my room with the college pennants on the wall. We sipped the whiskey-laced sodas.

"So what's it like being an Indian? Bet you hate us whites for stealing your land," I said.

I was high and didn't know what I was saying.

"Some of the tribes are getting even, with the casinos on federal lands. Lots of jobs and lots of money."

I told him a joke that was going around school.

"The Bureau of Indian Affairs said they found another Mohican. So all those book titles gotta be changed to 'The Next to the Last of the Mohicans.'"

He laughed along with me. He had perfect white teeth and his thick lips were sensuous.

I gulped the drink and was higher than a kite.

"Joe, you got a hot body. I'd like to see the rest of it."

"You're drunk, paleface," he smiled.

Brazenly, I reached over and grabbed his crotch bulge. I felt his dick stiffen.

He didn't resist when I unbuttoned the metal buttons of his fly and tugged down his jeans. His big dick was semi-hard and in a horizontal position. Seeing that, and his beefy thighs, made my dick stir.

I sort of shoved him down on his back on my bed.

His brown eyes were glossy.

I climbed on the bed and straddled his legs. Bending down, I sniffed his piss-and-cum-stained white cotton briefs. I licked his shorts until they were wet and the outline of his fat, circumcised prick was clearly visible. I nibbled on his dick through the cotton and it throbbed.

Hooking my fingers in the waistband of his briefs, I peeled them down. His dick was even bigger than I had imagined, a solid eight inches. He had plump balls and a lush black bush.

I grabbed hold of his hot, throbbing dick and sniffed his musky, ripe smell. I nuzzled my face in his pubes. I licked them until they glistened with spit.

Clutching his dick, I licked his dangling, smooth nuts in their wrinkled sac. I sucked both of them into my mouth, then spit them out.

Cradling his veiny shaft, I flicked my tongue on it. His mushroom dickhead was rosy and spongy. I gripped his shaft and swabbed his bloated dickhead. Clear pre-cum bubbled out of his piss-hole. I lapped it up, savoring its sweet taste. I dug my tongue into his piss-hole.

"Oh, yeah, suck it. Suck my big fat prick."

This was the first cock I'd ever played with besides my own. I wanted to see

110

how much of it I could get down my throat. I wrapped my lips around his dick and sucked on the knob while I stroked the shaft. Letting go of the shaft, I plunged down on it. I gagged. I tried again. I gagged. I tried again. Finally, Joe helped me. He clasped my head and thrust his dick up into my throat. Tears stung my eyes. I almost choked on his massive meat, but I got control again. I bobbed my head up and down on his dick. He kept pushing my head farther down until his dick was speared into my throat and his pubic bush tickled my nose.

"Suck it. Take it all."

I slurped on his dick, drooling spit down onto his bush and balls. He rubbed my head and controlled the rhythm of the suck job. "God, you're good!" he cried.

I kept at it for several minutes. Then he stopped me. "Oh, yeah, I'm fucking ready." But I wouldn't stop. I knew he was coming and I wanted it. I wanted to take it all.

His big totem pole was hard as a rock and throbbing in my mouth. Suddenly it started gushing cum. He let me keep my mouth on his meat until I thought I'd drown in his cum. His stringy cum was even dripping out of my nose. I swallowed every drop of it that I could. It was like white syrup and tasted just as sweet.

His dick softened and I took my mouth off it. Flaccid, it was a plump five inches.

"God, I've never had anybody take my load before," he said.

"Oh, it was great, Joe," I said, wiping excess cum from my mouth.

I had a raging hard-on from sucking Joe, but I had to get an up-close look at his butt and touch it, taste it. I roughly rolled him over onto his belly. His dick was beautiful, no denying it, but his ass was one of the seven wonders of the world, as far as I was concerned.

Just the feel of his muscular red-skinned butt cheeks sent jolts of ecstasy through my body.

He glanced over his shoulder with his smoldering brown eyes, really bedroom eyes. He didn't try to stop me.

I spread those twin globes. I looked at the sparse black hairs, the pink gash, and my dick throbbed wildly and oozed. I simply had to try it with Joe.

I dove into his crack. I licked it, slobbered on it, tasting his tangy hole. I darted my tongue up his pucker until I had to come up for air.

Spit and butt slime covered my face. I had the biggest hard-on of my life, a woody that wouldn't quit.

Looking at that cherry Indian butt hole, I poked my middle finger inside. It was like a fiery furnace. I finger-fucked him for a few moments. Then, in the heat of the moment, with the taste of his tart butt hole in my mouth, I ripped open the metal buttons of my fly. I slid down my jeans and shorts.

My throbbing dick sniffed the air and bubbled precum.

Holding my dick, I slapped it against those butt cheeks and basted them with

clear precum.

"All palefaces wanna fuck Indians," he joked.

He didn't say no and he didn't try to stop me. I rubbed my randy prick in his steamy ass crack. I nudged the crown and it popped into his hole.

"Whoa! Oh shit!"

His elastic ass-ring snapped around my dick. I stayed still, not wanting to hurt him, but not wanting to take it out either.

When he backed up on my dick, it slid up his chute.

I sat back on my heels, with my jeans and shorts tangled below my knees and his pants down on his muscular thighs. I watched my dick move in and out of his hole and felt the delicious sensation that made me shiver and made him moan. He no longer watched over his shoulder, but clutched the pillow.

I lay down on top of him. I smelled his recently shampooed hair. I licked it and chewed on it while I slowly humped him. I licked his ear and sucked on the lobe. I bit into his neck. I clutched his shoulders while I rammed my dick in and out of his fiery butt hole.

"Finish! Fuck faster," he wailed.

I pulled out all the stops. I pistoned his ass, mercilessly, with my nuts banging against his ass cheeks. I worked up a full head of steam, sweaty and panting.

Suddenly I felt my balls rumble. The cum rushed up my shaft and squirted inside him, creaming his guts.

I collapsed on top of him. I saw stars. It was the best feeling I'd ever had in my life, coming inside him.

Just when I thought I'd died and gone to heaven, I was rudely bucked off.

Before I could even comprehend what was happening, Joe had reversed positions and mounted me.

Somehow I had never considered that. He was much stronger than I had imagined. He took complete control.

Glancing over my shoulder, I saw him drool spit into my crack. His brown eyes were wild.

"Oh, no! You're too big," I protested weakly.

He didn't listen to me. It was payback time, revenge, whatever.

I just hugged the pillow, which was damp with his sweat and spit. I waited for the inevitable.

His massive dick felt like a hot poker in my crack. In a flash, he shoved it up my ass. He lay on top of me and ravished my asshole. I begged: "Yeah, Joe, massacre my ass. Oh yeah, fuck me, fuck my ass like I fucked yours. I wanna feel that big motherfucker cum inside me."

I humped back and he relentlessly rammed my ass like a pile driver. He huffed and puffed.

"Oh, yeah, I'm coming!" he screamed. His dick exploded up my ass. I felt my teeth rattle and my eyeballs cross. He shot so much hot cum inside me that I thought it would come out of my ears.

His heart was thudding in his chest against my back.

He clung to me until his dick softened and slid out of my abused asshole.

When it was over, I let my eyes close, exhausted. To my shock, I felt him roll me over and begin lapping at my spent cock with his rough tongue. It was much too soon. No way would I be able to get aroused again so quickly. That's what I thought, anyway.

But Joe was merciless. His tongue kept at it. He made happy moaning sounds to show me that he was enjoying the taste his ass juices and my orgasm had left on my cock. He sucked lightly on it and nibbled gently on my balls until I felt I was erect again. It was incredible. I had never even believed it was possible. But there it was, happening to me.

This time my climax lasted even longer and felt even better than the first. When it was done, he started in again, kneeling between my splayed thighs and touching my ass lips with the swollen head of his erect penis.

I didn't think I'd be able to receive him so soon, especially since I had just come, but when he thrust slowly forward, my asshole seemed to open up and positively suck him in all the way.

Joe fucked me for a long, long time. He'd bring himself to the edge of climax and then slow down or pull back to postpone it.

Finally, when neither of us could stand it any longer, I begged him to come. As he slammed into me one last time, I think our cries of passion could have been heard around the world, or at least throughout the neighborhood.

I fell asleep, and when morning came, I found myself snuggled comfortably in Joe's muscular arms. The first words out of Joe's mouth were reassuring: "Your folks go to many seminars?"

I smiled. "I never know when, but yes, they do a lot of traveling." Pleased with that reply, he hugged me to him. He was hard again....

I guess I don't need to tell you that we had many powwows after that.

This tale has been adapted specially for this collection from material that originally appeared in *Playguy* magazine.

THE BOY ON THE BENCH
by John Patrick

"In front of one of the most palatial hotels in the world, a very young man was accustomed to sit on a bench which, when the light fell in a certain way, shone like gold...."

From "Malcolm," a novel by James Purdy, whose protagonist is a well-built teenager

Luke and Victor are happy now. The boy is naked at last they all are. There are no words, only the sound of flesh upon flesh, of whispers and grunts and the slither of bodies on sheets.

The boy, a slim blond of indeterminate age, is sandwiched between them. He leans back against Victor, cushioned on his broad, hairy chest, Victor's arms around him, hands busy palming the pecs while the younger one, Luke, kneels over the boy and arranges his legs to his liking. Then he buries his face in the boy's crotch. His tongue is precociously skillful and the boy cries out as Luke finds his most sensitive spot. He looks up in alarm, scared he has hurt him. Such a kind young man, that Luke. The boy smiles at him.

"Please fuck me," the boy begs in his broken English.

These are words Luke understands. He kneels up and leans back to display his standing cock. It is an incongruous sight against such a pale and slender frame. The big bulb glows an obscene and meaty red and the cock thrusts out from his body like another limb. Behind the boy Victor says something coarse as Luke spits on his hand and oils his big penis.

"Hurry up," the boy hears himself saying and Luke laughs.

Then all laughter is forgotten as Luke slips the head of his organ between the boy's waiting ass lips and slides it sweetly home.

It is thrilling while it lasts. Luke tries to control himself to begin with, slowly working his tool in and out, savoring every tantalizing second. But his excitement has been building for such a long time, the seemingly unattainable lad beneath him is his to enjoy as he pleases and his lover is urging him on. For a frenetic few minutes he drills into the lad's ass, grunting and groaning with animal delight as the boy wraps his smooth legs around him. His balls smack against the underside of the boy's ass cheeks as his hard cocks slams furiously in and out. Then it's all over as, one, two, three, he squirts his juices deep inside the boy and collapses on top of him.

But there is to be no rest. Now Victor wants his turn; he has been patient long enough. The boy, too, has yet to be satisfied, and his cock is hard and he is stroking it.

Luke is pushed to one side and the boy turns his attention to Victor. He kisses Victor eagerly, his tongue slyly flicking into his hungry mouth. The boy pulls Victor to him, his hands on the curve of his hips, Victor's cock pressed flat against the boy's hard belly. They explore each other urgently. The boy seizes Victor's fat cock, peeling the foreskin down over head and swooping down the stubby shaft to cup the balls. They connect easily now, Luke having prepared the ass with his cum.

The boy rolls beneath Victor's broad brown frame and spreads his legs wide to accommodate him. Victor enters the boy, roughly, showing no mercy, and sets a steady rhythm. As Victor fucks him, the boy strokes his cock, building the fire between his legs, urging Victor on. Victor doesn't understand him, but who cares? He is lost in his own private erotic moment. The wanton behavior of this cute stranger has turned him on and he laughs out loud, delighted with his youthful enthusiasm for the fuck.

Later, after the men have showered, the boy, dressed now, drops to his knees before them. First Luke, then Victor, then Luke again, the boy swallows the swollen members, rubbing the sensitive flesh against the roof of his mouth, jerking his hands on their shafts with the time-honored skill of a young, yet very experienced masturbator.

It would be nice, the boy thinks, to take both of them in his mouth at once. He presses the two shafts together, wanking them in a double-handed grip, but the two just won't fit. Never mind; to lick and suck and hold them like this is fun. He's never done this before. Not exactly like this.

Still working the two cocks eagerly, he lifts his head. The men are leaning against each other for support, all laughter gone from their faces. Victor's eyes are still filled with desire. His hand descends on the top of the boy's head and roughly pushes him back to his task.

Now the boy begins to suck and squeeze with a steady rhythm, switching from one prick to the other, trying to gauge their levels of excitement, desiring now to take each load.

It is Luke who finishes first, his big cock spraying spunk into his face like water from a garden hose. Then, with both hands on Victor's cock, he cleverly sucks the sperm into his mouth. Then he leans back on his haunches and raises his smiling face up to the two sated lovers. He grins up at them, happy in his victory. As he does so, he wipes his face, and their juices mingle.

It is late afternoon. The sun is still hot on the bleached shutters of the hotel.

In their room, nothing stirs. Victor sleeps happily next to Luke. They intend to sleep until it is dark, then seek another boy to excite them.

Meanwhile, outside the hotel, on the bench, the boy waits. He still aches a little from last night. The men were so eager, so in need. Maybe they will come out of the hotel and see him there and invite him back to their room. He leans back on the bench and pushes his crotch toward the sun. He tries not to attract

too much attention to himself. He has learned to be discreet but sometimes it's not easy. Still, no matter what he does it seems, when he is on his bench, adventures just come to him.

IN THE HEAT OF THE MOMENT
by Sonny Torvig

The first time had been a disaster. The moment contrived, and then handed away by yours truly. A sudden rush of failed courage had led to my hasty retreat from the scene, and I have spent hours since that moment wondering how things might have turned out if I hadn't lost my nerve, imagining what I might say to Martin if I were to meet him again. And in the end, all the analysis only added to the intense frustration of a lost opportunity. The daydreams I had, the things I imagined trying with Martin, they were all left shattered, and a bitter pill to swallow. And it was all down to me.

I am not a brave man, I'm usually the one who's the shadow in the corner at parties. Yes, I've set eyes on a few men who have made my insides turn over, but never had the courage to turn that lust into an approach. But with Martin it had been subtly different. We had passed each other in the everyday flow of the office, and one day, by chance, ended up in the same bar after work. There had been something special about Martin, a calm sureness in himself perhaps, or his openness to friendship, but whatever it was it had given me the courage to blurt out my longings, and he had listened! Not only that, he had been honest about his own brief sorties into the world of men. The tension in the air that night was enough to have me straining the buttons on my 501's. We'd made it to bed too, after much discussion of equal expectations and respect for changes of mind, and until we got our shirts off, the night was promising to be the answer to all my prayers.

The intensity of my fear in the face of actuality had turned me cold, frozen me like a deer facing headlights. Faced with naked flesh, black hair curling around large, dark nipples, down from his navel to the button of his jeans, I had lost it. I had felt sick with the raw sexuality of the moment, and backed off. The fruit there for the peeling and I had walked away from the tree! I skipped work for a week, I found another job.

But here it was again, here *he* was, and a chance to put right all the frustrations of the last two years. He sat opposite, over a coffee, and talk eventually turned to partners. I felt the same old, icy chill beginning in my stomach, and shouted, loud in my head. My face never registered that deafening inner cry for courage. My hopes began to rise. My cock began to rise. And so did the bill when we decided to string things out awhile. No places to go and time on our hands. The gods were giving me a second chance!

"Do you ever think back to that night?" I couldn't believe I had just said that, heaven knows I had practiced it often enough, but never for a moment thought I'd manage to utter it. He looked up at me over his cup.

"Why?"

I breathed out as if discovered in a lie. "I've always wondered what you

thought of it, whether you were glad I'd bottled out, or if I'd gone and left you frustrated."

He frowned, swirling the last of the coffee in the cup. "I thought you were a shit!" He downed the dregs and cupped his hands around the warmth left behind. "I was left feeling used."

I muttered an apology, suddenly wanting the ground to swallow me up. "Yea, I owe you one." I fell silent for a moment. "I was so scared suddenly. It was all so new, so strange and, well, to be frank, just too exciting for me. Anyhow, I got my courage back a day later, but I didn't dare call you to apologize."

There was a silence. It grew uncomfortably long and I squirmed. "Want another coffee?"

He shook his head. "No, I'm swilling in caffeine already. I better get myself organized and catch a ride home." That was it, I had blown my chance.

I felt my car keys, cool against my eager fingers.

"Can I give you a lift?" I rushed that one, he was already rising to leave. It stopped him for a second. "Honestly, it's no problem."

We stepped out into the cool of the afternoon, the sun making a brave attempt to warm the street. "Not weather to be waiting for a ride," I told him. I felt awkward now, and full of a growing regret that I'd screwed up, again. Thankfully the journey was short, and little was said.

We came to a quiet halt outside his small flat, and I turned off the engine rather than leave it running. I wanted him to sense I wasn't just waiting for him to get out, and then go. He gathered up his bags and held them on his knee for a while before he said anything, unaware of my watching his distorted look in the rear view mirror. "I'd ask you in for a coffee, but I think the cafe saw to that." He looked over to me. "But do you want to come in anyway?"

I smiled; I felt as if somewhere inside a bottle of champagne had been uncorked.

"Well, yes. Yes, I would. I don't want the afternoon to end on a sour note. I feel bad now about....about then." Shut up, I warned myself. Don't keep apologizing for Christ's sake. The voice inside my head was getting loud again. He'll think you're a real arse hole! I bit my lip.

By then Martin was already out of the car. He leaned in before he closed the door. "Hurry up then."

I jumped out, slammed the door, watched him walk up the pathway, and locked the car. By the time I reached his flat he had vanished. I walked slowly in and closed the door behind me.

I leaned on the cool wood, took a deep breath, and looked around. It all looked just the same as I had remembered. I glanced over to the bedroom door, a chill of nervous excitement beginning in my stomach. Martin appeared in the kitchen doorway; his look could almost have been triumphant. He gestured to the room in general, "Make yourself at home. You said you had nothing to do this afternoon, but I have." He moved into the bedroom, and out of sight.

120

I sat down and waited for his reappearance, and that wait grew longer. In fact it became painfully so. The silence, the strange mood of the moment, the lack of any sound.

"You know you said you owed me one?" I heard his voice. He made me jump. "Well, you can settle that debt now." Silence. "Right now."

I fidgeted, waiting for him to come back in. The silence grew ever louder.

"Maybe you didn't hear me, but I said you could settle your debt now." His voice had developed an edge of annoyance, and I felt the fear in my stomach growing more intense.

"Yes I know, but how?" I rose from my seat and moved nervously to the bedroom. I peeked round the door, and felt sick. Martin stood beside the bed, and he was nude. Gloriously nude. My eyes fixed on the throbbing length of his cock, the reddened tip peeking out from the semi-drawn foreskin. His dark hair curled down his belly and chest. There was a clutter of items on the bedside table. I swallowed hard.

"I quote, 'I owe you one' unquote. Now get your arse in here and strip."

I looked at his face, I looked at the cord looped on the bed, and my cock began to swell.

"Martin, I...."

He took one step toward me, and I knew from his face that there was no going back, that I had handed myself over to him the moment I had asked about my failure that last time. "I said, strip!"

I kept my eyes on him as I unbuttoned my shirt, the soft material stroking my shoulders a warm farewell as I pulled it back. His eyes wandered over my body, hungry eyes, ownership eyes. He nodded assent as I looked up, and I felt cooler air touch my belly as even warmer jeans slipped away from me. I saw his cock twitch eagerly as I undressed

I hesitated when left with just my jutting briefs to preserve my modesty. I shrugged in desperation, my excitement as painful as I could bear, hoping for release. None came, only the sharp command to do as I was told. I eased the taught fabric down over my own rampant erection, and stepped out of its fallen concealment.

"Now, turn around and bend over, right over!" I bit my lip, and did as I had been told. The slap, when it came, was stinging, and I whimpered in surprised hurt. There came another, harder. "Quiet!" I gripped my shins tightly as he rubbed my stinging skin. "Now reach back and part those cheeks, wide." I felt something warm and firm against my virgin ring, and thought for a moment I was going to be raped there and then. Instead, I recognized the pressure to be a slippery finger, one that slid inevitably inside me. My muscle tightened around it in protest.

More cool fluid was spread over my crack, more slippery invasion. I groaned involuntarily as the finger withdrew. "Straighten up and give me your hands."

I began to turn around, my hands reaching out, the nausea in my stomach intensifying further as soft cord bound first one wrist, then the other. A harsh

push sent me spinning face- down onto the bed.

I looked over my shoulder in real fear now. "Come on Martin, this has gone far enough. What is it you want to do to me? I've said I'm sorry!"

His naked weight was suddenly pinning me down, his hot breath on the back of my neck. "You think that makes everything just fine, do you? Well, I'm afraid not. What I want to do is everything. Everything I wanted to do last time, only now I'm making sure you don't suddenly run away and leave me with a huge, very stiff cock and nowhere to put it!"

I felt the ropes tighten and drag my arms above my head, there to be secured. His weight shifted to my lower back, and fresh cords were looped around my ankles, to part them as widely as he could. I felt the cool of the air across my moistened rosebud, the hardness of his fingers gripping my ankles, the pain of my own rigid cock twisted into the bedcovers. He moved back to my neck, a hot tongue lapping at my ear. "So here we are, and at last I can get rid of the head of steam I had when you ran out on me. But before anything else, here is who's boss tonight."

I felt the rampant heat of him between my spread cheeks, sliding up and down my crack, touching its wet tip to my virgin hole. And there it stopped.

I relaxed when nothing more seemed to happen, beginning to bask in the heated sensations of his lust. The hard weight of him pressed down warm against me, the wet heat of his cock nudging my slippery tightness. I closed my eyes.

The pressure on me increased, his cock slowly beginning to force entry. I hard on the duvet as I felt him slide very slowly inside my wetted hole. His hot tip slipped into me, waited while I relaxed, and then slipped out again. I groaned in some discomfort, but more from excitement, only to sense that he took this as a license to completely fill me with his sex. Slowly at first, but with greater urgency, Martin roughly pushed his way into me, until his belly pressed me down hard, and his hairy bush ground against my wet buttocks.

I was in shock, the full enormousness of another man's cock filling my hole with its urgency was setting me on fire. The painful stretching of my insides and ring was focusing my whole attention on the hard flesh buried deep in me. I desperately tried to relax around him, to twitch under him, feel that thing move a little. Martin just lay in me, his cock twitching, throbbing with a steady pulse against my insides. I groaned into the duvet, the sensations were so incredibly intense. Then he began to withdraw. I began to feel him slowly sliding out, a lack of sensation left deep inside me. The slippery noises followed as I squeezed first the base of his cock-head, then the diminishing circumference of him made me cry out in loss. It hurt. It hurt because I had been invaded by something bigger and more powerful than any dildo or finger, and it ached because I wanted more of the same which I got!

With a groan and a rush Martin's weight crashed back down onto me, the full length of him rushing powerfully upward. I screamed into the silencing fabric as he pounded against me. "This is for last time!" He pumped as deep as was

122

possible, new avenues of pain and pleasure rushing through my belly and cock. "And this is for now!" I squeezed my eyes shut in expectation. And was rewarded by withdrawal to the ridge of his cock, quickly followed by a new onslaught into my heated bowels. I moaned, I screamed, I cried out for mercy, and then for more fucking as again and again Martin pounded me into the creaking bed. His panting breath on my neck, his nails raking my shoulders, sweat slicking my back. Faster and faster grew his frenzy until, with a stiffening of his motions and an arching away from me, I knew I was about to be filled with his cum.

Martin was moaning curses in a language of his own, panting and swearing hot breath on my neck. His thrusting grew jerky as, with gushing and slithering noises, hot jets of cum pumped deep into me, then flowed warmly out. It brought a slow, creamy trickling down over my balls and thighs, the heady smells of sex and sweat. I cried then, cried for the pain, and for the pleasure so long wanted.

Martin fell onto me, his breath ragged and hot. "God, but I needed that." Some moments passed as I lay beneath his hot body, then teeth bit into my earlobe. "I feel better now, and the debt is paid." I squeezed myself tight around the softening flesh inside me as a reply, and was suddenly aware of how wet the bed was beneath my belly.

With no great haste Martin left the room and I heard the shower begin. I lay in my own cum, warm and wet against me, and focused on the new feelings I had. I ached from his fucking, and yet I ached for my hole to be filled again, and again. My cock was beginning to swell against my groin, the foreskin pushed back between bedding and flesh. I tried to ease myself up a little to free the discomfort.

A hand gripped one ankle and loosened the tie there, but the other remained fixed. I felt them being bound together then, but loose from their moorings. I flexed my legs to ease the growing discomfort there. My hands were next, systematically tied together and then freed from the bed-head. Martin dragged me over onto my back, the blood rushing through my arms a distracting relief. He was glistening with droplets of water, rivulets still running down between his thighs. He wrapped one hand around my urgent cock and rhythmically squeezed and rubbed it into a fiery intensity of want.

I almost cried as he let it loose, but swallowed hard as he climbed up onto the bed, his own glistening erection jutting and bobbing before him, dripping cool water onto my hot belly. He leant over me and luxuriantly licked my lips, "I'd guess that was a first for you?" I nodded, dumb. "Do you want to be introduced to another?" I suddenly felt sick with excitement, powerless and in his strong hands entirely. He saw the flicker of fear cross my face and grinned, his wet heat pressed against my chest, rigid cock tensing against my leg. A hot tongue lapped at my ear, a low whisper of promise sending shivers through my entire body. "I have made you ache in one hole, so now I shall broaden your education." His hot tongue pushed between my teeth lapping about my own tongue and tickling

123

the roof of my mouth. "But with something bigger than that!" His voice had changed again, from temptation to demand in a split second.

To my surprise he worked himself down my body, nipping and sucking at my nipples and belly button as he descended. A wet and hungry mouth enveloped my rampant cock, and drew a gasp of urgency from my wet lips. He let me slip from his heated suction and reached over to the table, taking a tube of something and anointing my straining length, drawing back my aching foreskin to cover my pulsing cock head.

I looked down in total rapture as he positioned himself over me, reaching behind him to hold the tip of me against his tight ring. Slowly and deliberately he allowed his weight to increase, forcing my cooling cock past his resistance, and deeper into his clinging heat. Down and down he slipped, tighter and tighter the grip on me became. Until, with a sigh of pleasure he wiggled his hips, fully impaling himself. And so he remained, his head thrown back, his eyes tightly shut. And tight around my cock I felt his hot muscles tense and relax. I groaned in ecstasy. I twitched my hips to feel him the better. Then he slowly rose, his muscles squeezing my cock in their wish to remain full. I groaned again, the intensity of the sensation lifting me to a new plane of experience.

I wanted Martin to pound my desperate body into the bed, to wring my balls dry as I pumped into the very depths of him. I followed his hips with mine, trying to remain so deeply embedded in his hot hole. His weight crashed me back into the bed, and he leant forward to bring his face to mine.

"You don't do anything until I say so! It's me running this show, and don't forget that!" His teeth bit my chin before he sat back.

I closed my eyes in frustration at his lack of movement.

"Just for that insubordination, you can get your sweet lips around this."

He gripped his cock with one hand, my shoulder with the other, and began dragging me into a sitting position while lifting my arms to loop around his neck. With some careful angling of his body over my cock he leant back, pulling me nearer to his engorged and luscious prick. It almost winked at me as I found myself being forced to gulp its length into my virgin mouth.

My breathing become labored as my mouth filled with all of that throbbing solidity, the softness of the skin against my lips, and the lushness of his pubic bush as my nose made contact. I gagged at first, but after drawing back for a moment I felt the reflex give way a little. I pushed myself farther. The wet head of him hit the back of my throat as my face ground into his belly, and my hot breath became even more labored. Having a throat full of cock, I drew back a little and began to suck and lick at him, the noises and smells of his sweating sex swelling my enthusiasm. I noticed him tighten around my own cock as I reached his tip, my lips pushing back his foreskin as I drove my face down his wet abundance once more. He groaned. An arse full of rigid cock and his own deep in the hot and wet mouth of an eager learner. I hoped he was in heaven as I slavered and squirmed in my own moist frenzy of awakening.

Things were getting more heated, Martin's nails raking my shoulders as he

124

began to buck in my lap. His cock cramming my hungry mouth on the upswing, my cock swelling his hot, wet hole on the down. The rhythm grew faster and louder as I began to reach my own levels of ecstasy.

My cock was throbbing and aching inside him and his in my mouth was tasting of something new. I felt him begin, his panting growing ragged and his movements fevered. The pounding began to slow and become more trembling as at last he cried out in surrender, my own moans stifled by the mouthful of gushing prick. Hot juices jetted against the back of my throat, and as I eagerly swallowed back I tasted both his sex and my initial distaste. I gobbled and sucked, the taste now seeming less unpleasant. In fact I wanted the sensation of pumping juices invading me far more than I might have dreamed. Noisily I milked him dry, my lips and chin running with his seemingly endless cum.

With an involuntary closing of my jaw around him I felt my own hot cum gush up and around my cock, the orgasm shaking my very foundations of self-restraint. "Fuck, Fuck, Fuck!" Our writhing and pounding only intensified the sensations as my reserve cracked and splintered. "Oh shit, but that feels fucking...wonderful!"

I jerked as deeply inside him as I could, the last of my cum slithering and squelching from his relaxing hole and oozing downward over our joined bodies. My face ran with his cooling cum and I licked my dripping lips of warm and salty ooze. Martin's head was thrown back, his eyes tight shut, my arms locked behind his neck.

At last, at long last, I felt able to pull him to me, take his full lips to mine and anoint his face with his own juices. His tongue mingled with mine in our frenzied savoring of the fruits of our joining, my hole feeling suddenly empty and longing for more of him.

The afternoon flew by much too quickly, as we lay hot and sticky together on the damp and cool bedding, silently caressing each other's lust, slicked body, licking at the remains of our fucking. My ties were not uncomfortable, but I was desperate to be free to enjoy him. In contradiction, he kept me at his will, which only served to keep me almost permanently hard, the power he had over me maintaining his own prodding enthusiasm. My nostrils filled with the smell of sex sweat and cum, my mouth salty and clinging with him. I bathed in sensations new to me. My arse ached, my cock ached, my jaw ached. And I wanted them all, all to overflowing again and again.

"Lick me clean." He pushed my face towards his erection. "All of me."

My head began to swim with excitement. Perhaps he was going to fuck me again, fill me to my belly with jetting cum, to dribble from me in slow trickles of afterglow.

I managed to begin at his face, licking my dried juices from his stubble, tasting the salt on his neck. His nipples when I reached them were hard and cool against my hot tongue, and I nipped and sucked there to try and encourage him further. He moaned as I began to lick my way to his bush, thick and heavy with the smells of man sex. I nuzzled and licked around the base of his towering

cock, lapping my way up its length, all the while growing drunk on the tastes and smells. I cupped my bound hands around the jutting flesh and drew back the skin to reveal his reddened and swollen head. It slipped into my mouth as if we were old friends, and I tasted the salt and sweat that so fired my hunger for more.

I crooned my way down to his balls, by which time his eyes were rolled back in his head and his breath was snatching and irregular. I even managed to get him rolled over, and began again at the base of his neck.

This time, I knew the ball was in my court, so to speak, for his groan of frustration lent power to my loins. I writhed my way over him and let my weight fall on his back, lapping at his spine like a kid with an ice. His back was well defined, with a lovely curve around his tight buttocks. I surreptitiously nuzzled my hard cock against his wet hole, all the more fired up by his arching back against me.

I crawled awkwardly farther down, licking all the while, arriving at the glistening bud as quickly as I could without hurrying. For some reason that made me think of Zen, as I passed my hungry tongue down the sweaty crease to its desired home.

He was tight at first as my tip tickled over him, the taste of cum and arse heady and forbidden. I took to it like a horse to a salt block, murmuring and slurping as he spread his legs farther for me. I gently nipped at his inner thighs as my nose pushed against him, nuzzling, feeling the muscle slowly relaxing. In a flash I took advantage of the moment and buried my tongue to the hilt inside his heat and taste. My jaw ached, my breath was hard to get, and my tongue cried out in distaste. I had my taste buds rammed up another man's anus, for Christ's sake. How sick could I get! To hell with sick I thought, I was loving every minute of this, and suddenly desperate to experience all there was to have of sex, sex and more sex with Martin. There was now only raw desire, and balls aching to overproduce as soon as possible. My body was on fire and my mind whirling with new landscapes of possible choices in my life. My fear had vanished in the heat of the moment, burnt out when my arse filled with another man's eager cock. I had been welcomed into the world of men, baptized in a way no church would condone.

A SEASON OF PLEASURE
by James Lincoln

The interval knob had been rotated to the highest speed but it did little good; the flurries sluiced at the Saf-T-Glas, filling it in before the wiper blades could finish one pass and stroke another. When the blades came back ... well, there was just no time.

I stomped the brake pedal. No squeal of tires, just a sloshing sound as the car skidded across a sheen of snow, plowing dumbly ahead. A tremendous whump! and the smack-crunch of the windshield as something kissed it. Then the car was gliding off toward the trees.

The tires dipped into the soft shoulder and the whole car slid absurdly down a steep knoll, tipping, rolling, crunching. Twenties and fifties were flying all through the car. I remember thinking I was in some sick game show where you had to grab as much cash as you could before the car stopped its violent reeling.

Wham! It was over. I had smashed against the base of a tree with a tremendous sound. The car was upright, for whatever that was worth. The wipers continued, beating a thump- thump, thump-thump pattern into the night.

I turned off the car, wipers stopping mid-salute. The glass filled in quickly, white as altar linen. Christmas miracle, they were calling it the snow. Curse is more like it.

I opened the glove box and rattled my hand inside, pulling out the flashlight. My door was against a tree and crushed inward; I climbed over awkwardly into the passenger seat and pushed open that door. The wind snatched it from me, threw it aside. Now I worked my way up the hill, grabbing onto whatever tree roots and small growths I could find to pull myself up out of the ditch. The snow was really falling down hard, big damask sheets.

I got back up on the road and looked back to where I had come from. Over there, by snow-flocked forest a lumpy, indistinguishable bundle. The windswept flurries were swarming like a horde of angry white gnats around me.

I got a weak beam from the flashlight, winking in and out. Shaking it made the beacon flush brighter. I hoped to see a deer lying on its side, snow accenting the rack of antlers, blood seeping from its muzzle and steaming in the snow. In fact, for a moment, I forced myself to see that. But only for a moment. Then the deer turned back into what I didn't want it to be.

A teenage boy.

I held my jacket lapels tight around my neck with one hand, shivering.

"Oh, fuck."

What the hell was I to do?

The flakes were dashing horizontal now as I slogged up toward the body, walking as upright as the buffeting gale would allow. I played the light across him. He was lying on his chest. Seemed to be about 5-feet 8-inches, kind of

lanky, wearing faded blue jeans and high-top sneakers and a down jacket. Short jet black hair though he was very fair-skinned. I couldn't make out his age.

I bent down and laid the flashlight on the road. His wallet was in his rear Levi's pocket. I plucked it out and opened it and pulled out his driver's license. Did the math. The kid was eighteen, almost nineteen. Name of Tanner Loiseaux. Photo. High cheekbones, small mouth, thin black eyebrows. He looked ill-humored, no doubt frowning at some DMV fool behind the camera. Couldn't make out his eye color in the photo though it said so on the license: gray. I flipped it over, saw he'd filled out the anatomical gift part. I supposed somebody was about to collect.

Slipping the license back into the wallet and pocketing it, I felt at the guy's neck, trying to find a pulse like I knew what I was doing.

"Unnnn ..."

"Christ!" My feet slipped out from under me and I fell backwards into the road on my ass.

The guy sat up, cupping a hand to his head.

"Don't move," I yelled. "You're hurt."

"No shit," Tanner said, wincing, pulling his hand away and looking at the small drops of blood there on his fingertips. The wind moaned and blew swirls of snow around us.

He looked up at me with cool gray eyes. "You the guy who ran me over?"

"The same."

"Where's your car?" he asked.

"Ditch," I said, reaching over and grabbing the flashlight and scrambling to my knees. I pointed the flashlight at his face. The kid had grown some since the driver's license picture. Not much, though. Head wound wasn't too bad just a cut up in the hairline.

"Where's *your* car?" I asked.

"Up the road," the teen said. "Dead."

"You should be," I told him.

"I ran out of gas," he explained, getting up to his feet and nodding off to the snowy shoulder where a red gas can lay. "There's my ... oh, shit!"

I reached out a hand, catching the kid under the arm as he fell over. "You all right?" I asked, steadying him. He was holding his right foot in the air. Now he gently put it back down until enough pressure was applied to make him wince and suck air through his teeth. He fell back into my arms. "Damn, that hurts when I do that."

"Then don't do it," I said.

"You've had medical training I see," Tanner Loiseaux said dryly, looking up at me with those keen gray eyes. I was overwhelmed with a sudden urge to kiss him. Instead I pushed him up and held him at arm's distance. "Look, what's the chance of another car coming along?"

"Well," he said, "there was like a one percent chance a car would come along when I started walking toward town. Then you came along. I'd say next to

128

nothing now."

"That's why I picked this route, actually, it's utter isolation. It's almost a trap street."

"Huh?"

I had been talking to myself really, looking around, trying to figure out a plan. My eyes went back to Tanner, his eyebrows raised in question, lips parted slightly. The guy was cute as all hell. "Trap streets. Cartographers ... ah, I mean map-makers."

"Oh, I know what cartographers are," he said, and giving me the same look as on his driver's license.

"Yeah, well they put in fake streets to trap people that plagiarize their work. Little isolated things that don't bother anyone usually, only give people away who copy their maps."

"I follow you," Tanner said, trying to keep his balance on one foot.

"Come on," I urged. "Let's get going." I acted as a crutch and brought him over to the edge of the ditch. We looked down at my car. It was already cooling and snow was beginning to cling to it.

"You go get the car," Tanner said. "I'll stay here."

"Funny. Now sit," I ordered and gently put him down. Then I went back for his gas can, grabbed it out of the snow, and headed back down the hill toward my wrecked car. I slipped the last few feet, falling in the cold, wet snow, and actually felt a tingle of embarrassment; this kid was cute, did I mention that?

I got up and undid the gas tank and stared at it and the empty jug as the snow kept falling, dusting my shoulders and hair.

"Maybe if you concentrated real hard," Tanner was saying. "The gas will jump from your car into my can."

"Shut up."

"Look, let me help," he said, sliding down the hill, keeping his foot off the ground.

"Just stay there. I think I've got a hose in my trunk."

"You ever siphon gas?"

"You?" I asked defensively.

"Yep. I used to filch gas from a neighbor's truck for a go-cart I used to have. Lemme; otherwise you'll get a mouthful."

And so I let him, holding the flashlight on him as he put the hose into the tank and then sucked on it, hollowing out his cheeks, drawing up the fuel and moving his lips away just as the gasoline began to flow out. I'll tell you this now: it turned me on, both in the obvious way, and also in the sense that this eighteen-year-old kid was taking charge. I could feel blood gushing to fill my cock as I stood there in the cold. I worked a hand surreptitiously into a pocket and moved my hard cock in my underwear so it wasn't so painful.

I could smell gasoline strongly in the cold air. I let him fill the can while I ducked into the passenger seat and gathered up my money and stuffed it into the duffel bag it had come out of. Then I reached into the glove compartment and

pulled out the first-aid kit and stuffed that into the bag, too.

"Okay, let's get moving," I said, slamming the door and coming up alongside the kid. Tanner handed me the can and I helped him up. He draped an arm over me and we made it up the hill. That in itself was a chore and we paused at the top, heaving, breath visible in the cold air. The snow was hurling itself down hard now and the chill wind felt like one long indignant slap.

"I don't suppose you'd care to know the name of the kid you ran over tonight?" he asked.

"Tanner Loiseaux," I told him. He looked shocked until I handed him his wallet.

"At least you aren't a thief."

"Yes, well...."

He paused his hobbling and I waited for him to poke the wallet back into his pants. He never even opened it to see if the money was there. Then we plowed ahead.

As we walked, Tanner explained how he came to be walking down the middle of an isolated road with a gas can. The Holly Ridge Tree Farm was a few twists and turns off this road, and he had gone to pick up a previously tagged Christmas tree and pay the remainder on his deposit.

"I don't know why I bothered," he said, limping like Tiny Tim, me holding him tightly against my body. The money-filled duffel and gas can were in my other hand. "I mean, I'm going to be spending Christmas alone. My lover just left me. Good timing; he doesn't have to shell out money for a present. Me, bought his Christmas present like two months ago what?"

"Huh?" I asked. Apparently I'd made some kind of face or smiled or something. Must have been when he revealed the gender of his lover.

"Anyhow," he went on, "I'd already put down a deposit, so what the hell; my parents are in the Caribbean and the house is empty so I might as well bring another living thing inside to wither away and die."

"You're breaking my heart," I said.

"Only fair I think you broke my ankle." He grinned at me, a kind of cockeyed smile that made his gray eyes twinkle and turned me on even more. My raging hard-on was back, even in the chill.

"What do you know? Still there."

I looked up and saw his car, a late model Escort. On the top was the tree wrapped tautly in mesh netting and lashed to the roof with frazzled green twine. Its coat of needles ruffled in the blustery gales like the breast feathers of a plump mourning dove.

"Virginia pine," he said. I let go of him and he leaned up against his car, holding that sore ankle up off the ground. I put in the gas and we climbed in, me driving. That was understood; it would have hurt too much for him to apply pressure to the pedals.

"Okay," I said. "I guess we're pointed in the right direction."

"Yep," Tanner replied. "So, what's your name? You know mine."

130

"Jack Frost."

I eased out into the road. The way the wind was whisking the snowflakes at the windshield, there appeared briefly the illusion of great speed. But we were going real slow; any slower we'd be going backwards.

"Jack Frost? I bet people used to tease you," Tanner said, voice full of sympathy.

"I was kidding."

"So was I, shit brains," he retorted and grinned again. "It's called playing-along. You know, I think that's what I'll call you. Shit brains. At least until you give me a real name."

"Pete."

"Pete?"

"Yeah. Pete Moss."

"Okay shit brains, be that way."

"I'm serious," I said. "It's Peter Moss."

He looked at me, narrowing his gray eyes. "You *are* serious, aren't you?"

I tried to look piqued but it didn't work and I broke out into a devious smile. Tanner slapped me on my arm and giggled. "You asshole." I looked over at him, admiring his pale skin glowing eerily in the greenish light of his dashboard. A weighty hush filled up the car.

"Uh," Tanner said, obviously feeling it too. He clicked on the radio. "How about some Christmas music? Put us in the spirit." He clicked it on.

"...indeterminate amount. K-9 units were used to track the suspect and determine if the box contained an explosive device. Police be..."

I reached over and snapped it off. "You want me to listen to three hundred Mormons screaming hallelujah? I think not."

"Bah humbug. Turn here."

A break in the trees and a road appeared. I eased onto it, trying not to fishtail. There were a few houses on this road, though they were tucked far back. Although most of the houses were dark inside, multicolored lights blinked from the eaves. Illuminated polyethylene Santas, wreaths with pine cones and red ribbons, the whole bit.

"It's better now," I remarked, looking up into the night sky. "The snow. Before, you couldn't see your hand in front of your face." I looked down at his hands. Pale, soft, small. I tried to imagine his fingers moving gently through my hair, his hand in my palm. Then I tried to imagine those fingers wrapped around my dick.

"Watch it."

I'd almost gone off the road again.

"Now, make a left," Tanner Loiseaux said, pointing, getting his arm in my way.

"I'm not dyslexic," I explained, pushing his arm back on his side. Just touching him made me hot.

As the car turned onto the street he'd pointed to, I glanced at a nativity scene

131

in a neighbor's yard. One of the thermoplastic wise men had been blown over. "I don't remember that part," I said.

"Oh, sure. Lemme think. In Matthew. 'And verily, lo, one of the wise men from the East doth falleth face-first in the virgin snow.'"

"'Verily?'"

"Yep," he said. "There. That's my parents' house."

I looked up at a nice two-story clapboard home tastefully decorated with white lights. I pulled into the driveway and shut off the car and handed Tanner his keys.

"You will help me in, won't you?" he asked. "I mean, you did run me over."

"Enough with that," I said. "That was like fifteen, twenty minutes ago."

I left the tree on the car and helped Tanner inside to the living room. I peeled his down jacket off him and then gently laid him out on the couch. I put his jacket and mine in the closet and laid the duffel down. Mistletoe had been hanging over the front door but I'd missed it on the way in. I looked up at the leathery green leaves and waxen berries, then looked back down to Tanner on the couch, who was gently placing his foot in different positions, wincing, trying again. He found a spot and rested it and then relaxed and let out a long sigh.

"Comfy?"

"I need something to drink," Tanner said. "There's some wine in the fridge."

"Wine?"

"It's Christmas. Besides, it's not every day somebody runs "

"I know, I know. You just won't let up, will you. Glasses?"

"Above the sink."

I slipped into the kitchen and got an opened bottle of red wine and two glasses and came back out, setting them down on the coffee table. I poured us some and handed him the glass, then proceeded to get his shoe off and take a look at his ankle. He shook his head, swallowing his mouthful of wine. "No, not yet. It's cold. Get a fire going."

I obeyed. I grabbed some wood from the hearth and piled it on, then threw one of those fake logs on top and lit the ends with one of those long wooden matches. The fire bathed the living room in warm colors. Then I spied a blanket folded neatly in an old rocker and shook it out and laid it over him. Tanner snuggled up under it and smiled dreamily at me.

"Tell me a story," he said, playing little boy.

"I don't know any," I admitted. The fire was getting bigger, sparks licking up the chimney like red-hot fire.

"Come on," he begged, making his voice tiny and childlike. "Just a little one. You did run me over you know."

"All right. A story. Once upon a time...."

"When?" he asked restlessly.

"I don't know. Let's just say a few years ago when this guy was your age."

"What guy?"

"I'm getting to that. His name was ... Graham. His name was Graham and he

132

was your age and he kept looking in the mirror and seeing someone else."

"Weird," Tanner said, snuggling into the couch. "Go on."

"Well, it just wasn't him. He didn't like the guy in the mirror at all. Couldn't stand to look at him."

"So what'd he do?"

"What could he do? He tried to be himself but he couldn't. There was really no recourse but to be the guy in the mirror." I looked off at the fire for a moment then sipped some of my own wine. "I'm not good at this."

Tanner frowned.

"Sorry," I said. "Make up your own ending."

"Happily-ever-after," he said. "That's how all stories end."

I patted his arm through the blanket. If only. "Well, let's get you fixed up." I gently began to undo his laces on his right sneaker.

"Back there," Tanner said, rising up to his elbows, "when I told you about Alex?"

"Alex?"

"My lover, shit brains."

"Oh, right."

"That's really not the right word. I mean, I loved him, and I thought he loved me, but, well, we weren't ... I hadn't slept with him yet."

"Oh," I said. "Brace yourself." I very carefully removed his shoe and then pulled down his sock, revealing a beautiful bare foot and a slightly swollen ankle. "Sprained, I gather. We'll need to put some ice on it."

"How about some head."

"What?" I asked, looking at him in astonishment.

"My head," he said, pointing to the cut. Apparently he hadn't said what I thought he did. I scooted over next to him and brushed his damp hair back. Nothing special. I cleaned it and put a Band-Aid on top of it and let his hair flap back over it. "Good as new."

I got up to get some ice from the kitchen.

"So shit brains, you want to tell me your name now?" he hollered at me.

"Yeah. It's Tanner Loiseaux."

"That's taken," Tanner said.

"What? We can't share?"

"We can't *both* be the same people," he said.

Somehow that disappointed me.

I found a Ziplock bag in one of the cabinets and opened it up. Then I put crushed ice into the baggie from the refrigerator. It ground up the cubes, a relentless gnawing sound, then spit the shavings into the plastic. I grabbed some paper towels and wrapped it around the ice-bag and came back into the living room.

Tanner smiled up at me, firelight playing in his eyes. I locked on his eyes and couldn't pull myself away. I knew it was too long but it was like I was being hypnotized. Finally a large pocket of pitch exploded in the fireplace like a pistol

shot and we both looked over to it.

"Well ... uh, the ice," I said, sitting down and putting it on top of his swollen ankle.

"Ow, shit!"

"I'm sorry. Here." I let him take the ice-pack and reapply it. His pants legs kept getting in the way. "You know ... maybe you ought to take those off. Get comfortable."

No response.

I reached down and unlaced his other shoe and pulled it off, then stripped that sock free of his bare foot. His toes wiggled in the air. Then I moved aside the blanket and reached up and undid his pants, pulling the zipper down, parting them to reveal a triangle of white briefs. I looked up to him. He looked back with damning trust. Then I proceeded. I pulled his pants down, him lifting his hips so I could get them under him. I was careful around his ankle and together we worked on ways to extricate his foot through the leg. Minor wincing and gnashing of teeth. Finally he was free and I laid the jeans down carefully on the floor. He'd pulled the blanket over him before I could get a good look at his smooth, sleek legs and the bulge in his tight jockey briefs. He shivered. "Thanks."

"Well then," I said. "Keep the ice on it."

"It's cold."

"That's the idea," I said and tousled his hair. "Constricts."

"Oh, right your medical training." He grinned, then bit his lower lip. Something expanded and filled the room. An electricity. The same thing that had filled the car in that moment of awkward silence. It scared me. I had to go. I gently patted the ice-bag lying on his ankle and started to stand, to get away. His hand came out and touched mine and I was frozen, unable to move.

"You know you're supposed to kiss it to make it all better," he said quietly, nodding toward the ankle. His voice quavered and broke with fear; he cleared his throat awkwardly to cover his nervousness.

I swallowed hard.

Now Tanner lifted the ice-pack, exposing his swollen ankle.

"Well, if that's what I'm *supposed* to do...." I said and trailed off. I leaned over and dutifully planted a kiss on the cold skin. "There."

"Here too," he said, pointing to his forehead.

I licked my lips. My breathing quickened. "Okay."

The wind whistled through the eaves as I leaned over and planted another kiss on top of his Band-Aid. Then I pulled back. "There you go. All fixed up."

"Here," he said, softer still, almost mouthing it. His eyes looked down and I followed them to his finger, which was pointing back to his ankle, only a little higher, away from the ice-pack. "Make it better," he urged.

I did. A wet kiss on his soft ankle. His flesh tasted heavenly. I think he moaned somewhat when I did this, let out a stuttering exhale of air. My dick plumped up in my pants and I felt flush.

"Now ... there," Tanner said and lifted up the blanket a little to reveal more of his alabaster legs. His finger designated another spot on his calf.

"I don't see anything wrong," I heard myself saying. Jerk.

"Internal injury, shit brains. Now kiss."

My lips touched his smooth skin, planted another peck on him where he specified. His finger moved again, to his other leg. I followed it, kissed again. Now higher, above the knee, somewhere on his inner thigh. A long, warm, loving kiss. The other leg again, back down toward his foot. I kissed once more.

"Here now," he said in a husky whisper. He completely removed the blanket, tossing it over the side of the couch. His finger was dangerously close to his bulge.

I climbed up onto the couch and worked my head down and kissed him, pressing my lips there, smelling his groin and the sweet odor of his sweat. Then I pulled away. My dick was massive now, as hard as a rock.

"Here," Tanner said almost croaked it pointing to his groin. His cock was outlined in tight white under shorts, pushing through, semi-hard. I leaned over and kissed it through the flimsy material of his underwear, felt it pulse and rise to my lips. My own cock throbbed anxiously. Then I backed up and looked at his wet, gray eyes.

My own eyes narrowed, suddenly concerned. He was crying. "What's wrong?" Behind us the Duraflame log crumbled in the fireplace, spitting sparks, but neither of us turned to look.

"I've never done it," he admitted. He seemed to be apologizing.

"You're cherry?"

"Yep."

"I see...."

Suddenly he sat up and grabbed me and pulled me close. "I'll give myself up if you give yourself up," he said with urgency.

"What?"

"You can take me, but only if you turn yourself in."

I looked at him hard. "So you know."

He nodded.

I frowned. I was confused. If he knew, then why was he trying to seduce me? I was no good.

"I could just rape you," I said, trying to scare him, to be ugly.

He squirmed. I looked down at his dick poking up. It was leaking pre-come, staining the underwear. I watched his bare legs rub against one another, his hips move. "You wouldn't do that," Tanner replied after a moment. His fingers reached out and lambently played with my arm and shoulder, fingers walking up and down the sleeve, picking off imaginary dust. "I'm not afraid of you."

So damn sure of himself it made me mad.

Mad because he was so damn right.

"Okay."

He blinked, simian eyes. "What?"

"I said okay."

"You could be lying, just to get in my shorts," Tanner reasoned. His hand moved up and touched the back of my neck affectionately.

"I could be," I admitted.

"Was it a real bomb?"

"Just a box. You go in, put the box on the counter, say it's a bomb, ask them for the money. I would never hurt anyone."

"I know that," he said and leaned up and seized my face in his hands and pressed his irresistible lips to mine hard. I completely tuned out the steady hiss of flames, the pops of resin bursting in the hardwood, the mewling wind. There was nothing but my blood coursing through me, my pounding heart, his smell, his delicate lips mashed against my own. I didn't even hear the ice-bag fall off his swollen ankle, forgotten.

Tanner worked his tongue at my lips now; I opened them and let it in my mouth. The kiss went on forever. Then we both pulled back for air at the same time.

Tanner smiled sublimely and pulled off his shirt in one swift motion. I was about to do the same but I hesitated, daunted by his beauty. A perfect, blameless body.

My mouth dropped open and he averted his gray eyes and looked bashful. That look made me hornier than I'd ever been. My dick rose to full erection. Quickly my fingers found the buttons of my shirt and undid them. I deftly got out of my shoes, pants, socks everything except my briefs. "I'll show you mine if you show me yours," I said giddily, like a kid.

"You first," he said. Of course.

That made me uncomfortable. But I nodded and obeyed. My thumbs went to the waistband of my shorts and in one able gesture I'd gotten them over my dick and out from under each leg. My huge cock seemed to fill up even more now that it was given room to breathe.

Tanner gasped audibly and his eyes widened, focused on my large meat. I could see his own dick throb beneath his underwear.

"Okay," I said. "Your turn."

"Take them off me," he beckoned enticingly.

Again, I obeyed. Kneeling beside the couch, taking hold of his shorts, I gently pulled them down and let loose his own raging hard-on. It was a slender, upward-curving dick and it rose up to meet me as I worked his shorts down his silky legs and cautiously pulled them over his sore ankle. Then I took him all in, admiring his dick dribbling come from a beautiful pink head. His body was smooth and virtually hairless, save for a small thatch of black pubic hair. I'd never seen such magnificence, such perfection, not in real life anyhow.

Now he lifted his left leg up, foot resting flat on the couch cushions. His inner thighs were mouth-watering.

"Suck it."

It was a command, a question, an invitation, a plea.

136

I bent down right next to his cock, cherishing its thinness, its seductive arch, its bulging crest. My hands went to it, grabbed him lightly around the base. He nearly hit the ceiling at my touch. Then he relaxed his body while his penis stiffened and swelled in my hand. I leaned it and breathed on it, hot, seductive breath. Tanner moaned and squirmed his hips. Then my tongue came out and tapped it gently, tasting it. Sweet. I let my tongue stay on it for a moment, pulled it back. I did that a few times, then breathed lightly again, warm breath across the places I had just moistened.

"Suck it," he said again, this time a little bolder, forcing his dick up into my face.

I considered it, then looked to him looking down at me expectantly, biting his lower lip. I pulled his tool back toward me like I was pulling the slots, and then licked up his length, tracing his veins with my tongue. "Mmm," I said. "That's good." I wetted my lips, then licked up his shaft again in one long, drawn out, full-tongued swipe. Then I circled his head, licked around the corona. I got his whole prick wet and slick, lapping at it. Blew on it again. More pre-ejaculate dribbled out and I caught each running bead with my tongue and licked it back up and off. I kissed his piss hole. Then I popped him into my mouth and clamped my lips tight around him.

"Oh fuck!" he said, unprepared for that.

I went down on him, then slid back up him with my tight lips, then went down again.

"That's it!" He sat up and his hands clasped the back of my head and forced me down on him. I sucked him, trying to swallow him, get his stiff head past my tonsils. Then I bobbed up and down, making my mouth a tight, wet circle. He let go of my head and fell back in a delirium. Tanner's hands didn't know where to go, moving up and down his thighs and across his flat stomach as his body writhed beneath me and he whimpered. I reached out and grabbed each wrist and held them down against the couch and then picked up the pace with my blow job. He rotated his hips under me, pushing his insatiable prick up into my mouth from various angles, pulling it out, pushing it back up. It was covered in my spit and his own pre-cum. His breathing was coming in short gasps.

I let him poke it into me like that, up and in, sliding it back and forth through my tight "O" of a mouth. Then I removed my grip from his wrists and wrapped my right hand around his cock again, pumping him up and down into my mouth as he clutched the couch with clawed hands. "Oh fuck yes!" My left hand went to his drawn, hairless balls and gently fondled them. Then my enveloping fist grew tighter around his cock as I moved it up and down, speed multiplying. He tensed up, squeezed his ass muscles, lifted himself, arched his back, sticking his teen cock deep into my mouth.

"Here it comes!" he announced loudly.

He wasn't kidding. I felt his cock shoot, sort of drawing back and then discharging like a cartoon cannon. Tanner pressed his head back against the couch and cried. He came and bucked wildly and it was difficult to keep my lips

around him and swallow it down. My hands grabbed his waist and I tried to hang on, letting it go down my throat, a warm, sliding load.

Some spilled back out but I got most of him down. He finally purged himself completely and went slack.

I pulled away and swallowed what was left in my mouth. Tanner suddenly rose up, grabbed me, and gave me an ardent kiss, letting his tongue slip in and lick my tongue and steal back some of his juices. Then he collapsed back onto the sofa, smiling, radiant.

All was quiet, save the wind outside, still whistling from time to time, pushing rippling drifts up against the house then laying them elsewhere like a finicky decorator. The fire was a subdued sizzle, much smaller now.

"Well," he said, out of breath, "that almost makes up for running me over."

"Almost?"

"Throw another log on," he told me, "and get me that tube in the medicine cabinet."

I obeyed. My dick was still hard and led the way. I put another log on and poked around with the stoker. I could feel his eyes on my ass as I leaned over to do so. Then I went to his bathroom, clicked on the light, and opened the medicine cabinet. My dick had gone semi-flaccid. Tube, tube ...what tube? This was the only one.

I read the label.

My dick stood at attention.

I was back down in a second, beaming like an idiot.

"You found it," Tanner saw, rolling carefully onto his stomach and revealing his perfect ass to me in the flickering warm firelight. "Now fuck my virgin ass."

My cock nearly exploded right then and there, spraying come all over the living room.

I got down beside him and started to squirt lube into my hands but then thought better of it. Putting the tube down, I ran my hands over his smooth bottom and leaned in and kissed each cheek, then licked them, and then let my tongue slip down into the groove as I lightly spread his cheeks apart to get to his pucker. "Oh," he said with surprise; he repositioned himself against the cushions to accommodate a growing hard-on of his own. His ass wriggled in my face and I went for his perfect flushed hole. My tongue touched it and wetted it. The hole seemed to wink at me, eager for attention gimme, gimme, gimme. I blew on the wet spot and he tried to worm away from it, unable to handle the sensation, but I held him down.

Now I licked all over his hole, sucked the ring of muscle. He was moaning with each of my ministrations, pitch and volume changing depending on what I did, a kind of "getting warmer/getting colder" game. I knew I'd won when I made my tongue stiff and pushed it up into the hot hole, his sphincter muscle opening up and closing around it.

"Oh my God, is that ... oh shit," Tanner said. It was clear he never imagined in all his sex fantasies and solo-play just how incredible this could be; I was almost

138

afraid of being *too* exhaustive in my rimming for fear of making him faint dead away.

"No, no," he said as my invading tongue slipped out of his zealous ass. Then I squeezed out some lubrication into my hand. I applied two fingers, working the goo up into the crack, tracing the split between those precious pale cheeks, lightly going over his puckered star. He gasped when I did. I pressed on the lips of his teenage asshole with my middle finger.

"Oh, yeah," he said receptively. I pushed in. My digit seemed to be swallowed up. Nice and warm and moist. I coated him while finger-fucking his ass. He loved it. Then I pulled it out and wiped lube on my cock-head and down and around the shaft. Tanner looked back at me eagerly, firelight playing in his eyes.

"Tell me if I hurt you," I warned and lifted his hips up so he was on his knees. I got behind him. I grabbed my dick and aimed and pressed against him. He recoiled. Then his small fingers reached under and found my cock. Again I almost blew it all, him holding my dick like that in his gentle warm hand. I let go of myself and he took me tightly. I let him guide my cock head into his rear. He stationed me right against his hole and then naively tried to pull me in with one yank. "Oh," he said with surprise.

I held his hips steady and pushed. His hand fell away and gripped the couch and prepared for my entry.

My cock head squeezed hard against his ass-lips. Impossible resistance, groans and cries, and then that grand miracle where the impossible occurs, when something so large can get in through something so small when my dick is not only allowed entry and is encircled eagerly by his ass, but is almost swallowed whole.

"Oh God yes!" he cried. "It's huge!"

I waited a moment, let him get used to it, then pulled slowly out, lube letting me slide smoothly back. Then I slid back up him. "Oh yes," he said, spreading his legs apart a little to get the angle just right and accommodate more dick.

Again I pulled back, almost to the point of losing my bulbous cock-head, having it squeezed on out, but I slid back in before that could happen, knowing he'd be devastated by such a loss, however brief. I picked up my pace, an even pace, in and out. He dropped his head, closed his eyes, experienced it. "Oh, that's sooo good."

How long did we go on like that, me riding him? It seemed forever. Then I decided to try something different.

I stopped.

He raised his head, looked back.

I smiled and, with hands on his waist, guided him back, sliding him down my length. "Oooh," he said. Then I pushed him away from me, sliding him back forward. He waited for me to resume fucking him but I stayed still and he got the idea shortly. Now he pressed his ass back against me, leaned forward off me, pushed back again, and in no time he was doing all the work. I lifted my hands from his waist and put them on my own hips as he fucked my dick with his

139

asshole.

Tanner was going wild now, squirming his ass all around me, flexing his chute, squeezing backward against me until his cheeks pressed against my pubic hair and his gobbling asshole threatened to swallow up my balls. He bent his head down so that his shoulder blades rose before me. Back and forth he slid on my pole as I stayed still. Then, finally, I began to join in, and we created something like the impossible perpetual-motion machine a marvelous harmony that outstripped the both of us, multiplied our rhapsody a million fold.

Tanner cried out, going frantically now, forcing me to go faster, and I felt myself about to give way.

"I think I might oh shit."

Impossible to stave off, my come shot in a ceaseless torrent, a fire hose in his ass. I paused, felt it well up, then came again in more spurts, a geyser of creamy juice spouting off in endless waves. His ass gulped it all down.

Then I was out of come and my body went droopy. I started to withdraw my cock from him slowly. He held his breath as it came back out slowly. My dick seemed even longer than I remembered. Finally the head was squeezed out and he fell on his stomach.

I leaned back, exhausted. Then Tanner turned around and hugged me, falling on top of me.

"You're incredible," I said. We hugged tightly, me cupping the back of his head, smelling his boyish scent and our own commingled sweat and love-juices. My eyes went to the window where outside the snow continued to fall. It was like being on the inside of a snow globe.

"I love you," I suddenly whispered and then regretted it.

"I love you too," he said and I didn't regret it after all. Tears welled up and spilled out the corners of my eyes and trickled down my cheeks.

He pulled back away from me and our eyes looked into each other. His searched mine I could feel them probing my depths. He looked concerned. "You're crying."

"Tears of joy."

"No such thing," he said. "'Tears of joy' are actually a release of pent-up sadness, done so at a time where you feel safe, usually at the end of some ordeal. So it could be a joyful moment, but technically speaking "

"Tanner?"

"Yep?"

"Shut up and kiss me."

He did just that and then slid down me through my arms.

"Hey, where are you going?"

He pulled out from under my tight, loving embrace, crawling down my length. He stopped crouched over my waist. Now Tanner leaned forward, bangs falling over and tickling my abdomen, and I felt him kiss my soft cock. He pulled back and looked at it with curiosity. I felt my dick twitch; he smiled. His doing, he realized; there was pride, plus the childish fascination with cause and effect, the

140

realization one has power.

"Oh, Tanner, I'm not going to be able to ..."

But yet here it came, my dick filling up with blood at the sight of him crouched down there staring at it with wonder and ideas in his head. It inflated, rose up, and he grinned excitedly like some kid on Christmas morning. He grabbed it with both of his small hands, one over the other. "Oh my God," I said, pulsing against his gripping, delicate fingers. He hoisted his hands up, pulling my skin against my rod, then jerked down so that my purple cock head poked up through his interlocked fingers. He yanked upward, brought his hands down again. Now I was oozing pre-come and it trickled over his fingers. Tanner felt it, removed his hand, looked at the glistened juice, then licked it off his hand before wrapping those fingers back around my dick.

I threw my head back against the couch and braced myself. Now his hands pumped me up and down with abandon.

"Not so hard ... oh hell, yes, hard," I said. I could feel my dick getting sore but it was a good sore. I looked up at him working me, saw my purple bulb appear and disappear quickly in his fisted hands, saw bits of my length, reddened down, saw pre-cum slathering everything. Then I saw him lean over me and open his mouth wide just over the top of my dick and move downward.

I threw my head back again in preparation for the most awesome experience of my life.

I felt his narrow lips wrap around my dick and he continued pumping me. He sucked on me good, then pulled back, a thread of pre-ejaculate connected from the tip of my cock to his lips. He brushed it away, went down on me again. I shuddered uncontrollably as he sucked and pumped, going faster and faster, and rough with eagerness. I strained to look at him as he jerked hard on my shaft with both hands, crouched over me, something feral, intransigently devoted to getting my come.

"I'm going to come," I said with some strange, third-party detachment. "If you don't want to swallow ..."

He pulled his lips off me and removed his left hand, going down to his own dick which I saw was fully erect again. He pumped us both madly.

I was a little disappointed he didn't want to swallow but seeing him crouched there like that, jerking himself off over me and jerking my cock up and down furiously, I couldn't have asked for more. But then I watched awestruck as he leaned over my cock and opened his mouth wide and beat me even harder, trying to get me to squirt into his target of a mouth like a clown's head at a carnival game.

That was just too much. Nothing could have stopped me. It welled up in my balls and erupted in one giant spurt of clear-white fluid. It hit him with incredible force and he closed his eyes. Most of it getting in his mouth, a lot of it on his face. He stuck his tongue out to get it all as I shot again. At the same time I was spraying him I felt warm stuff hit my chest and then neck and now my own face. It took me a second to figure it out; Tanner was coming too, pumping

141

his dick out onto me, assaulting me with wads of his juice like a paintball game.

We came all over each other simultaneously, spurt after spurt, a silly string fight. Finally he collapsed into my arms once more, face sticky with come, a wide grin on his slick lips.

"You did say you loved me, didn't you?" I asked.

"Yep. Shit brains."

"Graham."

"No duh," he said and snuggled up against me and laid his head on my come-sticky chest and closed his eyes and smiled contentedly.

I hugged him tightly in the firelight as the wind whined plaintively outside and the snow drifted down gently.

He fell asleep in my arms.

- - -

He was still asleep. I got out from under him and put the blanket over his body, like covering up a work of art. I could see the steady lift and fall of his small chest in the waning firelight.

I got dressed and looked at the duffel bag filled with that unspecified amount of money. I looked back at him. Then I grabbed the phone from the kitchen, dialed "O," and stretched the cord around the corner into the dining room so as not to wake him.

"Police department, please," I asked. "Non-emergency."

The operator connected me. I could hear the phone ringing, a purring sound.

There was a large antique mirror with an ornate frame in the dining room of the Loiseauxs' home. I was looking in it. And I liked what I saw.

142

HOOKED
by . M. Orlando

I was stunned by the sensations of intense pleasure that were overtaking my body as Eric's lips pressed against mine with a hunger an urgency I had never experienced. No woman had ever kissed me with such enthusiasm, such animal lust. He kissed the way I kissed: aggressively, with a desperate need for more.

I was surprised when the familiar tingle swept through my groin, causing my dick to stir and swell in the front of my 501s. I had never expected to become aroused by the kiss of another man, yet here I was slowly surrendering to him.

One minute we had been leaning against the side of my car, just chatting. The fishing had been so lousy at the lake that Eric and I had given up and decided to head back home. But then we got to talking about life and everything that goes with it. The next thing I knew, my back was being crushed against the door, while Eric's lips clamped over mine.

His tongue repeatedly slithered into my partially open mouth, exploring, probing every corner of my being. Our tongues danced around one another, licking and tasting, as his arms wrapped around my waist and pulled our bodies close, so our horny dicks were mashed together.

I held my hands away from him at first, resisting the intimacy, then surrendered, hugging him close to me and smelling his musky cologne.

The feel of his unshaven face against mine caused tiny drops of precum to ooze from the hooded tip of my now fully erect dick. The warm, wet spot in my white jockey shorts continued to grow and began to seep through the front of my jeans. I longed to reach down and free my aching boner from its denim prison, but I hesitated.

His right hand crept under my t-shirt, his fingers pushing through the coarse black hairs, tickling me. Goosebumps formed on my skin as he grasped my left nipple between his thumb and forefinger, squeezing gently at first, then tugging more and more roughly at the already-erect tip. No one had ever fondled my nipples, so I didn't know how exciting the sensation would be. But Eric did.

We were both breathing heavily by now as we continued to kiss. At first I wasn't aware that Eric had unzipped his fly and was grinding his naked rod against me harder and faster but then I felt the sudden wetness. His lips were still clamped tight over my mouth as he made his final lunge, and his hot, sticky load of man cream exploded onto the front of my jeans.

He quickly released his hold on me and backed away, fear showing in his deep green eyes. "I'm sorry, Marc. I didn't mean to," he pleaded, still backing away from me.

I looked down at the sticky goo soaking into my faded Levis. "Oh shit," I grumbled, reaching into the car for the roll of paper towels I kept on the floor in the back.

While I mopped up Eric's spunk, he turned and ran off into the woods.

"Eric...." I called, but he ignored me and continued to flee. I knew he was afraid of my reaction, but I wasn't angry. What I was was frustrated. I stood there with a raging hard on struggling to escape from the confines of my tight jeans. I hopelessly, desperately needed to get my rocks off. But I had been abandoned before I even had a chance to respond to his advance.

I reached down and squeezed my meat, contemplating whether I should whip it out and whack off right there in the woods. Then the realization hit me: Eric would run home. My place was the only refuge he had since his father had thrown him out. He'd moved in with me, sharing my apartment.

Well, it would take him a while to walk home from here, I thought, so I might as well have a smoke and think about what I would say to him.

I lit a cigarette and sat on the trunk of my car, considering the possibilities. I had never thought about another man the way I was thinking about Eric fantasizing about the feel of his throbber mashing against mine and wondering what it would be like to hold his cock in my hand the smooth shaft, the wet sticky head, and the vein pulsating as the blood rushed through the length of his spongy cylinder.

I had known Eric was gay when he moved in with me, but in the six months we had been living together, there had never been any discussions about it, much less any sexual contact. Yet here I was deciding how I would approach him how I would satisfy my curiosity.

I took a few more drags on my cigarette before dropping to the ground and crushing out the smoldering red tip, then jumped in my car and headed home. Eric had apparently hitched a ride because he was already at our apartment when I arrived, hurriedly stuffing his clothes into a trash bag. Immediately I challenged him. "What the hell are you doing?"

He looked up at me, that frightened expression returning to his face, as I stood in the doorway of the bedroom we shared. "I'm sorry, Marc. Please don't hurt me. I'm moving out, and I'll never bother you again."

I didn't speak, just stepped into the room. For the first time, I noticed how well Eric's firm, round ass cheeks filled out his tan Dockers, and I wondered if he'd ever been ass fucked. He continued to desperately shovel his clothes and possessions into the bag. "What are you? Some kind of dick-teasing prick?" I demanded, grabbing his hand.

He tried to pull away, but I held tight. When he looked up at me, I smiled, and he quit struggling. "I didn't mean for it to happen," he said, softly.

"I know," I replied, releasing his hand and placing mine on his shoulder.

With that tiny gesture, Eric slipped into my embrace like he belonged there. I wrapped my arms around him and pulled his solid body to mine. My lips instinctively pressed to his partially opened mouth, shoving my tongue between his lips and exploring his insides.

The smell of his cologne was overwhelming, and I couldn't resist as his fingers once again crept under my t-shirt and fondled my nipples, twisting and pulling, sending wild sensations sweeping through my body. A tingle, then the

144

familiar throbbing, returned to my groin, and I gasped for air.

Eric's hands moved downward, following the path of dark hairs, and began to fumble with my fly. When the buttons popped open, he tugged at the elastic waistband of my white Jockeys until his fingers contacted my fiery flesh. His mouth was still clamped over mine, while he yanked my dick out where he had easy access to it. He pulled back the foreskin and ran his thumb lightly around the rim, then began to stroke the length of my meat. His grip was firm and sure, unlike any touch I had ever experienced (except my own).

I hesitated, afraid to let my hands drop down to the telling bulge in the front of his pants. I had never touched another man before, and though I wanted to feel his hot, horny organ in my fist, my fear was more powerful than my desire.

He released his hold on my dick, unzipped his pants, and freed his throbbing monster from the restricting fabric. His arms slithered around my waist as his tongue continued to probe the insides of my mouth. Then he cupped my ass-cheeks in his palms and ground his naked flesh into mine.

"Oh, God," I moaned as our dicks met for the first time.

The sensation of his wet, sticky hardness gliding alongside my own brought me that much closer to an explosive climax. My heart thumped in my chest when he kissed my neck, his hot breath on my flushed skin sending shivers down my spine. He tugged my t-shirt off over my head and let his fingers push through the coarse black hairs moving slowly, tickling me with his light touch.

His mouth crept lower, gnawing on each nipple, nibbling and sucking until I was sure I would lose my load all over him. He dropped to his knees in front of me, and I watched as his full, pink lips inched nearer to my thick eight-incher. I gasped at the feel of his tongue flicking at my exposed glans, causing shock waves to course down my engorged shaft.

My balls contracted, their pent-up load begging for release. He lapped at the spongy dick meat, his finger probing my piss-slit and scooping my precum up, then smearing it around my dick. As his tongue lapped below my corona, his finger skated on my slick surface.

"Suck it, please," I pleaded, unashamed of my body's betrayal. But he ignored my plea and began to lap at my big, hairy ball sac. My knees were getting weak as he worked my balls, sucking first one, then the other into his moist, warm mouth.

"Man, that feels so good," I groaned. "No one's ever done that for me before."

He looked up at me, freeing my sensitive ball sac, and grinned. "There are a lot of things I could do for you, if you'd let me."

I nodded my consent, and he led me to the bed, each of us quickly shedding the remainder of our clothing. We lay side by side for a moment, his hand gently caressing my nakedness; then he reached over and opened the top drawer of the nightstand.

"We'll need these," he said matter-of-factly as he tore open a foil wrapper and placed a condom on his horny dick meat.

I watched him roll a condom the length of his seven-inch shaft, then slide one

onto me. Watching him cloak my tool was arousing. "What are you going to do?" I asked, beginning to get nervous.

He grinned down at me. "Relax and enjoy, Marc. It'll be better than you ever imagined."

I spread my legs wide and allowed him to kneel between them, then he reached for a bottle of baby oil that he kept on the nightstand. I had been curious, but not brazen enough to ask. Now he poured some into the palm of his hand and began to massage it into my thigh. He kneaded my muscular thighs, then moved up and rubbed some oil into my fur-covered abdomen, completely avoiding my painful boner. "Roll over," he whispered.

I turned over on my stomach, my latex-covered pole being mashed into the mattress beneath us, while he straddled my ass and squirted the cold liquid onto my back. Each time he leaned forward to rub my neck, his hardness slipped into my furry ass-crack. His powerful hands palpated my tense shoulders, then made their way down my spine, halting just before they reached my mounds of ass-flesh. I closed my eyes and relaxed until he shifted his position, so that his smooth ball sac was dangling between my thighs, and his slippery fingers were inching closer to my virgin chute. My eyes opened and my muscles contracted.

"Hey, just relax. It'll feel really good. Trust me," he reassured me.

"I don't know...."

"Here," he said, as his index finger pushed against the unyielding sphincter muscle until it gave way, allowing the squirmy finger to sink into my body.

"Ohhh," I groaned as he slid his finger in and out, stretching me gently. Then, as I squirmed beneath him, he inserted a second and a third digit. It felt so good as he finger-fucked me that I began to hump upward to meet his thrusts.

"Oh, yes," I moaned. I closed my eyes, the incredible pleasure filling me to overflowing. Still I was not prepared when his fingers were withdrawn and his cloaked dick invaded the heat of my insides. It only hurt for a moment, when the thickness of his dick pushed through the tight ass-ring. Then the thrill of having him inside me, satisfying the long-unfulfilled emptiness, made me light-headed. I moaned and squirmed as he began to withdraw his weapon until only the mushroom-shaped head remained inside me.

He thrust slowly at first, inching his dickmeat into my tunnel, but was soon overcome by his own desperate need. He slammed harder and faster, driving himself deeper into my body than I thought possible. His balls slapped against my ass-cheeks, and his curly bush was crushed to my crack with each forward lunge.

I was so disappointed when he pulled out, leaving my gaping fuckhole abandoned, that I cried out in frustration. But he slipped his arm around my waist, flipped me onto my back, and quickly reinserted his tool.

"I want to see you come," he commanded.

I opened my eyes, looking first at my twitching dick, then at Eric's face. I had never looked in a mirror when I came, and had never seen another man locked in the throes of passion, but Eric was a man consumed by the hunger. I could see

146

by his enraptured expression that he was close, and so was I. I stared in disbelief as my climax came to me. I had not touched myself, but still I watched as my dick jerked and the condom was filled with my juices.

Eric smiled, then he thrust one last time. His entire body shuddered as his balls launched their creamy spew into the condom buried deep in my gut.

He slumped over on top of me, while his softening dick slid out of my initiated man pussy. His lips brushed against mine, and he flashed one of his disarming smiles. "Maybe you can do me next time," he offered.

It had been a bad day for fishing, but it looked like Eric had still hooked a big one.

MORE THAN FRIENDS
by L. M. Orlando

"I wanna fuck you."

Dana's words echoed through my mind as I tossed and turned in my bed that night. I could hear him sleeping soundly in the next room and thought about waking him to talk, but I didn't really know what I would say to him.

We had been the best of friends since we met in high school. After that, we had gotten together whenever he came back to our home town for a visit and had remained as close as we had always been. Now he was home to stay, and was sharing my apartment until he could find a place of his own. But I wasn't sure I was ready for what he had in mind. I just knew there was no one in the world I would trust to take my virginity more than Dana. My breathing became heavy and a tingle of arousal swept through my groin as I considered the possibilities. I recalled one night back in high school when Dana and I had a close call, a chance encounter that could have led to a lot more than it did.

We were the last two guys in the locker room after a game and I had walked into the shower to find him slowly soaping up and jerking off his huge slab of manhood. The soap was oozing from between his fingers as his fist slid slowly along the thick shaft from the curly black hairs at its base to the hooded tip. I was hypnotized by the smooth strokes, the skin stretching taut along the eight-inch shaft. I couldn't take my eyes off the angry red cock head when he yanked back the foreskin and ran his thumb around the rim.

My own cock hardened and bobbed against my belly as I moved closer to get a better view of the explosive release I knew was only moments away. I was anxious to see the sizable load that was held prisoner in his oversized basket.

"It feels so good," he moaned.

Without thinking or considering the consequences, I reached out and cupped his crinkled nut sac, massaging his tender orbs. It was then that I felt his left hand wrap around my aching boner, his vise-like grip jerking me off with him. I didn't resist, didn't pull away. Instead I continued to play with his balls as he rhythmically stroked the solid cylinders, bringing us both closer and closer to eruption.

I thrust my hips forward to meet his touch as his stones contracted against his body. I watched, mesmerized, as his hot, sticky wad burst free and splattered the shower wall in front of us. I was more excited than I had ever been as I fucked his hand, the slippery purple head poking out of his clenched fist. Seconds later my dick began to jerk and twitch, my load coursing through me and exploding onto the wall just below his dripping cream.

He wrapped his arm around my waist, mashing our bodies together, and crushed his lips against mine. My heart raced when our naked flesh met for the first time and my body shuddered. His tongue slithered into my mouth, probing

and tasting, and stirring emotions I had never felt before. Then he released me. He didn't say a word, just finished washing up and walked away. Nothing had ever been said until tonight when he had confessed that he had always fantasized about me, about that night, and wished that things had gone further between us.

My fingers curled around my fully erect member and began to stroke it slowly, as I remembered the feel of his hand whacking me off and the sensation of his hot cock mashed alongside my own. I hadn't realized it then, but there had been a hunger, a desperate urgency to his touch, to his kiss. I imagined what it would be like to have Dana's full lips locked around my throbbing meat. He would lick the sensitive glans, then deliberately and methodically tease me to the most intense orgasm of my life.

While I continued my fantasy and fisted my meat, I slipped a finger up my virgin butt hole to get an idea of what it might feel like to have his monstrous cock meat plowing into me. I had never finger-fucked myself before, so I didn't know what I had been missing. The pleasure was so overwhelming that I shoved a second digit inside the warm, tight cavern. I could feel my load boiling, ready to explode from my horny dick. That's when I knew. I had to talk with Dana had to tell him I wanted him to fuck me. And there was no time like the present. I was so hot I would literally do anything to achieve orgasm.

I crawled out of bed and crept through the darkness, my heart pounding in my chest and my wet, sticky cock head slapping against my smooth belly. I inched closer to his bed, wondering if I was doing the right thing. I hoped we would not ruin our friendship by becoming lovers.

I turned down the covers and slithered into bed next to him, our naked bodies touching for the first time in twelve years. Erotic shock waves shot through me as I let my fingertips brush lightly across his furry abdomen and push through his coarse pubic curls until they contacted his soft flesh.

I wrapped my fingers around the deflated weapon and began to squeeze and massage it, awakening it from its slumber. It responded to my touch immediately, hardening and lengthening in my hand and quickly reaching its full size.

I tugged back the foreskin, exposing the tender head, and began to tease it as I had watched him do that night so long ago. I let my thumb gently circle the rim before lightly caressing the very tip of his helmet with my open palm. Tiny drops of pre-cum oozed from his slit easing my movements across and around the spongy head.

Dana moaned and began to hump against my hand in his sleep, while I continued to play with my new toy. I wanted him to be as hot and horny as I was, to want it as much as I did at that very moment.

My fingers again curled around the slick shaft and stroked it in long, slow motions, the kind I knew would work him into a heated frenzy. The loose hood slid back and forth beneath my fingers-- first covering the mushroom-shaped cock head, then exposing it. I massaged from the swollen helmet to the furry base, then let my hand drop down to that heavy ball sac. I rolled the fragile

150

stones between my thumb and fingers, releasing them when I discovered his tight pucker hole hidden between his succulent ass cheeks.

I wondered how he would react if he woke to find himself being finger-fucked. I pressed my index finger against the unyielding muscle, forcing my way into his love tunnel, then I easily inserted a second, stretching him farther.

As I invaded his body, he woke.

"Cody?"

"I made up my mind, Dana," I whispered into the night.

He reached out and switched on the light, then looked into my eyes. He was silent for a moment. "Are you sure?"

"Yeah, I am. I was thinking about that night in the locker room. Maybe it should've happened then, but I was scared. But I'm not afraid any more."

"I... well, I just want you to know how much this means to me. I've dreamed about you about us for so long. For so very long!"

I didn't know what to say, so I simply brushed my lips across his. He pulled me close, holding me in his reassuring embrace. Though I wasn't sure exactly what I was feeling toward Dana, I knew I felt safe in his arms and I never wanted this moment to end.

I felt his hot breath on my neck, igniting tiny fires on my skin. "I want you, Cody," he said softly. "I really do."

My fingers had remained motionless inside him, but now began to wiggle and twist, causing his body to squirm. His strong hand reached out and captured my painful erection, squeezing and yanking on it until I thought I would shoot off all over him. His touch was so sure so arousing so similar to my own, I could hardly stand it.

The room was quiet except for the sound of our ragged breathing as we both moved nearer and nearer to a powerful release.

"Let me suck you off," he begged. "You've got such a magnificent cock. And to think I've wanted it for so long. To feel it and taste it," he moaned.

I let my fingers slide from his stretched manhole and lay back on the bed. He picked up his jacket off the foot of the bed and retrieved a crisp foil wrapper from the pocket. I watched as he tore it open and applied the black condom to my sticky cock head, sliding the protective covering seductively along the length. He stared at the pulsating mass of cockmeat poking into the air, as if he were worshipping it, before grasping it in his fist.

I felt weak and my head was spinning as he began to kiss it, starting at the sensitive tip and moving down the engorged pole until his nose was buried in my curly blond bush. He cupped my huge balls in the palm of his hand, massaging them carefully before he pressed his lips against the crinkled flesh. My body trembled as he tongued the loose skin until my nuts glistened in the dim light of the bedside lamp. I gasped and squirmed when he sucked first one, then the other into the warm wetness of his hungry mouth.

"Oh, that feels so good," I moaned, my body wriggling as he managed to take both balls into his mouth at once.

"You like that, huh? Well, I'll bet you'll really love this."

He wrapped both hands around the thick stalk and guided it into his mouth. Slurping hungrily, he expertly engulfed the entire seven inches.

I thrust upward, forcing it even deeper into his throat. As the passion built up within me, I grabbed a handful of his dark hair and manipulated his head to and fro rhythmically, my horny member sliding in and out of Dana's ravaged mouth.

"Oh yeah, take it all," I moaned, slamming more forcefully against him as I came closer and closer to the most powerful orgasm of my life.

I could feel the hot wad escaping my churning ball sac and coursing through my shaft, then it was launched into the latex shield. My body convulsed as the passion swept over me, and still he held me in his mouth as if he were expecting more.

After he was satisfied that I was completely spent, he retrieved a second condom and lay down beside me on the bed, his impressive pecker bobbing from side to side as he positioned himself. The deep purple head peeked seductively from beneath the foreskin, sticky and wet with his pre-cum juices and drawing me to him. I wanted to touch him to taste him-- and to feel that stiff prick in my mouth and up my ass.

He handed the shiny wrapper to me and I tore into it, anxious to cloak his horny cock so I could get at it.

Once the protective covering had been applied, I cautiously, and with my heart thumping in my chest, lowered my lips to the beckoning wand. I flicked my tongue against him, tasting the rubbery sheath, and feeling his hardness and the heat of his arousal. I licked his stock, running the tip of my tongue along the pulsating vein until I buried my nose in his groin, drawing in his musky, masculine scent. I was feeling things I had never felt before, and the excitement, the thrill, was nearly more than I could bear

"Suck it, Cody, please," he pleaded.

Though I was frightened and inexperienced, I wanted to please Dana, get him off like he had done for me. I parted my lips and let them slowly circle the sensitive glans of his uncut cock head, then let it slide onto my tongue. He moaned when my mouth closed around the shaft, letting his length inch into me until the tip banged against the back of my throat. I nearly gagged, but pulled away long enough to catch my breath, then went back down on his throbbing meat.

He began to hump upward, trying to force his cock even deeper into me, but I resisted him carefully controlling my first blowjob. I slurped on his wand as it slid in and out of my mouth, letting my tongue swirl around the rim.

He looked surprised and disappointed when I let his cock slide out of my mouth and moved away from him.

"Cody, please," he begged.

I looked down at him and grinned mischievously. "I thought you wanted to fuck me," I teased.

He smiled and his dark eyes seemed to devour me.

152

"There's some KY jelly in my bag. Grab it and grease me up. Then you can sit on it. It'll make it easier on you if you do it yourself the first time."

I stared at the menacing member, wondering if my big mouth had gotten me into more trouble than my ass could handle. I retrieved the lube and spread it onto the smooth latex sheath. When I was satisfied that he was adequately lubricated, I squeezed some of the jelly onto my fingertip and rubbed it onto my tight butt hole, hoping to make this experience as painless as possible.

I straddled him and carefully lowered myself onto his pole, the thick head forcing its way passed the unyielding muscle ring and sinking into the heat of my body, taking my cherry. There was pain as I was stretched to accommodate his monstrous meat, but then there was an incredible feeling of fullness an overpowering excitement I had never felt before.

My dick hardened a second time and bounced against my hairless belly when I began to move letting his pecker slide almost entirely out of me, then slamming down so that it repeatedly invaded my narrow channel. I was so hot, I could barely breathe.

His eyes were closed and he thrust upward, burying himself deep inside me. We moved together as he came closer and closer to eruption and my cock jerked and twitched between us. I was shocked that I was getting ready to shoot off again. I had never cum more than once a night with any woman I had ever been with. My entire body was on fire more aroused than I had ever been. I had never imagined it would be so satisfying to have a stiff dick plowing into me.

His body tensed beneath me and I felt his snake pulsating within me the latex cloak being filled with his creamy load. I could hold off no longer. The urgent need could not be controlled. My body shuddered as white goo shot into the tip of the protective covering, filling it nearly to overflowing.

I collapsed on top of him, our lips meeting in a long, passionate kiss, our tongues dancing around one another. I was so glad Dana had finally been honest with me about his feelings because otherwise I would never have experienced the wonderful world of man-to-man sex.

"I love you, Cody," he whispered.

"I love you, too," I replied, surprised that I was not embarrassed or ashamed to admit my feelings for him.

I knew this was a new beginning for both of us, a chapter of our lives that had been a long time coming, and I couldn't wait to see what would happen next.

8 1/2 INCHES
by ill Nicholson

"Hello, sir!"

This jerked me from my daydream and back to my surroundings, the private lounge of The Falcon, in Market Oldham's center, on a mid-May evening. I was seated on a bar-stool, and someone had come through the connecting door from the public bar behind me. I looked around to see who had spoken, and met the smiling face of a handsome, dark-haired young man. I recognized him immediately, but my look of surprise made him say, "You don't remember me, do you, sir?"

I hastened to reassure him. "Of course I do back row, fifth form in my music class. Harvey Stephen Harvey, isn't it?"

He positively beamed at the recognition.

"Right," he said. "Fancy you remembering."

...So begins the most vivid of all the "videos" of my mind. You know what I mean; when perhaps the brain makes a subconscious "recording" of precious moments, to be brought out and replayed in times of loneliness, hopelessness or despair? Whatever the reason, I know that, as inexorable time draws me ever closer to the allotted "threescore years and ten," these cherished moments are recollected more and more frequently. Some are paraded to act as the stimulus for the occasions of self-pleasure (nice euphemism!) that, even at my age, my body sometimes demands. It is strange how some things that happened long ago can stay clearer in the memory than the events of last year, last month, last week even.

So those two apparently harmless words, "Hello, sir!", are the "switch" that sets this "video" to "replay."

"Fancy you remembering," he had said.

How could I forget, I thought. *Why would I forget possibly the most attractive fifth former of his year?*

"Why would I forget?" I said, aloud. "It was my first year of teaching at the Grammar School. You don't forget your first year. But you left at the end of it, didn't you?"

"Yes", he replied, "straight after 'O' Levels. I didn't see much point in staying on and Dad thought it was time I started earning some money."

"So, what are you doing now?" I asked.

"I'm an apprentice at Hardy's, the engineering firm," he said, "and I go to evening classes at the Technical College, until I get qualifications."

I looked round.

"Are you in company? Or waiting for someone?"

"No, I just came in to see if any of my mates were here. It's only my second time in here. I was 18, just last week."

"Well in that case," I said, "have a drink. What is it?"

"A pint of bitter," he said, "but it's all right, I'll get it."

"Nonsense it's my treat, a birthday drink," I said, and ordered it from the barmaid.

When it arrived, I suggested that we sit on the wall seats by the window. We did so, and "Cheers," I said, clinking my glass on his. "I wish I were 18 again."

He smiled and drank, then.... "Have you been swimming, sir? Your hair looks wet."

"Dear me, no," I replied. "I swim like a brick. I stayed back after school to play tennis with Tony Shaw. You remember Mr. Shaw, the French master?"

"Oh, yes," he said. "He's a good bloke like you."

I decided to ignore the compliment, and said, "We had almost two hours on the courts, and I really needed a shower."

"Oh."

A pause.

"Did Mr. Shaw go in the showers with you?"

(Why ask that? I wondered.)

"No he said he had a date with his girlfriend, and had to dash off."

"You're not married or anything, are you, sir?"

"No, I'm not married or anything." I stressed the last word. "And I think you can drop the 'sir', now, Stephen. Call me 'Bill'."

He smiled.

"OK," he said, "but it'll seem queer."

I smiled inwardly at the choice of word.

"And you can call me Steve; only Mum and Dad call me Stephen."

"Deal," I said.

There was a pause, after which he made a surprising comment. Why, he asked, had I not played more opera in my music appreciation lessons? I replied that opera, in my opinion, seemed unlikely to gain many converts among lads steeped in the latest "pop" songs.

"Well, I like it," he said, and went on to enlarge. It appeared that the films of Mario Lanza had been his starting point, especially "The Great Caruso".

"Colin Brooks, the lad who sat next to me in class, likes it too."

"Then you should have told me so. Who knows, we might have converted one or two Philistines."

Then I made the offer that set the wheels of Fate in motion. I told him that I had several complete operas on LP, and he might find that tenors such as Bergonzi and Gedda were certainly Lanza's equal. He was welcome to visit for an opera evening whenever he wished.

"I expect you know I live in Shelbourne," I said. "It's only a 20-minute bus ride."

"Great. I'd like that," he said. "I go only once a week to the evening class,

156

tomorrow Tuesday. Is this Friday too soon?"

"Not at all."

I felt in my pocket for a letter I had received that day, removed the contents and handed him the envelope.

"Here's the address; book to the Red Lion, and my street is third on the right, in the direction the bus is going."

I finished my drink and set down the glass. He reached for it.

"Another, sir ... I mean, Bill?" he asked.

"Thank you, no, I'm driving home."

I rose to leave.

"I'll catch the 6:30 on Friday," he said. "See you then."

"It's a date," I replied, and went to the door, giving him a wave as I disappeared.

- - -

I found myself awaiting Friday eagerly, and when it came, bought a 6-pack of bitter beer from the "off license" and put it in the fridge. I told myself that he probably wouldn't come.

However, at just before seven there was a knock at the door. A smiling Steve was on the doorstep.

We had the planned musical evening, and I was able to produce every tenor aria he requested, to his surprise, even though Lanza did not feature.

After an hour or so we had a break and I produced the cans of beer. As we drank, Steve told me about his home life. He lived with his parents and a 9-year-old brother, Dean, and had a 21-year-old sister, Stella, who was married, and lived with her husband nearby. He complained a little about the large slice of his weekly wage that his mother demanded for his "board," something that later assumed more significance.

We took up the music again, and as the time for his departure drew near, he asked if it would be possible for him to meet me at "the old school" for a game of tennis sometime.

"Yes, of course," I said. "I just have to arrange with the caretaker to have the key to the gym."

He said he wasn't very good at tennis, and didn't have his own racket. Were there any available? I said that there were a few in the cupboard in the changing room.

"What about Monday?" he asked. "Or are you seeing Mr. Shaw again?"

No, I wasn't, I said, and Monday was fine, as far as I was concerned.

"I can be there about 6 o'clock," he said.

"That's all right," I said. "When I'm staying back, I take a flask of coffee and some sandwiches. I'll have them while I wait."

Thus was our second rendezvous arranged, and Fate's wheels were well and truly oiled.

- - -

Monday was, fortunately, a warm and sunny day. After lessons, I repaired to the gym, changed into tennis gear and had my coffee and sandwiches in the sun. I'd also brought a novel I was reading, and immersed myself in that until Steve should arrive.

He appeared at close to six, carrying a sports bag.

"Hi," he smiled, "a good day for it."

I agreed.

"I'll go in and change," he said.

I waited for a couple of minutes, then followed him in, to show him the selection of rackets. I found him with his back to me, pulling on his shorts. I noticed that he was wearing no underpants, and a neat pair of buttocks was disappearing into his shorts. He turned when he heard me come in, zipping up as he did so.

As he sat to put on socks and tennis shoes, I opened the cupboard door.

"The spare rackets are in here," I said, "but I can't promise that they're up to much."

"Neither am I, as I told you," he said. "You'll probably beat me hollow, but the exercise will do me good."

I watched him as he bent to fasten the shoelaces. The dark fringe of hair fell over his forehead. It really was a very nice face below, I thought. In profile, the nose was almost Roman, the lips quite full, yet not in the least feminine, and the chin firm.

He finished the laces, stood up and brushed back the fringe with one hand in an oddly endearing, boyish gesture. Then he went into the cupboard and selected a racket.

"Right! Let the battle commence," he said. We went on to the court and began.

He was right about his tennis prowess he wasn't "up to much.". I am no great player, but soon had him racing from one side of the court to the other, losing point after point. After about half an hour, his fringe was sticking to his forehead and the underarms of his T-shirt, visible when he served, were darkened with sweat. As yet another game finished, he leaned, panting, on his racket and suggested a break.

I agreed, and as we went to sit at the side of the court he pulled off the shirt. After only a few seconds, he lay back and rested his head on his hands, shutting his eyes against the sun. He was still breathing heavily, chest rising and falling. I took advantage of his closed eyes to feast my own on the view presented to me. A slim but muscular torso, completely devoid of hair except in the armpits, where a luxuriant, dark growth glistened with beads of sweat; a pair of prominent, pointed red nipples encircled by brown, pimpled rings; a neat navel of the "outie" type; and below it a small bulge in the white shorts. What delights

158

lay hidden? "Stop it, Bill," cried an inner voice, "that way madness lies." Heeding it, I closed my eyes, but the image persisted.

Suddenly Steve's voice broke the spell.

"Told you I was useless," he said. "Do you mind if I concede defeat?" His breathing was back to normal.

"No, if you want to pack it in, I don't mind."

"There's something else I'd rather do," he said.

Before I could start imagining what that could be, he had risen and gone back inside. Again I followed him, and he was this time disappearing into the gym proper. I pushed open the swing door and found him, hands on hips, surveying the room.

He turned and said, "This is the sort of exercise I really like."

He ran and pulled a vaulting horse into the middle of the room, followed by one of the rubber mats. Then he pulled off his tennis shoes and socks, throwing them aside.

"I've missed this," he said, and went into a series of vaults. They began simply, then progressed into balancing and rotating exercises on top of the equipment, each time ending with a flip that landed him upright and poised perfectly on the mat.

"Not bad, eh?" he grinned.

"I'm greatly impressed," I replied. "You don't need to be good at tennis."

He went on to demonstrate his ability on the ropes and parallel bars, while I sat leaning against the wall, lost in admiration. The only worrying thing was that my own equipment was beginning to show its appreciation; there were definite stirrings "down below."

They hadn't subsided when the demonstration was over, and Steve said, "Shower time?"

"Err ... I suppose so." I delayed standing up. "After you."

Steve went to the door, pushing it open with a knowing smile, while I mentally willed, "Get down, go down, you bloody thing," to my excited member. It didn't want to obey, as I followed him into the changing room. I felt my cheeks redden.

Once in the changing room, Steve quickly discarded his shorts. He stood stretching, naked. There it was at last, that wonderful body, revealed to my eyes in the bright light from the windows, hairless on arms, legs, chest and belly, luxuriant only in the pubic area, as his armpits had been. From this thick bush hung a cut cock, roughly the size of my own when at rest. As the damned thing wasn't now, curse it! I was surprised to see that Steve was circumcised, like me, as it seemed to be the exception to the rule in our country. There had only been one other "cut" lad in my class in the days when I attended this school myself.

"Well, what's the matter? Are you shy or something?" said Steve.

"No, not really. It's just...." I dithered.

"I know what's bothering you," he said. "I can see the bulge. Do you think I've never had a hard-on?"

I took off my shirt.

"My, we are hairy, aren't we?" said Steve. "Come on the rest."

I sat down, slipped out of tennis shoes and socks, then, still sitting, my shorts. I felt like some Victorian bride, cringing and shy.

"For god's sake, stand up," said Steve.

"What the hell?" I thought, and did so. I knew that I had a "semi" on. When I raised my eyes, he was staring fixedly at my crotch.

"There now," he said, "that wasn't so bad, was it? We both know what the other's got. What's the big deal?"

He went to the showers and turned them on. They were in a double row, six faucets on either side, with an extra one at each end, at right angles to the others. Steve adjusted the temperature and went in. He was halfway down, and I stayed at the single faucet at my end. I'd collected my soap and was using it when he turned.

"I didn't think about soap," he said. "Can I borrow it?"

"Sure," I said, handing it to him.

He went back to his place and, with his back to me, began soaping. Though he reached round to his back occasionally, he seemed to be concentrating on the front of his body. I didn't know to what extent, until he turned and walked back to me, holding out the soap. I took it, but my unbelieving eyes went elsewhere. His cock, roughly the size of my own when "at rest," had grown to what? 9 inches? It dawned upon me that Steve had what I call a "telescopic" cock, one that swells in erection out of all proportion to its normal size. It pointed at me, throbbing with his heartbeat, a thick vein running along its upper surface, the whole wonderful organ curving towards his left thigh.

I just kept staring until he said, "What do you think?"

"I think," I said, "that you've got some of my share. What is it, 9 inches?"

"Nah. Only 8 1/2," he said, "but it does well enough."

He went back to the mid-point of the showers and lay down on the duckboard that formed its floor. The jets began to wash away the soap from his body, but the cock remained as proud as ever, standing clear of his belly and still pulsating. He began to assist it by working his muscles and making it buck violently, grinning the while. The spectacle made my own tool reach its inferior maximum. I went to him and knelt down between his legs, which were apart. I looked at him. The quizzical look seemed to imply, "Do whatever you want." If I was wrong, he could at worst push me away. I "went for it," lowered my head and began to kiss his smooth scrotum. When there was no objection, I began slowly to lick it.

There was a slight groan of contentment, I hoped so I increased the pressure, lifting and releasing each testicle in turn. The satisfied groans continued.

Thus encouraged, I allowed my tongue to attempt the whole journey, from the scrotum, slowly up the throbbing column, until I reached the frenulum, that ultra-sensitive region just south of the helmet. There I lightly flicked my tongue back and forth. This produced more deep groans and involuntary twitchings of

160

Steve's impressive joystick. My tongue made the same journey several times more, occasionally passing the height-of-ecstasy spot to complete the ascent and probe the piss-slit. His groans turned to staccato breaths and he began to writhe. I looked up to see that his arms were above his head, hands interlocked as though wrestling with each other. His eyes were tight shut, his mouth wide open, and his head rocked from side to side. My own tool was squeezed between my belly and the smooth wetness of the duckboard, and had found one of the thin gaps between the laths. My ministrations to Steve's body had been enough to bring me to the brink, and I knew that only the smallest slidings would result in orgasm.

I had never sucked a cock to the point of coming; maybe I was ready now, I thought. I reached up with both hands to Steve's nipples, and squeezed them between the nails of thumb and middle finger. A lusty "Ow!!" came from Steve's mouth. I went back to the bucking cock, holding it almost perpendicular with both hands, and buried its head in my mouth, sucking hard to create a vacuum.

"Oh, god!" Steve cried desperately, thrashing. "I'm going to ... I'm going to...."

At the last second, I chickened out. I took my mouth away and instead stretched the skin of his cock, still pointing toward the ceiling, down towards his balls, which I saw were now drawn up in readiness for delivering their sticky load.

There came a great cry which anyone could have mistaken for unbearable agony, and the volcano erupted spectacularly, its lava spurting a good two feet in the air before splashing down on its victim's chest. Secondary gushes followed, and as I worked my hips. my own ecstasy flooded my loins, so that there was a duet of gasps and groans.

We lay spent and gradually returned to sanity.

Steve was the first to speak.

He raised himself up on his elbows and smiled as the still- running water began to wash the jism from his chest.

"Great lesson, 'sir'!" he said.

- - -

Before we went our separate ways, it was arranged that Stephen would come to Shelbourne on the Friday again, for another music session. I bought another pack of beer and awaited his arrival, as I had done the previous week, but this time with fewer doubts about his appearance. Sure enough, he turned up at precisely the same time.

We didn't speak of our Monday experience; the knowing looks we exchanged were all that were required. I decided to try some other operatic excerpts on him, those that I thought would be unfamiliar. A tenor aria from Verdi's "Il Corsaro" seemed to appeal particularly.

"There's plenty more for you to discover," I assured him.

Then he asked if we could break for a half-hour television program he liked to watch, a sitcom at 8:30. I had no objection, and at the appropriate time switched on, having broken into the 6-pack of beer and produced glasses. We sat side by side on the settee and began to watch.

In my case, it was more "half-watch," as I kept glancing at his attractive profile. He was sitting on my right, and after about ten minutes I put my glass on the floor and my right hand on his neck. I ran my fingers through the hair on the nape of his neck, then stroked it with a circular motion. Then I eased closer to him and brought my left hand to his chest. My middle finger found the gap between two shirt buttons and went inside, reaching the smooth flesh.

Suddenly he jerked his head round. He was scowling, and his eyes flashed with what? Not hate, surely? No, perhaps not that, but resentment, yes.

He said, in a grating voice that was new to me, "Do you *have* to paw me?"

I took away both hands as though I had received an electric shock.

A few seconds elapsed before I said, "No. No, of course I don't have to do anything you don't want me to do."

I picked up my glass and moved to the nearby easy chair. I took a drink and put the glass on a small side table. Suddenly I felt cold.

The comedy program went on, but I wasn't listening. I took another, longer drink.

At last, Steve turned to me again. The harshness in his voice had gone as he said, "I'm not really ...."

In the pause, I completed the sentence for him.

"Not really gay?"

A longer silence; then, "Not really in the mood."

I decided against a reply. The TV program went on, complete with "canned" laughter. I had the feeling that Steve too was not really listening. For some reason, I felt like hitting myself.

The show finished and I switched off.

"More music?" I asked. "There's time, if you're going home at the same time as last week."

"Sure, why not?" he replied.

I opened two more cans and we went back into the music room.

"Let me try a bit of orchestral music on you, for a change," I said, and put some Tchaikovsky on the turntable. "He may not realize its significance," I thought, "but I do." It was the last movement of the Fourth Symphony, with its wrestling against Fate. When it finished, he said that he had enjoyed it.

His bus time arrived. I walked with him to the door and said, "See you sometime, then."

To my surprise, he said, "Can I come on Monday?"

The wind out of my sails, I said, "Do you want to?"

"Yes! Otherwise I wouldn't be asking."

"All right, if you're sure. Same time?"

162

"Fine," he said.

- - -

I could have dizzied myself all weekend, thinking about Steve's blowing hot and cold, but forced myself not to. What was it that Doris Day had sung in a recent film? Oh, yeah: "Que sera, sera".

Monday came, and I was still in the same frame of mind. Whatever happened, I would not lay myself open to rejection again. My cheeks reddened as I thought of it.

He arrived, and we went back to square one, an evening of records and alcoholic refreshment. I behaved impeccably, and neither of us referred to Friday's events. I remember introducing him to Mendelssohn's "Italian" Symphony and the "Liebestod" from Wagner's "Tristan und Isolde".

As his usual departure time arrived, I accompanied him to the door. It had started to rain heavily.

"Do you want to borrow a raincoat?" I asked. "It's tanking down."

"No, its OK," he said. "It doesn't go past the skin."

"As you like," I said. I paused, then, "Do you want to come on Friday?"

"Yes, thanks, why not? The usual time?"

I nodded, and he was gone. I locked up, shaking my head.

I went straight to bed, as tomorrow was a work day.

- - -

A hammering on the door dragged me back from the edge of sleep. I felt for the switch on the bedside lamp, switched it on and waited, to be sure I wasn't mistaken. The knocking came again.

I jumped out of bed and took the bathrobe from its hook. In those days I slept naked. Pulling it on, I switched on the landing light, went downstairs, undid the door chain, turned the key and opened the door.

Steve stood there like a half-drowned rat, rain pouring down his face and dripping from his nose and ears.

"The bus hasn't come," he said, "I've waited and .... "

"Get yourself inside," I said, "before you catch your death."

He came in and I made the door secure again.

"Go upstairs and take those wet clothes off. The bathroom...." but he was already halfway up the stairs.

I followed and watched as he stripped. I took a bath towel from the airing cupboard and handed it to him.

"Put your clothes in there," I said. "They'll be bone-dry by morning." He did so, and began drying his hair.

I went back to the bedroom, put the bathrobe back on its hook and got into bed. I heard the sounds of vigorous toweling, then that of the hand basin filling.

163

Soaping and splashing noises followed. After a while the bathroom light switch clicked off and bare footsteps approached.

Steve came naked to the bedside. He stood in the light of the lamp, and I saw his penis was not at its minimum size. It hung down heavily, swaying slightly. He flicked it casually.

"I've given it a good wash," he said, "in case you feel like a snack before you go off to sleep."

I didn't reply, and he moved nearer.

"Kiss it, Bill," he said, almost pleadingly.

I raised my head, leaned over and complied, the clean smell of soap reached my nostrils.

"Get into bed," I said. It was almost an order.

He leaped over me, rather than walking to the other side of the bed, and stretched out beside me. I was content, for a few moments just to feed my eyes on that slim, boyish body, hairless except for the thick, curling pubic bush, the rib-cage that emphasized the flatness of the belly below, the proudly pointing nipples and the semi-tumescent penis resting against one thigh. This, I thought, was true beauty, a painter's or sculptor's dream. I couldn't keep my hands off it for long.

"Do I take it," I asked, "that you are in the mood tonight?"

His long-lashed eyelids, closed until then, opened and he turned his head to gaze at me with deep blue eyes.

"What do you think?" The eyes closed again; he stretched, then relaxed again with a half-smile playing around those full lips.

I turned on my side towards him and began my ministrations with just the right hand. Very, very lightly I stroked his lips, then moved slowly down his chin and throat, pausing at the Adam's apple. His skin was as smooth as a baby's.

"Do you shave, Steve?" I asked. "Your chin and neck are very smooth."

"Not so's you'd notice," he said. "But we can't all be hairy apes."

He reached over with his left hand and connected with my chest, running his fingers through the hair there, then moving to my belly.

"You've nearly as much hair on your tummy as on your head," he said, "but I quite like it." He brushed past my dick, which was by now showing considerable interest in the proceedings, and reached my scrotum. He stroked it.

"Gawd, your balls are like a pair of coconuts," he sniggered.

"All right, all right," I said, "I can't help it. It's something to do with hormones."

"Don't go pouty," he said, "I've told you I like it."

He gave my balls a gentle squeeze and took his hand away.

I had decided how the scenario was going to proceed, so I jumped out of bed and made for the bathroom.

"Now where are you going?" he asked.

I collected a bath towel and came back without answering.

164

"Spread your legs."

He did so, and I doubled the towel and laid it between them, on the bed sheet.

"We don't want starched sheets," I said. "Lie back and relax."

I took up my position between his legs, shuffling down until my face was directly above his equipment.

"Fasten your seat-belt," I said, and went to work with my tongue, repeating the performance from the school showers. There'd be no "chickening out" this time, I'd decided.

After only a few long, slow licks, Steve's impressive flagpole was at full attention. I sucked his right ball into my mouth, swirling my tongue round it. The groaning started. I transferred my mouth to his glans, holding that glorious prick upward, as before. I went down on it as far as I dared, knowing that, inexperienced as I was, I would "gag" if I tried to be too adventurous. No way could I swallow the full 8 1/2 inches. However, what I was managing seemed to be quite enough for Steve. The heavy breathing started, as did the writhings of the body. I felt upwards, and again located his rubbery nipples, which I squeezed quite hard. I felt his heartbeat accelerate.

"Oh god, oh god, oh god...." he panted.

I felt down with one hand, and knew for the second time that his scrotum had hardened and drawn up in readiness.

"It's coming, it's coming...." A cry of willing desperation.

My mouth stayed clamped on the raging organ, which bucked and reared, begging for release.... Finally he came. A gushing, a spouting, an eruption of pent-up force hit my throat. My mouth was flooded, my tongue drowned, with the sticky elixir of life. I swallowed and swallowed, momentarily panicking. I'd read somewhere that orgasms averaged a teaspoonful. Surely not? From far off came the sound of Steve's moans, a marriage of agony and ecstasy.

I joined in.

- - -

The crisis over, both of us back in the world we knew, I realized that my own orgasm had wet the folded towel that was between me and the bed. I gathered up the towel and wiped my sticky belly, then returned to the bathroom, throwing the towel into the bath. Picking up a dry face cloth, I took it into the bedroom and threw it on Steve's chest.

"Dry your donkey dick with that," I said.

He put his hands behind his head and closed his eyes again.

"Can't be bothered, I'm tired. You do it."

I took the cloth and gently wiped his tool, which was still in a "semi" state. He shifted slightly as I moved over the glans. It was still sensitive, obviously.

I finished the job, put the cloth on the bedside table, switched off the lamp and settled down beside him.

"We'll have to get up at about 7 o'clock," I said.

The only reply I got was, "Mmmmmm."

- - -

I woke at 7 a.m. A glance told me that Steve was sound asleep, looking even younger than his tender eighteen years. He was lying on his back, and a second glance revealed a bulge in the bedclothes, farther down. I got out of bed and very gently pulled down the sheet and counterpane. As I thought, his cock was "piss-proud," as we'd called it in my National Service army days. His prick was pulsating gently, in unison with his heartbeat, clear of the smooth belly, and the usual two inches above the navel. Now was no good, though; daylight and work called. I replaced the bedclothes softly, which called forth only the slightest stirring.

I washed and shaved even more quickly than usual, then went downstairs, switched on the kettle, put tea in the pot and prepared my cereal, starting to eat it before the water boiled. I made the tea and popped two slices of bread in the toaster. I put two mugs and plates on the dining room table, with milk and sugar, and went back upstairs. Steve was still asleep. I drew the curtains, then pulled back the bedclothes, vigorously this time. The succulent 8 1/2 inches were still aloft.

"Hands off cocks and on socks," I shouted, "Time to raise your whole body, not just that throbbing piece of meat!"

Steve woke and raised up on his elbows. Squinting in the sunlight, he asked, "What time is it anyway?"

I grasped his cock in my right hand, "Time to get up," I replied, pumping it with each syllable.

"Get off, you dirty old man," he said, half-heartedly brushing away my hand. But he was smiling.

I let go.

"You know where the bathroom is. Your clothes are dry. Get them on and come down."

I went back down and he followed shortly afterwards.

"Corn flakes? Toast? A boiled egg?" I asked.

Still bleary, he said, "Just a couple of slices of toast. I never eat much breakfast." He poured a mug of tea while I saw to the toast for both of us. Bringing it in, I said, "Will you go home before work? What will your parents be thinking?"

"They won't be worried, I've stayed out all night before."

I thought of asking when and where, but refrained.

He went on, "I'll see them at tea-time, before evening class."

"You won't be in trouble?" I pursued. "I seem more worried than you are."

"It's all right, I tell you. If you're so concerned, I'll come tomorrow night to convince you."

I agreed to this. Steve finished his breakfast and stood.

166

"Ready when you are," he said.

We drove to Oakham and I dropped him off near his work place.

"Tomorrow, then," I said. He nodded, got out of the car and walked away. I went on to school.

The next day, Wednesday, he arrived. He said that his parents were "dodgy" about it at first, but seemed reassured when he told them about the non-arrival of the bus, and his knocking me up after I had gone to bed.

"Do they know who I am?" I asked. "I can understand their suspicion, if they know I'm your ex-teacher...." I paused, "and not married."

"You worry too much," he said. "I've told you: it's all right."

We went into the music room and I chose some records.

"I haven't any liquid refreshment in the house tonight," I said, after about an hour and a half. "I forgot all about it."

"Doesn't matter," he replied, "unless you'd like to go out for a drink."

"We can, if you like," I said. "I'm a member of the club just down the road."

"Yeah, why not?" was his response, so I switched off the lights and we left the house.

At the club, I signed the visitor's book for him, gave him the ticket and led him to the bar. I ordered the drinks and we sat down to enjoy them.

I don't remember all the details of the conversation. It was a mixture of the music I'd played him, plus reminiscences of the boys in his class at school. Did I remember Colin Brooks, who'd sat next to him? He liked opera, too. Did I remember the two "clowns" who sat at the back of the class with them? Those who had no interest in good music, and whom he and Colin had told to "belt up" when they were whispering in my lessons?

Our glasses were empty.

After one of our pauses came, "Bill, I can't buy you a drink tonight. I'm always short on Wednesdays. In fact, I haven't even the bus fare home."

"Don't worry, visitors aren't allowed to buy drinks; it's one of the rules," I said, and went to the bar for refills. Bringing back the glasses, before I sat I brought out some loose change. I put it on the table, saying, "Is that enough?"

He looked at it and then scooped it up.

"Yes, thanks. Look, I'm sorry...."

"It doesn't matter, really," I said.

When we had finished the drinks, it was time for his bus.

"It doesn't matter," I had said, and it really didn't. So little did it matter that Wednesday became another regular meeting day, along with Monday and Friday. What did it matter if Steve couldn't pay his turn? His company was enough. Wasn't it?

- - -

August arrived. By then I had hatched a plan whereby Steve and I could spend an uninterrupted spell together. One of my colleagues possessed a country cottage, at which he and his wife spent weekends now and then. He let it out to friends occasionally. After I had ascertained Steve's holiday period, I enquired as to the possibility of my hiring the cottage for a week.

I put the idea to Steve. If he wished, we could spend his holiday week together in the cottage. It was out in the wilds of Yorkshire, and we would have to fend for ourselves, but it might be fun. What did he think?

He thought, "Why not?" Accordingly, I arranged to go with the owner of the cottage to be "shown the ropes" one Sunday afternoon. The building stood some way from the road, surrounded by fields. It had been, in years past, a farm laborer's dwelling. There was no electricity, so I was shown how to prime a gas lamp, to be hung from a hook on the ceiling to provide light. There was also no gas mains supply, so cooking must be done on a stove fuelled by a liquid gas canister. If more hot water was required, the fireplace must be laid and lit. (There was a plentiful supply of logs in an outhouse.) There was, though, a bathroom, which had obviously once been a pantry off the kitchen, but hot water would be provided for it only if the fire was lit and a metal plate pulled back so that the flames would heat the boiler. It was all delightfully primitive; not to be endured for long, but fun for a short time. (Very "Wuthering Heights", I thought.) There were two bedrooms, one large and one small. We must take our own bedding. I assumed that we would be using only the one bed, so packed enough for that. The date for our departure was arranged.

I had made other preparations. I had never had another man "inside" me. I had wondered enough about the possibility to experiment, first with a finger in the bath, then with a vibrator well lubricated with "gel." After initial discomfort, it felt quite good. My vibrator was, though, both shorter and thinner than Steve's endowment. Could I manage that? Or indeed, would the opportunity ever arise? Oh well, take the gel and extra towels anyway. "Be prepared."

We were to leave on the Saturday. Steve told me on the Wednesday that because of this, his "babysitting" of his young brother had to be brought forward a day, to enable his parents to have a night out a day earlier than usual. Accordingly I planned a quiet evening, but at about 9.30 I began to miss his usual Friday company, and decided to go down to my club for a drink.

At 10.20, a couple of acquaintances came into the bar, where I was standing. They ordered their drinks and said, "Hello Bill, We've had a pub-crawl in Oakham. Started at the Station Hotel, and worked our way down to the market place, a drink in each pub. We finished up at the 'Queen's Head.' Your mate was there Steve, isn't it? with his girlfriend."

I turned to look at him.

"Well," he went on, "I *say* 'girlfriend'. It certainly wasn't his sister, the way they were wrapped round each other."

168

He picked up the drink his friend had bought.

"Cheers, mate."

He took a gulp and faced me again.

"Oh, yes," I lied, "he said he had a date tonight."

The two men started talking to someone on the other side. I finished my drink and left. There was food for thought on the way home.

I picked Steve up on Saturday lunchtime, as arranged. We drove to the cottage and unpacked. Last night's events would wait.

"First things first," I said. "The village is about a mile and a half down the road. We'll have to get food in."

"You'll have to do the cooking," he said. "I'm useless. I'll do any other things necessary. Oh, here...."

He handed me a note.

"For food, for the time being."

I took it.

We drove to the village and I bought milk, cereals, eggs, potatoes, sugar, tea, salt and some meat. I'd brought bread and butter from home.

"What vegetables do you like?" I asked.

"Any," was the reply, so I added carrots, turnip and peas to the order. I paid and we left, Steve acting as carrier.

Back at the cottage, we unloaded and I set about discovering the peculiarities of the oven. Regardless of fuel, they all have them. I presented Steve with some potatoes, carrots and turnip, together with a knife from the kitchen drawer.

"You *can* peel things, I suppose?" I said. "Besides yourself?"

Taking the knife, he said, "What's this? A working holiday?"

"Get on with it," I said, and set about seeing what cooking utensils were in the kitchen cupboard.

An hour and a half later, we sat down to our first meal. After a few mouthfuls, I asked if the chef would be satisfactory, or would he rather take over?

"You must be joking. No, it's great, really."

After a couple of minutes, I asked, casually. "How was last night?"

"Last night? What do you mean, last night? I told you that I was minding Dean while Mum and Dad went out."

"Oh, that's right," I said. "I'd forgotten. Only the 'telly' for entertainment, then. Anything worth watching?"

"No, not really just the usual. What did you do?"

"I had a short record session, then went to the club for an hour," I said. "Oh damn, I've forgotten all about dessert. Should have bought some fruit, or at least biscuits."

"No, it's all right. This will fill me up, with a cup of tea afterwards."

"I hate to spoil things for you, but your other duties include washing up," I said. "The best chefs don't do such things."

"Oh my gawd," he replied, rolling his eyes. "Oh, all right,- but not before a 'cuppa' and a rest."

I had brought my transistor radio, battery powered, which I switched on as I brewed the tea.

"You can't choose your music tonight," I said, "so it's pot luck, or listening to the sounds of nature."

We drank our tea, after which I said that we had better see to making the bed. Steve hadn't realized that bedding had to be provided. I carried the sheets and blankets upstairs to the larger bedroom and he followed. We laid the bed. I had packed pillows and pillow cases, which I plunked down.

"There," I said, "a virgin couch."

"If you say so," was the reply. "What are we doing tonight?"

I said that we may as well try the village's only pub. I wasn't going to drive, so we'd have to walk there and back.

We did so, on a lovely sunny evening. The landlord, his wife and the "regulars" made us welcome, as I think only Northern people can do. We told them that we were vacationing nearby, and after correcting the assumption that Steve was my son, things seemed to go smoothly enough.

On the walk back to the cottage, I said, "Now that they know you're not my son, what do you suppose they think I really am?"

Steve, none too steady on his feet after the night's drinking, said, "I dunno. Does it really matter?"

"I suppose not, but maybe we should have prepared some explanation. I could have been an older brother, or your uncle."

"Who cares? Do you?"

At that moment I couldn't honestly say that I did.

We reached the cottage in twilight. I unlocked the door and we went in. Once inside, it was quite dark.

"I don't feel like fiddling with the lamp," I said. "Unless you want some tea before bed?"

Steve flopped down in a chair. "No, not really," he said.

"I'll just go for a piss." He rose and went outside and I heard the sound of splashing on the grass. He came back in, fastening his flies. "I'm off to bed," he said.

"Here I've brought a torch," I said. "Don't try breaking your neck on the stairs."

I turned it on for him, and he went unsteadily upstairs. I too decided to relieve myself outside, rather than grope in the dark bathroom. Coming back inside, I locked the door, though there was probably no necessity. I went upstairs, guided by the faint light from the torch, which Steve had set down on a chair. His clothes were in a heap on the floor, and he appeared to be already asleep. I stripped and climbed into bed beside him, switching off the torch. I too was soon asleep.

We both slept late the next morning, but I woke first. It took a couple of seconds before I realized where I was. I looked to my right, where Steve's head was on its pillow. My right hand was exploring in his direction, under the sheet. It met his hip, and crept farther, but no sooner had it reached the crisp pubic bush than it encountered the warm stiffness of that seemingly permanently tumescent penis. Did it never sleep? I began to think that possibly I'd invited Priapus himself on holiday, or at least his reincarnation. I explored its divine length with two trembling fingers.

Then I stopped and memories of Friday intruded. Had this "girlfriend" been where I was now? What had happened after they left the "Queen's Head"? Why had he felt it necessary to lie to me? Why, indeed, was I lying beside this yes, this youngster? Maybe the whole idea had been a mistake.

I rose quietly, went downstairs and began breakfast, as I had on that Tuesday at home. After the cereal, I had some tea and a cigarette. Then I went in to wake him.

It was another fine day, so we explored the surroundings on foot. I began to wonder if Steve would not soon become bored in this quiet spot. I'd also forgotten that it was Sunday, with no possibility of buying in any more food until tomorrow. Luckily, we had enough to tide us over.

In the evening, we walked to the village and renewed our acquaintance with the owners and clientele of the pub. There were a few who hadn't been there on the previous night, including a middle-aged couple with their daughter, a pretty girl who soon attracted Steve's attention. We eventually found ourselves engaged in a friendly game of dominoes with them, which passed the time pleasantly. At closing time, we said our good nights and set off back to the cottage.

We had some tea and then went to bed, again dispensing with the lamp.

Steve seemed restless, unlike the previous night. After a period of his tossing and turning, I said, "What's up? Are you by any chance wanking over that girl?"

"Not really," he said. "She was all right, though. Whatever the reason, I've got a hard-on."

"So, what's new?" I laughed. I couldn't believe how horny he was. I decided to chance his being "in the mood," and felt across until I reached the flagpole. My fingers closed on its warm length, and I gave it a series of gentle squeezes. He gave a contented sigh. As far as I was concerned, it was the "green light", and I felt for the towel and tube of lube I had put on the bedside table on my side. I unscrewed the cap, felt for his cock and squeezed some of the gel on the helmet, smearing it downwards.

"Bloody hell, what's this?" he said.

"If you don't like it, tell me to stop."

"No, it's ... ooh," he said, as I went down his full length again.

I put the nozzle of the tube in my ass and squeezed again. The cool gel entered my rectum. I put the tube aside and wiped my hand on the towel. Now I'd find

out if I could take it.

I knelt astride him, felt for his dick and guided it to my entrance.

"What are you doing?" he asked. "You're not putting it...?"

"Somewhere tight and warm," I said. "Relax."

"But I've never...."

"Neither have I," I interrupted. "A new experience for both of us."

I pushed down and his cock head was past the sphincter.

So far, so good; the vibrator had been farther than this. I bore down again and another couple of inches were swallowed up. Steve began to make appreciative noises. I took a breath and went on, forcing myself to relax. More, more.... Then there was some discomfort; not exactly pain, but his prick was reaching unplumbed depths now. I felt behind with one hand and discovered that Steve's endowment had all but disappeared. There was a new pleasure/pain sensation as my prostate responded. At the same time, Steve began to groan like a soul in torment. He grabbed my shoulders and dug in his nails as his pelvis began to gyrate. I remained still as he took charge of the operation. Pleasure now had the upper hand of pain, and my hands sought his nipples, found them and squeezed hard as my own erection grew. He began to thrust wildly, panting as though struggling for breath.

We reached the peak. Steve's cries were stimulating me almost as much as his pistoning rod. As his gushing release, accompanied by what can only be described as a howl, spurted deep within me, my own jerking dick erupted onto his chest. Our hearts hammered out a duet that was a rhapsody to ecstasy. I fell forward, our burning cheeks pressed together, and thus we stayed until our bodies recovered from their delicious torment. I felt Steve's steel rod soften, as my own drooped between our bellies.

Eventually he let out a "Whooooo," followed by, "that was something else. Nearly as good as...."

He stopped

"As a woman?" I finished the thought for him.

"Well...."

I climbed off him, reached for the towel and wiped my cock and ass. I felt for the torch and switched it on. His prick and chest glistened. I threw the towel down beside him.

"Here, clean yourself up."

He did so, as I fell back, my hands under my head, watching the ceiling. Then I covered my face with my hands, pretending to sob dramatically.

"Daddy tried to warn me against men like you," I wailed. "You have taken away my virginity, and I am undone."

"Give over, you great fool," he said. "You led me into your wicked, wicked ways. Shame on you."

I took my hands away and turned to look at him. He turned too, and after a couple of seconds we simultaneously burst out laughing. He'd finished with the towel, so I took it away from him, threw it on the floor and felt for and switched

172

out the torch.

We pulled the bedclothes up and settled down to sleep.

I leaned over, found his head and kissed the warm, full lips gently.

"God help me, I love you," I whispered.

Nothing was mentioned by either of us over breakfast the next day about the previous night's events. Somehow I didn't want to broach the subject, and Steve didn't do so. We drove to the village and I bought in more provisions, not forgetting some fruit and biscuits this time. As there was no fridge in the cottage, milk had to be bought daily, the bottles kept in a bucket of water to keep them as cool as possible. Steve left the choice of meat to me, so I chose lamb cutlets for today's dinner. We both smoked so I stocked up on cigarettes.

When we got back and the provisions had been unpacked, we had some coffee and biscuits. The day was hot and sunny, so we took a couple of chairs outside on to the grass and I switched the radio on. After a while Steve removed his shirt, and shortly afterwards decided that lying on the grass would be more comfortable than sitting in the chair. The radio began to play a Schubert symphony, and soon I decided that this aural pleasure, allied to the sight of Steve's young torso, was the perfect combination. I had the urge to kneel down beside him and run my hands over his chest, but I stifled it. I think that this was when I realized that things couldn't last.

I cooked dinner, which called forth more praise from Steve.

"We're living like kings aren't we?" he said, patting his stomach appreciatively.

"Something like that," I replied.

We walked to the village again that evening and spent more time chatting and drinking. I felt like part of the community.

Later, in bed, I moved my leg across until it met Steve's. He pulled it away. I waited until he spoke.

"Look, Bill, do you mind waiting until I feel like making the running?"

"No, whatever you like," I replied, and turned away from him.

He turned the other way, settled down.

I didn't fall asleep as quickly as on the previous night.

- - -

On Tuesday evening, the weather broke. Thunder had been threatening all day, and at last materialized. Suddenly we were marooned on an island encircled by lashing rain, with jagged lightening followed at intervals by cracking thunderbolts. It crossed my mind that it was even more reminiscent of "Wuthering Heights" than formerly.

There was no question of going out that night. The only source of entertainment was the radio. I switched it on, to find that a Promenade Concert broadcast was beginning. It was an all-Brahms concert, beginning with the

"Tragic" Overture, to be followed by the second piano concerto. This latter was only half-way through the first movement when Steve jumped up.

"I'm going out," he said.

"Out where?" I asked. "You'll be drowned."

"Down the pub," he almost shouted. "Rain doesn't go past the skin, remember?"

He pulled on a plastic mackintosh, pausing at the door to say. "Don't wait up."

The door slammed.

During the interval of the concert, I made a cup of tea. I drank it and ate two or three biscuits, then listened to the second part of the program. It consisted of the first symphony. The opening doom-laden drumbeats seemed apt.

I didn't hear Steve come in; I was fast asleep.

- - -

The next day, the storm had dwindled to a drizzle, but it was much colder. Steve decided that a fire would both heat the place and provide hot water for a bath, so he set to work to produce a roaring blaze. By two o'clock the water was rumbling in the cistern....

"I'm off for a bath," he said, disappearing into the bathroom.

After a few minutes, I pushed the bathroom door open. He was naked, making a bit of a show, I thought, testing the water with one foot. Looking up, he said, "What do you want?"

Slightly taken aback, I said, "Oh, nothing really. I guess I just came in to watch.... or maybe join you?"

He gave me a violent push. "Get the hell out," he said, "It's not a fucking public peep-show."

I tried to shrug it off. "Could've fooled me," I said under my breath. As I started to leave, he pushed me out, slammed the door. Rebuff number two.

I went back into the main room, sat down and lit a cigarette. I had two more before he appeared, wrapped in a towel. He looked at me. No doubt my face told all.

"What's up with you?" he said.

"Nothing," I replied. I could hardly utter the truth, that I was, yes, sulking.

"We'll have to drive to the village for more food," I said. "and, by the way, the money you gave me on Saturday ran out a while ago, so I could do with some more." This was true.

His face changed.

"I'm not making this up," I said. "'Living like kings', remember?"

Eventually he said, "Well, to tell you the truth, I'm about out of funds."

Now was the time I had been waiting for.

"Oh, really?" I said. "Maybe things would be different if you hadn't spent so much on that girl in the 'Queen's Head' on Friday?"

174

His jaw dropped.

"How did you...?" he began.

Ludicrously, I said, like some agent in an espionage film, "Oh, I have my sources."

"You never said...."

"No, I didn't. Now get dressed, and we'll go shopping. A few tins will do for the rest of our stay, I think."

- - -

Friday, we returned, and I dropped him off near his home. He got out of the car with his luggage.

"When will I see you again?" he asked. Even now I couldn't be gracious; things still rankled.

"When you have some money," I said.

His jaw set and he gave a curt nod. "Yeah, right," he said, and then he walked away.

- - -

Somehow I knew that he would never come back. I did see him once again, however, some thirty years later. By then, I was teaching in another school, several miles away, and had stopped calling at public houses in Oakham.

I had been shopping there one day, and boarded my bus for Shelbourne. Glancing out of the window on my right, I saw Steve. He was sitting on a bench at the next platform, obviously waiting for another bus. His back was towards me, but I would have known that head and neck anywhere, even though there was now a sprinkling of grey hairs among the thick black ones. For a few seconds, I toyed with the idea of leaving my bus and going to speak with him, but quickly dismissed it.

My driver boarded the bus and we rolled homeward.

GEOMETRICAL FIGURES
by Tim Scully

"If it's so bloody important, I wonder why you don't ask if I can go with you," said Danny.

"It's only some sort of letter," I said. "Just an envelope with some papers, according to Mr. Parsons."

"But important. What would happen if you had an accident or a heart attack or something like that?"

"Thanks a lot! Anyway, you've got a football match that weekend."

"I can always say I'm sick. Anyway, I quite fancy a trip to Germany. That is, if you want me to come."

"Of course I'd like you to come. You'd be company. I just never thought of it before."

I saw Mr. Parsons on the following morning and mentioned the (unlikely, I hoped) possibility of my being struck down on foreign soil whilst carrying an important document. I rather expected him to smile and wave me away.

"Good thinking," he said. "Tell Mr. Taylor to see staff travel and get his ticket booked. They'll handle the hotel. Don't go too wild with the firm's money, will you?"

I was quite sure I was being involved in a shady deal of some sort but I'd got to know the armaments industry pretty well. I could guess what it was all about. It would be an order for some pretty nasty missiles to be delivered to some small but friendly nation. From there they'd be exported to a much larger and distinctly dangerous nation, described on the manifest as crop spraying equipment.

I told Danny about my misgivings some three days later. "You might not want to get involved," I explained.

"I'm not involved. I'm just coming with you to keep you company. That's what you said."

"Sure. I just wanted you to know there's almost certainly something fishy going on."

"Doesn't worry me at all." He continued to read the paper and then looked up again. I was sitting at the dining room table writing my luggage labels.

"Where does Michael live?" he asked.

"No idea. Why?"

"No reason, just wanted to know."

"Yeah, my ass! I know you, you're plotting something."

"Well, we could tell him we're coming to Germany. We might be able to meet him."

"He's probably miles from Munich. It's a huge country. Anyway, I expect he's got more to do than come and see us."

"It's worth a try. You've got his address."

"I don't think so."

"Yes you have. It's on the envelope of his last letter. A purple one. It's in the rack with the telephone bills. I saw you look at it the other night."

I rummaged through the bills and found the envelope. "Markt Schwaben," I read. "Goethestrasse 28, Markt Schwaben."

Danny reached over to the bookshelf and pulled out one of his library books. He riffled through the pages and then read "Markt Schwaben, Bavaria. Originally a small village outside Munich. It is now a suburb of Munich.' Ha! We'll be right on the boy's doorstep. If you write to him now I'll go and post it for you."

"Why this sudden desire to see Michael?" I said.

"Oh, I don't know. He's a good laugh. It would be good to see him again."

Two minds with a single thought! I missed Michael, too. He'd stayed with us in the previous summer, officially to improve his English and widen his vocabulary. That wasn't the only thing that had been expanded although we had, between us, taught him the difference between 'hard' and 'hardly' as in 'Let me make it hard' and that a blow job was the opposite to what he imagined it to be.

"Could do I suppose," I said.

"Of course you could. Get up there and start typing."

That didn't take very long. The letter had already been composed. I just had to insert the date and time of our arrival and change 'I' to 'we'. I sealed the envelope, put a stamp on it and Danny took it to the post.

Nine days later, we were on our way. We took a taxi to the hotel, which was in the centre of Munich right next to the railway station. "Ideal if he's coming by train," said Danny. "Which room do we use as a base?"

"They'd given us two rooms next to each other. Each had a vast double bed.

"This one, I should think," I said.

"Funny when you think about it," said Danny. "When Michael first came to us we were making all that pretense about me sleeping in your room to give him one of his own."

"That's right. So we were. If he wants to stay overnight here, he can free of charge. He can use the empty room."

"With me." said Danny.

"Or me," I replied. "That is if he comes at all, which I doubt. Anyway, we ought to go out to see Herr Huber and get this mysterious envelope. Let's attend to the business first."

"You go. I'll hang on here," said Danny.

"I thought the idea was that you were to take over if I have an accident."

"You won't. Take a taxi. The firm's paying after all."

"I'd have to anyway. I don't know where the Maximilian Strasse is. Sure you don't want to come?"

"No. I'll be okay."

"Give me the key then or I won't be able to get back in."

The address I'd been given turned out to be a bookshop. I was mystified at first. Fortunately the man inside spoke English. Herr Huber was a lawyer and his office was on the second floor.

He didn't look like a shady customer. He looked quite normal and his office could have been a showroom for the very latest in business furniture. He wanted me to prove my identity. Fortunately I had my passport with me. He took the envelope out of his safe. His secretary typed out what was apparently a receipt for it. I signed that and went downstairs. I'd been in his office for not more than ten minutes.

Getting back to the hotel was a nightmare. I didn't know about the famous Munich rush hour. The traffic was horrendous. People rushed past me, pushing me aside. It was as if the city was threatened by the plague. It took over half an hour to get a cab and then we were held up in one traffic jam after another.

Clutching the precious envelope I went up in the lift, along the thickly carpeted corridor to our room. It's always a moment of panic with me when I'm in a hotel. "Are you quite sure this is your room? What if the rooms on each floor are numbered in the same way?" Daft really.

This really was our room. The key slipped into the lock easily enough. I pushed open the door and was just about to say, "Hi! I'm back!" when I realized that Danny was not, as I expected him to be, lying on his bed watching the television. The television wasn't on but he was lying on his bed naked and not alone. One glimpse of the long legs splayed out under him, the wrists and hand, which clutched the side of the bed and the close-cropped head on the pillow was enough. Michael had received the letter. Worse, the open tube of lubricant on the bedside table was the stuff Michael preferred. I'd bought it in England at least a month previously, just after hearing that Mr. Parsons wanted someone to go to Munich. I wrote to Michael that night, telling him about the proposed trip.

Understandably, neither of them greeted me effusively. I think they realized I was there but they were both too far gone to care. For a moment I stood there watching them. Danny's ass wasn't rising and falling; it just tightened and relaxed rhythmically and slowly, almost as if it were a separate organism breathing for itself. It was doing the trick though. I had been amazed when Michael stayed with us that such a slim person could take Danny's eight and a bit inches but he had and was doing so again and enjoying it.

He gasped and sighed alternately. Danny was panting. Each contraction of his butt was accompanied by liquid, squelching sounds. Michael wriggled slightly and seemed to be trying to lift himself off the bed not to escape from the shaft that impaled him so much as to force it even deeper into his ass.

Suddenly, Danny stopped. "Good?" he whispered.

"Oh yes. Very good. Tim has come."

"So will I in a minute. So will you. Ready?"

"Sure. Make it well."

"Do it well. Make it good. How many more times?"

"Many times I hope," said Michael. "Oooh! Oh!"

Danny's butt went to work again; more slowly this time with a long pause between each contraction. Michael exhaled loudly with every one. Feeling very much the unwanted guest, I sat in the basket-work chair in the corner and placed the envelope on my lap. This was not so much a question of security as to cover the rapidly rising mound under my trousers. I slipped a hand into my pocket, found it without difficulty and couldn't resist giving it a few encouraging strokes.

Danny nibbled Michael's ear. Michael turned his head. Danny licked his neck and then nibbled the other ear.

Who came first? I honestly don't know. They both went tense at the same time. Deep dimples formed in Danny's butt. Michael's legs kicked as if he were having some sort of fit and they lay still and panting as if they'd been running a race.

"Better than ever!" Danny exclaimed after a few seconds had elapsed. "Stay still now. Don't move an inch."

"It feels more like a metre!" Michael gasped.

I watched him clasp the pillow as Danny lifted off him. Inch after greasy inch of the monster I enjoyed so much came into view. Finally it was all out and nodded up and down as if to express its own appreciation of Michael's lithe body.

Michael climbed off the bed and walked towards me, dripping semen onto the carpet as he did so. He shook my hand, which seemed a strange thing to do in the circumstances.

"It's good to see you," he said.

"Oh, it's good to see you too, Michael. If I were you I'd have a shower. That's going all over the carpet."

"Oh yes. Good idea. Danny was fucking my ass."

"Oh, is that what he was doing? I thought it was a Sunday school outing."

"Excuse me?"

"Nothing. Just making an English joke."

"Sunday school inning actually," Danny shouted from the bathroom.

"But today is Friday," Michael said, frowning.

"And we're here till Sunday evening," said Danny. "Come in here and get cleaned up. You can talk to Tim later."

I put the cap on the cream tube. Laughter and whispers came from the bathroom. Danny had a bit of a cheek I thought. He could have waited till I got back. I had no objection to him screwing Michael at all but it would have been nicer to have got over the social niceties first. And to rummage through my bag for the cream I had bought was a bit much.

I put it and the envelope in my bag. Danny and Michael emerged from the shower.

"Michael can stay till Sunday afternoon," said Danny.

"My parents give the special permission," said Michael, smiling. "When I say

180

that Danny and Tim are coming to Munich they are glad. They wanted that you stay with us but I said you have much business. My mother want that you Sunday have lunch with us."

I said something about it being a very kind offer. I wasn't too enthusiastic.

"I'm hungry. Lets eat now," said Danny. He's the most amazing person. Sex always makes him hungry. I've known him get out of bed and make himself a snack. I looked at my watch. It was nearly eight o'clock and neither of us had eaten since the journey.

"You'd better get dressed then," I said. "You can't go to the dining room like that."

To be truthful, I could have sat looking at them for hours. I loved Danny's body when it was slightly damp from a shower and looking at Michael was better than admiring any work of art. It was his slimness that really got to me, and his extraordinary gracefulness. His long legs and a very substantial cock were a few feet from my eyes. His pubic bush seemed to have grown and expanded a bit since the summer. Otherwise he was the same very beautiful boy I'd enjoyed so much in the summer and intended to have after dinner. My cock twitched at the prospect.

Dinner, as always with Michael, was a riot but the business of the lubricant was still niggling. Danny is no fool. He would have known, the moment he saw that cream tube, that I'd been planning to see Michael. Sooner or later he'd want to have it out with me and I'd have to confess to my deviousness. Getting it had involved a half hour drive.

"What are these, Michael?" Danny asked pointing to an item on the menu.

"It is what do you call them in English? And they are stuffed with... I don't know the English word."

"I'm none the wiser but I like stuffing," said Danny. "You do too, eh?"

"Excuse me?"

"Stuffing. You know." Danny made an explicit gesture pushing a finger between the thumb and forefinger of his other hand.

Michael grinned. "Oh. I understand. Yes, I like the stuffing very much, especially the English stuffing."

"And how about English cream?"

For a moment, Michael looked blank. Then the penny (or *pfennig*) dropped. "Ah! Last summer," he said. "I remember me. It tastes to me not so good."

Danny had told me about the incident. He'd got carried away and persuaded Michael to try a new experience. It ended up with Michael kneeling on the bed looking like a gerbil with full cheek pouches before he choked and then coughed. Danny got the whole lot back all over him.

"The soup is cream of asparagus," said Michael. "You like that?"

"I prefer cream of Michael, but guess I'll settle for asparagus for the moment," I said. He laughed.

There was some confusion at the end of the meal as to which room number the meal was to be charged to. Michael left us to have a word with the head

181

waiter.

"By God, that boy's as good as ever," said Danny, wiping his lips with the serviette.

"Yes, you looked as if you were enjoying yourself," I replied.

"So did he," said Danny.

"I guess I should apologize," I said, trying to precipitate the inevitable recriminations over the cream tube.

"Oh, don't worry about it. You had to turn up sooner or later and you didn't put me off my stroke." He laughed.

"So I noticed. You were good."

It was a strange feeling. It really had been great to watch him in action. I felt a sort of proprietorial pride, like a father must feel when his son has won a race. Danny had no experience at all when we first met.

Michael came back. "That is arranged good," he said. "What want you to do now?"

I could have told him. He'd obviously bought some new jeans since we saw him in England. The slight bagginess at the rear had gone. The new ones could have been molded onto him. I looked at my watch. It was still early and he probably needed a bit more time to recharge sufficiently. Everyone is different. It's just as well they are. Danny is remarkable. Give him a twenty-minute rest and he's as randy as a March hare again. With me it takes a bit longer. Michael, as we'd both discovered during the summer, needed at least a couple of hours. Don't get me wrong. He'll oblige quite happily. I'd screwed him once immediately after Danny had him but it was a disappointing and listless performance.

"We could have a drink," I suggested.

"Good idea. But not here in the hotel I think," said Michael. "The beer here is very expensive and the bar is - how do you say it in English? High nosed?"

"Toffee nosed or stuck up," said Danny.

Michael laughed. "Nobody there can be stuck up," he said. "They are all old men and they have the toffee noses. I show you the pub I go at with my friends. It is not far. We can walk there."

The walk was a delight in itself. It felt good to be out in the fresh air and I kept falling back to enjoy the view of two perfectly rounded buns rolling under the denim.

The pub was not a bad place. Unfortunately, one of Michael's friends was there. At any other time I would have been glad to spend the evening with him. His name was Martin and he was strikingly good looking with all the attributes that I liked. Long legs; a nice tight butt and, from the length of his fingers, I guessed him to be pretty well endowed in front too. His English was remarkably good. Phrases like "Notwithstanding the current climate of opinion" rolled off his tongue. I wondered why Michael had taken the trouble to come to England to learn English when he had a friend like that at home. I'm glad he did though. We just had one drink with Martin. He seemed determined to dissect British

182

politics with us. We had other things to think of.

We paid the bill and left. "What now?" Michael asked.

"Silly question," I replied. He turned his head to look at me and grinned. There was no mistaking that look. Michael was in his mischievously randy mood.

"Ah! You wish to do the stuffing," he said. "First you must catch the bird."

We were passing a sort of arcade at the time. One or two of Munich's stolid citizens stared at the spectacle of a laughing young man chasing a giggling boy round the pillars. Michael was incredibly fast and, even when I'd got a hand on him, he was like an eel and soon escaped again. Finally, by hiding behind one of the columns, I managed to grab him and hold him fast. We were both out of breath. I felt his cock, hard as steel, pressing against me.

"And what will you do to me now?" he asked.

"What do you want me to do to you?"

"You wish the cream or the stuffing?" he asked.

I dropped a hand down to his buns and kneaded them through his jeans. "The stuffing, I think," I said. "I'll have the cream some other time."

Danny followed us into my room. "Just picking up my bag. I'll sleep in the spare room," he said.

"Oh you can stay," said Michael, already peeling his skin- tight sweatshirt up over his torso. "I like it better when both of you are here."

"Danny wants to get some sleep," I explained. I was quite sure, in fact, that Danny would spend most of the night with his ear pressed against the wall and his hand on his cock.

Danny looked from one of us to the other and picked up his bag. "Come and see me in the morning, Michael," he said.

"At what time?" said Michael, tossing the sweat-shirt onto the floor. He sat on the bed to pull off his sneakers and socks.

"Whenever you're ready and Tim's had enough. I'll be waiting for you. I'll leave the door unlocked."

"It is better I think if you come in here. To visit with you I must put on my closes."

"Just put a towel round your middle. That's what I would do if I visited you." He looked again at our faces. I tried to look distinctly inhospitable. I must have succeeded. "Well, good night," said Danny. "I won't say 'Sleep well'. You won't."

"It's much better with just the two of us," I said when I had finished undressing and was sitting on the bed.

"I think maybe Danny feels we don't want him," said Michael. "I think we three are a tringle."

"A what?"

"A tringle. Like they say the ends of a line go more far apart and a tringle is closed forever."

"Oh! You mean a triangle. Yes. That's quite a thought. Quite philosophical.

Come here. Let me do that."

He grinned. I undid his fly. Seconds later he had stepped out of his jeans and under shorts and I was nuzzling his cock and his balls, burying my nose in his soft mat of hair.

It's funny how you forget things. I'd forgotten how sensitive Michael's nipples were. He had to draw my hands up to them. I'd forgotten how slowly he warmed up. For a moment or two I was quite worried about the slackness of his cock. I needn't have been. By the time I'd spent a few minutes working on him, it was steel hard. I could actually hear his heart thumping.

His thighs were warm and (I thought) more hairy than they had been but I had forgotten the extraordinary coolness and the smoothness of his buttocks. It all came back to me as, with one hand parting them, I wormed a finger between them to apply a dollop of the expensive lubricant.

He was much easier to penetrate than he had been. I didn't know whether to thank his Uncle Otto who, years before had done the groundwork, before being found out, or to blame Danny for taking advantage of him whilst I was out.

Just as he sank down onto the bed and I pushed the last centimeter into his warm, soft passage, a pigeon landed on the window ledge outside and stood staring in at us through a red- rimmed eye. I was obviously fated to perform before an audience! If Danny had been there he could have shooed the damned thing away.

The pigeon cooed. Michael sighed. I suppose I was breathing pretty heavily. Just holding the boy tight and feeling his warmth was enough to send me into ecstasies. Shoving into him and feeling round him to hold his cock made me forget all about the pigeon or anything else. Michael started to squirm under me and to groan. Cool, soft flesh rubbed against my groin whilst my fingers clasped a very hard, warm penis, which was already starting to weep copiously.

As always, I tried to make a conscious effort to make it last but that didn't work. He groaned as I thrust into him and shot my load. He sighed lightly and then much longer and more loudly. I felt it spurting, warm and sticky, through my fingers.

"Aaah! That was so good!" said Michael and the pigeon cooed its agreement.

My cock was still streaming when I came out of him. Some landed on the back of his thigh.

"I think you make more than Danny," he said in a husky voice as I wiped it away.

"I've been waiting longer," I said.

We cleaned up together in the bathroom. By midnight we were both in bed. Me with a beautiful, tapering, uncut teenage cock in my mouth like a baby with a comforter. Much later; some time in the early hours of the morning, Michael woke up to give me a mouthful of the tastiest drink in the world.

I must have been asleep when he got up. I only realized he wasn't there when the telephone rang. I put out my arm to reach over him and he wasn't there.

"Yes?" I answered, sleepily.

"Danny. You got the cream in your room? I left it on the bedside table."

"Eh? Oh yes. It's in my bag."

"What the hell's it doing in your bag? Can you bring it in?"

"What's the time?"

"Six o'clock."

"Sod you. Can't you come and get it?"

"No I bloody well can't. Stir yourself."

I put the phone down and, cursing, got out of bed. The cream tube lay on top of everything else so finding it was no problem. I was furious with Danny though. Wrapping a bath towel round my waist and making sure the door was on the latch, I nipped out of the room and tapped lightly on his door before pushing it open.

Michael was lying on his front on the bed. Danny met me with outstretched hand. His cock was in a similar condition. It was obviously not the time to start a row as to who owned what and the propriety of opening other people's luggage. I handed it over.

"Thanks," he said.

"Tell Tim to stay," said a muffled voice from the bed.

"He can if he wants," said Danny.

"The triangle," said Michael.

"What?" Danny asked, walking over to the bed.

"I'll explain later," I said. Danny's room was identical to mine in every respect. I moved a pile of his clothes from the basket-work chair and sat down. At that moment I was unmoved but watching Danny and listening to him very soon caused a tumescence to appear in my towelling sarong.

Danny obviously felt no guilt over the ownership of the cream but he did give due credit to Uncle Otto.

"Your uncle certainly knew a nice ass," he said. Michael splayed his legs farther apart. Danny put some of the cream on his finger.

"How old were you then?" he asked.

"Oh. Very young. Mmm. That feels me good!"

"Better than Uncle Otto?"

"Much better. Uncle Otto never...."

"This is going to feel even better," said Danny. He rubbed his sticky hand up and down the shaft of his cock, turned round to smile at me and then climbed onto the bed.

Once again, Michael gave a long, drawn-out sigh as Danny guided his cock slowly down into the boy until it was buried completely between the milk-white hemispheres of Michael's butt. The cream tube, I was annoyed to observe, had been dropped, still open, onto the floor. I got up with difficulty, retrieved it and the cap, re-sealed it and put it on the bedside table. By the time I was back in the chair, Danny was hard at it. Hard in it too. By watching his ass carefully I could pick out the movements of the muscles. They tightened and, whilst still tense, jerked. Then they loosened again and the cycle was repeated.

185

Michael groaned and kicked his legs. I hadn't realized what big feet he had until I saw them waving in the air. 'Big feet; big cock,' I thought. Of that I caught just an occasional glimpse when Michael lifted himself off the bed. Danny was holding it as I had done, massaging it slowly.

That time, they came together. There was no doubt of that. They both sighed simultaneously and sank down together, a tangle of legs and arms. A pungent smell of sweat and semen seemed to fill the room.

I left them at it and went back to bed. Predictably, they did not appear for breakfast. They came down for lunch looking the picture of innocence. You'd have thought they'd been out for a stroll.

Michael felt tired, which was hardly surprising, and went back to bed. Danny and I sat in my room waiting, I guess, for him to wake up again.

"Sorry about disturbing you so early in the morning," said Danny.

"Oh, that's okay."

"Why the hell didn't you put it in my bag?" he asked. "It was open."

I was astounded. "Because it's mine, that's why. I bought it."

"No, it's mine! I...." He started to laugh.

"I don't see what's so damn funny," I said. "You had a bloody cheek...."

He looked me in the eye. "Did you go out and buy a tube when you heard you were coming here?"

"Well, yes."

"And so did I," he said. "You remember when staff travel rang to say that I was going?"

"Yes. I was with Mr. Parsons."

"And I told you I'd better go to the dentist in the lunch break about my dodgy tooth in case it flared up here?"

"That's right. You did."

"I didn't go to the dentist at all. I went to that sex shop."

I couldn't help laughing. In fact we still laugh about it even now.

"You're a devious little bugger!" he said. "I thought it was odd when you said you didn't remember where Michael lived."

"And you just happened to have borrowed a book about Bavaria," I said. "Shit, you're as bad as I am!"

Danny laughed. "What was that about a triangle?" he asked. "Are you teaching him math as well as English?"

I explained. Danny said it was a profound thought, which I suppose it was.

"I don't know how you feel about it," he said, some minutes later, "but it might be an idea not to use the spare room any more."

"You mean the three of us...."

He nodded. "That's what Michael seems to be hinting at. I don't mind. What about you?"

I didn't know what to say. Watching him fucking Michael had been a terrific thrill and an incredible turn-on. Michael seemed to want both of us together. I just didn't know how I would react to the idea of Danny sitting and watching

186

me.

He didn't. That afternoon, I was the one sitting but I wasn't just watching. Michael supported himself on the arms of the chair. Danny pushed into him. I had my hand under his balls and his cock in my mouth. It was an amazing feeling. Every thrust from Danny drove Michael forward. His belly was pressed so close to my face that I could hardly breathe. By reaching farther between his legs I could reach Danny's balls. He liked that. All too soon, Michael gave his familiar sigh. His cock was too deep in my mouth for me to taste him. That was a bit unfortunate. Spurt after spurt ran down my gullet.

That night was even better. Michael's long legs were draped over my shoulders. I'd never had him in that position before. He felt quite different. Slightly slacker perhaps. I don't really know. He loved it though. He squirmed and wriggled as Danny kissed and licked his cock before taking it into his mouth. I came first but was still inside him when Danny got such a copious helping of cream that some of it trickled on to Michael's bush and his thighs.

On Sunday morning, we all stayed in bed. Michael lay between us, sometimes facing me and then turning over to face Danny. By the time we got up, as Danny observed, there was really no need for him to take a shower. He'd been licked clean. He did, though, and the three of us left by taxi to visit his parents.

Lunch at their house was a strain. For a start, not one of the family spoke any English. This meant that Michael had to translate. That might have worked had his English been better. An added embarrassment was that the conversation was mostly about him.

Neither of us knew he had a younger brother. Hans Peter was his name and he was fifteen. He sat there, unsmiling; the picture of the boy who'd been told "You will be at the table to meet the two Englishmen whether you like it or not." A pity really. He was a nice looking kid with the same slender build as his elder brother but with longer blond hair and (I just happened to note) long fingers too.

Herr Schweiger said something. "My father says he is very thankful that you fill my needs," said Michael and then, realizing what he'd said, he blushed and added "when I come to England to improve my English."

Danny didn't improve things by saying it had been a pleasure to have him.

Herr Schweiger said something else. "My father says before I come to you I am always a hard boy," said Michael. "Always things must be forced into me." He bit his lip but even he couldn't help laughing.

The rest of the Schweiger family looked on uncomprehendingly as all three of us laughed.

"Tell your parents that we always found you very willing," I said, "And you'd better say something about a private joke."

I think he told them something about work. I heard the name of the firm being mentioned. He went on for some time and then they all joined in the laughter.

"Hans Peter also wishes to go to England," he said. "At the moment he is too young."

"Is he a hard boy too?" asked Danny with a mischievous smile.

Michael thought for a moment. "Maybe he could be," he said. "I don't know."

"Well, tell him and your parents that when he is old enough we shall be very happy to fill his needs," I said. "We both like hard boys."

I think we were both too excited to sleep on the plane going home though we were both tired. We spent the entire journey reliving the weekend in conspiratorial whispers.

"With all the luck in the world," said Danny, leaning back in his seat, "our triangle could become a quadrilateral some time in the future."

"Both are nice figures," I replied.

COMING ON LINE
by Peter Gilbert

To quote the phrase Henry uses to describe the event, John Martin Bramwell came on line on the 20th of May 1978. He was still just a teen.

Henry is a scientist who works in the Research and Development laboratory of a huge pharmaceutical company. He's a very respected member of the little rural community in which we live. None of the people he drinks with know his secret. Henry is addicted to boys in their mid teenage years. Nothing wrong with that. So am I and so are Frank and the two Richards. The difference between us and Henry is that, in the days I'm writing about, we were thankful for anything that came our way. If you gave me a teenage cock, preferably uncut, to play with I'd be as happy as a lark. The same went for the others but whereas we were content to stay in the village and talk about it, Henry went looking for it.

He went off in his camper almost every weekend. It was a luxuriously appointed vehicle. We took to calling it the "passion wagon." It had everything a man with Henry's tastes might need: a huge double bed; a well-stocked drinks cabinet and a cupboard full of those little necessities that he hoped might be needed. More often than not, they stayed in the cupboard, for you will know probably better than I, of the thousands of boys out there, some can be persuaded to satisfy people like me. Few, very few, are prepared to 'go the whole way'. And, I have to say, Henry's figure can't have helped. Sitting for hours on end designing chemical plants had given him a pronounced paunch that wasn't helped by the amount of beer he downed to drown his disappointment on Sunday evenings.

We'd sit there amazed. "Any luck this weekend, Henry?" one of us would ask.

"Bloody awful weekend. Found this lad. Sixteen he was. Lovely build. Ass like a big, soft ball."

"Made use of it, did you?"

"Did I buggery! Licked round it once or twice. Then it was the usual story. "No! Not that!" All he wanted me to do was suck his cock!"

I leave you to imagine the effect of conversations like this on four guys who considered what he had done as the pinnacle of bliss. Our experience on most weekends was limited to a good look at a boy at the local pool and a wank afterwards.

Then he struck lucky. Graham was the name of the boy. Young man, really. He was eighteen. I've seen pictures of him and can confirm Henry's opinion. Graham was certainly no oil painting: He wore thick glasses and his front teeth protruded. He was, though, extremely well hung. The four of us drooled over that aspect of him.

He lived in Bournemouth. Henry had parked the camper in a field and was just about to set off into the town when he spotted the boy in a corner of the

field. He had a basket in one hand and kept bending down, picking something and putting it into the basket. The bending down bit attracted Henry's attention. He got the binoculars out of the cupboard and sat at the window to get a good look. Those binoculars of his are powerful. He could read the maker's label on the boy's jeans with ease but he couldn't see what he was doing. So, naturally enough, he left the camper and went over to find out.

"I saw you from my camper. What are you doin'?" In fact there was no need to ask the question. The basket was half full of mushrooms.

"Pickin' mushrooms. What's it look like?"

"Oh, yes. I hope you know which ones are edible and which ones aren't."

"Should do. Been doin' it for long enough."

They chatted away. Henry, of course, knew all about "mycological toxicity", his phrase, not mine. Nonetheless, he persuaded Graham to point out which fungi one could eat only once and which ones were really edible. Graham followed him into the camper. Henry made him a coffee and laced it with Scotch. They spread the mushrooms over the table and Graham continued the lecture.

"These are good," he said, picking one out. "Trouble is they're few and far between. Used to be a lot of 'em when the old oak trees was 'ere. Now they've gone and cut the trees down to make this camping area, you don't find so many of 'em."

Henry picked up a mushroom and smiled. "What does this remind you of?" he asked.

Graham grinned. "A cock," he said. "Not a bad'n either is it?"

"A very substantial one indeed," said Henry. The mushroom was enormous. "That'd give some girl a nice surprise if she were to sit on it."

"Or a bloke too," said Graham. "Can I have another coffee?"

"Sure." Henry stood up and took the empty cup over to the coffee machine.

"I wouldn't have thought there were many blokes round here who'd relish something like that in their backsides," he said as he poured a slug of whisky into the cup."

"You'd be surprised," said Graham mysteriously.

"Not you?" Henry asked.

"Happened a long time back. Curate down at All Souls he were. Nice bloke. He roped me in to be an altar server and before you could say 'Jack Robinson' he was in me ass.

"How old were you at the time?"

"Oh! Let's see." He held up his hand and looked at his fingers. "It was three years back. I must have been fifteen."

"If it was anything like the size of this mushroom, it must have hurt like hell," said Henry.

"At first. You sort of get used to it. To be honest I miss it a bit now. And he used to give me a quid a time."

"What would you say to someone who offers you five pounds a time?"

190

"Five quid! You, you mean?"

Henry nodded. "Well... sure," said Graham. "When?"

"No time like the present."

"I'd better get these home first. They get stale quick. I'll be back in an hour."

Henry could believe neither his luck nor the boy's promise but he stayed in the camper just in case. It was as well that he did. There was a tap on the door. Henry's heart was thumping. It beat even harder when he opened the door and Graham stepped in. He was in swimming trunks.

"Farver 'arris liked me to wear these," he said. "You can wear 'em under a cassock and nobody in church knows. Then in the vestry it's easier for 'im. He used to say my ass was like an exotic fruit. He was a great one for fancy talk was Farver 'arris."

"I should say Father Harris was quite a connoisseur," said Henry reaching out to feel the boy's ample buttocks. "Soft, juicy exotic fruit and just ripe...."

We, of course, got all this secondhand. I'd never seen Henry so happy. He was positively glowing.

"He was tight, but not too tight if you know what I mean," he said after downing his second beer. "Absolutely glorious. He stayed in the van overnight. I had him five times in all. Every position you can think of. There was only one problem."

"What was that?" Richard asked.

"He's so bloody slow to come. He wants to. You can tell that. I'm not particularly fast on the trigger myself but Graham's slower. I'd shoot my load, stay in him for a bit and then when I pulled out I had to suck him off. Every bloody time."

"Sounds like paradise to me," said Richard Dyson, who'd had a strange and exciting experience that afternoon that I shall come to in a minute.

Now it happens that one of Henry's drinking pals is a guy called Phil Morrison. Phil is not the most popular inhabitant of Hardwick Parva. I loathe the man. He's straight; aggressively straight if you know what I mean. According to Phil, homosexuality could be wiped out overnight if its practitioners were flogged. Unemployed youngsters are all work-shy and should be sent to work in coal mines. Hitler had quite a lot of good ideas. You know the type. What Henry saw in him I shall never know. A source of free drinks, I think. Phil is pretty well loaded and quite happy to buy drinks all night for anybody patient enough to listen to him.

Henry had been down to Bournemouth for three consecutive weekends when he went one evening to the 'George' for a drink. He'd had a busy day at work. Phil was propping up the bar as usual.

"Aha! Doctor Langford! The beloved physician. Welcome. What'll you have?" he said.

For the umpteenth time, Henry explained that his doctorate was in chemistry and had been awarded for his work on the hydrogenation of fatty oils.

"No matter. At least you work for your living. Bloody medical doctors these

days haven't got a clue. All perverts or reds. They get at them at university, you know. There was an article in the paper about it. This local bloke is totally useless."

"He's very well qualified," said Henry who happened to know the local doctor very well.

"Went down to see him because I've been feeling a bit run down and he told me to get more exercise," said Phil indignantly. "I pay a massive premium for private medical insurance to consult a man who doesn't know what to prescribe. Ought to be locked up. What do you take?"

"How do you mean?"

"Well, you're on something. You can't kid me. You're happier than you were. You look fitter and slimmer and didn't I see you on a push bike the other day?"

"Oh that! Yes. I got it out of the shed and I've started to use it again."

"So what's the wonder drug, old boy? You can tell me."

Henry took another sip of his beer. Some ran down his chin. He wiped it away with the back of his hand. The action brought back a very clear memory of Graham in the camper....

"It's an organic preparation," he said.

"You couldn't get some for me, could you? I don't care how much it costs."

"Mmm. I don't know." Henry's brain was working fast. At work he had access to the pilot freeze drying and encapsulating machines that were used for experimental products. If it was freeze dried and put into capsules, Phil would never know that he was taking a daily dose of spunk. The thought was hilarious.

"I'll see," he said. "Of course, it's still in the experimental stage."

"I don't mind that. By the time this bloody government gets round to validating it, I'll be in my box. They had the right idea in the old days. These apothecary chaps. When they discovered something it was on the market the next day. Business acumen. We've lost it now. All everyone wants to do is sit back and take it easy...."

Getting a container of liquid nitrogen and some collecting vials from work was no problem. Graham turned up and was duly fucked. He was a bit disappointed to find that he was expected to shoot his load into a tube every time but when Henry explained that it was for medical research and had absolutely nothing to do with hygiene or the taste, he did all that was required and Henry drove back with half a dozen samples. His pilot capsule-filling machine at work was cleaned and oiled and, after a little experimentation, worked like a dream. He managed to produce fifty capsules. They gleamed in the box like pearls.

Three weeks later, Phil telephoned. Henry had stopped going to the George in the evenings. He found cycling much more beneficial.

"Bloody marvelous, those capsules," said Phil. "Can you get some more?"

"I'll try. How many more?"

"Need enough for fourteen other people and a box for me of course."

"Fifteen! Well, I can't promise but I'll try my best."

In fact, of course, it was Graham who had to do the trying. By Saturday

evening, there were seven samples in the steaming flask and Graham was exhausted.

"It's no good," he said. "I'm right buggered," which was true. He had been. Six times. Even Henry couldn't raise the energy to fuck him before he produced the seventh.

"I need more," said Henry. "Quite a lot more. It's for a special research project. Maybe you'll feel better tomorrow."

"I will. No doubt of that but I can't do it more than seven times a day. I'll tell you what though...."

"What?"

"There's a lad I know. He'd fill a few tubes for you; only he's straight. He's short of the ready. If you was to give 'im something, I reckon he wouldn't mind wanking into a bottle."

Graham went out to fetch him the following morning. Peter was seventeen and stunningly beautiful. Henry explained what he wanted and told Peter it was in aid of medical research. He showed the boy how to release the gas pressure, open the hatch, drop the tube in and re-seal the container. Then Henry and Graham went into the town for the morning. When they returned, Peter had managed four ejaculations. Henry paid him. He left and, by that evening, Graham had provided another four. Fifteen samples proved to be just enough. He felt slightly guilty as Phil paid up especially when he heard that one box was going to Mrs. Goldsmith in the village. Mrs. Goldsmith was crippled with arthritis. However, Phil said he was paying so it didn't seem so bad.

Henry had never really thought about psychosomatic medicine. He knew about it of course but even he was surprised, a few weeks later, to see Mrs. Goldsmith walking along Horseshoe Lane. Phil said he was feeling younger and fitter. A young relation of his was doing better at school but, predictably, there were failures

It was at that stage that we heard something of what was going on. Never one to keep quiet, Phil collared us one evening. It was Sunday and we were waiting for Henry to return.

"Been helping Henry with his medical research," said Phil proudly. I said I wasn't aware of Henry's latest project. Phil said it was some sort of wonder drug.

"Been some failures of course," he said. "We expected that. I've listed all the results for him. Done it on the computer. Got the print-out here."

At that point Henry came in and we had to suffer a half an hour of Phil's pseudo-science and Henry's very real knowledge. We were dying to hear about Henry's weekend and the most amazing things had been happening in Richard's house. I will come to that eventually. Stay with me.

Phil realized that he wasn't really wanted and went back to the bar to trap some other poor soul. Henry sat looking at the print out.

"Well, how did it go?" I asked. He didn't answer.

"Didn't he turn up?" Frank asked.

"Eh? What? Oh yes."

"Well, let's have the details," I said. I needed something to wank over that night and a secondhand account of someone else's adventures was better than nothing. Mind you... that boy of Richard's....

"In a minute," said Henry. He took a calculator out of his pocket and tapped in some numbers. "Amazing!" he said. "Exactly eleven to four."

"Henry, what are you on about?" asked Richard and that's when he told us. The thought of Phil swallowing his daily dose of semen had us practically rolling on the floor with mirth. Henry, as ever, was far more serious. "The fact is," he explained, "that from these figures, Graham's spunk has got something that Peter's hasn't. What the hell can it be?"

We didn't see him for some two weeks. He was at work until late in the evening. He went down to Bournemouth again, collected more samples and analyzed them in every way known to science. He put them through gas chromatography, infra red spectrometry, microscopic examination, even something to do with radioactive isotopes but the mystery ingredient remained elusive. He continued to supply Phil. He even got us to take an occasional capsule. I think I must have had Peter's. It did nothing for me. On the other hand, as I said at the time, if he could produce the boy and let me take my medicine from the fountain so to speak.... Out of the question.

Which (finally) brings me to Richard Dyson. Richard is a technical translator and he works from home turning out Russian versions of scientific papers from (among others) Henry's firm. He lives in a semi-detached house in Horseshoe Lane. His neighbors, the Bramwells, are nice people and they have one son, John Martin Bramwell. When John Martin was a little boy he was the bane of Richard's life. His parents had erected one of those raised swimming pools in the back garden for him. It was only about three feet deep. Richard would go into the garden trying to formulate the Russian phrase for, say, 'peristaltic interference has been recorded as a minor side effect in some geriatric patients' and there would come this voice from the other side of the sparse hedge.

"Hello, Mr. Dyson. Do you want to play with me?"

"Hello, John Martin. What are you today?"

"I'm an otter and you've got to catch me."

"I don't think I really want an otter," but, nevertheless, Richard crossed over and spent an hour trying to grab an extremely active and very wet small boy.

The years went by. John Martin was twelve when his name was first mentioned in the 'George'. "That kid is growing up to be a real beauty," said Richard. "If he's not very careful, one of these days his games are going to tempt me to do something I shall regret."

We didn't know until months later about the incident that happened when John Martin was sixteen. I do recall a Sunday evening when Richard was quieter than usual. I think it must have happened that afternoon.

Richard was cutting the hedge. John Martin was lying on the lawn next door sunbathing in a tiny little slip. "It just about covered but only just, if you know

194

what I mean," Richard said.

Richard asked where his parents had gone. He'd heard them drive off early that morning. John Martin said they had gone to see a relation of his father's.

"Why didn't you go too," asked Richard, continuing to snip away.

"I wish I had now. It's really boring being on my own."

"There must be something you could do. A game or something?"

"I hoped you'd say that. What shall we play?"

"Well, actually, I...."

"We were learning about pig farming the other day at school. Did you know that hardly any of a pig is wasted?"

"No I didn't."

"That's why being a pig farmer is such good business. I know, you can be a pig farmer and I'll be the pig."

"Don't you think you're a bit too old for animal games?"

"Course not. You were much older than me when we played otter catching."

"I hardly ever managed to catch you."

"Catching a pig is easier. They're not so fast. Come on. Can you get through?"

"Just," said Richard, laying down the shears and pushing through a gap. "Now then, o pig. Time you were caught!"

There was something about the way the boy grinned; something about the way he dodged from side to side that told Richard that this was not a case of arrested development. John Martin was deliberately teasing him and egging him on but why? Did he suspect that Richard might be gay? If he did, what was the motive?

It was easy enough to corner the boy and grab him. A bit too easy. "Got you!" he gasped as he gripped John Martin's muscular upper arm.

"And now what?" said John Martin with another mischievous, tempting grin.

Now, the ultimate temptation as far as Richard Dyson is concerned is a boy of sixteen. If you ply him with enough drink to loosen his tongue he'll go on for ages about their slim hips; their long legs; the hardness of their bellies and the softness of their buttocks. Being a very professional man living in a small rural community, he contented himself with photographs and the books he bought on his trips abroad. Small wonder that actually holding one caused his self-control to slip. He knew that he ought to bring the game to an end and return to his hedge cutting. He didn't.

"I guess I shall have to find out if you're ready for the table," he said.

John Martin grinned again "Or the...." he said.

"Or the what?"

"Nothing. I forgot. Pigs can't talk."

"Just as well. Endless conversations about acorns must be very boring. Now then. Mmm. You look all right."

"You can't tell by looking," said John Martin.

"So how do I know?" Richard asked. His voice sounded breathless.

"Well, I suppose you'll have to feel me all over."

"Like this?" Richard ran his hand over the boy's chest.

"Yes."

"And this?"

"Well yes. You can buy belly of pork. I've seen it in the butcher's."

"Leg of pork too," said Richard. "I'd say this pig had very nice legs. They didn't have any hair on them the last time I touched them."

"It's grown in the last year. Hadn't you better feel for the ham?"

"If the pig doesn't mind. Oh yes! Very nice. Very nice indeed! Soft and fleshy. Good enough to eat one might say...."

John Martin wrenched his arm out of Richard's grasp and ran. For a moment Richard was dumbfounded. It seemed he'd been wrong. Then he realized that, instead of running into the safety of his own home, the back door of which was open, he'd run through a gap in the hedge and was standing in Richard's garden.

"What are you doing in there?" Richard called.

"What do you expect a pig to do when you tell him you're going to eat him?"

Richard scrambled through the hedge. John Martin opened the door of the house and ran inside. By the time Richard was in the kitchen he was nowhere to be seen.

"Where are you?" he called.

"That's for the farmer to find out," came a voice from upstairs.

John Martin had only been in the house about twice and never upstairs. Richard climbed the stairs, stopping on the landing to take a deep breath and make some sort of adjustment to the front of his trousers. "Talk about playing with fire!" he muttered and then climbed the remaining stairs.

He expected to find John Martin in the bathroom but he wasn't there. Neither was he in the study. That left the box-room in which there was hardly a square inch in which to stand or the bedroom. He opened the door. John Martin was stretched out on his bed.

"I must close the sty-door this time," said Richard. He shut the door.

"And the curtains," said John Martin.

"Pigsties don't have curtains."

"Someone might see."

"Depends what there is to see. Anyway, the people over the road are away."

"Close them all the same," said John Martin. Richard did so. The sunlight was strong enough to light the room.

"Now then," said Richard, sitting on the edge of the bed. "Where was I when the pig escaped?"

"Feeling my backside."

"Ah yes. The hams. They certainly pass muster. I think I'll just have another feel."

John Martin turned over onto his front and buried his face in the pillow. Richard placed a hand on his behind. John Martin mumbled something.

"Pardon."

John Martin raised his head. "You can take the shorts off if you like," he said

and slumped down into the pillow again.

I wasn't there of course. I can only tell you what Richard told us.

"I hadn't realized what I'd been missing," he said. "Books and photos are all very well but the real thing! It was absolutely beautiful! So white and soft! And those lovely long legs! God, he was a feast for the eyes!"

Only, apparently, for the eyes and hands - at least at first.

The 'pig' obligingly opened his legs for the 'farmer' to get a good look at his 'stuffing hole'. Richard tickled it. John Martin grunted and wriggled slightly. Richard tickled it again, delighting in the cool feel of the boy's cheeks against the back of his hand. John Martin wriggled again and opened his legs even wider. Richard was able to run a finger from the boy's spine right down into his cleft. John Martin lifted his head again.

"That's nice," he said. "Tickle it some more." Richard did so. The wriggling became frantic squirming. John Martin lifted his head from the pillow.

"Do you like sausages?" he said.

For a moment, Richard was baffled. "Yes. Do you?" he said.

"Do you want to feel the pig's sausage?"

Richard stopped tickling. "Is it hard?" he asked. "I only like sausages when they're hard."

"Very hard. It'll burst soon and the juice will come out."

"Then I think I'd better look at it."

"Take your hand away then." John Martin turned over "There!" he said.

Six and a half inches of rigid flesh rose from a bed of brown, bristly hair. The foreskin had retracted slightly. A bead of moisture oozed from the slit and ran down the vein-covered shaft.

"Now that really is a good sausage," said Richard.

"Feel it. Rub it up and down. That's right. Oh! That's great. Don't stop."

Richard had no intention of stopping. He couldn't have stopped if he'd wanted to. He remembers wondering if the boy in one of his books was really sixteen. His balls were much smaller than John Martin's. John Martin's balls jiggled up and down in time with his hand.

"Oh that's really good. Much better than when I do it!" he gasped. Richard's wrist began to ache. John Martin heaved himself upwards, moaned, and sank back again. For a moment Richard thought he'd had an orgasm and stopped.

"Don't stop. Don't stop. Keep on!" John Martin gasped. Richard changed hands.

"Ah! Ah! It's coming. There!"

A little arc of semen shot about six inches into the air and splattered down on the boy's groin and belly. Another lot ran out over Richard's fingers.

"That was good!" said John Martin. "Did you like doing it to me?"

"Yes I did. You don't feel bad about it?"

"No. You're a really nice man. I like you a lot."

"And I like you."

"I shot. Did you notice?"

"I couldn't help noticing."

"I've never actually shot before. It usually just runs out. I suppose it's the way you do it. It's much better with you than it is when I do it."

"That's nice of you."

"Can we do it every weekend?"

"Sure. Now, there's another thing about pigs."

"What's that?"

"They need regular feeding. How about getting dressed and we can go into town."

"The new burger place?"

"Why not?"

"Great! This pig could do with a burger."

Now I emphasize that none of us not one had the slightest idea of what was going on. We all gathered in the 'George' on Sunday evenings and when it was Richard's turn to relate the events of his weekend he invariably said that he'd been stuck on a translation for the entire weekend. I remember that I caught him out once.

"Not the whole weekend," I said. "I happened to walk past 'Big-Burgers' this afternoon and the boy you were with was rather attractive. I quite fancy blonds myself. Come on. Admit it."

"Oh him!" said Richard, laughing. "That's John Martin Bramwell, my neighbors' son. The parents went away and I had to look after him. You can cross him off your list of possibles. I suffered the saga of his girlfriends for two solid hours."

There were some Sunday afternoons when I walked past the house with the neatly kept garden in Horseshoe Lane and noticed that the curtains in the front bedroom were drawn. I just assumed that Richard kept them that way or was having an afternoon doze after working on his translations. In fact, as we learned much later, it was all happening behind those curtains. Sometimes John Martin was the pig. Sometimes it was Richard. John Martin called him 'a hairy old boar' but found the process of bringing the boar to a heaving orgasm fascinating.

Then, as the months went by, John Martin became a dairy cow and delivered cream straight into the farmer's hungry mouth. We, of course, had no idea of what was going on. In retrospect that amazes me. There was the Sunday afternoon when I decided to cut back the old apple tree in my garden. Richard has practically every garden tool imaginable so I called him.

"Sorry to disturb you. Were you working?" I asked.

"Yes. What is it?" he sounded strangely breathless.

"You know those things you cut branches off trees with?"

"Secateurs."

"That's right. I want to prune my apple tree. Can I borrow yours."

"When do you want them?"

"Well, now really. It's a nice afternoon and I've got nothing else to do as usual. I can pop round for them."

198

"No. No. Now isn't a good time. I lent them to somebody. I'll tell you what. I'll collect them from him and give them to you in the 'George' tonight."

"Give me the name and address and I'll nip round and get them myself," I said. "I really want to do this job today."

"No, I can't really do that. Anyway, I think he's using them all the weekend. I'll give them to you tonight. Now I really have to get back to work. I've still got a fair bit to do."

The 'fair bit', as Richard admitted much later, was lying on the bed, fondling his saliva-soaked cock to keep it hard until John Martin returned.

And then there was the Sunday evening when we were all sitting round our usual table in the corner waiting, as usual, for Henry to join us.

"How old should a boy be before you actually fuck him?" Richard asked. He was the picture of innocence I thought.

Frank said it all depended upon the boy. The other Richard agreed. I chipped in, relating an experience I'd had years before with a very young lad in Tunis. "I don't feel a bit guilty about it," I said. "He was willing enough."

"That's what I wanted to know," said Richard. "How do you know when a boy's ready for it?"

"How old is the boy in question?" the other Richard asked.

"Oh, I'm not thinking of anyone in particular. It was just a hypothetical question."

We believed him. The other Richard, Frank and I discussed our dream boys and what we'd do with them until we were practically slobbering into our beer.

"A nice slim ass. Not too rounded. I like them a bit flat myself," said the other Richard. "You can get deeper into them and they're beautifully tight."

"Oh no. The rounder the better. A bit of fat on them. Feel it slapping against you. That's a great sensation," said Frank.

"That's where the younger ones score," I said. "Now this boy in Tunis...."

"You're not answering my question," said Richard. "How old does the boy have to be?"

The general opinion was that if a boy would take a lubricated finger or preferably two, he was ready for a cock. It was a form of release for four men who hadn't had as much as a finger tip on, let alone in, a boy for months or so I thought. We didn't know until much later about the conversation that had taken place behind those closed curtains in Horseshoe Lane a few hours earlier.

"Mmm. Your hands are cold."

"They'll soon warm up. Open your legs a bit more if you can. You're not a pig or a cow now."

"What am I then?

Richard slid his hand over the boy's buttocks. "An oyster I think. Yes. A tightly closed oyster; but slowly, ever so slowly, you'll open up. It just takes a little bit of pressure to open an oyster."

"Oysters are supposed to make men randy, aren't they?"

"I believe so." Richard had never eaten an oyster but this particular one was

pretty effective.

John Martin put out a hand and groped for Richard's cock. "I wouldn't have thought you needed any oysters," he said. "This is stiff enough for anything."

"Like what?"

"Anything the farmer wants to do."

"Anything?"

"If you want. Tell me about oysters."

"Oysters. Well, oysters are juicy and succulent inside but you have to part the shells to get at them. Like this." He parted John Martin's buttocks and lowered his head.

"Now what?" said John Martin.

"Then you put your tongue in between the muscles."

"That doesn't sound very nice."

"It is though. Oysters love it."

So did John Martin. He spread his legs as wide apart as possible. "I wish you had shaved first," he said and those were the last coherent words he spoke for some time. Richard's probing tongue transformed him. In the past the 'pig' or the 'cow' had never lost its facility for making the odd cheeky quip or suggesting something new the farmer might care to try. Now he just grunted. His soft flesh pressed hard against Richard's face. He pushed upwards. The tightly knotted orifice was on the tip of Richard's tongue and the boy's musty odor swamped his nostrils. John Martin raised his rump, pushing Richard backwards. Then, supported on his knees, he reached round and pulled his ass cheeks even farther apart. Richard pushed harder with his tongue. He felt it begin to open slightly. He put his right hand round the boy's waist and seized John Martin's throbbing penis. That, as he admitted much later, was a mistake. John Martin came. He came with such force that it spattered over the bed-head and the wall.

He sank down and straightened his legs. It was all over. Literally all over. A split second later Richard's aching glands could hold their load no more and John Martin's back, bottom and legs were spattered with pearly drops.

They lay on the bed for some minutes. John Martin was still panting. Then, when his breathing had subsided and Richard had wiped most of the spunk from his prostrate form, he spoke.

"That was the best," he said.

"Do you think so?"

"I've never come so much. Sorry about the mess."

"No matter. It'll come off."

There was a long pause. "It felt really nice," said John Martin.

"Glad you enjoyed it. I certainly did."

"I'll bet something else would feel even nicer." John Martin turned over and stared at the ceiling.

"What for instance?"

"This," said John Martin, and he caressed Richard's flaccid cock.

200

Now, at this point, I can bring these two narratives together. Thank you for your patience. We still didn't know where the fingers wrapped round Richard's beer glass had been a few hours previously.

At that time, Henry was going frantic trying to get enough samples to keep Phil and his friends satisfied. The word had got round fast. It wasn't fair on Graham, said Henry, besides, it was affecting his sex life but money was money and if people were stupid enough to part with such large sums....

"How much do you sell them for?" Richard asked. When Henry told us the figure I nearly dropped my glass.

"Well, what about us?" said Frank. "I'll gladly wank into a jar for a fiver a time."

"No good," said Henry. "I put some of mine in the last batch. It was useless." It was the first time I'd seen him blush. "It's got to be a youngster," he added, "and, it seems, a special kind of youngster."

"I know a boy who might help," said Richard.

"Do you? Who?" I asked.

"My neighbors' son. The boy I have to look after at weekends. You saw me with him once in the burger bar."

"Oh yes. I remember. The blond boy."

"Do you think you could persuade him?" Henry asked. "Tell him it's for medical research."

"I think so."

It was arranged that Henry would deliver a nitrogen flask to Horseshoe Lane in time for the coming weekend. To help him in his quest for the mystery ingredient, he asked Richard to write the exact time the sample was taken on each tube before putting it in the flask. "It could be something to do with the time of day. Body clocks and all that," he said.

Richard brought the flask to the pub on the following Sunday evening. Phil was there, which was a bit unfortunate.

"What've you got there? An atom bomb?" he asked. Richard explained that it was something to do with Henry. The publican wasn't too happy. I don't blame him.

Henry duly arrived. Graham had done his stuff again and there was another, similar flask in the passion wagon.

"John Martin did four tubes," said Richard. "I've got them here and I've written the times on the tubes as you asked and on this paper."

Henry took the paper. "One eighteen p.m. Two twenty four p.m. Five eleven p.m. and six fifty-five p.m." he read. "Why the three-hour gap?"

"He had to do his homework," said Richard.

Two months elapsed. Life went on as normal. Henry spent most weekends in Bournemouth. The other Richard had found a flooded quarry somewhere in Dorset where boys swam naked, so he went there with his binoculars. Frank was hanging around a boy in the next village for whom he had high hopes. I spent most of my weekends chatting up the two farm lads over the road and dreaming

of impossible adventures with them. Richard said he had done nothing and gone nowhere. That's what he said.

The story was blown at the end of July. Henry had the print- outs in front of him.

"I can get to the bottom of most things," he said, "but not this."

John Martin's samples had been most carefully tested on a range of people of all ages. Two of them had no effect. The other two; the later samples, had worked.

"There's no doubt about it," said Henry. "These days I record every tiny thing. It isn't psychosomatic as I thought at first. There really is a mystery ingredient. Graham has it. Peter hasn't. I accept that but I don't accept that the same boy, on the same day, can produce two duff tubes and two potent ones. I really do need to know the truth."

And so, blushing furiously, Richard told him.

"It's much better when you suck it," John Martin had said.

"I can't do that. My friend explained. The saliva might get into it. I have to do it with my hand."

"Oh, okay then. Do it slow. That's right. Mmm. That's nice."

"And so are you. How old were you when I first saw you in your pool?"

"About ten. Why?"

"These weren't so big then."

"You never saw them. I had shorts on."

"I know but they can't have been so big as this. They're lovely and they're making lots of delicious spunk for me."

"For your friend you mean. Go a bit faster but keep on tickling them. I like that. That's right. Oh! Ah! Better get the tube ready. Oh! Ah! Any min.... Now!"

"Well done!" said Richard as it spurted into the tube. "That's a lot." He looked at his watch, wrote the time on the tube and put it into the flask.

"Now what?" said John Martin, wiping his sagging member.

"How about going out for a meal?"

"Burgers?" said John Martin eagerly.

"We'll go there tonight. How about trying that new place in Hardwick Magna? The steak place. I've heard it's very good and it's not too far.

"Okay then. I'll get dressed."

The amazing thing about John Martin, Richard thought as he watched the boy eating, was that he was every bit as attractive when clothed as he was naked. Every inch had been in his hands or his mouth but John Martin's jeans were tantalizingly tight. The 'V' shape of his open collar framed his face to perfection. Richard wondered what lucky star he'd been born under to find such a perfect boy. Like all of us, he'd seen Henry's photographs of buck toothed Graham and hadn't been greatly impressed. Graham was well endowed but who in his right mind would prefer Graham's massive nine inches to John Martin's smaller but aesthetically more pleasing penis? He had nothing to envy Henry for save, of course, that Henry fucked Graham.

202

"If he'll take a finger, he'll take a cock."

"Be a bit liberal with the lubrication. Specially the first time. The stuff I use...."

"Your lunch is getting cold," said John Martin.

"Oh, so sorry. I was lost in thought."

"What about?"

"Nothing much. We ought to be getting back. I'd like to get another sample."

"Again?"

"My friend wants as much as possible."

"Oh well, I suppose so. Why don't you give some of yours? I could do it for you if you know what I mean. I like doing it to you."

"No, that's all right. It's got to be someone younger."

- - -

"Are you horny again?" asked Richard when they were back at the house.

"Silly question," said John Martin. "Feel this."

It lifted eagerly to Richard's touch, straining to be released. "I think we ought to go upstairs, don't you?" said John Martin.

"This seems to be pointing in that direction," said Richard. "After you."

Getting that second sample was, Richard said, the most difficult thing he had ever done.

"Don't get me wrong," he said. "John Martin was as good a gold and as randy as a rabbit. *I* was the problem."

He had hardly been able to contain himself as he followed the boy's denim-clad butt up the stairs. Knowing what might happen to him at any moment, he left John Martin to undress himself and Richard did likewise.

"He likes me to be naked, too," he explained. His face flushed as he continued. "Actually, I was close to coming myself and I'd rather spatter it over him than my clothes."

Apparently that had happened one or two times in the past. If only we'd known!

He asked John Martin to do it himself but John Martin wasn't having any of that. "It's better when you do it," he said.

So, poor old Richard, horny as hell, had to wank the boy, trying desperately to concentrate on anything other than the stiff shaft in his hand. The nitrogen container was ready on the bed. He read the instructions on that twice and he noticed that one of the curtains needed sewing up. He made a resolution to have the bedroom re-decorated before the winter. All the time his hand was moving up and down, and John Martin gasped instructions.

"Bit slower. You're going too quickly. That's better. Tickle my balls a bit like you usually do. Ah, that's good. Oh yeah! That's really nice. Get the tube ready! Not long now... Ah! Ah! Aaaah!" And then it shot out of him, filling the little tube to the brim. Some even spilled over the sides.

He noted the date and time and popped it into the container. Then he licked his fingers dry.

"You're pretty close," said John Martin, putting his finger on Richard's cock head.

"Very close," Richard admitted. "Leave it alone for a bit."

"That's not very fair. I have to shoot when you want. Why can't you when I want?"

"It'll be better in a minute. Let's have a rest first, eh?"

They lay there for a long time. Richard made sure their bodies didn't touch. They talked about football and school. John Martin wanted to hear what Russian sounded like so Richard recited a long passage from Gorki he'd learned at university. When he had finished that, John Martin appeared to be asleep. Richard didn't disturb him but lay there thinking. Should he?

"The rounder the better.... A bit of fat on them. Feel it slapping against you...."

John Martin's behind wasn't exactly round, he thought. It was beautifully curved but more elliptical than round.... Oval, like an egg and, coincidentally, the whiteness of his buttocks and the brown of his thighs both reminded him of eggs...

"You ready to come yet?" John Martin asked. His eyes were still closed.

"I thought you were asleep."

"No. I leave the sleeping to old men like you. You snored just now."

"Did I? I didn't think I'd dropped off."

"You often do it. Old men do and let's face it, you are rather ancient."

"Thirty-three isn't old."

"It is to me. Really old. Let's see. You must have been born in 1945. That was the year the war ended. You're a historical relic!"

"Rude boy. I shall have to seriously think about smacking your bottom."

"You and who else? You don't want to exert yourself at your age."

"That deserves another smack."

"Not a terrifying prospect. A boy at school says that all gays are limp-wristed."

"Does he indeed? We'll see about that."

He turned John Martin over. That was easy. Too easy. Much too easy.

He delivered two playful slaps on the soft flesh of the boy's buttocks. John Martin lay still for a few moments and then spoke.

"What?" Richard asked.

"I said you can do it if you want."

"Do what?"

"You know."

"And did you?" Frank asked. All four of us craned forward over the table to get every word. The other people in the bar must have wondered if we were terrorists planning an attack. Richard didn't want to say any more but Henry, I am glad to say, insisted.

"I was a bit disorganized," said Richard, blushing. "I had to go to the

bathroom you see and, well, to be honest with you, I'd never done it before."

He explained. There was a tube of lubricant in the medicine cabinet in his bathroom. He's bought it way back in the sixties when a friend persuaded him to go to Naples with him, promising Richard any number of olive-skinned teenaged boys. But then Richard went on an advanced language course in Russia and had a brush with the police there because he'd met a delightful boy named Ivan and taken him out for a couple of meals. The experience shook him up so much that he canceled the Naples holiday.

He left John Martin, rummaged through the medicine cabinet, found the tube and returned to the bedroom. The tube, of course, had never been opened and he had to find something to pierce the inner seal. His fingers were shaking so much that he could hardly manage to do that.

"You are sure?" he asked.

"Course I'm sure. Aren't you ready yet? The sausage will go off if you don't get a move on." John Martin's voice was muffled by the pillow.

"And then?" said Frank.

"I told him to spread his legs a bit. Are you sure you need to hear all these details?"

Richard and I said "Yes" in unison. Henry explained that he really needed to know everything. Frank's name describes him perfectly. Frank will come out with things that other people feel guilty about even thinking.

"Describe his ass for me," he said, licking beer foam from his lips. "He's got long legs. You told us that and they're hairy. Go on from there."

Bashfully, Richard tried to do so. It was only the lower part of John Martin's legs that was particularly hirsute. There were a few fine golden hairs on his thighs. His behind, round and soft-looking, was milky white and smooth. Parting the cheeks with his left hand, Richard tried to insert the tube. John Martin winced. Richard pushed the tube farther in. John Martin tensed his buttocks, squeezing, them and a large amount of the grease went everywhere save the place it was supposed to be.

"So I gave that up and put some on my finger," said Richard. "I should have known."

Poor Richard! He'd never so much as seen a sixteen-year-old boy's asshole before, still less experienced its tightness. The situation wasn't helped by three quarters of a tube of sticky lubricant that was seeping down onto the boy's balls and into the small of his back.

"I had to use my handkerchief to wipe it away," he said. Only then did he get his first look.

"Tell us," said Frank. I was beginning to think Frank might shame us all by coming in his pants.

It was the smallness that first struck Richard. A tiny little puckered spot. "Like an insect bite. Same color too," was how he described it.

Wondering how anything as big as a human penis could ever manage to enter it, Richard tried gently to insert his finger. He couldn't. John Martin yelled out

loud at one point and he stopped.

"Try again," said John Martin, after a few seconds, "but do it gently this time."

Fascinated by its neatness and symmetry, Richard ran his finger up and down over it. "That's much better," said John Martin. Richard tickled it gently with the tip of his finger. "Oh yes! That feels good!" John Martin gasped.

Somehow, he couldn't explain exactly, Richard became aware of a relaxation.

"Lovely feeling, that is," Frank interrupted. "Feeling a boy's ass cheeks slacken and his little entrance to paradise opening slowly. God! I envy you."

Richard ignored him and continued. John Martin had begun to breathe more heavily and he stopped talking, which, for John Martin, was unusual. He didn't even answer when Richard asked if should try to get his finger in again. Taking this as silent assent, Richard pressed against it firmly and, suddenly, the tip of his finger slid into the boy.

The pressure on his finger was uncomfortably tight. Richard thought he might ease it by rotating his finger slightly. "A bit selfish of me when I look back on it," he said. To his surprise, John Martin groaned slightly. "Do that again," he breathed and so Richard did. The last visible remnants of grease vanished as he did so and, as if his finger was some kind of screw, it went in farther and, this time, John Martin didn't yell. He gave a low moan; shifted position slightly and lay still again.

Richard waggled the finger from side to side in the boy's warm, damp channel and, to his surprise, John Martin began to wriggle. It was as if he was trying to coax more into him.

"He was," said Frank. "They all do that sooner or later. That's the time to go for it."

Richard didn't need to be told. He pulled out his finger, wiped it on his already-greasy handkerchief and got up into position. John Martin's head lay on its side on the pillow. His mouth was open and his tongue was hanging out; quite different from the talkative teenager with a ready wit he was used to.

Gently, he lowered himself down. The tip of his cock brushed against John Martin's soft behind, found the cleft as if it knew where it was going and pushed down between the smooth buns. John Martin tensed up slightly. Richard murmured something about not wanting to hurt him and continued to lower himself.

"I couldn't find it at first. Lack of experience I guess," he said. But then he did and saw John Martin's face grimace in anticipation.

"And after that it was easy?" Frank asked.

It hadn't been that easy. John Martin yelled; a long drawn out yell as Richard's cock head pushed through the opening and slid into him. He went in as slowly as he could. Then came a time when he was almost all the way when he felt some sort of obstruction. At first he thought it was shit but John Martin's reaction banished that idea.

"He seemed to go crazy for a second or two," said Richard. "He was writhing

206

and squirming. He kicked out with his legs and moaned. I thought I was hurting him so I stopped. He put his hands behind me and tried to push me in farther."

"Aha!" said Henry, who, like us all, had been listening intently. "Then what?"

"After that it was great. I held on to his shoulders. His hands were on my backside and I fucked him. God! What a wonderful feeling that was. It's a funny thing but I remember making a resolution as I came that I wouldn't do it any more. It might be a bit like visiting some place you're fond of. The second visit is always a disappointment."

"Absolute balls!" said Frank. "Keep him going while you can. It'll take him a good six months to get to his peak performance. They have to be trained for it in the same way they train for everything else. It takes ages to take them to come at the right time for instance."

Without knowing it, Frank had voiced Richard's chief worry. His cock was limp and wet when he pulled it out but John Martin was still squirming against the bedding. Suddenly remembering Henry's vial he managed to turn the boy over and brought him to a climax by hand.

"And that's sample number three, is it?" said Henry. "Five eleven p.m.?"

"That's right. And the last one was just an ordinary wank. I think he wouldn't have minded but, like I said...."

"I think you've solved the problem," said Henry.

"How?"

"Look, let's have another drink first."

Our glasses were empty but nobody wanted to go up to the bar. I couldn't have gone. My cock was rigid. I guess the others were in the same state.

"Deceitful bastard," said Frank. "I don't blame you though."

"All those weeks of 'Nothing much happened,'" said the other Richard. I could have come round and taken some photographs."

"No way," said Richard.

"And that day I wanted the secateurs. Were you...?" I asked. He nodded.

Henry went to the bar. Richard's account seemed to have done little to him. Mark of the true scientist I guess. He returned, put the full glasses on the table and then sat down again.

"Stimulation of the prostate," he said. "I'm no physician, despite what Phil Morrison calls me. Not everything is known about the jolly little prostate gland. It secretes a constituent of semen. We know that much. I suspect that, after being massaged, it secretes something else; our mystery ingredient. The wonder healer."

He drew a crude diagram on a beer mat. "That's what I must have felt!" said Richard. "That's when he went into those odd jerks."

"Precisely," said Henry. "You've put your finger on it as they say. Your cock too. Graham has been fucked. His spunk is potent. Peter hasn't. His doesn't work. John Martin hadn't and produced ordinary semen but afterwards; with a little help from Richard...."

"Not so little," said Richard with a laugh. "It was amazing how it went in

though."

"And I want it to go in again," said Henry. "When are you next seeing him?"

"He said he'd come round tomorrow after school but I don't think...."

"Do it in the interests of science," said Henry. "I'll deliver a flask in the morning."

"Do it for his sake," said Frank. "Keep the pot boiling."

"Don't waste a golden opportunity," the other Richard advised.

I don't think I said anything. I was too jealous to speak.

Richard took their advice. John Martin was fucked every evening of the following week and several times during the ensuing weekend. Henry didn't go to Bournemouth. It was just as well that the people in the opposite house were away. They might have wondered what Henry was doing, picking up a flask from the doorstep, substituting it for another and driving off again. And he was right. That spunk worked wonders. Mrs. Goldsmith now walks for miles. Phil's idle relation went to university and got a first class degree and several people wrote letters of appreciation.

We've come a long way from those early times. Langford and Partners made a substantial profit last year. Phil Morrison is an excellent sales manager and although the chemical formula is on the side of every packet he still doesn't know the source. John Martin is grown up now and has three sons of his own all of whom have been promised. It's amazing what a powerful stimulus scientific success can be. Frank succeeded with the boy from Newton-Peverell. He came on line within weeks of John Martin. Unknowingly, my two farm boys confirmed Henry's theory. Jim would only let me suck him, which was pleasant enough, but he provided as many samples in tubes as we needed. Paul, the other one, proved to be much more cooperative. The other Richard has had quite a lot of success too and of course, one boy tells another boy and the word gets round effectively but very discreetly. We are able to pay them well now and that helps. Some weekends the phone rings continually. Henry had a grandiose vision of a special factory and bus loads of boys arriving every weekend. We soon put that notion to rest, especially when he said he was designing a machine to massage their prostates more effectively. We set him to work on another project: designing a nitrogen flask that didn't look like a nuclear bomb.

It's much better the way we are. You'll find us every Sunday evening in the George. Just look for five men sitting round a table littered with beer glasses and cryogenic flasks and all with satisfied looks on their faces. And now you must excuse me; Trevor is upstairs waiting to come on line.

SOMETHING WONDERFUL
by Rudy Roberts

The day hadn't started off well. Not only had I overslept, but I'd also left the window open in my study all night and the rain had blown in and soaked a batch of test papers. I spent the next hour struggling with the blow-dryer, trying to mend the damage. But some were irreparable; the ink had run into bruised blurs across the page. Fortunately, though, I'd already marked and recorded them. Now all I had to do was explain it to my students. And then Billy, my cat, had managed to sneak a mouse in, plunking it neatly with its head half-chewed off, at my bedside. And, as I always did, I stepped right onto it, making the poor dead thing's eyes bug out. And if that still weren't enough, a light bulb above the bathroom sink blew suddenly while I was shaving, startling me, causing me to slice my chin open.

And so, with a shred of blood-spotted toilet paper stuck to my face, I proceeded to get ready for work. Of course, spending an hour drying essays put me dangerously close to being late for my first class. So, I skipped breakfast except for a strong cup of coffee and raced through my habitual routine. Clean-shaven, yet somewhat disheveled, I roared off down the street towards school.

Up the hills I plodded. My car was temperamental at the best of times but was particularly cantankerous on cold, blustery days. Just when we got used to the cold weather and the snow of early November, we got hit by a mild spell that sparked rain albeit icy sending damp shivers through to the very bone.

I spotted several of my students as I chugged along. I didn't dare stop for fear of being unable to get going again. There, defiantly bare-headed to the weather, was Ian McCallum the consummate jock. I'd seen him several times at track practice and around the pool. I don't ever recall boys being built like that when I was his age. And there was Andrew Carrigan, a soft-spoken yet articulate scientist with azure eyes and chestnut hair. And a butt like Baryshnikov's. And, of course, always with an arm around some girl or other, was Steve Hislop big, built, brazen and bullish. Not very bright, sure, but packing something powerful in his pants. With a quick readjustment and a squeeze, I pushed my own pecker back down.

"Not now," I told it, bringing my focus back to the leaf-strewn streets. The wipers beat out a perfunctory rhythm as I sputtered along.

I knew the dangers involved in showing special interest in a student. Not only could I lose my job which should have been the least of my worries but I could also be arrested. Just two years before, in fact, Milton Inverness had been arrested during the middle of one of his music classes dragged out right in front of all the students amidst loud protestations and jeering. Milton had been less discreet than most not only eyeing every girl with anything larger than a B cup but also slipping his hands against the occasional buttock or thigh. What brought

the hammer down for Milton, though, was the testimony of three students who had watched in disbelieving horror from the hallway as he openly fondled the breast of one of his students. He has another year left to his sentence but should get out in a few months on good behavior.

Milton brought us all into line, though. The ones on staff who blatantly looked, who made comments and jokes about some of the young stuff that strutted through our halls, thought twice after Uncle Milty, as we called him from that day forth, got pulled from class. For the rest of us, though, it was still a shock. We had to think twice about everything. Even placing a friendly hand upon a student's shoulder in sheer congratulations or encouragement could be misconstrued as sexual misconduct. I certainly didn't want that rumor to get around. I think only one other teacher knows about my particular proclivities and that's Elaine, the girls' gym teacher. And she's got her eye on Belinda Smythe these days the head cheerleader. Belinda's got knockers that could smother a person. So, I don't think Elaine's about to blow my cover for anything. But we were on guard nevertheless.

Despite my caution, though, I liked to look. There was usually one special boy every year that caught my attention. I suppose I go for those strong, silent types. This year, oddly enough, there wasn't one that really spun my dials. Sure, there were the usual, good-looking ones with the physiques and the handsome faces. But there weren't any with whom I could talk about much more than school. Just as well, I suppose. A jail term wasn't something that looked all that great.

The rain didn't look as though it would let up all day. Once inside the school I'd parked in the middle of the largest puddle in the parking lot and had soaked both my feet upon climbing out of the car I squeaked into the office to pick up any messages and mail.

"Mr. Corbin," the head secretary called in that pinched voice of hers, speaking in a tone as though everything were an emergency, "Mr. Ashburn would like to speak with you for a moment before class!" And she continued typing at lightning speed, as though she were in competition for Secretary of the Year.

"Thanks, Myrna," I muttered heartlessly. Ashburn was a pain in the ass at the best of times, and I certainly wasn't in the mood right then to put up with his stodgy banter. Regardless, one doesn't say "no" to the principal. And off I squeaked down the hall towards his office.

"New shoes, Michael?" Ashburn attempted to joke. I knew he was up to something. Ashburn never joked unless he was up to something.

"Oh, you know the rain, sir," I said, forcing a smile. I've never been able to get over the formality of calling Ashburn "sir", as though I were still a high school student myself.

"Well, have a seat, Michael." And he even pulled out the chair for me.

"What can I do for you, sir?" I asked, looking at my watch, running later by the second. All I wanted to do was get out of these goddamned shoes and into something warm and dry.

"I won't keep you long," he said, sounding insincere, propped on the corner of

210

his desk like a business tycoon, his arms crossed. "You've got a new student in your home room by the name of David Lennox."

I racked my brain but found no significance in the name. I thought that perhaps it was one of those insufferable brats belonging to one of the board trustees. I must have looked sufficiently bewildered because Ashburn filled me in without having to be prompted.

"He's from England. His parents were just transferred here. I trust that he won't have too much trouble fitting in." He smiled at me with overwhelming condescension, looking more like a television evangelist than a high school principal.

"Well, England isn't exactly Red China, Mr. Ashburn. I think he'll adapt."

"Yes, yes, yes," Ashburn replied, tapping a finger against his front teeth, almost knocking the plate loose, "but he's a rather ... shy boy. He's almost painfully quiet and reserved but very, very bright. He comes to us highly recommended. His academic records are very sound indeed. And so I thought you might keep an eye on him and lend a hand where possible until he gets somewhat settled into his new environment. It would mean the world to his parents, Michael."

"And should I know who his parents are, Mr. Ashburn?" I was becoming obviously agitated as the meeting progressed.

"Oh," he said, as if realizing that he'd forgotten the most important detail I knew he hadn't, "well, yes. Of course. His parents are in the diplomatic service. That's all I'm at liberty to say, Michael."

I looked at Ashburn with a steely gaze and sighed heavily, exasperated. "I see. Special kid, special care."

Ashburn's smile was toothy. A light sheen of perspiration had broken out along his brow. "Precisely. If you would, Michael." And he gestured for me to leave.

I hurried through the halls towards my class, pissed off at having been prevailed upon to show special treatment above and beyond the call of duty. Ashburn was notorious for this kind of behavior, though; I shouldn't have been surprised. I made a quick stop in the English office, changed into a spare pair of socks and shoes and grabbed my day-book from my desk.

The bell was right above the door to my home room. I often felt like disconnecting it because of its harsh sound. Somewhat out of breath, I arrived just before it ceased. A dozen or so students scurried in all around me, making their way to their seats. Dropping my books onto my desk, I looked up and around the room for this new face.

And there it was. I found myself looking into two of the darkest, brightest eyes I'd ever seen. He seemed older than the other seniors, taller and physically more adjusted. He was broad-shouldered, with sharp, dark eyes, pouting red lips, large, still hands, clear unblemished skin and jutting cheek bones. I instantly felt a twinge and became suddenly aware of the rest of the class.

"You must be David," I said to him, not once taking my eyes from his. I just

wanted to hear him speak. He nodded instead.

"Okay, ladies and gentlemen," I said, raising my voice above the normal cacophony of jabbering teenagers. "May I have your attention? Folks, we have a new student in our midst. David, perhaps you could tell us a little bit about yourself."

Without prompting, David stood up, smoothed his hands over his thighs and cleared his throat, addressing his fellow-classmates. "Hello, my name is David Lennox. As you can tell by my accent, I'm from England. My parents have just recently been transferred here to Canada. I like reading, sketching and swimming. And I've got an unfortunate weak spot for chocolate." There were only a few snickers as he sat down, his face never losing its indifference, as though he were reading a financial report. He seemed almost depressed but I mistook his pout. I engaged him for the briefest moment with a warm, friendly smile and returned to the lesson.

"Well," I began, "will wonders ever cease? I've finally got a student in my class who admits that he likes to read." I faked a grimace. The other students groaned and opened their books.

At the end of the class, I asked David to remain behind for a moment. As the others flocked out, he approached. He was almost my height, I noticed. I'd found his answers to some of the questions posed during the class refreshing and thoughtful. I only hoped that he would become involved more in the school to share some of that knowledge and insight.

"David, the principal has asked me to help you out while you get adjusted to your new surroundings," I said, standing closer. His eyes bored into mine, almost defiant. But there was a subtle smile playing with the corners of his mouth. And I proceeded. "So, if you'd like to stop by after school, I can help you get accustomed to the way things work around here. I know that it's going to be difficult at first simply because it's so different from the British system, if nothing else."

"Thanks," he said, lowering his eyes and offering the slightest, sweetest smile. "So, you want me to come by tonight, then?"

"Yes, that would be fine," I said. "The English Office is just down the hall. That's where you can always find me. Okay?"

"Good," he replied, his voice deep and resonant. "I'll see you then." And off he trotted. I watched as he exited from the room. Even from behind, he was something to behold. I knew that I had to be careful with this one.

"So, I hear you've got a new student," Elaine said during lunch. My colleague had approached from behind while I waited in line for a bowl of vegetable soup. My stomach growled fiercely. Her voice was subdued. Students often saw our closeness and thought us to be involved romantically something that worked to both our advantages. We decided to let them think whatever they pleased.

Turning around, I greeted Elaine with a warm smile. With a lowered voice, I replied, trying not to sound too excited, "Have you seen him?"

"No, but I'm told that he's a rather splendid-looking young fellow." She reached past me for a bagel. "British, isn't he?"

I chuckled and nodded.

"So, what do *you* think?" she asked, discarding the cellophane and tearing a piece off the bagel, popping it into her mouth.

"Dangerous," I said, wary of those around us, maintaining the semblance of inane chatter to the rest of the world.

Elaine broke into a mischievous grin and chewed. Her eyes sparkled devilishly. "Signed him up for any extracurricular activities yet?"

"I wish," I responded, chortling at the insinuation. "Ashburn's asked me to keep a special eye on him for the first while. And who am I to disobey the wishes of my superiors?!"

Elaine laughed and then, half-serious, half-joking, almost whispering, she slowly said, "Just be careful."

"Always," I replied.

David was promptly at my door after the last bell. I looked up from the pages of *A Midsummer Night's Dream* to see those eyes glittering at me. He seemed slightly more relaxed than he had been that morning; his smile was invigorating and ever so slightly provocative.

I rose to my feet and smiled. "David, come on in!" I pulled an extra chair out and placed it next to mine. He entered, pulling the door closed behind him. He walked with tremendous confidence and grace, almost like a ballet dancer. He crossed his legs and placed a binder in his lap. I sat back down and shuffled through some papers on my desk absently, using them to appear busy and professional to disguise my nervous excitement.

"It really *is* organized," I said, noticing the smirk on his sweet face. "I know where everything is, honestly." Then I pulled a page out from beneath a pile of strewn papers. "Ah, here it is. So, how was your first day?" I asked, casually reading the notes to myself.

"Not bad," he replied. "I like your class the best so far."

"I'm flattered. And why's that?"

"Well, I like the way you teach. I like the questions you ask. All these other subjects are so cut and dry. Literature is entirely interpretative and I like that. But I suppose I like your class best mainly because I love books. I want to be a writer, you know. I guess I'd have to like my literature class, then, wouldn't I?"

"You're not obliged to, by any means, but I appreciate the compliment all the same. What other courses are you taking this term?"

"History, which is all right. Mr. Perkins is quite knowledgeable, but a bit dry, I find. And Social Science with Mrs. Reid. I feel a bit lost in that class because they're talking about Canadian cultural differences and I'm not quite up on all that yet. And I'm in Mr. Lawford's Physics class. I find Physics boring but I do well at it. Which I can't quite understand, really. I mean, doing well with things I don't enjoy."

I was surprised at his candor and the frank, albeit astute, observations about his classes and his teachers after just one day.

"Now, you'll probably want to take some time to get settled," I continued, "but when you do, I thought that you might be interested in joining some teams here. That is, if you have the time or the inclination. Do you work during the school year?"

"No, I won't be working this year. I'll have enough adjustments to make, I think."

"Well, let me just tell you about some of the teams and clubs you can join here. Okay? First, there's the Debating Team — which can occasionally be interesting, despite what others might tell you. But unless you're interested in seeking a job in public relations, then I'd say your talents could be better used elsewhere. Like the school newspaper, maybe. The Yearbook Committee. Or the Drama Club. Now, you said you like swimming, too? You can always join the Swim Team but they've already selected their regular team members for the year. You'd only go on as second string, you understand...."

"I wouldn't mind writing for the newspaper," David broke in. "And maybe I could offer my services to the Drama Club. But I'm not competitive in my swimming. I just do it because I like the water."

"Oh, sure, of course. I'm just making some suggestions, you know. Our Drama Club has a pretty good reputation in town for the work it produces. We don't have huge budgets so can't put on too many extravaganzas. But we do manage a few solid pieces every year. And there's a regional competition that we enter every spring. I sometimes direct, but the club itself is in other hands. Anyway, I'd imagine that you'd find it rather interesting and rewarding."

He nodded in agreement, momentarily losing that smile, looking straight into my eyes. He seemed about ready to speak but nothing followed. After a brief pause, I took it upon myself to accelerate the process.

"Did you have something else to say, David? You look like you're...."

He interrupted, erasing that momentary stare, his face blossoming once more with that beautiful smile of his. "No, no. Sorry, I was just day-dreaming."

I cleared my throat and shifted in my seat, momentarily abandoning my notes. "So, do you have any brothers and sisters?"

"No. Well, I *had* a brother. A younger brother, who died before he was a year old."

"Oh, I'm sorry to hear that."

"My parents didn't want any more after that." He seemed far away suddenly, perhaps remembering something painful and hidden.

I decided to change the subject. "So, what kind of stuff do you write?"

Fortunately, it worked. He returned a sparkling grin and we talked for another hour about books, films and theatre, and occasionally chocolate, before we both decided that we should get home. I offered to drop him off but he declined. Fortunately it had stopped raining.

214

The days passed slowly. And David became adjusted to the school quickly. He rose to the top of the class, in fact, within no time. His essays were remarkably insightful and provocative. And the work he produced for the school newspaper was formidable. There was little doubt in my mind that this boy would become a writer. And his comic genius in skits at school assemblies soon brought about a sense of familiarity and belonging both for him and the other students.

And, with each passing day, our own friendship developed into something I hadn't felt for a long time. But and I constantly had to remind myself he was only my student. I couldn't let myself lose sight of that for a moment. Certainly he was a favorite of mine. But we maintained a distance. And that seemed to work. For a while at least.

The cold weather had also returned and Christmas was only two weeks away. The last day of classes before the holiday was spent passing small trinkets back and forth. Our Home Form had drawn names for gifts. I'd selected a rather dim-witted, pimple-faced boy who would have appreciated a six-pack of beer over anything else. But I got him a hard-cover copy of *King Lear* instead. He had no idea what to do with it and claimed later to have accidentally left it behind. Disappointed, I retrieved it later from the trash can.

To my pleasant surprise, though, David had selected my name from the hat. But he had to give me my present after school, he said, somewhat embarrassed, claiming that he'd forgotten it at home. I'd waited fifteen minutes after the last bell and was about ready to leave when David finally showed up, out of breath, ears red from the cold.

"Sorry I'm late," he apologized, handing me a handsome package wrapped in embossed, red foil paper. As soon as I saw it, I knew it had to be a book. I opened it to find an ancient copy of Dickens's *David Copperfield*. Startled at the quality of the text, I smiled wide-eyed at David.

"It's lovely! Where did you get it?"

"Oh, this little shop in Oxford. They've got everything there. You just have to know what you're looking for. And there's this little old man there must be about a thousand years old who knows everything, absolutely everything, about books well, at least about British authors. He's always got some little treasure or other tucked away somewhere. Go ahead and open it up. I think you'll find that it's a bit of a collector's item."

I opened the front cover and saw an ancient and elaborate scrawl from a father to his son, passing the book along with his blessings. Shocked yet thrilled and deeply touched I thanked David profusely for such a precious gift.

"And what did you get?" I asked, setting the delicate book down.

"Oh, nothing really," he replied, unbuttoning his duffel coat.

"Who gave it to you?"

"Kenny, the village idiot." And he rolled his eyes. We both laughed aloud.

"I shudder to think what he got you," I said, sitting back down.

David smirked and removed his coat. "It's a penny bank, battery operated, in

the shape of a coffin. You know, you place a coin on a certain spot, press the button and a glow-in-the-dark skeleton's hand comes out and pulls the coin inside. Oh, it's beautiful." He spoke with biting sarcasm. I laughed as his description progressed.

"Well, thank you very much for this gift. It's wonderful. It's probably one of the nicest things I've ever received. I mean it, David. Thank you very much." And I reached out and touched his arm warmly.

I wasn't sure what that look of his held but he seemed to be comfortable with such intimate contact. Other guys would have run away screaming "faggot" with the slightest touch. I'd sensed for some time now that David wouldn't be one of those. I still had to be careful, though. And I couldn't allow myself to confuse my intentions, no matter how sensitive, bright and mature this boy was. Still, he didn't shy away. And I took note of that.

"And I want to thank you, too, Mr. Corbin," he said, looking away. I took this as a cue to remove my hand. "You've been wonderful to me these past few weeks and I want you to know how grateful I am for all you've done. You've encouraged me when I've felt particularly inept. And you've shown faith in me even when I lacked it. It means a great deal to me to count you as one of my friends if I may be so bold."

"Of course you can," I replied softly. "Ours is a special friendship. It's something rarely felt between a teacher and one of his students." Although I was trying to choose my words carefully, I felt as though I'd betrayed my true emotions. Trying to recover myself, I continued, "I hope that we can still get together and talk about books next term even though you'll no longer be in my class."

"I hope so, too, sir," he replied.

I paused only slightly. "Call me Michael," I said. And then, quickly and emphatically, "But only when we're alone. All right? Not in front of the others."

His smile was infectious. "All right," he replied, "Michael."

"Merry Christmas, David," I said, laying a hand upon his.

"Maybe we could get together you know, over the holidays and go to a movie or something," David suggested. It seemed that he didn't want to leave. But I didn't want to risk anyone's walking in and finding us like this. So, with great difficulty and against my own wishes, I rose and crossed to where my coat was hanging and proceeded to dress for the outdoors.

"I don't know," I said, wrapping my scarf around my neck, "I'm pretty busy over the holidays, what with visiting relatives and friends. What about you? Don't you have lots of things to do over the holidays?"

He shook his head, looking somewhat dejected. "Not really, no. I don't really want to spend time with any of my classmates outside of school. I know that sounds particularly elitist and arrogant, but I don't. It's just me and my parents. The rest of my family is overseas. So, Christmas this year is probably not going to be very exciting at all for me."

"Well, you've certainly made *me* happy," I said, holding his treasured gift

216

aloft before putting it safely inside my briefcase. "Shall we go?" And I turned the lights off behind us and locked the door.

It was Boxing Day when I saw him again. I'd been out for a drive after the Christmas Day snowstorm we'd had, taking in the sights of the blanketed countryside, when I came upon a familiar figure trudging along the side of the road. I pulled over and cranked the window down.

"David!" I shouted. I caught his attention and he trotted up alongside the car. "Good God, what the hell are you doing way out here?" I asked, unlocking the door.

He took the invitation and climbed inside, rolling the window back up and removing his gloves. "I was just out for a walk." He didn't seem to be in a great mood.

"Out *here*?!" I asked with some disbelief. "This is a good two miles from town!"

"I just needed some air," he replied, mysterious, silent and out of breath.

I could tell that he didn't want to talk about whatever was bothering him. So, we drove along for awhile, continuing the scenic journey.

"I take it you're in no rush to get home?" I asked.

He shook his head abruptly, looking out the window at the rambling countryside.

"You look cold," I noted, my voice softening, reaching for the heat controls. He shrugged. "Should we maybe go get something to warm us up?" I suggested. "I know I could sure use a hot chocolate right about now. How about you?"

"Sure," he replied, noncommittal, shuddering at the cold as it crept up his spine. He pulled his collar up around his ears and stared blankly ahead.

I drove carefully back to my apartment. Billy was huddled on the doorstep, waiting for me to return. I introduced him to David and that seemed to break the ice that had frozen David's otherwise reserved demeanor. Inside, I doffed my coat and boots and padded into the kitchen.

"You live here alone?" David asked, following me in his socked feet, carrying Billy.

"Yep," I replied, not wishing to make too much of this fact. "Hey, Bill," I said, noticing how content he was to be held aloft, "you don't usually go for that kinda thing. You must have the magic touch, David, because Billy usually hates being held. By anyone but especially me, it seems."

"I think he's just cold," David replied, scratching Billy behind the ears. "He'll probably want down soon enough once he warms up some."

"Cocoa?" I asked, holding the fridge door open, looking blankly inside.

"That'd be great, thanks."

I set about making the hot chocolate while we continued chatting. "So," I said, "did you get anything marvelous for Christmas?"

"Well, my grandmother sent me a wonderful copy of D.H. Lawrence short stories from that same little shop in Oxford where I got your Dickens. It's quite

a handsome volume, actually. She also sent a basket of chocolates and tea. She's great fun, my grandmother. You'd never know she was seventy from the way she carries on. And then my Auntie Louise sent me a beautiful sweater they've got such amazing wool in England. Oh, and my parents bought me a computer."

"A computer!" I exclaimed. "Hey, that's fantastic! Now, you'll be whipping off those assignments in double-time. I just hope we can all keep up with you."

He didn't respond to this. Instead, he asked, "What about you?" And, as predicted, Billy decided that he'd had enough and leapt down onto the floor and scurried off in search of the secret wonders of the feline world. David pulled up a stool to the island in the middle of my kitchen and propped his chin in his hands.

"Oh, I wasn't quite so fortunate, I'm afraid," I replied, stirring the milk atop the stove, heating it through. "My family never knows exactly what to get me. My mother always buys me towels or sheets and they're usually always hideous. I've got a closet full of them. But we had a nice dinner. And Uncle Art didn't drink all *that* much this year. We usually have to pull his face out of his plate."

"Your family sounds ... amusing," David said, chuckling at my story.

"Ya," I agreed, pausing slightly, carefully, "and frustrating at times. But they're my family. And I suppose I should be glad of that." I poured the milk into two large mugs.

"My parents had to work yesterday," he admitted then, his face losing some of its light. "But they left me with a TV dinner with all the trimmings, of course."

"Your parents work a lot," I commented. "It seems odd to me that they'd have to be called out to work on Christmas Day." I handed a steaming mug across to him. He cupped his large hands around it, warming himself.

"Ya, well...." And that was all he said. I could tell that this part of our conversation was definitely over. After a moment, though, he effectively wiped the worry from his face, sitting up straight and beaming across at me. "So," he said, looking around, "I like your flat."

"Well, thank you, sir. It ain't much, but it's home." And I sipped, silently toasting him.

"So, are you and Miss Carruthers really dating, or what?" he asked, a deliberate and mischievous smirk smeared across his face, one brow cocked.

I chuckled at his boldness, sensing that my defence was quickly being peeled away. "Is that what everyone thinks?" I asked, postponing the inevitable.

"Well, I don't see it myself," David replied, "but that's the rumor, yes."

"Miss Carruthers and I are friends and colleagues no more. You can rest assured."

"So, are you seeing anybody right now?"

I found his questions to be rather uncharacteristic of him. He hadn't struck me as the meddlesome, gossipy type. And I was cautious about letting a student any student get too close. But he sat there, face expectant and brilliant. And gorgeous. I had to give him some sort of reply.

"Not right now, no."

218

"Not that there are lots to choose from around here," he replied. Then, suddenly, as if having offended me, he added, "Don't get me wrong. It's a lovely town. It's just not ... well, I'm accustomed to London, I suppose. I've been spoiled. Anything pales in comparison."

"Ya, what's it like these days growing up as a teenager in London?" I asked, hoping to divert our current line of conversation.

"It's an exciting place," he replied, looking wistful. "And dangerous at times. You've got to be careful where you're going. And who you're going with."

"I guess you must miss your friends," I said, noting his reactions.

"Oh, yes. It's difficult at times because I'm not the sort who has many friends sticking out all over the place. I'm very selective about my friends, as I'm sure you've noticed. I mean, after all, you're the only real friend I've got here."

"And I'd like very much to be a better friend than I'm afraid I can be. The school board doesn't look too kindly upon teachers befriending their students."

"Ya, I know. I've heard the stories about Uncle Milty." And he took another sip, smiling sweetly.

"Well, it's a rule that protects us all, I suppose you against any kind of misconduct and me against any temptations. It's tricky business regardless. And not particularly pleasant for those involved, I might add."

"And have you found yourself ... tempted before?" he asked, his mug resting on the counter, his face cradled in his cupped palms. His lips were moist and dark. His cheeks and ears were still ruddy from the frosty cold.

"Well, I'd be lying if I said no. We're all human, after all. We're all tempted by something or other throughout our lives. We just have to know when it's ... appropriate *if* it's appropriate ... to follow through."

"And you've never given in," he added, more a statement than a question. He took one last gulp and wiped his mouth with the back of his hand.

"As a matter of fact, no, I haven't," I replied, somewhat proud of my record but wavering wildly.

"My guess is that even inviting a student in for a mug of cocoa could be seen by some as misconduct."

"Some people might see it that way, yes." I was becoming rather uncomfortable with these questions now and tried to find some way out.

"Well, don't worry, Michael," he softly said, reaching across and laying a warm hand upon my forearm, "I won't tell anyone. The cocoa's our little secret." And he smirked and winked.

I gulped, hoping that he didn't sense my nervousness. But I found his face difficult to turn away from. And I couldn't read it any more. The smile on his face could have been sarcastic. And it might have been seductive. Or merely friendly. I just couldn't tell any more.

Suddenly I remembered the movie I'd planned watching on television. And I broke away excitedly, heading into the living room.

"Have you seen *It's a Wonderful Life*?" I called back, hitting the Power button on the remote.

"A couple of times," he replied. "Is it on now?"

"Ya," I said, momentarily ignoring him, focusing my attention on the television. "Wanna watch it with me?"

"Sure," he said, sitting next to me. He tucked his feet up under his butt and snuggled into the sofa. I sat back and pulled a cushion up between us. Smiling, I turned back to the television screen.

"Did you maybe want to stay for dinner?" I cautiously asked, a few minutes into the film. Young Mary had just whispered into young George Bailey's bad ear: "George Bailey, I'll love you till the day I die."

"Ya, I think I would."

"I managed to snag a whole whack of left-overs from yesterday's meal turkey, cranberry sauce, gravy, sweet potatoes. My mother makes the world's best stuffing. And my Aunt Lydia makes a wicked mince pie."

"Oh, I love mince pie!" his voice betrayed his huge smile.

I looked across at him then and said, "Don't they give you mince pies with your TV dinners?"

He laughed then, tossing his head back, his apple bobbing enticingly. In the background, a grown-up George Bailey exclaimed, "I wish I had a million dollars! Hot dog!"

We ate and talked until about nine-thirty when we decided that it might be best that I drive David back home. The streets were deserted. Strings of coloured lights flickered in snow-laden trees and hedges. The occasional ice patch sent us skidding. And there, up ahead, was his house a large, forbidding, Tudor-style home with a wrought-iron gate at the mouth of the driveway. From the looks of it, nobody was home.

"Well," he said, having resumed his former gloomy posture, "I guess I'd better be going." And he let out a pitiful sigh.

"Well, I'm glad that I ran into you today."

"Listen," he replied, momentarily allowing a sparkle of wit through, "the way you drive, I'm just glad that you didn't run me *over* today. Just kidding."

I laughed at his words, not taking any offense whatsoever.

"I mean it, Michael," he continued, becoming serious once more, "thanks for everything. I had a wonderful time today." And then David did the unbelievable: he leaned across the seat and kissed my cheek. Then he quickly leapt out of the car, slammed the door and raced up the snowy driveway, not once looking back.

School went in on a Wednesday after the New Year began. We had to buckle down because the end of term was rapidly approaching. And that meant exams. Dozens of kids came into my office after school for additional help and advice. I had no time alone with David until the middle of January, the afternoon after the English exam.

He came knocking at my office door while I was busy marking some papers. I looked up to see his timid face peering around the corner. "May I come in?" he

220

asked. He seemed pale and nervous.

"David," I said, pleasantly surprised, sitting back, "please!" And I pulled a chair up beside mine.

But he didn't want to sit. He stood about six feet away from me, in fact, not looking further than his feet, obviously nervous and upset about something. He spoke quietly and carefully. I had to strain to hear his every word.

"I just wanted to apologize for what I did that night back over Christmas. It was really stupid; I don't know what came over me. I hope you don't think any less of me now that I've acted so foolishly. I'm sorry. I really don't know what came over me. It's just so very important to me that I have you as a friend. I don't want to think that I did something that might jeopardize that." Despite the rehearsed sound to his speech, it was fraught with emotion. I knew that this hadn't been easy for him.

I tapped my pen against the pile of papers in front of me. God, how I wanted to draw this boy into my arms and ease the pain and the suffering he'd been putting himself through. Obviously, however, his emotional turmoil didn't interfere with his studies because he'd pulled off the highest mark in the class not to my surprise. Yet I had to be careful.

"There's no need to apologize, David," I replied, my voice deep and friendly. "Why don't you sit down."

He looked up at me sheepishly and approached, sitting uneasily in the chair beside me.

"I thought that what you did that night was very sweet. You'd obviously had a rather disturbing holiday; I can understand what our time together must have meant to you. I often wish that we could all show our true feelings as honestly and openly as you did that night. You're a very sensitive and bright young man, David. I just hope that life won't take that away from you."

David then looked up at me, eyes glistening, his face quivering, holding back tears that threatened to erupt.

"And don't worry about jeopardizing anything. Because nothing's changed. We're friends, you and I. And what happened that night only served to show me that you're comfortable with me, that you trust me, that you respect me enough to show a part of yourself that isn't always so readily endorsed by others especially in small towns. I don't want you to change, David. Please understand that. I like you just the way you are."

A sob caught in his throat then and I thought that he'd break down on the spot. But he held back, rubbing at a stray tear with the heel of his hand. His lower lip quivered delicately, within moments ceasing as his emotions settled. I realized that my words were a tremendous relief to him. They could also be easily seen as a declaration of my true feelings for the boy.

"You don't hate me?" he asked, incredulous, his voice breaking.

"Of course not," I softly replied, smiling warmly. "Why would I hate you?"

"You didn't ... mind my ... kissing you?" He said "kissing" in a subdued voice, almost a whisper. I felt as though the walls had ears and became suddenly

very aware of our surroundings.

"Perhaps it would be best if we continued this conversation elsewhere," I suggested, scraping all of my marking together and plopping it into my briefcase. "Do you have some time?"

He didn't even check his watch. He merely nodded rapidly, taking a deep breath, and rose, thrusting his hands into the pockets of his coat.

"Then, let's go for a drive."

We were out in the country within minutes. There was no place inside the city limits that was more than ten minutes from countryside. It was one of the nice things about living in a small town. Looking around, I saw what the recent deep freeze had done to make everything snap and gleam. We drove silently for several miles, making turns down side roads, skirting the town. All the while, I was trying to find the words to say what I wanted. Finally, with my courage gathered about me like extra blankets, I managed to speak.

"I thought that what you did that night, David, was extremely brave. And honest."

"I was almost sick when I got inside the house," he confessed, "I was so upset. I thought that you'd never speak to me again."

"I know that it's difficult to show somebody else how you really feel. And sometimes there's no real way that you can be sure that the other person feels the same way."

"It's not as though I do this sort of thing all the time, you know," David explained, trying to justify his actions.

"David, you don't owe me an explanation. Okay?"

"But don't you think I owe *myself* one?" he asked, turning in his seat towards me. "Michael, I think I'm in love with you."

His words almost forced me off the road. I quickly checked my rear-view mirror and pulled off to the side of the deserted roadway. With the engine still running and the heater still generating I turned to face the young man beside me.

He was visibly upset, no longer holding back the tears that had threatened to erupt earlier in my office. I was so utterly torn. I was really the only one who could reach out and help this boy and yet I was reluctant to do so because of my position as his teacher. If any of this leaked out, I'd be in the cell next to Uncle Milty, no doubt. The thought was almost perversely funny. But laughter at this point would have destroyed David. I decided to comfort him the best I could under the circumstances.

"I find that sometimes a good cry is the best thing for you," I said, encouraging him to release his emotions. The crying came full-force then, tears flooding down his smooth cheeks. I reached past him, wary of contact, for the glove compartment from which I abstracted a packet of tissues. He took the offered tissue and swiped at his eyes and nose.

"You think I'm a fucking idiot, don't you?!" he spluttered, congested from crying.

222

"Not in the least," I replied, remaining firm.

"It doesn't bother you that one of your students a boy, for Christ's sake is in love with you?!" The crying had subsided now; he blew his nose vehemently and wiped his cheeks.

"You're not the first person, you know, to be in love with another man." I spoke quietly but deliberately, regretful and exhilarated simultaneously.

"What do you ...?" he said, breaking off in mid-sentence, in disbelief. Then, whispering, "You?!"

I nodded, maintaining eye contact regardless of how difficult it was, of how delicate the situation had become, of how dangerous all this could potentially be. But David needed somebody supportive right then. From my own experience, I wish I'd had somebody to help me through the coming-out stage. I'd vowed long ago never to push somebody else away like I'd been pushed away all those years ago.

"I guess it's too much to ask if you feel a little something for me, too?!" he asked, fearing rejection. He sniffled loudly.

"It's not too much to ask," I replied, "because I do."

His face was instantly transformed into one of confusion, although pleasant. "What?"

I took a deep breath before continuing. "David, when I first laid eyes on you, I said to myself that here is an absolutely stunning young man. But you're out of reach. I can't act on my feelings. I'm your goddamned teacher. Often, I find that the beautiful ones are ... well, generally more self-involved and arrogant than I care for. But you ... you've proven me wrong. You've shown me that you're not only very attractive, but also intelligent and witty and funny and sensitive. And I've grown to ... well, I don't know if I'd call it love just yet, but I've certainly become more and more attracted to you over the past few weeks. Even though we haven't had much time together since that ... fateful night last month." And I smiled, tipping an eyebrow.

This time the well-placed bit of humor did work. David chuckled and began to relax once again.

"I'm frightened, though," I continued, returning us to the reality of the situation, "and with good reason. I'll be honest with you. We can't let this thing get out of hand or I could stand to lose my job."

"I won't tell," he admitted.

"It's not you I'm worried about," I said.

We both sat there for a long while, neither one speaking, only letting out occasional sighs of exasperation. There we were, finally having proclaimed our feelings towards each other, and we couldn't do anything about it.

"So, what do we do now?" David asked. "Because I can't stop these feelings, Michael. Well, no, that's not true. I could, I suppose, but I don't want to."

"I don't either," I whispered in reply. I looked hesitantly across at him then out of the corner of my eye and saw that he was doing the same back. And we laughed, finding the situation increasingly silly.

"What do we do?" he whispered, placing a quivering hand upon mine. Even through our gloves, I could feel the heat and the strength in his fingers.

I boldly wrapped my fingers around his then and squeezed his hand tightly. "I don't know, David. Even we teachers don't have all the answers."

After a brief pause, David asked, "May I kiss you again?"

I checked the rear-view mirror for cars and, upon finding us to be very alone, I turned back to him. His face was flushed and perspiring. I then realized that the heater was working overtime. I shut it down a notch and removed my gloves. He quickly followed suit and we had our fingers locked again -- without the barrier of heavy cloth this time. With my other hand, I brought it up to his silken face and cupped it in my palm. He leaned into it as though it were a pillow and closed his eyes. His long lashes fluttered. My heart quickened. I could hold back no longer. And I leaned over and kissed him, sweetly, tenderly, gently on the mouth. His lips were strong and soft. I was transported.

I kissed the tip of his nose and shifted closer on the seat, becoming increasingly uncomfortable; the middle seat-belt was jabbing me in the hip. Not to mention the discomfort of my confined and increasingly aroused genitals.

Suddenly, urgently, David grabbed my hand and pulled it towards him, placing it on his thigh, pressing it against his denim-clad leg. He felt hot to the touch. I looked from his hands to his face; he hadn't taken his eyes off me. He was smiling now, content finally to be doing what he'd wanted for so long, what he'd obviously wanted to do on Boxing Day when the only one getting anything was George Bailey and that run-down Building and Loan.

"You are so beautiful," I whispered, almost inaudible. I almost felt like crying now myself, the moment was so tender and precious to me. "Where on earth did you get to be so goddamned gorgeous?"

He blushed and lowered his eyes. Part of me had said that just to make him lower those luscious lashes again. I pressed my hand, palm flat against his leg, upwards along his thigh, slowly, torturously. Our breathing had increased. The windows were fogging over. I absently flipped a switch and the windows began to clear.

"I can't guarantee anything, you understand," I said, inching closer all the time, our lips brushing together like two butterflies vying for the same flower.

"I know," he rasped. "I don't care. I just want you." And with that, he pressed his lips against mine in a moist and passionate kiss. His tongue slithered into my mouth, finding mine. They agonizingly entwined, writhing within our mouths. His fingers were fumbling with my coat, feeling for the heavy zipper. I slid my own hand up under the hem of his coat, feeling the heat of his crotch just fractions of an inch away. Then he rammed his long, pleasing tongue forcefully into my mouth, almost down my throat. I was hot and hard. And I couldn't wait any longer. I lunged for his crotch, kneading the heavy, hard mound of flesh beyond. He had a button fly and I deftly worked away at each button until the flaps were pushed aside. His moaning reverberated throughout my jaw. I slurped on his tongue as though it were a miniature penis. This boy was hot and

exciting. And, as it seemed, experienced beyond the realm of sexual novice.

I quickly delved past the open fly and fiddled with the opening in his boxers to the molten dick-flesh that sprang to life beyond. I felt a sharp pang in my side as the seat-belt jabbed into me. This car wasn't meant for such activities; there simply wasn't enough room. We had to go someplace else. And so I stopped, agonizingly pulling my hands away and pressing his face unwillingly back.

"What's the problem?" David asked, licking his lips. "Did I do something wrong?" His face seemed confused and desperate.

"Oh, no," I said, breathless, smiling, "nothing at all. I just had to stop before it got too far."

"I see," he said, not understanding.

"No, no," I insisted, trying to explain, "I just can't do this in the front seat, that's all. Not with all these clothes and so little room. We have to go back to my place." I gulped loudly, regaining my composure, my breathing settling.

"Great!" he beamed, sitting up straight, reaching into his lap to re-button his jeans.

"But we have to be so very, very careful that nobody sees us together. Okay?"

"Yes, Michael," he returned, impatient, "I understand."

"Well, I just don't want us to forget for one moment, or let our guard down. Because we'll pay the ultimate price if we do. You realize that." I threw the car into drive and sped back off towards town.

"Does it still count once I've ceased *being* your student?" he asked, slipping a hand across the seat to rest upon my thigh.

"Unfortunately, yes," I replied.

"Do I at least get an A," he asked, "for effort?"

"Oh," I suddenly remembered, not answering his question but recalling something else I'd meant to tell him, "I've got some more good news for you."

"What?"

"You got ninety-six per cent on the exam today."

"Is that all?" he smirked, not in the least surprised.

"I just hope you apply yourself to ... other things as thoroughly," I replied. Then I laid my hand upon his and pulled it farther towards me, pressing it against the inside of my thigh to rest flatly upon my own mound of crotch.

"God, it's big!" he exclaimed, eyes wide. And he gulped.

He really was a good actor. When we returned to my place, he nonchalantly climbed out of the car, pulling his collar up to guard against the icy breeze. Then, as if he'd already planned it, he launched into a conversation about school -- in case there were any eavesdroppers, I suppose.

"So, you're telling me that if our school wins the regional drama festival, we go on to the provincial finals?!"

I had brought home a box of books in order to make lesson plans for the beginning of the next term. With a mischievous smile on my face, I grabbed it from the trunk and handed it to him. "You think we stand a chance of getting

that far?" I asked.

He chuckled and looked away. "I sure as hell hope to get far," he said under his breath.

And we crunched up the driveway to the front door. Inside, I saw Billy racing madly through the kitchen, chasing something only cats ever seem able to see. I put my briefcase down and quickly worked my boots off. David shut the door behind him with an elbow and kicked off his boots before entering my apartment and putting the box down on a nearby chair.

We turned to face each other then, expectant, nervous, as though it were our first time all over again. When he broke into a wide grin, my breathing increased. I couldn't believe that this was happening.

"I guess we'd better take our coats off," David said, matter-of-fact, slowly undoing the large, wooden buttons of his duffel coat.

I hung my coat on a peg on the wall. He hung his beside mine, our arms brushing together. Our touch was electric. My fear was quickly becoming overpowered by my excitement. There was nothing left to say right now. I simply motioned for him to follow me, leading to the stairs, oddly hoping in the back of my mind that I'd cleaned the bathroom.

He was right behind me on the steps, resting his hands upon my waist as we ascended. At the top of the stairs, I reached behind me and he took my hand. Wordlessly we walked down the hall to the bedroom.

The bed was rumpled, unmade. Then, turning around to face him, I placed my hands on his shoulders, feeling the firm bone and muscle beneath his sweater. And I didn't hold back any longer. Our mouths mashed together forcefully, our arms flailing about clumsily as we nestled into an embrace. Our breathing became frantic as our fingers pressed and probed and petted each other's body. Sinking slowly, I sat down on the edge of the bed, bringing him along with me, our mouths still clamped together in a frenzied struggle for territory.

"God, but you're hot!" I managed, lips wetly smacking against his.

"That's because you've got me all worked up," he replied, arching his body down towards mine. His knees were locked, his legs curving. His body was taut, arched like a gymnast. And he held himself steady with extended arms, one on either side of me.

I floated my palms along his sides, down to his waist. Our mouths broke momentarily, our lungs filling with air as we stared hungrily into each other's eyes, panting. His tongue was busy behind his smile. And his eyes glistened with dark mischief.

"You've obviously been with somebody before," I said, licking my lips. I brought one hand around to the small of his back, pressing lower to the swell of his buttocks.

"Once or twice, yes," he said, smiling proudly, accepting the compliment graciously.

"Then I take it you won't need too much coaching?!"

He snickered. "I shouldn't think so." And he arched himself lower, pressing

226

his firm crotch against mine, rubbing.

And his lips returned to mine, at times soft, at times insistent. He lapped at my mouth like a dog. I was fully and painfully erect. I had both hands firmly planted on his ass then, kneading the solid, pert flesh, pressing his groin lower, feeling for his erection with my own through layers of clothing. Then I slowly dragged my hands upwards, catching the waistband of his sweater, pulling it up. Taking my lead, David raised first one arm and then the other as I pulled the sweater up and off, tossing it onto the floor heedlessly. All that separated me now from the flesh of his solid, stream-lined torso was a thin, striped, button-down shirt.

"Your lips are incredible!" he said, breaking away again. "I've never kissed anyone like this before."

"No?" I asked, disbelieving.

David lowered himself onto his knees then, resting his hands upon my outspread thighs, continuing that sensual eye contact. Without being asked, I crossed my arms and drew my own sweater up and off. He reached up then and fiddled with my tie, tugging on the silk, undoing the knot.

"Did you have a boyfriend back in England?" I asked, ruffling his hair, resting my hands on his firm, rounded, muscular shoulders. "Is that where you learned how to do all this?"

He smiled. "I met a young man who was a student at Oxford; I was working on a school project for my literature class. It only lasted about a fortnight, our involvement, but we had a wonderful time getting to know each other." As he continued to tell his story, he unbuttoned my shirt with tremendous care and lethargic seduction. "His name was Ryan. He was tall and handsome with dark hair and pale eyes and creamy skin. He was beautiful. We met at a symposium on William Blake in a washroom, of all things."

I giggled. "You slut!" And I playfully gave his shoulders a shake.

"Well, it wasn't quite that seedy, I'm afraid. I was using one of the toilets when I heard somebody drop a pocketful of coin. And several of them rolled under my stall. Well, I gathered them up and, when I was finished with my business, I came out and saw this guy, Ryan, on his hands and knees picking up the rest. And so I gave him the ones I'd collected. And, well, one thing led to another and we started laughing about the whole incident. And he asked me out for dinner after the symposium. My folks were away as usual so I didn't have to clear it with anybody first. And, so, we went out. He didn't seem to mind that I was only a schoolboy. He said he preferred younger guys anyway. He was quite open about his sexuality. Well, and so was I back there it didn't matter as much, it seemed. Small towns are a very different thing altogether, though."

"Ya," I agreed hastily, "tell me about it. So, where did you get together for dates? I mean, even *your* living arrangement couldn't have offered all *that* much freedom." I, too, was slowly unbuttoning his shirt, seeing the promise of a smooth, built body beyond.

"He had a flat that he shared with another fellow at Oxford. But this guy was away most of the time drinking and partying, what have you. And, so, we would

go there. It was wonderful. I'd had sex before that, but I wasn't very good at it or comfortable with the whole procedure. And so he acted as a kind of teacher, I suppose. And he graded me accordingly." With an impish grin, he leaned down and kissed my thigh.

"Did the roommate ever come home and find you two going at it?" I asked, curious and increasingly horny.

David chuckled, remembering. "Yes, as a matter of fact, a couple of times he did. I mean, he knew the score and all. Usually, he'd just turn around and leave. But one time, I recall, he stood in the doorway and watched Ryan in the midst of fucking me. It was actually kind of exciting."

"Sounds it," I remarked. His shirt slid off his shoulders now and I leaned over to kiss a mole at the base of his neck.

"So, I'm somewhat well-versed in the standard activities, shall we say." He selected his words carefully, never losing that wicked smile or that glint in his dark eyes.

"Ryan must have been a good teacher," I commented, slipping a hand down over his chest, fingering a taut nipple, exhaling slowly.

He moaned lightly. "It's like your fingertips are live wires," he whispered, eyes partially closed. "You really turn me on, Michael!" And with that, he reached up and pulled my shirt-tails out of my pants and opened my shirt wide, revealing my well-groomed and hairy chest. His fingers went immediately to my pectorals, rubbing them, feeling the hardened nipples and the coarse hair against his palms.

I slowly pulled him up on top of me, lying back, bringing his mouth back down onto mine. Our tongues were demanding, almost separate beings from the rest of our bodies. We quickly and somewhat clumsily pulled our shirts completely off, our torsos grinding together as we writhed atop the rumpled bed. I found my hands unwittingly drawn to his tight buttocks, roughly fondling them through his jeans. Then, as though doing a push-up, he raised himself, arms straight, taking in the view of my naked torso.

"You're really built," he rasped. "I like your body!"

I, too, managed to get my first real glimpse of his young, hot body. His chest was hairless, with smooth, round muscles and startling definition. I couldn't wait to get my tongue against the rippled flesh of his washboard stomach. I then noticed a thin trickle of dark hair snaking its way down past the waist of his jeans. And the corners of my mouth twitched.

"Wet spot?" he asked, noticing my reaction and focus.

"What? Oh, no," I replied, "I was just looking at your body. It's ... well, it's just about as beautiful as the rest of you."

David then sat up, sitting on his haunches, effectively pinning my legs down. And he reached for my belt, deftly unbuckling it. His fingers were firm and slender, working rapidly at my zipper. I absently stroked his ribs, rocking my pelvis back and forth as he continued.

And he reached inside my pants like a kid digging for the last cookie in the

jar. His face lit up with excitement when he made contact. "Jesus!" he gasped. "It's huge!"

"I wouldn't say it's huge," I countered, "but it does the job."

"Don't be modest," David replied. And he pulled my rigid eight-inch cock out into view, tugging on it with expert fingers. "Shit, but it's fucking lovely!"

I giggled and closed my eyes, savoring the sensations of his hot, young fingers tugging on my erect, shimmering cock. I wanted more, though, and could only stand this game-playing for a short while before reaching for his crotch.

He stood up then, momentarily relinquishing my cock, his hands reaching for his own fly. I quickly bolted to the edge of the bed and stopped his lightning-quick fingers from proceeding.

"Please," I said, looking into his glorious eyes, "let me do it." And, without awaiting a reply, I pushed his hands away and worked the buttons undone. Shortly, the flaps of his jeans having fallen aside, I pulled the tight pants down over those slender, smooth hips. All that separated me now from his fully naked body was his boxer shorts.

I could see the wet spot he'd mentioned before about the size of a silver dollar, off to one side. I could make out a sizeable shaft of flesh beyond the opening. With delicate fingertips, I pried past the flap and dug for his hot, moist cock. And there it was, fully erect, proud and steaming. I groped him for the briefest while before pulling his boxers off. He stepped gracefully out of them, reaching down for my hand as I returned it to his stiff pecker.

"Oh, shit!" I repeated several times. "Christ, but you're absolutely the most gorgeous boy I've ever seen!" And I leaned forward to pop the head of his glistening dick into my mouth.

"Oh, ya!" David exhaled. "Oh, this is what I've wanted for a long time. A *long* time." His hands cupped my head and pulled me farther down onto the length of his tasty prick.

I moaned loudly, sucking sloppily, greedily. But nothing could have made me pull that precious cock out of my mouth. All I wanted was to taste his sweet, young essence. Nothing else mattered at that point. The entire staff of the school could've been in my bedroom that afternoon and I wouldn't have cared.

"Suck it!" he hissed. "Suck my cock!"

I tugged on his heavy balls with one hand, reaching between his slightly parted thighs with the other. I brought a rigid finger up against his puckered asshole. And he twitched as I made contact.

"Oh, yes! Michael, yes! That's it! Yes!"

Without the slightest effort, I jammed my index finger up his tight, white-hot ass. And I sucked his cock to the root all seven fat inches of it. Saliva dribbled out of the corners of my mouth, matting his pubic hair. My throat constricted and hugged the plump dick-head. I was in ecstasy.

"Oh, God, you're good!" he said, his thighs weakening, quavering beneath the strain. "But I think I'd better pull out before I shoot off." And, reluctantly yet firmly, he pushed my face away from his pungent crotch, leaving me gasping for

breath on my knees before him.

"My turn," he whispered, looking down at me with such lascivious looks on his adorable face, like a fallen angel. And, with a smirk, he reached down for me. I slowly rose to my feet, my own cock sticking straight out in front. And I simply rested my hands on his strong, broad shoulders. He didn't look away. He just reached down and wrapped his large hands around my cock and started to jerk me off.

"God, you feel good," I said, regaining my voice.

"I've never been with a guy with a cock this big," he confessed, although this fact didn't seem to bother him much. "I can't wait to feel it inside me."

"Mmm," I hummed, cupping his shoulders, pinching his nipples. "Me neither."

And slowly he dropped to his knees, his mouth leaving a trail of saliva across my chest, down to my crotch. He took the shaft of my dick in one hand, carefully scrutinizing my pecker, and then, after licking his lips and swallowing, he opened his mouth and took me inside. It had been so very long since someone had blown me. (I'd been on the outskirts of town the previous August giving head to campers in the dark seclusion of the forest.) But this kid's mouth was hotter than any I'd remembered. His tongue was experienced. He knew precisely what he was doing. And the size didn't seem to pose much of a problem for him at all. After careful consideration, he pressed his face up against my body, his nose embedded in my dark, curly pubic hair. I almost screamed at the feeling of his oven-like mouth and throat sucking and slurping against my piston-like pecker. I grabbed his head with both hands and forcefully pulled him even closer.

Then I started pumping my cock in and out of his mouth. He didn't even let out a gag. He just moaned and sucked fiercely. His fingers didn't even dent my thighs as he held on for support. Saliva drooled out of his mouth, dribbling to the carpeted floor below. His chin was slippery with spit. His dark lips curved around my fat poker. All I wanted to do now was shoot all over him.

Things were progressing far too rapidly, I realized, and I was closer to orgasm than I'd anticipated. Like David, I wanted to enjoy this experience a while longer and so I hesitantly pushed him away.

We stood, face to face, panting with lust and fatigue, staring into each other's eyes with such longing. And then we were in each other's arms once more, precisely where we belonged. I cupped his perfect ass and made a silent prayer that I'd be able to taste it before long. He held onto me as though he'd fall if he were to let go. Then, as though he could read my mind, he wrapped both his legs around my waist, our cocks grinding painfully together, full and ready to explode, slick and hot from the oral assault they'd just received. And I turned him over towards the bed, carrying him, lowering him onto his back.

I lowered myself onto him, kissing him hard, pressing my insistent and greedy tongue into his mouth. His cock was hard against his belly. I rubbed the length of the shaft with the flat of my hand. He moaned.

230

"Sit on my face," he implored, barely audible. "Michael, please."

I stopped only briefly, looking into that sweet, innocent face of his, not expecting to hear such guttural requests. And with such pleading, he was irresistible.

"Oh, God, please!" he repeated. "Sit on my face!"

Silently, smiling, I climbed up, dragging my balls across his chest and chin. His lips were waiting for them, sucking them both into the hot cavern of his mouth. I held onto the headboard to steady myself. Then, pulling my balls free, I brought my dark, twitching asshole closer to his ravenous lips. He grabbed my thighs again and held me steady, pulling my butt-hole down onto his face. His tongue was a wet, steamy snake rimming my butt with expertise. His breath was hot and exciting against my slick skin. He was incredible.

Holding on with one hand, and arching my spine back, I reached for his hard, throbbing cock. Carefully, so as not to pull myself away from that incredible mouth and tongue of his, I held every muscle in my body rigid until I had that cock in my hand. His moaning was muffled. I wanted so much to taste his young cum. Being unable to hold back any longer, I rose suddenly, turned around, planted my ass back on the boy's flushed face and, facing his pecker, leaned down to suck its length back into my throat.

I knew it wouldn't be long now. I could feel his balls churning wildly in their sack as they prepared a fiery load for me. And his thrashing tongue and nibbling lips only served to make me more excited, more urgent.

Then, suddenly, with a muffled scream of ecstasy, he shot his first thick stream into my mouth. I instantly pulled back to taste it. String after string of hot, young cream sprayed from the nozzle of his dick. It was sweet and nutty. And abundant. I swallowed valiantly but still couldn't get it all. His legs were writhing beneath me as I slid his cum-slicked pecker back into my throat. The sensitive dick-head was hugged by my expert throat muscles; I made him wince and moan uncontrollably.

"Fuck!" he screamed. "Oh, Jesus! Suck it!"

My own cock was hovering above him then; I'd lifted my butt as I took the final plunge. Without prompting, he grabbed my cock and fed it into his hungry throat. And within moments, I was spraying his tight throat with a steady stream of cum. God, it felt good to be shooting off again in somebody's mouth! It had been so long!

After our mutual orgasms subsided, we kissed and petted as we made our way to the shower to clean up. Beneath the spray, soaped up, his skin was golden, his cock erect and proud. I reached for that pecker again and held it warmly in my hand.

"I'm glad we finally did this," David said, snuggling into my embrace, licking my neck.

"You're not alone, there," I replied. The water was spraying against my back. Steam billowed around our heads.

"What are you doing for dinner?" he asked, not relinquishing my neck.

"Oh, I don't know," I said. "But if it's half as good as the appetizer's been, then I won't care *what* we do."

I knew then that this was the beginning of something wonderful....

SELFISH PLEASURES
by Rick Jackson

I was sitting on the beach last night, feeling sorry for myself. I'd just broken up with my third girlfriend in six months and was feeling low, alone, and unloved. I was also completely clueless about what women wanted from men and me in particular. I had tried everything to make my last relationship work; but the harder I tried, the faster she back-peddled. She said I was too desperate, for chrissakes. Of course, I was desperate. I was 24, and feeling low and unloved.

I realized suddenly, though, that I was no longer alone. I wanted to be, of course. I had taken a walk on the beach to feel the sand work its way between my toes and the ocean breeze carry away my gloom. I watched the sun set and the crescent moon ripple off the water and felt even more alone as I sat by myself on the vast stretch of beach. I was minding my own business, but the character showed up and had to sit beside me.

After checking to make sure he wasn't a knife-wielding druggie, I ignored him. The last thing I wanted to do was talk. Somehow, he understood. He sat beside me, also wearing cutoffs, for almost an hour before he reached over and put his hand onto my knee.

I had been dreaming around and almost forgotten he was there, so I know I jumped. He gave me a goofy, engaging grin and said, "It's okay." It wasn't okay, of course, but I didn't argue. For one thing, the guy made me feel strange. He was acting almost as though he knew me, but I was almost sure he didn't. Maybe he had me confused with somebody else? He was a good-looking guy and obviously spent a lot of time working out to be so tanned and muscular, but he had a peculiar intensity that I didn't know how to react to.

His hand moved up six inches or so from my knee and gave my thigh a little caressing pat of approval. I was still trying to figure out what was going on when the character said, "I'm Jeff. You look bummed" just as his hand slid over to my crotch. I must have jumped again. I should probably have popped him one, but somehow I didn't really mind as much as I should. As he rubbed his way along my dick, I felt my tool thicken and start to pump up against his hand.

By now, I knew what he was and what he wanted. I couldn't keep girlfriends and now, for the first time in my life, another man was hitting on me! I wasn't even sure exactly what gay guys did with each other. My new buddy Jeff didn't seem to care. He just looked happy I hadn't run screaming into the night. I thought about moving on, but I hadn't the energy. Besides, if he was moving towards sucking me off, why not? The girls I had dated never much liked to, and it figured that gay guys would know how to operate a dick. What did I have to lose but a few minutes and a long overdue load?

I leaned back to lie on the sand and went back to pretending I was alone. Only

my dick knew better. After a moment, Jeff slowly unbuttoned my trou and my lizard leapt up to flash into the moonlight for a moment before it smacked down against my belly. I had never felt so hard which made me feel even stranger and more depraved and turned on all the more.

I sneaked a look down at my crotch and found Jeff's face hovering just above my dick, watching the thing as though he had never seen one before. I gathered he had, though, when he wrapped his fingers around my foreskin and eased it down across my throbbing purple knob. The breeze brushed against my tender flesh, quickly drying and cooling my swollen head and driving it to even more frantic throbs. It wasn't until I felt so naughty and excited that I realized he was the first man who had ever seen my knob with the `skin off.

From the way Jeff carried on, maybe I should have shown it around before. Once he had pulled my `skin back as far as it was going without surgery, he brushed it upwards again until I was out of sight again, but definitely not out of Jeff's depraved young mind. Again and again he worked my cock sock up and down not jacking me off; it was too slow and sensual for that. More than inspecting, he almost seemed to be worshiping my big stiff dick. God knows my dick needed all the attention it could get.

I was so engrossed in how Jeff was making my crank feel, I didn't notice right off that his other hand was cupping my nuts. I hadn't even beat off in five or six days, so they were full and heavy and sore, but he didn't care. As my big dick became more an old friend than a new discovery, he juggled my balls faster and harder in his hand until he was almost scrunching them. Despite my resolve to play possum and not show any enjoyment as he did what he wanted with me, I couldn't keep my hips from wiggling against his hand.

Jeff hardly needed any encouragement. Not ten minutes after he had started, he had worked my shorts off and left me lying naked on the beach for a moment. Soon, though, I wore his face like a jockstrap as his mouth yawned wide and ate my hairy balls the way a hippo would handle a canapé. You have to understand what a revelation that was. I had to beg to get my girlfriends even to suck my dick. Jeff was eating my nuts and moaning and cooing to himself about how savory they were. If I had needed the injection of a little self-esteem, Jeff pumped me full to overflowing. .

His mouth was wet, but nice and eager and deliciously strange like everything else about him. After a minute or two, he gently dropped my nuts out of his mouth and rolled a rubber down my dick. His face followed in no time, tugging at my tender head and grinding his fierce lips across a hundred million exposed nerve endings. The rubber might as well have not been on for all the good it did to cushion his blow.

My hips bucked upwards, driving more of my meat into his eager mouth as his hand clenched harder around my balls. Those lips and his bumpy tongue and, at last, the dangerous edge of his teeth moved gradually across my knob and down my shank. They followed their own relentless schedule using my tender dick as if it were the most marvelous toy in the world.

234

Almost as though it were destined, my knob ended up in Jeff's powerful throat. As his gullet ground and sucked at my helpless knob until I was past frantic, his tongue fluttered up and down my cum-tube and threatened even more devastation. My pelvis pounded upwards, bucking my bone farther and harder into the Jeff's phenomenal throat, but he was able to take in stride every wide inch I had.

As his head pounded along my shank, I couldn't help moaning out like a whore and putting my hands onto the back of his head. My legs automatically spread wide to give his hand more room with my nuts, but he took advantage there, too sneaking his fingers down into the crack of my ass and prodding into matters even I have never seen.

Jeff's head twisted in my hands, working my dick ever-faster until I found myself threatening to spew. At the very last second, he pulled his face off my crank and let it fall against my belly. Instead of diving back between my legs, he licked his wicked way up my belly along the furry crest that leads from my pubes to my navel and then, slowly, gently, remorselessly, on up to my swollen nipples.

I had never thought of a man's tits as anything special before, but when Jeff's spit-slicked lips flew up and down my tender tit-stalks, I learned how much potential I had been squandering. The sadist switched off, sucking and slurping and licking first and one and then the other. Each eventually grew blasé, but by the time he had tormented the other, it was ready for more delicious abuse.

His hands were busy, too coasting feather-light across my naked flesh, worshiping the cut of my muscles and the way one flowed into the next. Those hands reminded me in passing of one of those characters who plays glasses by rubbing their rims until the glasses vibrate and howl to whatever tune the maestro demands. Jeff's hands rubbed me the right way and I loved it, but my abandoned crank threatened to rupture from neglect.

After a time, Jeff's full, salacious lips moved upwards to nibble colt-like at my neck. Then, as his palms caressed my awakened nipples, he brushed his lips across my own in a promise of more to come. He sucked gently at my ear and trilled his way deep inside until I knew I was going mad and craved only more of the madness. The harder I squirmed and thrashed and screamed, the faster and deeper his tongue flicked about my ear as though it could taste my very brainstem.

Then, all at once, he hopped back between my legs and chugged my dick down his gullet again with a new ruthless determination that made me wonder for a moment what I had gotten myself into. The second time around, he sucked and gnawed my bone with a savagery I had never dreamed possible with sex. His hands were as vital as his throat, only they ravened my flanks and tits and thighs while his face slammed up and down my dick like a creature depraved.

I couldn't keep my hands from shoving his head down against my crotch any more than I could still the relentless bucking of my hips or the automatic way my ass clenched and ground into the sand. The harder I fought to concentrate on

having the time of my life, the more full consciousness drifted away from me, leaving behind only a golden glow of building satisfaction.

Once again, after ten minutes or ten hours, I felt my guts churn to liquid and threaten to blow. I yelled and screamed and thrashed, but this second time around, Jeff was a changed man. His wet lips stayed locked around my shaft as his throat cranked into all sorts of gears and his suction powered up into overdrive.

I couldn't think or breathe. All I could do was blow my load up into Jeff's wonderful throat. My dick throbbed and pulsed with glob after glob of jism; but even while I was spewing the biggest, most rapturous load of my life, I had very little to do with anything. My hips lashed upwards. My head exploded. Mostly, Jeff's face sucked my seed up from my balls as his fist squeezed them dry and his face tore the leavings from my head. My own jism felt for all the world like some sinister parasite being ripped relentlessly up through my dick and out through my shattered knob.

I spewed and Jeff sucked and the world spun on for what seemed half past eternity until I ran dry. Jeff squeezed and sucked gamely on, but even he couldn't milk out another drop. I lay naked and panting on the beach as he pulled his face and rubber off my dick. The next thing I knew, he was squeezing my load out of the rubber, splashing it into my mouth and onto my chin before I could react. For the first time in my life, I tasted a man's jism and it was my own and not half fucking bad.

I knew at last that my idiotic worries about my troubles with women were a thing of the past. If other men could do half what Jeff had done to me and make me feel a tenth as good, I was set for life. Jeff pulled me into his arms and held me tight and safe as we lay together for a moment. He kissed me deeper and taught me how perfect a man can feel.

When I confessed to him what a revelation he was, Jeff looked stunned for a moment and then smiled that my work wasn't done after all. He slid another rubber down my dick still amazingly stiff and eager and lifted his legs towards the stars. I was slow on the uptake; but, once I was between his legs and shoved my stiff dick past his firm, clenching glutes, instinct took over and guided me home where I belonged.

I eased my throbbing dick through Jeff's shit hole as gently as I could, but his impatient heels soon spurred my ass into action so I gave him the kind of humping I had never dreamed of giving anyone. Our bodies crashed together in a brutal, almost bestial frenzy, both of us growling and screaming out every blasphemy we knew. As I looked down into Jeff's glinting eyes, I suddenly realized how really handsome he was and what a physical turn-on men could be.

His muscles rippled as I used his body for my own selfish pleasure, his dick danced between us, and his hands on my back kept us from flying apart like colliding galaxies. I should have taken an hour to nut again so soon, but Jeff's guts were so tight and hot and eager and the revelations cascading through my consciousness were so blinding that within ten minutes, I pumped another frothy

236

load of jism this time up into the secret recesses of his ass. I didn't blow and run, though. I pounded his ass to pulp and then fucked the leavings even harder.

When I had plowed all the rich bottom land I could, I eased my way out of his seeded furrow and collapsed back into the welcome of his strong, safe arms. Now that I was wiser, I emptied the rubber myself and took my time to relish every slick taste of my load. Jeff looked so gorgeous and virile holding me, that I went crazy and asked if he wanted to fuck me, too. He smiled and said he wasn't sure I was ready for that just yet, but we could at least take a swim to wash the sand off my ass. Then we could see.

As it happened, Jeff was too big and I was too tight that night. He showed me how to use a flavored rubber and suck dick, and I discovered I'm pretty good at that.

Tonight we have a rematch at my apartment this time. We will have all the time we need instead of all the sand we don't. Who knows? Jeff may just get lucky. It's about time now that I've met him and learned what really makes me tick, I am as lucky as anything mortal can get.

A FEAR OF PLEASURE
by David Laurents

*"...the realization of oneself is the prime aim of life,
and to realize oneself through pleasure is
finer than to do so through pain...
It is a pagan idea."*
Oscar Wilde

I. Marvin's Room

Marvin Goldstein was dead, to begin with. Of that there was no doubt.

And there was no way for Scott Murphy to forget this fact, especially at this time of year, as one year was drawing to a close and another was about to begin. He remembered the last Christmas he and Marvin had shared, the party they threw with Marvin's friends, in the hospital room, knowing it was to be Marvin's last. Marvin was in rare form that night, kvetching and sarcastic as only a Jewish person can be. "Here's something for you to remember me by literally," Marvin had said, bitter and ironic, and gave all his friends yahrzeit candles as his final Christmas present. This was characteristic of Marvin's sense of humor, giving a Jewish object yahrzeits are part of the Jewish ritual of remembering their dead, candles that burn for days, which are lit each year to mark the anniversary of the death as a Christmas present. He didn't know if any of Marvin's other friends ever lit their candles, but each year, although Scott was not himself a Jew, he lit the yahrzeit to remember Marvin.

He did not light them on the anniversary of Marvin's death, the day itself, in the Christian calendar. Instead, he lit the yahrzeit on Hanukkah, the Jewish celebration of lights. Marvin had always hated how commercial Christmas had become; Hanukkah was not a major holiday in the Jewish calendar, but because of the secular prominence that Christmas had, Hanukkah was elevated, in terms of marketing and packaging, to a greater priority, to have a Jewish counterpart to Christmas.

Each year, Scott would place eight yahrzeits on the windowsill, and like a menorah, each night he would light another candle, until all eight burned.

Yes, Marvin was as dead as a doornail now, thanks to AIDS. And Scott had not had sex since his lover's death, seven years ago.

Not that he hadn't had offers. Why that very afternoon, Christmas Eve day, while working late at the office on a project when everyone else had already gone home to their families and celebrations, one of the assistants had again tried to pick him up. Fred had been after Scott for some months now never overbearingly, but persistent in his pursuit.

Scott was all but oblivious. Sure, he noticed the attention, and Fred's

intentions, but he had long since forgotten how to act in this situation, and more importantly, he had long ago lost the desire to do so, to follow these encounters through to their intense, heated climaxes.

Scott was a man who was afraid of sex. He was afraid of his desires, which were not so frightening as desires went sexually, he liked men instead of women, a very simple thing.

But Scott no longer had sex not with a lover, not even with himself. He had so given up any sexual activity, he had now forgotten how to enjoy the intimacy of another body, the slide of skin on skin. He could not even arouse himself.

An erection, for Scott, was nothing more than a bodily quirk these days, something he awoke with each morning. It was not at all sexual, but his body's mechanism to keep him from pissing in his sleep, and once his cock softened to allow him to relieve his bladder, it stayed soft, all day and all night.

And Scott's asshole, which once had brought him so much pleasure, now was clenched tighter than Scrooge's legendary, miserly fists.

Scott was dead to pleasure, and nothing, it seemed, could wake the dead.

Scott had been raised to believe his desire for other males was an abomination, and he could not help but fear for his soul whenever he felt this desire. And what's more, he could not help but fear for his life, for how could he enjoy sex when he was constantly afraid of AIDS?

Scott had managed to overcome his religious upbringing and love men, physically and emotionally. He had put aside his upbringing so totally that he "married" a Jew.

And the price he paid for this love was to bury this lover. Scott could not face loving another man again, not when he couldn't know if this man was or would become sick and leave him, as Marvin had. He could not face sex with another man when he wouldn't know if that man would infect Scott, accidentally, for they knew so little for certain about this disease. That risk was just too great for him.

When Fred came into Scott's office and said, "I saw the lights on. What are you doing here still on Christmas Eve?" Scott did not hear him until he began to speak.

"You startled me," Scott complained, not quite turning away from his work to look at his visitor.

"Would you like to come to my place for some dinner? I'm spending the Holidays alone myself, and I know I could use the company."

Though sexual tension still lurked underneath the gesture, Fred's offer was simple and genuine enough. He would be happy simply to spend the Holidays with another warm body, even if they did not have sex.

Scott had no use for companionship of any sort any longer.

"I have work to be done, and I don't celebrate the Holidays any longer." He measured the distance between two walls on the page before him.

"Well, a Merry Christmas to you," Fred said, undaunted, unwilling to give up so easily. "Here's my number in case you change my mind." He wrote on a

scrap of drafting paper on Scott's desk, then left the office, leaving Scott alone.

The security guards came through at 10 p.m. and kicked Scott out of the office, so they could close the building and go home to their families. Scott gathered up all the papers on his desk, intending to continue working on them at home. He had a drafting table set up, and would be able to work uninterrupted by the phone or coworkers tomorrow.

At the apartment a co-op he'd inherited from Marvin Scott rifled through the mail, an assortment of bills and unsolicited catalogs and advertisements. One catalog, advertising men's underwear, caught his attention for longer than he cared to admit, and the inkling of a memory began to bum within his brain. Scott ignored it. "Waste of trees!" he declared. He gathered up the offending papers, and went out into the hallway, to drop them down the chute to the incinerator.

As he opened the chute's little flap on the wall, however, Scott could swear he saw the face of his dead lover, Marvin, staring back at him. Scott blinked, trying to clear the image from his eyes. He thrust the papers down the chute as quickly as he could, and slammed the little door shut. The sound seemed to echo through the entire building.

Scott hurried back to his own apartment, and threw the dead bolt once he was safely inside. He stood, panting with an uncommon fear, leaning against the door as he mused upon the image he thought he had seen in the chute. Impossible, of course, for Marvin was long dead; Scott had buried him himself.

Not in a Jewish cemetery; they wouldn't accept the body.

Scott remembered quite clearly how Marvin had acted it out, upon learning his sero-status was positive. "The thing I've always been afraid about with tattoos," Marvin had said, "is that most of the designs I like won't age well. Things I'd regret when I'm sixty or seventy. But that's not a problem now, is it?"

Marvin had gotten a tattoo of Winnie the Pooh on his biceps, and later a band of geometric designs around his calf, and these kept him out of the Goldstein family's cemetery.

Scott heard a sound behind him, through the heavy door to the building's hallway. It was as if a doorbell was being rung, as if every doorbell in the building were ringing at the same time. His own bell began to buzz, but Scott ignored it.

He stepped away from the door as he again heard something in the hallway behind him. His buzzer continued to sound. Scott was afraid to look through the peep-hole, as if he might accidentally let whatever was out there into the apartment if he pulled aside the metal shutter to peek through the glass lens.

It didn't matter. Scott watched as whatever was out there making such a racket passed through the heavy door into his apartment.

"Marvin?" Scott said, his voice a whisper. "Can it be you?"

The apparition continued forward, and Scott took a step backward for each that it advanced, until he tripped on the edge of a rug and fell onto the sofa Marvin or rather, the ghost of Marvin, for Scott could see right through the

image of his dead lover continued to approach.

"What do you want from me?" Scott cried.

The ghost smiled. "What have I ever wanted from you, dear?" The apparition reached down into Scott's crotch, and the hand passed through the fabric of Scott's clothes to fondle his genitals. "It's been so long since we've had sex, don't tell me you're not in the mood. "

Scott leapt up from the couch and crossed to the other side of the room. He clutched his head between his hands, rubbed at his eyes, not believing what he saw before him.

The ghost sighed. "Please don't tell me you have a headache. Such a tired excuse. After seven years, after I come back from the dead no less, just to see you again, don't you think I deserve better than that?"

Scott's head did not merely ache, it felt as if it were about to burst asunder with incredulity and disbelief. What was he to do?

"You doubt your senses," the ghost continued, "because you have not used them to feel anything in so long. But I am quite real, have no fear of that. I am not what you should be afraid of at all."

"What do you mean by that?" Scott demanded. He took a deep breath, calming himself, as he waited for the ghost of his dead lover to answer.

"You are more dead than I am. Just look at you. When was the last time you got laid? Better yet, when was the last time you even jerked off? You're dead as a lump of coal, for all that you're still breathing. No pleasure, no feelings. I've known tombstones with more human warmth than you give off."

"How charming. How *very* charming. You came all this way to harangue me for my sexual habits. What's the matter, not getting enough ten feet under? Serves you right for all the times you cheated on me when we were together!"

Scott tried to turn away from the ghost, but found he could not quite turn his back to the phantasm; some part of him still feared his dead lover's upset ghost, and some part of him, too, hungered for a last vision of him, even if Scott was positive this was a hallucination.

"Still so petty, I see. Nice to see some things don't change. We wouldn't want any emotional growth, now would we?" The ghost heaved a great sigh. "I didn't come here to have a fight. I came to tell you that you are wrong. I came to warn you, so that maybe you can change your future."

"What are you talking about? What do you know about my future."

"My time is short, so I'll cut to the chase. Dickens got a lot of things right. Only I'm a Jew, so let's forget about Christmas. Instead, let's teach you about your dick. You remember the story, I'm sure: three ghosts, starting when the clock strikes One."

Marvin's ghost stood.

"But wait," Scott began. "I...."

"You had your chance," Marvin said, meaning so much. "I've pulled some strings to get you a second one. Don't mess up. Use it or lose it." The ghost turned away from him, then turned back. "And that applies to both the second

chance *and* your dick."

And with that, Marvin disappeared.

Scott crossed back to the spot where Marvin had been standing. "He was just here," he whispered to himself, hardly believing it was true. "His *ghost* was just here," he muttered, correcting himself.

Scott was afraid to go to bed. He brewed a pot of coffee. He would stay awake and greet the ghosts with a cup of coffee for each (they could at least smell the aroma even if ghosts couldn't drink liquids anymore). He would show them he wasn't afraid of them (especially since he knew they were coming).

But then he changed his mind and poured the coffee down the sink. He was more afraid not to follow the rules of the story. He brushed his teeth and flossed them, staring at himself in the mirror. He wasn't as inhuman as Marvin had said he was. Was he?

Scott pulled on his flannel pajamas, and double-checked the deadbolt on the front door before climbing into bed. He left the bedside light on just in case.

A thumping sounded from against the wall he shared with his neighbors. At first, Scott was afraid it was another ghostly presence, having arrived early. But then a woman's voice cried out, a howl that hovered between pain and ecstasy, and he realized it was just the woman next door having sex with her latest boyfriend. She went through a new one each month, more or less, because she wore them out so quickly.

"I'll never get to sleep now," Scott muttered, knowing from past experience that she could go on for hours. He wondered, for the first time in a long time, exactly what they were doing on the other side of the wall....

And, still musing on those images, Scott fell asleep.

II. Sowing Wilde Oats

Scott's alarm went off, but Scott tried to ignore it. He was in the middle of some dream he didn't quite know what it was, just that he was certain it was something he wanted to keep dreaming, just a little while longer. Then he could get up and go to work.

"I suggest you do something about that infernal racket," a voice to his right said.

Scott bolted awake and upright, staring about the bedroom. A man stood over his bed. Scott rubbed sleep from his eyes. The man looked like a young-ish Quentin Crisp. Only Crisp wasn't dead yet, Scott was pretty sure, so his ghost couldn't be standing in Scott's bedroom.

No, it wasn't Crisp, Scott decided as he stared more closely at the stranger. Just someone with his same outdated (not to mention outlandish) fashion sense. The face was plainer, more rounded, almost owlish.

The stranger was unfazed by Scott's mute appraisal. "The machine to your

left, I believe, is what you're looking for."

Scott stared at the alarm clock on his nightstand, which increased its insistent buzzing as the timer continued to tick, then turned back to the stranger in his apartment.

The visitor rolled his eyes, and exasperatedly demanded, "Silence that contraption already!"

Scott jerked alert and hit the snooze bar.

"Thank you," the ghost said. He moved around to the other side of the bed. "May I?" he asked, indicating the chair.

"Sure," Scott said, wondering what he'd eaten that gave him multiple hallucinations like this. Or, as Marvin might've complained: What have I done to deserve this?

Whatever it was, he still had to deal with the here and now.

Scott stood up. He didn't like feeling so out of control of the situation, so helpless. "So," he said, sitting on the edge of the bed, directly across from the spirit. "You must be the Ghost of Christmas Past."

"Indeed, you impudent pup."

Scott waved his arms. "Come on, old man. Let's get on with it, shall we? What have you got to show me?"

"There was a time you showed more respect of your elders," Oscar Wilde's ghost said, sternly. Scott could not help staring into the ghost's eyes, feeling himself lost in them. "Or have you forgotten?"

The room about him faded black. He could see nothing but the man's face, his eyes, his dark hair spreading outward and seeming to envelop him in a cocoon.

Scott blinked, and when he opened his eyes he was standing in the Mineshaft. The ghost stood beside him, looking completely out of place, with his foppish scarves and billowing sleeves, amid the macho clones and leather daddies who prowled the bar's darkened rooms.

The phantasm nodded toward one corner, and Scott turned to follow the ghost's gaze. With a start, he saw a younger version of himself, not even twenty yet, down on his knees before a trio of older men. His hands were cuffed behind his back. Each of the men wore chaps, with nothing on underneath; their heavy balls and cocks dangled before his young face. A harness crossed the wide chest of one of the men; the other two wore leather vests. The young Scott was sucking off one of the men, hungrily wolfing down his swollen cock, while the others stroked themselves and watched, awaiting their turn. The young Scott let the cock drop from his mouth to catch his breath, but one of the other two grabbed him by his hair and pulled his head toward their crotch, guiding their dick into his warm mouth.

Scott watched, amazed at his younger self's eagerness, his willingness to service these men, to do their bidding. He had hungered for their attention, for the way they forced themselves on him. He begged for it, and these men, these daddies, made him beg, made him voice each plea.

Scott felt someone cop a feel through the flannel of his pajamas, and glanced

244

away from the escapades of this younger version of himself. An elaborate lace ruffle brushed against his leg as the hand was withdrawn from his crotch. Scott looked up at the ghost, to express umbrage at the liberties that had been taken, when he realized that he had an erection. He'd gotten hard from watching his younger self blow that trio of older men.

"Pity an old man?" the ghost asked Scott, mockingly, while fumbling with the fastening of its trousers.

Scott opened his mouth to protest, but no sound came forth. He looked back to the corner. There, his younger self groveled before three men in their late forties or early fifties, men who, at the time, had seemed impossibly old.

"Yes," the ghost said, as Scott watched one of the men prepare to fuck his younger self up the ass while another continued to thrust into his mouth, "we remember now the respect that is due to our elders. Look at me when I talk to you, boy."

Almost against his will, Scott's head swiveled drawn by the ghost's power, and also by the authority in that command, by the memory of days when he desperately craved being in the hands of someone who would tell him what to do, someone he felt he could trust, who would protect and nurture him. Scott stared into that ghostly face, a face he could almost see through, as if it were a smoky pane of glass a face whose eyes were a window onto another world, the world of Scott's past, the things he had done in his wilder youth.

"No," Scott said, and turned away from the ghost's eyes.

The scene around them had changed. They were in his first Manhattan apartment, year's before he'd met Marvin, which he'd shared with three other young gay men, all of them newly moved to the Big Apple from the Midwest. Kevin was from Ohio, and Jordan and Edward were both from Kansas.

"You cannot escape from the pleasures of the past," the ghost reminded him.

Scott could not forget.

He knew what scene would unfold before them now. That first Christmas in the apartment together, the four of them threw a wild and raucous party for all the friends, tricks, and others they'd made since moving to that urban gay mecca.

Scott watched, unable to turn away, as old friends got drunk and slowly began shucking their clothes. He couldn't help wondering how many of these men were still alive. He hadn't thought about them in so long.

Soon, they were all naked, nearly twenty men in their twenties, having sex in a wild, messy heap.

Scott watched as this younger Scott threw himself with abandon into the fray, losing himself in the madding crowds, the press and crush of bodies and cocks, of willing mouths and asses. His younger self was intoxicated with pleasure, thrusting his cock into any nearby hand or orifice.

He watched the young Scott cum, time and again, in some youth's mouth or ass. And even when his cock was too tired to rise again, the young Scott continued to play with the men around him, greedily sucking on their limp

245

cocks, trying to coax life back into them.

"Yes, those were the days, the glory days of yore," Scott said, turning to look at the ghost who stood beside him. "The glory hole days of yore," he quipped. "But they're gone now."

"Yes," the ghost whispered, as the world faded black around Scott once more. "They're gone now. But you cannot pretend that they never were."

"I don't " Scott began, but he silenced himself as he knew his protestations were untrue. He turned away from the ghost's black eyes, but the world stayed dark. "Ghost, where are we now?" Scott cried out.

But as his eyes adjusted to the dimness, Scott knew where they were, as he had known the apartment they had just revisited, and he felt a dread foreboding in the pit of his stomach. They were in the showers of the Chelsea Gym, years later. In many ways, not so very different from the bathhouses he used to visit: a roomful of naked men, saunas, showers, sex. But the situation was different.

Scott knew what scene was to unfold before him. This was the trendy, fashionable gym, where Scott worked out three times each week, back when he still cared enough about his body to put effort into it. When he cared about his body but had grown afraid to use it.

For months, as he worked out, he had lusted after one dark-skinned Latino, with broad shoulders that tapered to a slim waist, a classical V-shaped torso. Scott didn't know the man's name, but he knew that body so well, had memorized every curve and shadow of it. In his mind, he had taken his pleasure from that body for in those days Scott still took pleasure from his body. But only alone, always alone. He was afraid of other men, though he wanted them, desperately craved them.

On this day that unfolded again before Scott's eyes, though he tried to block out the visions, to lose himself in the steam and mist to no avail this man who he had lusted after for so very long, who quite literally had become the man of his dreams, sat next to him in the steam room.

The vision-Scott's dick began to fill with blood at the mere proximity of his idol.

And his idol took notice. The man reached down and held the vision Scott's thickening cock in his dark hand.

Scott's own cock stood at attention as he watched, again, the beginnings of this scene he had imagined so many times. Scott had jerked off to this scenario for months, hoping and praying, but never quite believing this day might come true.

And when it actually did happen, Scott was afraid. His mind had rushed forward, to those images of sex with this man that he had fantasized so many times before. But being presented with the real thing, the man himself, his body touching Scott's, was too terrifying for him.

The pressure of the man's fist around his cock felt wonderful, but that feeling was not enough to combat the overwhelming fear that made Scott's dick go soft.

246

Scott gently lifted the man's hand off his dick, smiling ruefully.

The Latino shrugged, and turned to the man sitting on the other side of him, who'd grown hard watching Scott and the Latino play. Scott watched, aghast, as the man of his dreams slipped through his grasp, hating himself for letting this opportunity disappear. He could not stop watching as these two men groped each other, fondling crotches, tweaking nipples, nibbling the flesh of each other's arms and neck.

They did nothing "unsafe." Scott could as easily have been doing these same, "safe" things with this man.

But he was afraid. Afraid of sex. Afraid of intimacy. Afraid of pleasure. The price of fear was regret, eternal and everlasting. He would always remember having had this opportunity, and having botched it out of fear.

Regret, his sole companion of his advancing age.

"No," Scott cried out. "No. No!"

He awoke, in his bed, as he sat bolt upright. His cock spasmed again. Cum squirted against the inside of his pajamas, which were tented out in front of him from his erection. His pubic hair was matted down with ejaculate.

"No," Scott whispered still. He did not want to face his fears. It was easier for him to ignore sex.

But he stared down into his lap. Could he ignore sex again, after what he'd been shown? Could he ignore sex again, now that he remembered?

His groin was suffused with the pleasurable afterglow of release.

But he was also sticky with his own cum and sweat, all that messiness of sex.

He stood up and went into the bathroom. He cleaned himself off, pulled on a dry pair of pajama bottoms, and climbed back into bed.

III. (Saint) Nick

Scott woke with the knowledge that he had just finished a dream, though he did not remember what it was. He lay in bed, eyes still closed, and thought about the events of that evening. Without opening his eyes, he reached out and pressed the snooze button, for he knew that even though the alarm was not set, the clock would buzz at two am and rouse him. Scott had always been good at waking a few minutes before the alarm went off, to spare himself its shrill tones.

He listened to the darkness of the room about him as he lay in bed, wondering who the next ghost would be, and when it would appear. Scott realized he could hear something, a sort of fizzing sound, like an Alka Seltzer in water. He wondered if it was the ghost, already.

"Might as well wake up and find out," Scott muttered.

He rolled onto his back and threw the covers off of him. He had a piss-erection, he noticed, though he'd taken a leak just before getting into bed an hour ago, when he'd awakened after the *last* ghost's visit.

He didn't feel like he had to take a piss again. But he did reach down and feel his hard cock, marveling at how good it felt simply to hold his erection in his hand, and trying not to think about how long it had been since he'd last done so.

A bead of pre-cum stained his pajamas, where his cock head pressed up against the fabric. The rough cotton felt so good sliding against the sensitive glans.

"I see we've taken a head start on things," a voice said from the foot of the bed. "Or should I say a hand start." The voice laughed.

Scott looked up, and saw that the television was on. There was no station, just static the crackling, fizzing sound that had woken him and an image of a naked man, who was talking to him.

While Scott had become, over the last seven years, insensitive and impervious to sex and sexual pleasure, he was not completely unaware of the sex going on around him. So he recognized the naked man on his television screen, as the first truly famous porn star bottom: Joey Stefano.

"Bring that over here, big boy, and I'll give you a helping hand myself."

It was a corny line, Scott knew, but not many men were propositioned like that by an internationally popular porn star. Someone Scott had actually jerked off to, back in the days when he was still masturbating, if not having sex with other men.

There was something intoxicating about being approached sexually by this star so many men had desired. But at the same time, he wondered if a ghost could infect a person with HIV.

What harm could it do? Scott thought, as he stood up and walked to the television set. He unbuttoned his fly as he walked, and pushed his erect cock so that it poked between the folds of fabric.

"That's my boy," Joey Stefano said, reaching out from the television set to grab hold of Scott's cock. He squeezed the shaft sending shivers down Scott's spine, and then tugged Scott by his dick into the television set.

They were now both the same size, in a small hallway.

"Pleased to meet you," Stefano said, shaking Scott's dick, which he still held. "You can call me Nick. All of my friends do." Scott remembered hearing about Joey's real name after his suicide. Nick Iaconna, that was it. There was a whole book about him now; he'd seen it in the window of a porn store he passed on his way home from work though, of course he had not stopped to examine it.

"I can't believe I'm talking to you." Scott looked down at his dick, still being squeezed in Nick's palm. It felt like it belonged to someone else for all the connection he felt to it. "I can't believe I'm doing *this* with you. I have friends who would kill to be in my place right now." He thought how he could make a killing from people he knew, who'd pay exorbitant sums for the chance to be where he was now.

"Actually, most of your friends are having enough fun on their own. Look for yourself." He pointed behind Scott.

They were staring out of a television screen at Scott's co-worker, Tim. The

248

glass was like a window, through which they could look out at Tim's bedroom.

"He can't see us," Nick said.

"I can't believe this, you're a ghostly peeping tom! We both are."

"We're peeping Tim, in this case," Nick corrected. "Peeping at Tim's pee-pee."

Scott couldn't help glancing out at the organ in question. Tim was masturbating, completely naked on his bed as he pulled his pud with one hand, the other massaging his ass.

"I think this is more information about Tim than I wanted to know."

Tim had a small dick, much smaller than average. Which was surprising to Scott, who had just assumed that Tim's prick matched the rest of his large, over-muscled body. He began to wonder if Tim had used steroids, which were said to make one's genitals smaller.

"Why are we watching him?" Scott asked. Not that he could stop himself; he was mesmerized by his co-worker's actions, comparing it to how he would jerk off. He grabbed his own dick, as if for reassurance. "If I'm supposed to get off from these visions, wouldn't it be better to show me some well-hung stud?"

"Anyone can find pleasure in their bodies," Nick said. "Besides, it's in the script."

"The script?" Scott asked. He looked at the ghost, and suddenly realized he was talking with the Ghost of Christmas Present, and all the rest of the story. "Oh, I get it, now." He struck his forehead with one palm. "I can't believe I walked into that. Tiny Tim."

Scott stared out of the television set at his co-worker. Then he turned and looked over his shoulder, and saw they were in a porn set. "Hey, you're in here twice," he said, tapping Nick on this shoulder.

Behind them, Joey Stefano was lying on his back on a picnic table, getting fucked by Ryan Idol.

"I know," Nick said. "Tim's got good taste."

Scott kept looking back and forth, between the scene on the picnic table and the one outside the television set. Tim had pulled a dildo from under the bed, and was using it now to fuck himself as he watched the screen and jerked off with his other hand.

Scott's hand was moving in time to Tim's, he realized suddenly, and for a moment he felt as if Tim were watching *him* jerk off, not the other way around. Scott was the star, the hot body that everyone lusted after, that Tim, with his small dick, was fantasizing about at this very moment.

Nick slapped Scott across the butt, hard. "Wake up. You're taking this all wrong. You need to learn to take it," the ghost said, "up here." He shoved a hand between the cheeks of Scott's ass, pressing upward.

Scott woke up, as ordered, in his own bed again. But not without one last image of Tim through the television's screen:

Tim was happy as a clam, despite his tiny prick. He screamed and shouted with pleasure, not caring what the neighbors might think as he reveled in the

sensations flooding his body. His cum was shooting onto his stomach, pooling in his belly.

Scott's own stomach was slick with semen. Another wet dream, from this second ghost.

He reached down and pushed his wet pajamas down. He ran his fingers through the drying jism, smearing it over his body. He didn't quite have the abandon he'd seen in Tim, thrashing about on the bed, but Scott was enjoying himself. Which is what, he thought, the ghost had wanted him to learn.

He lifted his hand to sniff the cum-soaked fingers, and then put them in his mouth. For the first time in years he tasted cum, his own cum, still safe, but reminding him of how much he'd liked the taste of cum, its sweet/salty funk.

Scott left his pajamas on this time, and slightly-sticky, rolled over and drifted happily to sleep, one hand clutching his warm, softening cock.

IV. The Last Offering

Scott stirred as Marvin lifted the covers and climbed into bed beside him. The ghost snuggled up beside Scott, wrapping his arms around his lover. It felt so comfortable, Scott almost believed it was a decade ago, when Marvin was still alive, still felt so real as he did right then. Scott didn't want to do anything to break this moment. But he also couldn't help wondering.

"What happened to The Ghost of Christmas Future?" Scott asked, half-asleep.

"I am the ghost of your future," Marvin said.

"And I am the ghost of your future," a second voice said. Scott looked up, startled by this newcomer. There stood Steven Willis, the first boy he had ever fooled around with, wrestling by the lake at camp one summer and accidentally touching each other's cock, and deciding they liked it, and touching them again on purpose.

"And I am the ghost of your future," a third voice said. Robert Sutton, his boyfriend from college.

"And I," said the voices, one after another, as every man Scott had ever made love to, had ever dated, had ever sucked off in some tearoom or back alley, had ever fucked or been fucked by, claimed him again.

"But you can't all be dead!" Scott cried. "I know you're not all dead. Eric, I got a Christmas card from you last week, even if I did throw it out. You can't have died between now and then. I didn't even know you were sick!"

"Oh, I'm not dead," Eric said, "but I am a ghost of your future. Every time you have sex, you remember all the other men you've had sex with."

"You cannot escape from your past," Marvin said, "nor should you try to. Whenever you make love to another man, I will be with you. And, through you, I will again enjoy the pleasures of life that are now denied me."

"Your abstinence denies not only your own pleasure, but ours as well. We are

250

the ghosts of your future," they cried in unison, every man he had ever loved before, as they climbed into bed with him and ran their fingers, mouths, and cocks across his body.

Scott screamed. It was too much for him too much sensation, too much pleasure, too much everything.

But the ghosts did not stop. Voracious and insatiable, they licked and stroked him, holding him down as he struggled beneath them, trying to break free.

His cock was swollen with exertion and excitement, almost despite himself. He did not want to be aroused right then, did not want to be having sex.

But he had no choice. The ghosts took their pleasure from his body, making up for seven long lost years of enforced vicarious abstinence.

They teased and caressed his body, stroked and pleasured him. And, at last, they let him come. It was a blindly overwhelming orgasm, which knocked him senseless.

When he awoke, daylight shone through the window. It was Christmas Day. He was naked, atop his bed. Semen, which he had earlier splattered his chest and stomach, had now dried. "A white Christmas," Scott muttered, and smiled. He lay on his bed, trying to make sense of his memories of last night, then got up and showered. He got dressed and went down to the street.

The city was trying to close down all sex establishments the peep shows and buddy booths, the erotic video arcades and burlesque houses.

Scott had once upon a timed approve of these measures, feeling that such things didn't belong in public, so garish and obvious and present. Sex was something for people to do behind closed doors, if at all. But his attitudes about sex had changed now. Or rather, changed back, to the way he used to feel.

Scott was glad the city had not succeeded in its attempts to shutdown the porno shops, as he headed to the one located just two blocks from his apartment. It was open, even on Christmas, for all the dissatisfied and lonely souls, needing some quick release on this stressful day.

As Scott entered the XXX-EMPORIUM, he decided to draft plans for a more upscale porno shop. Part of the city's problem, Scott thought aside from the fact that these stores acknowledged that sex, and especially queer sex, existed was the cheap, no-frills, sleazy way in which they presented and promoted themselves and the entertainments they contained. But if these stores were repackaged, Scott wondered, would they stand a better chance of staying alive?

It was worth a try, Scott thought. Even if his plans didn't work, they might get people thinking. It would be his way of contributing to the fight to keep these stores from being forced to close.

Scott bought a dildo to give to Tim Tiny Tim, he couldn't help recalling, and laughing at the irony of it all. The dildo was easily four times the size of Tim's own cock, but that wouldn't bother him at all, Scott was sure. Tim was a piggy little bottom, Scott knew from having watched him masturbate, and his eyes would light up when he unwrapped the Christmas gift.

He wondered if he'd use it with Tim sometime. Back when Tim first joined the office, he'd hit on Scott, and Scott had, of course, ignored him at the time.

Now, he wondered what it might be like. He considered sex with Tim, even with his tiny prick. Scott was pretty much a bottom, although he was afraid of getting fucked these days, even with a condom.

But Tim had fun during sex, that was obvious. Maybe they could have fun together, two bottoms in bed. And, of course, Scott did sometimes like to fuck, and as he stood in the porn shop with his newly awakened sexuality, he felt like he wanted to try everything again.

But thoughts of Tim could wait until later, Scott realized, as he bought the store's largest bottle of lube and a box of condoms for himself. He brought his purchases back to his apartment and put them on the small table just inside the hallway. Scott sat down at his drafting table and rifled through the papers he had brought home to work on that day.

At last, he found what he was looking for, and reached for the phone.

"Fred? It's Scott Murphy. Merry Christmas! I was wondering if that offer you made last night was still open...."

THE PLEASURE OF HIS PRESENCE
by Austin Wallace

From the moment I had started working at the restaurant, I noticed him, fantasized about him, pictured him naked. Nearly every moment of my day I furtively watched his every move. I was totally in lust, yet my fear of rejection kept me from ever making a move. Sure, we had chatted now and then, but it was the usual jabber of work-related nonsense, sports and general mindless talk. I was always a good boy around him, but I wanted to be bad, really bad with Ryan. He was such a stud, I thought. He was tall, close to six feet, solidly built, with deep set brown eyes. His black hair was in a Caesar cut, framing his face and highlighting his strong, square jaw and aquiline nose. He had dark hair covering his taut arms and legs which I noticed whenever he wore shorts and short sleeves when working as the bartender.

He knew I was gay (hell, *everyone* knew I was gay), but it never seemed to be an issue for him. I was convinced he was straight, but sex was never discussed between us, though I did manage to throw in an innuendo now and then and he just good naturedly laughed them off.

The turning point in my relationship with Ryan came when I gave my notice at the restaurant. A friend of mine in California had been trying to convince me to come for months now and I had reached the point of frustration, both sexually and professionally, that it finally seemed like a good idea.

My last day happened to be a Sunday and I was pulling a double shift. Things were much busier than normal but I was exhilarated with the thought of moving to California.

I was delighted to see Ryan was working that day: I could have my fill of him before I left. I began staring at him as soon as he started on the dinner shift. He was in shorts that were even tighter than usual and his strong hairy legs attracted my rapt attention as usual. He moved easily behind the bar, mixing drinks, chatting with customers, taking orders, his body moving confidently from one task to the next. I had just put in an order and stood at the end of the bar watching him. I fear I was staring at him more intently than usual, noticing his hunky form from the neck down, swept up in the thrill of his presence. When I worked my way up to his face he had stopped working and was standing there staring back at me; he smiled slyly. Stunned, my face dropped and I quickly turned away, embarrassed by my lasciviousness.

I went steadily about my work, but my lust kept returning; my eyes darted his way every chance I got, and each time my gaze was returned with that same sly grin.

Confused, but turned on, I tried as hard as I could to focus on my work. Finally, closing time arrived and I began my side work so I could leave.

As we ushered the last customer out the door the manager called me into the

back. When I entered the lights were off and as I turned them on, everyone yelled, "Surprise!" It was a going away party and I said, "You shouldn't have," but, secretly, I sincerely loved it. There was cake and wine so we all set about partying.

It started getting late and the party was breaking up. I said my farewells and Ryan came over, wished me luck, shook my hand and then took off. How anti-climactic, I thought, but it was just as well; the last thing I needed now was a complication in my life. I collected my things and headed out the door.

I raced across the parking lot towards my truck. As I inserted the key in the door a car pulled up beside mine, the lights blinding me. I turned to see who it was. The engine was shut off, then the lights. As my eyes focused I saw Ryan get out of his car. He closed the door and leaned against it, staring at me. I sighed, and followed suit. Silence passed between us as we stared intently at each other.

"So you are really going?" he said.

"Yeah, I need a fresh start. I need to get out of this town."

"I can understand that, man. I've thought about getting out too."

"So why don't you?"

"Oh, I will sooner or later."

The wine and the conversation had made me sleepy. I shook myself awake. "Well, I guess I'll be on my way...."

He stepped over to me, touched my arm. "I noticed you staring at me tonight, even more than usual," he said flatly.

I glanced at him without comment.

"I've seen you watching me since the moment you started working here," he said.

"Uhmm, well, I'm sorry if it bothered you. At least you know it won't happen again."

"I never said it bothered me, I just said I noticed you doing it."

At that my right eyebrow shot up. I thought, what the hell am I doing here? I just need to get in my car and go. I repeated that over and over in my mind as a mantra, yet my feet remained rooted to the ground.

"What, no comment?" he asked.

"Well, Ryan, I'm not quite sure what to say. Actually, no, I can think of a lot of things to say. I just don't know if I'm ready for the answers I'll get...."

"Well, you never know."

"No, I guess not," I said quickly as my hand shot out towards him. Realizing my foolishness, I began to pull my hand back and he suddenly grabbed for it. Our hands clasped each other, his thick, strong fingers stroking my hand. I was glad it was dark as I felt a flush envelop me from head to toe.

"This is totally unexpected," I stammered.

"Well, let me make this even more unexpected," he said and pulled me towards him, meeting me halfway. Our faces were inches apart and I felt his warm breath on my face. The anticipation of this moment was overwhelming.

254

His other hand reached behind and firmly grasped my neck. His mouth met mine and I felt his tongue slip past my lips to share his warm wetness with mine. He let go of my hand and ran his fingers through my hair. I felt the sensation of falling and we landed with a hard thud against the side of my truck. We both started to laugh and our lips unlocked. He continued leaning against me as we grinned uncontrollably. I could feel his erection pressing firmly against my waist as my own rubbed his leg.

"So, now what?" I reached up to stroke his face.

He reached down and grabbed my crotch, squeezing my hardness softly. "Oh, I think we both know what happens now," he leered as he lowered his mouth to mine again and our tongues began to search each other's mouths heartily.

He suddenly pulled himself away and said, "Follow me." "What? Where?" I said.

"Hey," he put his hand on my cheek, "just trust me, okay?"

I paused only momentarily as he let me go. He got into his car. I tried not to seem too anxious as I jumped into my truck and followed him for what seemed like miles.

We finally pulled into the driveway of a townhouse. As I got out he was already unlocking his front door. I came up the steps, "Nice place," I said. "You must make more than I thought you did."

"Oh, I do okay," he laughed. "And I have two roommates."

"Oh? And just where would those roommates be at this hour?"

"Well, one is at his girlfriend's house and the other's out of town. Convenient, don't you think?" he leered.

"Yes, yes it is," I said. "My last night in town and all...."

"Better late than never...."

As soon as we came through the door he grabbed me and pushed me against the wall, his mouth once again smothering me in deep, wet kisses. His hands reached behind me and began slowly kneading my ass. My goodness, I thought. My erection sprang anew and my mind reeled, not believing this was really happening. His mouth worked its way toward my ear and he began nibbling at the lobe. My eyes suddenly rolled back in my head as this was one of my erogenous zones. I could just feel myself getting wet below with precum and I pushed him off me to catch my breath.

"While this is great," I said, "I don't relish the thought of getting fucked up against the wall, or at least not this wall by the front door."

A toothy grin crossed his face and he reached his hand down and grabbed my belt. "I didn't think it mattered to you as long as you were getting fucked, but if it makes all that much difference, come with me then." He began pulling me down the hall and I took his hand off my belt and held it as he guided me up the stairs to his room.

"I don't know, Ryan."

"Sure you do. You've been wanting it for over a year."

"But why did you wait so long?" I stammered.

He stopped, pulled me into his arms, crushing me against his heaving chest. "I wasn't sure if I'd like it, but then I heard you were really good at it, so...."

He kissed me, but I couldn't concentrate on it. I was trying to imagine who would have told him about me. The only one at work I had had anything to do with was the other bartender who had only worked for two weeks. After he'd quit, he showed up at my door and suggested we go out for a drink, which led to my going back to his place and ... but I didn't think I'd been very good that night. I really didn't care for him and just lay there, letting him have his way with me, which maybe was what he wanted. Anyhow, I had no idea he was friendly with Ryan.

Ryan let me go and pulled me into a dark bedroom, and he closed the door behind us. His arms encircled me, his mouth nipping playfully at my neck. He quickly unbuttoned my shirt and pulled it down over my shoulders. Next came my belt and the sound of my zipper going down. As my pants fell effortlessly to the floor, my hard cock strained against the white cotton briefs. His tongue started on my neck and began working its way down my chest.

"I know this is going great," I said, "but after working all day I feel I need to take a shower."

"Ohhh," he moaned, "now that sounds like a great idea." He stood up and began removing his clothes.

"Wait," I said. "Do you mind if I see you in the light?"

He reached over and turned on the lamp by his bed, "Not at all," he chuckled. "You've waited long enough."

I sat down on the edge of the bed and watched as he untucked his shirt and pulled it over his head. A mass of black hair covered his full chest, running down in a straight line to his navel. His nipples seemed to stand out at full attention and I gave in to my temptation to touch them. He grinned and unfastened his shorts as I squeezed playfully. He was wearing boxers, which I immediately grabbed and pulled down. His erection sprang out at me pointing at my face as if to say, "Take me, take all of me." It wasn't an exceptionally long one, in fact its length was rather average, but the width was startling. Not as big as a tin can mind you, but it was close. I leaned back and sat on the edge of the bed to take in the full view of him naked. His cock throbbed in my face. God, it was beautiful, a thick, stubby club, arrow straight and stiff as a steel bar, very strong and sturdy looking. Its glans was the same width as the shaft, i.e., very thick. His body wasn't overly muscular but he was firm all over, the black, soft hair covering him in all the right places. "Oh, stop drooling," he said. "C'mon."

I leapt up and followed him dutifully into the bathroom and took in the backside view as he leaned over to turn on the water. "Hmmm," I sighed. He was gorgeous all over.

When the temperature was just right, we both stepped in and got wet. The steam from the water and our passion fogged up the glass doors within seconds. I turned and stood with my back to him and began to relax as his hands worked their way over my body, massaging my shoulders and neck, with a combination

256

of rubbing and kissing. I leaned back into him and felt the soft wet hair of his chest on my back. His hands worked down my chest, stroking and pulling at my nipples, sending tingling shivers down my body. I moaned with delight as his firm hands kneaded my buttocks. I stroked my cock up and down slowly from the tip to the bottom of my balls. I pressed closer into him, feeling his hard cock press against my lower back. He reached for the soap and lathered up my body with confidant even motions. I felt myself approaching climax but I wasn't ready, so I turned to face him, grabbed him by the shoulders, and pushed him against the cool tile. I pressed my mouth firmly on his and worked my tongue inside, searching over his teeth and gums, tasting as much of him as I could get.

I left his mouth and tongued my way down his neck, biting and licking his moist flesh. I worked down to his chest, taking his hard left nipple between my teeth, chewing lightly until a moan escaped his lips. I continued licking my way down the hairy trail heading for his hard cock. The water beat lazily down on us as I teased the tip of it with my tongue. Darting over the firm head and in the slit, tasting the salty flavor of his precum. I looked up to see he had his eyes closed, enjoying the moment as much as I was. I opened wide and took the whole bulging shaft in my mouth. I reached for his balls, pulling down while sucking furiously. He took me by the ears and helped guide my head up and down his thickness. I couldn't get enough of him in my mouth. I pushed down farther, pressing my nose into his pubic hair and taking his balls in with his penis. My hands moved around to massage his firm, slightly hairy ass. My fingers worked their way in towards his hole, poking and prodding, increasing his heightened sexual senses and bringing him closer to coming.

I came up for air and looked up at him. He was staring down at me. "Don't stop now," he pleaded.

I grinned lewdly and said, "I want you inside me."

He seemed to pause slightly, then carefully pulled me up and kissed me long and hard. He leaned back and said, "Okay."

We toweled off and headed for the bed. I jumped on top, pressing my body into his, feeling his warm and smooth hair against my skin. Our mouths and tongues met again in deep, wet kisses. I felt his fingers playing with my wet hole and I sat astride him, positioning myself so his thick penis was pressing into my crack. "I'm going to need a little help to get this in," I said as I grabbed his dick. He reached to the bedside table and opened the drawer pulling out a bottle of lube and a condom, "I knew these would come in handy someday," he smirked.

I chuckled and went to grab them from his hand but he pulled back saying, "I can do this, you know."

"Oh, I can see you know what you're doing, but even doing this I like to be in control," I said.

"Well, maybe you just need to relax...."

Oh yeah, I thought, this is going to be fun. He made a quick move and suddenly our positions were changed and I was under him. I put my hands behind my head and nestled into the pillow. He slid back a little, popped open

the lube, and squeezed some in his hand. I laughed loudly and said, "Oh, I am going to need a lot more than that."

"I heard you had one tight ass," he snickered.

"I hate people who kiss and tell."

"Oh, but then I wouldn't have made my move if he hadn't told me. I'm a shy guy, you know."

"Yeah, sure." I sat up and put my hand on his face. "I want you to fuck me. I want it more than you'll ever know," I said intently.

He tilted his head and gently kissed me on the lips. "Okay," he said calmly, "now lie back down and relax." He squeezed more lube into his hand and reached to saturate my already wet and anticipating hole. He slowly poked his finger inside me, first one, then another, loosening me up for the coming attraction. My dick seemed like it was getting harder and harder. I closed my eyes as he rolled the condom on his penis. I felt him grab the back of my knees and ease them toward my head. His dickhead pressed against my hole and I let out a breath to relax further as he pushed his way in.

A feeling of pleasure and pain coursed through my body, causing me to arch my head back into the pillow. He paused and asked, "Are you all right?"

I nodded.

"I'm not hurting you too much, am I?"

I kept my eyes closed and replied, "No, I'm fine. Sometimes a little pain is a good thing."

I heard him chuckle as he slowly pulled back, then pushed in again.

"Oh, god...."

He continued in a slow, even motion, in and out and back in again until he was completely in me. I tingled all over; I didn't recall ever being stretched so. As he pushed in and out, I opened my eyes to gaze at him. His eyes were closed and he appeared to be enjoying it as much as I was.

Soon my need to be in control again overtook me; I lowered my legs till they were resting on his shoulder and I began to push him down until I was sitting atop him again. It was a move that would have made a Chinese gymnast proud as his dick still remained inside me. I started riding him, pushing into him, helping his hips move in unison with mine. I asked him to take my cock in his hand and stroke it. I put my hands on his chest and tugged at his nipples. I could feel myself getting closer as his motions speeded up.

Up and down we went, his dick going deeper and deeper into me till I swear I could feel it pressing against my insides. I closed my eyes as the pace of our motions increased. This moment was all that I wanted it to be and more. Bucking up and down, my hands rubbing his chest, his hands jerking me off, I wanted this feeling to last, the ecstasy racing through my body, more and more. Reaching a peak of energy, I moaned loudly and my warm cum shot out over his chest. A feeling of calm release overtook me as he continued pumping with his hands and hips, getting every drop out of me, watching it dribble across his knuckles. As my eyes unrolled from the back of my head, I opened them to look

at him. I stopped his hand before he rubbed me raw and said, "Now it's your turn."

He slowly pulled out of me, took off the condom and we changed positions again with him sitting atop me. I grasped his hard cock and put some lube on it to increase the friction. I worked him up and down in a furious motion, pulling him closer to climax. I reached my other hand beneath him and stuck my finger in his wet hole to massage his prostate and almost immediately his cum poured out, flowing like a river over my hand onto my stomach, forming a small pool. He implored me to keep going until it was all out and then he collapsed on me, covering my face in soft kisses as we embraced in the afterglow.

We cuddled and stroked each other's wet, sticky body. I started to rise to get a towel but he pulled me back down. "Not just yet," he said. "How do you feel about another round?"

I paused briefly and stared deeply into his eyes. "I guess I'm up for it if you are," I said.

He looked down at my dick, which was rising again. "I can see that," he snickered.

I looked down and saw he was also hard. "Looks like we're both ready."

And then he rolled on top of me, covering my mouth with his, forcing his tongue inside as we exchanged salty wet kisses and much more, deep into the night.

I awoke the next morning with bright sunlight streaming through the window into my eyes, the memory of the night before still vividly fresh in my mind. I looked over at Ryan and watched him sleeping peacefully beside me. I reached over and slowly stroked his hair, locking this image in my mind like a photograph. I thought, or maybe I realized how perfect this moment, last night, and generally everything seemed right now, and I knew in order for it to remain that way I needed to remove myself quickly and quietly. After all, I was leaving and I wanted to go with no strings attached. I got up and dressed and softly made my way downstairs. I found a piece of paper and wrote Ryan a brief note, thanking him for what will always be the most gratifying and memorable going-away present I have ever had. I taped it to the mirror and calmly walked out the door feeling more alive and sure than I had in months. I got in my car and made my way home to finish packing for my long trip out west.

The next day went by quickly as I rushed to get everything done. Before I knew it a day had passed, the alarm was going off, my truck was packed, and I was hugging my father goodbye. I hit the road with one more stop at the grocery store to pick up some supplies. As I pulled out of the parking lot I heard someone's horn blaring. When I looked around I couldn't see anything, so I kept going. As I hit a stoplight the car horn got louder and came up behind me. I looked in my rear-view mirror and it was Ryan. He was signaling me to pull over. I spotted a McDonald's and pulled in the lot. Ryan jumped out of his car and came up to mine as I was getting out. He stood about two feet from me and

watched me as I closed the door and leaned against my truck. I felt a twinge of familiarity as this reminded me of the other night.

We kept staring at each other for an eternity before I finally spoke. "It's going to be a long drive...."

"You just left," he said.

I stared at the ground, "I did leave you a note," I replied.

"Yeah, and I spent the last day and a half tracking you down. You could have at least left a forwarding address or something," he said.

"Well, I guess I just thought you might want a clean break or something. I mean I told you I was still going and this seemed the best way to go," I said.

I looked up to see he was studying me intently. He paused a long moment, then let out a sigh, "Yeah, you're probably right. It's just that I thought maybe we could have had one more last goodbye."

A grin crossed my face, "Oh, I think the other night was a pretty good one, don't you?"

He started to chuckle.

I reached out my hand to him and he grabbed it and I pulled him toward me until he was leaning against me. I stared into his eyes, "Look, we had moment. Okay, we had a really, really great moment, that I will never forget. It was more than I could ever have dreamed. As a matter of fact, the night is forever etched in my brain." I reached up to stroke his face, "I'm sorry also, because you are right, I should have stayed, said goodbye and thanked you properly. It's just that sometimes I do things on the spur of the moment that seem right at the time. Sometimes they work out, sometimes they don't. I...."

He put his finger up to my lips. "You know, you talk too much," he said.

"I'm sorry."

"You should be." He leaned his head down and pressed his mouth to mine and kissed me long and deeply right there, in the light of day, in the parking lot of McDonald's.

After forever passed and we finished, I said hesitantly, "I really have to go now." I opened my door and reached in and pulled out a pen and paper and quickly scribbled down my future address and phone number and handed it to him. He took it and folded it into his pocket. "If you want to call or visit or whatever, feel free," I said. He stepped back, then reached his hand up to touch my cheek and gave me a wink.

I leaned my face into the warmth of his hand for a brief moment then pulled away. I reluctantly got into my truck. As I pulled out of the parking lot, I rolled down my window and playfully blew him a kiss.

Halfway down the street, tears welling in my eyes, I looked in the rear-view mirror and could just make him out still standing in the lot next to his car. I was sure he was smiling.

THE PLEASURE IS SUDDENLY SO GREAT
by Antler

Most boys don't think about
what to do with their hands
while being blown.
They just let them rest at their sides on the bed
or on the arms of the chair,
Or hold their arms up to their chests,
hands open or folded as in prayer,
Or perhaps unconsciously
stick a few fingers in their mouth,
Or sometimes fold them behind their head,
looking dreamy,
Or over their face, one arm or both
gracefully thrown,
Or stretching their hands over their head, as far as possible
while stretching their feet far as possible
in the other direction,
Or at their request tied spread-eagled and blindfolded
to bedposts,
Or holding the nudie magazine
no longer turning the pages
having chosen the girl whose cunt
is your mouth.
The pleasure is suddenly so great
they let the magazine go
and place both hands lightly
on your bobbing head,
Or if they're sucked standing up,
hands poised proudly on waists,
Or cupping their rump
or spanking themselves with joy,
Or feeding their cock to your mouth
offering it with both hands,
Or putting their thumb and forefinger
around your lips as you suck,
Or, sometimes, while you suck,
grabbing their own balls with one hand
and pumping their cock with the other,
Or they reach over and start pumping you,
jerking you off boyish style,

Each nuance of your mouth
inspired by and inspiring
the virtuosity of their hand,
Or stroking your shoulders, neck or back,
or gently placed there throughout,
Or running their fingers through your hair as you suck
and cradling your head
as they come.

The photo on the preceding page from the archives of one of STARbooks' all-time favorite authors, William Cozad.

Re-live a time of sexual surprises...

SUMMER CAMP

Edited by **JOHN PATRICK**

A Series of Raunchy Tales

STARbooks Press
Sarasota, Florida

Contents

Anonymous

IN THE TENT
K. I. Bard

"...The exalting freedom of nudity, solitary or in company, releases naturally *not* perversely the freedoms of the mind, the spirit and the body. A smooth, untimid eruption of these freedoms, as natural as an errand-boy's whistling, surely must lead to moral health (if that's what moral means); their constriction, to deformities of the spirit."
— *Michael Davidson, in his memoir "The World, the Flesh and Myself"*

INTRODUCTION:
A SERIES OF SEXUAL SURPRISES

John Patrick

"Generally summer camp was a series of sexual surprises," recalls Samuel R. Delany, writing in the book *Boys Like Us*. "The afternoon of my very first day in Bunk Five, a young camper from Florida explained to the bunk that the way to have the best summer was if the big boys (like him) regularly fucked the asses of the smaller boys (like me) and proceeded to use an interested and willing me to demonstrate how it was done.

"Five years later, on my very last night in camp, half a dozen of us were cavorting in the altogether after lights out in the bunk next to our own when the flashlight of the returning counselor flickered across the porch screening. Big, rough Berny, whose foreskin was as long as his four-syllable Italian last name, lifted up his covers and whispered, 'Quick, Delany! Get in!' and I slid in to be enfolded by his arms, my naked body pulled against his, where his cock, already rigid, began to rub against my belly.

"In that same landscape between these first and last moments, fell some half-dozen more of those twenty-two incidents that constitute the field of my childhood sexuality. One of the oddest was when, in my third year of camp, I noticed a boy hanging toward the outside of the circle of campers and counselors that we formed every morning before breakfast for Flag Raising.

"When he thought himself unobserved, Tom would dig in his nose with one thick finger or the other and feed himself the pickings. Watching him gave me an erection. There was little specificity to the desire, neither to emulate nor to share, though if he had offered me some I would have accepted, pleased by the bold self-confidence and inclusion of his gesture. (At five, in school I'd been roundly embarrassed out of the same habit by public ridicule, led by Miss Rubin: 'If you are hungry, young man, I'm sure we can arrange for you to get something to eat. But *stop that!'*)

"My response was to make every effort to befriend Tom and, once the friendship had been secured, to explain to him that I had no problems with the habit I knew must have caused him, now and then, at least *some* social pain; he

should feel free to indulge it whenever we were alone together. He did, at first with some trepidation, though less as time went on. We ended up taking long walks through the woods, holding hands (another nail biter, he), talking of this and that. While he dug and ate, we wandered along beneath the leaves, pushing aside brush, crunching twigs, and climbing over logs, I in a haze of barely presexual ecstasy.

"The same years contained three fairly enduring (for weeks in each case) heterosexual experiments which, while they were pleasant enough physically (all three involved everything, as they say, except penetration), nevertheless registered with a complete emotional flatness and a lack of affect, save the immediate frisson of trying something new a flatness and lack whose prevailing sign is the lack of detail with which I recount them here. (The four girls' bunks occupied two bunkhouses outside the Tent Colony on the other side of the Knoll across from a red-and-white barn, gray inside and housing a Ping Pong table and an upright piano, called, rather eccentrically, Brooklyn College.) Although the word *love* was spoken repeatedly and, I suspect, sincerely by the young women (and even a few times by me, to see how it tasted on my tongue), my silent judgment was that if this was all that accrued to these 'normal' adventures very much socially approved of by both the male and female counselors they just weren't worth it. In two cases, the lessons learned were among the more negative ones I took from these early explorations. One affair ended with a fight between me and a rival named Gary over the affections of a young woman who could not, or would not, make up her mind. 'You decide which one of us you like better,' Gary and I agreed, 'and the other one will go away.'

"'But I don't want to hurt anyone,' the young woman lamented repeatedly behind Brooklyn College, while Cary and I repeated our request, then shoved, repeated our request once more, then-finally, to avoid any hurt feelings bloodied each other's noses. A feminist critic to an earlier account of this incident suggested, 'Perhaps she wanted you both and was as stymied in her ability to get outside the status quo response as either of you.' It's possible. Probably we were all social dupes. The other girl, the other boy both may have been acting under the impetus of an always-excessive heterosexual desire. But if some idealized social norm is villain in the piece then I represent it since, though I sincerely liked the girl and equally sincerely disliked the boy, I found both without sexual interest. My actions were determined purely *from* my knowledge of social norms and had none of the creative energy, enthusiasm, or invention that sexual desire can sometimes lend. I've no clear memory of what any of us did afterward. I don't think much of it was with each other."

"Most people don't understand the difference between guilt and shame," Dr. Charles Silverstein says in the same book. "The distinction is central in the lives of gay men, particularly those over thirty. I often masturbated in my adolescent years and felt guilty about it. Guilt means one has done something wrong, which could have been avoided. It's a matter of will; I could have chosen not to jerk off. In reality, it made no difference whether I masturbated or not. The toxin was

within me. What I was, not what I did, resulted in my deep sense of humiliation. My homosexuality was the shame built into me, and embarrassment over my condition created self-hate. It made no difference that I bedded women. I knew the truth. That's what shame is about, and I learned it well.

"...In Boy Scout camp, I fell in love for the first time. It was 1951. I was sixteen years old and a junior counselor. Steve was fifteen and a camper. He was tall and slender, with dirty blond hair, a magnetic smile, bright blue eyes, and a charming personality. I loved him more than anyone else in the world. I often saw him nude, when he and the other boys changed before and after swimming, and I wanted to touch him.

"One night, after taps, while the boys in the cabin were talking, I slid my hand under Steve's blanket and touched his penis; then, with supersonic speed, withdrew my hand. Steve just went on chatting, cheerful as ever. I often wonder how different my life might have been if I had left my hand on the taboo object, softly rubbing his dick and as much of the rest of his body as I could reach. Thoroughly inhibited, trained to substitute shame for desire, terrified of exposure, I lost my chance with Steve. Not that I didn't have others.

"After camp we became best friends. Every Saturday, we went to the movies, talked for hours, ate together, complained about our parents, and attended Scout meetings. For years, we took overnight hikes, or slept at his house or mine in only our underwear. That was the most painful pretending that the occasional contact of my body against his in bed was an accident, keeping up our teenage repartee when I wanted to look into his eyes, feigning sleep when Morpheus himself couldn't temper my excitement. I sometimes sneaked out of my house in the early-morning darkness, long after everyone in my middle-class Brooklyn neighborhood had gone to bed, walked to Steve's apartment house, up one flight of stairs, down a long, very wide hallway, the white octagonal tiles magnifying the sound of my footsteps, and sank to the floor next to Steve's door where I sat in the blue, ugly fluorescent light for hours, accompanied only by my memories and fantasies. There were about six or eight apartments on the floor, and I knew from experience that no door would open until daylight.

"What did I do there? I dreamed.

"I was walking through Steve's *front* door, down the long hallway that led to his living room, turning left, into his bedroom. There he was, in T-shirt and shorts, as I had seen him so often in camp, lying on his bed, arms raised around his head, smiling at me, 'Hi, Charlie.' 'Hi, Steve. You know I love you.'

"He opens his arms, his eyes saying everything. I sit on his bed, like I did in Scout camp, and softly touch his chest, then slowly (perhaps not so slowly) move to his genitals, his dick already like steel. And all the while, Steve is smiling at me -lovingly, warmly. When he sits up, he puts his arms around me, making me feel safe and protected. We kiss tenderly, falling together in a heap on the bed, an endless embrace, folded into each other's arms, and sleep.

"Sitting in that cold hallway, I embraced myself, imagining Steve was with me, that I was holding him. At home later, I would embrace my pillow

(something I still do). Steve never knew how often I spent the night outside his door. Our friendship ended when I left for college. Furious at me for abandoning him, Steve refused to speak to me again.

"What an absurd situation: Two young men, each feeling the stab of abandonment, each crying over the end of an intimate relationship, each blaming the other for the rejection. I'd hear this scenario many times as a therapist, from couples struggling for love. The wound has never completely healed in me, though forty years have passed."

Our favorite "camp" is a nudist camp, of course. It was interesting to note that not long ago the Associated Press carried a story which revealed that even Cap d'Adge, on the Mediterranean Sea in southwestern France, surely the world's finest such camp, has been cleaned up. Is nothing sacred?

"A few years ago, Cap d'Adge got a very bad reputation," Claudine Tartanella, who runs the Cypress Cove Nudist Resort near Kissimmee, Florida, told the Associated Press. "They had a gay group and another group of exhibitionists that got together down on the far end of the beach. It was like a red light district, you know, and groups of people would go down there and watch.

"But they cleaned it up completely. As far as their behavior they have really straightened out their act." Darn!

CAMP HADRIAN

Peter Gilbert

One summer many years ago, I had been persuaded to go to camp by Rob, my best buddy at that time. One afternoon he wanted to play tennis, but I wasn't too keen on tennis. Rob went off to play, and by the time he returned later that afternoon I'd been screwed by a bishop!

The holy man was there for just a few days as a visitor. All the staff and boys were accommodated in tents. In my own case I had to share with five others. Showers and toilet facilities were crude in the extreme. The bishop had brought his own mobile home; a huge thing that was parked in a corner of the camp site. I was on the way to the shower tent when I encountered him. He agreed that the showers were not very good. Something would be done about the problem before next year he said, and invited me to use the shower in his 'waggon' (I think he was Australian but can't be sure.)

I can't remember much about that afternoon. I remember having the shower and him bringing me a towel. I remember being shown some pretty graphic pictures in books: not at all the sort of books you'd expect a bishop to have. Then there was the business of locking the door and going into the bedroom. The ice-cold feel of some sort of jelly being put into my ass and then the anguish as what felt like a telegraph pole invaded. I guess it was all over in a hour or even less.

In the succeeding days I spent the money he had given me and watched with amusement and a certain amount of envy as a succession of other boys visited the bishop. Rob was a pretty constant visitor.

There followed years of hard work and the acquisition of this piece of land. Now, Camp Hadrian is an established business and a good business. There are sixty-eight boys down there at the moment and twenty three men. I can see the site from this window. The boys' tents are surrounded by the trailers and mobile homes almost as if they were expecting an Indian attack. Sometimes I walk round the site in the evening, listening to the rhythmic squeaking of vehicle springs and the gasps and moans of the inmates.

We bill it as a multi-cultural, multi-ethic camp and run it from June through to September. The boys, of course, pay nothing and genrally come on recommendation from a friend. It goes without saying that they leave with considerably more money in their pockets than they had when they arrived!

I started with three, all of whom I had picked up in various places. Colin was the first. He was a lanky lad with a cock like a pick handle. Then came David. He was eighteen at the time and a telephone engineer. He came to install my fax machine, stayed to dinner and then for the night. He hadn't got much in front but his was the nicest ass I'd screwed for years. The last of the three I shall never forget him was Richard. Now the odd thing about Richard was that he wasn't

gay. I didn't believe him at first but he's married now with about five kids so I have to accept that he was telling the truth and yet he couldn't get enough of it. Three times a night was nothing to that boy and afterwards he wanted his ass whipped. I don't mean 'deserved'. He really did plead for it. I had to buy a succession of bamboo sticks to keep him happy.

So the first Camp Hadrian was born. Len, my auto salesman buddy from Phoenix, had David. Mike who was (and still is) an antique dealer had Colin. Simon, professor of English Literature, kept Richard happy with his all British cock and an all- American rawhide belt. All three are really nice guys and still enjoy 'Honored Client' status here. Me? I was too busy spending the money those three guys had paid for a two-week stay! They paid for the bathroom extension in the house and part of the cost of our super-Olympic-size pool.

The three boys found five more. The word soon got around the adult community and Camp Hadrian was born.

Why Hadrian? Everybody asks that. I'd read about him. He was a Roman Emperor and fell in love with this young guy Antinuous. It seemed a pretty appropriate name for the establishment.

How do we get the boys? Well, as I say, they come on recommendation from someone usually a buddy who has been here before. They have to fill out a form. Usual things: name, address, telephone number (Some of them come from under privileged backgrounds and don't have a phone at home.) I spend an enjoyable three months every winter traveling all over the States interviewing. We never take anyone under sixteen but it's amazing how many of them bring a parent along to the interview. Fortunately, our color brochure with its testimonials from clergymen, doctors, professors and diplomats puts their minds at rest and that leaves me to interview the lad privately. Usual questions at first but very important. Sports? Swimmers are the best. Swimmers have muscles where other lads have soft fat. Footballers are okay. You have to be careful with cyclists. Some of them have delightful asses but they tend to suffer from horribly knotted leg muscles. Best of all, surprisingly, are the 'no sports at all' boys. You'd be amazed how enthusiastic and active a bespectacled study-fanatic can be when he's undressed and in somebody's bed.

Then the thousand dollar question. It really can be a thousand dollar question for a good boy. Does he really know what's expected of him? There are going to be men there. At least one of those men is going to want to get to know him pretty well, to be his buddy. Of course he will get paid and of course nobody will know about it at home. Exactly what he does and does not do is up to him but the big bucks go to the boys who drop their inhibitions with their pants.

Generally speaking, they get the message if they haven't already heard it. One or two like to think about it but not before I've taken my two polaroid shots. One of the front and one of the rear. The customers like to know in advance what the goods are going to be like. Incidentally, if you are thinking of going into this business, take a tip from me. A limp cock is much more tempting than an erect one. A client likes to imagine what it's going to be like when he's got

272

his hands or mouth on it and there are cocks which can be disappointing.

The months go by in a flurry of preparation here. The swimming pool has to be cleaned, overhauled and filled. Tents for boys who don't bring their own have to be gotten ready and, in particular, food has to be ordered. I have three cooks sympathetic to the cause who give up their vacation time each year to come and help. A randy teenager is a hungry animal and nobody gives of his best when he's hungry.

Finally, the opening weekend comes. The boys arrive first. On Friday and Saturday they come by bus, car and motorcycle. Boys of every racial group you can imagine. The site suddenly comes to life. If it's a good weekend they tend to gravitate towards the pool. It's there where I meet them. Some are old hands which, when you consider that their hands are probably their least interesting aspect, is a stupid phrase. It's the new ones I am interested in. So, I guess, would you be. They tend to form a little group at the end of the pool talking nervously to each other. Fortunately, the others manage to put them at ease. I am against nighttime invitations and teenage initiation ceremonies. I like the lads to be at their best for Sunday but there is very little one can do about it. There is no doubt, I'm afraid, that one or two asses lose their virginity on the Friday and Saturday nights.

On Sunday the road that had previously carried a procession of beat-up old jalopies and noisy motorbikes sees the arrival of the trailers and mobile homes. Huge things, some of them, worth thousands of dollars. Three of my regular clients have had theirs custom built with king size beds and transparent shower cabinets.

It's a great time. A time of reunions and introductions; of hand shakes and protective arms round shoulders, sometimes even a furtive kiss planted on a fuzzy cheek. I often wish that my critics the people who send me anonymous letters and make abusive phone calls could be there on Sunday. I love to see how the new boys lose their shyness. To hear some kid from a slum home calling a captain of industry or an ambassador by his first name; to see them together in the pool or walking round the edge of the site deep in conversation gives me a real thrill. Why, three of our lads have gotten good jobs and a secure future as a result of meetings made at Camp Hadrian. When I think of Jose Gonzalez, who arrived here seven years ago in his only set of clothes and with worn trainers, and compare him with the Jose Gonzalez, who now occupies a position as a clerk in the United Nations; or of the streetwise, Bronx kid Leroy Fuller, now Mr. L. Fuller in the sales department of a large multinational, my blood boils. Mobile brothel indeed!

Most assignations are made at the pool. I knew they would be. That's why I installed the viewing gallery with its glazed windshields and comfortable seating. I will have nothing to do with selection parades or numbers on the boys' backs. If a guy wants a boy, it's up to him to make the first move, to plunge, literally, into the deep end. I confess that quite a few of the boys who've been here before make a few bucks on the side from introductions, but the idea of

lining them all up at the side of the pool go, a firm 'No' from me when it was first proposed. And, incidentally, we do not stage poolside orgies despite what you might have heard. I don't deny that, on a fine summer evening, the pool might be a more pleasant spot to fuck a good- looking lad than the stuffy interior of a trailer. I don't deny, too, that one grunting, moaning couple can attract others. Indeed, they seem to pop up from nowhere, but despite the pleasure they give to our guests and the lads, they are never organized in advance.

And, you know, we've never had bad weather on that first Sunday. Proof to me that whoever is up there is on our side. I generally get down there just before lunch time and join the guests in the viewing gallery and enjoy, with them, some of the most beautiful sights this world can offer. No painter or photographer I know of has captured sunlight scintillating on the drops of water on a boy's back or the delighted smile of a boy who has just found his first adult friend. As for the physical aspects of our young campers: it's small wonder that very few of the guests want to break off for lunch when they've got butts of every conceivable shape and degree of roundness and intriguing bulges in swim shorts to contemplate.

By degrees, the pool empties. By early afternoon it is nearly empty and hands that are used to wielding dictating machines, expensive pens, scalpels or even a crozier get their first real feel of something much more exciting. Tongues that have been restrained for a year are loosened. Accents from every part of the states and some foreign countries are whispered into damp ears as loving hands towel them down.

"What you got in there, boy? A python?"

"Guess you'n me are goin' to have a real good time together."

"Now that is what I describe as a delectable bottom." (Simon of course. He talks like that all the time.)

"I sink you like what I have for you, nicht war?"

It won't have escaped your notice that the number of boys and young men exceeds the number of guests by quite a margin. There are guests who find one boy and stick with him for the whole time but they are in the minority. Most like a change of company and some seem to prefer a crowd. Simon for example. He'll invite three or four boys together. It has to be said that Simon's preferences are unusual. He smacks them. I'm not kidding. I've told you about young Richard. I thought then that Simon was only pandering to the kid's masochism but he wasn't. He picks the youngest looking, marches them over to 'The Paddle Steamer' as he calls his trailer. Apparently (I get a lot of information from the boys) they all have to line up and confess to their various misdeeds at home or college. Then they have to strip and, one by one, they get thrown over Simon's lap to be slapped or paddled as he thinks fit. As most of the boys discard swim shorts after about the third day of camp, it's pretty easy to spot the ones who have kept Simon entertained. Those rosy pink marks are an instant giveaway. The one to watch for, I'm told, is the one with the lightest marks. He's the one who stayed behind after class to have better behavior drilled

274

into him.

I guess I shouldn't be telling you about the secret tastes of three good buddies but, like the man in the quiz show says, 'I've started so I'll finish.'

There's Len, the auto salesman. He, too, appreciates a nice ass but he doesn't waste time with the palm of his hand or a paddle! No sir! And yet the funny thing and he'll kill me if he gets to read this is that David the telephone engineer was the first boy he'd ever fucked. He told me some years later. Imagine that! He was twenty-three then. David had to tell him what to do. You wouldn't believe it if you were to see him at Camp Hadrian. One by one the really big guys, twenty-one years and older with huge pecs and bulging asses, get invited to spend a night in the very latest mobile home.

As for Mike... Well, Mike believes strongly in the therapeutic properties of semen. To him it's the elixir of life and God knows how many other high-falutin' phrases. Whether he's right or not I couldn't say. He certainly doesn't seem to look any older as the years go by. Mike doesn't seem to care much what a lad looks like. If he's got a big cock, it won't be long before Mike is slobbering on it. This year's camp is only nine days old and he's had twenty-three of them already. I can see his trailer from this window. Paul, the big blond lad from Minneapolis, is in there with him now and there's another waiting patiently on the step.

And me? I guess it's only fair. Well, of course I have to let the guests pick first but I never do too badly. In fact, my third so far is lying on the sofa bed behind me while I write this.

His name is Michael and he is eighteen years old. He comes from Tampa and he's a delivery boy for a pizzeria. His mom left him years ago and he lives with his alcoholic dad and his three younger brothers. But perhaps you aren't as interested as I am in his background. I spotted him at the first pool party. So, as a matter of fact did a certain diplomat from a South American nation but I managed to divert his attention to another lad who spoke Spanish. It's so much more convenient (as Simon would say) when they speak each other's language.

The dark blue swim shorts he was wearing accentuated the whiteness of his skin and his butt. He has a neat, tight little butt just the sort I go for, and long legs. He also has an appreciable cock. One look at that lump in the front of his shorts and the perfect hemisphere of his backside was enough for me. He is also very slim, dark and, more important, very nervous.

Let me explain: Michael has been around. He was telling me earlier how he and his buddy the one who coaxed him into coming here tossed each other off when they were in school together and how he once wanked into an unpopular customer's pizza. But nothing bigger than a thermometer has ever penetrated his asshole yet.

I believe that sex with a beautiful boy should be like a good meal and savored slowly. First you have to select what you're going to have. I've told you about that. Then comes the preparation. He turned up on the doorstep in jeans and T-shirt. I gave him a drink. He told me about his life. Then....

"Well, we'd better get started. Let's get you undressed."

He wanted to do it himself. I wasn't having that. The tee shirt came off. I noticed that he'd gotten slightly sunburned on the shoulders. Then the trainers. His jeans peeled off with a slight struggle. Finally came the moment of truth you might call it. I slid his under shorts down and off. One can be disappointed at that moment. I wasn't. It was every bit as good as I had anticipated. A really nice uncut cock, rubbery then and a milky white butt. I have a perfect view of that at this moment in the mirror on the wall above this word processor. The next stage, you see, is preparation. He's been well oiled. A tiny fleck of oil is gleaming on his right buttock.

And now the meal must be well cooked! In my view the most important stage. Cooking time varies. I'm giving Michael an hour and a half giving me time to write to you. Time for the lubricant to trickle right down, which is why he is lying on his front.

He wants, he says, to get it over. He must have said it at least six times since I started this. He's got some picture books to look at. Close-ups, in the main, of extremely large cocks (infinitely bigger than mine, I have to admit) going into tight assholes. All part of the plan. When I switch off this machine he'll look up anxiously. They all do. I shall see that in the mirror. When I touch him he'll shiver slightly and when I turn him over his cock will be just right. Not too hard and not too limp. He'll be cooked just right and his cock will be delicious. Nervousness sure adds to the flavor. I don't know how but it does, and if you're one of those guys who can't even wait to put the cap on the grease bottle, take a tip from me: A boy who's been frightened fucks better. Again, I don't know why but it's true. Maybe it's the trembling; that little bit of extra resistance. Michael's butt muscles will be as hard as steel at first. They'll soften as I go into him. And he's going to love it as much as me. So will all the others.

"Aren't you ready yet? I'm supposed to be at the pool."

I am. And I think he is. Excuse me.

AT THE SCOUT HUT

Thomas C. Humphrey

Clay Fordham anxiously eyed the entrance door as he chatted with a group of fans. It was nearly time for him to get ready for the game, but he was waiting to talk with Kenneth before he went downstairs to the dressing room. He had been wanting to get Kenneth alone for several weeks, ever since the slightly built blond cadet had started coming to his basketball games and cornering him to talk every time they ran into each other. From the hungry looks Kenneth gave him, Clay had begun to dream of having that tight little ass that set him on fire every time Kenneth walked away from him.

He silently prayed for Kenneth to show up. He had things all planned out for the night. Kenneth had to come; if he didn't show, all of Clay's preparations and lies to his parents would be wasted. As he thought about that possibility, a frantic emptiness gnawed away in the pit of his stomach.

When he finally spied the first Harrison Academy uniform at the door and then saw Kenneth in the midst of his usual clan of cadet friends, he quickly pried himself away from the group of admiring kids and old men around him. Heart pumping rapidly in his chest, his knees weak and trembling, Clay sauntered over to meet him, struggling to appear casual.

Kenneth Kreger had thought of Clay continuously since the Tuesday night game, and the intervening three days had dragged on forever. A shiver of excitement ran through him as soon as he spotted Clay moving toward him. He had been coveting this big, good-looking farm boy for weeks and anticipating what he could entice him into, once he had him worked into a frenzy of desire. So far, he had not had the balls to try him.

Kenneth had been in town only a few months, having transferred to Madison Academy from another military prep school for his senior year after the provost had made it known he was not welcome to return. From the beginning, he had felt that this little town was not like those other places, where he had seduced dozens of local guys, as well as other cadets, a hobby that had gotten him booted out of a couple of other schools. This time, though, he had had to admit that, as much as he wanted Clay, he was afraid of what might happen if he tried and failed.

Academy students did not fare very well in Wilkinson, especially barracks cadets. It was a small rural town with only two high schools, the Academy and Pelham County High. Although they did not compete against each other in athletics, an intense rivalry existed between them. Even local boys who attended the Academy were bombarded by insults from the county high students about their "monkey suit" uniforms and military haircuts.

The barracks cadets were the ones who really caught it, though. They were outsiders, foreigners, many of them even Yankees, an obscenity to the redneck

teenagers who rode around in pickups displaying Confederate flags and bumper stickers proclaiming "Forget, Hell!" The local teens were violently protective of their women, and any cadet who tried to make a move on one of them might very well wind up in the hospital. Kenneth shuddered at the thought of what could happen to a faggot cadet who tried to make the star high school basketball player.

Before the previous Tuesday night, Kenneth had done little more than speak to Clay, whose slow drawl and country demeanor spelled danger to him, despite the way Clay's towering, muscled physique turned him on. The few times they had talked, they both had been tongue-tied, although Clay's eyes had clearly communicated an interest that Kenneth had been afraid to follow up on. Now, finally, something was going to happen at Clay's initiative, he just knew it was. He had relived the Tuesday night episode dozens of times, and he was sure he had interpreted it correctly.

He had been sitting two rows up from court level when, in the third period, Clay had sailed out of bounds after the basketball, flipped it to a teammate, and wound up with his six-foot-six-inch frame sprawled over Kenneth and his friends in the stands. His head rested briefly on Kenneth's chest, the mop of sweaty, brick-red hair spotting his shirt. As he slowly extricated himself, his hand slid up Kenneth's inner thigh and fleetingly squeezed at his crotch. Then he sat up, with a broad smile on his face, and gave Kenneth a quick wink before returning to action on the court.

"You guys save me a seat," Kenneth said to his friends as Clay walked up. "I'll be right with you." He turned to look up at Clay with a smile and an almost unbearable visceral excitement.

"Hi, Kenneth. I didn't think you were coming," Clay said, dropping his gaze shyly, suddenly unsure of himself.

"You should have known I'd be here. I like watching you," Kenneth said.

"Uh, look, uh, I've got to hurry, but I wanted to know: what are you doing after the game?" Clay stammered.

"Probably stop for a quick burger and then back to prison," Kenneth said. "Why?"

"I thought maybe... I'd like to talk to you."

"I'm riding with a friend. You got wheels?"

"No, but it's not that far to the Academy. I'll walk back with you."

"Okay, but it's cold as hell outside."

"You won't freeze. I guarantee," Clay said, his voice filled with innuendo that sent both their hearts racing.

"Clay! Coach says get your ass downstairs!" a freshman third-stringer interrupted, tugging at Clay's shoulder.

"I got to go. Wait for me in front of the classroom building. It won't take any time for me to shower and dress," Clay said, moving away.

"I'll be there," Kenneth called after him. "I wouldn't miss it for the world," he added under his breath.

278

- - -

"I'm freezing!" Kenneth protested when Clay finally pushed into the tiny alcove where it seemed he had waited for an hour, muscles trembling involuntarily against the biting cold, which his thin tunic could not seal out.

"I'm sorry. I hurried as much as I could," Clay said, stepping closer. "You are cold; your teeth are chattering." Impulsively, he wrapped his arms around Kenneth and pulled the smaller boy against his chest, his big frame swallowing him in his embrace.

Kenneth nestled his cheek against the rough fabric of Clay's athletic jacket, luxuriating in this unexpected intimacy. This was promising to be easier than he had imagined.

Clay shifted slightly and unbuttoned his jacket and wrapped it around Kenneth. "Here, put your hands inside," he said, pulling Kenneth tight against him.

Kenneth ran his hands around Clay's sides and wrapped his arms around his back. He felt the heat radiating from Clay's body. His cock surged to life with a force that threatened to rip through his trousers. He groaned slightly and ground his erection against the taller boy's thigh and discovered Clay's own hardness pressing into his abdomen.

Although Clay had never kissed a boy before, caught up in the moment, he lifted Kenneth's chin with his fingers and leaned down to part his lips, thrusting his tongue deep into Kenneth's mouth. As Kenneth avidly returned the kiss, Clay reached down and cupped the rounded spheres of Kenneth's buttocks in both his big hands and kneaded hungrily.

"Whew! I thought you wanted to talk," Kenneth said when they finally separated.

"Looks like we don't need to waste time," Clay said. "I think we both know what we want."

"We can't do much besides talk here," Kenneth said.

"Come on, let's go," Clay said, stepping back and re-buttoning his jacket.

They walked silently about a half mile toward the Academy, keeping their distance, afraid to touch in the glare of cars zooming by occasionally.

"Where're we going?" Kenneth asked when Clay cut off the road onto a nearly obscured path into a pine woods. "It better not be far. I'm freezing my balls off again."

"We're almost there," Clay answered, putting an arm around Kenneth's shoulder and pulling him close.

A few hundred yards into the woods, they came to a darkened log cabin set in a small clearing. Clay withdrew a key ring and fumbled with a padlock on the door.

"What's this place?" Kenneth asked as they stepped into the room and Clay closed the door behind them.

"Boy Scout hut," Clay replied. He moved familiarly through the room, struck a match, and lit two small camp stoves. "These'll warm the place up pretty fast," he said, stepping up to embrace Kenneth again. "In the meantime, I'll do my best to keep you from freezing, like I promised."

In the faint blue light thrown off by the stoves, Kenneth could make out the features of the room, the American and Boy Scout flags against one wall, the ordered rows of chairs against another, the camping equipment neatly stashed on shelves along an end wall. Just beyond where they stood was a thick pallet of sleeping bags framed by the two stoves. Clay obviously had things well planned. This discovery of premeditation sent shivers of excitement through Kenneth.

"You're still a Boy Scout?" he asked as he began to unbutton Clay's jacket.

"Explorer," Clay said. "We don't have a separate troop, so I meet with the younger guys as a sort of Assistant Scoutmaster. I'll get my Eagle rank soon, and I want to stick with it at least until then."

"I don't think I've ever corrupted a Boy Scout before," Kenneth said.

"This Boy Scout plans to do the corrupting," Clay said, removing Kenneth's tunic and draping it over a chair.

They hurried out of their clothes and crawled naked into the top sleeping bag, huddling and shivering and deep-kissing until their body heat thawed out the kapok padding.

When they had warmed up, Kenneth threw back the covering and explored Clay's body. Up close and completely naked, Clay was even more imposing than Kenneth had realized. His hand could not half encompass the firm biceps. Clay's broad chest displayed prominent pecs with a small thatch of brick-red hair in the valley between them. His nipples were big as half dollars, the nubs firm and erect. Kenneth leaned down and took one in his mouth and sucked and nibbled as one hand slid down Clay's chest and hard abdomen for what seemed like two yards until he entered the forest of wiry hair and reached for the prize he had lusted for.

"My god! What is this thing?" he whispered as he wrapped his hand around a cock thicker than any he had ever created in his hungriest fantasies. Sliding his hand along the shaft, he quickly realized it also was the longest he had encountered. He stacked one, two, three handbreadths up the rigid pole before he reached the rim of the cowled glans.

Clay responded to Kenneth's question and tantalizing hand movements with only a loud groan. He knew the exact dimensions of his appendage, and, though he was proud of the stares and comments it evoked in the shower room, he had come to wish he were not so well endowed. Both a blessing and a curse, his huge cock had caught the attention of a few local kids, who eyed it and licked their lips in desire. But when they had it in their mouths, they could not do much with it. When he had tried to screw a couple of them, it had terrified them when he barely started in, and he had backed off, afraid of hurting them and of having them talk later.

He had sensed that Kenneth was more experienced than the local kids, but

Kenneth's awed response to his cock dampened his hopes that, at last, somebody would be able to provide what he had come to consider the ultimate experience. Since he had first noticed the way Kenneth's tight round ass molded his uniform trousers and undulated when he walked, his desire to plunge full-length into it and stay there for hours had become something of an obsession.

Kenneth squeezed the base of the big rod with one hand and peeled back the foreskin with the other, freeing the dimpled head, as big as a small apple. As he slowly eased the foreskin back and forth, he wondered what he was going to be able to do with this prize now that he had won it. Deciding to find out, he bent down and took the bulbous crown into his mouth and began nibbling and tonguing it. As his excitement grew, his mouth relaxed and he gradually eased down until the tip of Clay's cock rested at the entry to his throat. Then he paused to regroup, his mouth stretched open wider than it had ever been.

Clay quivered in faint paroxysms of anticipation as Kenneth sank farther and farther down on his cock. All the other kids had backed off gagging after they took little more than the head in, if they could manage that much. When Kenneth stopped after absorbing close to a third of him and did not take his mouth off, Clay reached with one hand to explore between Kenneth's legs. With the other, he cupped the back of Kenneth's head and firmly coaxed it forward. The one hand located a longer-than-average, thin, cut cock, but at the moment it did not hold Clay's interest. He was intent upon burying his complete rod in the warm pleasure point of Kenneth's mouth.

"Yeah! Suck my cock! Take it all!" he growled roughly, increasing the pressure on Kenneth's head.

Kenneth pushed against Clay's thighs and twisted his head away, breaking free. He coughed and struggled for breath. He was a little anxious at the way the night was turning out. With all the other kids in all the other towns, he had always been in charge. As much as he was turned on when he finally got in some kid's pants, after toying briefly with his newly found prize, he selfishly concentrated on his own needs. More than a few times, he had carried some virtual innocent almost to orgasm, only to flip him on his stomach and callously fuck him. With Clay, however, he sensed that he was not at all in control.

As exciting as the challenge of swallowing more of this huge tool was, a little prickle of fear warned him that, as big and strong as Clay was, he could easily overpower him and force his cock down his throat, unconcerned about choking him.

"Let me do the work," he said when he found his voice. "I want to try to take it all, but I'll have to go slow. I don't know if my throat will open that wide."

"Okay, I'm sorry," Clay said. "But, god, it felt good!" He went back to fisting Kenneth's cock and gently rubbed his back as Kenneth took him in his mouth again.

After several attempts, Kenneth's throat finally relaxed enough for the huge cock head to slide past, and with a sense of victory, he gradually eased it on down his gullet until Clay's pubic hair tickled his lips. He felt like shouting, but

all he could manage was a gurgle. With Clay trembling and writhing around beneath him, fighting the urge to drive in even deeper, Kenneth began a steady sucking with his lips, matching their movements at the base with rhythmical contractions of his throat around the middle of the shaft. Then he withdrew to breathe and work on the head awhile before gradually swallowing it all again.

Clay was almost delirious with pleasure. For the first time, somebody was actually sucking his cock instead of just licking and tonguing it. As exciting as it was, though, it was not what he had dreamed of doing.

As Kenneth kept flicking his tongue around maddeningly and diving down to the base periodically, Clay reached to squeeze Kenneth's ass cheeks. He rubbed the tips of his fingers through the crack between the two firm globes and circled the ring of Kenneth's ass with his moistened forefinger, gradually working it in to the first, second, third thick knuckle. Kenneth sighed with pleasure, thrust his ass into the air, and contracted his sphincter around Clay's finger, which was rotating as deep inside as he could probe.

"I want to fuck you," Clay said, matter-of-factly. He withdrew from Kenneth's mouth and crouched beside him, rubbing and kneading his ass. "Come on, let me put it up in you," he insisted.

Kenneth's good sense battled his growing excitement. His ass was far from virgin, but it had never been invaded by anything close to the thick timber between Clay's legs. The thought of being trapped beneath Clay's big body, unable to move while Clay impaled him on his monster cock, sent waves of panic through him. Overriding the panic, though, was a newly born desire to be dominated by this big farm boy, to gain a new form of pleasure in knowing that he had been used to the fullest by Clay, instead of using him, as he had originally intended.

"I don't know; that's the biggest dick I've ever seen," he hedged.

"I really want to fuck you," Clay said, a tremor of excitement in his voice.

"It would take lots more than spit, but I don't think I could handle it no matter what you used," Kenneth said.

Clay reached over his head for a first aid kit, placed in readiness near the sleeping bags. He opened it and took out a small jar of Vaseline. "I've got something to use," he said, handing the jar to Kenneth.

Fired by the knowledge that Clay had dreamed about this and prepared for it, Kenneth rolled onto his side and dabbed big gobs of the jelly into his opening while Clay kneeled before him and rubbed his ass cheeks, almost panting with desire.

"Grease me up good, too," Clay ordered, thrusting his cock toward Kenneth's hand.

As he worked the thick Vaseline up and down Clay's long shaft, Kenneth had a strong urge to back out, to grab his uniform and flee to safety. He knew, though, that they had gone too far for that. Already, Clay was lying tight against him, maneuvering him onto his stomach. Kenneth knew that Clay could take him by force if necessary.

282

"Lie on your back," he said, breaking away from Clay and pushing against his chest. "I want to try sitting on it until I get used to it."

Clay rolled onto his back and Kenneth crouched over him, holding his cock upright with one hand. He wiggled around until Clay was centered beneath the target and gradually eased his weight down onto the rigid pole. Clay lunged off the floor and his huge cock head shoved through Kenneth's muscular barrier.

"Damn! Use your dick instead of your fist!" Kenneth said, flinching away from the intense pain of intrusion.

Clay was in no mood to joke. For the first time, he had penetrated a guy's ass, and he single-mindedly focused on burying the full length of his cock in this delightfully new, soft warmth. He grabbed Kenneth's slim hips in his big hands and shoved down in one hard push, until Kenneth's ass cheeks caressed his thighs. "Oh, god, it's in there. Wow, I'm gonna fuck your ass!" he cried out in near disbelief.

Almost in a panic, Kenneth winced in pain and tried to raise himself off the huge firebrand that seared his insides all the way through his abdomen. "Stop! You're killing me!" he begged.

Caught up in the fulfillment of a long-denied goal, Clay was unmindful of Kenneth's pain. He tugged downward on Kenneth's hips while bucking his own ass a foot off the floor in rapid staccato thrusts, pile driving Kenneth's ass. Fighting back tears, Kenneth collapsed forward onto Clay's chest and pushed himself upward to soften the onslaught.

It was over almost before it began. Clay lunged forward with several quick, short jabs, crying "Shit! Oh, shit!" on each one, and then collapsed against the sleeping bag. "Damn! I shot off too quick," he complained.

"Not for me. You were splitting me open," Kenneth said, moving to extricate himself.

"Don't get up. I ain't through," Clay said, grabbing him by the hips again. He twisted onto his side, arched his body, and gradually rolled Kenneth onto his back and lay heavily on top of him, his cock still fully erect and fully embedded.

Accepting the inevitable, Kenneth wrapped arms and legs around Clay's big frame, heels digging into Clay's buttocks. "Go slow," he whispered. "You don't realize how big that thing is."

His driving lust partially cooled, Clay settled into a gentle, leisurely fuck, intrigued by the novelty of the position he had accidentally discovered. All of his failed attempts had been with him crouched behind some kid on hands and knees. He had never even conceived of doing it lying atop a guy, face to face.

He softly thrust only part way and rotated his hips in broad, circular motions, relishing the velvety warmth gently embracing his huge cock. The stimulation on Kenneth's prostate overrode the pain, and soon he was lifting up to meet Clay, clenching his ass tightly to create resistance on his upswings.

"Oh, yeah! God, this is great!" Clay cried. "You're the only one who's been able to take it. You're the only one, and it's so fuckin' beautiful!" He raised up on elbows and craned his neck down until he could lock his mouth on

Kenneth's.

Kenneth's entire body trembled with the newfound excitement of lying completely submissive beneath Clay and offering himself for Clay's pleasure. His restless hands twisted in Clay's hair and roamed down, kneading the flexing muscles of his back and on down until they grasped his powerful buttocks and tugged them toward him, coaxing even more of Clay's cock inside. His own cock throbbed and thrashed around between them until, finally, the stimulation became too intense.

"Oh, god! I'm gonna come!" he cried out. "I'm coming!" For the first time in his life, he exploded without anyone having touched his cock, and he exploded in torrents, his body convulsing as if he were being drained all the way from his toes.

All the time, Clay continued the attack on his ass, fighting to drive his rod past the rapidly pulsating muscle. Just as Kenneth's last spasms faded, Clay cried out a long, "Aaaah!" and lunged forward, burying himself as deep as possible. His huge cock bucked and fought against Kenneth's confining walls and washed them with wave after wave of his hot cream.

Afterward, Clay was as affectionate as a puppy, almost childlike in his euphoria. He dipped steaming water from a pan Kenneth had not noticed on one of the stoves, cooled it from a nearby bucket, and cleaned Kenneth off with towels he had laid out, pausing regularly to kiss and caress Kenneth's body.

Kenneth languidly reclined on the sleeping bag, thrilling to Clay's gentle touch, amazed at the complete contentment achieved through his submission. He was certain that sex had never been more pleasurable.

"What time do you have to be back?" Clay asked, thrusting them both back into reality.

Kenneth strained to see his watch. "Oh, hell! I'm already locked out," he said.

"I didn't mean to get you in trouble," Clay said.

"My roommate's making bed check. He'll cover for me tonight," Kenneth said. "I'm all right as long as I make roll call tomorrow morning, but I don't have anywhere to stay."

"Oh, yes you do," Clay said, tumbling on top of him and grappling in a bear hug. "We'll stay here together. I think I can keep you from being bored."

"More likely, you're planning to bore me all night," Kenneth joked, "but don't you have to go home?"

"I lied to my parents that I was staying with a friend," Clay said.

"That's not a lie," Kenneth said, kissing him lightly, "but what would you have done if I hadn't come here with you?"

"Spent the night here alone and jacked off thinking about you, I guess," Clay admitted.

"That would have been a real waste," Kenneth said, reaching for his huge cock.

Clay fucked him twice more during the night, with no diminished enthusiasm

284

or pleasure. Although Kenneth did not come again, he finally drifted into sleep as contented as he had ever been.

He awoke suddenly in the first light of day with Clay's mouth wrapped around his stiff cock. It came as a complete surprise; he had supposed that Clay always would seek only his own pleasure. He lay thrilling to the warmth of Clay's mouth and let his hands drift idly over Clay's broad back. Clay's inexperience was obvious, but so was his enthusiasm. With some instruction and lots of practice, Kenneth knew, he would become a master. Kenneth intended to see that he got both.

After Clay had taken his load and spit and rinsed and spit some more, Kenneth pulled him down between his spread legs, encouraging him to fuck him. "I'm all tuckered out," Clay said. "I just wanted to pleasure you this morning."

As they prepared to leave, Clay tossed Kenneth a heavy lined flannel shirt he dug out of a backpack. "Here, I don't want you to freeze before you get to the barracks."

"If Boy Scouts is always this much fun, I think I'll join," Kenneth said as they walked arm in arm toward the highway.

"I'm holding a private session for new members at the Scout hut Sunday afternoon," Clay said. "Think you can make it?"

"I wouldn't miss it for the world," Kenneth said, pulling Clay's head down for a kiss.

THE SHOOTERS OF SHOOTING CREEK

Thomas C. Humphrey

The cool grass caressing my lower legs and tickling my balls, I settled back on my haunches and waited uneasily for my next instructions. As the fleeting fingers of a mountain breeze teased across my bare body, hardening my nipples and tingling through my groin, I strained to catch even a glimmer of light beyond the tight blindfold or the slightest sound from my companions. This wasn't turning out anywhere near what I had envisioned when I sneaked out of camp with Todd, Chet, and Bo as soon as it was good dark.

"All right, Jeremy, start strokin' it," Chet spoke from over my left shoulder.

"Aw, come on, guys," I protested.

"You agreed to a circle jerk, remember?" Chet said.

"Yeah, but...."

"So, we make the circle and you jerk," Bo said, half-snickering.

"You gotta do it if you want to hang with us," Todd said. "Get at it. We don't have all night."

I did want to hang with them, in the worst way - especially with Todd. But it was only the second day of summer camp, and, as I slowly started fingering my limp dick, it struck home that I didn't even know these guys, not really. For all I knew, this was some cruel trick they were playing on me, like having half the camp run in laughing just about the time I shot my load, or sneaking off and leaving me to find my way back to the cabin without a stitch of clothes. As excited as I had been when we left camp, I doubted that I could even get a hard-on, not under these conditions. But I had gotten myself into this fix, I knew, so I had to see it on out.

Spending a month at Shooting Creek Wilderness Camp in the foothills of the Smoky Mountains hadn't been my idea of the perfect summer vacation from the beginning. I had wanted to stay at home and play baseball and goof around and party with my friends. But Mom and her new boyfriend and almost certainly my soon-to-be stepdad had insisted on camp, mostly to get rid of me for at least a month. After I had fretted and fumed and pouted that I'd had enough artsy-craftsy crap and was too old for little kid stuff, they had settled on Shooting Creek.

The Wilderness Camp idea did sound interesting on paper, I had to admit. From the base camp, small groups would go out for days at a time, partially living off the land while learning to scale steep mountain cliffs and rappel back down, maneuver across deep gorges on rope bridges, and shoot white water rapids of a nearby river in canoes. I had always liked the outdoors and had done my share of camping out, but always in the piney flatlands of south Georgia. Mountain camping would be a new challenge. I actually had left home filled with excitement.

Reality quickly intruded my first day at camp. I was put in an eight-man cabin with a bunch of dorky, whiny kids two or three years younger than me, and I caught on right away that I would be stuck with some of them the entire time, even when we left base camp. I gloomily resigned myself to a miserable month.

My spirits weren't lifted any when I had a run-in with a hulking, dumb-jock, football-lineman type who tried to shove ahead of me in the chow line the very first day. He was older than me and outweighed me by a hundred pounds, but I'd never backed down from a fight, and we were squared away and ready to go at it until a counselor stepped in and sent the fucker to the back of the line. His angry glare as he turned away from me made it clear that he planned to kick my ass the first chance he got.

The only glimmer of light that first day was Todd MacCarton, a lithe, good-looking blond kid. He caught my eye right off, as we checked in and filed physical examination reports and received cabin assignments. He was seated at a desk collecting paperwork, and I assumed he was one of the counselors, although he didn't look much older than me. I found out later that day that he was a senior camper, back for his third summer, along with his buddies Chet and Bo.

That afternoon, everybody had to take a swim test to see if we needed lessons before tackling the river. As I stood around waiting my turn, I couldn't keep from staring at Todd, who was assisting the swim instructor with the tests. Some of the kids around me whispered among themselves that he was a state champion swimmer from a big high school in Atlanta.

In the brilliant glare around the pool, Todd's evenly tanned body glistened and the sun's rays haloed through his tightly curled hair. His hard, lean body was hairless, except for an almost transparent tangle on his legs, which also glowed in the sun. His blue bikini was molded to his firm flesh and provocatively outlined his rounded, up-thrust ass and the ample bulge in front. I had an almost irresistible urge to reach out and trace the contours of his chest with my fingers. By the time I stepped up for my test, my breathing was shallow and I was fighting against an erection that kept straining against my jock strap.

"Ready, slugger?" Todd said with a wink. "Let's see if you're as eager to swim as you are to fight." He flashed a broad smile and reached to punch me on the arm.

With that encouragement, I dived in and swam four lengths of the pool in what, for me, was record time. I knew then that I would do almost anything to earn another smile and touch from him.

The rest of that day and most of the second, as I went about the daily rituals of camp life with my dorky cabin-mates, I was always aware of Todd's presence. I noticed right away that he and Chet and Bo were inseparable and didn't have much to do with the other campers. While I was gleaning this information, though, Todd didn't even acknowledge that I was alive.

Late that second afternoon, during a free-swim period, we started a tug-of-war

contest, with the bigger guys carrying a smaller one on their shoulders. The riders would grapple with each other, attempting to topple the other and, if possible, the one who supported him, into the water. The last team standing would win.

"Come on, Jeremy; be my partner," Todd surprised me. I didn't know he even knew my name.

It was great fun for a while. One after another, Todd and I dumped our challengers into the pool. Todd maneuvered so quickly, his legs and body were so powerful, and I was so excitedly determined to win that we appeared unbeatable.

Then, with nobody else left standing, another kid and I were grappling directly over our partners' heads. As the kid pulled forward and Todd strained backward, I was rocked back and forth on Todd's shoulders. With each forward tug, my crotch jammed into Todd's neck. In the midst of intense competition, I realized that I was getting a hard-on, and I fretted that Todd would feel its firmness against his neck. I twisted and squirmed, trying to relieve the pressure, and momentarily lost my concentration. The other team sidestepped and rushed forward suddenly, and both Todd and I were dragged backward into the water. We came up sputtering.

"Well, partner, somebody finally beat us," Todd laughed.

"It was my fault. I'm sorry," I said, my face flushed with embarrassment.

"No big deal," Todd said, draping his arm across my shoulder. "Come on, let's challenge them again."

"I don't think so; I'm pretty tired," I said, feeling my cock swell even more under Todd's touch. I stepped out from under his arm and swam to the side of the pool and waited for my erection to subside before climbing out.

Toward dusk, as I headed for my cabin after mailing a letter at the canteen, I saw Todd and his buddies lounging under a tree. I was pretty sure that Todd pointed to me and whispered something to the others. Then he held up thumbs and forefingers of both hands and measured off a good six to eight inches. All three of them burst into laughter. Immediately, my face flushed and my heart started drumming. I had walked past them without speaking when Todd called to me.

"Hey, Jeremy! You don't even speak to your old tug-of-war horse, huh?" he said lightly.

"Hi, Todd," I said, retracing my steps to stand beside him.

"How do you like your cabin assignment?" he asked after introducing me to Chet and Bo.

"It's a crock," I said. "Nothing but a bunch of crybabies."

"We're stuck with a real dork, too," he said, "but we're shipping him out. How'd you like to maybe bunk with us?"

"Are you serious?" I said, my heart beginning to pump with excitement. I already knew that, as senior campers, the three of them were completely on their own in a small four-man cabin without a counselor.

"Yeah, maybe," Todd said. "Course, we'd have to vote on it. Chet and Bo and I go way back together, and we don't want just anybody bunking with us. We're looking for somebody special."

"That's right," Chet said. "We liked the way you squared off against that dickhead in the chow hall yesterday. That's one point in your favor."

"And I liked our game in the pool today. That's another point," Todd added, a broad grin spreading across his face.

"But we need to know you ain't a pussy," Bo said. "We're looking for somebody who'll bend the rules a little, somebody who's willing to experiment and try new things."

"Yeah, like, we're not supposed to go up to the lake after dark, but we do. Are you willing to go with us?" Chet said.

"Yeah, sure," I said hurriedly. I was prepared to walk barefoot across hot coals for the chance to bunk with them and be around Todd for the next month.

We sneaked behind the cabins and into the woods. As we headed up the trail toward the lake, Todd filled me in on some things. "We've known each other since grade school," he said. "We have sort of a club. The three of us are permanent members, and every summer we choose somebody else to join while we're here at camp."

"We had another kid from Atlanta we thought would make a good member this summer," Bo said. "But the doof broke his arm last week and had to cancel out on camp. I was looking forward to initiating him into the club, too."

"Initiating?" I said. "What does that involve?"

"Oh, not much," Chet said.

We walked on quietly for a while, and then Todd hit me with a question. "You ever jack off, Jeremy?"

I swallowed hard and made a split-second decision to tell the truth. "Sure, all the time. Doesn't everybody?"

"A month's a long time, and you don't get much chance to be alone here. You're almost always with at least one other guy," Todd said. "You ever been in a circle jerk?"

"Sure," I exaggerated. The only thing I'd ever done besides fantasize was to jack off with my friend Jimmy, who was so uptight he wouldn't consider doing anything else. He wouldn't even let me see him shoot his load, and every time after we finished he swore we were going to hell and vowed never to do it again.

"A circle jerk is mostly what the initiation is," Chet said. "That way, we know you're not some mama's boy who's gonna cramp our style for a month."

"So, what do you think?" Todd asked. "You ready to get initiated tonight and move in with us tomorrow?"

"Yeah, sure," I said, having to force my words through my tight throat, my dick swelling in my shorts. I was going to jack off with Todd! God was in his Heaven, after all!

Then they sprang their surprise on me. "Okay, take off all your clothes except your sneakers," Chet told me.

290

As I undressed, they stood and watched, instead of stripping themselves, as I expected. When I slid my shorts and briefs off and stood up, exposing my nearly stiff dick, Bo commented, "We knew you had balls after you didn't back down in the chow hall, but now I see you've got a nice cock to go along with them."

"I told you, didn't I?" Todd said.

Chet pulled out a thick band of cloth and walked behind me. "Now, we blindfold you," he said, fitting the cloth over my eyes and securing it behind my head.

"Now, let's go for a walk," Todd said, grabbing my elbow and guiding me through the woods. We walked for a good while, twisting and turning until I was completely disoriented. Finally, we stopped in some ankle-high grass and they told me to kneel down and start jacking off.

Despite my concern that it all might be some kind of prank, my cock rose to the occasion, as always, and I kept stroking it with a steady rhythm, not knowing whether they had crept off, leaving me stranded. Straining my ears, I heard from in front, then to my left, then my right, the faint, rhythmical susurrations of flesh sliding against flesh. They were jacking off along with me, matching my rhythm stroke for stroke.

I had an almost irresistible urge to snatch the blindfold off so that I could feast my eyes on their equipment and watch their faces contort with ecstasy as they neared their peak. The fact that I couldn't see them especially Todd became a real torture. But it was a delicious torture, as, one by one, they began sighing and finally moaning with approaching climax. It all fired me up almost to the point of explosion, and I groaned, "Aah! Aaah!" and really started pounding my rod.

"Tell us when you start to shoot," Todd instructed from directly in front of me.

"Uh-uh," I managed. Then, after a couple more quick strokes, I knew I couldn't hold back. "Now! I'm coming! I'm coming!" I groaned.

Just as the first spurt escaped from my cock head, splat Todd's load blasted into my face. I instinctively reached to wipe it off, turned my dick loose, and started to stand up. Strong hands on each of my shoulders held me in position, and somebody I guessed Todd grabbed a handful of hair and tilted my head back as his load sprayed over my nose and lips and chin and dribbled down onto my chest.

My own cock was swinging and swaying and spurting like an unmanned fire hose, in the most intense climax I'd ever experienced. As it began to subside, more blasts of cum washed across my chest from both sides as Chet and Bo directed their loads onto my body. When they were completely spent, somebody snatched the blindfold off my eyes.

As I blinked and adjusted my eyes to the faint light of a quarter moon, my first impulse was to come up swinging. As good as my climax had been, I was pissed at the way they had used me and felt befouled by their sticky cum all over my body. But Todd was standing with a big, happy grin on his face, dangling in

front of me a perfectly formed, creamy-white cock with its head just retreating into its protective covering. It looked so beautiful that all my anger evaporated.

I turned to my left for my first glimpse of Bo's naked body and his rather short, cut cock as big around as my wrist, a dick in perfect symmetry with his compact, tightly-muscled build. To my right, Chet's lank, nude frame towered over me, and he still fingered his exceptionally long but thin shaft, crowned with an outsized head. The two of them were completely different, but, I unhesitatingly decided, both turned me on in their own way. Todd, however, had already captivated me, and seeing him nude intensified my desire for him. I quickly turned my attention back to him and his beautiful dick.

He stepped close between my legs and reached down to swipe at my cum, which had sprayed over my stomach and soaked into my pubes. "You shot a hell of a load," he said.

He started saying something in a dialect I didn't understand, but which I later learned was an ancient Scottish clan oath he'd learned from his grandmother. As he recited, it was if he were dubbing me into knighthood, except he dabbed some of my cum on my forehead and then onto each of my cheeks, which he had already sprayed with his own semen. Chet and Bo collected some of their cum from my chest and repeated the ritual Todd had performed, intermingling the essence of all of us on my face.

When they finished, Todd pronounced in a very formal tone, "Welcome. You have proved to be a worthy shooter. You are now a full-fledged member of The Shooters of Shooting Creek. You are duty-bound to get off at least once every day, with one or more of us, if possible."

Chet and Bo lifted me to my feet and, with broad grins on their faces, they all shook my hand and said they were glad I had gone through the initiation.

Bo and Chet went down to the lake, which was only a few steps away, and washed their hands and then started getting dressed. Todd made no move for his clothes, and I didn't even know where mine were.

"We'll go on back and cover for you two while you get cleaned up," Chet said, stooping to tie his sneakers.

"Yeah, but don't take all night, Todd," Bo cautioned with a smirk.

After they disappeared down the trail, Todd and I walked into the frigid water and he helped me clean off the accumulation of cum, which was now dry and flaky all over my face and chest. "Sorry about the mess," Todd apologized, "but it's a real rush to cream on somebody when they don't expect it."

"I don't know," I said. "Not being able to see you jack off was the worst part of it. You don't know how much I wanted to snatch that blindfold off."

"Don't worry. You'll have plenty of opportunities to see all you want of all of us. No more blindfolds. You were a good sport about it, but I was sure you would be."

After I cleaned up, Todd suggested that we swim awhile before heading back. I matched him stroke for stroke until we were a good way out into the lake, but I knew I couldn't maintain the pace he had set.

292

"I'm turning back," I called.

When I was about a quarter of the way back, I turned and saw Todd treading water where I had left him. Suddenly, he began swimming with powerful racing strokes, almost gliding through the water, eating up yardage. I began pulling as hard as I could toward the shore, but Todd sped by me and then disappeared about the time I touched bottom and stood up in waist-deep water.

I looked all around without seeing Todd, and then I felt him pushing his body through my legs from the rear. One hand cupped around my cock and balls as he wiggled through and turned to face me, still submerged. His warm mouth engulfed my shriveled cock, which hardened almost at once. I had dreamed about having my cock sucked as much as I had fantasized about having other guys' rods in my mouth, but in my wildest fantasy, I had never imagined it happening for the first time with someone as overwhelmingly attractive as Todd. My legs almost buckled beneath me, I was so excited.

He finally came to the surface and pressed close against me. His hands roamed over my slippery back hungrily, and he ground his erect cock into my groin. With one hand, he lifted my chin and leaned in to kiss me. His other hand strayed down my back and massaged my buttocks. I pulled him even tighter against me and reached for his cock, which bucked and throbbed when I touched it.

"Let's get out," he said hoarsely.

We paused under a tree for another long kiss, then dropped onto the thick carpet of grass, arms and legs entwined. Todd rolled me onto my back and planted light, quick kisses on my forehead, nose, chin, and throat. His hand strayed over my chest and abdomen and on down to my engorged cock. His lips moved to my chest, his teeth played at a nipple. I lay in near ecstasy, my hands frantically rifling through his hair and burrowing into his shoulders.

His exploring lips moved downward. I held my breath in anticipation, my thighs quivering uncontrollably. When Todd's mouth engulfed my cock, I emitted a quick breath and raised up off the grass to meet him. He began a series of delicate movements with lips and tongue that set me on fire. I had never felt such intense pleasure before. My balls tightened up until it felt like they had retreated into my abdomen, and I knew I couldn't bear the acute stimulation much longer.

"Quit! Not yet!" I groaned, shoving at his head and twisting away from his ravenous mouth.

I flipped him onto his back and grabbed his cock. As I bent toward it, I muttered, "I've never done this before. I hope you won't be disappointed."

Then I eased my mouth down on his shaft until his cock head brushed against my tonsils and I had to back off to keep from gagging. As I got accustomed to having him in my mouth, I relaxed and tried to duplicate some of the things he had done to me. My tongue hungrily explored the sericeous texture of his long shaft and probed beneath his foreskin and around the tender rim of his cock head. His trembling thighs and low sighs of pleasure told me I was doing

something right.

After what seemed like almost no time, Todd was rearing up off the grass, arching his back and thrusting deep into my mouth. He grabbed my hair with both hands and tugged me down on his cock. The thick tube on the underside swelled and throbbed against my lip, and he shot blast after blast into my mouth. Shocked by the unexpected force and unfamiliar taste of it, I tried to pull away, but Todd held me in position until I had taken his full load and he sagged back onto the grass.

"Whew!" Todd exhaled as I turned to spit out his cum. "That was the greatest! The best ever! And you're virgin? I don't believe it!"

"It's true. I've never done anything before," I said, snuggling close against him. "Believe me, I've dreamed about it a lot, but actually doing it was better than any dream." I reached for his softening dick. "I could fall in love with this thing."

"You'll get all the opportunities you want," he said, "but it's my turn now."

He pushed me onto my back and swallowed me down to the roots. I let out a cry of amazement and sheer pleasure as I felt my cock head slide past his tonsils. He shifted until he knelt between my thighs. As his tongue lashed my throbbing shaft, one hand cradled and squeezed my tight nut sac, the other explored my ass and one finger slid inside me. I set up a gentle hunching, driving my shaft deep into his throat time after time.

As our intensity mounted, it was as if I underwent an out-of-body experience and hovered somewhere looking down on the two of us succumbing to our passion. Then all of my being focused on my cock and the stimulation of Todd's warm mouth, and the rest of the world ceased to exist. I desperately wanted the experience never to end, but, inevitably, I passed the point where I could not sustain it any longer, and with several primal cries from somewhere deep inside, I erupted voluminously into his eager mouth.

Afterward, we lay in a languid embrace, our hands constantly exploring, lips barely touching. "I sure didn't expect this," I said. "I thought all of us would just jack off together."

"Jacking off's a poor substitute for other things we can do," Todd said.

"You've got that right!" I agreed. "But what about Chet and Bo? Do they...?"

"Yeah, we do all kinds of things together, and they're both gonna be waiting for a shot at you," Todd said. "But I've already staked a claim on you most of the time. I can't wait to work on that sexy ass and take your cherry. It's gonna be great sharing a sleeping bag on a cold night when we start our wilderness hikes!"

His talk and the promise of things to come made my dick rise up again. "Do we have to hurry back?" I asked. "Why don't you break my ass in now?"

"Are you sure?" Todd said. "I'm pretty big, and I don't want to hurt you too much. We should wait until we have some proper lubricant and all." His hand drifted to my buttocks and spread my cheeks. One finger again eased up in me. "But that is one hot ass! I'd like to take it now!"

294

"Then do it," I urged. "I want it to be you, and I want it to be now."

Todd again knelt between my legs and took my cock in his mouth. As he sucked me, he kept wetting his fingers and rubbing around my ass and working one, then two fingers inside me. When he had me relaxed enough, he lifted my legs onto his shoulders and lubricated his dick. In the faint light, it suddenly looked huge, and I almost backed out, but when he rubbed the tip of his cock head around the perimeter of my ass, it felt too good to give up.

"Just relax and push out," Todd advised. "It'll hurt a little at first, but then you'll love it, I guarantee!"

He gently pressed forward, and I opened up to accept him. The pain was sharp at first, but as he eased in farther and farther, I realized that the discomfort was only at the surface. Deeper inside, his thick cock set up a warm glow that spread throughout my abdomen. When he was all the way in, he began short, easy in-and-out movements and swiveled his pelvis from side to side. I reached back and grabbed his ass cheeks and pulled him into me tighter and faster until he was really pounding it to me.

I switched one hand to my own demanding cock and stroked it in rhythm to Todd's deep drives into my ass. We both were sweating and moaning and writhing around on the grass, and then I exploded all over my chest. Todd kept shoving into my pulsating ass, and with a few grunts, buried his cock all the way inside me. I felt it swell against my confining walls and then bathe my insides with his warm jism. When he was done, he collapsed on top of me and lay panting and fighting for breath.

"Thanks for the cherry. It was delicious!" he said as we walked back toward camp. "Next time, you get to be top, okay? I want that big rod of yours up in me."

"Glad to oblige, any time," I said. "I've got to uphold the Shooters tradition of at least once a day, don't I?"

"I've got a feeling once a day won't be enough," he grinned. "Maybe I'll change the bylaws to make it at least five times. I suspect it'll take that to drain a horny guy like you."

I stopped him and pulled him tight against me. "Think you're up to it?" I teased. "I wouldn't want to wear you out." Before he could answer, I pulled his head down and crammed my tongue in his mouth.

As we kissed, I silently thanked Mom and her boyfriend for making me the newest Shooter of Shooting Creek.

SO HARD, IT HURT

John Patrick

One day a letter would arrive in the mail, with directions about where my bus would leave, and my father or my mother would take me there along with a duffel bag that had all my things with name tags sewn on, and wave goodbye, not having the lamest notion to what sort of place I was being taken.

Now, I'm not saying my folks were negligent, but their indifference led to some uncomfortable situations. For instance, one summer I ended up being the only white boy in an all-black YMCA camp. Of course, I was much too young to fully appreciate all of the ramifications of this. The next summer I landed in a Christian Bible camp. Those had to be the worst weeks of my life. It was not until the next summer that my parents, without knowing it, of course, did me the greatest favor of my young life they sent me to Old Camp Myakka.

At this haven, our bunkhouse was situated at the top of the hill, surrounded by woods, and every morning we ran down to the mess hall for cocoa and pancakes, or whatever they had for breakfast. It was a pretty nice camp: all the activities swimming, baseball, crafts, meals seemed to take place on the field below, while the bunkhouses were notched into a steep, wooded hill. Our cabin was nothing but a lean-to, with a roof but no supporting walls. Once I lifted my head from my pillow in the early morning and saw a crocodile slither by, through the mist around the lean-to. "No more than six feet away!" I was hysterical. Then all the other boys pretended they had seen it, too.

One day the other boys went off to their first activity and I waited behind, hoping to talk to Chuck, our counselor. He had held me and soothed me when the croc had invaded our space and I felt a strange kinship with him. I knew he would return to straighten up the bunk and inspect the beds. At least that's what I assumed he was doing checking for contraband in our mattresses. He was probably just grabbing a few minutes by himself, to read a magazine I imagined he was jerking off to pictures in a *Penthouse* or something. I had no sense of who Chuck was, other than that he had recently gotten out of the army. He had a crew cut and amazing biceps, which the kids liked to see wobble up and down like Popeye's, and which he would let them feel, with the greatest of patience, whenever they wanted. I got the greatest number of feels, letting him know where I stood. He didn't tell horror stories like other counselors I'd had. He just came off as a decent guy, with mirrored sun-glasses, which I associated then with mystery.

Chuck was surprised to see me still in the bunkhouse. I told him that I had wanted to talk to him about something that was bothering me. He immediately suggested we walk down to the lake and sit by the bank, where it was quiet and more private.

We sat on an incline along the bank, at a place where the tall grasses had been

pressed down. So far none of us had ever been taken there; it was his secret retreat. Chuck listened to me explain my problem about my sexuality. I admitted to him that I thought I might be "strange, different."

He seemed to understand completely; at least that's what he said.

We entered a drifting state where we both let ourselves fantasize about what we would like to do with our lives. As we talked, we looked out at the lake, and I experienced for the first time a calm I had never known. Being so far away from the others, hearing their noisy screams from a long distance off, made me feel special. I was at last alone with Chuck. I savored every moment of it. I demanded to touch his biceps again. He let me. Then he let me touch him anywhere I wanted.

"Anywhere?" I asked, amused.

"Sure."

"Here?" I asked, my hand poking his crotch.

He laughed, then put his arm around me, pulled me close. He kissed the top of my head.

"Don't be afraid," he said softly. "I know what you want. It's okay to have feelings for another guy."

I hadn't mentioned it, really, so he seemed to be reading my mind.

His hand passed over my crotch, lightly at first. Then, feeling what his caring was doing to me, he began to squeeze. I was so hard it was beginning to hurt.

"Looks like you need some help," he said.

"Yeah," I said.

I laid back and he undid my pants. My cock throbbed in his face. He sucked it for a while, then started playing with my butt.

I was a delicate, slender boy, and when he spit on his finger and stuck it in, it hurt. "God, you're really tight."

"I know," I said, "I've never done this before."

"Jesus." He sounded upset somehow.

"I'm sorry," I said.

"I'm not," he said, happier now, putting more spit on it.

He went on like that, spitting and finger-fucking me, for several minutes. He was also jacking me off. He told me I had a big cock. I couldn't help it I came.

"Oh, yeah. What a big load! "

I was so proud of myself.

"Hey," he said, pulling down his swimsuit.

"Oh?" I said, as his huge erection throbbed before my eyes.

"You wanna suck it a bit?"

I didn't answer, just leaned over and started kissing it. Over the next ten minutes, he schooled me in cock sucking. He told me if they had a merit badge for that activity, I'd sure earned it that day. When he came, I saw his load was bigger than mine had been, and I dipped my fingers in it, tasted it.

"You're a sweetheart," he chuckled, hugging me. "We gotta get back."

He promised that would not be our last meeting down by the lake, but I didn't

298

see how that was possible, since we were due to leave in two days.

But, sure enough, the very next day, Chuck took me out in the rowboat to the far end of the lake. As we ran the bow into the shore, he asked if I wanted to work on another merit badge.

"Sure," I said.

After my T-shirt was slowly raised across my chest and onto my arms, Chuck's lips brushed my nipples and I moaned as his tongue moved roughly over one, then the other. My cock swelled rapidly inside the confines of my swimsuit. I flinched as he gently began to outline its growth. In a jerk, my T-shirt was removed and his lips went back to my nipples for a bit, then were brushing over my tight abs as they moved downward toward my navel. Finally Chuck's mouth moved to the bulge in my swimsuit, and my fingers began to rub his smooth, sweaty back. My cock was so hard it almost hurt as he revealed it. My swimsuit became bunched at my ankles and he lifted each of my feet to pull it off.

I shut my eyes and tried to relax, but there was something so exciting about being buck naked at the far end of the lake in a rowboat with Chuck that I couldn't rest. I didn't want him to linger over my cock, to tease me; I wanted to come, as I had the previous day. Coming was the only thing that would relax me. Just the thought of coming again sent me over the edge. As his lips skipped over the coils of my bush and his fingertips brushed lightly along the insides of my legs, I came. It caught him by surprise, and I groaned as his tongue lapped up the cum as it gushed from the cock head.

His fingers kneaded my ass cheeks as inch after inch of my cock found its way into the warm wetness of his hungry throat.

I was fucking his face with every instinct in me. His hands on my ass directed my movements.

I sagged as he let go of me. He had to grab me by the waist to steady me. He chuckled softly. "My god, you're the horniest kid I've ever met."

I succumbed to my first kiss from another man. My desire grew as I reached over and squeezed his cock. At that moment I wanted him, wanted him teach me and guide me.

He rowed ashore and grabbed a blanket. He laid me down and I instinctively spread my legs to let him get between them. Our lips met again in another passionate kiss as our fingers intertwined above my head. My heels found the divide between his ass-cheeks and my legs crossed over the small of his back in a scissors lock.

I felt his cock blindly probing past my balls. I suddenly remembered how big he was and began to tremble. As he ground his hips against my crotch, the head of his cock was posed at the entrance.

I broke away from our kiss and stared up at him with eyes filled with fear. "It's so big!" I yelped.

"I'll go slow and easy. You just push down as I'm pushing in." His lips pressed against mine again, silencing me.

I wasn't sure about this at all now, and I wanted to pull myself away, but his weight on me made that impossible. I could feel my ass lips spreading, opening themselves up to his prick. Desperately, I pushed down and he lifted up, helping me to breathe again.

Pain shot through me as the cock head entered me. I raised up and saw the cock slowly entering me. I reached down and felt the hard cock until it was all the way in.

Now that he was in, Chuck began fucking me. My cock jumped to attention at the new stimulation. "Jerk off while I'm doing it," he said, but I had already moved my hand to my cock.

He slipped into an easy rhythm, and kept plowing my ass as I shot a blast, then another on my belly.

"My god," Chuck said.

My cock stayed hard even though it was too sensitive for me to continue stroking it. My fist became fingers again and sought out Chuck's ass cheeks. He grinned down at me.

"Oh, god," I moaned as I felt his cock grow thicker deep inside me. I realized then his thrusts had grown shorter and shorter until only a little more than an inch of his cock was sliding between my ass lips with each lunge. His forehead became beaded with sweat. His face got redder and sweatier as he pumped, his eyes rolling up in his head.

He shuddered and his pubic bush stayed stuck to my anus as he sent blast after blast deep into me. "Oh, this is great!" he cried. I guess he was okay with me being a virgin. He didn't seem to mind that he had to work so much to get even a couple inches of his cock inside me. His body kept heaving on me and finally he shuddered and said, "Oh, yes."

Then he pulled his cock out of me and came some more on my thigh. He got off me and, out of breath, he finally asked, "Did I hurt you?"

"Not too much," I said, still stunned from it all.

"It'll get easier," he promised, and I knew he was right.

THE ROOKIE

John Patrick

It was muggy. It was muddy. It was perfectly miserable camping weather. But, oddly mercifully the constant drizzle must have been just enough to drive off most of the mosquitos. We did get off to a bad start though. When we checked in with the park rangers, they gave us directions to the trail head and the combination for the lock on the gate of the trail parking lot. So we drove five miles down to the road to the trail. Only the lock wouldn't open they'd given us the wrong combination.

So we drove five miles back, got the right combination, and then drove the same five miles again to begin our overnight camping trip. Along the way, Ricky, whom I nicknamed The Rookie since this was his first camping trip, learned some new cuss-word combinations. Ricky started off strong, tramping through the muck like a trouper in his new tennis shoes. He learned to follow the orange trail blazes, and got some practice reading a map. Each time we stopped to rest, I made him take two sips of water.

It finally stopped raining and the trail was beautiful, moving from open prairie to live oak hammocks and pine flatwoods. We got a thrill early on when a small deer bounded across the trail in front of us. It left perfect tracks on the muddy trail.

After a few miles, though, Ricky got tired and he said his feet started to hurt. He shed a few tears just before we reached the campsite, but five minutes later, with me rubbing his feet, he was fine.

We set up my old Sears tent. We pumped water from the campsite well, then filtered it to make it drinkable. We made and ate peanut butter sandwiches.

Ricky was feeling better by the minute. Stomach full, he got playful, reminding me why we had come out here: he wanted me to fuck him. I had avoided it for two years. I let him suck me at least once a week but then he read an article somewhere about what gay boys did together and he started practicing with his finger. I kept putting it off, thinking it would somehow upset things. I suppose I secretly thought that getting a blowjob from an effeminate little blond kid was okay, but to fuck...?

Anyhow, I never thought he'd actually go through with this camping trip. But I had not reckoned the strength of his desire.

Trouble was, everything about him was wrong. This was not what I wanted at all. I willed myself to say it, finally, to tell him, but my hard-on betrayed me. I watched him undress. He was not what I wanted really, but he was beautiful naked, all lean lines and tight muscles. He was lithe and young and pure. His eyes were on the bulge in my shorts. I knew he wanted to unleash that cock, wanted to free it, want to feed on it. He moved beside me and quickly helped me undress. I didn't mind that, now, he was the one who was in charge.

After bossing him around all day, I was ready to relax. I was docile as I let him unbutton my shirt and spread it out and away from me. His expression changed when he regarded the tip of my cock poking through the top of my shorts. He then bent down to kiss along my ribs and down the center of my stomach, trailing wet kisses all the way to the waistband of my underpants. Deftly, he slid these down my thighs and went to work with his tongue and fingers. He was the best damn cocksucker I had ever run into, not that I had known very many, you realize, but he was so good that if he spent enough time with his quickly circling tongue, if he stroked me any harder with his tentative fingers, he would make me come. I pushed him away just in time. Startled, he looked up into my eyes. He could see that I was ready now, ready for what we'd come for.

Ricky knew how happy he had made me. I was tired of nice and sweet and good girls. I was tired of chaste kissing at drive-ins, or while watching the sun set. The girls I knew didn't want to fuck or to suck my dick. I rubbed against them and that was about it. Then Ricky came into my life. He lived down the street with his mom and he enjoyed bringing me pleasure.

My cock, slick with Ricky's spit, shiny with my heat, seemed to glow in the dim light inside our tent. Slowly, he worked, loving my cock. I told myself I was doing this for him. And I had no problem doing this for him. I got pleasure from his pleasure but I was about to play rougher, too. I slid one moistened finger into the rosebud opening of his ass. He was so tight that I took a deep breath, a ragged breath. I was suddenly shy, blushing like a little kid. I really wasn't sure I could do it to him. I opened my lips to speak, but the words wouldn't come out of my mouth I couldn't even formulate them in my mind.

"I want you to stick it in," he moaned. I was thrilled at the urgency in his voice, the desperation. "I want to feel it all the way in me. Take me like you do your girlfriends. Like you do with Amy, and Betty, and Mary."

Ha! I thought, what a joke. He did not know it but those girls were all so boring. And not to be cruel or anything, but they were all sort of mousy. And I had never fucked any of them. Heavy petting was about as much as I'd done. I sighed, "Uh huh."

Ricky decided that the only way to do it was to sit on it. He took a tube of Vaseline from his bag and greased my cock. I couldn't believe my eyes as he climbed over me and did just that. As he began moving up and down on my cock, I slowly began stroking his body, along his shoulders, across his pecs, and down his belly.

Once he told me I wouldn't do it because I was afraid I would like it, and I guess that was true. My fears, I now knew, were justified. This was hot. Silence hung in the air around us, filled with thoughts and dreams and fantasies ... all of which were about to come true. I bit my bottom lip to keep from crying out, my cock vibrating amazingly inside him. God, it felt so good, first his tongue and then his fingers, now his ass muscles, the sensations building, the need rising. No more pretending. My cock throbbed inside him. He rocked back and forth as

I pulled out to the tip and then eased right back in. He bucked against me and I moaned louder, knowing that we would not be heard out here in the swamp. Now I pushed him onto his stomach and entered him again, not giving any thought to the repercussions, calling his name out, "Oh, Ricky, it feels so good!" Just then I came inside him. I hadn't even gotten it all the way in him and I came. I felt sorry about that, but couldn't tell him. He was busy, jerking himself off, his other hand on my cock.

Afterwards, we were warm and sticky, naked and sweaty, collapsed on the floor of the tent. I knew that I could talk to him about it now that something had changed inside. I was a different person, but it didn't seem as if he was into talking.

He wanted to play cards he won, of course and we tried out my new candle lantern. It was a little hot for snuggling, but I stroked his head as he fell asleep. In the worst of camping conditions, we had the best of camping times.

Before our hike back the next morning, Ricky insisted on being fucked again.

"Hunch up on your knees," I ordered him. This time I was going to get it all the way in. I smeared the lotion in his ass and then popped a finger inside. With one hand I pulled him forward against my body; with the other I lined myself up to stick it to him again. I felt him open up and then stretch wide as the head of my dick pushed through. Gradually, more and more of my cock was able to penetrate him. When I was fully and deeply inside him, he turned toward me and opened those angelic eyes and flashed his devilish grin. "Oh, it's all the way in, isn't it?"

I nodded as he began to rock gently back and forth. His chest rose, and with a low groan, fell. Our bodies glistened with sweat as he jacked himself while I screwed him. His whole body tensed and froze. His ass contracted around my cock as I continued to pump into him. We each fed off the orgasm of the other. His shot out and landed on the mat. I collapsed against him, my cum filling him. Under me I felt him shudder one last time.

I made no effort to withdraw, but soon my cock, which had been long and stiff for so long, began to soften, then slide out.

I straightened myself out beside him. Neither of us said anything for a long time. Then he reached over and took my wet cock in his hand. He bent over and kissed it. "Thank you, Steve," he sighed.

"No, thank *you*, Ricky. That was great. It really was."

We ran to the creek and washed ourselves. We splashed in the water like little kids, then he dropped to his knees and took my cock in his mouth again. Soon I was hard once more, and he sucked me until he managed to draw one more orgasm from me.

"God, I love it," he said, after he had swallowed my cum. He held my cock against his cheek.

"Better than Paul's? Better than Kenny's?" I could have gone on, naming all the guys I knew he had sucked, but I stopped. I didn't need to hurt him. I had beaten those names out of him, and he confessed. I was the only one who knew

who else he had sucked. But that didn't matter any more.

He looked up, tears forming in his eyes. "But you're the only one who's fucked me, Steve."

"And I'm the only one who's taken you camping, too."

"Right. And I'm not a rookie any more, Steve."

I smiled. "No, neither of us is a rookie any more."

After we packed up, we took shortcuts on park roads. They were just as muddy and puddly as the trail, but we were able to walk side by side holding hands, which was kinda nice. He looked up at me and said, "I'll only do it with you from now on, Steve."

I smiled. I knew he meant it at that moment but he would surely change his mind when he saw Paul or Kenny again. Still, it didn't matter, not as long as I got to fuck him whenever we could arrange it.

By the time we were back in the car, heading home, he was chattering away, reviewing the trip and talking about what we'd do next time. Next time.

SLEEPING BAG SEX

Troy M. Grant

Like most kids, my head was filled with sexual fantasies. I can't tell you how many times I sucked dick or got fucked, in my imagination. The very sight of another hot young stud caused a stirring in my shorts and sent my mind racing. I could almost feel my hands running over his hard, muscular chest, down over his firm abs, and into his shorts. I could picture myself dropping to my knees, pulling out his cock and putting it between my lips. It's no wonder I had a massive hard-on most of the time.

My fantasy life was rich, but I was still a virgin. I had masturbated more times than I could count, but I had never touched another guy. All that changed on a camping trip with some of my buddies. There were six of us, all from the senior class, and all eighteen. I didn't have the slightest indication that any of them were into guys, so the possibility of sex was far from my mind. Sure, I was interested, but it takes two and I just didn't think any of them were hot for guys the way I was.

I really enjoyed being around my group of friends — especially when we went swimming or engaged in some other shirtless activity. Each of my buddies were nicely built. Sean and Scott were blond twins. They were both on the swim team in school and they were hot! You can just imagine the fantasies I had about them. Chad had jet black hair and a body to die for. He and Dan, a brown-haired, gray-eyed hunk, were both on the wrestling team. I'd have wrestled with them anytime. The other member of our group was Brandon. Brandon had brown hair and eyes, just like me. He was on the soccer team at school and lifted weights. He wasn't as thickly muscled as Chad and Dan, but he was built. He had just the right amount of muscle everywhere, and not an ounce of fat. His body was a work of art, and he was cute as hell.

Things really got interesting that night. Everyone stripped down to their boxers or briefs and we settled into our sleeping bags under the stars. I had a massive hard-on and was looking forward to jerking off later in the night. It was getting chilly and the fire felt great. We lay around talking as the darkness deepened and the chill increased.

"Fuck, I'm getting cold. Why don't we double up?" asked Chad.

"Sure," answered Dan. They slipped out of their sleeping bags and zipped them together, making one big sleeping bag, just right for two. Sean and Scott did the same and Brandon and I put ours together.

It was warmer, but I had a problem. Laying next to Brandon, with his hard body actually touching mine, was setting me on fire with lust. I willed my erection away and was partially successful, but I didn't know how long I could keep it up. My mind was racing with wild thoughts, all of which involved Brandon's hard, hot body. He scooted closer to me, bringing his body into

contact with mine from shoulders to feet. It was awesome, but it was torture.

Sean started telling us about the last great party he attended. He spelled out in graphic detail how blasted he and his girlfriend were and what they did in a closet. This was not what I needed. I could just picture Sean getting his dick sucked and fucking the hell out of his girl. This camping trip was turning into a nightmare.

Just then I felt Brandon's hand on my leg. I was sure it meant nothing coming from him, just a place to rest his hand, but it sent a shudder of excitement throughout my body. Brandon started rubbing my thigh. I couldn't believe it. In fact, I didn't. There was no fucking way that....

Brandon's hand ran over my crotch. Mere seconds later it was back again. He was fondling me through my boxers!

I turned to face him and he raised his eyebrows and smiled. Fuck, he was really feeling me up. I didn't know what to do. I hadn't thought about something like this happening at all. It sure felt good though, and I was so excited I could hardly stand it. My cock was getting harder by the second. I reached over and felt Brandon's equipment through his boxers. He was hard, and boy was he hung! It was the first time I ever felt another guy. I was so excited I was ready to burst.

I trailed my hand up and rubbed Brandon's flat stomach. I keep feeling my way higher and higher, until I reached his chest. I massaged his hard, muscular pecs. I was in heaven.

"Okay, Troy, your turn," said Sean.

"Huh?" I said, quickly drawing my hand away from Brandon's body, although there was no way anyone could tell what was going on under that sleeping bag.

"Tell us about the last girl you had," said Sean.

"Oh, that," I said. I was on the spot. I hadn't touched a girl, didn't want to, but I wanted to be one of the guys. I made up a story on the spot. I kept it simple, but made it hot. Brandon kept fondling me and feeling my body all over while I talked. I had to struggle to keep my voice even, especially when Brandon reached into my boxers and starting stroking my throbbing cock. My voice broke. No one said anything about it, however. They were too wrapped up in my fictional sex-life. I was relieved when my story was finished and it was Dan's turn.

Brandon had my pole pulled out of my shorts and was gently stroking me. He kept jerking me off for a few minutes, then let his hands wander all over my body while I cooled down. Now that my story was over I let my fingers go walking, all over Brandon's hot, hard body, too. I paid special attention to his chest. I even tweaked his hard little nipples.

Of course, I also worked my hands into his boxers and examined his meat. Brandon was long and thick and oozing pre-cum. His nuts were firm and large. Man, this was hot!

I was afraid one of the other guys would notice what was going on in our sleeping bag, but the darkness was thickening and our friends' voices covered

up our heavy breathing and the sounds of our movements.

We were careful not to do much that could be noticed, but I'm sure what we were doing would have been obvious if it had been lighter. I was all over Brandon and I wanted to keep it up for hours. Brandon was all over me as well. If we were alone we would have done some serious fucking around. But as dangerous and frightening as it was, the possibility of being found out by our friends made it that much more exciting.

The fire died down to glowing embers and the clouds obscured the moon and stars. It was unusually dark and the other forms around us were barely visible in the gloom. The stories kept flowing and our hands kept roaming. I was so hot with desire I could hardly stand it. I couldn't believe I was taking the chance, but my balls were doing my thinking for me. I squirmed down under the sleeping bag and pressed my lips to Brandon's chest. I'm sure Brandon would have warned me off, but he couldn't exactly say anything without drawing the attention of everyone.

I licked his hard pecs. I loved the feel of his soft skin and hard muscle. I licked and kissed him all over and even sucked on his nipples.

Brandon whimpered a little, but quickly covered up the sound with a cough.

I ran my tongue all over his hard torso. His abs made me wild with lust. My balls weren't in complete control, however, and I played it cool.

I licked my way up Brandon's magnificent torso and chewed on his neck and ears. I pressed my lips to his and kissed him passionately.

We necked as quietly as we could while Chad recounted tales of his sexual escapades. I listened only for any hint of discovery. I couldn't care less about Chad's story.

Brandon slipped his tongue in my mouth and we Frenched each other for minute after minute. It was wonderful.

"Brandon!" shouted Dan.

"What?" said Brandon, after quickly disengaging from my mouth.

"Your turn. Aren't you paying attention over there?"

Brandon couldn't seem to find the words, so I stepped in. "Sure we are, Dan. Come on Brandon, tell us about your last time," I said.

Brandon started his tale. I wondered if it was true, or a complete fiction as mine had been. I didn't really care. I caressed his chest as he spoke. I squirmed around in the sleeping bag until I was head-downwards. I inched along Brandon's body, licking his firm young flesh as I went. I reached the object of my desires and fondled his manhood through his boxers. I drew out his long, thick prick and licked it. I wrapped my lips around his dickhead. I could hear Brandon's voice go up an octave as he continued his story. I pulled his cock into my mouth, little by little, exploring with my tongue as I went. This was my first cock. I relished the taste and the way it felt as it glided over my lips. I worked my way down the shaft as far as I could manage, then slid my lips back up. Up and down, up and down, each trip was better than the last. I drew in more and more of Brandon's throbbing cock with each trip.

The other studs around us had no idea that Brandon was getting sucked off while he told them his story!

Brandon had kept from making any noise so far. I knew he wouldn't be able to keep silent for long however. I listened so I could calm things down if he started to lose control.

Brandon was as smart as he was cute, however. He worked a blowjob into his story. He described it in intricate detail, no doubt inspired by my lips running up and down his dick. I tensed for a moment when I heard him begin to moan and groan, but then I realized Brandon had worked it into his tale. I was sucking his cock, he was moaning and groaning like crazy, and the other guys thought it was just part of a really hot story!

"You're making me hard, man," said Dan.

"Yeah," said Scott, "me too. Keep going."

I just knew our buddies were jacking off to Brandon's story. I didn't care; I had a mouthful of dick. I worked my lips right down to the base of Brandon's dick. His pubes were crushed against my nostrils and his scent drove me crazy with lust. It was hot being buried in that sleeping bag, pressed against Brandon's firm, young body. I was sweating, so was Brandon. The scent of sex was heavy in there. I loved it. I sucked Brandon harder and faster. His story was reaching a crescendo. I knew he was getting close. I worked my lips up and down his dick as fast as I could manage. My tongue massaged his long shaft every step of the way. Brandon was really moaning and groaning now. Just hearing it was hot. I'm sure Brandon wasn't the only one about to spill his load. I could hear some of the other guys moaning as well.

"Unh! Unh! Unh!" grunted Brandon as he unleashed his load down my throat. Spurt after spurt of his thick, fresh juice erupted from his pole. His cream spewed all over my tongue and down my throat. His jizz tasted sweeter than my own. I sucked him hard and more and more cum fired from his throbbing tool. He moaned loudly as each jet of cum shot forth. He thrust his hips toward my mouth as jet after jet of his cum spurted from his dick. I drank it down and sucked him for more. His cock was like a cum-shooting geyser! As soon as Brandon shot the last of his load, I quickly squirmed around so that I was right side up in the sleeping bag.

"That was an awesome story, Brandon!"

"Yeah, I just creamed my shorts!"

"Who's next?"

Scott told his tale as Brandon began to feel me up again. I hoped he would duck down and give me head, but I guess he was a little too scared. I didn't blame him. I couldn't believe I had just taken that chance. If one of the guys had flipped on a flashlight it would have all been over.

Anyway, Brandon's hand on my dick sure felt good. He pulled my pole out of my boxers and was jerking me off. It wasn't as good as a blowjob, but it was great. I got an idea and pulled Brandon around with his back toward me. I nestled up against him with my dick pressing into his ass. I pulled his boxers

down and my own. I rubbed my dick along his crack and began humping him. My cock felt great sliding along his firm little ass. I wanted to fuck him real bad, but there was no way in hell we could do that. I don't think anyone could get fucked and not make any noise that our buddies couldn't hear. Besides, humping Brandon's cute little ass was a real turn-on. I reached around his slim waist and massaged his abs. I let my hands wander over his muscular chest and down onto his growing cock. Brandon was getting hard again.

I was as hard as I'd ever been. It felt so good to slide my cock between Brandon's butt cheeks. He had one great ass. I wanted to moan with pleasure, but I kept myself under control. I was hard, however. I felt myself pushing Brandon onto his stomach. I mounted him and humped his cute little ass like crazy. We were taking a real chance, but unless one of the guys turned on a flashlight, they couldn't see us in the dark.

I slid my dick between Brandon's taut butt cheeks. It felt so good I can't even begin to describe it. I don't think fucking his tight little ass would have felt any better. I started humping him faster.

"What are you guys doing over there?" asked Dan.

I froze. I wasn't sure what to do. Then an idea occurred to me. "I'm humping Brandon's ass," I announced. "What did you think?" I heard Brandon gasp beneath me. He was so scared his whole body tensed.

"Yeah, right!" said Dan, "And I'm sucking off Chad!"

"All right, I'm jacking off, okay?" I said. "Like you haven't been doing it too."

The guys just laughed and I started humping Brandon's ass again. I wondered what the guys would think if they knew I really was humping the fuck out of Brandon's butt. I went faster and faster. I was so worked up I couldn't help myself.

"I'm getting close, guys. Anyone else ready to blow?" I asked.

"Getting there," said Sean.

"I'm on the fucking edge," said Scott.

"Oh yeah," I said. "Keep your story going, Scott. Make it hot!"

I started moaning and groaning now. So did the other guys. We were having a circle jerk, more or less, only I was humping Brandon's ass instead. The danger of being discovered and the excitement of doing it right under my friends' noses was such a rush!

I humped Brandon harder and faster. He was moaning too.

"Unh! Unh! Unh! I'm gonna blow!" I screamed.

"Me too!" yelled Sean.

I could hear grunts and groans from all around as one guy, then the next blew his load. My nuts churned and the cum coursed up my shaft. Hot, sticky cum erupted from my dick-head to plaster Brandon's cute little ass. I pumped his butt cheeks full of my cream. I grunted loudly as each spurt gushed from my pole. I kept coming and coming! I could hear the other guys getting off as well.

It was so hot with all us guys getting our rocks off at once. Spurt after spurt of

hot cream flew from my dick and coated Brandon's ass. Brandon moaned louder than ever. His whole body tensed and I could tell he had just shot his load into the sleeping bag. That thing would be smelling of cum for weeks. I shot the last of my load and crawled off Brandon. He turned toward me and gave me a quick, passionate kiss. We lay there innocently as Sean clicked on his light and added wood to the fire.

"You sure were going hot and heavy, Troy," said Scott.

"You have no idea," I replied. Brandon squeezed my cock under the covers.

As soon as this trip was over, Brandon and I would have to make plans to go camping alone together. You can bet I was looking forward to that! It was a cold night, but I didn't mind, not with Brandon's body in my arms. I fell asleep with his head resting on my chest.

CAMPING OUT

Ken Smith

The ship docked at Portsmouth. I was more than relieved for that. It had been a bitch of a week, force eight gales. Continuously riding the big ones can piss you off in the end, constantly being tossed from bulkhead to bulkhead, or into sailors you'd rather be shagging than saying sorry to. Paul was one of those I'd loved to have been riding, rather than fifty foot waves. I think he knew that but never let on. I'd been close enough to his cock to give it a cautious brush with my palm and slapped his bum in a playful manner many times, but a smile and wink was all he'd ever offered. I often wondered, when he jumped from his hammock in the morning with his stiff cock poking through the fly of his Hong Kong, floral boxers, dribbling cum, whether or not he was offering me that mouthwatering, massive meat which somehow appeared far too big for his small frame or just teasing. I hoped one day I'd find out. That one day I'd pluck up the courage and tell him I fancied him stupid.

I'd been a sailor for a year but, unbelievably, had not had sex since my school days, and then it was only a wank. But, now, as a sailor, I was obliged to go ashore with mates and play the hettie game, watching them box off with the birds. I often got strange looks because I wouldn't. And I could never let on to those sexy baby-sailors, who's sailor suits made their buttocks look even more horny, trapped in bum-hugging bell-bottoms, that it was only their pants I wanted to dive inside. Thus frustrated, I tossed myself regularly in the heads, in my hammock, in my office. Constantly I tossed myself, but always alone.

Below decks, those of us granted a pass were preparing to go ashore pressing uniforms; the older sailors, civvies. As always, Paul was close by his locker being next to mine. His pert white butt, trapped between tanned brown torso and thighs, was closer to my cock than was comfortable. In fact, I believe I felt my dick glide, semi stiff, over his right buttock cheek as I squeezed past, in order to reach the ironing table.

"I hope that was your finger," he giggled.

"You'd need something fatter than a finger to satisfy you," I teased.

"Bum bandit," parried Paul, then to the whole mess, "Smiffy's a bum bandit."

"Shut up and take it like a man!" a butch sailor bellowed.

I poked my tongue out when Paul turned to face me. "Yeah, take it like a man," I repeated.

"You got lovely, sucking lips, Smiffy," smiled Paul, grasping his cock, which looked stiffer than it should have. "If you get a couple blowjobs this weekend, come back and give me one."

"Anytime!" I winked.

Paul tucked his prick away and grinned a knowing grin.

"I'll have the other one," a cute, naked seaman called, jumping from behind

the lockers, wiggling his dishy butt and swinging his cock in a clockwise motion.

"I want a meal, not a morsel," I replied, deflating his ego and his four inches.

Paul scooped up his hold-all and scurried up the ladder, "Have a good one, Smiffy," he shouted, accompanied by an extremely sexy wink.

I waited until his butt was out of view before continuing to dress, contemplating whether sex with Paul was only a couple of days away. I'd already decided when I returned that I would offer him one or both of those blowjobs, whether I got them or not.

Not long after Paul had left, I hoisted my hold-all up the ladder and after I'd been inspected by the Officer of the Day, was trotting over the gangway. The first pub beyond the dockyard wall was my initial port of call. It was the usual thing we sailors did a quick pint and chat before catching our respective trains. The place was buzzing with sailors from various ships. I had a quick glance around for Paul but he wasn't about. After chucking a couple of coins in the fruit machine, I chose a windowed corner to sit and watch sailor boys and men get sloshed. I'd always found it fascinating how close men and boys could be, without there being any sex involved; manly arms slung affectionately over youths' shoulders or wrapped around waists or draped over cute buttocks. Men and boys can be really loving toward each other when women are absent.

I noticed a boy sailor a little worse for drink draped over a burly Bunting Tosser. Their cheeks were touching, and I do believe I glimpsed a peck on the boy's cheek. They wandered out not long after that, the older sailor supporting the younger. To where, I do not know. To bed, I hoped. Something I longed to do with a boy, one day. When I was more sure. When I was more brave. When....

The bar was beginning to clear, sailors leaving for their trains. Mine wasn't far off, and as I drained my glass, I began to think of the weekend break what it would hold, whether I would get that thing called a blowjob, whether I would meet that boy I longed for.

That may well happen, I thought, because we'd been at sea for three months and during that time my family had moved to a village close to Portsmout-Wickham. What Wickham would do for my frustrated sex life, I had no idea, but a sailor suit in places where they were not usually seen, often brought attention to oneself. Hopefully, that attention would be the kind I was searching for.

The train journey was uneventful, apart from being in the company of scruffy, loud schoolboys, two of whom had cum stains on their black trousers. I guessed I knew what they'd been up to during lunch break, or in my case, during lessons.

Alighting at a deader than dead railway station, my heart sank. Why on earth had my family moved here? I wondered. A short walk brought me to a large, empty square surrounded by several shops, a pub, and tumble-down cottages. What was noticeable was the people that was, their absence. Not a soul in sight to greet this youthful, would-be sailor-boy-lover. A solitary sports car did speed by, honking its horn, but it seemed the pilot was only too pleased to pass

312

through this peaceful hamlet in the shortest time possible. Had he known how I was feeling he might have offered me a lift back to my ship, to his home, even his bed!

I found a living person in the rickety Post Office. At least I thought she was living. She looked older than the building itself. My parent's new home, I was informed, was 'up yonder hill, about a mile'. Thanking her and purchasing a Coke for the extra energy I would need, I began my ascent of the tree-lined road.

Houses were few, I noted, as I climbed ever skyward; only fields of corn, grasses, and other crops spread for miles around. Thoughts of a new improved sex life, my first sex life, faded fast. And, then, like a God-given grace, I heard joyous sounds. In amongst the twittering birds and farmyard noises, I heard the voices of boys. I think I almost ran to the five-bar, wooden gate of the field they were coming from.

Cracking open my can of Coke, I rested my body, arms slung over the top bar, and absorbed the beauty of boys bouncing merrily around the field, kicking the usual bag of wind. Football crazy boys, spurred on by World Cup mania, pretended to be their heroes. It was a wondrous sight!

Lads, from youth to boy, chased each other, in pursuit of the ball, often using foul play I did see a pair of shorts brought to ankle height attempting to score that winning goal, in a goal without keeper. Shorts-clad boys, naked above the waist, kept my eyes and mind occupied for a good half hour. Dearly I wanted to trip across the field and join in, but being at least two years older than the eldest boy, I somehow felt too old.

For the last five minutes of playing spectator, I perched myself on the top bar of the gate for a better view. A misdirected kick sent the ball sailing in my direction. I stumbled slightly forward wondering whether to retrieve it with a kick and send it sailing back, but with my football skills I guessed I'd only make matters worse. But that decision was made for me by a youth who came charging after it.

Silver-stranded, wavy hair caught in the breeze above his reddened, puffing cheeks as he galloped toward me, his sunburned chest glistening in the sunlight as it teasingly rose and fell as he sucked in air. Instinctively my eyes went from face to crotch, and even from my distance I could easily make out a fine bulge in his grass- stained shorts.

I have no idea why he did it, and even the shouts from mates couldn't hurry him, but, after scooping up the ball, he turned and looked directly at me. A broad, sunshine smile erupted from his bright face, engulfing me in rays of warmth, sending tingling sensations throughout my entire body. His second glance, even more seductive halfway back to the other players caused me to stumble from the gate and him to laugh; a laugh more golden than the yellow corn surrounding me. In that instant, I believe I fell in love!

I think I caught his name in those lad's shouts Chuck or Chip or perhaps they were football terms. Whatever it was, my final ascent toward home was going to be brighter than any part of the day so far.

313

I left the boys to their football and their summer camp, and moved off. A farther quarter mile it was certainly the longest mile I'd ever walked, I would inform the Post Mistress - I turned left into North Lane, a road I can only describe as a dirt track. My family, it seemed, had moved into the outback.

A further sweaty mile along North Lane and I was in front of my home, if I could call it that. A shack of a building, built from wood, wood that looked as if it had been washed up upon a beach stood before my dejected face. Had my parents gone mad, or what?

The usual, excited, "Kenny! Kenny!" greetings came form brothers and sisters and parents. I accepted their cuddles in the usual way but somehow refrained from asking why they had moved from a lovely cottage into a cow shed.

Evening couldn't come quick enough, having answered a barrage of questions about my navy life, but avoiding those, "I bet you've found a girlfriend in every port!" interrogations. And as soon as the opportunity came one of those silent gaps after every question had been repeated and answered twice - I found an excuse to leave.

I freshened myself with a quick shower then re-dressed into my uniform. It was about seven and the pubs were open. I decided I would do the three day camel ride back to the village, beat up the postmistress for lying about the distance, then meet the local lager-drinking lads; although, in a place such as this, they probably drank Real Ale or brain damaging Cider.

Thankfully, neither of my folks drank and my brothers were too young. So, left to my own devices, I headed back along the dirt track, the pleasant evening sunshine beating on my back.

More relaxed now, I took in more of my surroundings cows, horses, squirrels, cottages I hadn't noticed them before and a variety of birds. Sadly, not a burly farm-hand, stripped naked to the navel, in sight. Turning right at the end of the track, my mind instantly flashed back to my 'sunshine smile' lad. I opened my ears, eager to hear the sounds of playful boys, but all was still. I was being silly, anyway. What chance was there of me picking up a youth who I didn't know? Picking up anybody, to be honest. And if I did meet him again, what would I say? After all, I was extremely shy and pretty thick in the chatting-up cuties department.

Moving down hill, I approached the five-bar gate, set slightly back from the road. Passing the old oak that shielded it from my view, my stomach tightened in a knot from my groin to my throat. 'Sunshine' sat upon the top bar, bare legs straddled either side, crotch in his shorts pushed up, silver hair sparkling in the evening sunshine, suntanned shoulders and back glistening boy sweat.

My body froze, surges of sexual desire stunning me like some scared animal!

Sensing my presence, Sunshine spun around. "Hi!" he beamed, tanning my face red with a single smile.

My stomach ached with desire, so much so, I even felt sick. "Hi!" I replied, not knowing whether to continue walking or stop and torture myself.

"You're not from around here?" he beamed again, breaking my body into

314

panic-ridden particles with his soul stirring smile.

"No." I felt awkward. Were one-word answers all I could come up with? I was older than him. More knowledgeable. More traveled. More most things. But his beauty and my desperate desire to engulf him in arms and legs left me speechless.

Sunshine spun his other leg over the gate to face me, opening his legs and offering a clearer view of his boy-bulge. "Like being a sailor?" he questioned, perhaps to draw me into a more meaningful conversation.

"Sure." Another one-word reply. God, how cowardly!

Sunshine continued to bombard me with smiles and erotic strokes of his brown thighs. "Off to the village?"

This was getting me nowhere and the pain in my eyes from absorbing bulges and beauty was unbearable. I had to say something more substantial or leave before I dived on him and devoured him whole.

Daringly, I moved closer, almost standing between his parted knees, my eyes wandering from face to chest to crotch and back. "Know where all the girls go in the village?" I inquired defensively, taking on a straight role.

Sunshine brought his hands to his hips. "Girls? What's wrong with me? I can do anything they can!"

I'd never been hit by a ten-ton truck before, but that confession had an equal force. And when I next moved my gaze back to his crotch, no longer was it a neat round bump but a straight and solid sex, scrumptiously stiffened down his left thigh.

Though I desperately wanted to reply, I just couldn't. Sunshine laughed, a real boy-laugh, leant forward, took my cap and plonked it upon his silvery hair, the wavy strands protruding sexily over his ears and forehead. "Come on," he encouraged, holding out his slender palm.

I took his hand nervously as he jumped from the gate. My cock crowded my bell-bottoms when he squeezed my palm intimately. He looked stunningly beautiful wearing my cap and I could easily visualize him dressed in the complete outfit. Should he join the Royal Navy, I mused, he wouldn't be a virgin for very long, but, somehow, guessed that perhaps he wasn't; even that he had had far more sexual encounters than I'd ever had. Indeed, it was Sunshine who was seducing me!

"What's your name?" he asked, dragging me across the road and toward the cornfield.

"Kenny."

"Ken. I've got a mate called Ken. We looked our names up in a dictionary one day. Did you know it means comely?"

I liked the way he emphasised *cum* of *comely* and had no doubt that coming was foremost in his mind. "What's yours?" I asked.

"Chip."

"And what does that mean?"

"Got lots of meanings but one of them has something to do with chickens," he

winked.

I had no idea what he meant by that but guessed it was sexual in some way. "It's a lovely name and you look as cute and cuddly as a little chick, but I've given you a nickname of my own: Sunshine. It's that smile of yours. As big and beautiful as the sun."

"Sunshine, eh? I like that." And giving another broad grin, he pushed me into the hedgerow and planted his smiling mouth onto mine. For that long, oh-so-succulent smacker, I stopped breathing. Never before had I been kissed by a boy, and I almost passed out from the euphoria of it. And during that magnificent mouth to mouth maneuver, I took the opportunity to grasp Sunshine's stiffened sex, holding it, so tightly, I never wanted to let it go ever!

"Can't wait, eh, Kenny Cum-ly. Still want to go to the village and find a girl?" he teased.

"Nah!"

Sunshine pushed me through a gap in the hedge, into the cornfield. Hand in hand we cut a swathe through the tall, golden stems, the ears slapping against my uniform and his naked chest. Twenty yards into the sea of gold I scuttled my ship, bringing Sunshine down with me; our bodies rolling playfully over and over as we flattened the corn around ourselves a bed for boys to learn about boys.

It was Sunshine's eager hand which was first to move between thighs, levering my dick into the warm evening air; and how incredibly good and refreshing that felt. But not as incredible as the hot mouth that unexpectedly swallowed my sex. Only three movements down to my black pubes and back, and I filled his mouth with cum, gripping his head tightly for fear he might pull away. He gulped down the fluid, fiercely flashing his tongue over my cock-head and into the eye. My brain spun and my eyes rolled back, my legs quivering and stomach knotting as the sensation became so wonderfully painful that I needed to pull away.

Sunshine's lips met mine, cum and saliva dribbling down his chin as he kissed me passionately. "I guess you needed that!" he delighted, and kissed my nose and forehead.

"Shit! That was... out of this world!"

"Your first time?" Sunshine smiled, knowingly.

I felt like an amateur by admitting that it was but Sunshine was pleased by that news, giving me a loving hug and saying that he was glad that it was his mouth to be the first to savor my virgin cum.

"I suppose cos you like girls, you won't want to suck mine?" he questioned, but still smiling. "I don't mind. But can I do it to you again, please?"

I didn't tell him that I didn't fancy girls but pushed him down into the corn and climbed on top of him, pressing my mouth onto his cherry-colored lips. Sitting upright, I could feel his young sex pressing into my bum as I rode my palms over his silken chest and up under his hairless armpits. Sunshine giggled as my fingers stroked the sweat in the hollows.

316

he siphoned the contents of his small balls in swirls of sweet spunk, filling my mouth to capacity and beyond, my lips dribbling the excess over my chin. How could such a minuscule ball sac contain twice their volume? I considered gulping gratefully (and gluttonously) gorging on his enlarged plum for the final remnants.

The dull dongs of a gong drifting over the cornfield caused Sunshine to jump to his feet and quickly dress. "Hell. Got to get back to camp. Supper gong," he informed, but not before kissing my cock and face for a final time. "Meet me here tomorrow. About ten. Bring some Nivea, or something!" he shouted as his cute butt disappeared, bunny-rabbit-like, through the hedgerow.

"Nivea!" I called after him. "Why?"

"You'll see!" he waved and grinned again.

I glided down the hill toward Wickham village, sparks of love igniting my insides like miniature firecrackers. My excitement was electric. I had made love to a BOY! I wanted to tell the whole world. I wanted to climb to the highest hilltop and shout it out loud. I wanted to do it again, and again. I wanted my euphoric state to stay with me forever!

The village pub looked drab from the outside but before entering I glimpsed a 7-11 across the square and trotted over. A youth stood behind the counter. Because of my flushed cheeks and dizzy state, I wondered whether he knew I had just made love for the first time in my life. I wondered, also, whether he knew it had been with a boy. I plucked a blue tin of Nivea from the medical section. Suddenly, becoming self-conscious of purchasing what I thought to be a feminine product, I replaced it and pulled a small pot of Brylcreem from the shelf above. But even as I paid for that more legitimate item, my self-consciousness grew, aware that I had no hair, at least not hair that required lacquering down.

Hastily, I exited the 7 - 11, to the wide grin of cherub cheeks, positive he knew that I'd been sucking boy-cock in the cornfield only minutes previously.

The pub was better in than out and contained the usual pub furniture: juke box, dart board, beer stained tables with wooden chairs beneath. Customers were few two farm-hands playing dominoes, an elderly couple, a group of posh, wealthy types, and a back-packing lad beside the unlit, log fire.

I slotted myself close by the back-packer I could never resist being beside good-looking guys. But little happened during my pub session, apart from me getting slightly sozzled; and not once did the back-packing youth get speared by the Cupid arrows I was constantly firing at him. Come eleven, I did the return camel ride back home, in a kind of zig-zag fashion, and was soon snuggled up in bed, wanking furiously over visions of Sunshine sucking and savoring my sex.

I must say, nine o'clock in the morning was a more civilized time to leave my bed than the usual six o'clock. I felt wonderfully relaxed and happy as I showered, and was pleased to see the sun beaming through the bathroom

318

window as I soaped my body, bringing my sex solid with sweet-smelling Camay bubbles and lather. I refrained from jerking myself off; saving it for Sunshine.

I dressed in shorts and tatty T-shirt for my meeting with my Boy Wonder-full. Sadly, my navy issue short were far from tantalizing or titillating, but I hoped Sunshine wouldn't mind. After all, what was beneath them was more important.

Excited, almost beyond control, I was soon heading along the dirt track and toward the cornfield Brylcreem bulging in pocket. Actually, it made me look like a very big boy indeed. Anyhow, I wasn't too bothered about being a big boy and was amply gifted, and when it came to other boy's cocks, I did prefer smaller ones. Sunshine's was just about right. Just perfect, in fact.

The cornfield was soon upon me, having almost marched the distance. Sunshine wasn't about and I was suddenly saddened but I made my way through the hedgerow gap and to our corn bed. My eyes lit and my face flushed bright when they were greeted by the vision of Sunshine sunning himself in the shelter of the tall corn.

"Did you bring it?" were his first eager words.

I rubbed the bulge beside my cock and smiled. "Yep!"

"Oh. I thought that was your cock," he beamed, bowling me over and on top of him with one of those smouldering smiles.

Swiftly we were licking faces, chests and nipples, then sucking tongues and lips and eventually cocks. And, somehow, that felt even more exciting than yesterday's passionate embraces.

"Get it out, then," Sunshine ordered.

He couldn't have meant my dick, that had already been rolling around his mouth for the past ten minutes, so I retrieved my shorts, while he continued to suck my balls and bursting bell-end, and passed him the Brylcreem.

Sunshine laughed, a deep, boyish, roar of a laugh. "Taking up hairdressing, are we?"

"What's it for?" I ignorantly inquired, my face slightly flushed from my naivete.

"You're going to fuck me," he laughed again, unscrewing the cap and dipping a finger into the white cream, then sniffing it. "But I didn't expect to get a new hair-do at the same time," he giggled again.

I'd heard all the banter on board about bottoms getting knobbed and the Golden Rivet stories, but I never ever thought that boys had actually did it to boys shoved their cocks up bums.

Desperate to hide my ignorance, but knowing Sunshine instinctively knew I was a novice, I humored him by saying, "Well, I thought I'd give you a descent parting at the same time!" spreading the cheeks of his slightly hairy butt wide apart and darting my tongue into the hole.

Sunshine just loved that and pulled on the back of my head, slinging his legs over my shoulder and wriggling delightedly against my stiff tongue.

Next, dollops of white cream were delicately drawn over my stiff shaft and bulging cock-head, and a larger quantity up into his dainty hole. "Don't do a

thing," he commanded. "Just lie there."

'And take it like a man!' suddenly flashed through my mind, and I laughed inwardly.

Sunshine placed his knees either side of me, one hand pressing on my tight tummy, the other holding tightly onto my lathered cock. Gently, he eased his cute, tight buttocks backward, guiding my cock head between them. I felt giddy with excitement, desperately wishing to push forward, to sink inside this boy and bury my cock into depths I had never dreamt of disappearing into.

A deep sigh slipped from Sunshine's mouth and his face grimaced, but only slightly. I felt my bulging cock-head pop into his tight hole. Like that first blowjob, I thought I would come instantly. Desperately, I wanted to drive my dick home but I could see that it was painful for him, and even thought that it might be the first time he'd been screwed.

Sunshine stopped briefly, then, with a slow backward movement, he sat right down, palms pressed firmly on my rising chest. My head exploded! I could no longer hold back my desire to thrust and withdraw. Gripping his buttocks in both palms, I pulled my cock out to the tip then rammed it back home. Sunshine yelped and fell onto my chest. Our mouths met and he sucked furiously upon my tongue, gasping, oohing and aahing, and demanding I fuck him hard. There was no need. My hips and buttocks were rising from the flattened corn and pushing all that I had into his relaxing butt.

Squealing now and shaking with excitement, Sunshine sat up and began driving down on my upward thrusts, all-the-while jerking his cute cock in rapid movements. His pretty boyish face brightened with pleasure. His fingers worked furiously over his own sex, the other hand diving inside my mouth and playing with my tongue and lips. A sensational feeling engulfed my cock. I was ecstatic!

"Sunshine!" I shouted, shooting several salvos of semen inside of him. "I've come! God, have I come!"

Sunshine leapt from my cock, cum dribbling from his bum-hole and my slippery solid sex, and scrambled quickly over my face. Still jerking off, he rammed his young tool into my mouth. Cum gushed, gushed, and gushed it seemed it would never stop down my throat, with so much force, the first jet didn't even touch the sides; shooting straight into my stomach.

Body quivering, Sunshine sat back up, grabbed my still-stiff sex and sent it back up his hole. Again he slammed into me and I could feel my own cum swirling inside of him. Moments later it was a repeat performance. I emptied my cock a second time into his delicious dark hole and he emptied his onto my lapping tongue.

We continued screwing until early afternoon, until the Brylcreem tub was dry, and had Sunshine not had to leave for a scouting trek, I think I'd have bought another pot and we'd have continued well into the night.

We said our goodbye's with more kisses and cuddles, sadly knowing that we would not see each other again Sunshine returning home, me to my ship. And with a final hug, kiss and wave, he returned to camp.

The taste of Sunshine's cum was still fresh in my mouth and the sensation of screwing him singing in my dick as I slung both my and Paul's hammocks. Having farther to travel, he would not be back on board till early morning.

I lay back in my hammock, pleased and proud I was no longer a virgin. Delighted that my virginity was lost to the most beautiful boy on earth. Slowly, I drifted into sexual fantasies of Sunshine and screwing, and soon I was asleep and dreaming.

My dream was so real, I could feel Sunshine's talented mouth working my cock down to the base and back.

As often with wet dreams, just as I was about to shoot, I awoke. But the sensation of rising cum was still prominent and getting better. I moved my hand to my cock to finish myself off. A cropped head was bobbing frantically up and down my shaft. "Paul!" I gasped, coming before I'd finished my sentence, "What are you doing!"

Paul gulped my cum, slurping his tongue around the dribbling head for a few moments before raising himself level. "Got a couple of blowjobs ashore. Thought you might want one, Smiffy," he smiled. Then, giving me a secretive kiss, he whispered, "Got one for me?"

My head disappeared into his hammock!

THE INITIATORS

John Patrick

(Inspired by an adventure by Guy Davenport)

Down by the river four boys were leading a fifth. Their campground was far behind them. It was a lovely summer's day: there were puffs of white clouds in the bright blue sky.

All of the boys wore skimpy swim trunks and the closer they got to the river, the more pronounced the bulges at the crotches of the four older boys became. Every attempt of the fifth, smaller boy, Gary, to break free was thwarted by blocking shoulders and quick footwork on the part of the others.

When they reached the riverbank, the leader of the group, Martin, told Gary to be still. Gary stopped fighting and stood, a worried look on his cute face. Martin told him to remove his swimsuit. Shaking, he turned his back to the others and took it off with a flourish.

"Put it in here," he instructed Gary. They were hidden from the camp completely now by a stand of trees. Martin's voice was calm and menacing as he opened the sack he had brought. "Here in the sack."

Gary dropped his suit in the sack. Then Martin pulled from the sack a dress; blue with white dots, a frilly hem.

"Ahhh, he'll look so pretty," Joey, the tallest, said.

"Looks more like a nightgown," said Bo.

"More the better," Joey laughed.

"You're going to make me wear a dress?" Gary asked.

"We told you not to talk," Martin said. "Stick your arms through the sleeves."

"It's only a game," Martin said. "Isn't it, Joey? Joey doesn't tell lies."

"Yeah, it's only a game," Bo said, "but a game with the rules backward. Like, you'll be It, Gary. And instead of you being the blindfolded, we'll be wearing them.

"Wow," Bo said, "except for the haircut, he looks just like a pussy."

"More the better," Joey laughed.

"Why...?" Gary asked.

"The more you talk," Martin said, "the worse it's gonna to be for you, squirt."

"You keep talkin'," Bo added, "and you'll wish you were dead."

Gary stood in the midst of them, feeling foolish in the dress. He started to cry.

"Yeah, we'll be blindfolded, you're not. If you were to get clean away well, shit, you can't go back, not in a dress."

"What happens when you catch me?"

"We told you not to talk."

Martin first bound Kurt's eyes with a scout kerchief he pulled from the sack. Kurt was the handsomest of the boys, Martin thought, and this whole scene was being played out so that Martin could get closer to Kurt, who was very shy.

Martin went around until they were all blindfolded, except Gary, who stood miserable and confused in his dress.

Laughing, they all moved like windup toys.

"You're there, somewhere," Martin said. "If you talk, or holler, we'll know where you are, and get you."

They began to seek Gary out, with stiff arms and open hands.

Giggling, Gary ducked and bobbed, avoiding the flailing gropes of the others.

"Everybody stand still. Blind people can feel what's around them."

Arms out, they began to turn slowly, all of them in close.

"We could hold hands, in a circle, and move in."

"If he's inside."

"He's inside. Aren't you, Gary?"

Silence.

He could see. They couldn't. No reason why they should ever catch him.

"Who groped my crotch?" Kurt asked.

"Probably Gary, getting anxious," Martin said, knowing better. He groped Kurt again, harder. Kurt, squirming away from Martin, made a wide opening in the circle, through which Gary raced. He ran down the riverbank as fast as he could.

"Bastards," he said out loud.

If his luck held, he could be a long way ahead of them before they caught on, then he could double back and get the sack, and his swimsuit. His breathing became labored and he fell on the rocks, only to pick himself up again. He didn't dare look back.

Running, he fell again, hurting himself. He'd cut the underside of two toes, the little one on his left foot, the long one beside the big toe on his right. His knees hurt. His shins hurt. He stumbled and fell sprawling.

He got up and heard voices in the distance. He forgot that his ankle wouldn't work, and fell again. Where were they?

He soon found out. They had him surrounded. His hands tightened into fists. Martin was breathing fast, his chest jumping as if he'd run farther and harder than Gary. He stood eerily still, waiting, with a strange expression on his face. Gary's knees were quivering. Bo had his hands on his hips, legs wide apart. Joey was licking his lips. Kurt, bashful, was looking away.

"Keep back," Gary said. "You fucking stupid shits!"

"Let's get on with it," Bo said, lowering his trunks to expose his hard-on.

"No," Gary said. "Please."

Joey got behind him, held him.

"Turn me loose...."

Joey pushed him down so that he was sitting on a rock.

"You'll love it," Martin said. "I fucking promise."

"Suck it!" Bo demanded.

Gary looked up at Bo like he was going to burst out crying, but then he dutifully took Bo's erect cock in his mouth. He pressed his lips around the head

324

and went back and forth over it. He knew how to do it; Martin knew about Gary's unusual talent for oral service, but the others did not. Gary had sucked Martin almost every night since they came to camp. Now it was time Gary got Martin's friends off as well. At first, Gary rejected the plan, but Martin said he would deny him his cock unless he went along.

Now Gary got Bo's cock halfway down his throat. He used his tongue on the underside of it. He put pressure on it and deep-throated it; he gagged a bit but continued. Bo looked down at his soft white shoulders and his bleached blond hair and his skinny arms. One of his trembling hands came up and he put it under Bo's balls and the other hand went around and held Bo's ass as he sucked.

God, Martin thought, he *really* knows how to do it.

Bo was gasping for breath, ready to shoot. Gary kept Bo's cock in his mouth for a couple of seconds, then he pulled his head back and Bo's cock slipped out. Bo came all over his face, cum dripping onto the dress.

Martin was all the while standing off to the side, jacking his cock. He grinned as Bo backed away from Gary and put his cock back in his swimsuit. Gary sank back on his ankles. Tears were streaming down his cheeks. He knew his initiation wasn't over. Joey came around and stood before Gary. "Take it out and suck it," he demanded.

Martin edged closer, delighting in the sight of Joey's huge prick as it was revealed in all its glory. For his part, Gary didn't seem to mind a bit as he brought his mouth to Joey's prick. Bo moved in closer as well and he and Martin stood tight against Joey while Gary did his thing. Bo was getting hard again, and Martin's eyes widened as he watched Gary suck Joey, then take both Joey and Bo in his mouth at once.

"My, god," he said, turning his head. "Kurt, look at this."

Kurt was standing in the water, avoiding the scene. "We shouldn't be doin' this," he grumbled.

"Oh, c'mon. Gary's queer, man. He loves this."

Martin left the action and went to Kurt. He saw that, despite his protestations, Kurt was hard. Martin playfully poked Kurt's boner. "C'mon, let Gary take care of that for you."

"I dunno, man."

"C'mon," Martin said, shoving Kurt towards the others.

Just then, Joey came, his cum joining Bo's on the front of the dress.

Kurt now stepped in front of him, and Martin moved close as Gary pulled away the fabric to reveal Kurt's fabled equipment. Martin thrilled at the sight of the upward curve of Kurt's incredible eight-inch prick.

While Joey's was longer and thicker, Kurt's was a sleek beauty. It looked like a missile pointing to the sky. Martin knew the best way to take it would be to sit on it, across Kurt's chest, facing him. It just seemed it would fit naturally that way. But sucking it was difficult, at least for Gary. Martin guessed the cock's curve and its extraordinary stiffness was making it difficult for even a young master like Gary.

After a few minutes of this, Martin said, "Lie down, so Kurt can fuck it."

"Oh, no, please. I ain't never been fucked."

"I dunno," Kurt said.

"Oh, c'mon, Kurt. You first, then me." He spit on his fingers and began fingering Gary's virgin asshole. Gary screamed as Martin skewered him. "God, maybe you ain't."

"No, I ain't. I ain't never."

This news seemed to turn Kurt on because he quickly got in position and his cock replaced Martin's agile fingers. Kurt was so hot for it that he rushed it, jamming his cock head into Gary's wet hole. As a couple of inches of shaft went in, Gary's face was screwed up in pain and he was gasping and letting out little sobs.

Martin knelt next to them as Kurt began to pump furiously. Mercifully, the fuck didn't last long. Kurt finally stopped screwing. His hips heaved a couple of times and he lay still on top of the skinny initiate. Then he got up, saying to Martin, "He's all yours, stud."

Martin got down over Gary.

What a feeling, Martin realized. It seemed as if Gary's asshole was sucking him in and he started pumping automatically. Nice, long, slow strokes and each of them got a little sob from Gary.

While Martin was pumping, Kurt got down in front of Gary, and presented his limp cock. "Clean it off, little buddy."

Gary was sobbing and shook his head no. Kurt grabbed him by his blond hair and pulled his head all the way back and said, "Suck it clean, you little faggot, or I'll break your fuckin' pretty neck."

Seeing Gary take Kurt's cock in his mouth once again was turning Martin on even more. He wanted to make his first fuck of Gary last several minutes at least but in a couple of seconds he was erupting inside the boy, his huge load joining Kurt's. Panting, he pulled out and stood up.

It was then that he noticed Gary was jacking off while he was sucking Kurt to renewed hardness. Just as Kurt started to come again, Gary came. When Gary was finally free, he tried to stand. His attackers forced him back against the rock.

Martin lifted him up and told him to take off the dress. He helped Gary get back into his swimsuit.

The sun was setting as the boys made their way back to the campground. Martin was carrying Gary piggyback and Gary bent down to whisper in his friend's ear, "Okay, was I good or what?"

Martin chuckled. "You were damn good. Maybe too damn good."

CABIN NO. 9

Mark Anderson

Two weeks at summer camp: a boy's dream. As a three-year veteran, I assumed the role of expert. It was the first year for my cousin Dave and a church friend, Hines. Excitedly, we unpacked in the assigned cabin number nine. Parents were already long forgotten. At the back of the cabin, the top left-hand bunk was my preferred spot for sleeping. I spread my sleeping bag. Eight beds to each cabin, mine had an overall view and abutted on the shit-house. From my spot, I could keep tabs on who sported the largest EMR that's camp talk for early morning erection. Our counselor would sleep opposite me, on the bottom bunk. From my spot, if I looked over the edge, I had a fine view of his bed. A born leader, I made introductions with each new arrival until the counselor appeared and our cabin was filled.

An hour later, assembled in the Recreation Hall everyone was given schedules for the two week period. Swim, dinner and camp- fire would occupy our first night. During the hour at the lake, I was able to check out potential fun buddies. One guy got my immediate attention. Slender, darkly tanned with black hair, he stood alone near the vacant lifeguard stand. His jockey bathing suit had a huge bulge. I found out that he hated cold water as much as I did. Under that pretext we became water buddies. The rule states campers must always swim with a buddy. So, Jim became my buddy; I liked him. He had an infectious laugh and a fun personality. We automatically gravitated to each other. I think he was aware of an undercurrent of trust between us before I was.

After dinner a make-up soft ball game was started in the back pasture. Jim, to my surprise, sought me out to go down and watch. Neither of us was interested in playing. Overhearing some of the counselors and leaders say they were going back to their cabins to change into something warmer for campfire, I suggested we do the same. Baseball game still in progress, we headed up to his cabin. Standing in his tight red bikini briefs, Jim searched for something to wear. I noticed how relaxed and composed he was. I wanted to touch his lithe, smooth satin skin. He announced that he had to take a piss, but did not want to use the shitter because of the smell. I suggested he piss off the back porch like I always did. Showing him what I meant, I opened the back door to the cabin, pulled out my cock and started to piss into the grass.

"Gosh, I never thought of that," he said standing beside me looking at my cock. "Ever jack off?"

"Sure," I said, "all the time. Why?"

"Because I do too, all the time I mean," he said, still looking at my dick, which was beginning to get hard.

"Wanna fool around?" I asked.

"Yeah, right now. I kind of feel horny." he said, pushing down his underwear.

Still looking at my dick, he commented, "You sure have a big dick."

"Well you have the biggest balls I've ever seen," I replied.

"Think so," he said lifting his balls up for our mutual inspection.

In his hand Jim had the fattest, roundest nuts I had ever seen. They were pulled up tight against his short, thick cock. The sac was a darker skin color-covered with fuzzy black hair.

"How far can you shoot?" he asked, while I watched his knuckles bang against his nuts as he fingered his dick.

"I don't know," I honestly answered. "Can I feel your nuts?"

"Yeah, that would be nice. Can I feel yours too?"

Feeling those hard, warm nuts in my hand, I started to stroke his dick. He then moved to face me and started to pump my cock.

"We'd better shoot fast before the others return," I cautioned." Yeah, you ready, 'cause I sure am."

"OK, you shoot your load and keep working my cock. I'll be there with you," I said excitedly.

"Oh, yeah, here it comes," he breathlessly said.

"So's mine. Keep pumping me!"

His cock got harder in my hand and white cum squirted out of the head of his dick. The sperm drooled over my hand. At the same time my cock shot cum all over his chest and belly.

"Jesus, you shoot far," he said still holding onto my cock.

"We better get dressed and fast," I said, knowing the baseball game would soon be over.

Jim walked with me to cabin number nine while I changed into warmer clothing, just as my cabin mates returned. Usually different guys were in and out of each others cabins all the time, so Jim being with me was not questioned. We all walked down the hill out back, across the pasture, to a wooded area where the fire pit was located. Giant logs placed in a circle had blankets placed around them with guys sprawled upon them in groups. With darkness and the cooler air we were glad of the roaring fire. Songs and stories lulled us into quiet moods. Stretched out beside me in the dark where no one could see us, Jim pressed his legs against mine. I was relaxed and content with my new friend.

Hot chocolate and oatmeal-raisin cookies were served in the mess hall after the campfire.

Tired, we were all ready for bed; it had been an exciting, but exhausting, day with promises of more to come.

"See you tomorrow," Jim said quietly.

"Sleep well," I said. "I sure wish you were in my cabin and we could sleep together."

"Me too," he said and smiled, as he went off to his cabin.

What a sweet face, I thought climbing up and into my large bunk. Alone in my sleeping bag, my thoughts of Jim tumbled in my head. Suddenly we heard the voice of one of the first-year campers in my cabin. He was lonely and afraid

to sleep alone. I pitied the voice that was honest enough to confess fear. Everyone else joked and laughed at him. He was in the bunk below me, so I heard a quiver in his voice, which no one else heard. I felt his hand on my hip and turned to look into the wide eyes, etched with fear.

"Can I sleep with you'?" he whispered. No one else heard him.

"Sure," I said, "come on up."

Even in the darkness, I could sense the silent relief come over his face. Quickly, the young camper was up beside me before I could unzip my sleeping bag to let him in.

"Thanks," he said turning his warm, sweet-smelling body against mine.

I couldn't help but spring an erection immediately. I turned toward his back prepared to sleep when he pushed against me. His butt rubbed and brushed my hard cock. "Hmmmm," he murmured and pulled my arm over him, to hold him tight. He was asleep in no time. For the first time in my life it actually felt good to sleep with another guy in my arms. I drifted into a wonderful sleep thinking of Jim in cabin one.

Always an early riser, I was awake before anyone in the cabin. My little friend, I discovered, had his face buried against my chest with his chin wedged into my armpit, his leg draped over my leg and his hip beside my thigh. Two clenched hands were pressed to his chest as he slept. How beautiful he looked with light brown hair falling over his eyes while he lay in a deep, peaceful sleep. I looked around to make sure everyone else was still asleep. I moved my trapped arm from under his neck. I pulled him closer. Closing my eyes, it felt great to just hold someone. I heard the rhythmic pattern of his breathing change. He was awakening. "Hmmmmmm," I heard him mutter and pull closer. How could I not enjoy our mutual need for warmth in the cool morning air?

"Shush," I cautioned him only to feel his hard dick jab at my side.

Feeling his hand slide down my chest and belly, I let him explore and find my obvious pleasure waiting for him. His hand touching my erect shaft, caused me to stifle a moan.

"Not now," I warned. "Later, when we are alone, OK?"

"Hmmmmm," was all I heard; then, I felt his hand clench tighter on my dick.

"We'd better get up," I said extricating myself from him.

I went to the john to wash. When I returned, he was dressed, sitting on his own bunk. He smiled and went to clean up. Cool morning air and damp grass saw two quiet guys head to the mess hall for coffee. I wondered what Jim was doing.

Eventually the three of us became fast friends. Jim and our new friend, Ken, from my cabin arranged all our activities together. That night after dinner when the scheduled baseball game started Jim was drafted to play. Disappointed we could not sneak away, I watched with Ken as Jim hit a home run, rounded the bases and, at home plate, slid into the catcher. The loud crack followed by a scream sent my friend Jim to the hospital with a broken leg.

Understandably upset, I suddenly realized I might betray my feelings toward

Jim. What we did together would remain our secret. Dave and Hines would be kept in the dark. It was none of their business why Jim and I were friends. Only Ken was informed, because he was to join us later that night for a jack-off session. I hoped Jim would write to me, because I knew he would not be returning to camp. Ken was loyal and understood my loss. I never heard from or saw Jim again.

From one till two every day was quiet time. Usually naps were encouraged. Ken and I continued sleeping together and no one thought anything of it. Dave and Hines opted for sports finding the cabin communal life not to their liking. I seldom saw them. Every afternoon, I would lie down on my bunk and Ken would cuddle against me with his back to the wall. Because, we were hidden in the large bunk bed we would doze with our hands down the front of each other's shorts. Cocks held firmly, we would drift to sleep for an hour. We went everywhere together. Our friendship and camaraderie was never questioned or made fun of. Every night one of us would wait for the other to join together in my sleeping bag. Often I was the last in bed. How nice it was to see Ken's smiling face snuggled down in my bed waiting.

After Jim's accident, Ken and I became water buddies. Lingering late one afternoon, we found ourselves returning to an empty cabin. Wet bathing suits tossed aside, we stood naked looking at each other. Our erecting dicks told us all we needed to know. I knelt before Ken, kissed his cock, and slipped it into my mouth.

"Oh, yeah, suck it," he gasped, then slammed his butt forward, so the entire long, slender shaft, shot down my throat.

Moaning, I held onto his ass while I worked my throat muscles along his buried cock. Holding onto my shoulders for support, he bucked about three times, yelled, and shot sweet jizz.

"Yes, oh yessss," he groaned against me, then pulled away quickly. "Let me have yours."

Standing, I said, "Here, take mine! I'm about to shoot."

"Give it to me. Give it all to me," he sighed and swallowed my cock as I shot my hot load.

"I knew it would be like this," he said standing up, licking his lips, smiling. "I wish we could do this more often."

"So do I."

I had never had a friendship quite like the one we had. Being together during the day was a joy, but to be able to spend the nights wrapped in each other's arms was pure bliss. The affection I felt toward him was returned in kind. We managed, without anyone knowing, to sneak away and have the hottest sex. I had yet to know. He enjoyed getting fucked as much as I loved fucking him. Often he would climax while my dick was buried to the hilt in his ass, without even touching himself. As the two-week period wound down, our sexual encounters became frantic. We knew we would be losing each other and were trying to make up for lost time.

330

"How and when will I ever see you again?" Ken asked at the lake one late afternoon.

"I don't know," I responded with honesty and looked into the saddest face I had ever seen.

His pain was my pain. Ken lived in another part of the country, making our meeting at a future date impossible for either of us.

"Letters, we'll write letters," I said.

"Then, in time, we could try to arrange a meeting or something," Ken suggested.

"Yeah," I said, hopefully. "But remember what we had was special."

"Yes, I'll always remember you."

The few days we had left settled into a wonderful caring for each other. Had I experienced the depth of feelings that I was searching for?

I held my tears in check, as I waved goodbye. He became a blubbering idiot getting into his family's car.

"You sure must have liked camp?" I heard his father say kindly.

His face stained with tears, his eyes wide, he waved from the back window of the car. I stared after him until the car was out of my sight. With a lump in my throat, I saw my parents drive into the parking lot. The ride home was made worse because I could not confide to anyone my feelings. Alone, I learned how to mask my emotions.

Ken and I would write great letters, enclosing photos of ourselves till the end of summer. Without any warning, his letters stopped. Mine went unanswered, until I realized our correspondence must have been discovered. Sadly, Ken would drift from my mind but not my heart.

Getting back into the swing with my neighborhood buddies was a little harder than I thought. Youth in summer grow and change quickly. Friendships click, squabble, break apart and regroup many times over. Friendships are interrupted by summer camp, family vacations and commitments that take us apart from one another. Some of my friends found that girls were suddenly more interesting than fishing, rafting on the lake or sleepovers in backyard tents.

My world narrowed. My interest in males became covert, with the need to survive in a straight world. Bruce, Donny, Ross, Bill and Philip found excuses not to be alone with me. If I talked about girls and had a date, then we would team up together for a show, or picnic, but never would we be alone together as in early summer.

Doug was a life-line for my sanity, but lived too far away. I had to make my own way in life. I found enjoyment in my porn collection, which grew larger as the summer dwindled to an end. I knew I had become two identities. The juggling had just begun.

NIGHT RIDING:
CAMPING WITH THE COWPOKES

Jason Carpenter

I've always had this thing for cowboys. When the rodeo is in town you'll find me hanging around trying to get better acquainted with some slim-hipped youths in tight blue jeans and wearing the sweet cologne of leather, sweat and horse manure. The experience I'm going to tell you about fulfilled all my fantasies and may have ruined me for life.

The Great American Cattle Drive, a re-enactment of an original cattle drive along the cattle trails once used to get beef to market in the eighteen-hundreds, started from Fort Worth, Texas in March, 1995. Doctors, lawyers and other professional people with a yearning to re-live history, along with numerous working cowboys, were taking a herd of longhorn cattle all the way to Miles City, Montana a trek expected to take six months. Attending the riders were cooks and well-stocked covered wagons for the supplies and food necessary to fuel the participants during their journey.

At each stop along the way people from nearby cities would go out to greet the riders. When I found out they were going to be camping for the weekend near my home town of El Reno, Oklahoma, I made certain I was there to welcome them.

The drovers got the cattle squared away on a rancher's spread while the cook set up camp and got a huge black pot full of beans boiling over an open fire. I went straight for the cook's wagon, while other visitors sought out riders to chat with. I'm bright enough to know that eventually all those hungry cowboys would make their way toward food. Sure enough, within minutes several men rode up and climbed off their horses. They slapped trail dust from their clothing with their hats, then squatted around the fire, some tearing at strips of beef jerky with their teeth, too hungry to wait for the beef and beans to finish boiling.

I caught one of these riders snatching glances at me from beneath the wide brim of his western hat.

I glanced back.

His thighs strained to burst the seams of his faded jeans and his well-muscled, hairy forearms bulged beneath the rolled-up cuffs of his brightly patterned, western-style shirt. He tilted his head back a little farther and our eyes met. His were the angry steel gray of prairie storm clouds. His nose was narrow and his lips, slightly parched from the wind and sun, were full and expressive as he shot me a knowing smile. The ends of his handle-bar mustache drew up as he blatantly winked at me! Damn, he was cute!

I lingered on the outer perimeter of the camp, afraid to approach him among the other riders. He must have guessed the reason for my hesitancy because he stood up from his squat, ramrod straight, and rolled his shoulders. I could hear

his stiff bones pop at a distance of ten feet. I hoped all of his bones were stiff. He ambled over to me with a bow-legged gait. I guessed him to be a couple of years older than my own age of twenty. He was taller than me by several inches, but the heels on his boots were two inches high. He rolled the right side of his mustache between his thumb and forefinger and looked me straight in the eyes.

"Name's Chance and, unless I miss my guess, you'd like to fuck me," he said in a soft Texas drawl.

"Go ahead and beat around the bush if you want to," I laughed. "I'm Jason ... and yep, I'd sorely like to fuck you. And vice-versa," I added.

"Okay. Follow me," he said, walking away from the campfire. Night had fallen, and once we were twenty yards from the fire it was pretty dark. If not for a zillion stars and a nearly full moon overhead it would have been black.

Chance stopped and turned to envelop me in his strong arms. We kissed deeply, tongues probing and twisting. His mustache was driving me crazy. We reached simultaneously for each other's crotch. I wrapped my hand around his thick cock and stroked him. He must have had ten inches pressing against his jeans. I dropped to my knees and unzipped his pants, then reached in and dragged his monster out into the moonlight. It was a white, circumcised, perfectly stiff dick, without any bend in it. I kissed his throbbing range-rod. He smelled of saddle leather and horse sweat, a heady combination that almost made me pop my load down my leg. I took him in my hand, lubricated him with my hot saliva, and stroked him. I heard him whistle. Seconds later his horse walked up behind me and snuffed, blowing air from its nostrils down the back of my neck. I'm surprised I didn't pull Chance's rigid tube right out of his groin.

"Get up," he said, taking me by the shoulders. "And take off your pants."

I did as he said, watching as he, too, dropped his jeans and underwear, then pulled them off over his boots. He fished a foil-wrapped rubber from his sock and, in one swift movement, he mounted his horse and stretched out his hand to me. I put my foot in the stirrup and let him hoist me to a position in front of him on the saddle.

"Let's go night riding. Lift up," he instructed, patting my ass.

When I leaned forward, Chance took his condom- covered meat-spike in his right hand and screwed the bulbous head straight up my puckered asshole. His unyielding poker pierced far up my anus, filling my rectum with cowboy cock. Once he had me speared, he put his hands around my waist and pulled me to a sitting position, impaled on his prick.

"Ungh," I moaned, as my own fuck tube swelled to its full nine-and-a-half inches.

"Hang on, little cowpoke," Chance said, snapping the horse's reins.

The beautiful animal began a slow walk, but Chance urged it into a canter. The rocking, bouncing motion of the animal's gait drove Chance's stiff tent pole up and down and around in my guts, reaming me out to perfection. Chance let go of the reins with his right hand and fisted me with his callused palm. The roughness against the soft head of my dick was too much. At the same instant I

334

felt Chance go stiffer and arch beneath me, spurting and gushing his hot cum up my butt hole, I also spewed my molten rush of creamy cock juice all over his hand and the horse's mane.

Chance kissed my shoulder, then yelled, "Hang on! Eeeehaw!"

He urged his horse into a full gallop and I bounced on his still stiff root until I thought I would faint. Chance, grunting and heaving, poured another load of night rider fuck cream up my willing anus.

Finally, having butt-fucked me until I was sure I was going to be bow-legged, Chance drew his horse to a sliding stop, kicking up dust beneath the Oklahoma sky.

We climbed down from the animal and Chance took a rolled, up blanket from where it was tied with leather thongs behind the saddle. Spreading the saddle on the cool night ground, he lay down and pulled me to his side. We kissed until I was rock hard again. If only he'd blow me, I thought, my fantasy would be complete.

As if able to read my mind, Chance twisted his body so that he squatted over my belly, his hard buttocks facing me. He took my pulsing, oozing beefsteak in his hand, rolled a condom down my shaft, and guided it to his mouth. He swallowed me whole! His mustache rubbed against the front of my balls and the bulging head of my dong was pressed and squeezed as it slid passed the back of Chance's tongue and down his throat! He bobbed his head rapidly, while stuffing a couple of fingers up my dark cavity, and I returned the favor by drilling three of my squeezed-together digits up his sweet brown canyon.

Oh, could he suck cock! His tongue and those slightly chapped lips worked like a good quarter-horse, cutting out a cow from the herd, instinctively knowing what to do to make me blow my wad -which I did, pushing upward, shoving my dick up to the balls into Chance's throat then blasting a ten-gallon hat full of steaming dick-honey into the rubber so hard I'm surprised it didn't burst. He could hardly breathe, but he sucked and sucked until every drop of jism was suctioned out of my balls and through my bulging shaft. I think I could have died a happy man at that moment, with no regrets.

Later, after we went back for our clothing, Chance took me to the campfire, where we had met. He rolled the end of his mustache again and gave me a dimpled smile.

"I'll be looking for you tomorrow, kid, if you want to go out night ridin' again."

I looked around to make certain no one was watching us, then took Chance's hand in mine and gave it a squeeze. "I'll be right here at seven o' clock. Thanks for the evening, Chance."

Those moody eyes, barely visible from beneath the brim of his hat, seemed to twinkle. He shook my hand and turned toward the campfire.

The next day went so slowly I thought my watch had stopped running. My part-time job at a local supermarket seemed to drag on forever as I swept, straightened canned goods on the shelves and stocked the produce section.

This last duty wasn't so bad after I got turned on stacking cucumbers. Every one of the long, thick vegetables reminded me of Chance's hot, bulging wrangler's meat. I caught myself stroking one of the green cukes when an elderly lady said "Ahhhhh!" at my elbow. I hastily set the cuke on top of the others I had stacked, afraid the woman would report me to the manager.

Instead, as I turned to walk away, I saw her pick up the same well-endowed cuke and place it lovingly into her shopping cart. Something told me the woman had found her

mate for the evening.

I knew I'd found mine.

Still the clock moved like a mule through molasses. Two hours remained until I would get off work and be free to prepare for my date with Chance. When the time finally came I whipped off my apron and tossed it in the dirty clothes bin in the back of the store, stamped my time card and headed for home, stopping once along the way for some last minute shopping. A little something for Chance.

I showered and dried off. Standing naked in front of my bathroom mirror, I blow-dried my red hair, brushing it until it was perfectly coifed, and shaved twice so my skin would be as smooth as Chance's was rough. I dabbed cologne everywhere I thought Chance's nose might get close to and a couple of places I could only pray for.

Dressed in jeans, a western-style shirt and boots, I looked about as much like a real cowboy as Mickey looks like a real mouse, but I knew I'd look good to Chance.

Seven o'clock found me standing at the perimeter of the

campfire, trying to look as if I belonged there. Chance wasn't anywhere to be seen. Then a hand slid between my thighs from behind and cupped my balls. A rough voice whispered in my ear as I leaned back against a lean, hard chest. "You look good enough to eat, my little drugstore cowpoke."

"Thank God!" I said, turning to look into those cloudy eyes. Chance had obviously bathed and changed clothing from the previous evening, but his face was still a darkly covered field of stubble. I touched his days-old beard with my fingertips and shuddered at the texture, imagining how it would feel between my thighs.

Reaching into my tight jeans I took the small gift I had purchased earlier in the day. "Hold your hand out," I said. "I have something for you."

Chance narrowed his eyes, but held his left hand out toward me. I slipped the knotted leather friendship bracelet over Chance's big hand and positioned it on his wrist. "To remember me by."

Chance moved the leather band on his wrist then said, with what I thought was a tiny catch in his voice, "Thanks, Justin. Nobody's ever gave me much before I appreciate it. And I'm gonna have more than this to remember you by before this night slips into morning."

I looked at the quickly darkening sky. The setting sun produced a rose-colored panorama in the heavens. "Good weather tonight," I commented. "Red skies at

336

night, sailor's delight. Red skies at morning, sailor's take warning and we sure have red skies tonight."

Chance nodded. "Did you know that little saying is from the Bible?"

I looked at him to see if he was putting me on. Didn't seem to be. "I've heard that saying all my life. You sure?"

He smiled. "Cowboys have a lot of time to read of an evening. Check out Matthew 16:2 and 16:3 sometime."

Chance led me to where his horse was tied. He removed his hat and dropped it to the grass. "Ready to ride again, partner?"

"Only if we can swap places," I said. "I want to feel my dick up your hard ass as we gallop off across the plains."

Chance began taking his clothing off except for his boots. I quickly followed suit, then mimicked his actions from the previous night, climbing into the saddle and rolling a condom over my bursting meat log. Chance took my proffered hand and mounted in front of me in the saddle.

I spread his taut, white globes and screwed my cock up his unprotesting ass. "Unhh," he moaned, leaning farther forward so I could ram all of my pulsing meat into his steaming insides. I urged the horse into a gentle walk.

The frenzied lovemaking of yesterday was exciting as hell, but I wanted a slower, more romantic evening this time. My arms were around Chance's waist and I held the reins in my hands near his flat belly. He ground his butt against me, massaging my dick with the muscles of his anus,

nearly making me spew my load. I held back, though, and gently kissed his sunburned neck; sucked his ear lobes, and let one hand free of the reins to stroke his protruding pole.

The easy swaying motion of the horse brought me to a slow, but powerful climax. My hot juice spurted in seemingly unending clots to fill the rubber with sex-scented spunk and I rammed all of my meat up Chance's love chute as far as possible. I didn't jack him off to climax, though, preferring to give him pleasure another way. I directed the horse back to the place we had left our clothes.

"You going to let me die here, you sweet fucker?" Chance asked, leaning back against me.

"Not a chance, Chance. Climb off."

He got off of my pole. A sharp sucking sound could be heard as my penis slipped out of him. He dismounted, as did I. I took the bedroll from the rear of the saddle and spread it on the ground. Taking a fresh condom from my boot I dropped to my knees in front of Chance and rolled it sensuously over the bulging head of his shaft all the way to his balls. He stood there with his hands on his hips staring down at me. I clasped my hands around his ass globes, took his cowboy cock head between my lips and eased him down my throat.

His fingers laced behind my neck and he pulled me closer. I licked his rod from tip to base and buried my nose in his wet tangle of pubic hair while I cupped and squeezed his nearly tennis ball-sized testicles in my hand.

He fucked my face with a vengeance, his cock sliding passed my uvula; down

337

my gasping throat. Then he was coming!

Even through the rubber I felt the steaming heat of his fuck juice blow into my mouth. The sweet scent of him made me dizzy. I sucked until his knees began to wobble and he fell to the blanket beside me. We kissed and touched, his mustache making me crazy. Beneath the stars we fell asleep, each holding the other's dick in his hand.

A couple of hours before dawn we awoke, dressed and rode back to camp.

He stayed in the saddle as we said good-bye. His fingers often touched the leather bracelet I had given him. "I'll never forget you, Justin."

"Do you have to forget me, Chance? Can't you come back after this trail drive is finished?" I asked hopefully.

"This drive is scheduled to take the better part of six months and I've already accepted a job from a rancher in Montana once we get there," he said sadly. "Maybe someday...."

I placed my palm on his thigh. "Good luck, cowboy. I'll dream of you."

He smiled, touched the brim of his hat with his finger, winked, then spurred his horse to make it rear up on its hind legs.

I'll never forget that stunning image of Chance silhouetted against a blinding moon as big as Texas!

— Adapted for this collection from a story that first appeared in Indulge For Men magazine.

338

COME JULY

...As the thousands of little gulags that dot the turbid, leech-infested fens of the Berkshires and Adirondacks echo with the cracking voices of hapless pubescents being warehoused for the summer, moms and dads can cavort uninhibitedly in any room in the house, with Stan Getz burbling from the hi-fi while they replenish their Martinis from a huge underground storage tank in the back yard.

At least that's the scenario I imagined at age eight, as I languished at camp, weaving lanyards and singing Bavarian roundelays while fending off the taunts of the kiddie Cossacks I bunked with. I could never understand why my parents, who touted me as their beautiful genius prince, could so easily pack me off to fend for myself among God knows what assortment of bedwetters and animal torturers.

I won't reveal the actual name of the camp I was sent to. Suffice it to say that it had one of those ersatz American Indian names synthesized from the first names of the owner's children (e.g., Natalie, Gabriel, and Kenneth yield Camp Na-Ga-Ken-Ken).

...I had to fight for self-respect at Na-Ga-Ken-Ken every day, and was most certainly not the proverbial 'happy camper.' I became friends with only two people that summer: a retarded dishwasher and a pockmarked, bucktoothed Alabamian counselor who promised, insinuatingly, to take me to see 'Yellow Submarine' someday, "just the two of us."

And then there was Bruce, a classic summer-camp archetype: older (he was nine), cigarette-smoking, beer-drinking, jaded, and a fount of forbidden wisdom. That summer, for instance, he had jock itch *(tinea cruris)*.

To the rest of us, that seemed wildly exotic as if he'd contracted some drug-resistant strain of venereal disease while banging hookers in Borneo. One day, Bruce held court at the horseshoe pit, regaling us with explicit details of the love act for many of us, our first introduction to the facts of life. I couldn't believe that my parents would do such a thing, and I remonstrated fiercely with Bruce. "What do you think they're doing right now?" he sneered.

Horrified, I ran to a counselor and insisted on an immediate phone call home. My mother answered, the dulcet inflections of Astrud Gilberto in the background. "What are you and Dad doing?" I demanded indignantly. "Making fondue," she replied. (To this day, 'making fondue' remains one of my favorite euphemisms for intercourse.)

Famed writer Mark Leyner, remembering summer camp for The New Yorker magazine.

WAS IT YOU?

Anonymous

The campground is quiet in mid-week, and the sun is warm through the trees. You slept very late after yesterday's hike, and now you walk to the showers, enjoying the mingled smells of balsam and fir, wood-smoke and frying bacon.

The building housing the showers is small. There are only two stalls and a reversible sign on the door for Men/Women. You knock on the door, as the sign shows the wrong flavor; getting no answer, you flip the sign over so it's right and go in. You are alone. You drop your clothes in the dressing area and take your soap and shampoo into the nearest stall.

The hot water feels marvelous coursing down your body and you begin to use the soap more as a lubricant than a cleanser, rubbing, smoothing, touching. Your eyes close as you begin to build a fantasy and feel the excitement rising. The sun coming through the skylight, the water running, the soap slipping it's all very sensual. You hear your own moans begin as your hands move around your ass, your shoulders, your thighs, your belly.

Suddenly a chill breeze hits your back; the curtain has been pulled open and you feel someone else come into the stall with you. You try to turn quickly to protest, but strong hands hold you in place and one hand covers your eyes. You feel warm breath against your neck and another warm breath at your crotch. So, you think, there are at least two. Part of your brain is sorting through options, wondering how to get out of here without getting hurt. It is frightening; nothing bad ever happens in the woods, does it?

Another part is fascinated. How did they know you were in here? Do they know you at all? Why are they doing this?

And another part is too far along in fantasy, the excitement too built up to lose it now. This part is urging back against the body behind you, bending a bit, still moaning under the sound of the water.

There is now one hand at your waist holding you, and only one other, over your eyes, still. The breath is still warm on your genitals, arousing you even further. You feel more soap now, on your legs, around your crotch, on your ass, working into the crack and you think, "No! Not there! Oh god, no...." but you don't say anything because by now you need to come very badly. Hands begin to work the soap over and around your crotch, bringing you very close to orgasm. Fingers are working at your asshole, working the soap in, moving you gently back and forth.

You bend over farther, wanting more, wanting it now. You feel your climax starting from the handwork in front of you and urging back even farther moan, "Now, please... now...oh, please...." Your wish is granted. You feel a hard cock slide gently into your ass, begin pumping in time to your own coming. You come wildly, as strong as you ever remember, groaning with the joy of it.

By now, the hand is away from your eyes, but the warm water still pours down, obscuring your vision. And you don't *want* to look. You keep your eyes closed, feeling the cock fucking you, harder now, wondering when it will be done, wondering if you *want* it to be done, keeping your eyes closed, not knowing who is in front of you or who behind. Soon enough the man in your ass begins to spasm, pumping you full, leaving you sated. The hands in front are gentle now, coming down. You slump against the back wall for support as the cock slides out and away.

By the time you open your eyes and turn off the water, you are alone in the building. You wonder if it was only a fantasy, but then you finger your ass and feel the cum dripping out. It was real.

Walking back to your tent, you look curiously at the other campers. Was it you? Or you? Or perhaps you?

IN THE TENT

K. I. Bard

It wasn't what it became,
not at first, especially,
because at the start
it wasn't anything much.

His name was John
and he was twelve,
a smiley kid
two years my junior.

He acted nice,
kind of silly
the way kids his age
so often are.

We joked a lot,
teasing one another or
making fun of others,
a riot of laughs.

I don't remember
who's idea it was,
he says it was me,
who insisted.

Did I insist
we sleep together
that spring camp out
in Scouts?
I don't remember
wanting it,
but I wasn't unhappy
it happened.

Neither was John,
and maybe that's why
I like to think it was
his idea as much as mine.

One thing I know.
I didn't start anything.
In fact, I was surprised
when he grabbed my hand.

We'd been whispering
in the dark,
each in his own bed roll,
when suddenly he took my hand.

It was really strange,
feeling my hand in his.
Boys don't hold hands together.
Hands have other uses.

My head felt dizzy
from him playing with
my fingers,
all he did, at first.

Then, slowly, my hand was drawn
inside the warm confines
of his sleeping bag,
dragged deep inside.

I had to adjust my position,
wondering when he'd stop,
wondering what he wanted,
wondering why.

He halted, pressing my hand
against his belly
at the juncture of tummy
and the elastic wall barrier.

On one side innocent gut.
On the other
his not so innocent part,
straining.

Did I feel its heat?
Was I drawn to John's
unvoiced wishes?
I reached.

344

He sighed,
pushing and guiding my hand.
It wasn't as if
he didn't want me to.

What happened wasn't much,
hardly worth remembering until the next day
when John confessed.

Abuse.
He said I'd abused him,
forced and tricked him
against his will.

He told our Scoutmaster
and his parents,
who hurriedly called mine
and filed a complaint.

The police came.
I had to go with them
and make a statement.
A lawyer was called.

I was fourteen
on the outside.
Inside, I was old
and cold and dead.

Frozen in time,
I tried not to feel
by clamping down
on everything.

The drugs helped.
I felt sleepy,
hardly ever got hard,
not like before.

I went into counseling.
We moved.
My life went on,
but not as before.

All that was over,
ended in a confession
that made John a hero
and me an offender.

Sometimes (I can't help it)
I find myself
trying to remember what happened
that night.

I try to discover
what was so important
it had to change my life,
leaving me alive, but dead inside.

Steamy sex among the filthy rich...

THE PLEASURE PALACE

**An Erotic Novella by
Kevin Bantan**

One

I had been friends with Mike since early in freshman year at the university. It was now summer break, and my friend had surprised me by inviting me to stay for a few days at his house. He had a pool and more, so we'd have fun, he said with a wink. I wondered if that meant sex. We had come out to each other early in our friendship, but we'd never dated or had sex. Mike had dirty blond hair and eyes the blue of the sky on a sunny day. His ready smile was enhanced by straight, white teeth. He was nicely built, too. Although Mike wasn't my type, I knew that we could still have a good time together.

I consider myself fairly good looking as well. My brown hair is cut close, my eyes the color of emeralds. My cheeks dimple when I smile, which all of my boyfriends liked. I have a pretty strong chin over a smooth, muscular body. Those same boyfriends I mentioned described me variously as "beautiful," "gorgeous," or "adorable." Well, yeah, I do like what I see in my bedroom mirror, clothed or not.

So, I was thinking that the visit would be fun with maybe a little sex thrown in.

Mike had instructed me to take a taxi to his place and told me that he would pay the fare. The house was in the valley, but the street name didn't sound familiar. That wasn't surprising, because I had never had a reason to travel to that wealthy part of town. As I remembered it, there were some pretty impressive homes there. I gave the driver the address, and the guy looked at me with a what in the world are *you* doing going there? Look. I wasn't shabbily dressed, but Mike had told me to wear comfy casual, as he put it. I thought that my big black T-shirt over baggy khaki cargo shorts with black sport sandals qualified. Screw the driver. I had been invited, not him.

"This was the address, right," the driver asked.

"Yes," I said, with a slight tremor in my voice. I was awed.

The 'address' was that of a massive colonial-style house with five gables punctuating the roof. As the cab made its way up the tree-lined circular drive, I saw a large wing off the rear of the house. Well, a mansion.

Instead of ringing the bell as I was told, I paid the driver with my own money, just to show him that I belonged at such a place. I didn't feel that way, but it was none of the man's business. I gave him a deservedly modest tip, picked up my knapsack and exited the vehicle.

Mike answered the door wearing only a pair of long yellow shorts. He greeted me warmly. I explained that I had paid the fare, which made him cluck.

"Well, everything else is on me, including your first treat. Come on, I'll show you," he said, surprising me by kissing me on the cheek and taking my hand.

We walked down the wide central hall to a room on the left. I was impressed with the rich furnishings and rugs along the way. But nowhere near as much as when we entered the room. My mouth dropped open when I beheld the tapered back of a tawny-skinned boy with the highest, roundest ass cheeks I'd ever seen.

"Marcus, your date is here."

The boy turned around and smiled. The smile widened as his hazel eyes focused on me, my breath having suddenly vanished at the sight of the rest of him. His tautly muscled body was as finely proportioned as a classical sculpture. Calling his face striking would have been a lame start in describing the power of its beauty. His scalp was shaved, but hair would have been a needless distraction on that body. His nose was slightly flared and his lips were still full, despite being stretched across his teeth. His smile was dazzling. He wore a black leather thong as a necklace, and nothing else. His dusky cock curved elegantly from his body. Geez, it had to be eight inches, at least.

"Very pleased to meet you, Jeff," he said, extending an elegant, long-fingered hand to me.

"Likewise. Really." I tried to sound as sincere as I felt. I was in the presence of my first certifiable Adonis.

"Marc is going to be your chaperon, at least for the first part of your stay. He *is* more your type, I've gathered."

I blushed and almost stammered. "Beauty like his isn't a type. It's universal." That made Marcus grin wider.

Just then, arms appeared around Mike's waist. I followed them to find them attached to a short, adorable boy of oriental extraction. "Well, hello love. This is Cecil. He's Thai. I can't pronounce his name, so I call him that. He adores it."

"I do," the boy said with a heavy accent, as he undid Mike's shorts from behind. They fluttered to the ground. I couldn't help staring at Mike's short, fat member. If it weren't for the prospect of spectacular Marcus, I would have been happy to suck Mike for the duration of his stay. However, Marcus was a far more compelling presence.

Once Cecil had made Mike naked, he took his hand, grinning. The boy was nude, too, and wore only gold earrings, a necklace and matching waist chain. He, too, was hung, or at least appeared to be, given his short stature. I doubted that Cecil was anywhere near his majority. Or would be for years. I was so addled by the unexpected nude male beauty that I thought that my head would go into spin cycle.

A servant appeared, wearing a white satin vest and brief, and bearing a silver tray with fluted glasses of what turned out to be mimosas. "Thank you, Ferdinand. Taste it, Jeff. You'll love it. The orange juice cuts the champagne bite nicely. After all, we haven't had lunch yet. Or breakfast in one case," he said, winking at me. "Well, Cecil and I have some business to attend to. I'll leave you two to make your own entertainment. I'm so glad you came, Jeff."

"I haven't yet," and immediately reddened at my slip of the tongue. I gave Marcus a sheepish smile, and it was returned with a wide, affirming one. Mike and Cecil were gone.

"Well, would you care to see my secret hideaway?"

"Very much."

The nude boy took my hand, and we walked up the thickly carpeted stairs to

350

the second floor. I watched in building arousal as my companion's cock swayed sexily as we mounted the stairs. And I noticed that the cock and balls were ringed by another length of black cord, too. Cool.

The bedroom was large and at the front of the house.

"I thought we could get to know each other before we ate and I showed you around the place. That is, if you want to."

"I do. I meant what I said. You're absolutely gorgeous, Marcus."

"And Mike did not lie. You're to die for, Jeff."

"Let's die together, then."

Marc kissed me after he removed the T-shirt and knelt to unfasten the sandals. Those full lips lit my fire, which my partner found out, when he unfastened the shorts and they dropped to the ground. Now our erections pressed between us, our arms in pursuit of soft skin over hard muscle. I didn't care if I did die making it with Marc at that moment, because I couldn't imagine a more beautiful creature on the face of the earth.

We actually kissed and caressed until Marc's smooth right leg humped the short hairs of my left, signaling his skyrocketing excitement and impending orgasm. His leg on mine felt wonderful. We moaned into each other's mouth but kissed on, the shared passion too wonderful to interrupt. Mark's leg action became so erotic that I began to see scatter shots of color exploding behind my closed eyes. Our tongues and lips met as old lovers, irresistible to each other. Our cries of orgasm were joyous but muffled by our kissing as our knees buckled, and we wetted each other's torso. Marc's leg was now wrapped completely around mine as our essences commingled and trickled down our bellies.

We opened our eyes and looked, heavy-lidded, at each other. Then we exchanged a chaste kiss.

"Man, I didn't know that just kissing could make this happen," I said, feeling a sense of awe for the second time that day. Well, third, if you count meeting the beautiful creature named Marcus.

"Not in my lifetime, except that it just did."

"Wow. Can I propose to you?"

"Yes, but you might want to wait to see what other earthly delights lurk here before you do."

"None could be better than you, Marc. You're exquisite."

"Thanks. So are you, Jeff."

Our foreheads were pressed together, when the knock came on the door. I jumped, feeling panic being naked and a visitor standing outside. "It's okay," Marc cooed to me. How? We were not only nude, we were wet with each other's come. "Come in." Another boy did, wearing a satin vest and matching thong, like the boy, who had served us the drinks downstairs. He laid a tray of food on the table near one of the windows. Marc thanked him. He smiled and bowed. Then he grinned and winked before leaving. I watched his cute brown ass cheeks leave. They framed the tiny white back strap engagingly.

"You're really hot, you know that, Jeff?"

"Me? You made me come by kissing me."

"Don't forget that I came, too. So what does that tell you? And, just for your information, all of the wonderfully clothed servants are Filipino and off limits, unfortunately. And completely desirable in those uniforms."

"Yeah, they're sexy as hell. A little mystery, as they say."

"You got it. And you'll get to see some more after we eat."

"Seeing you is enough. And there's still plenty of mystery about you."

"Keep flattering me, and you won't get past that door for your entire stay."

"I'm glad that's settled."

After lunch, which was caviar, spiced shrimp and clams casino, we showered together. It was a novel experience for me, and a very enjoyable one. It was great to have my body lathered, especially my genitals, which were ready for a comeback. When we returned to the bedroom, we finally made it to the bed and lay on luxurious satin sheets. Marc let me have my way with him. First I sucked on the irresistible long toes of his wide feet. That got him squirming as I fellated each digit as if it were his cock. I licked the smooth, pale soles, which made him shiver. By the time I was ready to feast on his dark member, it was already beginning to bloat. I made it glisten with my spit and completely harden with my lips and tongue. I had never seen what I considered a perfectly formed penis before Marc's. It was no surprise that it was as beautiful as the rest of him.

With a lot of difficulty, I managed to take its length into me without gagging. It felt enormous. My other lovers had been puny by comparison. I moved up and down, savoring the taste and feel of it. He began to moan. I shifted into higher gear on it until his opening spurted cream into my mouth and throat. Then I lifted his legs, entered him with my own considerable endowment, and fucked the stunning boy with youthful urgency.

This was the most handsome body I could imagine, and, unbelievably, I was tightly sheathed in it. As if mesmerized by that fact, I slowed down in spite of myself and caressed his silky light brown skin. So beautiful. So sexy.

"Ride me, stud. Give me your best shot."

With that I picked up momentum and fucked Marc into a frenzy of groans and whimpers. "Oh, god!" I yelled as I came for the second time.

Two

Lying with my head propped on my arm and making circles around Marc's small, dark areolas with my index finger, I asked what his heritage was.

"Several," he responded. "Quite a melting pot, from what I gather. Mike's uncle bought me when I was a young boy, so I don't know. I've been kept ever since."

"Really? He owns you?"

352

"He owns one of those towers downtown, too. He's filthy rich. But I'm just one of his art objects now. The uncle has new toys. Mike and I make it from time to time, but usually it's with the other boys, who are around. You're different, Jeff."

"How?"

"You can speak in sentences without 'you knows' and 'know what I means'. You know?" We laughed.

I was feeling completely relaxed with my partner and was prepared to stay in bed forever, and said so.

"Trust me, I feel the same way. But you shouldn't be denied the other sights in the house."

"None will be as good as you."

He kissed me on the nose. "And you're sincere, too. That's refreshing. But reserve judgment."

Marc gave me a white silk fundoshi to wear. He helped to fit it on me, including tucking the front flap inside the waistband. He cupped and rubbed the sensual material against me as he kissed me. When I saw myself in the large door mirror, I did feel self-conscious about the prospect of having my buns exposed to other people. And that Marc was naked, all of a sudden.

"Do you ever wear clothes?"

"Sometimes, depending on who the guests are. But sometimes I like to dress in clothes just for the change. You know, I live my life nude, otherwise."

"With good reason; your body's so beautiful. But would you mind putting something on now? For me?" That elicited a show of perfect teeth and a "Sure." He donned a matching skimpy loincloth. I liked what that said. Then Marc pulled us together, crotch to silken crotch and said, "I put you in this, because I didn't want the sexhounds to see how hung you were. A little mystery, remember."

"With all of the material down there in front, my secret's safe."

"Exactly. Feel good?" he asked rubbing his crotch against mine.

"Dynamite," I said and kissed him.

We went past the staircase and turned right to go into the rear wing, the one I had seen upon arriving, I assumed. Most of the doors were open, and the first room was occupied. In it, a tow-headed youth, wearing only tall engineer boots and tight black gloves, was holding a leash that was attached to the studded leather collar encircling an Oriental boy's neck. He was mimicking a dog sitting up on its hind legs. His leather-covered sex was pointing up in excitement. God, that looked so sexy. When the dog boy's owner was satisfied with his performance, he let him go down on him. I had never seen another guy getting blown, except for watching myself get done, and I was thankful for the blousy crotch of the silk garment, which hid my renewed excitement. We stood, hand in hand, as the pup eagerly finished off his master. The young man patted his head as the boy covered the shaft and head with kisses. Then Marc tugged on my hand to continue our walk.

"Man, that was hot."

"You're in the lap of depravity, Jeff. Fortunately you have me."

"All I need."

"We'll see."

In another room, three nude boys were going at it on a large bed as two others watched. A white boy was fucking another white boy, while a black boy straddled the other and sucked his cock. He, in turn, was being rimmed and jerked off by the fuckee. "Jesus," I muttered under my breath at the sight of the urgent male need. One by one they came in an orifice, except for the black boy, whose little cock only twitched in pleasure.

The next scene shocked me. A young, black woman, clad only in beige stockings and panties, had her hand inside the nylon tricot undie and was diddling herself while fondling a round breast. "Mike's uncle gives her drugs, so he can have her son. He was the one in the middle back there. He lives here." I just shook my head. I had thought that I was pretty worldly, having begun to experiment with sex with guys at age twelve. I had been fucked and sucked by the time I was thirteen so often I had lost count. I had acquired my first steady boyfriend, Keenan, at fourteen, but I would never have guessed a world like this existed.

On the way down the carpeted back stairwell, two of the Filipino servants were doing it on the stairs, their lustrous satin thongs lying beside them. They ignored the two of us passing them, as the one urged the other to fuck him hard. At least that's what I thought he was saying. The fucker had pretty cheeks, I noted, but they paled next to Marc's.

In the huge kitchen, servants scurried about, no doubt preparing the evening meal. After what we'd had for lunch, I couldn't imagine what kind of feast that would be. All of the servants were cute and displayed engaging smiles. None as nice as Marc's, however.

The area just beyond the patio was dominated by a swimming pool. On its terrazzo apron, boys in bright, abbreviated swimsuits were sprawled on cushioned chaise lounges. Some napped. Some chatted. On one lounge chair, a tanned blond sat on a black blond, moving his hips deliberately as his erection bobbed tantalizingly. We stopped to watch the coupling. The young black man would molest the hard-on with his fingers for a few seconds at a time and stop. "Yeah, that's it. Fucking tease my hard prick while I fucking keep yours going fucking crazy in my tight boy cunt." A leisurely fuck, I thought, understanding now what that meant.

A couple of boys turned to see us standing there and one whistled and said, "Wow! Hey, you gonna, you know, share the babe, Marcus?"

"Not a chance."

"Shit. You're a fuckin' selfish bastard, know what I mean?"

"And a confirmed bastard, at that." The boy snorted. "Come on, Jeff."

"Whoa, this is serious, girlfriend. Marcus has clothes on!" Catcalls followed us.

354

"Ignore them. They're jealous."

We walked past the sunbathers, and my eyes widened again. Not only were the 'suits' brief, they were all exhibitions of obscene beauty. "Their crotches," I whispered in hoarse excitement.

"Uncle likes their maleness shown to best advantage. So they wear double cock and ball straps to accentuate what nature gave them. Whether they're big or puny, they all make delightful statements in their little briefs."

"I'll say. Those baskets are really hot looking."

"Yeah, it's a real turn-on to see all those beautiful male bulges!"

All of the skimpy briefs were brightly colored and shiny, the integrity of the sleek material challenged mightily by the harnessed genitals. Yellow, red, blue, white, gold bikinis glinted at me in liquid metallic provocation. And every one of the wearers of these was handsome and deeply-tanned. The image of fully-displayed, iridescently feathered peacocks came fittingly to mind as I ogled the scantily clad, bronze-skinned boys. Even in repose, I felt an aura of cockiness emanate from the muscular bodies. The skimpy suits, sitting seductively on their narrow hips, glistened in sexual invitation, their revealing postures practically demanding, "Suck me!"

This was the human male equivalent of a candy shop, I thought. Except that these candy bars were far more tempting, and the sour balls under them promised a liquid reward at the end of a good suck. My mouth watered at the thought, reinforced by the sight of the steaming glossy bodies.

As we walked past the pool, a lone youth in yellow was lazily backstroking his way through the water. The grace of his movements enhanced the allure of the taut muscles hugging his slim frame.

On the far side of the pool a walnut-skinned youth was intent on getting darker still, lying naked on a blanket. His discarded metallic silver suit had side buckles for closures. His silver cock strap lay on top of the brief. He opened his eyes at our approach and greeted Marc warmly. "Is this Jeff," he asked, and reached up to shake hands with me. "Great to meet you. Mike wasn't lying. You're an absolute doll." Embarrassed, I thanked him. But, curiously, I wasn't embarrassed by the boy's nudity, I had seen so much skin already. Nor by the yellow-thonged white boy, who now emerged from the pool and walked wordlessly to the dark youth. He knelt between his spread legs and took the uncircumcised ebony cock into his mouth, as if it were a scene being played out in an erotic movie. We watched as the nearly black shaft lengthened and swelled and gleamed from the hunger of the insistent moist lips and mouth. The supine boy stroked the brown five o'clock shadow bobbing rhythmically above his abdomen. We watched with growing excitement and fondled each other's silk-covered cock. The boy's moans became a kind of mantra as the talented mouth drove him toward orgasm. A final loud groan signaled his essence's surrender. The boy captured all of it, licked his lips and then lay down on the cream giver and began to kiss him as he humped him.

"Darryl's one of uncle's favorite new toys. Adam's, too, evidently. Darryl's

355

trying to see how close to ebony his skin can become for uncle. He's into the contrasting pale and midnight looks in bed currently, for some reason. Maybe he's running out of fantasies."

"Darryl sure is one."

"Yes, but they all are in their own way."

"Can't argue with that."

We walked down a gently sloping, manicured lawn toward a formal garden of rigorously-trimmed boxwoods, arborvitae, privet and other bushes. We came upon a tall, leanly muscled boy with golden hair and skin, wearing tan work boots. And something else, I noticed. A tan and brown lace, which matched his boot laces, was tied behind the head of his cock. The ends hung down to nearly his ankles. My cock responded to the sight of the tantalizingly swaying penile embellishment. Marc greeted and introduced the boy as Romulus. He smiled widely and shook my hand. "The guest of honor, I presume. Welcome to our hovel of hedonism, Jeff."

"It's hardly a hovel. The bushes are beautiful, too."

"Thanks. If you want to compliment me and my brother more later for our expert work, we live over there in that cottage," he said, pointing to a low, peaked-roof building hardly visible in the distance for the foliage.

"Not a chance, Rommy. Where is Remus?"

He jerked his head toward the center of the garden. "In the cathedral. Didn't get enough in bed last night, the shit. Go have yourselves a look." We thanked him and did.

"The cathedral?"

"You'll see."

The edifice was a large circular hedge about ten feet tall, made of Canadian hemlocks impeccably clipped into verdant walls. As young as they were, these gardeners were good, I thought. And at least one of them was entirely desirable. There was an entrance in the wall formed by inner and outer rows of bushes, creating an open, curved hallway. Under our bare feet, the grass had been mowed close, as if it were a putting green. It felt great. The opening at the end of the hall revealed a much larger expanse of soft green, and something else, which made me do a double-take. I swore that I was looking at Rommy. Jeff smiled and whispered, "Yes, they are." Romulus and Remus. Identical twins.

He was standing in the center of the cathedral. Two boys with short blond hair were kneeling fore and aft of him, worshipping him. The two youths, both Asian-looking, wore red silk thongs with gathered pouches. Remus's boot lace was tied securely around his genitals, and the boy sucking on him was delighting in the result. The one in back was holding the lace ends tightly while he rimmed the sweaty ass and licked the round cheeks. Both boys were rubbing the delightful silk of their pouches against obvious erections as they pleasured the other gardener. His eyes were closed, and he was playing with his little, brown, raised nipples.

"The ones in red are uncle's personal servants. Both of them are named Peter,

356

so their boss refers to them as Pete and Repete. Not original, but he isn't known for his wit, just his ability to make money and for his decadent lifestyle."

Rommy, evidently having had enough of his brother's infidelity, walked past us into the outdoor sex room. He smoothed the hair of Repete, and the gorgeous face smiled up at him. Without a word, he untied the lace from the head and repositioned it to encircle Rommy. Then he went down on him with gusto. Remus, sensing his brother's presence, opened his eyes and leaned into his twin's face, kissing him.

As I watched the identical brothers being brought off side by side, I had another revelation; Pete and Repete were identical, too. Man, it was even more of a turn-on to watch this oral sex in duplicate. Marc ran his right hand over my smooth cheeks as we waited for what would be thundering orgasms, the two bodies spasming as their sperm jetted into the mouths of the kneeling boys.

"Man, that was hot."

"Sultry, even."

When Remus opened his eyes and saw us standing there, he smiled. He introduced himself to me as Ream and also extended an invitation to the cottage, despite the fact that he had just capitulated his libido to Pete. Marc told him to behave, and introduced me to the Asian twins, whose smiles were unmistakable leers, telling me that they would like to perform the same ministrations on me that they had on Remus. However, their social graces kept them from voicing the desire.

Remus kidded Marc about wearing the pouch as his brother's and his laces were refitted behind their cock heads. Marc told him that he was impossible and said goodbye to the four youths. My head swam with the images of their male beauty.

"Man, the term bronzed beauties fits this group to a tee. But Romulus and Remus?"

"Uncle must have read a book on Roman history once. Actually, I'll take Marcus Aurelius."

"It's a beautiful name."

"Thanks, cutie."

"But none of 'em is nearly as stunning as you."

"Flattery will get you back into bed in a hurry."

"And you're a really nice guy, too."

"Okay, you win." We chuckled.

A couple of the boys not dozing in their tanned, young splendor made lewd comments as we passed. And one, who had not been there before, and possessing shiny black hair and eyes and miles of lashes, smiled and winked at me. He wore a tiny white suit with bows tied on the sides, which rode high on his slim hips. The fabric strained to contain him. "His name is Angel. I'm surprised his legs didn't go straight into the air and part at the sight of you. He's really sweet and fun to play with, though. He loves to suck and be fucked."

"He's gorgeous."

"Yeah, he's one torrid little Latin body."

I agreed, my mind eagerly conjuring up the image of being coupled with the boy, but I was just as soon distracted by the rise and fall of Marc's impossibly sculpted cheeks. That was what he was. A living sculpture. A mixed-race David over whom Michelangelo would have salivated at the chance to chisel his perfection into a block of marble.

The two contrasting blondes were still connected in easy lust, evidently making an afternoon of it. I didn't know that guys could possibly last that long. The black blond was holding the other's cock and making its slit wink at him. He blew kisses to it as he manipulated it.

On the patio, we met a younger boy coming out of the house. He wore only an orange G-string, which was much fuller than I expected it to be. The harness, I remembered. The youth looked vaguely familiar, for some reason. He smiled at me and winked. Then I made the connection. "Angel's little brother, Raphael. He mostly likes to watch and get sucked off, but I suspect he'll be a chip off his brother's block one of these days. He is so sexy already." That he was, I thought, as I watched the boyish hips sway seductively as he walked away from us toward the pool.

"Where did they find a harness to fit him?"

"Two little gold cock rings. They look quite fetching on him." No doubt. I wanted to see them bad.

The two servants were gone from the stairwell, but a previously vacant room now had a short, very muscular and handsome boy spearing a thin brunette while standing and holding him. The latter's legs were locked around the muscle boy's slender waist. They were kissing in real passion as the lean boy rode on the other's pole with the help of the rippling arms. Seeing him masturbate himself with the other youth only heightened my own desire.

The young woman was moaning in drugged ecstasy as we passed that room. Neither of us looked in.

Another room was now occupied by a couple wearing red and blue bandannas, respectively. An hispanic youth, this one with a mustache and vertical rectangle of hair under his lower lip, was plunging his lengthy, studded-leather-harnessed erection between the cheeks of a standing white boy, who was furiously pulling on his own double-strapped sex. He was grimacing in pleasure/pain from the long rod. Still, the youth urged his tormentor on as his back arched sharply and his erection throbbed in his hand. Pairs of glossy red and blue briefs lay limply at their feet. Two of the pool boys. The mustachioed boy saw us and gave us a smirk, not missing a beat of moving the boy's hips back and forth on himself.

In the room where the threesome had been going at each other, the two former observers were now on the bed, as the other three boys stood beside it. The two white boys wore red and blue patent leather straps; the black boy wore a ring of silver filigree behind his glans. One of the new participants was lying with his legs pulled all the way back next to his head, his lower torso and ass up in the

358

air. The other boy was lowering himself onto it. Half of a translucent pink dildo protruded from between his cheeks. Slowly he eased the head of the toy into the doubled-over boy, who urged on the coupling. Once connected, they pumped their rods leisurely, letting the blood flow into their harnessed shafts. The top boy's was silver leather, the bottom's, gold. I looked around to see if their suits matched, but they must have been on the other side of the bed. However, I did realize that their very short hair matched their straps, so I'd bet their briefs did, too. Once their cocks were engorged, they speeded up their hand movements. Dueling pricks, I thought. I began to fondle Marc, who was already responding nicely to this action. The tanned beauties were feverishly pumping themselves, desperate for an orgasm. We watched as one, then the other shot his load, white come spewing, geyser-like, from their slits.

Then we stayed to watch the top youth ease off his partner and straddle the now prone boy with the ersatz cock sticking lewdly out of him. He wiggled his ass for effect. His partner pulled the rest of the long device out of him slowly, prolonging the impaled boy's pleasure, and said, "That was way cool." I thought so, too.

Lastly, we passed the room of the leather boy, who was fucking another leashed boy now as the puppy sucked him off. Both boys were wearing steel manacles with chains on their wrists and ankles. They were fettered to each other by a thick genital chain locked onto them. Something about their joint helplessness was a turn-on. I also couldn't wait to have at my partner now, so I stopped him in the main hall to feel those marvelous lips on mine. "Remember what happened the last time," a breathless Marc said, pulling off my slickened lips.

"Yeah, a happening to remember forever." We giggled.

Marc undid the flap of my fundoshi, and let it trail like a tail from the rear of the waistband. Then he knelt and took me into his mouth. He was moaning in happiness on my rigid sex, when the knock came on the door. It opened, and a browned, long-haired blond in white bra, panties, stockings and heels looked at us with his mouth forming an 'O'. He recovered to say, "Sorry, Marc, I didn't know you had company. And unbelievably gorgeous company at that." I was so shocked by the boy's appearance that I didn't even think to cover myself. When the youth made no move to leave, Marc said, "You knew very well that Jeff would be here."

When the pretty boy remained standing there, Marc said, "We're busy, Randy."

"Oh, sure. Sorry." But he continued to stare at me with deep brown eyes.

"Leave, Randy. Now," Marc said, getting to his feet. The boy did, closing the door, quickly.

"Is he one of your playmates?"

"Does it bother you?" Marc asked. I shrugged. It did. "That's no answer, Jeff. Look, I've been sexual all my life. I was taught to perform just about every sex act in just about every position and costume imaginable. If that turns you off,

I'm sorry."

"No, I am. This is all so much to absorb. All the beautiful naked and nearly naked bodies, all the sex. I mean, it's great, but I guess I'm on overload."

"That's understandable. Why don't you kick back in bed and forget what else is happening here. It's just the two of us for now, okay?" He positioned himself between my spread legs and took the base of my penis into his hand.

"I told you that was all I wanted."

"I know. I'm glad you still do."

"I do. You're worth a hundred of the pool boys."

"But some of them are worth a lot."

"I'll take your word for it."

"You won't have to," Marc said and went down on me. What did that mean?

The smooth friction of the moist lips was electric on my head and then my shaft. In spite of having come twice already, I felt myself rising quickly. Marc's mouth was as talented as it was beautiful, and my desire was stoked not only by him, but also by the erotic sights I had just seen. I thought briefly of Angel and Raphael, but I banished them in favor of watching the stunning face moving on me. "That feels great." Marc winked at me. God, what curved lashes. It was hard to believe that this splendid creature was making love to me. And was he ever. I petted the smooth skin of his scalp as my lover changed to a slower pace before speeding up again. Suddenly I was coming. "Oh, Marc!" Every last drop was sucked from me, and I felt that my strength had left me along with my essence. Marc lay down beside me.

"Can I keep you?"

"I'm hoping so."

"Are you serious?"

"Yes. Are you?"

"You bet I am."

"Good. It's mutual. But the day is still young; a nap is in order."

"Not until I take care of you."

My last boyfriend had taught me some of the finer points of lovemaking, like kissing more than just a mouth. Licking and nipping and sucking, too, which I really came to like. By the time I had finished kissing Marc's elegant neck, including planting the hickey there requested by the Adonis, I was erect again, against all odds. I ignored it because Marc's body was irresistible to me. I continued down the torso, ministering to the concave navel, exploring the ridges of the abdomen and licking the indentation above the trembling, erect shaft, where his pubic bush would have been. However, Marcus's body was smooth, a seemingly endless delight of soft, glowing skin unmarred by hair.

And the best of it was now in my mouth, filling me with its impressive size. I knew what I wanted to do with this magnificence, but I doubted my ability to take it. None of my boyfriends had endowments anywhere close to Marc's. Still, I was game, because I wanted his male perfection inside me. I slicked my partner as best I could and then knelt, straddling the incomparable boy, and

360

impaled myself on the cock of my dreams. It went in surprisingly easily, and even the feeling of fullness felt good. I let it sit in me to enjoy the unusual sensation. Then I ended up riding him effortlessly as Marc stroked my sides and smiled at me. I liked having my sides fondled, I found out. And I moved faster, as a result. "Make me come, baby," Marc whispered. "Make me give it up to your beautiful body."

And he did, his hips bucking, sending him all of the way into me as his boy cream surged into the bowel encasing him. I was stunned. For the first time in my life I had felt someone coming in me, and I was entirely pleased with the experience. More importantly, it was Marc's seed surging deep inside my boy-cunt.

I eased off the spent organ and lay down next to him. Marc reared up and kissed me tenderly. "That was great, Jeff."

"I couldn't help it. You're so fuckin' hot, and playing with you is so much fun."

"It's going to get a lot more fun."

"I can't wait."

We slept until nearly supper time. Then we showered together again, and I liked it as well the second time. And getting dried off with the impossibly soft, thick towel. Within minutes one of the vested-and-thonged Filipino boys brought in our supper. He poured red wine into our glasses, bowed, smiled and left. I watched the brown cheeks with interest.

"Sorry, they're off limits?"

"What? Oh, no. I have my hands full, as it is."

Dinner was broiled sea scallops, filet mignon, a stuffed potato, and green beans almandine. The wine tasted very good, even if my palate was a neophyte on the subject.

"So, who's Randy?"

"Uncle's son."

"Really?"

"He's a widower, left to raise his sons on his own. And free to indulge in his favorite sexual activities with young males."

"You said sons."

"There's also Trey. He's the leather boy."

My jaw dropped.

"And Jeff," he went on, "he's been dominating other boys and men since he was ten. And Randy's his cross-dressing opposite."

"Man. They seem to be too young to be into their different lifestyles."

"Again, they started very young. It's second nature now."

We talked more about the two completely different boys as we ate dessert, which was a rich, multi-layered chocolate cake with mousse between the layers. Marc told me about the business partner whom the uncle blackmailed by allowing little Trey to seduce him, and eventually get the man to kneel before him and suck his dick while he had a whip laced around the man's neck. It was

361

all on videotape. The man was ruined and soon not a business partner anymore, either.

Similarly, Randy lured a potential client into bed, the man thinking he was a girl. Randy was straddling him, playing with the guy's nipples, when he felt him up and realized that he was in bed with a boy. Randy pulled down his panties to confirm the fact, and another man was under uncle's control.

"Either way the asshole was dead meat. But Randy is awfully pretty. He makes a convincing Lolita, don't you think? Which reminds me," he said, looking at an antique clock on the high boy across the room. "There are some more things I want you to see. Understand that the first one is strictly forbidden, except that we've been granted an exemption."

We walked back to the rear wing and stopped at Trey's room. He was now in a studded, full torso harness and thigh-high engineer boots. His studded cock strap matched his harness. Hanging from chains fastened to the ceiling was another golden blond. He wore a black leather collar and garter belt, black stockings and knee-high stiletto-heeled boots. A black mask covered his eyes, but even with his head down, I knew that it was Randy.

We watched as Trey used his brother, twisting nipples, pulling hard on his cock and balls, hurting and humiliating him in numerous ways, playing his body like a cruel musician. He would stroke his brother's shaft to pulsing erection and then let go of it and watch it wither. And as it did, Randy would beg his brother to masturbate him to climax. Once Randy was flaccid, Trey would kiss his brother hard, while caressing the boy's nylons. That achieved the same result, only to have the organ go limp again, when he ceased doing it. I suspected that Randy was really wanting at that point.

Finally he went behind his brother and entered him. He rode him with casual indifference, using him for his pleasure. He tortured the already sensitive nipples. I was amazed by Randy's total surrender to his brother. And there was something about the incest that was a real turn-on, because I was hard again.

As Trey fucked Randy harder, he removed the mask. The boy looked up to see us witnessing his degradation and then hung his head, seemingly in shame. Trey cried out in triumph as he marked his brother as his own. Then he jerked off his brother, while nuzzling his neck. There was an expression of ecstasy on the boy's face.

Marc moved us on down the hall. All of the rooms were empty. Even the woman was gone. Where, I wondered. At the end of the corridor, we looked out the window and saw the pool boys dancing on the patio, wearing only their cock bands. Some had erections waving in front of them. Some partners were holding or stroking each other's rigid sex as they undulated to the music. It was a torrid sight to see the naked, muscular bodies adorned only with the colorful twin straps.

I saw that my friend, Mike, was reclining on a chaise, Cecil sitting astride him, watching the naked dancers. No doubt sheathing his erection, I thought.

"Where's the uncle?"

"Out of town. He took Kerry, an adorable redhead, with him. He's as pale as Darryl is trying to be dark. He would have taken Darryl, too, but he's working on his color, so that he'll be as close to black as he can be, when uncle returns. Besides, he doesn't lack for sex, which you saw. Frankly, I think he prefers younger guys, specifically Kerry. They make a beautiful couple."

"Will I meet them? The uncle and Kerry?"

"I doubt it. But that's not why you're here anyway." He kissed me on the cheek. "You're here to be physically entertained."

"And you're doing a great job, trust me."

"It seems we all are," Marc said, taking hold of my renewed erection.

"Well, it is a beautiful sight."

"So are you. And I have a little surprise for you."

"What is it?"

"You'll see shortly."

"I can't wait."

"You don't know how right you are."

Three

We engaged in some tender kissing and fondling on the bed, again as if we had known each other for years instead of hours. I wondered what the surprise was but didn't have to wait long.

There was a soft knock at the door. It opened and a seductively smiling Angel, trailed by an equally captivating Raphael walked in. They padded into the room barefoot, both golden bodies still clad in their tiny white and orange suits. Angel was wearing a necklace and ankle band made of white pukka shells. They were dazzling next to his skin. As was the fancy swimsuit, which flattered his slim, desirable body.

The boys moved with sensual grace toward the bed. Angel stopped next to me and bent to kiss me. I couldn't resist cupping the rounded crotch. The lustrous fabric felt sensuous to the touch, almost as if it were a liquid. But the protrusions behind it felt even better and made me stir. As did the kiss, delivered with all of the sensuality the pouty lips could muster.

As our lip action escalated to include our tongues, I took hold of one of the tied ends and pulled on it. It came loose, and the suit gathered at Angel's crotch. Then I undid the other one, and it fluttered to the floor. I groped for the boy's penis. When I found it, I felt it in disbelief. It caused me to come off the ripe lips in order to see the maleness that hung pendulously between his legs. Angel smiled, put his hands on his hips and posed in all his glory. The presence of the white cock strap made his endowment look even more alluring. I looked up at Angel.

"You're beautiful. All of you."

"Thanks, so are you. Even more than Mike said. If you're interested, this body's yours."

I looked at Marc, who winked. Go for it, stud. Raphael was standing apart from him, arms folded, posing strap full, smirking. I wondered if I would get to see those golden enhancement rings of his and hoped so more fervently now. But why look a gift body only in the mouth? Angel was mine for the taking. I rubbed the boy's prick to erection. I kissed the wide slit. Then I slid farther into the bed on the satin sheets, and Angel climbed onto it, his rigid sex swinging proudly. He kissed me again, before moving down my body to take my penis into his hand and mouth. As he sucked and I became fully tumescent, I thought, guiltily, how good a cocksucker Angel was, as if I were betraying Marc with the thought. The boy's succulent lips came off me and were replaced by his playful tongue. He feathered it up and down the shaft and over the taut skin of my scrotum, my balls in full retreat from the concentrated attention. The teasing action of the tongue tip drove me crazy with need. I whimpered in pleasure as my cock jerked in response to its tormentor. Suddenly Angel stopped. Roundly disappointed, I opened my eyes.

"I think that this beauty is more than ready to take me." The rock-hard organ he was holding supported his statement with mute eloquence. He kissed the sensitized shaft, which twitched in response to his loving gesture. Then he lay down next to me and pulled back his legs.

Not missing a beat, or losing my raging erection, I quickly positioned and guided myself into the unexpected slipperiness of Angel's snug private place. The muscle hugged me with a firmness that my already-afire nerves were helpless to last against. I concentrated on the magnificent sight of Angel's brown cock straining under the milking motion of his elegant hand. Instead of taking my mind off my own soaring passion, watching Angel masturbate only intensified it.

"I'm close."

"Me, too," the flawless youth said, pumping himself harder. "Fuck me hard, Jeff."

I did, slamming into him for less than a minute before I froze and released myself into his bowel. He followed, arcs of white shooting from him to fall on his chest and belly. As spent as I was, I found the sight of the sperm highly erotic. I slipped out of the snug, warm cavity and bent to lick up the small pools of Angel's cum, as the boy petted my head. Once I had cleaned my sexmate, we kissed lightly.

"That was great," Angel said.

"Yeah, you're one sexy boy."

"I'm not the only one," he said and smiled at his brother. The return smile was directed at me, as was Raphael's provocative posture. His legs were spread, feet turned inward, his hips thrust forward to present his unmistakable excitement to me.

Not missing the cue, I climbed off the bed and went to the younger brother,

364

eager, hungry to see what lay behind the shimmering orange pouch. I knelt before the boy and kissed the silky material before pulling the narrow hip straps out and down, revealing a handsome small cock and sac adorned with bright round gold rings hugging the base of the little penis and encircling him. It was a beautiful sight. Raphael's hand guided my head toward the jeweled organs, wanting to be engulfed by the warm mouth inches from his boyness. I took him in one motion, my lips kissing the shaft ring and savoring the metallic taste of the shiny constrictor. Raphael hardened quickly under my enthusiastic adoration, and the juvenile urged me on. "That's it. Suck it fast. Do me now, man. I promise I'll come in your mouth." I smiled inwardly. I liked Raphael. That was the problem. Like Angel, I also found the little brother irresistible. Like just about every other male I'd seen since coming here. It was something close to boy heaven. I wondered what it would be like to do it with Darryl. Then I returned to the dick I was sucking. "Swing on it hard, Jeff. Make me come," he said, breathing heavily. I ran my hand up the soft, young skin of his belly and chest, then down his side to his leg. "Oh, yeah. Make me come, man. Make me shoot." I did. "Oh, fuck!" The small amount of effluent shot into the back of my throat. I sucked gently, keeping the boy inside me, his hand on the back of my head, wanting me to stay there. I wanted to stay on his small maleness and suck it all night.

"Rafe, you look so fucking pretty when you come," Angel said.

"Yeah, but it's easy when you've got a stud making you feel that way."

"I'll second that," Marc said.

I had forgotten the other boy's presence once I began my liaison with Angel and then Raphael. The adonis was sitting in an easy chair covered in mauve velvet, hands behind his head, legs straight out and spread. His semi-erection rested comfortably on his abdomen like a contented, slumbering baby. "Well, I want to paint my nails and see what other hot scenes I can find," Raphael said, adjusting his ringed genitals in his stretchy G-string. "Thanks, Jeff, that was cool." He stood on his tip toes and kissed me. Then he left.

"You game to stay with us, Angel?"

"You even have to ask? Best invitation I ever had," he said, running the toes of his left foot up his right leg. God, he was sexy! "That okay with you, Jeff?"

"You even have to ask?"

We decided to go down to the kitchen for ice cream. Angel let me wear his sexy little swimsuit. He was very hands-on in fitting me with it, roving them over the slinky fabric as he positioned it to tie the sides. When he was finished, he pronounced me too cute for words. He and Marc wore the silk fundoshis.

The kitchen was vacant, although there was still some activity on the patio from the sounds of it. While Marc was getting the ice cream and Angel the bowls, I wandered into the long central hall. The first room I came to was the dining room, although it was much larger than any I'd seen. As was the table, which was lit by candelabra flanking an elaborate flower arrangement. The candles cast all of the illumination needed for me to see clearly that the action

on the long table was not eating, unless you considered the body receiving the footlong hot dog entering it, consuming it. A medium brown-skinned boy with light brown hair lay on his stomach. His handsome face was turned to me, eyes closed. The candles made his curved eyelashes look extraordinarily long. The one with the huge endowment was a reddish blond boy with barely a tan. His profile was to me, but it showed a nice, straight nose and prominent lips. I noticed that the black boy's were, too. I licked my own. Man I would like to see these two in a kissing marathon, I was thinking as I watched the white boy's genetic blessing sink between the high, dusky cheeks. Braced on his hands, he moved his hips to enter the other youth fully and then withdraw almost all the way.

"Oh, god, that feels so good, Ryan."

"Same here, Ty. Man, you're so tight."

"Just the way you like it."

"You know it."

I felt guilty being a voyeur, but the scene was too compellingly erotic for me to break away from it. The candle light, the contrasting muscular bodies, the connectedness of the two by more than just a cock. Which had to be more than twelve inches, I figured, the longer I watched. Ty moaned as Ryan picked up his pace and showed his sexual athleticism. Slim, but powerful hips they were. With help from his washboard abs. Ryan was grunting and dripping sweat, which glistened on Ty's back in the soft light. The grunting and moaning rose together into a carnal hymn before Ryan froze and let out a long uhhhh. Ty's eyes were closed tightly, no doubt enjoying the feeling of the come hitting the end of his transverse colon. I left before they were aware of my presence and returned to the kitchen.

"Well, somebody sure doesn't need a cock harness to show off in my suit."

"Thanks, Angel, that was nice of you to say."

"It's the truth."

"It is, Jeff." I kissed them both.

"Thanks. Man, there were two guys doing it on the dining room table. White guy had a horse cock."

"That's Tyler and Ryan. Here," he said, handing me a bowl piled with ice cream. "I'll tell you about them upstairs."

As we passed the rooms, we could hear noises behind doors, which were now closed. "For some reason, they like their privacy when they pair off or whatever at night."

"They like to sleep with the doors locked," Angel said. "They don't trust each other, probably with good reason. Being pretty doesn't mean you're honest."

"But I'll bet you are," I said.

"You meant that. You're sweet, Jeff. But, yes, Rafe and I keep to ourselves most of the time."

"Do you and your brother, I mean...."

"Uh, huh. He's kind of like Trey, in that he's into the power thing with

366

watching and having guys suck him. But he likes to make love with me. How could I ever turn down such a cute fawn?"

"Put a ring on that finger of his as soon as you can, Angel. He's going to be as gorgeous as you one of these days."

"Flattery will get you sucked, Marc."

"I'm counting on it."

We sat on the bed, digging into the heap of Rocky Road Marc had scooped into each bowl. "Okay, let me tell you about Tyler and Ryan. They aren't pool boys. They're people uncle met at a party in New York. They come here from time to time to visit. They're models, and exotic dancers, I think."

"With his endowment, Ryan is sure to be a hit."

"Well, Tyler isn't far behind. He has eleven and Ryan almost fourteen. They're a beautiful couple, and they've become taken with each other, which is neat. I hope they fall in love. Naturally, the pool boys don't leave them alone, so they try to be where they aren't until it's bedtime. I'll bet they knew that the dining room was safe."

"Except from me."

"True, but pool boys never go in there after dinner. They use the rear stairways all the time. So the boys had every reason to believe that they'd have their privacy. Still, I'm glad you got to see Ryan in action. He said that they had jokingly decided that if it works out, they'll become Ryan Tyler and Tyler Ryan. Cute, huh? And, although I'm not a betting boy, I predict that a year from now those will be exactly what their names will be."

"Neat."

"Marc is a romantic, Jeff, in spite of the fact that he should be the most jaded of us, having been a sex boy all his life. Go figure."

"Surprise. But as lovey-dovey as they are, I did extract a promise from Ryan."

"A promise?"

"Later."

"Oh, Miss Mysterious," Angel said.

When we finished the ice cream, Angel said, "I don't know about you guys, but that stuff made me cold. I think a nice, hot shower would warm me up nicely." He winked. That eye movement melted something in me each time he did it.

Marc and Angel disrobed me by pulling the bows apart. Then we went into the bathroom. Marc turned the water on to a pleasantly hot temperature and the three of us stepped into the soft-sided enclosure. Marc sat down against the side of the stall. Angel wasted no time going down on all fours and gulping his cock. Marc jumped and shouted, "Your mouth is still cold, fool!" Angel giggled over his little gambit having worked. Then he stood up and let the shower spray warm his mouth. After raising the temperature, he turned and spit the water onto Marc.

"Creep," Marc laughed. "Jeff, you have to understand that if there were one person in this house I would fall madly in love with, it would be *Angel*."

"Oh, yeah, same here. But I have Raphael, so I'd be a fool to kick him out of my bed. Besides, Marcus Aurelius's stunning beauty notwithstanding, incest is best."

Now Angel knelt on all fours and took hold of Marc's beauty and pleasured him deliberately. I shook my head. The kid sure could suck cock.

"Jeff, the liquid soap there is hypo-allergenic for goodness sake! It won't hurt Angel."

So I slathered myself with the thick, honey-colored liquid and massaged my prick to life, then knelt behind him. First I inserted my index finger into Angel, who playfully shook his ass for me and raised his cheeks higher for my entry. Then I eased in and took full measure of the boy, holding his hips and pulling them to me, the way I'd seen the Hispanic youth do to his partner. And best of all, I was feeling Angel while seeing the god of the house being worshipped by its demigod. That was all the incentive I needed to fuck Angel's brains out, although Ryan had gotten closer to that organ in Tyler than anyone else in the house could hope to. Even the three of us present in the fogging enclosure. Marc was caressing Angel's flattened black hair as the boy moved up and down on him like a barber pole. He opened his eyes and grinned at me. The smile said that, even though we weren't directly connected physically, we were sharing this. I smiled back and reached down to squeeze the big toe of Marc's right foot to confirm it. He flexed the toe and blew me a kiss, which I returned in kind.

It was as if we were on the moors of England as fog rolled in. Visibility was problematical, but the various noises we uttered told each other that we were close to reaching nirvana. I fucked Angel hands-free now, because I wanted to pleasure the boy's rod. It was rock hard and after only a few pulls on it, Angel cried out on Marc's cock and came. "Oh, god, Angel," Marc said and came, too. The sphincter clamping down on me made me lose it seconds later.

When we emerged from the bathroom, as dry as we could get, liquid smoke billowed into the room with us. How the water had stayed hot, I had no idea. However, I did promise the conservation gods that I would pee twice before flushing from now on. But it had been worth the waste of water to feel the heat and see the glistening bodies in passion.

"Care to stay the night, Mister Rivera?"

"You know I would. But I have a personal investment to protect. On second thought, if you did give me that pair of seamed, black, silk stockings, I might still marry you."

"I'll keep that in mind."

"And in the meantime, I'll keep Raphael."

"You do that."

"Goodnight, Adonis," he said, pecking him on the lips.

"And the same goes for you, Jeff." He kissed me longer.

We got into bed, sated and ready for sleep. We snuggled together, our warm bodies happy for the contact.

"Quite a day, huh?"

368

"Quite. Man, I've never come so many times in a week, let alone a day."

"I doubt that."

"It's true. Well, probably. Can you actually buy silk stockings?"

"If you can, I haven't found them yet, and believe me, I've tried."

"You have?"

"Uh, huh. I've been in love with Angel since he and Raphael came here. You don't want to know how old they were then. Uncle fancied Angel for a while, but, like with me, he lost interest eventually."

"Man, what a waste."

"I guess middle age can do weird things to a psyche. But I think Angel prefers being a slut. As does Raphael. Not husband material."

"And I am?"

"We'll see."

"I hope so."

"Me, too."

Four

I squinted in the bright morning light. I gazed upon Marc's creamy white skin. He was turned away from me, so I kissed the exposed shoulder. He stirred.

"Sorry. I didn't want to wake you. How'd you sleep?"

"The sleep of dead men."

"But not of dead cocks."

"I don't know. I don't remember dreaming."

Mark reached his hand back. "Trust me, it's not dead." We chuckled as Marc held my hard-on. "Go take care of your duty, stud. I'll be here."

I did, and when I returned breakfast was waiting. I resisted removing the silver keeping cover from the entree until Marc had taken his turn. Which turned out to be a huge western omelet and thick slices of buttered rye toast. There was also a bowl of melon chunks. Marc poured me coffee.

"Thanks. Man, I almost never eat like this. I'm a starving college student."

"Starve no more," Marc said, and winked. God, his wink was sexier than Angel's. Something else melted.

"Seriously, doesn't anybody here worry about cholesterol?"

"No, we live for today. However many hours that might be."

"Well, I have to admit that this sure is the way to go."

"Maybe."

"Maybe?"

"Sometimes starving makes you appreciate food more."

"Yeah, I guess it does."

I loved being with Marc. He was easy to talk to, intelligent, and surprisingly literate for someone bred as a sex object. Well, he certainly was, but he was a

subject, too, which I found really cool. After the meal, he suggested that we take a walk. Although I was becoming comfortable in my nudity, especially because Marc and Angel said they liked my body and big cock, I was more than a little relieved when Marc said that he had picked out our dress for the day. It turned out to be a shiny red thong with a narrow waist and what he said was a micro pouch. "It's a Rio suit, and it has this elasticized opening that your equipment goes through to show you off to full advantage."

"Like the pool boys."

"Like that."

"I thought you didn't want to show me off."

"I don't, but to hide you forever would drive the pool boys wild. And they can be."

Well, I didn't have to worry about my endowment being misunderstood. It was out front and personal. We both filled the narrow, vertical pouches to lewd distention. When we kissed before leaving the room, we rubbed them together, they were so obscenely beautiful.

Marc led me to the left at the cross hall, instead of to the rear wing. In a way, I regretted it, because I wanted to see what Trey was up to. I'd hoped to see the beautiful Asian puppy in his leather collar and excited genital sheath. I'd never thought about leather as enhancing sex, but Trey had changed my mind in one day. I entertained thoughts of letting the boy dominate me the way he had his brother. I also thought about Randy and his female attire and decided that it had looked sexy on him. I tried to picture Angel in the seamed stockings, and what I saw was beautiful. The image stirred me. I was taking a crash course in different sexual cultures and loving it.

It turned out that there was a mirror wing on the other side of the house. In the last room on the patio side was a gym, where the pool boys were curling and pressing weights, doing crunches and variously admiring themselves in the mirrored walls. I spotted the stud from yesterday, who'd masturbated himself with the other boy's body. He was pressing weights as big as Saturn's rings.

All of the boys were wearing jock straps of the same material as their swimsuits, and the same as Marc and I had on. The fabric was incredibly sensual. Marc said that it was a very expensive nylon/spandex fabric, and I could easily believe it. We left the sweating, buffed bodies and walked downstairs. This stairway ended behind the pantry, so I hadn't seen it the previous evening.

When we walked out onto the patio, I saw four of the boys playing in the pool. Two of them were on the others' shoulders.

"They're playing cavalry."

"Cavalry?"

"You'll see."

As we walked past, I saw that the youths were nude in their harnesses. And something else. The participants stopped to behold the glossy maleness we sported in our rude swimwear. They whistled and hooted, which I suspected was

370

probably indicative of the IQ level of pool boys, given my limited experience.

"How many pool boy brains can you fit on the head of a cock?"

Marc thought that was funny. "You're catching on, Jeff."

"Um. Did I see right? Did the two on the bottom have tails?"

"Uh, huh. You're pretty observant. They're the horses in the game. The tails are butt plugs with fake hair. You could plug an appliance into these guys, and they would love it. They might even manage to run it, somehow." I laughed.

We walked toward the formal garden, where we saw Angel and Raphael. They were walking hand in hand. Then they stopped. Raphael embraced his brother and kissed him. He lifted his left leg and ran it up and down Angel's leg. Their full lips seemed to be causing enough friction to singe the other's. I began to harden quickly at the enormously erotic sight, but I watched the passionate scene now in frustrated arousal, my cock trapped by the narrow pouch. However, it was quite evident that the two very beautiful brothers were very hot for each other.

"It looks as if maybe someone else needs to buy Angel the seamed stockings, Marc."

"It sure does look that way. I guess I was way wrong. And if Raphael keeps rubbing his smooth leg over Angel's, I'm going to need to jack off bad." The crooked leg rode higher onto Angel's thigh now. They were in complete lust, kissing and grinding their crotches together. I was ready to drop my thong, too.

Then they stopped and held each other tightly. Angel's lips moved. Raphael looked up at him. His lips moved. They kissed tenderly. And smiled. Raphael melded into his brother's body, closed his eyes and smiled. Angel kissed the black silk of his brother's hair. Marc led me out of view of the two boys.

"I think we've just witnessed what that relationship really is."

"They're in love."

"Looks like it. I think the ring is coming soon."

Now we walked back toward the garden, hand in hand, and were met by the lovers, similarly attached. We smiled and exchanged warm greetings. I couldn't help noticing that they were helplessly sporting erections, the work of their genital chokers. I noticed, too, that Raphael had not lied about painting his nails. They were orange to match his bloated G-string. Both boys winked at us, each probably unaware that the other was.

Instead of going into the garden, Marc steered us toward another one off to the right. It was rioting with flower blossoms.

"I thought you might like to see the perennial garden."

"I would, but next to you, it pales."

Marc kissed me and looked into my eyes. His own hazel ones tended to shift from having a light, wet sand quality to a dark molasses hue. They were wonderful, expressive eyes. "Thanks for saying that, Jeff."

"I mean it. How many times do I have to say it?"

"I can't tell you."

"What is that supposed to mean?" Marc shrugged. That was no answer, either,

I thought.

The garden was fragrant and brilliant in the morning sun. We walked from bed to bed, admiring Romulus and Remus's handiwork. Then another couple appeared, the sight of them making my heart jolt. It was Tyler and Ryan. In the clear light, they seemed to be unearthly in their beauty. Ty's short flat top appeared to be an even lighter brown next to his milk chocolate skin. His wide nose flattened into elegantly flared nostrils. Ryan's unruly straight hair glinted reds and golds. His wide, straight nose supported beguiling eyes of greenish blue. His skin held the wisp of a tan. The contrast of their features, given their similar body types, was appealing.

They, too, were holding hands, and they smiled at Marc and me and stopped.

"Hi, Marc. Hi. Isn't this great?" Ty asked.

"It is. Ty, Ryan, this is Jeff." We shook hands. "He's visiting for the week." Week? I thought it was just for a couple of days.

Ryan scrutinized me and smiled. I had an unexplained urge to kiss that comely wide nose. And suck on the full red lower lip. Although I also wanted to put my tongue up Ty's nostrils and have my lips swallowed by the young man's oral buttresses. Both faces were celebrations of close to perfect male beauty but in vastly different ways. Their minor flaws contributed to their apparent flawlessness, somehow.

I was in lust with both of them. So different, yet so beautiful. Together, they could make love forever, and I would watch the video until I died. I really felt inadequate in their presence. Especially seeing the fullness of the bikini briefs that they wore. Theirs were even more revealing than ours, eleven and fourteen being the lucky numbers. The two models said they hoped to see us later and walked on to admire the rest of the garden. I smiled inwardly. I could imagine Ryan Tyler and Tyler Ryan. I squeezed Marc's hand and smiled at him. I had thought I saw a sheen of tears on his eyes. There were. Why?

"I feel guilty for what I saw last night now."

"Oh?"

"They really are in love."

"Is that why you didn't check out their asses?"

"No, I saw them last night. Besides, yours is better."

"Really?"

"Hadn't I told you that?"

"I don't think so."

"A bubble butt of sculpted granite."

"Not marble?"

"Granite's harder."

"You sweet talker."

"No, plain talker."

Marc managed a little smile. "Thanks."

"For telling the truth?"

"You want them in the cathedral?"

"Lead the way. Are you okay, Marc?"
"Never happier." Then why the tears?

Five

The dew had evaporated, but the heat of the day was still in abeyance as the sun struggled to move higher in the sky. As we entered hemlock haven, we heard a human voice. We stopped and listened. We heard it again and looked at each other. Curious as to who was in the sex cathedral, Marc crept to the opening and looked in. He smiled and motioned for me to join him. I peered over his shoulder.

In the center of the velvety green lawn, the puppy from yesterday was lying on his back in a dog pose, his leather penis pointing up in excitement. Trey was on all fours, a tightly gloved hand rubbing the puppy's hard belly. He bent and kissed his pet. They rubbed noses and laughed. I sensed that this scene was private, even to us, because it appeared that Trey and the other boy were engaging in actual lovemaking. That was a first, Marc seemed to say by shaking his head. He'd said that Trey was always emotionally unattached to his partners, although he suspected that he loved Randy on some level. Still, it was interesting that he brought the puppy, whose name was Skipper, here. And rubbed noses with him, no less. After several more minutes of watching the leather hand caress the boy intimately, and the lips claim him, Marc decided that we'd better not force our luck. Sooner or later one of them would feel our presence. And he didn't want to deal with Trey's attitude. Having seen him work over Randy, I didn't either.

Still, we were both dying to see how this scene would be played out. I was because I was fascinated by the fact of this young guy being able to bend other guys' wills to his. It had to be more than his looks, although I was ignorant of how one did that. Maybe it was in some guys' natures. Like always wanting to be fucked. Skipper, the puppy, was completely submissive to him. I'd have to ask Marc about that. And I knew that Marc was curious to watch, because Trey was showing a side of himself he had never seen.

He waved for me to follow, which was unnecessary. I was ready to follow him anywhere. We walked hurriedly, clear around to the other side of the natural structure. He got down and duck-walked for several feet before pointing. Then he got onto his stomach. I did the same next to him. And there it was. A small opening at the base, which the twins had pruned too zealously, or perhaps on purpose to satisfy voyeuristic tendencies they had. Then what did that say about us?

Skipper was now lying flat on the natural emerald carpet. Trey was still kissing him and fondling him, leather on soft leather. The Asian boy was standing at aching attention, his body squirming from the intimate touches he

was receiving. I tried to picture Trey running the soft leather of the skin-tight glove over my body. That fantasy wasn't helping my poor trapped sex.

Trey stood up, and Skipper knelt before him. He bent down and kissed the insteps of the boots before kissing the flared head and then taking his master's cock into his mouth. He really was an enthusiastic cocksucker. I wondered if he were as good an oralist as Angel and Marc were. I guessed that Trey thought so, because Skipper seemed to be his favorite pet. And the fact that he was hard already from the boy's mouth on him. I didn't think I'd find out, because that would mean submitting to the boy's power. I would have to give him my ass, at least, to have a chance to feel Skipper's hot cavity on me.

When the puppy had made the cock into a twitching erection, he lay down on his back and retracted his legs so that his calves and toes were pointing straight up. Trey's thighs pressed against the other youth's cheeks and he slowly fed his meat into the hole eagerly awaiting it. Skipper closed his eyes and smiled. When he was in to the hilt, Trey bent forward and began to kiss him intensely. The puppy locked his ankles around his master's neck. We watched as he pummeled the young ass and scorched his lips. Marc and I looked at each other. If that wasn't lovemaking, it didn't exist.

Skipper moved his legs to Trey's back and replaced them with his hands, holding the blond's mouth to his. I didn't know how long we'd been watching, but it seemed like a hell of a long time. Ah, the endurance of youth. What was I thinking? I was still a teenager, for crying out loud. Even from that distance we could hear the mewling sex noises they uttered as their coupling became overheated. It was a beautiful sight. Two handsome kids joined in the intimate male act. Trey's hips were moving at breakneck speed now, and it sounded as if Skipper were begging for the hard fucking or for his come, but lips and tongues got in the way of perfect enunciation.

Then they stopped kissing, although Skipper continued to hold his master's head. Trey's body froze. Both had their eyes closed, focusing on the warm pleasure of the tow-headed boy's orgasm. When the rush had passed, Trey knelt upright and took his puppy's leather penis into his hand. He stroked it several times, and it gave up its white cream. Then he bent and sucked on the opening. Then he began to clean Skipper's belly and chest. We looked at each other again. This was completely unexpected. When he'd lapped up his partner's come, he moved his head forward and rubbed noses with his animal. They laughed.

We got up, unsteadily, our bodies aroused and tingling because of what we had witnessed.

"Man, what a scene," I said, a safe distance away from the circular sex place.

"Yeah, it was unmistakably real emotions cutting loose. Although for all we know the open door sex is a show. Maybe they get amorous behind closed doors all the time."

"Man, such young guys making love so well."

"Better than people twice or three times their age know how."

374

"It was really neat."

"Yeah it was. Let's check something else out, considering how early it still is."

We walked toward the cottage, which was really a small house with a dormer. It reminded me of the witch's house in 'Hansel and Gretel'. I thought of our encounter with Tyler and Ryan and chuckled.

"Going to let me in on it?"

"I was remembering Ryan and Tyler. They were wearing what appeared to be regular bikinis, and they still looked lewd. Thank God."

"Maybe we can find out where they dance and go to New York and see them sometime."

"You mean it," I asked, enthusiastically.

"We'll see," Marc said, seeming to regret that he'd brought it up now. What the hell was going on, all of a sudden? "Yellow looks great on Ty. And blue on Ryan."

"Yeah. To go with those green/blue eyes. They're gorgeous. But so is Ty. Where are we going?"

"To see if the brothers identical are up."

"Why?"

"Because I want to see if they're screwing."

"Really?"

Unfortunately, we were met on the path by the twins coming out of the cottage.

"Morning, guys. You come by to let us have at Jeff?" Remus asked.

"Not on your life, you degenerate."

"Degenerate?"

"You fuck your own brother."

"But I'm monogamous."

"Yeah, like yesterday," Romulus said.

"That was an exception, and you know it. Besides, how could I resist the incomparable handmaidens of the queen throwing themselves at me?"

"Uh, huh."

"I shared."

"Finally. So, why did you guys come to our humble abode?"

"To see if you were being monogamous," Marc said.

"Later. In the cathedral. About ten. We wanted to get an early start on the lawn, considering it's been pretty rainy."

"We'll see you then." I watched them walk off, their penile laces dancing between their hard, bronzed legs.

"Why do they wear the boot laces on their cocks?"

Marc shrugged. "Makes them feel sexy, I guess."

"Sure makes them *look* sexy."

They looked even sexier with their golden skins glistening with sweat. They were already on the close-cropped grass, getting aroused. Their cock adornments

were cast aside.

"How can you tell which is which?" I whispered.

"Rommy's earring is in his right ear. Ream's, the left. Their mother had it done to tell them apart."

"Huh. Smart woman."

Who had produced two abundantly desirable boys, who found their mirror image irresistible. It was evident as their hands feverishly explored the identical body next to his, and their matching cocks crossed between them. Ream reached for his brother's, and when he found that it was as stiff as his, he broke their oral contact and got up on all fours over Rommy. He took the sun-darkened rod into his mouth and lavished it with love. He inhaled the familiar musk as his head moved faster on his twin. Rommy sucked Ream's glans into his mouth and used his tongue to torture the sensitive underside of the hard prick. I wondered if either of them was fantasizing that he was sucking himself. Why bother, maybe. I wondered at the sheer narcissism of it, two guys loving themselves. One thing was for sure, it was one of the most erotic sights I'd ever seen.

Ream came off the spit-soaked cock, taking him out of his brother's mouth at the same time. He straddled his twin and guided him into his body. He moved gracefully but excitedly on the shaft, his own sex captured by his brother's hand, which jerked him fast. They thrashed together in lust, taking the short way home. "You're fucking gorgeous, Rommy. Fucking gorgeous. Fucking...god!" I didn't know whether he actually meant that his brother was his god, or if it was an exclamation announcing his orgasm, because both boys' faces screwed up in intense pleasure at the same time. Then Remus scooped up his come and offered it to Romulus, who accepted it, sucking in his brother's tongue. When he had deposited the last, they kissed and laughed.

"Well," Rommy asked, smiling.

"Too hot for words," I said.

"We are," Remus said, with the same grin.

"Thanks, guys. We must do this again," Marc said.

Instead of waiting for the brothers to leave, Marc led me out of the cathedral, to my severe disappointment. My erection was raging, trapped in my pouch, egged on by the elasticized ring pressing on it. I looked down at mine, then at Marc's and did admit that we looked sexy as hell the way our pouches were distended dramatically.

"Where are we going?"

"I thought I'd show you the stables. Uncle keeps horses. I'll introduce you to the two stable boys, Toby and Yancey. They're dolls, but who here isn't?" He had got that right.

We walked past the cottage, and beyond a small grove of trees we came upon a showy, whitewashed, barn-like structure, which I knew was the stable. As we approached the wide, open doorway, Marc stopped us. I could see two boys with dark five o'clock haircuts, eyebrows, and lashes. One of them was braced against the wood-planked wall, legs spread, knees bent, ass out. The other was

kneeling behind him, his face nestled between the boy's cute butt. Both wore black bandannas as sweatbands and high, black leather boots. "Oh god, that feels great. God, Toby, don't stop. Fuck me with that long tongue of yours. Do me with that fucking tongue."

It was obviously a talented tongue, however long it was, because Yancey was pointing up at the wall. I had never seen anyone come by being rimmed, but then I had never come by being kissed before Marc. I hoped this would be a first, too. Toby was hungry, that was certain. He moaned in delight as he kept his face buried in the crack, causing his partner to quiver and move his ass desperately into the other boy. Finally, Yancey cried out, "Oh, fuck, Toby! Oh, oh, fuck!" and splattered the wall with his come.

Toby got up and they kissed. Then they walked over to a stack of hay. Yancey lay on a mat of it. Toby lowered himself onto his stablemate's face and sat on it. He pulled on himself as Yancey returned the anal favor on him. "That feels rad, Yance. I'm jerkin' hard so I don't smother ya, man." And he was doing just that. "That's it, blow in me. Yeah, suck some more. I'm close! Oh, yeah. Oh, Yance. Suck, man. Oh, mama, I'm coming!" He emitted a soft keening sound as his cock erupted. Beautiful, I thought, as I watched the white fluid sail up into the air and fall harmlessly to the ground. Marc pulled me out of sight, before the boys saw us.

A minute later we walked into the stable, and he introduced me to them. Both guys were about five-seven or eight with blue eyes. Yancey's were a crystal blue, while Toby's were deep cobalt. I wanted both of them to fuck and blow my ass with their mouths, and anything else these beautiful creatures wanted to do with my body. They showed us the horses, which didn't mean much to me, except that horses are beautiful creatures, as the stable boys were. They had evidently saddled the horses before their male need overcame them.

After a couple more minutes of visiting, during which they seemed completely unselfconscious about their tanned, lithe bodies being nude from the kneecaps up, they announced that it was time to exercise the horses.

As we walked away, I wondered what it would feel like wearing only a pair of boots and riding a horse without a saddle, holding onto its mane and feeling its smooth coat on my bare skin.

"Man, they sure are anal, aren't they?"

"But not retentive. You pretty much see it all here."

"Marc, I'm really hurting. Can we go back to the cathedral now?"

"Sorry, Jeff, I forgot to tell you that I need to do something. Why don't you go back to the room, and I'll try to join you shortly."

"What is it you have to do?"

"Just a chore. You go on."

"Please, Marc?"

"You'll get relief soon. Promise."

Six

I did as I was told, but in the upstairs hallway I stopped. Someone was outside our bedroom door. It was the short, muscular boy from yesterday. He was wearing a tangerine thong which looked like it had been painted on him. His crotch was indecently beautiful. This only worsened my heightened state. Approaching him, I also noticed that the boy wore gold rings on the second digit of each foot. And another on his right pinky.

"Sorry, I didn't mean to startle you. My name is David. I think you're the hottest thing I've seen here, and I was wondering if you'd, like, you know, to get it on."

"Well, I'm supposed to wait for Marc."

"This won't take long."

"I don't know."

"Look, man, you're hot. Marc won't know, you know? I'll make it fast."

Looking at his exaggerated basket made him irresistible to my hormones. They made me ask, "Will you fuck me the way you did the other guy yesterday afternoon?"

"Sure. Any way you want it. Come on."

We went to David's room, where he removed my suit. "Man," he said, when he saw what I had. He peeled off his own form-fitting suit to reveal a tangerine harness. I dropped to my knees and took the short, fat prick in my mouth. Within seconds it rewarded me by lengthening to a respectable five or six inches. The head was purple with lust and hard as a door knob from the tight, bright straps magnifying his engorgement. "Okay, climb on me and wrap your legs around my back. I'll do the rest," he said, standing in a crouch. I complied, and soon David was lowering me onto the thick cock. I sank all the way onto it and sighed. He moved me on the swollen member as effortlessly as he had the other boy. I could not believe how strong he was. "Danny loves taking it this way. That's who you saw me dicking yesterday. We're fuck buddies. That's what my pinky ring means. That way the other assholes leave us alone." David moved me up and down, the fullness in me stimulating, although not to the pleasing extent that Marc's cock had been. Then I wondered why David was fucking me, if had a thing with Danny. Well, he had said how desirable I was. "Man, you're fucking tight, Jeff. Nice and tight, you know what I mean?" I knew what he meant, and it felt good. And also to have my body used by another handsome male for his pleasure. There was something further arousing in knowing that. David kissed me as he masturbated himself with me, though not as passionately as he had with Danny. Not surprising, if Danny was his fuck bud. David moved me faster and announced, "I'm gonna fuckin' come in you, gorgeous." True to his word, seconds later I felt the organ bloat further as it released the contents of his harnessed balls into me. He held me fast in coitus but lifted me off after he stopped spasming. "I gotta go, man," he said pecking me on the lips and

378

stepping into his little suit. I enjoyed watching him arrange himself for maximal exposure. The front of the brief was seamless but seemed to be contoured to accommodate him. Then he was out the door, no doubt heading for the pool, so that Danny wouldn't see the wet spot on his little suit.

As I watched him leave, I longed to have my cock nestled between those tan cheeks. Standing alone in that room now, I felt somewhat used. But all David had promised was a quickie. And had delivered. I did feel guilty, as if I'd cheated on Marc. And with one of the pool boys at that. I picked up the glossy red thong and managed to get myself into it with difficulty. I wished that Marc were doing it for me. I seemed to be in a constant semi-tumescent state at that point. I considered jerking off to relieve my need, but I wanted to save it for Marc. And I still wasn't ready to be roaming the halls naked, although the idea of letting my cock swing free for the pool boys to salivate over did have a certain egotistical appeal. So, once more harnessed in my sexy brief, I left the room where David had, in fact, cheated on Danny.

When I turned the corner into the main hall, I saw the two boys with the red silk pouches coming toward him. "Just the guy we were looking for," Pete or Repete said. "Marc asked us to tell you that he's going to be busy for a while and for you to amuse yourself. But why not do it with us? We'd both like to entertain that gorgeous body of yours."

What was happening here? Where was Marc and what was it he had to do all of a sudden? I asked.

"He's probably with a client of Master's."

"Sometimes he has to entertain, you know?" No, I didn't know.

"But we're willing to keep you company."

Reluctantly, I went with them, having no better plan. And I as I walked down the hall, I realized that I was more than a little pissed that Marc had left me for someone else. No doubt screwing a complete stranger. For uncle, the bastard. Considering that he was kept in this place, he was nothing but a prostitute, exchanging sex for room and board. The most beautiful whore in the world, but a whore nonetheless. Realizing that, I was happy to be in the twins' company. And I'd finally get off, no thanks to the whore.

They led me into their rooms in the main wing of the house. The sitting room was bathed in satin in the brilliant hue of a male cardinal. Their favorite color, or their master's? Probably the latter. Although he seemed to like lots of different skin colors. That being the case, he certainly had tons more possibilities for sex partners than if he limited himself to one race. Smart man, I thought. But I still thought he was a bastard.

Once inside the room, the boys began to fondle my slick crotch. I returned the favor, delighting in the feel of the silk loosely covering them. And of their little endowments behind the slinky fabric. These hardened quickly, tenting the material slightly. I was able to wrap the silk around them and masturbate them with it. They squirmed under my touch and planted kisses and soft touches on my torso before sucking on my nipples. When they had the little nubs saluting

379

them, they changed to licking them and flicking the sensitive skin with their tongues. I was breathing harder, which no doubt pleased them immensely. When I was nearing the point of pleasure turning to pain, they stopped.

They dropped to their knees fore and aft of me to perform fellatio and analingus on me as they had on Remus. Before they commenced, I asked, "Guys, can I ask a favor?"

"If it's to fuck us, the answer's no. We're virgins. Well, officially."

"Officially?"

"We've never been fucked by anyone other than our brother. Master doesn't consider that having our cherries busted."

"I see. No, what I'd like is for you guys to be naked, too."

"Sure, why not. Okay, Pete?"

"Yeah, that's cool, bro."

They stood and sloughed off their silk G-pouches, and my eyes lit on Pete's penis. It had a ring sticking out of the head of it with a large teardrop-shaped red stone hanging from it. I turned to see that Repete was similarly pierced. He grinned at me. "Cool, huh?"

"Yeah, it is. More like a real turn-on."

"We think so, too. Actually, we like to be nude in our rooms, because the jewels feel great when we walk."

"And play with each other."

"Right. We'll give you a little demonstration after we take care of your needs."

Which they did with enthusiasm. Man, I had never been with two guys like this before, where I was the center of their attention. Feeling my rosebud and cock being loved simultaneously flooded me with acute pleasure. At the same time, Pete was massaging my calves as Repete did the same to my thighs. The lower part of my body was awash with elation. The twins were relentless in their attentions to my body, and my sphincter actually clamped down on Repete's tongue as I filled Pete's throat with my cream.

"Man, that was great."

"Thanks. It works out fine for us, because I'm a rabid cocksucker, and my brother's anal."

"Well, it sure worked out fine for me."

"Glad you enjoyed it."

Repete carried several red satin-covered pillows to the bed and piled them up.

"Why don't you get comfortable on these, while Pete and I sex each other for you," he said. I did and watched the twins mount the bed and kneel facing each other. Their rings and jewels glinted in the afternoon sun. Man, that would have had me hard in no time, if I hadn't just come.

They kissed, loosely holding each other, careful to keep their bodies apart so that I could enjoy seeing their adorned sexes. They quickly hardened, probably liking no lips and tongue better than their identical brother's. Once erect, they stopped and pushed back their asses, overtly to give me a different view of their

380

erections sporting the rings and gems. But it was then that I saw that they had another ring on their tailbones with a matching stone hanging from it. Now I was starting to respond to the decorations on their beautiful sleek bodies, against all physical logic. They didn't respond after I uttered, "Absolutely gorgeous," but they resumed kissing and now each took his brother into his soft hand. Their masturbatory actions were intensely sensual. Slowly they worked up to the point of making each other hump the other's hand, frantic to get off. Their orgasms were shuddering in their intensity. A boy's best friend is his identical twin's hand, in this case, I thought.

They let me kiss both of their rubies, which is what they told me they were. I didn't doubt them, the stones were so dazzling. Then they called down for supper for us and pulled their pouches back on. "The servants are never allowed to see us naked," Pete said. Only a select few were, I suspected. It was then that I realized that I was famished. I hadn't eaten anything since breakfast.

The cute servant brought in a large tray and set it on a table across the room. I started to get up, but the boys told me to relax on the pillows. I felt like a pampered sultan, when they brought the food to the bed and took turns feeding me and each other. The first course was lump crabmeat in a dilled mayonnaise. Then medallions of pork in a rich, dark wine sauce. Finally they fed me chocolate mousse. Wonderful. As were they. So exotically beautiful, but All-American boys of Chinese descent, they told me.

After dinner we retired to an adjacent room, which was carelessly strewn with huge pillows covered in red satin. They were scattered over a luxuriously-piled carpet the color of champagne. The focal point of the room was a big screen TV, the largest I had ever seen.

One of the twins, I couldn't tell which one, because there were no identifying marks as were the earrings on Rommy and Ream, turned on the TV and VCR as one of the Petes and I made ourselves comfortable on the plush pillows. Now I did feel like a sultan. Pete wiggled out of his pouch and walked toward us, his ruby moving and glinting on his modest sex.

The screen was still blank, so I asked, "How come you two don't wear something to distinguish yourselves from each other?"

"Why? It's not important to Master."

"Besides, we're the same person. We came from the same egg. We're just two halves of one being."

The screen came to life, and I wondered what kind of movie we were going to watch. It wasn't *Heidi*, I could tell immediately. The title of the movie was in Chinese or Japanese characters. "It's a Japanese ritual. These people worship a golden cock as their god," one of the Petes said. As the movie opened, a handsome teenage boy was being escorted by two men in white, kimono-like robes trimmed in gold. The boy was nude, except for wide golden bracelets and anklets. His body was leanly muscular. His uncircumcised sex swayed as he walked. The robed men led him into a kind of chapel, where another priest waited at an altar. Behind him sat a statue on a base of white marble. The

sculpture was a tall, wide phallus made of gleaming gold. In the cleft of the glans was a brilliant, clear-faceted stone. It looked like a diamond the way it glittered from the flames burning in a broad, shallow golden dish at its base.

The boy was taken by the head priest to the phallus, where the youth leaned forward and kissed the base of the ersatz cock. He took the teenager's penis in his hand and began to masturbate him slowly, sliding the foreskin back and forth over the sensitive nerves. The boy closed his eyes, obviously enjoying the manipulation. The priest had the boy erect, but he still took his good old time sexing him. It seemed that he wanted the teenager to receive the fullest enjoyment from this sex act. The attractive chest rose and fell faster, even though the priest kept up an easy pace. The boy's mouth opened. He was getting close. The monk milked him now, causing jolting pleasure, and his semen spewed from the slit into the flaming dish, where it hissed in death, the fruit of his malehood his offering to the god.

He was led to the altar, where the priest took a chalice and held it under the boy's cock. He raised it so that the shaft was inside the cup. When he lowered it a minute later, the skin shone with wetness. Then the boy mounted the altar and knelt. He was given another chalice to drink from, which he did, fully. Then he lay on the altar, wiggling himself onto a small, angled butt plug, which was part of it. Then his bracelets were clipped to rings at the corners of the altar, further immobilizing him. He seemed to be drugged from having drunk from the cup, his head lolling to one side.

The head priest had a small, thin golden knife with a diamond-encrusted handle. He proceeded to grasp and cut away the boy's foreskin, expertly excising the skin flap in seconds. He swabbed the raw area, and I was amazed that whatever he applied prevented bleeding. Then he deposited the skin in the flaming dish and bowed to the golden idol. Next he took a gold band and worked it past the head of the boy's penis to nestle over the wound. "The ring has a bunch of sharp points inside, so the spongy tissue and skin will grow into them, making it a permanent part of his body." Oh.

When the youth came to, he seemed ecstatic to be circumcised and adorned. He was unshackled, lifted off the plug by the priests and positioned at the end of the altar, where the three of them took turns fucking him. He seemed deliriously happy to receive the other banded cocks up his ass. Man, I thought about Joey Tibault, an altar boy I had wanted to blow while he was sitting on the altar at church. That was an enduring fantasy, because Joey was as pretty as the school day was too long. Dark curls and lashes, eyes of sapphire, a girl's lips. Joey had been the embodiment of sexual desire to me at age ten. Then I thought of the other boy on whom I'd seen a ring. The black boy in the three-way the day before. The one whose mother rented him for drugs. How beautiful his boyness was with the sexy silver filigree ring on it.

When the men had their way with the novice, others approached the altar, all young, good-looking and naked, save for their own gold rings, and proceeded to have *their* way with him. There must have been a dozen of them. By that time I

382

was playing seriously with Pete and Repete, and they were returning the favor.

Once the marathon fucking ended, a golden plug was put into the boy to keep the copious amount of viscous liquid inside him. He was helped off the altar and led to the statue, where the chief priest masturbated him again, this time as a circumcised, bejeweled youth. This act took longer than the first, but he seemed in sexual ecstasy, perhaps because of that. He seemed to be in no pain and a lot of pleasure. Maybe worshipping a golden phallus was the way to go, I was thinking. Lots of sex and an ornamented cock thrown in for good measure. The boy spasmed in happiness, giving up a surprising amount of himself the second time.

"Man, that was hot."

"Yeah, kind of quirky watching a boy lose his skin, but it was. Those Japanese sure know what to worship. The next one's even kinkier."

That scene opened with another beautiful dark-haired teenage boy sitting naked on his bed, petting a large black dog with a sleek coat. The kid was very pale, so the contrast between their colors was profound. Then it became clear pretty quickly that this was no mere boy and his dog story. "I love you darling," he said as he smoothed the short fur in long, slow, sensual caresses. The dog licked his face in brief strokes in response to the declaration of love. He nuzzled the dog as he patted it. It was evident that I was watching two males engaging in foreplay. Their tongues then met in long, lingering licks. The boy's hand went down to the dog's haunch, where it dallied before moving inside the leg. The dog raised his paw and lowered it onto the boy's crotch. "Yes, Rex," he said. "I belong to you."

Rex closed his eyes and panted as he was being fondled intimately.

Then the boy said, "Let me give you even more pleasure." With that Rex removed his paw from the boy's crotch so that the human could lie on his stomach and bury his head in his partner's groin.

I watched, incredulous, as the boy sucked off the dog while making happy sex noises. The dog's paw rested proprietarily on the youth's back.

After a while, he came off the canine tool so that we could see his handiwork. He told Rex how delicious he tasted and went down on him again.

Several minutes later, Rex pawed the boy and growled softly, and he removed his mouth from the raging hard-on again. He got onto all fours and turned his cute ass to the dog. Rex mounted him, sinking the rewards of the boy's labors between the round white cheeks. The dog's paws clutched the slim, hard chest as he humped his human lover with feral sensuality. The boy's eyes were closed, his attention focused on the animal organ filling his bowel. "Oh, Rex, fuck me. Fuck me, darling."

The dog licked his face as he rutted furiously in the comely boy, wedded in passion, the youth his sexual possession. It was such an erotic sight to see their contrasting bodies joined like that. And further, to see the kid's cock begin to grow as a result of the pleasure being rendered to his boy cunt by man's best friend's own maleness.

He continued to beg his sexual master to take him until he cried out in orgasm. His come shot from him like bullets from a gun. Rex yowled and shuddered in release as he flooded his sex slave with his own male effluent. When his tremors ceased, he pulled out of the boy, who turned over and collapsed onto the pillow.

Rex lapped up his lover's essence and then licked his spent cock, gently, thoroughly cleaning him. Then he sprawled onto the boy's body, and they engaged in post-coital caresses, nuzzling and licking. "I love you, Rex," he said, before the scene ended.

"Man, where do you guys get these nutty movies?"

"It's a secret. Want to see more?"

"God, no! I'd rather do it with you two again."

"That'll be even better."

I ended up on all fours, but there was no dog present, thank goodness. I wasn't sure I loved them that much, but I admit that the coupling had been really arousing and piqued my curiosity about what it would feel like to take a long canine organ into me. One Pete was on his back under me, sucking on my cock. The other twin let me get his brother hard again before impaling himself on the cock identical to his. Which he did after unhooking the ruby from the glans ring. The fuckee had to be Repete, who loved everything anal. I bent my head and took him into my mouth as he rode his identical brother's pole. The jewel felt weird and wonderful at the same time, but it was a welcome challenge to pleasure him that way. Repete played with my hair as I sucked on him. I liked that. And also Pete making me light up down there. At that moment I knew that I didn't want to leave this palace of pleasure, where it seemed that I could have anything I wanted. Right now this was what I wanted, to be joined to these young twins in lust. Repete came soon after Pete surrendered to his mirror image. I gave myself to Pete, his mouth was so frantic on me in orgasm.

We lay down again on the pillows, and I fell asleep with the twins nestled against me.

The dream was perhaps the strangest I'd ever had. I was in Santaland at the department store, standing in line with dozens of other boys. Elves flitted around us, wearing green tights, red jerkins and floppy hats. They leered at us as they passed, because all we were wearing were droopy caps like theirs. And every one of them sported an erection that was boldly outlined by the stretchy tights. Seeing them in arousal made my wee wee tingle, and I liked that.

As I got closer to Santa, I could see that he wasn't the jolly, old, roly poly Claus I had been expecting. He was young and muscular. His skin was the color of peach ice cream. I saw this, because he was wearing only his black boots and white fur-trimmed red velvet hat. His hair was long, but it was as black as his boots, as was his trim beard. His dark eyes expressed the same lust as his helpers as he talked to each little boy. I watched as he would lift the boy onto his thigh to straddle it, lowering him onto a black dildo strapped to his leg. The boy would sit impaled on the ersatz penis as he told Santa what he wanted for Christmas. The young toy deliverer would take his time with each youth,

stroking him, and all of them reached down between Santa's legs before being kissed and lifted off the device.

When my turn came, Santa smiled widely at me with unexpectedly full lips. He put his hands into my arm pits and lifted me effortlessly into the air. He lowered me onto the warm anal plug. I felt no pain, only a strange heat spreading throughout my abdomen as I told the handsome St. Nick what I wanted for Christmas. As I talked, I was unaware of what the warmth below had caused. Santa was, though. He smiled and whispered in my ear that I would get everything I wanted and more. His fingers brushed my wee wee, and I looked down to see that I was stiff. His fingers felt oh so good on me and made me twitch with unexpected good feelings. For some reason, I looked down to see what Santa looked like there. It was huge compared to mine, and it was sheathed in red velvet with white fur trim imitating a cock ring. It was pointed up at me like a missile. He encouraged me to feel how soft the velvet was. And it was; a delight to touch. The velvet second skin made his hard boy thing look beautiful. At his insistence, I continued to stroke him until he gave a strangled cry. I thought I'd hurt him, but when he opened his eyes, he smiled widely and kissed me with the full scarlet lips. His tongue parted my teeth and invaded my mouth. I sucked on it as if it were a lollipop. It was sweet but had no discernible taste otherwise.

His hand was caressing my wee wee more urgently now, engulfing it in his big, soft hand. I writhed on the dildo from the strange pleasure emanating from my little dick. He withdrew his tongue just before I cried out and convulsed on my black impaler. He grinned more widely and repeated that I would get everything I wanted, and more. I already had, I thought, just before he kissed me again.

Seven

When I woke up, the feeling of the dong and tongue persisted, as did Santa's warm hand on my wee wee. Only it was actually one of the twins I was sucking on, the downy skin of his belly pressed against my face. The other was buried in my crotch, I realized as my awareness grew. But the pressure in my rectum was a mystery, albeit a pleasant one. I knew that the bejeweled cock I had in my mouth belonged to Repete, given that his twin loved giving blow jobs more than just about anything. And mine was paradise, he'd said the previous evening. Evidently he hadn't seen Ryan's yet.

I forgot about what was in my rear end, concentrating instead on the handsome, jeweled erection in my mouth and the soft, pleasant scent arising from his heated crotch. Repete shifted upward, allowing me to move on his hardness. I took his cheeks into my hands and kneaded them. Then my right index finger teased his rosebud before sliding past it. He gave an approving sigh

at being invaded in his favorite place and began to fuck my face, moving his hips in an up-tempo, fluid motion. I managed to keep my finger inside Repete, letting him ride it as if it were a small penis.

My cock strained and throbbed in Pete's mouth, helpless to stem my impending orgasm. Sensing this, his lips scorched my head, and he brought me off. Repete, feeling my rising moans on his cock, squirmed as the added pleasure vibrated onto his sensitized nerves. He froze, mewled and washed my throat with his thick essence. He pulled out and wiped himself on my nose. We both laughed. Pete brought himself off while still milking the last of me, and my body bucked in response to his animated oral declaration.

"Man, it's great making it with you, Jeff," Repete said and kissed me.

"At least," Pete said and did the same. Then I remembered the fullness in me.

"What did you guys put in me," I asked, reaching to feel behind me. Repete took my hand away.

"Get up and look in the mirror, man."

I did as I was told and saw a thick, lustrous brown tail arcing out from between my ass cheeks.

"Way cool, huh? We figured you're hung like one, so we decided to make you look more like one. Besides, they're our favorite animals, and we love to ride them."

"You want to ride me?"

"Only for sex, because you're one of our favorite animals, too," Pete said, and winked. "But you look even more beautiful and desirable with the tail." Evidently the servant, who brought us breakfast, agreed. He eyed me furtively, but I could see the lump in his shiny thong begin to grow. I moved my hips to make the tail swish and almost laughed out loud, when he caught the movement and gulped. He exited quickly.

"You know, I think I could get used to being a horse."

"And you'd be *even more* popular than you already are!"

"And Toby and Yancey would demand to groom you." That was a prospect I could handle quite easily. I definitely could get used to being a horse, if they would be my trainers.

Then I thought of Marc and felt the stabbing pain again. An almost overwhelming feeling of missing him welled up in my heart. Part of it was guilt, I knew. I hadn't thought of him once, when I was playing games with the twins.

"I should get back to the room to see if Marc's there."

"He won't be. He's still busy."

"How do you know?"

"We know everything that goes on here. We have to as Master's servants."

"Sit down and eat, Jeff. We'll make sure you're occupied."

"Look, Marc has no choice in what he's doing. He has to, because he's Master's slave. He has to obey and do what he's told." I didn't like hearing the word 'slave', but Marc himself had used it. Face it, Jeff. That's what he is. A thing to be used for another man's pleasure. The twins showed me how to sit so

386

that my tail hung over the back of the chair. And it was a much fancier one than the pool boys had worn in the pool, I noted.

After the hearty breakfast, the brothers decided that we would check out the wing where Trey's playroom was.

"But shouldn't I wear more than a tail?"

"Why? Everybody else but us flaunts it. Besides, if he's there, he'll be delighted to see your horse tail. And cock. You can't be feeling all that cock-shy at this point."

That wasn't completely true, I was surprised to admit to myself. In spite of my time spent naked there, I was still a little bashful about letting other people see my stuff. So I left the haven of their rooms, reluctantly, wearing only the long, elegant tail. Maybe I would have the same kind of effect on some of the irresistible numbers I'd seen by the pool as I'd had on the Filipino servant. There were several pool boy bodies I would be happy to put my equine endowment into.

The door to Trey's room was open. He was lying on the bed, clad in his boots, leather chaps and a matching pouch and gloves. He was watching his puppy taking care of a boy dressed in a motorcycle police officer's uniform. Tight black boots gave way at the knee to even tighter black uniform pants with white side stripes. His black uniform shirt was open, and he was playing with his nipples with black-gloved hands. A black-brimmed white helmet completed his authentic look. It was contradicted by his youthfulness, but that only made him that much more alluring. He had short, light brown hair. I envied Skipper his meal. As always, his leather-covered sheath was sticking up as he hungrily swallowed the boy's cock. He really was into oral sex, and from what I could see, this one was certainly worth having in his mouth.

Trey saw us watching the action, smiled, and motioned for me to come over to him. He reached out and played with my tail and said, "Cool."

Then he continued to manipulate it as he watched his puppy pleasure the young 'cop'. Who opened his brown eyes and stared at me with a frown, as if daring me to want him. I didn't need a dare, because I did. Then he shut them again and concentrated on the blow job and torturing his nipples.

Trey was now running his left hand down my shaft. "Way cool," he said and winked. The soft leather of his gloves felt that way, for sure. He stopped just to admire it hanging in slight arousal. "You are a horse," he said and smiled. No, Ryan was a horse. I was, well, pleasantly hung.

The boy playing cop came, holding Skipper's head fast to him as he emptied himself into the boy. When he let go, he patted the puppy's scalp as he was being rearranged inside his pants and zipped him back up. He told him he was a great cocksucker. Smiling, the boy got up to go to Trey, but when he saw me he knelt and kissed my cock head, acknowledging me as desirable, I guess. Trey leashed him and he knelt with his legs apart so that we could see his proud, shiny, very black erection. Instinctively, I liked him, even though we'd never exchanged a word. I was also happy that Trey did have genuine feelings for this

most attractive boy.

The cop came over to where I was standing and gave me the look again. He wasn't a pool boy. Was he one of Trey's middle school classmates? I doubted that Trey went to school. Oh, well, he could leer all he wanted, because we wouldn't be getting together, I was sure. However, his sex did make a pleasing outline in the tight pants, even at rest.

Pete announced that we had business, and Trey bade us goodbye. "See you, gorgeous," the cop said, and I knew he meant it.

None of the rooms was occupied as we made our way down the long hall. When we stopped at the window overlooking the pool, it seemed that all of the pool boys were in or around it. Six of them were playing the cavalry game nude. The rest of the boys were swimming or lounging.

"Why doesn't your master let them go around naked all the time?"

"Because he likes tan lines on white boys. Except for Kerry, whose skin color is even. So those guys are only nude at night. Not that Pete and I care. Most of them aren't worth more than their beauty, which is all master cares about. Marc and Troy are the big exceptions. They're beautiful and in love. They're a joy. Nice guys and hot, to boot. Danny and David are nice, too, but watch out for David, because he'll want to get into you, as striking as you are." I decided not to admit that David had already had me.

"Jeff, why don't you rest in your room for a while. We'll make sure you're occupied in Marc's absence." Whatever that meant, but I didn't ask.

I wish they hadn't mentioned his name. I hurt again. I thought that I was falling in love for the first time in my life. I actually hungered for Marc's presence. But I would have to continue to settle for gorgeous in the absence of stunning. At the door, Pete made me bend over, and he removed the tail. "Later," he said, and they both winked. I watched their juvenile cheeks move seductively was they walked down the corridor, hand in hand. Yes, later.

Eight

My next shock came when I opened the door to discover that the room was not unoccupied. Specifically, the black boy was lying on the white comforter, smiling at me.

"Hi."

"Hi. Have you been waiting long?" What a stupid question. I might as well have said, do you come here often?

"It was worth it, you're so beautiful."

"Thanks." He patted the place beside him, and I joined him on the bed. He moved his body against mine. "I'm Jeff."

"I know. I'm Andrew." Instead of shaking my hand, he kissed me. I was immediately under his spell. I put my arms around him and that's how we lay.

388

His little penis looked so cool with the fancy ring encircling it. Close up, I could see the fine ornamentation of the filigree.

"That's a beautiful ring."

"Thanks. Actually, it's a harness!"

"It is?"

"Yes." He moved his shaft onto his belly, so that I could see that the ring didn't go all the way around him. It left his sensitive underside exposed. On either side were little silver balls. "See them," he asked pointing? Yes, I said. "They're attached to a straight bar inside me. The thing's called a barbell. It holds the ring on me. It's called a frenulum harness."

A young boy being pierced and harnessed? Amazing.

"Does it hurt?"

"No. Only when they did it, a little bit. It feels way cool to be harnessed."

"Can you get hard?" I already knew the answer to that, having seen him in action.

"Sure. No sweat."

"But what happens when you get older and grow?"

"They just fit me with bigger rings and bars. I'm already permanently pierced, so it's no problem. I got my first little ring jewelry when I was six." I didn't know what to say. He had been here since that age?

"Uh, where's your mother?"

"Oh, you know. At our apartment. Probably all coked up or grooving on heroin. She likes both. And she went home with a good supply. I'd rather she get stoned and play with herself there. I like it better here. It's a lot nicer than living with her. Besides, I belong to Mike's uncle, not to her. All he has to do is keep her in drugs to keep his end of the bargain."

"So you really do like it here?"

"A lot. I mean, I really like making it with the other boys, even if they are older and can come. It's fun. My pretty little cock is real happy here."

"It is pretty." He was lazily playing with it, making the light glint off the ornate harness. I kissed his soft lips and felt his downy skin. Heaven. He looked up at me and smiled. His lips were tantalizingly full. I noticed that his eyelashes curled around his dark eyes. He was pretty now, but he was going to be in Marc and Angel's league, when he grew up. Uncle had made a wise investment. Andrew was irresistible. "Can I suck you, Andrew?" I couldn't believe my ears, but I'd said it.

"You want to? Yeah, I'd really like that, Jeff."

I settled between his spread legs and took the small ebony member into me. I decided that I wanted him in my other opening, too, when my lips felt how smooth the uneven surface of the ring was. I caressed his chest, sides, hips and thighs as my lips encouraged his black boyhood to hardness. When I'd accomplished it, I held him and looked at his jeweled cock, at the balls which helped fasten it to his shaft. He grinned at me. "Man, I never thought that the god would make love to me."

"Oh, yeah? Then why were you waiting for me here in bed?"

"It's a secret." He could have told me to eat shit, and that grin would have convinced me to take a dump and feast on it for him, he was that desirable.

"I'll take your word for it." And sucked his boyhood back inside me. In a few minutes he was thrashing on the bed. "Suck me, Jeff! Suck me! Ohhhh! Oh!" I felt him pulse, his head swelling from the constriction of his harness. His body went rigid. He was in orgasm. I looked up to see his face screwed up in pleasure. I was glad that he'd learned about sex early, because he obviously enjoyed getting off.

After I let him savor his climax while resting in my arms, he wanted to masturbate me. He played with me, using his hand to excite my nerves. The skin of his palm and fingers was exquisitely soft. "Man, you're humongous, Jeff." I almost mentioned Ryan.

"Thanks, Andrew. I'm glad you like it."

"I do. I wish I could take this, but that's a no-brainer, considering the size of it. In fact, nobody's allowed to fuck me, even the guys with little endowments. Not until I can come, at least."

I planted kisses on his shiny brown face as he played with me. It felt so good that I wanted to show him, in addition to telling him, how great he made me feel. He liked that and smiled a lot. I thought about how much happier he was to be here, where the main activities seemed to be sloth and sex. And posing, if you were a pool boy. I thought of one I had seen. Adam, who had blown Darryl. I almost used him as a fantasy and then wondered why. I had one of the best there could be stroking me. Andrew was concentrating on the area just under my glans now, and he was doing an excellent job of sending me into orbit with his touch. He seemed so adept that I wondered if he had engaged in sex since he arrived at age six, or if he was also just a piece of art, as Marc had called it, until weekly sexing of his little organ finally revealed that he could have an orgasm.

He felt me harden further and left my arms to put his mouth over my head. I filled it with my cream and watched as it dribbled out of him and rolled down my shaft. He was urgently swallowing and swallowing, trying to keep as much of it as he could inside him. When I ceased producing, he began to lick me like a lollipop to get every bit of it he could. When he was satisfied that ninety-nine percent was sitting in his stomach, he turned and smiled at me. I laughed. "What's so funny?"

"You have me all over your face." He licked the sides of his mouth. "Come here, Andrew." He crawled up to me, and I gently licked his silky face, cleaning it. Then we kissed. A long, loving kiss. God he was sexy.

We were interrupted by a servant delivering lunch. He was the same one who had brought dinner the first night I was there. I watched his cheeks leave the room again. I think that they looked especially good to me, because they were forbidden fruit. I still didn't understand the logic of our not being able to have sex with the servants. But there was more than enough other ripe fruit available. Namely, Andrew.

390

"Have you seen Marc?"

He shrugged. "He's busy. You like him, don't you?"

"At least."

"Yeah, I'm not surprised. Marcus is our star. He's owned by my master, like me."

"I know. And Kerry and Darryl?"

"No. He didn't buy them. They're just his favorites right now. I wished that he still liked Marc. I think he's sad that he's pretty much on his own now."

"Except when it comes to entertaining uncle's friends."

"That's even sadder, Jeff." He sighed. "Some day that's probably what I'll do, when he gets tired of playing with me."

"He does now?"

"Oh, sure. But just to play with my wee wee, mostly. And feel my soft skin. Like I said, no one is allowed to fuck me. Period. I'm too little."

"Who's the cop?"

"One of Trey's friends. His name is Shane. He likes uniforms and power trips. He's not *that* much older than I am for crissakes." He shook his head. "He is awfully sexy, though. In a smoldering kind of way. It rolls off him. Like Trey."

I laughed. "You have a surprisingly good vocabulary for a boy your age."

"Thanks. I'm pretty smart. And don't forget most boys my age aren't interested in sex yet. They could probably make themselves hard, but they don't even think about it." He shrugged again. "I guess I'm lucky, because I'm one of those boys who has been able to get it up for years. That's why master bejeweled me, he was so pleased that I could."

"Your cock is beautiful. Like the rest of you."

"Thanks, Jeff. That means a lot to me."

"So what do you have planned for the rest of the day?"

"Spending it in bed with you. I mean, if you want to."

"Are you kidding? That's a no-brainer, too." His grin was priceless.

I understood the danger in doing it. I could easily fall in love with Andrew, as I knew I was with Marc. Maybe I would and that would prove that it was nothing more than lust with him. Besides, he hadn't even broken away from his who-knew-how many trysts to even see how I was doing. But he had seemed so sincere. And so taken with me. Maybe I was too young to recognize love. Maybe I deserved to be burned for my stupidity.

Andrew was snuggled on top of me. In answer to my question, he said emphatically that my finger inside him was not considered fucking him and, further, that he loved it. It was so peaceful lying there with him squirming on my digit from time to time, kissing tenderly and just talking. I wondered if he had anyone to talk to. Really talk to.

"Your finger feels great, Jeff. Thanks for making my cunt feel so good."

"My pleasure, Andrew."

"More mine." He giggled and kissed my nose. Then he moved down my body a bit, so that our cocks were touching. "Stay in me, okay, Jeff?"

"Buried to the hilt." He smiled that gorgeous white smile. Marry me, Andrew.

He began to rub himself against me. Most of it was his body, but his small endowment was lined up against mine. "Is my harness hurting you?"

"Nope. All I feel is your silky skin and the smooth balls."

"Great." He continued to arouse me with his movements. I'd never had sex like this, cock to cock, and his on mine felt incredibly arousing. Here was what I guessed to be a nine year old boy teaching me a new way to make love. "Feel good?"

"Feels great. You're really talented."

"Well, I am a sex slave in training." That didn't come close to explaining him.

"God, Andrew, you're going to make me come."

"Yeah, do it, man. Make cream for me." He was rubbing frantically now. "I love the taste of your cream. Oh, close. So close. Oh, mommy!" I held him tight with my free hand as we spasmed together in pleasure.

"That was awesome, Andrew."

"Thanks. Frottage is so cool." He explained that was what we had done, between lapping up what he could of me. He even ran his finger up his abdomen and chest and slowly sucked on it, all the while eyeing me, playing the boy seducer and a stunning one at that. He was wearing large silver hoops in his ears, and they only magnified his youthful beauty.

We ate another delicious supper. Those boys sure could cook. The seafood au gratin was loaded with shrimp, scallops and crabmeat. Everything else was good, too.

"So, why are the Filipinos off limits?"

"Mike said it had something to do with frat...frat...." He frowned. "Sorry, I can't pronounce it."

"Fraternization?"

"Yeah, that's it. Thanks. And those boys have pretty much paired off. They're happy with the way things are, so why have the pool boys mess things up? Hey, speaking of mess, you want to watch videos this evening?"

"Sure. Sounds like fun."

"Anything with you is." He batted his long, curled lashes. My heart leapt in response. God, what a sexy creature he was. "What I was thinking was we could go watch Sal and Mikey get messy. They usually let anybody watch, they're such sluts."

"What is it they do?"

"You'll see. Oh, and wear your red thong. I don't want any of the pool boys to get any more ideas than they already have."

"Andrew, David fucked me."

"He did?" He chuckled. "I'm not surprised, knowing David. That's cool, though. He's okay. He's trying to be faithful to Danny, 'cause they're kind of in love. But let him see an Adonis like you, and he strays. It isn't your fault that you're a god, and he is way handsome and built. As long as Danny doesn't know. He's such a sweet guy."

392

I felt guilty about cuckolding Danny, but I had loved feeling David's power over me, his strong arms using me to pleasure himself. But if they were in love, why did they let Marc and me witness their lovemaking the other day?

"David convinced Danny that they should let the other pool boys see how much they loved each other by doing it during the day for everyone to see. In addition to being sweet, Danny's dumb."

"You're pretty insightful."

"Thanks. You learn all sorts of things here in the pleasure palace."

"I'll bet. And it is that."

"Yeah, all you have to do is hang around Trey and Skipper for two minutes."

"I have. He loves Skipper a lot, doesn't he?"

He looked at me sharply before asking, "How do you know? That's the deepest, darkest secret in this place."

"Well, how do you know, then?"

"Trey told me, because he likes me. Well, and I let him tie me up. Skipper likes to do me, which is no surprise. But how do *you* know?"

"I was where I wasn't supposed to be and saw them making love."

"At the cathedral, I'll bet."

"Yes."

"Damn. Rommy and Ream are supposed to watch for people coming there, when Trey is in there with Skipper. Even they don't know that they're in love. But Trey is their boss, and they're supposed to guard his privacy. Assholes."

"They're awfully young to be in love."

"Jeff, Trey got Skipper as a pet when he was nine. Skipper was six, like I was. That was how Trey's dominant nature started to come out. By the time he was ten, he was wearing leather and Skipper was completely trained. It's just one of those things. Skipper adores Trey, and the leather boy loves his human dog more than anything. I've seen them, too, when they didn't realize it. It was such a tender scene. Not sex, but just real intimate. It was obvious. The rest is pretty much for show. Trey lets Skipper blow guys, as a treat. And Randy demands that his brother humiliate him, so Trey accommodates him. But otherwise they're hot for each other."

"Do you and Randy ever get it on?"

"Sure. We dress up and have sex. I look adorable in some of his outfits. Besides it feels neat to wear stockings and heels. I look cool in them, too."

"I don't doubt that."

"Well, let's get on down to the toilet. After you dress." Such as it was.

Nine

The toilet turned out to be a room in the wing with the gym. The door was open, and three other guys were looking through another open doorway. They

boy. And there's another gorgeous one, who likes to wear pantyhose with his swimsuits. Alex. I hope they'll end up being girlfriends, because they'd make a beautiful couple. And like I said, I like to wear fem things, too."

I found Andrew amazing. Like Marc, he didn't have much education to speak of, but he was smart and well-spoken, like the other guy I was in love with. I played with Andrew, lazily, as we watched the video we both liked. It wasn't overtly gay, but the young male actors in *Dead Poets Society* turned us on. Especially innocent, sweet Ethan Hawke. It felt so relaxing to be with Andrew, his body pressed against mine, his soft hand on my vulnerable organ. I had to keep telling myself how young he was. And I kept answering that he wasn't, in reality. He knew his way around the block.

Like another kid, who was a neighbor of Mickey, my boyfriend in high school at the time. Mickey said that the kid had psychological problems, but his mother refused to put him on medication. So, one time when I was visiting, the boy was naked in his back yard, acting out. He wasn't really good-looking, but he was the sexiest boy I had ever seen. Even more so than Mickey, although I didn't tell him that. He was built and surprisingly well-hung, and moved so sexily, that it was hard to believe that he was only ten. Both of us got hard watching him, he was so hot. Mickey said that he hit on older girls in the most graphic terms. He probably could have given them all they could handle from the looks of him.

In the middle of the movie, Andrew hit pause. I thought that maybe he wanted to make love. Instead he called down to order hot fudge sundaes. "With lots of peanuts and a can of whipped cream. Thanks, Pedro." He hung up the phone. "Was that all right?"

"Sounds perfect. Well, close. You are." We kissed.

Pedro, himself, brought up the sundaes. He was very engaging, and it was obvious that he liked Andrew a lot. What was not to like? He was gorgeous and a first-class cock tease. And the desserts did appear to have a can of whipped cream topping them. In addition to half a jar of maraschino cherries. And from the size of the bowls, a half gallon of ice cream each. Andrew looked at me and smiled. "We'll work off the calories." I had no doubt of that.

When the movie ended, we made love. I held him and kissed and nuzzled him. I sucked and licked his glorious chocolate brown skin. He was better than the richest hot fudge could ever be. We kissed for a long time, and it made me remember doing it with Marc to orgasm. That had been awesome.

"Something wrong?"

"I'm sorry. I love you, Andrew. I know that I could easily be in love with you, you're such a neat person. But I miss Marc."

"I understand," he said, caressing my face. "He's really special."

"I know. Do you and he make love?"

"Sure. We do it all the time. And it is lovemaking with Marc. With most all the other guys it's just sex. Which is cool, because that's what I'm into. But with him feelings are involved, you know?"

"Yeah, I do. Deep feelings."

"No surprise there, because Marcus is the prize here. Along with Kerry and Darryl and the Petes. And you."

I asked Andrew to fuck me, which did surprise him, but he was delighted by the request. I got him hard and then lay back and retracted my legs. He slid in past my sphincter, and the presence of his cock in my body felt wonderful. I said so. He beamed. "Fuck me, Andrew. Own me with that jeweled cock of yours, man."

I can't say that he exactly rutted in me, but he gave a pretty good approximation of it, his abdomen undulating so sexily to facilitate his taking of me. As he moved steadily faster, he wet his left index finger and began to stroke me with it where I was most sensitive.

I responded to the finger almost like a hair trigger, not believing that he had aroused me to aching in so short a time. I begged him to fuck and masturbate me, feeling completely helpless under this boy's control. He brought me off, and I was still spasming in orgasm, when he stopped fucking me and savored his own climax.

We nestled between the slick satin sheets and went to sleep with Andrew in my arms, his boy smell the smell of love.

Ten

At first I was disoriented, when he wasn't in bed with me upon waking. Assuming that he was in the bathroom, I lounged in bed. But he never came out. He was gone. My spirits plummeted. Another boy, for whom I was developing massive feelings, and whom I might not see again. I ate breakfast alone, not really tasting the pancakes, sausage and fruit. When I was full, I walked to one of the front windows beside the bed. It was another sunny day, but my heart wasn't. I missed Andrew. I missed Marcus. Whom I missed more, I didn't know. But I did know that I was alone in the big bedroom, and, curiously, I was as horny as hell, even after all of the loving Andrew had given me.

I showered, trying to think of what to do with myself. Leaving was a plan, but I really wanted to see Marc one more time. Maybe I could ask Trey to tie me up and hurt me, while Skipper gave me the best head of my life. Or be a slut like Billy, ready to give myself to any and every pool boy, who wanted a piece of my body. Andrew had said that Toby and Yancey had caught the cross-dressing soccer player in one of the stalls, certain that he was going to go down on one of the horses. Maybe I could find Billy. Or the twins. But they had abandoned me, too. Like Andrew and Marc.

I still hadn't decided what to do, when I came back into the bedroom. Something white caught my eye. It was lying just inside the door. I walked over and picked it up. It was a note. 'Meet me in the cathedral at ten,' it said. Marc! But why not just come in and lie on the bed to surprise me? Maybe he was with

one of those clients yet, and he had just enough time to pen the note and rush up to shove it under the door, while the guy was taking a leak. Or maybe one of the servants had delivered it. The cathedral. Where we had intended to make wild, passionate love. Marc.

My heart was beating faster now in anticipation. I knew then that I was in love. I looked at the note, again. I noticed that there was something else written on it at the bottom. 'Come naked, and use the door in the solarium. It'll get you around the pool boys.'

I went down the front stairs and walked down the central hall to the dining room. Beyond it were the satin-graced Filipinos and the kitchen. Once inside the dining room I saw a doorway in the near wall. It led into the solarium. I left the house by the door and walked past the wing of the house, keeping to a dense grove of what looked like fruit trees, so that I would be inconspicuous from the pool. Past that, the formal gardens began. I heard laughter and stopped. Curious, I walked toward the mirthful sounds and saw two naked boys in work boots, like Rommy and Ream, except that theirs were black. They were both dark-haired white boys, albeit with the tans of many black boys. They had a hose and one was cooling off the other, putting his hand over the nozzle to spray his fellow worker.

They didn't have laces on their cocks, but their genitals stood out, because they had no pubic hair. I couldn't make out what they were saying, but I saw one boy brace himself against a tree with smooth gray bark and spread his legs. Unbelievably, the other took the gurgling hose and inserted it into his fellow worker. I watched as his head arched back, a smile spreading onto his face as the water filled him. The other handsome youth pulled out the hose, and clear water emerged in a stream, like piss, from the enema boy.

When he was finished pissing out of the wrong orifice, he returned the favor to his partner. I watched the other boy hug the tree and begin to hump it as the hose was lodged past his sphincter, ensuring that his bowel would fill with cool, clear water. It seemed to be a sex act for him, the nozzle a cock, as he rutted on the smooth bark, the water surging into him. Then the other gardener yanked out the hose as the filled boy continued to couple with the tree, his anus squirting gallons of water. He cried out as the last of the clear liquid left his body. Panting, he relinquished his hold on the tree, and I could see his come darkening the light gray surface. I shook my head and turned toward the cathedral. Every kind of sexual expression could be found here. I smiled. I liked that, in spite of myself.

I had thought that I was pretty worldly, as I mentioned earlier, but I now realized that I was pretty ignorant. A little boy had taught me sex acts I never knew existed. I pictured both Andrew and Marc putting a garden hose up my ass and liking it. Maybe tying me up, too. And, at that point, Marc could piss and shit on my face, and I would like it. I would wear stockings and garter belts for him, and would no doubt love that, too. And the pony tail. Definitely. I would be his colt and let him ride me into the sunset.

Except that it wasn't Marc in the Cathedral, when I entered nearly breathless. It was Shane, dressed in his policeman's uniform. I have no doubt that shock and disappointment registered on my face, in turn. Then I felt betrayed by Marc, again, although he had never been involved in the first place. Shane was frowning at me, daring me to want him. All of a sudden I did. I walked over to him and knelt before him. I kissed his cock, outlined against his pants. Then I nuzzled his endowment, which was impressive at rest. And on a fifteen year old boy, if he were Trey's age? I kissed it again, giving him sexual power over me.

"Suck it, Jeff. Please?" That threw me. I unzipped him and carefully pulled him out of the stretchy pants. He was already hardening. I put my hands behind my back and swallowed him. He must have been all of seven inches, even then. I knew why Skipper had enjoyed him, although he was notorious for liking any cock. Shane's was pretty and long and dusky. As I was sucking on the lovely organ, I wondered if Trey let Skipper feast in order not to lose him. The master as slave. That was an interesting idea, but having seen them that day in this same place, I doubted that Skipper had a coercive bone in his body. He had been so happy to have Trey make love to him. As had Trey.

"God, that feels great. You're as good as Skipper." That kind of flattery could get you laid, I thought. Except that I wasn't coercive, either. I would gladly submit to Shane. I caressed his high boots as I made him more than hard enough to fuck me. I looked up at him, and he nodded.

Without any order, I got up and thrust my ass at him. He grabbed hold of my hips and slowly inched seven of them into me. I was being fucked by a teenage policeman in high boots, and the thought made me hard. It was the kind of erection where you're just glad to have it stay with you, because it simply feels good having it. Besides, Shane was filling my bowel quite nicely and moving in me at an easy pace. He was a good friend of Trey, for sure, and probably had gotten fucking down by the time he was twelve, as a result. What a place.

In truth, I loved having this beautiful boy using me in his uniform. All sorts of unnamed half-fantasies began to drift through my brain as he took me for his pleasure. Gay male sexuality, the delightful unknown. But he was knowing me, biblically, and I wanted his young seed in me.

"God, you're so beautiful, Jeff. Thanks for doing this."

"You're hot, Shane. Glad to. Fuck me good, sir." He liked that and got back into character. And I liked that.

"You got hot when you saw me straddling my cycle behind your car, didn't you, pussy?"

"Yes, sir."

"Wondering what else was between my legs."

"Yes, sir."

"Well?"

"You're big, sir. As big as your machine. It feels awesome in me."

"And it's as hot in you as the cycle's muffler. As hot as...as...oh, Jeff!"

He held me to him, keeping our intimate contact for several seconds after he

came. When he plopped out of me, he put himself inside his pants and zipped up. I turned and he held and kissed me. "Thanks, again. And for playing along. That really turned me on even more." I loved having his gloved hands run through my hair and over my body. Then he left, abruptly. I wondered if the sounds I heard were crying.

I stood in the middle of the outdoor sex palace feeling bewildered. Then I decided to lie down to feel the silkiness of the grass on my body. My thoughts were muddled, but I felt a kind of peace that the combination of sun and the soft, green surface imparted. I lazily stroked myself, remembering how good Trey's glove had felt, and regretting that Shane hadn't touched me with his. Then I got an idea. I decided to visit the stables, remembering how the stable boys had gotten off on each other's oral ministrations. Maybe I could get lucky with them.

What shocked me, upon my arrival, was the naked human with ebony skin, seemingly waiting for me.

"I'd hoped that you would get my note and come," Darryl said.

"I didn't find a note...from you."

"You didn't? Huh. That's strange. Well, at least you're here."

"How did you get so dark so soon?"

"Uncle is coming back the day after tomorrow, so I lay out all day the last three days to get as brown as I could for him. And besides, I was already close to Hershey's bittersweet, so less than a week in the sun...."

He did get the picture. Did I ever! I chuckled, because I saw that he was wearing riding boots. "I didn't realize you had on boots." He laughed.

"Well, now you do, smart-ass."

"Do you like being black, Darryl?"

"Jeff, I absolutely love my new skin color. And it'll contrast with Kerry's so dramatically. Come on, let's go riding."

"Riding?"

He held out a high pair of boots like his. "Bareback."

He also had a pair of sheer nylon socks for me to don first to facilitate putting on the boots. I was thankful for their slickness, it turned out. Darryl showed me how to hold onto the loops at the inside top, wiggle my legs and pull hard. It was a struggle, but the result was worth it. They hugged my calves and felt great. They looked really sexy, too. I thought of how desirable Shane looked in his police boots. These were going to be a bitch to take off. I wondered if Skipper pulled Shane's off. I wished he would do mine. Darryl interrupted my daydream about the puppy, to tell me that I looked too sexy and give me a generous kiss with his bountiful lips.

Toby and Yancey must have thought that I did, too, because they were all smiles, when they saw me. They helped me onto my horse. Whose name was Phallus, appropriately, they said with smirks. I liked them, although I couldn't give a specific reason. Well, they were really attractive, and looking at them, they were more handsome because their own beauty complemented their partner's. And I felt a kinship with them, considering that we were all naked,

399

save for the high boots. More than I ever wanted to make it, anally, with them.

I had never ridden before, let alone bareback, so I was more than a little leery of Phallus, although the horse had nuzzled me when I approached him and seemed to approve of me. At least that's what Toby and Yancey said. I had to take their word for it, being a novice, but they assured me that I would have no problems.

I wondered if Phallus was the same one they suspected that Billy was going to try to suck off. Actually, slut or not, I had found the boy completely appealing, to the point where I could envision us being lovers. And indulging him in his gender fuck. I thought of the way his dark hair fell over his forehead and the way he carelessly, and fetchingly, pushed it back with his slack wrist. Yes, I could like that. Love that, in fact. And he had looked so hot in his soccer outfit with the pantyhose. Honestly. Man, I was learning more about what could give guys pleasure in a few days, than I ever learned in eighteen years and half a dozen boyfriends. Further, that our world was not vanilla, and that was good, I decided. Except for those stuck on one flavor, whichever one it was.

As Darryl and I rode leisurely across the estate, I looked at him. His deep brown skin did appear black and turned me on something fierce. All of my boyfriends had been light-skinned to Marc's tawny, but not to Andrew's milk chocolate. I'd never seen anyone so dark in person. His black eyes looked bigger surrounded as they were by his heavy pigmentation. We chatted leisurely as we rode. I enjoyed the breeze hitting my naked body and the feel of the horse's coat on my skin. I asked where we were heading. A copse of trees near the eastern boundary of the property, he said. There was a stream running through the woods. And he'd brought along a blanket and some food.

I thought about my encounter with Shane and how much I had enjoyed his dirty blond beauty. The uniform added to the act, I admitted. Then it dawned on me that, like him, I was wearing tall boots, too. The idea of making it with Darryl, wearing them, was appealing. And the ride on Phallus was even more so. I had sprung an erection from the motion. I saw that Darryl had, too. He smiled at me. "Like riding bareback?" I grinned and nodded. "Sure do."

The wooded area was thick with underbrush. We dismounted and led the horses down a narrow path to a clearing next to a wide, shallow brook. It was peaceful and secluded.

"Come here often?"

"No. Just with Kerry sometimes," he said, taking me into his arms and kissing me gently.

"Do you love him?"

"Yes. And uncle, too, I guess. We're mostly a threesome. But I seem to like twosomes near streams with gorgeous men."

"Won't Kerry be upset?"

"No. He knew an Adonis was coming to visit. Relax. Let's spread the blankets."

There were two of them, which padded our bodies nicely as we lay and kissed,

400

intertwining our legs as well as the boots would allow. Our bodies were warm from the sun and fragrant with that fresh smell with which it imbues the skin. We were also mildly sweaty, allowing us to glide over each other with minimal friction and maximal nerve excitement. This got us highly aroused within minutes, and sweatier, continuing the exhilarating cycle. I was on my back, my lips being smothered by Darryl's, my body electrified by his caressing right hand. He pulled off my lips and said, hoarsely, "I want you."

"You got me."

"Turn and lift your leg."

I lifted it high in the air and felt him enter me, his long, black cock sliding almost all the way into my boy cunt. I'd never been taken this way before, but I liked it. His erect cock moved urgently in me. I moaned and groaned and emulated his thrusts with my hand on my own steely erection. Getting off was what it was about in our needy states. Going for the O, in unvarnished terms. Behind my closed eyes I saw the beads of perspiration form and drip from Darryl's beautiful face as he worked my body for his pleasure. One of uncle's prized boys was rutting in me. "Man, you feel so good, Jeff."

"You, too. Fuck me with that big black tool. Cream my insides."

"Your wish is coming true. Oh, man." We stayed coupled for several more minutes, until I cried out and sent arcs of come flying from my slit. Darryl lost it soon after, blasting my walls with his gooey white stuff.

He pulled out, and I lay down. He was still nearly hard, and my spit on him made his dark member gleam in the dappled sunlight. I put my hand around it, marveling at the contrast between our skin tones.

He kissed me lightly and thanked me for a great fuck. Thrilled, I gave him a gentle tug and told him he was welcome. We lay with his arm over my belly, content to share the silence. My thoughts were about life at this place. For all intents and purposes, it was ideal. For the first time I thought seriously about becoming a pool boy. I was certain that I would qualify to become one. I could quit school for a few years and enjoy the lazy life afforded these guys. Three squares a day, tanning, swimming and sex. I imagined Trey choosing bright lavender as the color of my shiny swim thong. And submitting to having the cock straps affixed to my organs, with Marc doing the honors. A skimpy, lustrous pouch during the day, and then nude in my leather harness until after sex at bedtime. I also would get to meet the other half of uncle's dynamic duo. Kerry, of the flaming red hair. I was dying to see him, because I'd never met a redheaded guy I considered really cute, let alone gorgeous. I thought of falling asleep, sated, with Angel and Raphael nestled against me. And regularly having sex with Marc and Andrew, perhaps becoming the boy of one or both of them. And satisfying Shane, when he visited and donned his uniforms. Being fucked by a sailor, a Mountie, a firefighter, but most of all, the cop. I could envision rooming with Billy and eventually wearing a pinkie ring to show that we had sown our wild oats and were now a couple. Brushing his hair back from his face and receiving his radiant smile in return. Kissing the full lips. Sucking on his

brown nipples. Roving my hand over his silky tanned flesh. Entering him to bond with his teenage beauty.

"What are you thinking so deeply about?"

"Honestly? Becoming a pool boy."

"Uh, uh. Not you, Jeff. You're too intelligent. And beautiful, I add, needlessly. Their existence is a numbing one, but there's little to numb up there, so they enjoy their lifestyle. You'd be bored to tears. And you can only have so many orgasms a day. No, it's not for you. Trust me."

"It seems so idyllic."

"For that certain type of person. Now, let's eat, because I want this monster for dessert." I almost said that Ryan was the one with the fiendish endowment, but I didn't. I did, however, fantasize taking every inch of it up my descending colon. Man. If I was going to let him tear me up, I wanted it to be in front of a mirror, so that I could see the impossible rape taking place. Yet Tyler seemed to revel in being speared with it. More power to him.

After shrimp salad, cole slaw, melon chunks and rolls, plus a nice fruity sauvignon blanc, Darryl treated my cock to his luscious lips. Curiously, I found myself wondering what Marc was doing at that moment. Did he have some dumpy, middle-aged guy's cock in his mouth? Playing the whore he was? But I loved that whore, in spite of myself.

"Whoa, Darryl. You're too good, man." He smiled and repositioned himself over my organ and slowly lowered himself onto it. He sighed when I was sheathed in him.

"The naked truth is that I would like to have this all to myself. As would at least a dozen other guys here."

"I'm flattered."

"You should be, Jeff. You're as gorgeous as Marc." Marc again. My ghost of Christmas Past.

"Thanks, Darryl. I appreciate the great compliment. I guess I wish I had been able to spend more time with him."

"You guess?"

"Oh, all right, I know so. But I'm delighted to be making it with you. Black is definitely your color." I played with his nipples as he rode me. Birds overhead chirped their approval of our union. My left hand moved to his navel, and I fingered the smooth outie there. My right hand caressed him to hardness and then began to jerk him off. We moved together, almost as if we were two parts of a machine. I had marvelled that Marc and I had been so in synch in our own lovemaking, as if we'd done it together for years. God, love hurt. Fortunately, Darryl was a dazzling distraction. I could get very used to being his lover, too. We were a great-looking couple. Like Marc and me. My finger left his belly button, and I stroked his right boot and thigh. "That feels really good. I can feel your touch through the tight leather."

"Do Toby and Yancey ever take theirs off?"

"Uh, huh. They have a boot fetish, so they're in heaven as stable boys. And

402

they like to smell each other's sweaty leg wear at the end of the day. It arouses them."

"Really?"

"Jeff, you can see just about everything here. And you certainly haven't seen it all yet. Jerk me faster." I did as he increased his movement on me. I could feel him build and waited for the stunning sight of his ebony cock spewing white fluid. It happened less than a minute later. I almost caught the first volley on my tongue, but it died a couple of inches away. I missed the other ones, because I closed my eyes against my own powerful release. Man, I could live like this, I thought as I lay spent.

We remained joined for several minutes, indulging ourselves in the afterglow of our orgasms. Then I realized I was in a hurting way. "Darryl, I really have to pee."

"Go ahead."

"What do you mean?"

"I mean pee in me. It's cool, Jeff. I want to feel your piss hitting my walls." I wasn't given to bashful kidney, thank goodness, but I had a difficult time coaxing my bladder sphincter to relax. When my need overcame its reluctance, I felt the vibrations of my urine bouncing off Darryl's insides. Then the liquid warmth settling around my flaccid cock in his bowel. And finally on my crotch and scrotum, as I trickled out of him. His face had a look of incredible ecstasy on it, so it must have felt awfully good to him, too.

We cleaned up at the stream. The cold water was stimulating. We let the warm air and sun dry us as Darryl answered more questions about the stable boys. He didn't give me much encouragement as far as making it with them. It seemed that their world didn't extend far beyond the horses. And their only contact with the house was when groceries and mail were delivered or when someone wanted to ride one of the horses. Which we did shortly after bathing, returning them to the stable.

"That was a lot of fun. Thanks, Darryl."

"It was. And I really liked getting peed in. You should try it sometime."

"I just might, because I liked it, too."

"I'll walk you back to your room." As we got toward the end of the formal gardens, intending to veer right and out of sight of the pool boys, I asked, "Who are the other gardeners?"

"The brunettes? Tim and Jimmy. Why?" I related their own version of water sports, which is what he called the enemas. "Hot, huh?"

"Yeah, it was. It was making me hard."

"There's a lot here that will. And already has, I might add."

"You got that right. It's been a workout. A very, very pleasant one."

"I'm sure you'll find more to occupy yourself before you go home. When is that?"

"Tomorrow, I guess. You know, I haven't seen Mike since my first night here."

"He's been preoccupied with his little Thai boy. He adores him."

"I'll bet. The kid seems like a pistol."

"Let's just say that sex fascinates him."

We had moved farther into the grove than I had gone, and I was able to see another formal garden over the rise of the hillock. There were paved paths through this one. I saw two pool boys rollerblading. I stopped to watch them. The gleaming black skates crawled up their calves. They had on helmets and hand, elbow and knee pads, but otherwise they were wearing only slinky black jockstraps. I hoped neither landed on his bare ass. "Slow down," I heard the one behind call.

"That's Troy and Mark. Troy's the blond."

"They're beautiful."

"Yeah, they are. But they're also in love and so cute together." An understatement. And they proceeded to show us how they were both. Mark, a brunette, undid three snaps at the top of his jock and let the flap hang down. He played with himself fast as he approached a slowing Troy. He let his erection wave up in the air as he drew close to the comely cheeks ahead of him. Then Troy widened his stance and Mark held onto Troy's left side as he guided himself into the boy with his right. They continued their slow movement as their tanned bodies engaged in intercourse. "Amazing."

"Well, they're pool boys. And you know, for some reason, rollerblades really turn me on."

"Me, too. I just didn't know how much." I did now, as I watched them kiss and fuck. Mark was masturbating Troy through the shiny black material. God, what a beautiful sight, joined like that, skating! They disappeared behind shrubbery, so we didn't get to see the denouement, but I imagined the pleasure on their pretty faces as they came.

"Jock strap fucking's a real turn-on to me, too, because the guy getting fucked is helpless, his equipment trapped in the pouch. The Petes have a video of guys doing it that way." They would. Except that the stretchy jocks the pool boys wore weren't nearly as constricting.

"You ever make it with the Petes?"

"Uh, huh. Only Kerry and I, and Marc and Andrew can. Pool boys aren't allowed near them, thank goodness."

Yes, as far as sex partners went, I felt in heady company indeed.

Eleven

We went into the mansion through the solarium, and Darryl showed me another doorway, which led to the back hall and stairs. As we walked down the east wing, I saw that most of the rooms were empty. One, which wasn't, had a lone youth in it on the bed. Seeing the careless straight brown hair, long black T-

shirt and stockings, I knew immediately who it was. My jaw dropped, when I realized what Billy was doing. Specifically, doing himself. He was one of those guys I'd heard about, who could contort himself and suck on his own cock. It also helped that he had a good eight or nine inches pointing into his face. He made happy noises as he loved himself. "Man," I said, under my breath.

"Oh, I think he's Narcissus personified," Darryl whispered. "He sucks all those other cocks for the practice, I think." My heart sank, watching him. That delightful fantasy was definitely out the window. Then I thought, strangely, that he couldn't have a much more handsome lover. I shrugged. Go for it, man. We stayed until he made noises on his tool and filled himself with his own essence. In spite of myself, I was responding to this scene of self love.

"Let's see if Trey is up to anything," Darryl said, perhaps to distract me, sensing my chagrin.

"Sure. That's always entertaining," I said, without much conviction.

However, it was more than that this time. It was shocking. "Fuck me with that big cock, Trey. Fuck me, man. Yeah, that's it. Oh, god, it's so big," I heard, as we neared the doorway. Okay, Trey did have a big cock for a kid his age. But that wasn't what I saw. Well, I did, but it was merely a spectator to the action this time. A boy with curly blond hair was bent over. He wore only a collar attached to a leash, which Trey held. Skipper stood by in his collar, sheath and his footed, leather leggings, watching Trey do it to the boy. With his hand. It took several seconds for it to register that his other hand was in the youth. Not only that, but he was actually moving it farther inside the boy, who kept begging for it, even when it was in him up to the elbow. Skipper looked at us and smiled, beautiful oriental puppy that he was.

"That's called fisting," Darryl said. Man.

"Doesn't it hurt?"

"Trey gave him a relaxant, so all it feels is good." Then just after he said that, Skipper broke a popper under the boy's nose. He inhaled deeply and sighed in happiness. His erection bobbed. That made Skipper sink to his knees and attend to it. As the boy's sex noises increased, Trey began to withdraw his arm from the youth's bowel. Then he slowly pushed the forearm all the way in again. Man, that was quite an experience. The blond convulsed on Trey's arm and in Skipper's mouth. We left.

We returned to the blessedly empty guest room. We helped each other remove the tight boots from our legs. Darryl noted that voyeurism could sometimes be a lot of fun. I conceded that it had been in the last half hour, because I didn't rollerblade well, let alone fuck someone while doing it, couldn't suck myself off, and had no desire to have Trey's hand up my ass. He laughed. When we were unshod, he kissed me goodbye and thanked me again for a great afternoon. I lay down to review the events of the day so far. It certainly had been another one filled with them. And then I wondered what would happen next. I didn't bother to cover myself, because I didn't feel embarrassed to be naked at that point, when the Filipino boy brought in supper. Three lobster tails were stuffed,

as was the potato.

I begin to think perhaps I would die of a heart attack before I left the place. I would be dying happy in that palace of pleasure except that I wasn't really all that happy. I missed Marcus Aurelius more than I wanted to admit. I had had sex with a bunch of gorgeous boys, but my heart always came back to him. I knew why, too. I would never meet a more handsome guy in my life. Nor a sweeter one, probably. Certainly not a sexier one, although Angel hung in there on all accounts pretty well. Andrew came even closer, beautiful little sexpot that he was. But I couldn't even consider my feelings for him, for fear of going into emotional shock.

I had just finished dinner and was trying to decide whether or not to seek out the identical Petes for more weird videos and carefree sex, when there was a knock on the door. Just what I needed. I knew it wouldn't be Marc. Or Andrew. Still, I was surprised to see Randy standing there. He was dressed in a red latex body suit with matching stiletto-heeled boots. Even though I'd never done drag, Randy looked good enough to do. "Hi, Jeff. I'm on my way to my semi-weekly humiliation at the hands of my beloved brother. I wanted you to meet my dress-up playmate, Billy." Who looked achingly desirable, attired in a French maid's uniform, complete with a lacy headpiece in his lustrous hair; hair I wanted bad to run my fingers through. "To clean up the gore," Randy said, by way of explanation of the costume. I said how much I honestly liked it. And his, because I did. "We sort of met last night. I really liked that outfit, too."

"Thanks, Jeff. That's about as butch as I get." He had a soft, appealing sibilance to his speech, which only added to his attractiveness. Also the hurt I felt over his already having a mate; himself. God, he was so desirable. And that incandescent smile made my heart go thump.

"And there's someone else you haven't met yet. Jeff, meet my other brother, Damien."

Another blond boy entered the room, as cute as Randy and Trey, at least. There were three of them? No one had mentioned the third brother at all. And he was in drag, too, in a way. Baby drag. His horizontally-striped T-shirt had snaps along the shoulders. He also wore a light blue corduroy short pant overall, matching socks and white baby boots. He was sucking his thumb, quite sensually, I thought. He removed it and said, "Hi." I couldn't quite believe that I was seeing a teenager dressed up as a toddler, but the proof was smiling at me.

"Damien's my baby. I thought that you could entertain him while I'm busy getting debased by the other brother I adore. Come on, Billy." I got one more flash of smile from the maid, and they left me with the big little boy.

"You're as gorgeous as everyone's been saying. And way hung, too. Do you like babies, Jeff?"

"I never thought about it. Except that the one standing here is the prettiest I've ever seen."

"Thanks," he said, coming up and kissing me and putting his arms around me. Mine encircled him and cupped his boyish cheeks. I felt the crinkle of rubber

406

over thick fabric. "Yeah, I wear a diaper and training pants. I was never potty trained, because Randy wanted me to stay a baby. Daddy agreed, if he would take care of me. He has. Completely." I took that to mean attention to his wee wee, too. "I like to play boy games, if you're interested, stud."

"Let's see what comes up."

"I know what I want to."

"And I'll bet you can do it."

"Let's just say that I've had a lot of practice living here." He stroked my face, lightly. I thought that perhaps he was even better looking than his brothers. "And Randy just changed and bathed me, and I ate right before that, so I'm safe."

"Your sphincters don't work?"

"Never had to. I've always been in a diaper."

He smelled of baby powder, which was strangely intoxicating. So were his ripe lips. We stood there and kissed for several minutes. That's all it took. He grabbed my erection and said, "I know where I want this. But first you need to undress me. Either Randy or Eduardo, and sometimes Billy, dress and undress me." He saw my expression. "I'm pretty much helpless. I mean, it's the way Randy wants me." He sat, and I untied his boots.

"Where did you get baby boots to fit you?"

"A mail order company. You'd be real surprised at how many adult babies there are. Of course, they have to unlearn their potty training, which is harder to do. Randy gets all my clothes from that place."

"Can you eat by yourself?"

"Yeah, that I can do. But otherwise...." He shrugged. He stood so that I could push down the straps of his romper. Then I unsnapped his shirt and removed it. "Beautiful," I said.

"Thanks, Jeff. It's mutual." Lastly, I took off his training pants.

He got onto the bed and lay down, still wearing his diaper. We began to kiss and fondle. His soft skin made me think of Andrew. I played with him through the cotton of his diaper. He liked that. So did I, because he sure wasn't a baby down there anymore. I put my hand inside the diaper and stroked him. He cooed into my mouth. He squirmed as I aroused him, rubbing him slowly with my fingers, up and down. "Ooh, that feels so good."

"Good, because I've decided that I like playing with babies a lot."

"Will you take off my diaper?"

"Can't wait. Why the pink safety pins?"

He sighed. "Randy. I let him. It's not worth fighting about with my fem brother. When Trey or Skipper changes me, he uses the blue ones. I think to upset Randy." I chuckled.

I actually lifted Damien by the ankles to raise his ass off the diaper to remove it. His crotch was smooth, just like a baby's. I figured that he might be too young to grow hair yet. He was the youngest. I thought that Randy was probably the oldest of the brothers. Anyway, he was as hairless as Marc. I frowned. And

407

Andrew. Damn. There was also a lot of powder, and the smell was stronger now. It caused distant memories to fight to surface but fail. I took his semi-tumescence in my hand and masturbated him with the baby powder. He sighed as I worked him to hardness. I wondered if I were as good as Randy, but I didn't want to know. "Fuck me now, Jeff."

"You sure?"

"Yeah. Take me on all fours."

He had a cute, smooth ass, which was also white. I fondled his cheeks, which he said felt good. I put my finger in his hole and was surprised to find him wet. "Randy prepared me." He spread his legs farther apart, signalling that he wanted me to enter him now. I stroked myself as I massaged the soft cheeks. When I was ready, I moved against him and pushed the head in. "Feel okay?"

"Feels great. Spear me, stud."

I did, sliding all the way in on his lubrication. I wondered if Randy fucked him or just jerked him off. Did Trey, the times he changed him? "God, your cock's so big, Jeff. It's all the way up my little boy thing. Make me feel it. Make your baby goo goo." I wasn't sure I wanted to hear baby talk, but I did want to fuck the tight hole of this beautiful baby.

"You sure I'm not hurting you?"

"No, I'm sure you are. My little belly's on fire. Fuck me harder. Make me hurt, stud." I complied, even though I didn't understand how pain could be pleasurable, sexually. Maybe it ran in the family, thinking back to witnessing Trey hurt Randy. I reached under him and was shocked to feel that he was bloated. From the pain? "No, rub my belly. It'll help make me come." I did, figuring that Randy had probably done that to him when he was a real infant as part of his molestation. Whatever it was, he liked it. I fucked him so hard that I came within minutes. Damien cried out several times, as if he were having multiple orgasms. When I pulled out of him, he informed me that he had. I didn't know that guys could. Especially not someone so young. But he hadn't come, because the sheets were dry. Huh. He kissed me and thanked me for the great fuck. Then he asked me to re-diaper him. I had just gotten the thick cotton under him, when he leaked urine onto it. He didn't comment, probably because it was a routine experience. It still amazed me that someone his age had no control over his functions. I finished pinning him and put on his rubber pants. We lay and talked for a while, before he suggested that we find out what Trey was doing to Randy. I agreed, because it would be another excuse to see Billy. And the nice legs covered in fishnet. I had noticed that his soccer socks had hugged great calves the night before.

I knew that my time at the mansion had caused me to become jaded, because I thought nothing of walking down the halls naked with a teenager in a diaper and training pants sucking his thumb.

When we got to the room, Trey was zipping up Randy's rear end and Skipper his front fly. Billy was sitting on the bed with his legs crossed. Even though it was pointless, I fantasized about those legs being around my neck.

"Hey, Jeff. Glad you came by. I have a proposition for you," Trey said.

"You'll love it," Randy said, and kissed me on the cheek.

"Thanks for everything, Jeff," Damien said, and the three of them left.

"So what's the proposition?"

"A little light pain in return for the legendary Skipper blowing you."

"I don't know, Trey." But I saw the puppy lick his lips. My resolve was fading. Especially since the master had on his very high boots and a full, studded torso harness. I thought now that he was the most attractive of the brothers. His cock looked so tempting. I gave in.

He put a plain black collar around my neck and cuffed me to what he called a Saint Andrew's Cross, which was in the form of an 'X'. The center of the cross bar had a hole in it for easy access. Lucky me. I soon found out that the light pain was just that. He affixed what he called tit clamps to my nipples. They did hurt, but the pain was bearable. In fact, I felt a little of the spreading fire, which Damien had mentioned. Trey weighted my sac with a ball stretcher, he called it. "There, you look like a properly adorned slave."

"You do. You look hot, Jeff," Skipper said. It surprised me to hear him speak.

They let me endure my mild suffering for several minutes. Then the puppy went into the bathroom and brought out a warm washcloth, which he used to clean both of us. "We know where this has been recently," he said, squeezing me. They both laughed. I guessed that it was a safe assumption that Damien and I had sex. That was probably Randy's plan, and he'd mentioned it to Trey.

After what seemed like hours, Skipper knelt and fellated his master. God, it was hot watching him go down on Trey. There was something about his enthusiasm that made the act even sexier. Once hard, Trey came around to the back of the cross and put his finger in me. He depressed it, opening me up, and slid his cock all the way in. He took the finger away, and my rosebud kissed the base of his shaft. Skipper assaulted me from the front, and I knew that I was going to receive the best blow job of my life. He began by licking the underside, running his tongue all the way up and then down the shaft. I jerked to life. Next he swallowed the head and held it there before teasing under the cleft with his tongue. The act was pure torture, and exquisitely so. When he had me squirming, he began to suck me in earnest, using only his red lips. This calmed my screaming nerves somewhat. I'm sure he did it so as not to lose me too soon. But then he was on me in earnest, probably because he heard Trey grunting. He was reaming me but good. I had never been fucked so thoroughly in my life. He was awfully talented for someone so young.

Trey reached his gloved hands around and stroked my abdomen. "You're so fucking beautiful, Jeff. Fucking Adonis. Fucking you silly."

"You are," I wanted to say. I could hardly stand it. I was getting the best fuck and the best sucking of my life. All I could feel were the ripples of pleasure they were sending back and forth to each other through my body. It was too much. I bucked and gushed into Skipper's throat. For a moment I thought I might choke him, but he kept me lodged there until I finished coming. Then he came off me,

his lips clamped on me as if he were draining the last of my cream out of me. He probably was. "Fucking gonna come in you, boy stud," Trey growled and lunged one last time.

We were on the bed now, Trey and I lying down, Skipper straddling his master/lover. Who was playing with his puppy's leather cock and balls. I told them that they had given me the best pure sex I'd ever had. They both seemed unsurprised by my admission.

"So, I take it you've enjoyed yourself here."

"That's an understatement."

"You sure had a lot of sex, from what I hear."

"Yeah. To last a lifetime."

"There are some great-looking guys here."

"True, but one would have been enough."

"Oh? Who?"

"Marcus. No offense, but his beauty is otherworldly."

"None taken. Skipper and I know that we're just simply gorgeous. Marc's an Adonis, like you."

"Thanks, but I'm not in Marc's or Andrew's league."

"So the studlet turned your head, too, huh?"

"Completely. I mean, they're not only beautiful, they're incredibly sexy."

"Yeah, they are. Dad has a way of picking them. Darryl's no slouch, either. Too bad you won't get to meet Kerry."

"Meeting Marc was plenty, thanks. I just wish I hadn't fallen in love with him."

As I left them after about an hour or so, Trey told me he had a going-away gift that he would bring by later. I thanked him, wondering what it could be.

Ryan, it turned out. He was lying in all his glory on the bed when I returned to the room. I felt myself stir at the sight of him, despite having gotten off twice already that evening. By now I was recharged and ready. Except that I didn't want to do it with Ryan.

"Hi."

"Hi, Jeff."

"I guess you're my going away present."

"Your what?"

"Look, Ryan, I think you're one of the most beautiful men I've ever seen. But so is Tyler, and I know you're lovers. And as much as I'm dying to find out what fourteen inches in my gut would feel like, I can't do this. It's not just making you cheat on Tyler. I realize that I've been acting like a sex fiend all week, because I was trying to deny that I had fallen in love. But a little while ago I admitted it." I shrugged. Tears formed in my eyes. "Thanks, Ryan, but go love Ty. He's well worth it."

"Gee, Jeff, I don't know what to say. Thanks, I guess. I was willing to make it with you, because you're so gorgeous, and as a favor...."

"A favor?"

410

"They wanted to keep you happy, while you were here."

"They did, but I was happiest the first day. Happy again later, but I knew what I was feeling, and a nine-year-old boy and I had no future together, either. Could I ask one favor? Could I kiss your cock? It's the most magnificent one I've ever seen."

"Sure." He got out of bed, the monster swinging so erotically. I kissed his big cock head. He pulled me to my feet and kissed me. He told me that I was a special guy and left.

Hardly. I was just a love-sick teenager. I had an arrow sticking in me somewhere, whose tip was soaked in love potion, and I desperately needed to find it and pull it out. I sat in the window well in the dark. Tears rolled down my face. With any luck, I wouldn't see Marc before I left. That would help. Maybe.

I think that I had just gotten to sleep when I heard the knock. I said come in and reached for the crystal lamp on the bedside table. I switched it on, blinding myself. Then I tried to focus on whoever had come in. I realized that the overhead light was on now, too, which didn't help. I tried desperately to adjust my vision. Please don't let it be an axe murderer, I prayed. It wasn't, in the least.

It was a vision in sparkling diamonds. Showy earrings, choker, bracelets, anklets; a rock the size of Gibraltar nestled in his navel. Even a diamond cock ring encircled his genital perfection. He was the most beautiful thing I had ever seen in my life. I had to be still dreaming. It couldn't be. But it was. "I love you, too, Jeff," Marc said. I jumped out of bed, and we met halfway, embracing each other tightly. Then we kissed, long and passionately and then hugged again.

"I told you I'd bring your going-away present by later," Trey said. "You thought it was Ryan. Fooled you. I'm so smart."

"Yes, we know, dear," Skipper said.

"Well, do you want him?"

"You mean it?!" He smiled and nodded. "Always," I said and smiled at Marc.

"I now pronounce you man and husband," said Mike. I didn't realize that he was there until that moment. And if Marc hadn't been wearing the twinkling precious gems all over his body, Cecil would have looked quite fetching to me. He had on a necklace of multiple strands of gold, which came down to his nipples. Another series of them formed a metallic loin cloth, although it didn't hide his sex well. Still, he looked tremendously appealing in it. But not nearly as desirable as Marcus Aurelius.

"But what about your uncle," I asked Mike.

"What about him?" Trey asked. "This is my decision."

"Yours?"

"Trey is the defacto head of state of the Undemocratic Republic of Debauchery," Mike said. "Marc's been unhappy here, since he no longer amused uncle."

"And it pissed me off, royally, that Dad did that to Marcus. So when Mike told me that you were an Adonis and dated only guys who weren't white, we decided to see if you two would hit it off. You did, but I wanted to make sure of

411

what you might be feeling for him. So, I arranged all of the other encounters to see how you really felt about Marc. And the guys kept telling me that you'd bring him up in conversation. And Marc begged me to hurt him to stop the plan, he wanted you so much. Our god is not into pain, by the way. So, maybe you'll take. I think that Andrew is the most disappointed, because he loves you, too."

"And I love him. I really do. But I love Marc more."

"He's non-returnable."

"You can bet your life on that," I said, which made them laugh.

After they left, he asked, "Will you ravish me?"

"I can't help doing it. Are those real?"

"Very real. My dowry."

"But they must be worth...."

"Tens of thousands of dollars each. Petty cash here."

I think that I kissed every part of his body as I slowly made my way down it. His scent aroused me all over again, as did his soft, lustrous, brown skin. I had him hard before my tongue even danced rings around his belly jewel, but I took him in me, loving the prettiest of maleness I'd ever seen, with all of the technique I could muster. It paled in the face of Skipper's, but Marc was moaning in delight. I moved to his scrotum and lovingly tortured that. Then I molested his pucker until he begged me to fill him. I did and felt whole again.

"It was agony being away from you."

"It was for me, too. Except with Andrew, I admit."

"He's a very special boy. He knows he's gay!"

"How can he?"

"Well, nine-year-old boys are screwing girls and fathering children. Why shouldn't Andrew know what he is, sexually?"

"Well, I guess you're right. Will you always be right, for godsake?"

"Ha! I doubt it. Come on, fuck me with that fire hose and then turn it on full blast in me, you big stud."

His ankles were crossed behind my neck, and I felt thousands of dollars worth of diamonds pressing against it. I leaned forward and kissed him as my rhythm in his tight boy place remained constant.

As my sap rose fast, Marc came off my lips to tell me that he was going to come, because of how great my cock felt in him. "Oh, god, me too, Marc."

Despite how much pleasure Skipper and Trey had given me earlier, my guy spot tingled after I came in Marc. Again, I realized. My penis was in a special place, and his name was Marcus Aurelius. We lay loosely connected and in love.

"That was fantastic, as always, Jeff. Now, one little matter we need to get out of the way. We've already been pronounced married, but I don't know what my surname will be."

"Your surname?"

"I don't have one, remember?"

"Oh, right. Sorry, I forgot. It's kind of mundane. My name is Jefferson Thomas. I guess that my parents thought it was a hoot doing the play of names

412

on the president. But I love my name. Jefferson, I mean."

"I do, too. Marcus Aurelius Thomas. I like that even better."

"Good, because that's your name now."

Twelve

Andrew, Angel and Raphael, Billy, Damien, Randy, Trey and Skipper were in the foyer to see us off. Andrew had tears in his eyes, having fallen for me, too. Trey and Skipper kissed me and hugged and kissed Marc. Randy followed, telling me I would look divine cross dressed. He had on a smart pink summer dress and heels with beige stockings. Damien was in pink and white togs, probably to coordinate with his diaper pins and his brother. He pecked me on the cheek and gave me a knowing smile. "Nobody's ever hurt me that much! Awesome cock! Thanks."

Angel whispered, "We'll live. But not as well."

"But you have Raphael."

"Yeah. Now if only he'll buy me those silk stockings." We laughed.

Billy was in a long, baggy black T-shirt, shorts, hose and low-cut Converse Chuck Taylor All Stars. He looked great in his butch drag. When he hugged me, he said, "If I hadn't found myself first, I would definitely want you."

Andrew said goodbye last, unable to keep his eyes from leaking. He simply held me and trembled. Then he looked up and said, "I love you, Jeff." I didn't doubt that for a second, because it was mutual. He hugged and kissed Marc, obviously not wanting to let him go and suffer the double loss. But he did and we left to embark on our new life together.

- - -

Although it broke my heart to leave Andrew, it wasn't the end of the story. What happened was that Mike's uncle died in bed soon after returning home from his trip, following sex with Kerry and Darryl.

Although a relatively young man, bad eating habits and stress evidently killed him. Trey called up after the funeral, as he told Marc and me that he would. "Well, I'm going to make some changes here. I'm going to let Darryl and Kerry stay and give them their own apartment. The pool boys I'll keep around for a while, anyway. They *are* nice to look at. And some of them to use, you know? Besides, Mike and Nok like them."

Nok? Oh, Cecil. What the hell was hard about Nok to pronounce? I shook my head. Mike.

"Skipper and I are going to let Mike have the master suite, because he will be my legal guardian for a few more months, anyway, even though I'm the one running the show."

Say what? The fifteen-year-old, who was really almost eighteen? I would never have guessed, he looked so young. But more like approaching fifty than eighteen.

"So, Mister and Missus Trey Beresford will move into the honeymoon suite." He chuckled. I appreciated his telling me their true relationship, and said so.

"You're welcome. But Skipper talked, when we did you. That was our clue to you." Oh, did they do me. And, yeah, Skipper had. I'd forgotten it. "And he called me dear, when we brought Marc to you, so that could have blown us out of the water, except that no one noticed. Which is fine. Jeff, surely you can understand that it's not your age, it's your maturity that counts, if you're going to commit yourself to another person.

And for me that's Skipper, as surely as the sun rises. Well, Zachary Beresford. My Skipper. He started out as my pet, but we're nine years older now and deeply in love. But we're keeping the cottage in the west wing for extracurricular activities. Have to keep up appearances, you know?" I laughed and said I did. "Now, there's one more very important matter, and it involves the unhappiness of a very special human being. I'm going to ask you a question, and I want you to think about it very carefully before answering, okay?"

"Okay."

"Do you want Andrew?"

My heart leapt. I covered the receiver. Marc had been watching me the whole time. "We can have Andrew!"

"We can?"

"Trey will give him to us!"

"Oh, god, Jeff, that's great!"

"I know!" We were kids on Christmas morning, we were so excited. I took my hand away from the mouthpiece. "Yes! Yes! Yes!"

We met Kerry, when we went to pick up Andrew less than an hour later. He actually was a gorgeous redhead, as promised. I was thrilled for Darryl. Well, both of them. Andrew was wearing a T-shirt and shorts, which didn't fit him. They were probably what he'd worn to the mansion three years ago. While there, he was always nude. He was so happy, he leaped into my arms and covered my face with kisses. And Marc's, as I held him aloft.

- - -

I would never have guessed in a million years that I would end up with not one, but two beautiful, loving mates. Andrew, Marcus and Jefferson Thomas are doing extremely well, thank you very much. And we owe it all to an invitation I received to the pleasure palace.

And the next one would be no less interesting.

414

The Contributors
(Other Than the Editor, John Patrick)

"The Wedge and the Voyeur" and "Cabin No. 9"
Mark Anderson
The author, who lives in Canada and winters in Palm Springs, has contributed to *Boys of the Night* and *Juniors*.

"The Pleasure Is Suddenly So Great"
Antler
The poet lives in Milwaukee when not traveling to perform his poems or wildernessing. His epic poem *Factory* was published by City Lights. His collection of poems *Last Words* was published by Ballantine. Winner of the Whitman Award from the Walt Whitman Society of Camden, New Jersey, and the Witter Bynner prize from the Academy and Institute of Arts & Letters in New York, his poetry has appeared in many periodicals (including *Utne Reader, Whole Earth Review* and *American Poetry Review)* and anthologies (including *Gay Roots, Erotic by Nature,* and *Gay and Lesbian Poetry of Our Time).*

"The Pleasure Palace"
Kevin Bantan
The author now lives in Bethlehem, Pennsylvania, where he is working on several new stories for STARbooks. His last story for STARbooks was in *Sweet Temptations*.

"In the Tent"
K.I. Bard
The poet and author, who lives in Minnesota, is currently working on several projects for STARbooks.

"A Day at the Beach"
Frank Brooks
The author is a regular contributor to gay magazines. In addition to writing, his interests include figure drawing from the live model, and mountain hiking.

"A Night with the Coach"
Leo Cardini
The celebrated author of the best-selling *Mineshaft Nights*, Leo's short stories and theatre-related articles have appeared in numerous magazines. An enthusiastic nudist, he reports that, "A hundred and fifty thousand people have seen me naked, but I only had sex with half of them."

"Camping with the Cowpokes"

Jason Carpenter

This Texas-based author is frequently published by gay erotic magazines under many aliases.

"Navajo Joe"

William Cozad

The author, whose work frequently appears in *Playguy* and other publications, has stories in most STARbooks anthologies. He lives in San Francisco.

"Sleeping Bag Sex"

Troy M. Grant

The author is a frequent contributor to gay magazines.

"Camp Hadrian", "Coming On Line",

and "Forbidden Fruits"

Peter Gilbert

"Semi-retired" after a long career with the British Armed Forces, the author now lives in Germany but is contemplating a return to England. A frequent contributor to various periodicals, he also writes for television. He enjoys walking, photography and reading. His stories have swiftly become favorites by readers of STARbooks' anthologies.

"At the Scout Hut" and "The Shooters of Shooting Creek" Thomas C.

Humphrey

The author, who resides in Florida, is working on his first novel, All the Difference, and has contributed stories to First Hand publications. His superb memoir of his youth on the farm appeared in *Juniors*.

"Selfish Pleasures"

Rick Jackson, USMC

The oft-published author specializes in jarhead stories. When not travelling, he is based in Hawaii.

"A Fear of Pleasure"

David Laurents

More of David's stories appear in STARbooks's *Smooth 'N' Sassy*, *Juniors*, and *In the Boy Zone*. A collection of his stories was recently published by Prowler Press in London.

"A Season of Pleasure"
James Lincoln
The author is new to the erotica scene. He has a number of supernatural tales slated for publication by various magazines and anthologies. Originally from New York, he says he currently resides in the deep south, "against my better judgement." More of his stories will appear in future STARbooks anthologies.

"Hooked!" and "More Than Friends"
R.J. Masters
The author, who lives in Maine, is a frequent contributor to gay erotic magazines under various pseudonyms. His first novel, *Foreign Power*, an erotic tale of sexual awakening, a young man's introduction into the world of S/M, was published by Nocturnis Press.

"Bi-Night"
Edmund Miller
Miller is the author of the legendary poetry book *Fucking Animals* (recently reprinted by STARBooks) and frequent contributor of stories to magazines and anthologies, is the Chairman of the English Department at a large university in the New York area. His current major writing project is *Icons of Gay New York: A Celebration in Words and Pictures*, a sonnet sequence with photographs celebrating the go-go boys of New York.

"My Latin Muscleboy"
Jesse Monteagudo
The author is a regular contributor to many gay newspapers and can be found on-line at the gaytoday.com website. His stories have appeared in STARbooks' *Intimate Strangers* and *Play Hard, Score Big*, among others.

"8 1/2 Inches"
Bill Nicholson
Born in the North of England and educated there and in London. His interests are music, literature, and the cinema. He has composed music which has been performed locally and poetry which has been published.

"The Punk"
Jack Ricardo
The author, who lives in Florida, is a novelist and frequent contributor to various gay magazines. His latest novel is *Last Dance at Studio 54*.

"Something Wonderful"
Rudy Roberts
The author, who lives in Canada, has contributed to many STARbooks anthologies, including *Naughty By Nature*.

"Geometrical Figures"
Tim Scully
The author, who lives in Europe, is a great pal of popular STARbooks contributor Peter Gilbert. He is working on more stories based on his pesonal experiences.

"Camping Out"
Ken Smith
Ken's work appears frequently in gay publications. His new book, *Virgin Soldiers*, has been published. He lives in England.

"In the Heat of the Moment"
Sonny Torvig
The author, who lives in England, also contributed a story to *Intimate Strangers*.

"The Pleasure of His Presence"
Austin Wallace
The author is a 10-year veteran of bookselling, having worked at Lambda Rising, Obelisk, and White Rabbit bookstores. He currently lives in California, and this is his first work of fiction, based, we are sure, on his personal experience. His previous story appeared in *Play Hard, Score Big*.

"Hide & Seek"
James Wilton
James has had several stories appear in STARbooks's anthologies, including *In the Boy Zone* and *Beautiful Boys*. He resides in Connecticut.

ABOUT THE EDITOR

John Patrick is a prolific, prize-winning author of fiction and non-fiction. One of his short stories, "The Well," was honored by PEN American Center as one of the best of 1987. His novels and anthologies, as well as his non-fiction works, including *Legends* and *The Best of the Superstars* series, continue to gain him new fans every day. One of his most famous short stories appears in the Badboy collection *Southern Comfort* and another appears in the collection *The Mammoth Book of Gay Short Stories*.

A divorced father of two, the author is a longtime member of the American Booksellers Association, the Florida Publishers' Association, American Civil Liberties Union, and the Adult Video Association. He resides in Florida.

in the park. He was wearing these really tight jeans, so tight you c
ring any underwear. "Excuse me," I said, having a hard time looki
nded by that bulge in his crotch, "but don't I know you?" "Maybe,
d of te about a
th Ray God, yo
oser? in?" he
. "Lil strong
body e on Gr
, he l I ever
p to t ny ide
aking e same
coul ry long
d rac e swe
with e in sto
go c behind
see u in pub
?" he vent to
acy. grabbe
rd. I
tracin t, so fir
it, ha
th my bing di
ng, I n cock,
sound of unzipping filled the small space. I don't know who's ha
t before I knew it, I had his rod in my hand, and mine was in his.
do?" he asked, his tone challenging. I knew exactly, and sank to